AN UNSUITABLE MOTHER

Sheelagh Kelly was born in York. She left school at fifteen and went to work as a book-keeper. She has written for pleasure since she was a small child, but not until 1980 were the seeds sown for her first novel, *A Long Way from Heaven*, when she developed an interest in genealogy and local history and decided to trace her ancestors' story. She has since completed many bestselling sagas, most of which are set in or around the city of York.

Visit www.AuthorTracker.co.uk for exclusive information on Sheelagh Kelly.

Also by Sheelagh Kelly

The Feeney Family Saga

A Long Way from Heaven
For My Brother's Sins
Erin's Child
Dickie

The Kilmaster Saga

A Sense of Duty
Family of the Empire
A Different Kind of Love

My Father, My Son
Jorvik
Shoddy Prince
A Complicated Woman
The Keepsake
Secrets of our Hearts

SHEELAGH KELLY

An Unsuitable Mother

HARPER

This novel is entirely a work of fiction. The names, characters and incidents portrayed in it are the work of the author's imagination. Any resemblance to actual persons, living or dead, events or localities is entirely coincidental.

Harper
An imprint of HarperCollins*Publishers*
77–85 Fulham Palace Road,
Hammersmith, London W6 8JB

This paperback edition 2009
2

First published in Great Britain by
HarperCollins*Publishers* 2008

ISBN 978 0 00 787489 7

Typeset in Sabon by Palimpsest Book Production Limited,
Grangemouth, Stirlingshire

Printed and bound in Great Britain by
Clays Ltd, St Ives plc

FSC is a non-profit international organisation established to promote the responsible management of the world's forests. Products carrying the FSC label are independently certified to assure consumers that they come from forests that are managed to meet the social, economic and ecological needs of present and future generations.

Find out more about HarperCollins and the environment at
www.harpercollins.co.uk/green

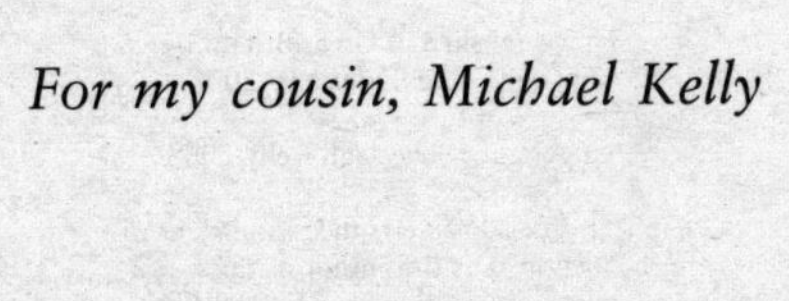

For my cousin, Michael Kelly

Acknowledgements

I am deeply grateful to my late aunt, whose lengthy nursing career provided the background for this novel. Any gaps were filled in courtesy of the archives of the *Royal College of Nursing Journal*. Though the places mentioned are real, I have taken the liberty of providing a fictional crew for the casualty evacuation train, and for both hospitals. I am also indebted to Leo Kessler for the use of his excellent book *The Great York Air Raid*, which spared me from trawling through any more old newspapers than was absolutely necessary; and to the staff of York Reference Library for providing me with countless volumes of historical material over the decades.

To relatives, friends and strangers who have contributed to my novels, I would like to say a belated and sincere thank you.

PART 1

1

What an intolerable burden, to be adopted by unsuitable parents. It was at times such as now that the holder of this view had a burning need to find the woman who had given birth to her. Whatever had made her abandon her baby, she could surely not be as insufferable as the one whose disembodied voice invaded this room.

Nell formed a weary reply to it now. 'Ye-es, almost ready!' When in fact she was not ready at all, but lounging on her bedroom windowsill, observing the newcomers moving in across the avenue; infinitely more fascinating than what lay in store.

'You needn't think dragging your feet's going to help,' inveighed Mrs Spottiswood. 'And please don't speak to me in that tone of voice! You're coming to Ronald's party, so get on with it.'

Some party, thought Nell, whose brown eyes remained fixed to the semi-detached house opposite, as yet another item of furniture was transported between the wooden rising-sun gates, and along a drive lined with hydrangeas. Her cousin's send-off to war promised to be the dullest affair. Never mind that all involved had pooled their rations to concoct a good spread, with Aunty Phyllis in charge it would hardly be an electric occasion. At least, though thought Nell with a resentful sigh, there would be a do of sorts for the son of the house. Her own mother's idea of a good send-off was to supply clean knickers, a flask of tea and a packet of sandwiches.

It was hard to believe there was a war on, with this dazzling August sunshine that lingered well into evening. No barrage balloons over York to mar the blue sky, nor even the faintest drone from one of the airfields that surrounded the city. Other parts of the county might be getting hammered, in southern skies British pilots battling desperately for what could be their final days of freedom, but the only bit of excitement around these parts came in the shape of foreign men seeking billets. None of them were around today, though, more's the pity.

Nell closed her eyes and tilted her face to the sun, whilst waiting for the newcomers to reappear, and dreamed of the venue she would rather be attending, had she not been dragooned.

'*Eleanor*!'

I am *not* an Eleanor, I am a Nell, came the irritated thought.

'Coming!' Sounding gay, but inwardly peeved at having to tear herself away, she went to grab a box of mascara from the dressing table. Spitting on the dwindling brown block inside, she worked it into a mud with the little brush. Then, determined not to miss anything, she repositioned herself by the window with her compact mirror, and began a hasty application to her lashes.

Whilst she was doing this, a figure entered her peripheral vision. In the hope that it was one of the new neighbours, and thus distracted, Nell poked herself in the eye. 'Ooh, sod and blast!' She was forced to cease everything, with a handkerchief pressed to her eye until the stinging receded.

And to cap it all, the figure had been no one important, only Geoff from next door, about whom she knew everything, for they had grown up together, though he was three years her junior. Fifteen: it seemed so long ago. She recalled herself at Geoff's age in her final year at school, the trip to the hairdresser to lop off her plaits and reduce her dark-brown hair to jaw length, in preparation of starting work. But surely she had never been so childish as this boy? Certainly she had grown up very quickly in these last three weeks. A secret smile twitched her lips.

Still waiting for her right eye to stop smarting, tweaked by thoughts of other things, she continued to watch Geoff with her left. In his Boy Scout uniform, he was practising lobbing grenades, ripping out the pin with his teeth, and generally playing the big warrior. Except that the grenade was a potato. Stifling laughter, Nell leaned again on the windowsill to maintain her one-eyed surveillance, as, time and again, Geoff cantered with manly strides up the path, like a spin bowler hurtling for the wicket, his mouth emitting an explosion upon hitting the target.

Then his mother came upon the scene. 'Geoffrey, what have I told you about wasting food?' And, much to Nell's further amusement, she cuffed him sharply round the head, ignoring his protests that he was only following orders.

Biting her lip in sympathy for poor Geoff's plight, though still tickled, Nell finally managed to adorn her lashes with mascara, and added a quick smear of rouge to her lips and cheeks. At her mother's further shout of impatience, she snatched a last look in the mirror, heaved in dissatisfaction for the tall and well-built figure reflected there, with its heavy breasts and thighs – such a big girl – then she prinked a dark-brown wave, smoothed the white sleeveless blouse and blue skirt, and tripped to the stairs.

But before she was halfway down, her mother witnessed a crime. 'You are not leaving this house with bare legs!'

'All my stockings are laddered!' With no need to impress relatives, Nell had been hoping to save her one decent pair.

'Then you can wear ankle socks!'

She turned back with a grumble. 'Oh, all right, I'll go and have another look . . .'

'And close your window whilst you're there!'

Nell's white sandals stopped in mid-track. 'It'll be stifling!'

'Why do you have to argue with every single request I make?' It was Thelma Spottiswood's turn to sound weary now. 'Close it! It'll be after blackout when we return, and I've no intention of leaving an open invitation to every crook in York. Anyone who'd stoop to pinching the light-bulb out of a public lavatory would have a field day in here.'

Nell wanted to complain that, if previous so-called family parties were anything to go by, they would be home well before nine thirty. Nevertheless, she went back to her room to don stockings and to pull down the sash – which was criss-crossed with brown tape as a safeguard against being shattered by bombs, even though York had been virtually free of those after almost a year of war – for it didn't do to upset Mother. Be prepared, that was Thelma Spottiswood's motto, as testified in her stock cupboards, her first-aid box, the stirrup pump forever at hand, and the thermos flask close to the kettle ready to fill with hot water in case of an air raid. So, being a considerate girl at heart, Nell did as she was told, finally arriving downstairs to present herself with a smile.

But her heart was to sink, as her father ordered dispassionately, 'You can get that muck off your face for a start.' Making ready for his stint as a member of the Home Guard, and changed from his shirt and tie into its newly issued khaki, Wilfred Spottiswood bent to put on his bicycle clips. But just because he would not be attending the party did not mean he would allow his daughter free rein. 'You look like a trollop.'

With no expectation that Mother would spring to her defence, a dutiful but inwardly hurt Nell rubbed at her lips with a handkerchief, hoping not to blot away too much of the colour. That was one of the drawbacks of having elderly guardians – no, positively ancient, thought Nell, who still found it astonishing that they had been children at the time of Queen Victoria's Golden Jubilee – how could one expect them to understand a modern girl's outlook? Father would quite gladly spend all weekend in his garden, or painting the house, and keeping both immaculate – but woe betide if his daughter should attempt to embellish her looks. Checking the pockets of his battledress for his identity card and his manual, and slinging a rifle over one shoulder and a gas mask over the other, he finally deigned to spare her another, rather resentful, glance. The fact that he made no comment informed Nell that she was classified as fit to leave the house.

Father, though, was the first of them to depart, saying, 'Have a good time at your party, but don't be too late home.'

'That's if we ever get there,' sniped his wife, with an accusing glance at their daughter.

Good time indeed! A grouchy Nell knew where she would rather be. Waiting now for her mother to don hat and gloves, she wandered to the window and watched her father push his bicycle to the footpath, where he paused to run a critical eye over his newly clipped privet. What could possibly be out of place? Why, it looked as if he had used a blasted spirit level on it! Then he cycled off, a grey, reserved and unhealthy figure, who spared not a wink of curiosity for the folk who were moving in. This was no surprise to Nell, for, outside work, the only human being to whom he paid lip service was her mother. Mother was a marvel at everything, possessing the ability to whip up a delicious meal despite this rationing, and would have it on the table the moment Father came in, and treated him as lord and master. As for their daughter, they seemed to think it sufficient that they were donating every material comfort that Father's good position at the insurance firm could endow: a room of her own in a well-furnished house;

a family car – even though it might be stuck in the garage most of the time due to wartime restrictions on petrol; elocution lessons to oust any trace of Yorkshire accent that they themselves retained; a grammar-school education, and a decent job to follow it. Yes, Nell was grateful for their sacrifices, and it was perhaps understandable when they had endured twelve childless years before adopting her that they wanted to be constantly involved. But did they have to be such old miseries?

'What are you sighing at now?' came the testy demand.

Made aware that she had been thinking out loud, Nell turned to see that her mother was ready: solid, large-bosomed and respectable-looking in her navy spotted dress, navy shoes, white gloves and white straw hat, she cut a shapely figure – but shapely in the manner of a cooling tower, thought Nell, everything rigidly confined and uninviting. She donned a smile, and explained, 'Oh, nothing, I was just envying those new people across the road their lovely French table.'

'So *that*'s what kept you so long upstairs!' Beads of perspiration had begun to seep from the menopausal brow. 'I don't know what there is to envy, they can't be so well off if they're having to do the removals themselves. Sunday night and still they're at it!'

Nell's focus had by now turned back to the street. 'Ooh, look, there's the lady of the house again! At least I think it is, but she looks far too young to have children – maybe they're not hers, maybe they're only nephews and nieces come to hel—'

'For goodness' sake!' Thelma Spottiswood came to smack her away from the window. 'I've already waited an hour for you to get ready, I've no wish to hang around further whilst you invent people's life stories.'

'I'm just interested . . .'

'That's obvious! I wish you'd show as much enthusiasm for your cousin as you do for the antics of strangers.

I don't know where you get your nosiness from – now go and fetch your gas mask then let's be off to this blessed party, Nebby Nora!'

Hurrying to comply, Nell wondered, too, from whom she had inherited her boundless curiosity in mankind, how she could be so intrigued with what went on in others' homes, not just in material concerns, but in their relationships, and how they coped with this war. Had her real parents been writers, artists, actors even? Often detached, her adoptive ones showed not the slightest interest in anyone outside their sphere. As anticipated. Thelma Spottiswood hooked her gas-mask container over her shoulder, and, in the same aloof manner as her husband, left the house with nary a peek at the newcomers or their furniture, discreetly nipping her daughter's arm when Nell turned to stare.

Few words passed between them as they walked along the tree-lined avenue to the nearest main road. In fact, the avenue ran between two main roads, one end being quite genteel, almost countrified in appearance, and enclosed in its view a quaint redundant windmill upon a rise – having once formed a village west of York, prior to urban spread. But with their house being situated nearer the more industrial highway, it was there they must head. Nell's aunt lived in the adjacent district, about a mile or so away. Before the war they might have walked there on an evening such as this, but now, with a thought to conserve shoe leather, they went only so far as the nearest bus stop.

Being Sunday, there was little traffic about, though still enough army vehicles to irritate Nell, who remained piqued at having her own jaunt vetoed. On the opposite side to the bus stop, behind a wall that extended from the carriage works, ran a vast network of railway lines, at this point in the road some of them bulging out from the main track, like an aneurism in a blood vessel, to serve another part of the city, before joining the chief artery again. Even today, the locomotives made for a great deal of soot, and Thelma

Spottiswood puffed gently at her white glove to expel such a fleck.

Nell had something to broach to her mother, but it might not go down too well. Anyway, the bus came then.

There was a wasp on board, floating up and down the aisle and generally causing a nuisance, until a grim Mrs Spottiswood rose and squashed it with her bag against a window.

Five minutes later, mother and daughter alighted, to undergo the rest of their trek along a straight, wide avenue that had lesser groves branching off to right and left, the occasional shade of a tree, and a variety of building styles, some Edwardian, but most of them modern semi-detached residences, with leaded lights and neatly planted beds of marigolds, roses, white alyssum and blue lobelia. The avenue was around a mile in length, though Nell and her mother did not have to walk half so far.

Upon reaching her aunt's gate, there was a warning. 'Stop making it so obvious you'd rather be somewhere else! I won't have your aunt and uncle offended. You never know, you *might* enjoy it.' With Nell tagging behind, Mrs Spottiswood approached a door not dissimilar to their own, Buckingham green, half-glazed, with a circular formation of stained glass, and a cast-iron letterbox. Singing could now be heard from behind it, which presaged a livelier affair than usual.

'Goodness, Phyllis,' Thelma Spottiswood announced above the rowdiness upon entering, with a smile to her sister-in-law, 'you do have a full house!'

Nell perked up too, there being several more guests than she had anticipated, her main focus being the young men in uniform who had commandeered the gramophone, and were leading a rousing chorus of 'Roll Out the Barrel', to which Ronald and his sisters and other relatives were happily singing along.

At such extraordinary sight, her mouth fell open. Whilst

she continued to gawp, her mother waved and smiled to family members, and enquired somewhat dubiously over the din, 'Are those Ronald's army colleagues?'

'Yes – at least two of them are,' mouthed her sister-in-law, a mousey dumpling of a woman, not half so smart as the other Mrs Spottiswood, with a kinder though less intelligent face. Then, unable to speak without having to shout, she drew Thelma and her daughter aside, and divulged, 'The others he met in town and just hit it off with. They were billeted in York after Dunkirk. Such grand young chaps. I don't think any of them is over twenty, I could weep when I think what a terrible time they must have had, but they're putting such a brave face on it – as you can hear!' She issued a quick laugh. 'And what with them being so far from home – from London, two of them – Ronald thought it would be nice to extend some local hospitality. He's such a thoughtful boy. Look at our Daphne and Margaret, can't even peel themselves away to greet you. I'm sorry about that – and the noise. I'm afraid they're all rather merry, let's hope they've left you something to drink – you should have come sooner.'

Missing Thelma's blameful glance at Nell, Aunt Phyllis tried to catch her husband's eye, waving above the sea of heads and summoning him. Eventually he came, holding his bottle aloft as he forged a passage towards the latecomers, a similar height and build to Nell's father, though less poker-faced.

But even as Nell returned his kiss, she was gazing intently over his shoulder at the others.

'Right, let me go and collar them!' Upon the final line being hollered, Phyllis wobbled back to the gathering. 'Settle down, boys, settle down!' Then, with order half-restored, she led forth her sister-in-law and the mesmerised Nell to introduce them. 'Ronald, I don't want to curtail your fun, but let me just acquaint your pals with Aunty Thelma and your cousin.'

Tall and bony, the image of his father, except with pimples, Ronald bade a cheery greeting to the new arrivals, as did his sisters – all three cousins older than Nell, in their twenties – whilst their mother turned to those in khaki and began counting them off on her fingers. 'Now, let me see if I can remember all their names – no, don't tell me, Margaret!' Her elder daughter had been about to leap in. 'This is George, Sid – no, Stan, oh, I'm so sorry! – John, Reg, and last, but by no means least, Billy.'

Nell's heart was already spinning, having flipped over in shock at her first glimpse of the latter, who epitomised the phrase 'tall, dark and handsome' – if a little chubby. Formally introduced to the young soldiers, she could only blush as Billy extended a confident handshake to her mother, his accent most definitely from the heart of London.

'Very pleased to meet you, Mrs Spottiswood!' Then, just as quickly, whilst Nell remained slack-jawed, he grasped her hand too and shook it firmly, smiling with genuine warmth – some might say impishness – into her face. 'You too, Miss Spottiswood.'

'Nell.' She managed to find her voice, and smiled as she withdrew her hand, which felt as if it had touched a live wire, then moved it along the row to be shaken by the rest, one after another.

'It's *Eleanor*,' corrected Mrs Spottiswood, though her exasperation was mild, and to her sister-in-law and the rest of the gathering she jokingly complained, 'Really, you give your child a lovely name and what does she do but adulterate it!'

'A rose by any other name!' Billy's eyes were warm and mischievous as they rested on Nell's blushing face, only to receive a mute warning for this blatancy.

But her mother seemed very taken with the tall and good-looking young man, indeed with all of those who surrounded her, beaming in that coy fashion which always embarrassed Nell. '*You're* not from round here, Billy!' She wagged her plump finger at him. Nell wanted to drag one of Aunt Phyllis's antimacassars over her head.

'Ah, I can see there's no fooling you, Mrs Spottiswood!' Billy, with his sparkling blue eyes, had one of those faces that looked as if it were permanently laughing, but there was such kindness in it too, that no one could take offence at its teasing. 'No, I have to confess I'm one of your perishing southerners – so is Johnny here.'

'Nonsense!' tinkled Thelma Spottiswood. 'We're very happy to have you in our midst, all of you.' Inconveniently overwhelmed by a hot flush, she shed her hat and tried to fluff up the dark-grey waves beneath, which were soaked in perspiration, at the same time wafting her face. 'Goodness, I thought it was hot enough out there – do excuse me!'

'I'll fetch you a drink of water!' Billy shot off, soon coming back to press a glass into her hand. A crimson-faced Thelma sipped at it gratefully until recovered. Following which, the bout of polite interrogation continued, most of it directed at the handsome Billy, with whom she was obviously smitten – as were Margaret and Daphne, saw Nell, for they clung on his every word.

'And are you and your friends liking it in York?'

'Oh, you bet,' vouched Billy, with a smiling glance at Nell. 'Not to mention it's a darned sight safer than the capital at the moment, what with Jerry creeping nearer by the day. Can't help worrying about my old mum, though.'

Thelma Spottiswood sympathised; Nell, too, managing to display similar condolence, as he looked at her quite brazenly.

At his mention of the enemy, Daphne's plain face had turned anxious. 'I heard some people at church this morning saying the Germans've already landed and the government's kept quiet about it.'

'Don't you think we'd have seen them by now?' Touring the room with his bottle, her father remained calm and kind, though there was a hint of anger in his eye for those who had caused such disaffection. 'Come on, I thought this was meant to be a party?'

With his words, it was back to another singsong, Margaret and Daphne swooping on their handsome visitor, one either side of him as they caroused. Provided with food and drink, Nell and her mother were to sway happily in time to the music, though Thelma didn't actually know many of the words. Despite being sandwiched between his hostesses, Billy seemed unable to keep his eyes off the attractive dark-haired girl who stood out from the rest, not only because of her height, and though she persisted in turning her back on him, Nell herself could not resist sneaking an admiring look.

'Well, I'm glad to see you've shed that maungy expression,' observed Thelma, causing her daughter's face to snap up from her glass. 'Kicking up such a fuss about wanting to traipse around town on a Sunday, looking into closed shop windows – I told you you'd have a much better time here. See? Mother knows best!'

Sorry for all the horrible thoughts she had entertained earlier, Nell smiled warmly for her mother – the one she genuinely regarded as Mother, and not the faceless one who had given her away – and had to agree that it was a more enjoyable evening than she could ever have forecast.

So enjoyable, in fact, that she and Thelma were still to be found there at ten o'clock.

Then – 'Hush, everyone!' A tousle-haired Uncle Cliff urged the roisterers to stop. And they heard that ominous wail that all had come to dread.

'Oh bother!' exclaimed Thelma. 'I was just about to suggest we make a move.'

But there were more fragile souls to be comforted, Uncle Cliff laying a firm hand on Daphne's shoulder. 'Don't worry, love, it'll only be another false alarm.'

'Will it, though?' Her pasty face had turned even whiter, and her behaviour nervy. 'This could be it.'

'Be assured, Daphne,' laughed her Aunty Thelma, a stalwart of the Women's Voluntary Services. 'In the unlikely event that they were to breach our defences, there are millions of us ready to take up arms before we'd allow them to get to our children. Your uncle's showed me how to use his gun, and God help the first German who tries his bullying tactics on Eleanor!'

Mimicking this bold example, despite her own twinge of nerves, Nell gave her cousin a reassuring smile, and assisted her to the exit.

With others taking care of Daphne, Cliff put on his tin helmet and herded everyone towards the Anderson shelter in the garden. 'By, it's going to be a tight old squeeze tonight.'

'Some of you'd better come in ours!' summoned a next-door neighbour, invoking the group to split in half and move after him. 'Bring your glasses with you if you like!'

'Er, not the bottles as well!' Cliff objected, but in vain. He uttered a groan, then, after going round turning off the gas and electricity supplies, hurried after the others.

It was dark outside. With those around her toting glasses of beer or sherry, Nell found herself guided by competent male hands towards the even darker interior of the shelter, which smelled of damp earth. Uncle Cliff had rigged up a light of sorts, but they couldn't turn it on yet, and as they filed in, everyone seemed to be tripping over everyone else's feet as well as the items of comfort that had been deposited here in case of a drawn-out siege: bottles of water, a torch, a paraffin stove, a kettle, cups, magazines, tins and boxes of essentials. Her mother's plump bottom directly ahead of her, head down and bent almost double, Nell shuffled and groped her way in, intending to take a seat beside her mother on one of the bunks that Cliff had fitted on two sides. But somehow, amidst all the fumbling, one of the young soldiers managed to engineer a place for her elsewhere, leaving her sandwiched between him and the one called Billy. Then, with ranks of bodies squashed together, the unnerving wait began.

The light had been turned on now, though it was still very dim. There was desultory chat as they sipped their drinks and waited. Nell herself remained speechless, for she had just felt the back of Billy's hand caress her thigh. Jammed into place, it was impossible for her to move out of range, and so she remained stiff as a poker on the edge of the bunk, hiding her discomposure in her glass and trying not to flinch, as the hand continued its secret stroking.

With no word to the contrary, Billy seemed to take this as an invitation to go further. To her shock, whilst casually chatting to the others, and unnoticed in the poor light, he worked his arm round behind her and tugged her blouse from under the band of her skirt, slipped his hand beneath it, and began to caress her bare back. Nell developed instant goose bumps, and dared not move as the hand grew ever more adventurous, stroking its way underneath her perspiring armpit and brushing the tips of its fingers against her breast. Outraged at his nerve, Nell immediately clamped her arm down on it to prevent any further indignation, growing redder and redder, and trying to retain her look of interest as Aunty Ethel related each step of her recent medical procedure.

Undeterred, a twinkling Billy – obviously greatly enjoying this assault – managed to release his trapped digits from beneath the moist heat of her arm, and diverted his efforts. Nell shivered in anticipation as his hand meandered seductively downwards over her spine and began to invade the waistband of her skirt. She bent forward as if to attend to some interesting morsel of conversation, though her intention was to prevent this rude foray. She half succeeded. The waistband too tight a squeeze, Billy had to content himself by wiggling a finger against the swell of her buttock. Then, a press stud burst with an audible pop. As alarmed as she, Billy quickly withdrew his hand and pretended to examine the sleeve of his battledress.

Everyone looked at him. 'Was that you, Billy?' laughed Aunty Phyllis.

'Yes, I don't think this uniform's quite up to my bulging biceps,' joked Billy, the object of some amusement. 'I shall have to get out me needle and thread when I get back to billet.'

Phyllis glanced around for her emergency sewing box. 'Oh, I'm sure one of us can do it while we're wait—'

'Thank you very much, but don't you go bothering yourself, Mrs Spottiswood!' he cut in hastily. 'They teach us how to do that sort of thing in the army – it's nothing much anyway. And if my seam's the only thing that explodes tonight I'm sure we'll all be heartily glad.'

But the ensuing ripple of laughter was curtailed upon the rumble of a distant explosion, and at once everyone's attention was back on the threat.

A faint burst of machine-gun fire had Daphne almost hysterical. 'What if there's gas?' In the claustrophobic surroundings, she was already gulping for air.

Those around were quick to douse her shrieks. 'You'll hear the rattle,' said her father calmly. 'And we've got our masks. Don't worry.'

Even so, the tension became palpable, each ear pricked for imminent disaster. With one arm tightly around Daphne, Uncle Cliff took quiet possession of his wife's hand and gripped it, each of the other men doing likewise with the woman who was seated next to him.

Billy went further. Appointing himself as Nell's protector, he clamped his arm around her soft flesh and leaned intimately towards her, whilst she was forced to sit there with a rapidly beating heart, as much intent on Billy as on the bombers, wondering what he would get up to next, and if her skirt would fall down when she finally rose to leave.

After what seemed like only minutes to a stimulated

Nell, but an interminable wait to the others, the all-clear finally sounded. Thoroughly relieved, the occupants dribbled from the musty shelter into the garden, breathing in sweet air, extending their upper limbs to a sky that was not black but a very deep and romantic shade of blue, stamping their cramped feet, and handing round cigarettes. A secret smoker, Nell was forced to decline as a packet was handed to her, knowing her mother would criticise. Still unnerved herself, not by the bombers but by what had occurred in the shelter, she deftly refastened the press stud on her skirt, and in kindly fashion enquired if her mother was all right.

'Of course I am!' announced Thelma with bravado. 'It'll take a lot more than that to frighten me – but thank you for asking, dear.'

Nell squeezed her mother's plump arm, but even as she did this, her eyes were darting around to pinpoint her impudent assailant.

He was behind her, saying in a quiet murmur to his friend John, 'Wonder if anyone copped it – sounded not too far away. I hope Ma's all right.' He spoke not of his mother, but their landlady on the other side of the city.

'We *really* must be going now,' Nell's mother was saying. 'It's terribly late and I want to make sure Wilfred's safe – he'll be concerned about us too.'

'Stan says he and the boys'll escort you home, Aunty Thelma,' piped up Ronald.

'Well, let's all have another drink first to calm the nerves,' motioned his father, still with his arm around his whey-faced daughter, and coaxing everyone else indoors to be bolstered with what little alcohol was left.

Lagging behind, so as to give Billy a telling-off, Nell found herself dragged to the rear of an outbuilding, where the boldest of kisses was delivered to her lips. Her protest stifled, she had no option but to kiss him back with equal passion, pushing her mouth against his and squashing her whole body against him.

It was darker behind the asbestos shed, but not so dark that their fumbling outline could not be seen. Though she was enjoying this with every fibre of her body, Nell soon broke free and rebuked him heartily, thumping his chest in playful dissent.

'You rat!' she hissed at his laughing face. 'You sat beside me only days ago and said nothing whilst I grumbled on about having to come to this blasted party instead of being out with you – why didn't you tell me you knew Ron?'

'I wanted to surprise you.' Billy giggled merrily at having incited such a display, then gasped and chuckled as she thumped him again.

'You certainly did that! I almost had kittens.'

'So you're not pleased to see me then?' Lower lip jutting, he rubbed his chest as if winded.

'You rotter, you know I am!' And she kissed him again, even more zealously this time, the heat of it travelling to her groin. Feeling his hand cup her breast, she squeaked from the side of her mouth, 'Behave – we might be caught!' But Billy only shook with mirth, and continued to press his ardour, and she to return it.

Drawing breath, Nell glanced around quickly to check they were still unobserved, then asked with eyes agleam, 'Did I do a good job of pretending we were strangers?'

'Impeccable.' He tugged her groin back against his, wriggling in pleasure.

'And no thanks to you!' She physically berated him again.

'Oy! I'll have you for assault and battery.' Billy faked offence. 'Your mother seemed to like me well enough. Maybe I should change the object of my affections.'

Laughingly dismissing this, Nell pressed her face into his warm chest and hugged his khaki-clad form for all she was worth, breathing in the scent of tobacco and beer and the man himself.

'Seriously, though, your mum did seem to like me,' put in Billy. 'Why don't we just –?'

'No!' Nell forestalled him. 'I know what you're going to suggest, and coming clean would be the biggest mistake ever. Don't let Mother fool you. She might well approve of you as a champion of our nation, and so might Father, but once they've been alerted that I have a chap my life will become even more regulated. And that's the last thing I want – oh, I still can't get over this lovely surprise! My dear, gorgeous Bill.' She hugged him tightly and he hugged her back, not one trace of self-consciousness between them, as if they had known each other for years instead of just three weeks.

It had been one of those breathtaking events that happen out of the blue. Nell had not gone looking for love at all. In fact, she had been quite disposed to spend that particular evening in more serious pursuit at her first-aid class. It was from there that she and two pals had been ambling home through town, heading innocently for their bus stop, when a group of soldiers had – there was no other word for it – a pounced on them, and, the boys linking the girls' arms in a firm hold, had commandeered their company for the rest of the night. They had been such a friendly, jocular lot that their cheek could not possibly give offence – not to mention that the girls were eager to seize any bit of excitement on offer, and had readily accepted the soldiers' invitation for drinks at Betty's – even though Nell had never entered a bar in her life.

It was to be the first of many dares she had accepted during this brief enthralling period. Madly in love with Billy, and being compelled to face her own mortality like countless others, Nell wanted to taste everything life had to offer. She had known nothing whatsoever about sex prior to meeting him – did not really know the whole of it even now – for neither her mother nor her school had enlightened her about such an unthinkable subject. But the passion he engendered within her, the overwhelming urge to discover, was almost unstoppable tonight . . .

Then, in a trice Billy's smile had faded, and his voice was reticent as he stroked her and admitted, 'I've another surprise, only part of it good, I'm afraid. The boys and me have been called back down south.' At Nell's utterance of dismay, he gripped her arms and drove the sombre expression from his face as he added, 'But at least they've given us a weekend leave before we go! It means you and me can . . . well, you know . . . if you want to.' His eyes probed hers, brimming with enticement. 'Will you come away with me?'

In that bittersweet moment, Nell did not know whether to cry at his leaving, or rejoice at this opportunity to spend the night together. She chose the latter, giving breathless reply. 'Oh, Billy, do you have to ask?' And her expression poured with willingness as she gazed into that fine-looking face that shone with love for her.

'I hoped you'd say that, so I've already booked a place in Scarborough – actually, a pal's arranged it for me, it belongs to his aunty. I got him to say we'll be on honeymoon.' He shared a grin with her. 'It's nothing posh, I'm afraid, and it's full of evacuees, but everywhere else is taken by the army.'

'It doesn't matter, so long as we can be together!' Nell performed a little dance of joy. There followed a brief run-through of Billy's secret plan – where to meet, what to bring – then Nell voiced her one worry. 'I'll have to fabricate an excuse for my parents . . .'

'Oh, well, that's it then, we'll have to call it off.' He was obviously joking.

She pressed herself against him, seduction in her eyes. 'Don't you dare! Seriously, though, it's going to be very cloak and dagger, they always want to know my every movement.' She had only managed to meet him by coinciding their assignations with her first-aid classes and pretending she would be staying behind to chat with female friends.

Billy thought of something else. 'Would they open any letters I might send?'

'What do you mean *might* send?' she scolded. 'I'll expect one every single day – that's how often I'll be writing to you.'

Billy grinned, and said that of course he would.

Nell told him then, 'No, they don't go so far as to open my mail, but one never knows what they might do if they're suspicious, so maybe you could send them via Mrs Precious.' This was Billy's landlady in York, with whom she was acquainted. 'Then I could collect them on my way home from work.'

But then her eyes misted over, and she clung to him, her joy over the weekend tryst overshadowed by the thought that it would signal his departure. 'Oh God, how am I ever going to exist without you?'

Billy was trying to quash her look of despair with a beer-flavoured kiss when a male voice called, 'Are you out there, Eleanor?'

Both of them instantly alert, Billy gestured for her to remain silent, then stepped from behind the shed and greeted the intruder. 'No, just me, I'm afraid, chum, enjoying the last of me fag.' He drew Ronald to him and kept him occupied, allowing Nell to sneak around the far side of the shed, and along the gap between that and the fence. On tenterhooks as her feet encountered dried and crackling branches, she finally managed to reach the outside closet.

A few moments later there came the sound of a clanking chain and flushing, and Nell emerged. Ronald turned at the sound and exclaimed, 'Ah, there you are! Aunty Thelma's keen to be off, I think.' Then all three went back into the house.

'We do have indoor facilities,' chided Aunt Phyllis when it was announced where Ronald had found her, obviously embarrassed at being thought of as the poor relation in front of visitors, and especially her sister-in-law Thelma, who always displayed the best.

Noticing bits of foliage stuck to her clothes, Nell brushed them away and looked flustered. 'I just thought as I was out there – right, I'm ready when you are, Mother.'

Stan moved forward to fulfil his guarantee, but: 'We'll all escort you,' put in Billy, and, grinning encouragement, he crooked each arm and invited the women to link theirs with him. 'Jerry won't dare harm you with us in tow.'

Nell felt a rush of warmth, but looked to her mother before making a move.

Thelma appeared similarly pleased, though tendered, 'Is it not out of your way, boys?'

'No! We'll be heading towards town anyway.' And so, at Billy's generous insistence, Thelma and Nell hooked their arms through his.

'How come you always get the girls?' teased his army pals as they made their exit, yawping goodbyes as they left.

With everyone slightly tipsy, weaving a rather uneven route through the blackout, the soldiers continued to be good company on the way home. With her mother obviously taken with their repartee, Nell sought to enlist the young men as support, and aired the topic she had been wanting to put forth for a while.

She began with a positive comment, trying to sound chatty as they ambled along with the others close behind and the whiff of cigarette smoke on the air. 'Mrs Benson thinks I should easily get my first-aid diploma. Apparently I'm one of her top pupils.' It was not in Nell's character to brag, but in her mother's case it always paid.

'I should hope so.' Thelma withdrew a handkerchief from her bag and dabbed it over her perspiring brow, adding to the man on her arm, 'Eleanor had a very good education, Billy. She was always top of the class – and head girl of her school. We're very proud of her.'

'I can tell that, Mrs Spottiswood.' Billy smiled through the dark, and secretly squeezed Nell's arm in the crook of his, as his sweetheart continued:

'She says, that it seems such a waste not to make full use of it, and that I should volunteer for one of the first-aid posts on an evening, but I've been thinking, I'd like to do something even more positive for the war effort – certainly do more than sit behind a typewriter.' Nell worked in an office of the civil service, but was still on the lower rungs of the ladder. 'You know, to feel that I was really doing something tangible to help – like you and father, and these brave chaps here. So what if I applied to become a nurse?'

'As a full-time occupation?' quizzed her mother doubtfully. 'After your father went to all that trouble to get you the job? Throw away your typing and shorthand qualifications?'

'They wouldn't be wasted!' Nell hated her working environment, but for now sought to cajole her mother with the premise, 'I can always return to the office after the war.'

'That's true, Mrs Spottiswood!' chipped in one of the squaddies from the rear. 'They're crying out for nurses. My sister's gone to be one, and very proud of her we are.'

Thelma glanced round briefly at the speaker, and then back at her daughter. 'Yes, but the training would take years, wouldn't it? The war might be over –'

'Oh, I don't mean to go on the register,' said Nell quickly. 'That would take years, yes. I just mean in an assistant capacity.'

Her mother tutted. 'Why not be a proper nurse? That's just like my daughter!' She glanced around to roll her eyes at the soldiers. 'Always goes for half-measure because she can't be bothered!'

Nell felt belittled, and was glad of Billy's support.

'I can't believe that, Mrs Spottiswood. She strikes me as very capable.'

'Yes, I agree, she is, *when* she puts her mind to it – and she'd want to be, the money that's been spent on her,' laughed the woman on his right, using his arm to steady herself as she tottered off a kerb, in spite of there being a white line to define it.

Nell jumped in, craning her neck around Billy to exclaim, 'Well, that's partly what swayed it, Mother!' She had to box clever here, for Mother was touchy on the subject of finances, there must be no intimation of poverty, even though any reduction in Nell's wage *would* mean hardship. The Spottiswoods had sacrificed much in their pursuit of their daughter's betterment. 'I wouldn't be able to pay my way if I had to fork out for the registration fee, the textbooks, the exams, pencils, et cetera . . .'

'And if you want her to go back to secretarial work after the war, Mrs Spottiswood –' began Billy.

'Of course we do, she has a fine career ahead of her!'

'Until she marries, naturally,' added Billy, receiving a swift dig from Nell's elbow.

'That will definitely be a long way off,' laughed Thelma. 'We've invested so much in her, the last thing we want is for her to throw it all away by tying herself to the first young man who comes along, and to become a dull little housewife.'

'But you're a housewife and you're not dull,' flattered Billy.

Nell's mother gave a simpering laugh. 'Oh, you're so gallant, dear! But no, Eleanor's father and I have agreed – he's very progressive that way – the further she climbs in her career, the more assured her future. If she does choose to marry, when she's much, *much* older, well, by then she will be able to raise her sights considerably.'

Billy seemed unfazed, laughing as he asked, 'What if she has other ideas?'

Again Nell dealt him a nudge that warned, *I'm going to kill you if you don't shut up!* But to her mother she said, 'We're getting off the subject here! As Reg said before, Mother, they're crying out for nurses of any variety. Mrs Benson tells me the time I spent helping you look after Grandma should ensure that I can attain my certificate of home nursing.' For the last couple of years until her grandmother had recently passed away, of her own volition Nell had helped her mother tend the bedridden old lady. It had been her own idea, too, to attend the first-aid course. 'I do so want to do my bit, and I just thought you'd prefer it if I kept my options open for after the war . . .'

With Mother still looking unsure, perhaps a little dig was warranted. 'Of course, with the wage being only two pounds a week, I realise that would leave you short –'

'It won't make *that* much difference.' Thelma turned airy.

'So you don't mind then?' badgered Nell.

'Oh, I suppose it's a reasonable enough suggestion,' decided her mother, wanting to leave the subject behind, for the lateness of the hour had just caught up with her. 'I'll speak to your father about it.'

'Oh, good!' Guessing it would have met with blank refusal had the soldiers not been there, Nell grinned at Billy in relief, and experienced a surge of enthusiasm at the prospect of taking a genuine part in the defence of Britain. 'I'll apply as soon as I can get my certificates and references then.' In fact she had already filled in the pink application form of the Civil Nursing Reserve.

Almost to the avenue where they lived, Thelma showed reluctance to leave the young soldiers. 'Well, boys, it's been thoroughly marvellous having your company, but we'll say goodnight to you here, so as not to delay you. Thank you so much for accompanying us.'

'The pleasure's all ours, Mrs Spottiswood!' Billy released her arm, and to murmurs of agreement from his friends, added, 'We hope to meet you again sometime – oh, I almost took this one by mistake!' Pretending that he had been about to move off with Nell still attached to his arm, he donned his wide, attractive smile and made great ceremony of handing the daughter over. 'That'd earn me a right ticking off, and no mistake!'

And upon Thelma's laughing agreement, he managed to slip a secret wink to Nell, before he and his friends melted into the night.

'They were nice sociable chaps, weren't they?' opined her mother, as she and Nell undertook the last fifty yards through the darkness unescorted. 'Especially Billy. And so good-looking – distinguished, even. I wonder what he did before the war?'

Her mind still crammed with thoughts of her loved one, the smell and touch of him, Nell responded without thinking. 'He's a carpenter.'

'I never heard that arise in conversation,' frowned Thelma.

Realising her mistake, Nell said quickly, 'I think I overheard Ronny mention it.'

Her mother issued a sage nod. 'Yes, I thought with that accent it had to be something, well, practical shall we say – not that it matters,' she added charitably, 'he's the salt of the earth.'

It would matter if you knew I was planning to marry him, though, came Nell's grim thought.

'With chaps like him we're sure to win – oh, thank goodness, your father's safely home!' Thelma had noticed that the gate was open. Her husband always did this, no matter how many times she went to close it after him, and in the knowledge that he was unharmed, her next comment was tinged with displeasure. 'I do hope he hasn't brought the stench of beer and cigarettes home with him again. Your Aunty Phyllis might not care that her upholstery reeks like a saloon bar, but I do. He seems to have gone completely wild since he joined that Home Guard.'

Nell clicked the latch behind them. 'Do you mind if I rush straight to bed? Or I'll never get up for work in the morning.'

As she headed upstairs, her mind and body were ticking over at the thought of her coming weekend with Billy.

2

It turned out that she was to be late for work anyway, but it didn't matter for so were plenty of others. The previous night's raid had been successful – for Jerry that was – sixty-nine houses near the cemetery being damaged, leaving two seriously injured, over one hundred and fifty with minor wounds, and causing all sorts of problems with the flow of traffic around York's narrow streets, mostly due to sightseers clustering to gawp.

Apart from twittering over the matter with colleagues when she finally arrived, for once Nell was to suppress her curiosity and focus on more pertinent matters. Hence, over the next few days and evenings, eager for change – eager for anything that might help the time up to meeting Billy go more quickly – she was to acquire her two certificates, plus the necessary references, one from her first-aid instructor, the other from her old headmistress, and then submit her application to be a nursing auxiliary. Applying personally in her lunch hour on Thursday, her keenness, intelligence and smart appearance being viewed most favourably, on the heels of her interview came acceptance.

It was with pride that she was able to announce to her mother that evening, 'I'm going to be working on one of the ambulance trains – I start a week on Monday!'

For once, Thelma was magnanimous. 'Very well done, dear!'

Basking in this praise, Nell chattered away about her new post whilst her mother carried on preparing the evening meal, which smelled delicious as usual.

'But won't your employer require a month's notice?' cautioned Thelma, looking suddenly distracted as beads of moisture sprang to her brow.

'No, they're willing to accept a week as it's such a worthy cause,' said Nell, her mind moving to Billy, with whom she had managed to steal a few hours on Tuesday evening after first aid, but who remained ignorant of her success. She couldn't wait to give him the news, and the thought of this made her clasp her hands. 'Isn't it exciting! But I'll miss my friends, of course.' Having struggled to devise a plan of how to gain parental consent to go away without them, she had now seen a way forward. 'Oh, before I forget, Barbara's parents have invited me to spend the weekend at their house in Scarborough. Was it all right to accept?'

Slightly hot and bothered as she went about the kitchen, Thelma paused in her preparation of dinner. 'Barbara . . . was that the girl you introduced me to in town the other week?'

'No, that was Enid.'

Her mother looked only slightly relieved. 'Good, she wasn't the kind I'd like you to spend time with. Very flighty.' She elbowed her daughter out of the way in order to transport a saucepan from the gas stove to the sink. 'Will you please shift? And hand me that masher – and lay the table, your father will be in any second.' Once assisted, she drained the potatoes, raising a brief cloud of steam from the sink, then began to mash them as she went on to ask, 'Well, who is this Barbara then?'

'Oh, just a workmate.' Collecting a handful of knives, forks and spoons, Nell tried to sound casual, but it obviously emerged as dismissive as she went to the dining room.

'Really, Eleanor! She might be only a workmate to you, but she obviously holds you in much higher regard, or why would her parents have been kind enough to invite you into their home for the weekend? Having said that, I'd rather have met her before you accepted.'

'She's a perfectly respectable girl,' replied Nell, 'you've no need to interrogate her.'

'I'd much rather form an opinion on that for myself – and don't be so insolent!' Thelma's cross response was due as much to the sweat that was streaming down her temples as to her thoughtless daughter.

'Sorry, I didn't mean it how it sounded.' Nell tried to be helpful, lifting the warm plates off the rack before tendering, 'So will you ask Father if it'll be all right?'

Her mother gave a snort. 'I'm sure he'll say the same as me – it will have to be all right, seeing as it would be rude to rescind your acceptance! Don't mention it at the table or you'll give him indigestion. I'll speak to him later. Oh, the things you land me with!' Having quickly drained all the vegetables and replaced them near the stove to keep warm, she went to throw open the larder door, tapping her lips thoughtfully as her eyes ran over the contents. 'Now, what do I send?'

'What do you mean?'

'Well, you can't arrive at someone's house empty-handed! Not in these times of shortage.'

Nell gave a negating smile. 'Barbara's parents won't need it, they're very well-off.'

This was rather condescending in her mother's opinion. But, before Thelma could object again, Nell added, 'What I meant was, it's not just me going, there's a whole group of us, half a dozen – it's a huge house apparently, so they can't be short of a bob or two.'

Her mother looked slightly relieved at not having to plunder her stock cupboard. 'Well, I've no wish to insult – but you must reciprocate. Barbara must come to us sometime.'

Nell gave a quick nod. 'Should I take my ration book,

do you think?' Billy had warned her that she would have to hand this over to the proprietor of the hotel. This might be difficult as her mother had charge of it, but she added now, 'Her parents might need it so they can purchase extra food.'

Returning to check on the bread sauce, her mother voiced scepticism. 'If they've got the wherewithal to have half a dozen house guests for the weekend they must shop on the black market.' Nevertheless, she undertook to relinquish the ration book come Friday evening. 'Oh, here's Daddy – right on time as usual!'

The next day, after a quick bite to eat, Nell hurried round to her lover's billet during the hour that had been allocated for dinner, to convey the good news that she could go away with Billy as planned. He wasn't there, of course. Every morning since he had arrived in York, straight from the beaches of Dunkirk and carrying only a mattress and a small bag of rations, along with wounded pride, a lorry had collected him and other infantrymen from their billet, and taken them to a camp for exercise. But Nell left a message with Mrs Precious, just so he would not fret that he might not see her again before being sent to London.

Then it was back to her typewriter, the rest of the afternoon feeling as long as a week.

Directly after tea, Nell asked that she might be excused, and ran up to pack a small suitcase, her mother calling after her, 'I've laid out clean underwear for you!'

Shouting merry thanks, Nell reached behind a row of books to retrieve the carefully folded package she had recently hidden there. Not daring to unwrap the silken nightdress, which had left her virtually penniless until next pay day, she slipped it directly into the case alongside her old one – better take that or Mother might be suspicious. Straight on top went a layer of suitable clothing and a bathing costume. Hidden though it might be, the nightdress provoked a momentary quiver. She was sexually ignorant in regard to the mechanics, though not so totally naive that she did not know the gamble she was taking. A man and a woman in the same bed . . .

But then her parents slept in the same bed, and they had no children – and at this moment Nell could not have cared less, for who knew how long they would all have to live? The excitement and urgency of being with Billy overruling any risk, she snapped the case shut, then it was back down the stairs.

'Let us look at you!'

Hurrying through the hall to the sitting room, a suitcase in one hand, her gas mask container slung over her shoulder, Nell answered her parents' demand, reduced to a schoolgirl again as she posed for their inspection.

Father had spread before him on a maroon chenille tablecloth the small arsenal he had accumulated. Some of it was from his exploits as an officer in the Great War, such as the Webley service revolver, the lethal-looking bayonet, and the Luger automatic pistol taken from a dead German. Other weapons were home-made – a brass knuckleduster and a garrotte. To Nell he didn't appear to be doing anything specific with them, but he just liked to exhibit them from time to time, as if to reassure his family that he would be ready to protect them if the Germans did land. But his attention was now for his daughter. 'That's more like the girl I know!' announced the grey face, with a pleased smile for her lack of make-up. Then he dipped into his pocket and pulled out half a crown. 'Here you are, my little chickadee, treat yourself.'

Nell reached out and thanked him with a warm smile.

'Better take a mackintosh in case it rains,' warned her mother, rising to go and fetch this, whilst Nell exchanged an amused but frustrated glance with her father.

'Let her do it if it keeps her happy,' Wilfred advised her,

as his wife folded the mackintosh over the crook of Nell's arm.

'Now, have you got everything – identity card?'

'Yes, Mother!'

'Let me check your case.'

'There's no time!' Nell dashed for the door. 'I've a bus to catch.' For once, she thanked providence for the rationing of petrol. There was no danger of Father offering to chauffeur her into town: he was saving all his coupons towards a decent family outing.

Her parents came to see her off, their exit disturbing a sparrow that was enjoying a dust bath amongst the geraniums, and drawing a tut from Wilfred over the desecration of his prized garden.

'Now, don't do anything to show us up,' warned her mother. 'And if you hear the sirens go straight to a shelter!'

'I won't – I mean, I will!' Nell called gaily over her shoulder, and hurried away up the avenue.

Not until out from under father's eye did she take a little cardboard pot of rouge from her gas mask container and smear some on her lips, checking her appearance in her compact mirror, before catching her bus, nerves gurgling in her craw all the way into town.

And there was Billy! As handsome as a film star, waiting for her at the prearranged spot. Waving frantically to him through the window, she jumped off the bus almost before it stopped, and rushed to meet him as he too accelerated forth. Thrilled by what lay ahead, they exchanged a quick bright-eyed kiss, then spurted to catch their connection to Scarborough, which was about to depart further along the kerb.

Once in their seats, holding hands and grinning like Cheshire cats, they spoke little to each other as the bus chugged jerkily on its way out of the city, for besides them being so keyed up, there were too many passengers who might overhear intimacies.

However, as the bus paused to give way to a tank, Nell did reveal her successful appointment. 'Guess who's to be a nurse?'

'Oh, when?'

'Monday week!'

'Good for you!' He gave her a commending pat on the hand, before appearing to have second thoughts. ''Ere, you won't be dealing with wounded soldiers, will you?'

'Why, would you be jealous?' teased Nell.

'I flipping-well would, if you'll be running your hands over their bits and pieces!'

She tittered at his rudeness, then moved up close to appease him. 'Well, you've no need to be. I'm led to understand that we'll only be used for evacuating civilians from London to somewhere safe up north.' Then she donned an optimistic smile. 'Maybe we'll be able to meet down there! You could take me to Bermondsey.' This was where he hailed from. 'I'm dying to see it.'

Billy had mixed feelings about this. 'Much as I'd love to see you any time, I'd prefer it to be well clear of London. The way things are heading, it's only a matter of time before they hit us.'

'Hmm, well, I don't relish being bombed either, but I hope I get to do something crucial, that's the whole point of becoming a nurse.' It was Billy who, in part, had inspired her decision. To be so young and yet so totally embroiled in the defence of one's country, he had put her to shame. 'Anyway, let's not talk about the war. Let's concentrate on enjoying ourselves.'

'Oh, I intend to.' Billy gave her his dirty grin as the bus started to move again, then added hastily, 'Speaking about that, you'd better put this on.' After a peripheral glance, and with a definite lack of ceremony, he withdrew a small box from his pocket and slipped it to her.

Taking his lead, Nell lifted the lid of the box in surreptitious manner, and though she would have preferred to exclaim and openly admire its contents, she was to sneak the ring quickly onto her finger and whisper only, 'It's lovely!' before tucking the tiny container out of sight.

But as much as she tried not to draw attention to it, the tips of her thumb and finger itched to examine the golden circle that adorned her wedding finger – not a fake one from Woolworths, as one might expect for an illicit weekend, but a genuine wedding ring – for which she beamed thanks to her lover.

'Only nine carats, I'm afraid.' Bill looked self-effacing, the restrictions of war and not parsimony having barred him from acquiring a twenty-three carat one, as he was quick to explain. 'But I'll be buying you a proper one when it's all over.'

'No you won't,' came her murmured instruction. 'I'll be keeping this one forever.'

Then, sharing a loving smile and a squeeze of each other's hand, they tore their eyes away, and for the rest of the journey were to watch the countryside whiz by, and to mull over tantalising thoughts about the coming night.

With the room in total blackout, and her senses all to pot, there was no way of telling when night became day. Nell gasped as, with the aid of a lamp and snatching a look over Billy's naked shoulder, she consulted his watch on the bedside table. 'You do realise it's almost nine o'clock?' Nine o'clock in the morning that was.

Her bed companion grinned and stretched luxuriously like a cat, sharing a long, loving gaze with her, before hugging her to him and dappling her shoulder with kisses between words. 'Well, the landlady did say to make ourselves at home. Anyway, we can stay in bed all day if we like, we're married.'

Nell chuckled adoringly and returned his hug, shivering at the touch of his lips on her skin. 'Oh, I wish we were, Bill, that we could fall asleep together every night, wake up together like this . . .' Intensely happy, she released her hold on him and extended her hand to properly examine the exquisite gold ring he had bought her, all shiny and new.

Averse to losing any contact with her, however brief, Billy repossessed her hand and kissed it. 'We will one day, I promise. You do believe me, don'cher?' And he beheld her with a face so earnest that it could not possibly tell a lie.

'Of course I do! That goes without saying.' They had discussed this in depth. Aside from her parents not granting permission, Billy had told Nell she was much too young to be left a widow.

'I saw what it was like for my mum after Dad was killed,' he had become serious. 'If anything should happen to me, I couldn't bear the thought of you strugg—'

'Don't!' Shuffling around quickly to synchronise her body to his again, she laid her hand across his lips, her eyes and voice pleading. 'Let's just put everything else aside and enjoy this chance to be together. I can't tell you how wonderful it is.' Totally spellbound, she cupped his cheek and stroked his brow, his ear, his smooth young jaw, feeling so intensely close, yet desiring to be closer still.

Billy agreed, his expression as blissful and contented as Nell's as he tried to pull her even nearer to him, and rubbed his hand from nape to buttock as they kissed again.

At length, he tendered, 'So . . . was it all right then?'

Nell glimpsed again the slight self-consciousness she had witnessed upon first entering the hotel room last night. She had been so worried about her own innocence that it had not occurred to her that Billy might be nervous too, but it had turned out that her lover was as inexperienced as she. 'More than all right,' she murmured lovingly, bestowing more kisses, to which Billy responded by burying his face in her neck, nuzzling around the back of her ear and into her hair.

'But we really ought to get up,' she was finally to say. 'It'll be embarrassing if the landlady sees the light under the door and comes knocking.' The rattling of pots could be heard from downstairs, and the thunder of childish footsteps on the landing as the evacuees returned from breakfast.

'She won't. She thinks we're on honeymoon, remember?' Billy assured her, his face still pressed to her neck, dotting it with kisses.

'Even more embarrassing! Everyone at the breakfast table knowing what we've been up to.' But her smiling embrace was to prove Nell didn't really care. Didn't care about anything but the boy she loved.

Eventually, though, they had to rise. Dressing quickly, with a fond smile for Billy as he too covered his nakedness, Nell waited for him to cease hopping about on one foot, before turning off the lamp. Then, rendered blind, she stumbled her way to the window and pulled aside the blackout curtains to let the sun filter through the network of masking tape. Even lit by sunbeams, the room was not much to speak of, with a cast iron bedstead – with very rumpled sheets – beige lino and two well-worn green rugs, a wardrobe, a washstand, and above this an unframed mirror, plus one or two pictures of moorland and sheep to punctuate the faded wallpaper. But to Nell and her lover it was heaven. Both adjusting their clothes, giggling and whispering to each other, they made their way downstairs to seek breakfast, trying to appear like an old married couple.

The landlady did not bat an eyelid upon announcing she had been keeping something warm for them, and almost immediately they were served with bacon, egg, toast and tea. At least the evacuees had gone off to play, so they were allowed to eat in peace. Tucking in, but remaining self-conscious in an otherwise empty dining room, it was not long before Nell and Billy had cleared their plates, and were escaping into the fresh air.

Despite the fact that Scarborough was under fortification, with barriers, minefields and concrete pill boxes thrown up around the town, and sections of the beach cordoned off with barbed wire, it remained the bustling place of entertainment it had always been – even more bustling, with so many servicemen and children competing for space along the front. Historically a place to sit in deckchairs and listen to the band, the genteel Spa was now under military requisition. Nevertheless there were pleasures to be had amongst the amusement arcades and shellfish stalls, and these Nell and Billy proceeded to chase, undeterred by the sandbags and wire-netting, barely letting go of each other all day – even managing to eat a saucer of cockles with arms entwined, as they bumped and weaved their starry-eyed way in and out of the promenading throng, absorbing all the raucous treats that were on tap.

And when the money ran out, there were self-invented pastimes to supply laughter – even without the glasses of beer partaken at lunch – Nell's companion so easygoing, a delight to be with. For her afternoon recreation he made up a guessing-game, which involved comparing passers-by to animals.

'I can't think what that chap might be,' mused Nell, when it came to her turn, swinging her leg as they sat on a bench along the seafront. 'He's not really like any creature, is he?' Billy was quick to gain points. 'He's a thatched cottage – has to be, with all that hair. Blimey, he's like Moe off the Three Stooges!'

'That's cheating!' She elbowed him laughingly, and drew away to accuse. 'You said it had to be animals.' Even this short gap between them proved too much, her eyes barely able to leave him for one second, as she watched a runnel of sweat filter from his dark hair to his brow, trickling through the creases at the edges of his eyes, then onwards down his firm cheek, before giving in to the urge to dab it away with her finger. 'I'd hate to hear what I remind you of.' But she shuffled back to him again, fondly laying her head on his shoulder.

Billy cuddled up to her, his voice deep and flirtatious as it murmured into her ear, 'I can answer that easy enough – velvet, and chocolate and cream, all soft and sweet.'

'Oh don't say that!' Nell looked and sounded disappointed. 'Not all sugar and spice and things that make one puke.'

'I didn't mean it like that!' Billy laughed. 'Gawd help us – how do you want me to see you then?'

'I'd much rather be thought of as a *femme fatale*.' She adopted an exotic air, her accent foreign and her voice theatrical. 'Dark and mysterious –'

'You're a ruddy mystery all right,' cut in Billy, whipping his jovial face out of reach as she pretended to clip him. Then he sought to explain. 'No, it's just sometimes hard to put a word to a feeling, ain't it? I think you're really nice-looking – that goes without saying.'

His subject flushed with pleasure, but made self-effacing comment. 'Not exactly dainty, though, not like that girl over there.'

'Who cares? Look at the geezer she's with, he's not built like me, is he? No, we're well-matched, you and me. I like something to get hold of.' To Nell's chuckles, he demonstrated this, before adding, 'What I meant about the velvet thing was, your face has this gentle, warm way about it, as if you're always concerned for other people, no sharp edges to it . . .'

'Pudgy,' contributed Nell.

'No! Stop running yourself down. It's a lovely mug. Your skin, it's all creamy, and those chocolatey eyes, it's as if they're reflecting candlelight . . .' His subject gave a squirm of delight, he an embarrassed quip. 'How's that for bleedin' poetry?' Moving on quickly, he asked, 'Okay, what do I remind you of then?'

Nell placed a finger to her chin and looked thoughtful. 'Hmm – a wet dog.'

'Thanks very much!' he sputtered laughingly. 'I needn't ask what you think of my hairy chest!'

Nell laughed too – her face ached with all the laughing she had done over the past twenty-four hours. 'Let me finish! One of my uncles has this black mongrel –'

'Oh, even better!' roared Billy, throwing back his dark curly head.

'– who loves nothing more than to jump in the river, and when he comes out he's all bright-eyed and laughing and boisterous, bursting with life and energy – that's what I love about you,' Nell managed to finish. 'You're so full of fun, and believe me there's such a dearth of it in our house. My parents are such old fogies.'

'Do you ever speculate over what your real ones were like?' asked Billy, who knew her life story.

Nell looked slightly taken aback, for she considered Wilfred and Thelma to be her real parents. They were the only ones she had known, and, perhaps due to their honesty in never hiding it from her that she had been adopted, she felt as secure as if she had been born to them. But then she admitted with a guilty smile, 'Only when my own are annoying me, I wonder if the others were film stars or something exciting like that. But I don't regard them to be real parents – after all, they gave me away, didn't they?'

'They must've been mad.' He squeezed her. 'Well, there'll be bumper fun when we get our own house – and lots of kids.' After sharing a tender kiss, his eyes, and Nell's too, drifted away from each other to watch the youngsters frolicking on the crowded beach with their buckets and spades. 'Shall we join 'em?'

And so they did, removing their shoes and emptying them of sand, then threading their way amongst an ever-growing colony of deckchairs to find an unoccupied patch of beach, where Billy spread his khaki blouse for them to sit on. Then, aware of other people only yards away – old men with knotted handkerchiefs to protect their bald pates and trousers rolled up to the knee, scarlet-faced wives in full corsetry, complete with handbag – in discreet but awkward fashion, both shed their clothes to reveal the swimming costumes worn beneath.

Once settled side by side, looking out to sea over their kneecaps, Nell leaned against Billy, lost in reverie. 'Where shall we live? London or York?'

'I don't give a fig, so long as I'm with you,' he answered, rocking her back and forth, their flesh stuck together in the August heat.

In total agreement, Nell imbibed a deep lungful of all the scents that wafted by – the brine, the shellfish, the donkeys, the frying of chips, the honest sweat – and felt her spirits soar as high as the brilliant sun. Squinting at its reflection glittering on the waves, she exhaled a rapturous sigh. 'We couldn't have asked for a nicer day, could we? I just wish it didn't have to end.'

'Me neither.' He squeezed her gently. 'But we've got most of tomorrow as well.' Then, as his eyes swept her curves, he became aware that her shoulders were quickly turning pink. 'Lord, you're going to have to watch it with your delicate skin.'

Raking her damp fringe from her brow, Nell puffed out her cheeks and fanned her face. 'Yes, I should've brought a hat.'

'Allow me!' said Billy, and, reaching to his pile of clothes, he pulled out his forage cap and stuck it on her head at a jaunty angle. 'There you are, Mrs Kelly! How do you like that titfer?'

The recipient looked proud at first, but then she sniggered and covered her mouth. 'Nelly Kelly – won't Mother be delighted!'

And they found themselves laughing gleefully again, as Billy exhorted, 'Come on, let's go for a dip!' And, ignoring their audience, they ran yelling into the ice-cold sea.

* * *

By the end of an exceptionally fine day, which was to include an abandoned spell of jitterbugging on the dance floor, whilst Billy's olive skin was to assume an attractive shade of tan, Nell found herself crimson. She had won a photographic award as the girl with the most sunburned back on the beach, but it didn't feel much of a privilege now. Even a hastily purchased pot of cold cream failed to ease the fire, and by bedtime she was radiating such heat that her lover could not get near without causing discomfort – hardly conducive to unrestrained passion. All the same, she vowed that there was no way this would prevent her from being in Billy's arms for their final night together.

Afterwards, reluctant to go to sleep, draped only in a sheet, for Nell's burnt skin could bear nothing more, they lay with the curtains apart and their bodies lit by the moon, loath to miss any expression on the other's face, holding hands and murmuring into the night.

'I'm dreading leaving you,' Billy voiced his mixed feelings, gently playing with her fingers throughout, 'but I'm rather glad to have this chance to see my old mum's all right.'

Nell softly agreed. 'You must be worried, and she about you.'

'Yeah, her little baby,' he grinned.

Nell smiled too, knowing that he was the youngest, almost twenty years younger than his eldest sibling. 'I'm more worried in case they send you back to Europe.'

His tanned body heaved a sigh. 'Well, they'll send us sometime, that's for certain. I'll almost be glad in a way . . .'

'Oh, Billy, don't say that!' She knew a little of what he had been through, for in their quieter moments she had coaxed it from him: how he hadn't known where he was going or what was happening, had just done what he was told and gone where he was sent, only to end up on a beach with thousands of his comrades, their backs to the sea; there to wait for days under murderous fire until the rescue boats came; and even more days whilst others boarded ahead of him, forced to watch them sail for England, whilst in the meantime he lost everything – his comrades, his rifle, his equipment, half his uniform, and all personal possessions, even a little china ornament for his mum. As the brave boats had continued to come, he had waded out until the sea lapped his chest, only to wade ashore again when there was no more room aboard; and when his wrung-out carcass was eventually hauled onto a craft and given the tastiest jam sandwich and the best mug of tea he had ever consumed, this was promptly interrupted by a dive-bomber, forcing him once more over the side to swim for his life . . .

At her first cry of anguish, Billy had lifted his head from the pillow. 'No, I mean, if I have to fight 'em, I'd rather it be over there than on our own doorstep – oh, I don't know what I mean, Nelly, it's hard to explain . . .' Allowing his tousled head to fall back, he hesitated for long moments, before proceeding to admit his shame over the benighted inhabitants of Belgium and France. 'Those poor bloody wretches, thinking we'd come to save them – well, we thought we had too,' he interjected a bitter laugh, 'lapped it up, I did, being thought of as a conquering hero, taking souvenirs off the girls – none of them as pretty as you, mind,' he added quickly.

Secure in his love for her, Nell showed this with her smile.

'Didn't think we'd be running for our lives with our tails between our legs,' added Billy, picking absently at the sheet that draped them, 'and leaving the poor blighters to their fate.'

'But you gave of your best, you've no need to be ashamed!' Nell felt tears prick her eyes. Hating that raw anguish, she tried to stroke it away, her hand upon his cheek.

He turned to meet her gaze for a second, love and pity

in his eyes, before averting it to the ceiling. For how could he tell her the real story? That it had been every man for himself. That he had stepped over dead and dying comrades in his haste to escape the blazing hell of Dunkirk. How could he violate such innocence of mind? How could he share with this tender-hearted young thing the sights he had seen: of men's limbs blown to fleshy rags, of their screaming pleas to be put down; how he had clamped his hands over his ears to try and block out their piteous cries of 'Mother' as they died; how he'd frantically dashed their blood and brains and bone from his uniform, as if that would erase the intense humiliation he felt as a soldier, as a man. The ceiling became a battlefield, the whole of it ablaze, he could taste again the smoke, his lungs choking with it, his ears filled with the terrifying shriek of the Stukkas and the hellish shrieks of men, his heart and body leaden with exhaustion and overwhelming loss . . .

All he could murmur now was, 'You've no idea how powerless I felt, Nelly. No idea, and I pray with all my heart you never do, my darlin'. Never.'

Her fingers encased in a grip of steel, Nell tried to ease them out so that she might comfort him, making Billy suddenly aware that he was hurting her.

'Oh, sorry!' He was immediately attentive, yet his face remained etched with atrocious memories.

'No, no . . . I'm not hurt.' And with her hand freed, she was able to stroke him tenderly, trying to impart that she understood, that she loved him more than any other person on earth.

Forgetting her burnt skin, a distraught Billy reacted by hugging her so tightly she could scarcely breathe. Then, just as quickly, he apologised again. 'I just love you so much, you make everything better . . .'

The minutes leaked away, their voices becoming drowsier. Gripped by an awful premonition that she would never see him again, that these were the last moments they would ever share, Nell refused even now to look away, for that would propel her towards the sleep she was trying so hard to fight.

Even after Billy had gradually succumbed, her eyes remained on his dear face, allowing every detail to be imprinted on her memory, gazing, listening to his breath, feeling it on her cheek . . .

She had fallen asleep after all. Her head felt like a ball of fire, and her eyelids were stuck together, but the blinding sun which pierced them told that it was morning. She turned away from the source in discomfort, but could not escape the punishing light that streamed in through the window, and so lay there for a second, rubbing her eyes and attempting to prise them fully open.

Then, feeling the heat of Billy close by, she roused him gently with a kiss, privately wincing under his instinctive caress, for her face was still as a beacon in contrast to the white linen pillowcase. Yet, they made love again, for it need not be said that this might be their last opportunity for a very long time.

'How long do we have?' she later enquired softly, cherishing every second.

Bill lifted an arm to grope on the bedside table. 'Oh, bloody Nora, me watch's stopped. I can smell breakfast, though, so it must be about seven.' With a hasty kiss, he rolled onto the edge of the bed, forwarded the hands of his timepiece, and began to wind it, chatting to her over his shoulder as he did so, before exclaiming, 'Sod it, now I've over-wound the perishing thing!' He gave the wristwatch a hearty shake, then tapped it on the table, but nothing could get it started again.

'Good!' beamed Nell, rolling across the mattress to imprison him. 'We can stay here forever then.'

''Fraid we can't!' Giving her a kiss, then an eye-watering slap on the rear that almost sparked a fight, Billy chivvied her into getting dressed, then both went down to breakfast. His guess had been imprecise, for it was actually closer to eight, and forty-five minutes later they were back in their room, reluctantly, to pack.

This done, Nell took a final look at the bed, her half-wistful gaze noting that the sheets were covered in black hairs from Bill's chest and arms. 'Gosh, it looks like a ruddy dog's slept in it!' And with a false laugh, she made a last-minute effort to brush them off.

'Here, don't forget your budgie box!' Billy noticed her gas-mask container and quickly hooked it over her shoulder. 'Whoops, sorry, forgot about the sunburn!' He gave an apologetic wince, then reminded her, 'Must get your ration book from the landlady as well.'

'Do I have to give this back?' Reluctant to depart, protective of the wedding ring he had given her, Nell was gazing at it now, still upon her finger.

'Are you telling me you want a divorce already?' he scolded with good humour, drawing forth a negating laugh from her. ''Course you must keep it – and take good care of it till we can use it for real. Here!' He took a chain from his pocket and pressed it into her hand. 'I bought you this so's you can thread it through and keep wearing it, even if it ain't on your finger. Don't do it yet, though!' he warned with a smile. 'Else the landlady'll be calling us a pair o' dirty dogs.'

'You are so romantic!' quipped Nell, despite her low spirits. Then she heaved a sigh. 'Well, I suppose we'd better go and catch our bus then . . .'

Downstairs, though, there was to be a reprieve. The landlady, who had shown such kindness all along, now proposed that she look after their luggage so they could catch a later bus, and so, 'Make the most of your honeymoon,' she whispered.

Though at first deeply obliged, and exhilarated at being allowed this extra time together, by the time evening came around the young couple were forced to accept that it might have been better to leave as planned. For this had merely been a stay of execution. Due to Nell's blistered skin they had constantly been forced to seek out shade. Not that it really mattered, for their spirits already resided there.

It was almost a relief to arrive back in York. When they alighted in Exhibition Square, it was to be surrounded by the dozens of airmen and soldiers waiting to catch their buses back to camp after an evening out, all extremely merry. Without aid of a street lamp, which were all painted black, Billy held on tight as he steered Nell towards her bus stop, there to wait with her.

'Leave you on your own and give one of these rag-bags a chance to interfere with you? I don't think!' And he insisted on catching the bus with her, even though it would mean a return trip to town for himself.

But it was merely prolonging the agony. Hand in hand, their pace becoming slower and slower as they followed the white line of the kerb to the end of her avenue, Nell finally drew to a halt and turned to him, her face saying everything. Wearing a similar expression, Billy gave a sigh, at the same time nabbing an automatic look at his watch, forgetting that it was useless.

He gave a mirthless little laugh. 'I'll have to see if Mr Precious can do anything with it – he does a lot of delicate work with instruments so he might be able to. Well, I reckon I oughta go . . .' Implanting a last wistful kiss, then holding Nell at arm's length and gazing into her eyes, he pledged that they would see each other before too long. 'Keep your chin up, gel.' Then, reluctantly, his hands released their hold, and their owner made tracks for his billet.

Unable to bear the poignant departure, her suitcase in hand, Nell immediately turned and hurried for home.

'Ah, the wanderer returns!' announced her father in a pleased manner as she entered. 'We can go to bed.' But as he turned off the wireless and rose, he thought to ask, 'Did you enjoy yourself?' Then he chuckled at her mother. 'From the colour of her face it certainly looks as though she did.'

'Oh yes, it was smashing,' replied the luminous Nell. 'But I'd better not keep you and Mother up any longer.' Case in hand, she made for the stairs. 'I'll tell you all about it tomorrow.'

'We'll look forward to it,' supplied her mother, rising to pat the cushions. 'Heavens, your skin does look angry – dab some calamine on before you go to bed.' Then she made a pensive addition. 'You know, you wouldn't think a weekend is long, but we *really* missed you, didn't we, Father?'

Touched, and rather guilty at deceiving them, and already pining for Bill, Nell felt her eyes start to burn. Hence, she increased her pace. 'I missed you too – goodnight then!'

A lump in her throat, she tried her best not to let it get the better of her as she undressed and climbed into bed. But the moment she laid her head upon the pillow, the image returned of Billy walking away. Then she buried her face under the covers, and quietly sobbed.

3

The next day it was boring old work as usual. Nell was thankful that there would soon be a new career to take her mind off things. But there was a week to get through before then.

How time crawled. It felt like a year had gone past and it was still only Monday teatime. Ever despondent over Billy's departure, Nell sat at the table, nibbling on the home-grown salad, trying to take her mind off him by watching her parents, wondering what was going through their minds as they ate in silence – had it been just herself and Billy at the table she was sure they would have never stopped chattering. Drat! There she was, thinking of him again already.

Only the clicking of Father's false teeth was annoying enough to lure her mind away. Mr Spottiswood had developed the ability to clean the underside of his artificial palette without removing the dentures. Using his tongue to whip any debris from beneath, he rolled the clackers from cheek to cheek and around his entire mouth, giving them a thorough vacuum before fitting them back into place again. Why did he persist in doing that, as if it were some sort of art form? Skilful it might be, but the way it warped his face, the dentures jutting forth as if to pop from his mouth at any minute and making him look like a camel, and that awful clickety-clacking they made, it was so uncouth. Did he assume he was being discreet in not actually removing his teeth, or did he just not care?

Nell's eyes flickered to her mother, who found it as irritating as she did, she could tell that by the slight flare to her nostrils. Yet her mother never dared criticise him, even when he did it at someone else's house. Poor Mother, dying to be considered as a pillar of the community due to her prominent role with the WVS, purchasing its uniform so she could stand out from lesser women, yet brought down to earth by a husband who did not know how to eat in polite company. And that was not all. Mother had tried to allude that it was not the done thing to sit at the table in one's shirt sleeves, but there was Father, lord of the manor, with his jacket off and his sleeves rolled up past his elbows. Nell could not say she blamed him in this heat, but it obviously grated on Mother. How awful to feel that way about someone you were married to: wanting to change them. Nell couldn't ever envisage being annoyed by anything Billy did. She loved the way he walked and talked and ate, the way his giggles shook his entire body – he was a proper giggler, her Bill – all his little fads, such as picking the strands of orange peel out of the marmalade before spreading it on his toast . . .

Trying not to sigh, she crunched the last radish on her plate, laid down her cutlery, and attempted to make conversation.

'One of the girls at work said they found a German parachute in the field at the back of their house after the other night's raid.'

'And would she know what a German parachute looked like if it fell on her?' enquired her father in a supercilious tone. 'No. You want to tell her to watch it, or she'll find herself locked up for spouting such rubbish.'

'It'll be fifth columnists who've planted it,' explained her mother. 'Don't let it frighten you, dear.'

Nell gave a nod and fell silent again. Then, when her

parents had also finished, she helped her mother to clear the table, whilst Father seated himself in his armchair with the evening newspaper.

Her mind far away, wondering whether Billy had reached London yet, she was helping her mother to wash the pots when a disgusted exclamation drew both women's curiosity, and they wandered back to the sitting room.

'What is it, dear?' Thelma asked her husband, tea towel still in hand.

Nell's father regarded her for a moment, the expression on his face turning from annoyance to disgust, as he announced in a tart and slightly melodramatic voice. 'I *was* going to ask what you enjoyed best about your weekend in Scarborough, but I won't trouble you now, for it's quite evident!' And he bequeathed the newspaper, suitably folded to display a laughing photograph of a group of young people in swimming costumes, with Nell at their centre, under the banner: *Girl with the most sunburnt back*.

Nell's heart leaped as her father stabbed a finger at the dark-haired man beside her in the photograph and mouthed sarcasm. 'One didn't imagine your friend Barbara to be so hirsute!'

Her frowning mother snatched up the press and exclaimed, 'Why, that's Billy!'

Wilfred turned on her. 'You knew what she was up to?'

'No! But I know *him* – he was at Ronald's party.' And his wife joined the attack on Nell, saying, 'Someone had better explain themselves!'

Nell twisted her fingers as she fought to deliver an explanation. 'I didn't enter the competition. The photographer just snapped –'

'That is not what we're objecting to, and you know it!' interrupted her mother. 'You didn't think to mention there'd be chaps amongst the group! Did you arrange this at the party, invite Billy along?'

'No!'

'Look at him with his arm around you,' stuttered her father, 'and you with barely a stitch on!'

'I'd never have let you pack your bathing costume had I known!' railed Thelma. 'You let me assume it was an all-girl group – although those other young *ladies* leave much to be desired!'

To Nell's astonishment, she realised then that her mother was under the misapprehension that the strangers in the photograph were part of the fictitious Barbara's group. This being so, things were not half as bad as they could have been. 'It *was* all girls!' she strove to convince her parents. 'We bumped into Billy by accident and he tagged along.'

'To ruin our daughter's reputation!' Wilfred was livid with Nell. 'What have we done to deserve this? There's our Ronald, doing his bit for King and country, his parents proud as punch, showing off the photo of him that appeared in the church magazine, and what sort of pictorial keep-sake do we get of our child? This decadent rubbish!' He slapped the newspaper onto the hearth. 'That's only fit for lighting the fire!'

'I'm ever so sorry,' Nell gushed earnestly to both, 'but it's this war! No one can afford to be serious all the time. Everyone has to grab their chance of having fu—'

'Don't blame Mr Hitler for your behaviour!' interrupted her father. 'Fun? Huh! The war seems to have become an excuse for all manner of immorality under the guise of fun!'

'Quite!' his wife agreed 'She's becoming far too wayward for my liking.'

Nell bit her lip. Thank heaven that neither of them had guessed that she had gone away with Billy alone, and even worse had shared a bed with him. Never in their wildest nightmares could they have conceived such a thing of their well-raised daughter.

'Well, there'll be no more! I'm going to write to this Barbara's parents!' babbled Thelma, hurrying to a bureau and taking out a writing pad and fountain pen. 'Here, you can jot down their full address!'

Nell hovered between panic and impatience. 'It's hardly their fault, I was the one who was snapped by the photographer! I didn't even enter the blasted competition.'

'And you can dispense with that language!' Her father pointed a warning finger that came dangerously close to her face. 'Apologise to your mother!' And after Nell had shown contrition, he added, 'What she said is right, the girl's parents are obviously lax and need to be reminded that they had someone else's daughter in their care!'

'It wasn't their fault!' protested Nell again, but more politely. 'They had as much idea as I did that I was even being photographed!'

'That's hardly relevant,' barked Wilfred. 'And stop arguing!' His scowl served to terminate any further protest. 'For God's sake, girl, you seem to have forgotten there's a war on, that men are out there fighting for their lives whilst you're acting like some –' He broke off with a growl of exasperation.

Don't you think I'm aware there's a war on? railed Nell silently. That I might never see my darling boy again? That all this kidding about of which you so disapprove is just a front to make everyone feel better? But she didn't say it, for she had been raised to respect her parents.

'And as for this chap!' continued her father, seizing the newspaper again and rapping the photograph of Billy with the back of his hand as if wanting to punch the man himself. 'If I catch him pawing you again I'll be writing to his commanding officer!'

'She won't be seeing him again!' pitched in her mother.

'I shan't,' mumbled Nell, eyes to the carpet. 'He's left York.'

'Good – and I forbid you to write to him!' shrilled Thelma. 'We'll be checking all your letters!'

'Right, get to your room!' came the abrupt command from her father. 'And stay there for the rest of the night.'

Packed off in disgrace, Nell flung herself onto her bed, lashing out at the mattress in frustration. These stupid bloody people, why could she not have been adopted by someone at least able to understand? They had no perception of her whatsoever. Dealing the mattress a last punch, she rolled into a sitting position and balanced angrily on the edge of the bed, glaring at herself in the dressing-table mirror.

Then, after a moment or two, she conjured up Billy's laughing face, made believe that he was looking back at her, teasing the bad temper from her with one of his jokes, and it forced her to blurt out a laugh – laugh, then cry, that she missed him so much already, and he had only been gone twenty-four hours. Face crumpling, and tears bulging over her lower lashes, she jumped up, snatched a brush and ran it viciously through her dark hair numerous times, to try to prevent herself from breaking down completely.

Well, her parents might think they had covered everything, but the letters wouldn't be coming here. In defiance, she hauled a stool up to her dressing table, and proceeded to write to her beloved, telling him what had just occurred. '*But you needn't worry*,' she assured Billy. '*Nothing and nobody will ever stop me loving you . . .*'

Once the envelope was firmly adhered, and its flap marked with '*SWALK*' before it was concealed in her pocket for tomorrow's post, Nell dragged the stool up to her open window, to take solace in the goings-on of the avenue, waving over her sill to the new people, whom she had yet to meet, and chatting to various neighbours until the light began to fade.

Words were terse and far between at the breakfast table the next day. Outwardly cowed, but secretly smug at having the letter to Billy in her pocket, Nell left at the usual time and posted it on her way to work. She was also to slip into the press office during her lunch hour and order two copies of the damning photograph – not purely from any sense of mischief, though certainly this was a bonus – mainly because she did not have any visual record of herself and Billy together, and it was such a good one. The prints would be ready to collect by the end of the week.

Despite having this to look forward to, though, she was, if anything, even more subdued upon coming home that Tuesday evening, for her visit to Billy's former billet had been fruitless, no letter arriving from his hand.

Still, the fact that she appeared so passive did go someway to healing the rift with her parents. And after all, it was early days, Billy had only been gone forty-eight hours. Undaunted, yet missing him dreadfully, Nell had no need to be ordered to her room that night, but went willingly, pulling her stool to the dressing table and pouring out her heart.

And to her joy, the next day her visit to his digs was to be rewarded by an envelope which sported the endearment 'ITALY' – I trust and love you.

Treasuring his letter, and the one which came two days later, she was to read them again and again throughout that week. And also to pore over that memorable photograph, a copy of which was swiftly despatched to Bill, who had said how much he would value it. Thus Nell was to keep herself happily occupied, whilst waiting for her new position to commence.

Finally, the important day came. Instructed to report at eight a.m. to the railway sidings in Leeman Road – which, being at the far side of the network of lines, involved a journey by bus to the station, and then a short walk – Nell arrived in good time, though she was to find two others had beaten her to it. She offered a friendly hello, but being taller and much younger than both, and sticking out like a sore thumb, she felt too self-conscious to say any more for the time being.

The first response was to come from a stocky woman with bobbed auburn hair and a quiet, but mature and amicable way about her, whose smile and the shrewd twinkling glint in her blue eyes more than made up for any plainness. 'I'm Beata Kilmaster,' she began, in a soft Yorkshire accent. 'Are you for the ambulance train as well?'

Before Nell could reply, the third in the group butted in knowledgeably, 'We're not meant to call it that, it's a Casualty Evacuation Train, they're totally different things.'

'That's me told then,' said Beata, with an arch expression at Nell.

Liking her at once, Nell was now assigned leave to introduce herself. Having done this, she turned expectantly to the self-appointed oracle, whose response was concise.

'Avril Joyson.'

Nell gave her a nod and a smile, but the latter was secretly for Bill, whom she imagined would have had fun describing this one. Avril's face was that of a goldfish, cheeks sucked in as if blowing bubbles, and protuberant blue eyes that lacked either warmth or animation. Her tied-back hair was extremely thick and coarse, the colour of hay, and with a tight natural wave. Nell had to bite her lip to prevent herself from bursting out laughing – a goldfish with a thatched roof, Billy would probably have it.

Based only on looks, she much preferred the former woman, who, with her fresh complexion and russet hair, was more like a trusty Cox's Pippin, and with whom she felt immediately at ease. 'I wonder which one's ours?' She glanced around at the collection of locomotives that chugged and steamed around them, filling the air with their sulphurous hiss. Her query was mainly addressed to Beata, for Avril seemed to be more intent on scrutinising her than the trains.

'Well there's one thing, you won't have any problem hefting patients about. Tall, aren't you?'

Embarrassed, Nell turned to the speaker, who was looking her up and down quite shamelessly, and tried to shrug off the accusation. 'Well, taller than average, I suppose . . .'

'I can't think why you'd want to make yourself even loftier with those high heels.' Avril continued to criticise. 'And they won't like that lipstick.'

Already unsure of herself, Nell's heart sank. Thank goodness she had one person who appeared to like her, as Beata smiled in rebuttal:

'I don't suppose the patients will care much, so long as we look after them.'

Thankfully there was someone else for Avril to look at soon, for at short intervals, the rest of the crew began to turn up: a portly mother and daughter duo named Green; a vivacious French woman, coincidentally bearing the surname of French, who could barely make herself understood; two more women of Beata's age; and seven men.

'Gosh, they've already got their uniforms,' whispered Nell, as two very aristocratic-looking girls made a tardy appearance. 'They look rather grand, don't they?'

But it turned out that the pair had few airs and graces, and from their chummy introduction it appeared they would be more than willing to muck in, even if they were hoping to qualify as state-registered nurses and not mere auxiliaries. One might have guessed from their mannerisms that Lavinia and Penelope Ashton were sisters, but never twins, marvelled Nell, for the first was dark of countenance, the other fair and blue-eyed, the only similarities their height and their wavy hair. During a brief chat with the rest – not instigated by Nell, but by the thoroughbred girls – she discovered that the men were Salvation Army bandsmen, who were to act as stretcher-bearers. All except Avril were very pleasant, decided Nell, as she smiled and shook hands with each in turn. There was no chance to discover much more about her fellow volunteers, for preceding Matron Lennox, Sister Barber came on the scene then, a pretty, delicate-boned woman with fair hair and a heavily freckled face, who grudged them a smile before warning them to pay close attention to what their superior had to say.

Despite the clanking activity from the railway that went on around them, all became attentive to matron, who was starched in dress though not in manner, with pleasant, rather birdlike, features. It was an old-fashioned face, kind, her hair parted in the middle before disappearing under the neat little white cap, conjuring for Nell the spectre of Florence Nightingale.

Upon ascertaining everyone's name, Matron Lennox was not to mince her own introduction. 'No woman should offer herself as a nurse unless she is prepared for hard work, self-denial, and to take her share of occupations that are repugnant to every refined and sensitive being.' Hands clasped before her, her periwinkle-blue eyes rested briefly but effectively on each and every female, allowing her sermon to permeate those ignorant minds. 'Whether it be your intent to fulfil a lifetime vocation, or whether your services were offered purely from a view of public-spiritedness and only for the duration of the war, the attributes you will need to fulfil your role shall be the same. To whit: –'

To whoo! Nell looked at her feet to stop herself giggling.

– presence of mind, gentleness, accuracy, memory, observation and forethought. No matter what rank you are to achieve, these are essential to the wellbeing of your patients. You may find the way ahead severely taxing, and be especially overwhelmed during your initial introduction to the wards, and fear that there is far too much to learn. But you will not be expected to know everything at once, and, in possession of those qualities, in no time at all you will reach a standard where you can rightly be proud of your title.' She finished on a smile, then briefly turned away. 'Very well, Sister, let us show them what they're in for!'

There followed a procession to the designated train, where Matron was to come to an abrupt halt.

Sister's eyes penetrated the nearest recruit, who happened to be Nell. But before the latter could grasp her meaning, Beata had stepped forth and opened the door of the van for their superior.

Crushed by naivety, and wondering how Beata could have interpreted Sister's mute instruction, Nell kept her head down as Matron ushered her group of nurses aboard one of the converted railway wagons, and proceeded to lecture them on what was required.

'As you can see, even though the workmen have done their part, it is somewhat in the raw.' Her declaration was unnecessary, for amongst a liberal sprinkling of sawdust were relics of its previous cargo: a wizened carrot and a shrivelled cabbage leaf. Matron began a slow tour, tapping the partitions that separated the 'wards' from the rest of the wagon. 'This will eventually be the doctor's office, this one for myself, this for the sister, and this is the nurses' mess.' She showed them how the stretchers would be installed in racks, one above the other. 'But before any equipment is installed it will need to be cleaned from top to bottom, and for this it will be all hands to the pumps – so, as I announced earlier, I hope none of you is afraid of hard work. If you are then you're in the wrong profession.' She eyed them all with a face that was stern yet fair, as if allowing them this last-minute chance to withdraw.

At Sister's prompting glare, Nell reacted a few seconds after everyone else. 'Yes, Matron.'

'Very well, I shall close by issuing a warm welcome to all, and leave you in Sister's capable hands!' And with this she departed.

With their superior gone, Sister Barber then proceeded

to give her new nurses all the do's and don'ts. And the don'ts seemed to be mostly for Nell's benefit. 'You'll be expected to turn up in more sensible footwear tomorrow, Miss Spottiswood, and without lipstick!'

Nell's humiliation was amplified by Avril Joyson's told-you-so look, as Sister continued, 'You won't feel half so glamorous when you're swinging the bedpans!'

Initially deceived by the warm smile of welcome and the freckled angelic face with its baby-blue eyes, Nell was quickly learning that this one would brook no nonsense. If Matron was Florence Nightingale, this was Florence Vulture.

'For those of you who have been nurturing some romantic notion, let me make it plain that you are here under sufferance, and in the most fundamental capacity. Although you may be credited with the title "Nurse", make no mistake, it is an honorary one. You are here as helpers. Some of you may go on to achieve distinction,' her eyes flickered briefly to the Ashton girls, before settling on Nell, 'others are merely here for the duration. But you are all starting out on the same footing, and there will be no lording it over others. I am here to see that you do not kill anyone. We must all of us make the best of it. But let it be known that I cannot abide giddiness or laziness. Neither will be tolerated.'

Having imprinted these opinions on them, Sister Barber began to interview them one by one. On discovering that the Frenchwoman had barely a word of English, she tutted in dismay to herself. 'What on earth have they landed me with?'

'Pardon?' The French woman cocked her ear.

Sister mouthed loudly at her, 'What are you doing here?'

'Zey send me!' came the strangled response. 'I nurse.'

'But in England – why are you in England?'

'Ah, *mon mari*.' Mrs French groped for words. *''E Anglais!'*

Sister heaved a sigh. 'Good Lord, I'll warrant you can barely count to ten . . .'

'*Mais oui!*' The other's face brightened, and she proceeded to count aloud with pride, 'Wan, doo, tree, four, fahve, sees, sevahn, ate, nahn –'

'Yes, thank you!' Sister held up her hand with a look of defeat, and moved on to the next in line. But she was to emit more frustration on encountering Nurse Green the elder, whose hair was snow-white and whose glasses were as thick as jam-jar bottoms. 'Dare one enquire how old you are? No, please don't tell me,' she uttered quickly, 'I'd rather not know.' Her expression declared what a bunch of misfits she had been landed with, as she proceeded to interrogate the next.

With one ear to the conversation, Nell was making examinations of her own. First, Beata – was that swollen ankle as painful as it looked? Those plummy girls, who had arrived already in attractive uniform, how would they cope with all the unpalatable things that would be required of them? And Avril Joyson – she had obviously taken against Nell for the crime of being too tall; would she continue to be so obnoxious? What had made her so? But in the midst of trying to fathom Avril's hostility, her reverie was to be interrupted.

'And what about you, Nurse Spottiswood?'

Nell snapped back to attention. 'I beg your pardon?'

Her face like a cold summer's day, Sister Barber gave an exasperated sigh and brandished a packet of cigarettes at her. 'You will address me as "Sister"! I asked, do you smoke?'

'Oh, I won't at the moment, thank you, Sister.'

The freckled face closed its eyes in lamentation of this gauche response. 'I wasn't offering you one! I was trying to ascertain if you smoked! For those of you who do, there will definitely be none of that in uniform!'

Why then, Nell wondered, did Sister herself have

cigarettes in the pocket of her own blue dress? As if the other had read her mind, there came a warning that forbade her even to think of offering defiance. 'The last thing a sick person needs is for his nurse to smell like a chimney!'

Unhappy that the pair of them had got off on the wrong foot, Nell tried to buck up her ideas, as she and the others were sent to a depot to collect said uniform.

Upon receipt, and out of earshot of Sister, Nell made salty judgement on the unattractive dress. It was much more basic than those worn by the aristocratic Ashton girls, with no separate white collar but a cutaway one of the same fabric as the dress, no long sleeves with white cuffs like theirs, but puffed short ones, and there could be no mistaking her for a 'real' nurse with the large letters NA emblazoned on her breast. And instead of a neat little organdie cap like Matron's, or a voluminous starched one with wings to either side like Sister's, the nursing auxiliaries' headgear was little more than a white triangle tied at the back. 'How unflattering,' scoffed Nell. 'Like a peasant's scarf! Still, I suppose we should think ourselves lucky we're not made to wear black stockings.'

'It's not a fashion parade,' sniped Avril Joyson. 'We're here to help the war effort. And I'm not surprised you got taken to task in those high heels.'

But as the one with the goldfish pout minced out of earshot, the trustworthy Beata Kilmaster smiled back at Nell and admitted, 'I'd love to be able to wear those, but I always have to wear sensible shoes with this leg.' Nell's eyes went straight to the other's distended ankle. 'And whatever type of shoes that one wore, she'd still be a pain in the arse – pardon my French.' Beata chuckled in afterthought of the French nurse.

Nell giggled, and knew immediately that despite the age gap they would be firm friends. 'I only meant about the uniform, when you're built like I am, you need all the attractive camouflage you can get. I feel like a bag of spuds!'

But there was no time for any more banter, for they had been instructed to return immediately to the train. Once there, enveloped in aprons and armed with mops, buckets of water, soap and scrubbing brushes, the squad was set to work, men on the outside, females within. Nell threw herself into this wholeheartedly, imagining what her parents would say if they could see their daughter on her hands and knees. However, there could be no quibble about social division, because, to her pleasure and respect, the well-bred girls mucked in quite enthusiastically alongside everyone else.

It was obvious, though, that contrary to Avril Joyson painting herself as the dedicated nurse, she deemed these elements of the job beneath her, and it had not escaped Nell's sharp eye that she had quickly volunteered for the easier task of wiping down the walls – meaning she did not acquire a crick in her neck from having to wash the ceiling, nor sore knees for scrubbing the floor, as Nell herself was suffering.

None the less, working her way along the wagon, with only a piece of sacking to cushion her kneecaps from the hard planking, the youngest one amongst them put in vigorous effort, moving her scrubbing brush back and forth along the dusty grooves, constantly scouring her knuckles and sending them redder and redder, yelping at splinters as she sweated and scrubbed alongside Beata Kilmaster. Her own joints being so punished, Nell marvelled at how poor Beata coped so well with her swollen leg. Casting a glance sideways now, as she uncoiled her aching spine, she noted that Beata's shoulders were trembling. About to touch her in concern, she then realised that her friend was shaking with mirth, and, grinning along with her, she asked, 'What on earth's tickled you?'

'It's ironic,' Beata arched her own back to relieve it, 'you come and be a nurse to save you from skivvying, and what do you end up doing? Skivvying!'

Nell shared her merriment, but wasn't certain that she understood. 'Do you mean you were a domestic servant?'

'Aye, for fifteen blasted years,' declared Beata. 'More if you count the unpaid ones.'

Nell frowned, but was too polite to ask how old the other was. All the same, she calculated that if Beata had been working for fifteen years that would make her around thirty. Realising that she was staring, she said quickly, 'I'm sorry, I didn't think you were –'

'That old!' Beata gave her chesty chuckle and finished Nell's sentence. 'It's all right, I know I must seem ancient to a young lass like you.'

'Oh, no!' Nell struggled to explain, her scrubbing brush dripping as it paused idle in mid-air. 'It's just that you don't talk down to me, as most of your generation would.' Her smile said how much she appreciated this.

The other rejoined with her affable air, 'I hate being patronised meself, so I never do it to others, no matter what age.'

Nell cast an impish glance to where Nurse Green and her snowy-haired mother worked side by side, and whispered to Beata, 'I don't mean to be rude, but Mrs Green looks, well, a bit like Methuselah's wife!'

Beata shared her mischievous laughter. 'Her daughter's about fifteen years older than me, so missus must be at least sixty-five. She'll get the elbow if they find out.' Though how she had managed to slip through with her grandmotherly looks was inexplicable to both. 'It'll be a shame, though, she's a damned good worker. She'd make three of Oh-be-Joyful.'

Guessing that she meant Avril Joyson, Nell rolled her eyes. 'Yes, I noticed she was swift to volunteer for the easier bits. I wonder which of us will be first for the chop. Sister doesn't seem to like me very much.'

'She's all right, she's just strict,' advised Beata. 'I've had much worse task mistresses in my time – mindst, I think she'll be getting rid of poor Frenchy before very long if her mangled English doesn't improve.'

Nell agreed with a laugh. 'It's a shame, she seems so nice. We'll have to help her.'

'You might be able to. I don't know any proper French. I don't know how she and Green got through the interview. I had a stinker.'

Nell then pointed out an anomaly. 'When I went for interview, they said we shouldn't have any domestic duties – at least that was the impression I was given.'

Beata confirmed this, but made a cynical addition. 'I've learned never to take an employer on trust.'

Nell pulled a face. 'I brought a notebook to write down everything I'm taught, as a reminder, but I won't forget this in a hurry.' She winced at the gritty block in her hand. 'Gosh, this blue-mottled soap's taken the skin off my hands.'

'At least there won't be any germs left.' Beata's application was that of an expert.

Nell glanced at her partner's leg and, with their characters being so harmonious, decided to risk an impertinent question. 'I don't mean to be nosey, but what's the matter with your leg? It looks very painful.'

'Lymphatic oedema,' supplied Beata, still working whilst Nell paused. 'They don't really know what causes it. I've had it since I was about ten. The doctor said then it was either heart or kidneys so I was probably a gonner. But I'm still here, so I reckon it's not so life-threatening.' Her grin belied how awful it had been to have such a threat hanging over her for years, until a more competent physician had taken charge. 'It just swells up from time to time. Bit of a nuisance, but there's plenty worse off.'

Nell guessed that her new friend was in more discomfort than she let on, and admired her stoicism. 'You don't complain much, do you?'

'Oh, I have me moments,' smiled Beata.

Nell was curious to know more. 'It must have been hard, being in service.'

'Not so different from this,' revealed Beata. 'As far as the hierarchy goes, anyway. I was always at the bottom of the ladder.'

Nell breathed a realisation. 'So *that*'s how you knew to open the door for Matron . . .'

'Quit slacking, nurses!' called Sister, interrupting her own task, her ire mainly for Nell. 'I hope you're not going to be a troublemaker, Spottiswood.'

'It was my fault, Sister,' admitted Beata. 'I was just explaining to Nell –'

'If she requires an explanation regarding anything to do with nursing – which is all you should be discussing – then she must come and ask me! And you can dispense with the Christian names, from now on it's surnames only.'

'Yes, Sister,' replied both subserviently, and launched back into their scrubbing.

But Nell was to protest when the gorgon was out of earshot, 'We've both got such long names – and it sounds so unfriendly, doesn't it? Do you think she'd mind if we shorten them?'

'Spotty and Killie – I don't think it'd inspire much confidence in our nursing skills, do you?' grinned Beata, causing Nell to laugh too. At any event, these names were how they were to address each other from then on.

At the end of a very long day of hard labour, Beata's leg blown up like a sausage and Nell's knuckles red and bleeding and still embedded with the odd splinter, the nurses were allowed to go home at five, with the promise from Sister that there was plenty more work and longer hours to come.

'So what are you going to be doing tonight?' enquired Beata, as the pair of them limped their way from the noisy railway sidings into an equally grimy road. 'If you've any energy left, that is. Have you got a boy to take you out?'

Nell ceased picking at her ragged fingernails, to cast a secretive smile at her much shorter companion. 'As a matter of fact I have – but I'm only telling you and no one else. My parents would kill me.' The twelve-year age gap was as nothing in this quickly established friendship, at least as far as Nell was concerned. 'But I won't be seeing him for a while, he's been sent to London.'

'You'll be like me, then,' Beata smiled up at her, 'just sitting with your feet up by the wireless.'

At this point a small group of their colleagues caught them up. Having overheard the last statement, the more forthright of the upper-class twins said gaily, 'No, we can't have that! We've just been discussing starting up a band with those Sally Army chaps – a modern one, I mean, not banging the tambourine or anything! Can either of you sing? We're going into town for dinner and to discuss names, come and join us.'

Nell observed that Avril Joyson had tagged on to the Ashton twins, seeming to enjoy the reflected status. The last thing she desired was that one's company, and neither, apparently, did her companion.

'Sounds fun,' replied Beata, 'but I can't sing for toffee. I'll be glad to come and applaud, but tonight I just want to get home, have a cup of tea, and rest my barking dogs.'

'Me too,' smiled Nell, affecting to collapse.

'Killjoys!' Lavinia's plummy voice denounced them, but its owner was only joking, as she further scolded Nell. 'Especially you – why, you're barely out of school, you shouldn't be such a fuddy-duddy!'

If only you knew, thought Nell, with a mind to her passionate weekend with Billy, but told her accuser, 'I've just managed to get back in my parents' good books. I daren't risk upsetting them. I can't really sing either.'

'Why, you are no use to anyone, Spottiswood!' Her detractor aped Sister Barber's strict tone. 'You should jolly well show more enthusiasm – can't you even help us out with a name at least?'

Recalling Sister's earlier admonition, Nell was swift to come up with one. 'How about the Bedpan Swingsters?'

'That's perfect!' Lavinia and Penelope fell against each other in mirth, and with even Joyson agreeing that this was a great idea, there was much good humour as they parted.

The last to break up, Beata enquired if Nell would be catching her bus from the railway station just around the corner. But Nell had other plans. With no opportunity to pick up Billy's letter at lunchtime, she had been forced to wait until now. It would mean travelling out of her way, but she would never sleep without reading his latest words. Feeling safe in confiding all of this to her new friend, she gushed, 'See you tomorrow!' then went to collect the prized letter and read it on the bus home.

'Ooh, here comes Nurse Spottiswood in her new uniform!' remarked her mother when Nell finally got in, her father having arrived just before her.

'Looking very pleased with herself as well.' After drying his hands, Wilfred took his place at the table, Nell doing the same.

'She must have had as good a day as I have,' surmised her rather frazzled but cheerful mother, placing a meal in front of both before serving herself. 'The washing dried in no time in this sunshine, and I managed to get every bit folded and ready for ironing tomorrow.' This accounted for the cheery mood, thought Nell, politely attending whilst her mother wittered on. 'So if I can make an early start before it gets too hot, then I can devote the afternoon to fruit-picking,' finished Thelma.

Father came alert at the thought of his territory being invaded. 'Er, I'll tell you when you can pick it, thank you very much!'

'Oh, I don't mean from your domain, dear.' Though

fruit trees grew in abundance in the Spottiswood back garden, Thelma would never dream of touching them without her husband's permission. 'No, I just mean those brambles by the railway – that's if anyone hasn't beaten me to it.'

Father looked duly appeased. 'Oh, well that's all right then. I just didn't want you giving our best quality stuff to the WVS. I've negotiated a decent price for it with a couple of greengrocers, you see – you can take all you need for ourselves of course.' He set into his meal, a good portion of it being consumed before either parent thought to ask about Nell's new job.

'So what type of girls are you working with?' enquired her mother.

'They're mostly very nice.' Nell lifted her attention from her plate, and proceeded to tell her parents a little about each fellow nurse, hoping to titillate them with her impression of the French one, though they did not guffaw as much as Billy would have.

'So you think you'll enjoy this nursing lark?' smiled her father.

'I'm sure of it!' When I get a chance, came Nell's grim thought, not revealing that her entire day had been taken up with scrubbing floors and getting splinters in her hands and her nails torn to the quick. 'It's hard, but worthwhile.'

But she did make it known how tired it had made her, and, after listening to the wireless for news of how the Battle of Britain had gone that day, she was to linger only for another ninety minutes or so with her parents, enjoying a serial, then some music, whilst helping to make firelighters from compressed newspaper. By eight o'clock she was on her way to bed with a cup of cocoa, secretly to prop up the photograph of her beloved – whose laughing face looked on whilst she read his letter again – and to compose another to him, relating in brief the events of the day, picking out things that might amuse him, and ending with the usual sentiment of how much she missed and loved him. Then, within five minutes of kissing his photograph, and hiding this and the envelope under her pillow ready to be posted in the morning, she fell asleep.

The transformation of the rolling stock took a couple more days, during which all the recruits twiddled with each others' surnames so as to make their address less harsh. There was not much one could do with some of the names, but in addition to Killie and Spotty, Nurse French was now Frenchy and Avril Joyson was Joy – but this was a mischievously ironic title. Sister made no complaint as long as they did their work.

Only after the wagons had been thoroughly cleaned and polished from top to bottom, and were fully kitted out, were the volunteers to learn anything related to actual nursing. First, there was to be a fortnight of lectures and training at a hospital. Though continuing to miss Billy dreadfully, Nell was intelligent enough to realise there was no point in moping, and so welcomed this opportunity to throw herself into learning her job, and thus be equipped with fresh material for her nightly penning. Even before this, Billy had seemed to enjoy all her mundane details. Now, though, she would have much more interesting news for him, which was good for her too, for this nightly ritual certainly helped to ease the emptiness – though, oh, how she yearned for him.

The County Hospital was in Monkgate, only an extra stop on the bus then a few minutes' walk under two ancient Bars. Beyond its Viking gates and medieval dog-leg alleys, York's suburbs had begun to encroach on one village after another, but inside its compact walls nothing was far away, and you could get from one side to the other in less than half an hour. There had been no need for Nell to rise early, yet she had. Thankful that the manual part was over, she rolled up at the hospital that morning raring to fill the pages of her notebook, as did her colleagues.

All were in for a shock. After their matron on the trains being so decent, her counterpart at the hospital was quite the opposite, making her feelings clear upon meeting the auxiliaries. Whilst Sister Barber had made it plain that she did not appreciate having amateurs foisted upon her, this woman was downright insulting.

'I gather that one or two of you will be applying to have your names included on the national register. Those I shall be addressing later. As to those others of more restricted intellect, I shall attempt to convey this as simply as possible. I do not, and never shall, subscribe to quackery, and will not permit it in this hospital. I may have been coerced by the powers-that-be into accepting recruits who are totally inadequate for the task, but that does not mean I will subject my patients to abuse by persons who are only fit for domestic service, factory or shop work . . .'

Flushed with indignation, Nell shifted uncomfortably in her new sensible shoes, as Matron proceeded with her waspish rendition.

'You might flatter yourselves that you are nurses – indeed, others might address you by such a term. I shall not. In these times of emergency the word has gained inflated value. If you were worthy of the title, you would have made the grade for it, whatever the effort. The qualifying examinations are prepared on a minimum curriculum, and if you cannot attain this simple standard, then your intellect is exceedingly limited.'

Nell could not help but emit a gasp. The matron's cold gaze rested upon her for a few seconds, though her lecture was to remain universal.

'Be that as it may, you should all be able to hold one rule in your minds. And it is a vital rule. Whilst you are in this hospital, never, I repeat *never*, presume to undertake actions that are beyond your capabilities. You may watch qualified nurses at their work, some of you *might* learn from them . . . as to the rest of you . . . I myself will attempt to inculcate the rudimentary syllabus.' A heavy sigh insinuated just how tiresome this would be. The way she looked down her nose and stared into each and every face was extremely unnerving. No one deserved such discrimination, the friends agreed later, once out of range of this termagant; even the normally docile Nurse French pouring forth a string of Gallic invective, after Nell had translated the gist for her.

'I've never been so insulted,' breathed a distempered Nell to the others. 'And I'm *not* stupid! I went to grammar school.'

'So would I have done, if we'd had any spare cash for the uniform,' muttered an equally incensed Beata. 'I passed the scholarship.'

'Same here!' lobbed Green the younger. 'What about you, Joy, did you pass?'

'Yes!' Joyson was eager not to be judged a dunce, though the way her eyes flickered told that she was lying, which made Nell feel a twinge of sympathy. Having got to know her, she had learned that, apart from the vice of laziness and her blunt opinions, there was no real malice to Avril.

'And so did me mam, didn't you, Mam?' finished Green junior.

Similarly nettled as the younger ones, Mrs Green's white head gave a nod of confirmation. 'My poor dad could hardly scrape the funds to feed us all, let alone for school books and pencils.'

'Well that's just it!' objected Nell. 'I don't think Matron's exceptionally bright if she couldn't even make any allowance for those of us who are unable to afford the exams. I've never been spoken to like that in my entire life – why, it's as if she regards us as scum!'

And, indeed, this was further exemplified at midday, for they were forbidden to eat in the dining hall – even though it was raining – and had to huddle under the bicycle shelter, with no means of alleviating their aching feet – though this was not to be endured for very long. 'Dinner-hour' being a luxury of the past, after wolfing down their lunches in fifteen minutes it was back to the grind.

During that most testing of fortnights, they were required to learn all the names of poisonous gases that might be used by the Germans, and to avoid these themselves by deploying their respirators in seconds. This latter seemed to be the sole functional thing they were allowed to do, for only those who were full probationers had any actual contact with the patients. But even in practising on each other, the auxiliaries were constantly reminded that they were the poor relations.

Or not so poor, as one of the 'real' nurses was quick to accuse. 'I think it's a disgrace that you're earning so much without a single qualification! We all had to spend years passing exams and paying our dues, and you swan in earning more than probationers – *and* no cleaning to do!'

'You could have fooled me,' muttered Beata, which is what young Nell would have said if she had not been so overwhelmed by the amount of antagonism.

All this being so, having made their protest, the trained nurses chose to tolerate the auxiliaries, and were kind enough to teach by example the various aspects of their work. Along with asepsis and antisepsis, and the precautions to obtain these, came methods of resuscitation, including those which took place in the casualty department. For some reason matron had not objected to these ignorant individuals coming along there, nor to the operating theatre. Nell thought perhaps she knew why: Matron hoped they would take fright at the horrible injuries, and thus she could be rid of them. Determined not to give this awful woman the satisfaction, she steeled herself not to faint at the bloody scalpels and bone saws, and was quite delighted that her friends managed to do the same – although all were very pale when they emerged. But these ordeals seemed to have no purpose other than for Matron's gratification, for in the main it was one lecture after another, and a lot of scribbling in notebooks.

After being previously lauded for her skills at first aid, Nell had to relearn almost everything she had been taught, any polite query seen as insubordination and earning a severe dressing-down. She certainly knew her place now, and that was as a slave to the authorities, for they demanded to know her every whereabouts – even after working hours, when she was expected to keep her superiors informed of her movements so that they could contact her in an emergency. 'It's worse than being at home,' spluttered Nell, only half joking. 'At least my parents allow me freedom to visit the lavatory!'

As a matter of fact, Thelma and Wilfred had been persuaded to allow a little more than that lately. The incident in Scarborough forgiven, if not completely forgotten, their daughter had been allotted leave to go and watch the newly formed Bedpan Swingsters perform on an evening. Had they known the chosen venue was a pub, undoubtedly they would have been less lenient. Not about to enlighten them, Nell kept a ready cache of peppermints to disguise the combination of stout and cigarettes that were consumed during the lively performance. Everyone agreed that it was such a delight to let one's hair down after Matron's authoritarian regime and obvious detestation of them.

The latter continuing unabated, it was a very long fortnight at the County Hospital – and to exacerbate Nell's misery, during that period there came news that the Germans had finally bombed London itself, in broad daylight. How she was to fret until Billy's letter arrived to assure her he was safe! Though her relief over this was to be somewhat short-lived, for that daring attack was only the beginning of a murderous blitz on the capital, and every night after this, as Nell perused her darling's latest letter before going to sleep, she was to dread it would be his last.

There was to be some respite on the work front, however, when the fortnight at the County Hospital came to an end and the recruits moved on to the Infirmary. This was only a short walk along the same route until the road diverged, yet miles removed in style from the handsome redbrick building of their previous post, the institutional block straddled between the brown River Foss and the cocoa works, both of which could be smelled on the air. Here they hoped to gain practical experience with the elderly. It came as something of a damp squib, though, to learn that this was the type of patient on whom they would be concentrating: hardly the romantic ideal some of them had treasured.

'It used to be the old workhouse till they changed the name,' whispered Beata, upon catching Nell's look of shock at some of the inmates they encountered on their way along the drab corridors that hummed of stale cabbage and decaying humanity.

Nell was glad to be taken under the elder's wing, for she felt very nervous under the vacant, sometimes malevolent, gaze of those whiskery old men with crumpled shirt collars and crumpled faces, grease-stained ties and baggy suits. But she tried not to show it, deporting herself with dignity as exemplified by Sister Barber, for she wanted to appear as mature as the rest. Did nothing faze those Ashton girls?

Apparently it did bother Joyson, though. 'I don't really mind,' she began, her expression telling, 'but I'd rather feel I was doing something for the lads who are defending us.'

'Some of these old chaps would have been soldiers once,' Beata told her.

'Maybe in the Crimean War,' scoffed Joyson, nose in the air as she bustled along, trying to act the professional. 'I doubt they'd know one end of a Spitfire from the other.'

'And do you?' came Lavinia Ashton's forthright demand.

Joyson grew shirty. 'I'm just saying what a great job the RAF boys have done, and I'd like to pay them back, that's all.'

The others shared a look here. They were well-acquainted with Joyson's penchant for airmen, having seen her flirting with squadrons of them around the bars.

'God knows we need them after that mess at Dunkirk,' she added, being immediately heckled for such a defeatist attitude.

Too fixed on her surroundings, Nell had not really been listening to Joyson's moaning, but this had her full attention. 'I admire the RAF too,' she shot back. 'But everyone's doing their part!' She envisaged poor Bill as he lay on that beach under fire, pictured him now as wave after wave of the Luftwaffe pummelled his home town, night after night, thousands of people killed and injured . . .

Perceiving her fears, Beata tried to dispel them, though in doing so she addressed everyone. 'Did you hear on the wireless last night, a hundred and eighty-five German planes shot down over London – in a single day! We've certainly got 'em on the run . . .'

But Nell was to remain apprehensive as the group made their way past vast dormitories of chronic infirm and the mentally ill, to rendezvous with the master and matron, wondering just how bad the superintendent of such an institution might be.

Surprisingly, and to everyone's great relief. Miss Fosdyke turned out to be as pleasant and fair-minded as their own matron on the trains, having the knack of not speaking down to them whilst retaining her own authority. There would be nothing to fear from this one, felt Nell, looking back into the kind, reassuring and ladylike face, which was directed at each girl in turn, not addressing them en masse, but asking each individual why they had not applied to go on the register – leaving aside the Ashton twins, who had.

When it came to Nell's turn, she replied that it was

purely the expense that was prohibitive. 'I should hate for it to be a hardship on my parents,' she told Matron respectfully. 'But, like everyone here, I just wanted to do my bit for the war.'

As usual there was some difficulty in ascertaining Nurse French's thoughts and feelings, but the others, who had by now achieved a certain camaraderie, helped by explaining to Matron what Nell had recently discovered for them: that Frenchy was in fact a fully qualified nurse in her own country, and it was only her inability to grasp the language that was the barrier – and only then the speaking of it, for she understood instructions well enough. Considering that as an auxiliary she would not be entrusted with drugs, and that her manner was kind and caring, her mode of communication was of little handicap.

Matron accepted all of their answers without criticism – and was even complimentary. 'I can tell you are all intelligent women. Perhaps once you are acclimatised you will decide to make that extra sacrifice to attain registered status. In any event, we are very glad to have you all here, short as your stay might be. The care of the chronic sick and elderly is a greatly neglected field, but it is very rewarding.'

They were to find that hers was a different persona altogether than Matron Lennox's quiet way, more outgoing and amusing, as she shepherded the group on a brief tour of the infirmary. 'And it will be brief, I'm afraid,' she informed her entourage. 'Our peripatetic MO is due to arrive for his rounds at any moment.' Even so, she did appear to have sufficient time to introduce the recruits to others along her nimble way, not merely staff but inmates.

'This is one of our longest serving residents – I do beg your pardon for walking on your nice clean floor, Blanche,' she said, as politely as to an equal, whilst steering her party around the elderly woman in the shapeless cotton frock and long bloomers, who was on her hands and knees scrubbing the corridor and mumbling to herself.

The old girl lifted a beautiless, wart-bedecked face, appearing not to notice the rest of her audience, but smiling brightly at the one who had spoken. 'You're all right, miss!' Then immediately going back to scrubbing the floor, jabbering to herself as the group moved on. 'Late, late, always late, never did a day's work in your life, not worth a candle . . .'

Her mumbling was fading into the distance, Matron explaining that Blanche had been born here, when she interrupted herself to accost another. 'One moment, Cissie Flowerdew! I can see you, trying to slope off.'

Mop and bucket in hands, about to run, her victim wheeled around to portray the aura of a simpleton, the face framed in cropped brown hair held with a grip at either temple, and her lumpish torso clad in a similar shapeless blue frock to the last woman. Then Cissie came hurrying up with a repentant smile, her head cocked to one side, as she gave an answer that was well-rehearsed. 'I wouldn't know him again, Matron! He had his hat pulled down over his eyes and –'

'– a long black coat to his ankles!' finished Matron Fosdyke with grim amusement. 'My word, this chap does seem to be a regular suitor, doesn't he?' Turning to the recruits, she offered an explanation, whilst encompassing the inmate in her reply. 'Sister tells me that Cissie is expecting another happy event in the new year, isn't that so, Cissie?'

'Aye, Matron.' There was no further attempt at guile.

Shaking her bonneted head, Matron issued a benign smile. 'We'll say no more about it for the moment. You may go back to work now.'

'Baby number four,' she explained to her party when the offender had clomped away. 'Cissie works as one of our ward maids, she's been with us for twenty years, entered when she was pregnant with her first child – someone took advantage of her when she was little more than a child herself, and it was deemed safer to keep her here for her own protection. How wrong we were! Every now and again she manages to give us the slip, and every time the same excuse: "Ah wouldn't recognise 'im again, nurse, 'e 'ad 'is 'at pulled down over 'is eyes an' a long black coat to 'is ankles!"' The group broke into a unified smile, much disarmed by Matron's feigned Yorkshire accent.

'Every one of the children has a different father, though,' Matron added, in her clipped fashion. 'It doesn't take a genius to work that out when you see them. They remain with us until they're old enough to enter the orphanage. You'll probably meet her last one in the nursery ward – right, onwards!'

Nell exchanged glances with Beata as the group surged off again, one of them hopping rapidly ahead each time they reached a door, and opening it for their leader to go sailing through. It was apparent that, despite her hearty kindness towards the inmates, Matron would condone no slapdash behaviour from those who should know better. For her arrival on each ward was met with much deference, and even when her eyes and mouth showed satisfaction, no one dared put aside their awe until she had gone.

Nell was by now feeling overwhelmed, and not a little dispirited, for not only did many of the occupants wear the identical and uninspiring uniform, but a similar expression. Even those not confined to bed could hardly be termed mobile, the odd one or two shuffling like tortoises from one end of the ward to the other, the rest seated on uncomfortable chairs. All wore the same look of resignation, as though condemned to a dungeon, their skin wrinkled and papery and slightly yellow, like plants deprived of sunlight. How bored the poor things must be, sympathised Nell, with only a square of sky to view, no pictures on the walls, not even a splash of colour to cheer them, just polished floors, crisp white linen, and endless rows of beautifully made beds.

Yet not all was gloom, for some of the old people still had their wits about them, and engaged the visitors in a few moments of playful chat. Then, after racing around in Matron's slipstream for a while, Nell and the other auxiliaries were to receive the honour of shadowing the visiting MO on his rounds. And even if forced to stand to the rear of those more worthy, they were to pick up much information, though some of it amusingly suspect.

'And how is Mrs Grant this morning?' enquired the eminent man, upon his satellites being gathered around the current bed.

Its elderly occupant leaned forward and summoned him with a bony finger, as if to pour some confidence into his ear. 'The city walls are made of shit.'

'Really? They've stood up to it well,' replied the doctor, without batting so much as an eyelid, whilst Nell and her friends tried not to choke on their mirth.

There were to be many such opportunities for amusement during that tour, some grossly embarrassing ones too, and some so intensely sad they made Nell want to cry, and to wonder if she was really cut out for such a commitment.

She was to pose this question to herself again later, when she and her fellows were handed to the care of their very own Sister Barber, under whose judicial eye they were to endure ward training. Many of the duties they had done before, such as bed-making, which was terribly frustrating when one wanted to get to grips with the real job. But as it seemed to be paramount on the list of rules, or at least as important as hand-washing, Nell proceeded to do as she was told. She must have done something right, for after first making up empty beds, she and the others were allowed to make one with someone in it. After showing her pupils the correct way to roll an infirm patient from side to side, to check for signs of pressure, and how to sponge the person down, Sister divided them into pairs, and instructed each to follow her example.

Nell would much rather have been paired with Beata than Joyson to undertake the blanket bathing of Mrs Wrigley, but without a choice in the matter she was determined to shine. Thankfully the elderly lady was compliance itself, and not one of those who screamed blue murder like the poor Ashton girls had been landed with. But despite her ruttly chest, Mrs Wrigley raised not a grumble, as she was manhandled about the mattress and generally used as a practice dummy. Thankful for this cooperation, Nell voiced appreciation to Mrs Wrigley whilst trying not to make her cough worse, wondering throughout if Sister would admonish her for gossiping. But Sister appeared to be content to let them go about this in their own way for a while, and a lot less keen on pointing out their faults at every turn, as she had done at first introduction two weeks ago. Though coming to know her so well, Nell had the suspicion that this was just a ruse, and that Sister was merely saving all her complaints for later. Thus attuned, she determined to rob her of any chance to grumble.

Sister had other ideas. Gathering everyone around the bed that Nell and Joyson had just stripped and changed between them, after first excusing herself to the patient, she prowled the scene, checking that all castors were turned inward, the corners of the sheets were all neatly tucked in, the top one was folded over the counterpane to the regulation measurement, and the dirty linen had been deposited in the bin. Finding no fault with any of these, she then canvassed the group. 'Do all of you consider that Mrs Wrigley has been satisfactorily provided for?'

Feeling nervous as her peers ran their eyes over her work, Nell was relieved that none of them spotted anything wrong.

'Nothing wrong at all?' queried Sister. 'Then where is Mrs Wrigley to deposit her sputum – on the floor? This is not a saloon bar!'

Additionally reminded by the old lady's chest noises, Nell realised with dismay. 'Sorry, Sister, I took the cup away to wash it and forgot to fetch it back. I'll go –'

'It's no good remembering it later! Mind to the task, Nurse, anticipate your patient's every requirement! If they should have to ask for anything then we are not doing our job.'

'Yes, Sister . . .' After paying such care to the handling of the old lady, and feeling proud of her efforts, Nell felt slightly less so now.

Sister Barber then turned her attention to the lower bedding, again excusing herself to Mrs Wrigley as she pulled aside the covers to emit a sound of accusation. 'This draw sheet is not taut enough! A few shuffles from Mrs Wrigley and it will form rucks!' She was levelling her criticism at Nell again. 'And what do rucks make?'

'Bedsores, Sister!' came the unified chant.

'And a bedsore is to be regarded as an abomination – there will be none on my ward!'

Nell's lips parted to object, and she waited for Joyson to admit that she had been the one responsible for not tucking her side in properly, whilst Nell had been more focused on the patient. But the real culprit merely gazed straight ahead and let her take the blame, as sister emoted, 'This is sheer laziness! Do it again, properly!'

'Just my luck to get partnered with *her*,' muttered Nell from the side of her mouth to her friend Beata, as the group was dispersed to other tasks. Having tried to discern over the past few weeks if there was more to Joyson than met the eye, she had soon discovered that there wasn't. She was as shallow and lazy as first impressions had implied. No matter that they enjoyed friendlier relations now, she would always let you down. 'The treacherous cat. I get into enough trouble without taking the blame for Joyson too.'

But despite that telling off, Nell was to learn a great deal that morning, Sister proving to be very informative as she instructed her pupils in the accurate taking of temperature, pulse and respiration; the cleaning and sterilisation of appliances and instruments; what to observe in a patient's posture, appetite, evacuations, colour of face, pain, effect of medicines; how different ailments required different management – heart and chest patients being propped up with pillows, others laid flat – and so on, these things being scribbled down in notebooks – for it was impossible to remember them all – and taking them right up to dinnertime.

Though not banned from eating inside this hospital, the recruits had already taken the contingency of bringing sandwiches, and now chose to eat these in the fresh air. At least it was fine, and there was a much nicer outlook here on the bench of a small nearby park – if a little chilly, for it was now well into September.

'Golly, it's a real eye-opener, isn't it?' exclaimed Penelope Ashton. 'Some of the old girls are fun, though, with the things they say!'

'Oh, and what do you make of Ciss?' interjected Lavinia. 'Four babies, how scandalous!'

'It's a blasted disgrace,' declared Joyson, opening her sandwiches. 'Allowing her to have one after the other like that! They should have her sterilised.'

Unsure as to her own stance, Nell looked to Beata, predicting a kinder opinion.

But, 'It's the poor little kids I feel sorry for,' said her auburn-haired friend, for once unable to defend the indefensible. 'There's enough illegitimate babies being produced in the so-called normal world, what with lasses throwing themselves at soldiers, without having to put up with it in there too. I'd keep her locked up permanently if it were up to me. It makes me boiling mad.'

'*La pauvre imbecile,*' murmured a dissident voice from further along the bench.

'Well, you'd expect that from her,' muttered Joyson under her breath. 'The French are always at it.'

Nell was examining her sandwiches without much enthusiasm, when she noticed her mentor frown and hold the miniature suitcase containing her own lunch to her ear.

'What's up, Killie?'

'I'm sure I can hear – why, it's like scratching.' Looking puzzled, Beata opened the case in cautious fashion, to reveal a seething mass of ants. With a yell of disgust, she threw it to the ground, the ants in a panic as they continued to swarm over the jam sandwiches.

'Well, that's my dinner down the swanny,' came her dismal utterance.

'No it isn't, you can share mine!' Nell offered them brightly.

'Nay, I'm not depriving you,' Beata tried to refuse.

But Nell exerted friendly pressure. 'Honestly, there are too many here for me. They're meat paste. I don't even feel like eating any of them, the stench in there has made me feel so queasy.'

'*Oui* it eez very, er, pongy,' agreed Madame, pinching her nose and making the others laugh with affection.

Despite her own geniality, Nell's face remained wan, and it seemed all she could do to nibble on her sandwich. 'I swear I've not felt right since I entered that blessed place.'

Grateful to be fed, Beata shifted from one plump buttock to the other. 'I wonder when those luncheon vouchers will make an appearance.' They had been promised some at the outset.

'To be honest,' said Joyson, viewing her own sandwich distastefully, 'I couldn't even stomach roast beef and Yorkshire pud, having seen the dirty habits of those old folk.'

Nell's face buckled in laughter. 'Yes, did you see what that old chap did with his business?'

'Ah, *non*!' Frenchy begged her not to elaborate.

'They can't help it.' Beata assumed her usual virtuous character, addressing herself mainly to Nell. 'You'll be old yourself one day. Just thank your lucky stars your family isn't impoverished and you won't end up in here. It's not very nice having to put your nearest and dearest into an institution.'

Nell looked chastened. 'Is someone you know in the Infirmary?' she tendered.

'My Aunt Lizzie. She went senile, started being a hazard to herself, so we had no choice . . .'

Having contributed to the mockery, Nell felt ashamed and silly, and innocent. 'Of course, I'm sorry if we offended you, Killie. My grandmother went a similar way, but we were able to nurse her at home.'

'Then she was lucky,' announced Beata, taking another bite of her sandwich.

Nell nodded thoughtfully over her own abandoned lunch. 'I'd never imagined there were people so unfortunate until today.'

'Aye, well, it's one thing to be forced to end your days in the Infirmary, another to have been born there, like Cissie's children. I don't know which is worse. But you can't allow your feelings to show in our job. If we treat them all with equal respect, then at least we can leave them with a bit of dignity. I always put meself in their position – the old folk, not the unmarried mothers,' she added hastily with a chuckle, then was serious again. 'I just think how I'd like to be treated. You know how you were mentioning the other week about not talking down to people just because they're younger than you – I hate people who treat the elderly like little children.' As Joyson rose to wander about the grounds to enjoy a crafty cigarette, Beata leaned towards Nell and muttered pungently, 'She's a bugger for doing that, I've noticed – pardon my cursing,' she added at Nell's sparkle. 'It just makes me mad.'

'You're very wise,' admired Nell. 'I think if I stick by you I won't go far wrong.'

Whilst the others went for a stroll around the compact gardens, she was to remain with Beata, who was obviously keen to rest her leg.

Having had her earlier questions answered as to the cause of Beata's swollen ankle, and many more personal ones besides during their three weeks together, Nell decided to chance another.

'I noticed when Matron asked us why we only wanted to be auxiliaries, you gave a similar answer to mine . . .'

'That I was too skint to go on the register?' Beata nodded. 'Well, I could hardly tell her the real reason.'

Insatiably curious, Nell sat up. 'What was that?'

'I wanted to join the WAAF but they wouldn't have me – I failed the medical.'

'Why, you surprise me! I think you'll make an exemplary nurse.'

Beata shook her head in self-doubt. 'I fought against it for years, and now look where I am.'

'But why?' pressed Nell.

'You're a nosey little bugger, aren't you?' But when Beata turned to her, the small blue eyes were twinkling.

'Sorry.' Nell formed a regretful smile. 'It's just that I'm interested in other people's lives – especially people I like.'

'Well,' her friend looked upon her warmly as she explained, 'I can't think it'll be all that scintillating, but if you really want to know . . .' And she proceeded to reveal how, throughout her life, from the age of ten, she had always seemed to be nursing one relative or another. 'Whenever anybody fell ill, it was always, "Send for our Beat". I got a bit sick of it at times, you know . . .'

Nell commiserated. 'But still, it's a shame you couldn't afford to go on the register and be a proper nurse.'

'Oh, I daresay I could've done the same as one of my sisters. She put herself into domestic service so's to be able to save up for her true vocation. My money always seemed to be frittered away – anyway, what constitutes a proper nurse? I might not have the right qualifications, the right uniform, but nobody could care more about a patient's welfare than I do – and I reckon you're the same type, that's why you're still here after seeing all those poor demented souls in there.' Her auburn head made a gesture at the Infirmary.

Pleased to be so well regarded, Nell thought she now saw the reason for Beata's unmarried state at such ripe age: she had been too busy caring for others to make a life for herself. But she did not press for verification, for it was a question too far, and much too personal, and she had no wish to point out that that was where she and her friend differed.

So, lifting her face to the sun, she closed her eyes, daydreaming of Billy, enjoying this moment of peace after the chaos of the former workhouse, only the drone of a Halifax bomber interrupting the quiet.

Finally, though, Beata glanced down at the case that had contained her lunch, and saw that the ants had completely left it, though she dealt it a final bash just to make sure. 'We'd better get back to work, else Matron'll have ants in her pants.'

Nodding, her young companion rose, and, along with the rest of the group, strolled back to the Infirmary, looking forward to the afternoon.

4

They were to see many more ants during the next few weeks, for the old workhouse was infested with them. It was as well that Nell soon grew too familiar with this small army for them to bother her, and similarly those old men who had so frightened her at first, for it appeared that she would be there much longer than anyone had expected. The casualty evacuation trains might all be ready, with beds made up and their crews fit for action with a mound of surgical dressings at hand, but there seemed little urgency to call upon their newly acquired skills.

Though these were still very modest, the probationers and auxiliaries were gleaning more knowledge by the day, being permitted to witness the work of experienced nurses, and to practise, practise, practise those things that would be expected to be second nature to them in weeks to come: the insertion of catheters, the administration of enemas and medicines, giving injections – though only the Ashton sisters were allowed to have a go at the latter – meting out food and stimulants, dressing wounds, making a poultice, and even helping to lay out the dead. Nell had already changed her mind about going back to clerical work after the war, having decided that this would make for a much fuller and more satisfying career one day.

For now, though, she and her fellows were still mainly confined to the routine of changing filthy bedding, washing backs, handing out false teeth, trying to interpret the barely intelligible language of the stroke patients, and listening to old people's objections over the food they had been given. Some might consider it drudgery, but Nell had made it her mission to get to know all the patients, to take an interest in their personalities and not just their ailments, and to converse with them as one might a peer, as she clipped their toenails and attended their bodily functions. Ditto the permanent residents, such as Cissie Flowerdew, whose situation had intrigued her so much that she had secretly delved into dusty ledgers to find out more about her. Sadly they had little else to tell about this poor simple woman, other than the entry 'imbecile' beside her name, and the date of entry. Yet by bothering to pause and chat with the subject herself, a persistent Nell had discovered that Cissie's hopes and dreams were not dissimilar to her own.

'I'm going to have a big white wedding!' a pregnant Cissie delighted in telling the listener. 'He's coming back to collect me any day – do you want to be my bridesmaid, Nurse? I'll need lots of bridesmaids.'

And instead of tittering, Nell felt quite sad that Cissie would never realise those dreams, and had answered kindly that she would regard it an honour. Any banter that might be exchanged was not at the expense of the victim, and any amusement lacked malice. On the contrary, she found herself looking forward to her next day, when she could give Cissie the length of gay ribbon she had decided would cheer her up. Indeed, there were to be many yards of ribbon handed out to brighten the other old ladies' drab lives, which used up most of Nell's pocket money, but was considered well-spent.

If there were any elements of this institution that Nell abhorred – apart from death, of course – it would be Ward Three, which housed the mentally deranged who could be violent, though none towards her so far, and the ward devoted to venereal disease. Just to find herself amongst such degraded individuals for the first time was sufficient ordeal. But horror was to be heaped upon horror for those compelled to watch as a man's private member was exposed – in itself enough to set Nell's cheeks aflame – and an instrument like a miniature umbrella then inserted into it. Face burning with embarrassment, unable to turn away lest she be dubbed a prude or a coward, Nell tried to bolster herself with the thought that it was far worse for the unfortunate victim than it was for any of his audience. But this did not make it any easier, and she hoped her experience on this ward would be brief.

What on earth would Billy have to say if he knew? Though she had no intention of telling him, or her parents. Nell doubted either of the latter would know of the existence of such horrific diseases, what with the upright lives they had led. Why, she herself had never guessed beforehand. This job had certainly broadened her education, though she would have preferred to remain ignorant of some things. Still, there was always humour to be found in any situation, and she could not help blurting an unintentional laugh in front of her friend Beata as they washed their hands for what seemed like the hundredth time that day.

'I'm just trying to think of an answer for when my mother asks what I did at work today,' she explained to her friend, who cracked a similar smile.

'Aye, it's not really polite conversation to say you watched a man have an umbrella shoved up his willy,' said Beata. 'Let alone recommend it as a spectator sport.'

'I could have died of embarrassment!' Blushing at the thought, Nell covered her face with the towel, before heaping admiration on her friend. 'Whilst you didn't even flinch.'

'Oh, don't go accrediting me with special powers, it's just that I've seen a lot of 'em – a lot of the same one, anyway,' Beata corrected herself, as Nell burst out laughing again. 'I had to nurse my bedridden uncle, amongst others, bath him and everything. So there's nowt much else can startle me. Not that Uncle Teddy had anything so horrible done to him as that poor chap.' Then she cocked her head and reflected. 'Mindst, some days I would've liked to ram a proper umbrella up him, the nasty old sod.'

Nell's eyes watered from merriment. 'Oh, I'm so lucky to be working with you, Killie, you're such a joy!' And her words were truly heartfelt.

But still, her main source of joy was in the receipt of Billy's letters at the end of the day. With no time to visit the Preciouses each lunchtime now, she had to wait until after work, travelling a mile out of her way in order to retrieve a few mundane lines of news. Yet she would have gone to the ends of the earth for the row of kisses that always embellished Billy's short letters.

It was immensely worrying, though, to think of him in that terrible blitz inflicted on the south. Though nothing in comparison, the air raids had become more frequent around York as well, and October had seen the first two deaths, though on the other side of the city to where Nell lived. Moreover, the bombs were getting to be a little close to home; last week one of them had descended quite near to Aunty Phyllis's, falling between two houses and half-demolishing both. And although, thankfully, the occupants had escaped with burns and fractures, it was all very unsettling, for Nell was personally acquainted with these victims.

Had England thought she had seen the utmost that Goering could unleash, there came a change of tactics, and the worst raid of the war, this time upon Coventry. Stunned from the news, the fledgling nurses were still discussing this during their lunch hour at a restaurant in town, none of them able to fathom the scale of the destruction, nor how it must feel to confront so many casualties. A thousand dead, God knew how many more injured, rank upon rank of them being ferried to the first-aid post, of which there was one at the Infirmary.

'I mean, where would one start with numbers such as those?' Lavinia Ashton looked anguished. 'Whom would one treat first? We've never been given any real practice – all right, we've applied one or two bandages, et cetera, but in the scheme of things they were small-fry. We've never been put to the test. I'm afraid I might not come up to scratch when faced with something so massive as Coventry . . .'

Nell was afraid of this too, and was deeply thoughtful as she devoured the contents of her plate. After two months of visiting the Infirmary, her senses were no longer so acute to the disagreeable sights and smells, and the queasiness that had initially marred her appetite had waned.

'Well, it hasn't put you off your meal,' reproved an amazed Joyson, breaking the serious atmosphere, having been studying Nell's gluttonous attack on the suet dumplings that Beata had left on the edge of her plate. 'By you can eat like a horse!'

Suddenly aware that everyone else at the table was eyeing her in fun, Nell reddened and paused in her lusty consumption. 'Sorry, I didn't mean to offend anyone . . . I'm just ravenous with all that hard work.'

'You eat all you like, love.' Between sips of tea, Beata stuck up for her.

'Yes, you jolly well deserve it,' chipped in Lavinia, backed by her sister.

'I'm glad to see them go, I never could stand suet.' Beata shuddered and grimaced.

'What did you order dumplings for, then?' countered Joyson.

'Because I wanted the stew that came with them,' retorted Beata. 'If that's all right with you?' She and Nell had been looking forward to this hearty meal, which could be had for only a shilling – including a pudding – and had attempted to sneak off by themselves. They had not minded Frenchy and the younger Nurse Green and even the Ashton girls tagging along, but Joyson was bad enough at work without having to suffer her at meal breaks. 'Eh, she'd argue with her own reflection, she would,' came her assertion to the others.

'I 'ate zem too,' declared the attractive Frenchy. 'I 'ate all Angleesh fud.'

Joyson turned on her. 'What will you be having for your Christmas dinner, then? frogs' legs and snails, I suppose?'

Whilst Frenchy struggled for a reply, the questioner was criticised by Green, though not for her xenophobic assumption. 'Heaven help us, Joy, it's over a month away!'

'Whatever it is, it'll be a damned sight better than t'other Christmas I spent with Uncle Teddy,' quoted Beata. 'Pork ribs and cabbage – eh, he were that tight he'd make Scrooge look like Good King Wenceslas.'

'Never mind, you'll be able to buy yourself something tasty with all these extra three and sixpences you're getting,' said Green. The auxiliaries had lately received a rise.

'Well, all *I* want for Christmas is to see some action.' Feeling self-conscious at being the only one left eating, Nell had laid down her cutlery and now sat back with a look of frustration. 'It's so annoying being all dressed up and nowhere to go.'

How she was to regret those words! For at half past eight that same evening, just as she was relaxing into a steamy bath, fantasising over Billy, her mother banged frantically on the door.

'Eleanor, your debut is nigh!'

Having shot upright, sluicing water from one end of the bath to the other and onto the black and white lino, Nell remained there for a second, suspended by shock and clutching the wedding ring that hung from her neck. 'Oh, Mother – what was that?'

'They've sent a messenger! You've to get to Leeman Road straight away – don't waste the water, leave it in for your father!'

Launching herself from the bath, a dripping Nell began rapidly to dry herself, stumbling and hopping over the putting on of her clothes, which clung to her still-damp limbs and much hindered her dressing. But it was all so exciting – she was needed at last!

'Have you any petrol at all in the car, Father?' came her breathless query upon rushing downstairs, clothes all awry.

'I don't want to waste it. You can borrow my bike, though!' he offered.

First came dismay – she was hopeless at balancing on two wheels – but then, 'Needs must!' Nell put on her hat and coat, and, with her father striding ahead to ensure the lights were turned off before opening the outer door, she hurried in his wake. Plunged into darkness, she held back whilst Wilfred tugged the awful contraption from the shed.

Hardly able to see what she was doing, trying to cope with the over-large vehicle, Nell had to stand on tiptoe to accommodate its crossbar, and swerved all over the road as she fought to work the pedals, 'Don't wait up for me, I may be all night!'

'A key! You'll need a key!' Thelma scuttled to fetch one, then raced to put it in Nell's pocket, causing yet more delay. But, eventually, with a helpful shove from her father, Nell somehow mobilised herself in ungainly fashion towards town.

With the traffic lights out of use and no policeman about, there was no option but to grit her teeth and hope for the best at junctions, and go careering into the black beyond, often forced to judder to an abrupt standstill by using her foot as a brake when a car almost flattened her, and nearly keeling over in the process. Only after a great many mishaps along the way did she get the hang of it, and finally sailed triumphantly into the sidings at Leeman Road, there to be met by a shadowy figure with a stopwatch.

A shielded torch was quickly flashed on and off in order for Sister Barber to read the time. 'You'll have to do better than this when it's the real thing, Nurse Spottiswood!' Once again there was disapprobation on the pretty freckled face, before it vanished into darkness.

Attempting to disentangle her leg from the crossbar, Nell tottered and almost capsized again. 'You mean . . . we're not going anywhere?' Her voice and expression told that she could scarcely believe this.

'No, this is just a dummy run to see how quickly we can be mustered in an emergency – and I have to say it's found us wanting,' Sister Barber added sternly to those other murky figures already assembled, all equally as dismayed as Nell. 'Very well, you can go home now.'

'To a cold bath?' muttered a displeased Nell to her friends, out of earshot of Sister, as she fought to heft her father's bike in the opposite direction and head off through the dark. 'Thank you very much, I don't think!'

'Bath on a Tuesday?' Beata called after her in amazement. 'By, you're posh!'

A couple of days after the test run Nell was able to laugh about it with the others, and to use it as a source of jollification for Billy. Since telling him about her tour of the city pubs to follow the Bedpan Swingsters, his letters to her had been quite tense, expressing the fear that she might be snatched from him by another soldier. As a result, she had immediately refrained from going again. He would be much happier to hear that her only company that Thursday evening would be the sensible Beata, with whom she had arranged to go to the pictures.

But, 'I'm a bit reluctant to divulge where I'll be, in case they spoil it again,' she whispered to Beata now, as, after a day of keeping the train clean and making more unused dressings, they put on their coats to leave work.

'I'm buggered if I'm telling them,' replied her friend more stringently. 'See you outside the Regal at seven!'

Laughing, Nell went home.

After a bite to eat and a change of clothing, Nell attempted to collect enough mascara for an application, scraping the little brush into every corner of its box, but all it produced was beige spit. Well, that was that. Unable to obtain more, she rummaged in the cupboard that still held a few childhood toys and brought out a paint box, pondering the feasibility of using one of its brown squares. But this was a failure. She would just have to rely on her natural lashes.

She had donned her coat, and was inserting her tuppence bus fare into her glove so as not to have to faff with her purse again, when her mother murmured confidentially in passing, 'I'll be going to the chemist in the morning. Would you like me to get you some things?'

Her days had been so consumed by hard work and writing letters to Billy, Nell had not noticed the absence of her monthly visitation, but now it immediately leapt to mind, and she turned crimson. By the discreet way her mother formed her lips to say '*things*', Nell knew she meant sanitary towels. It was a term neither of them ever used, except perhaps upon actually purchasing them at the chemist. Knowing how embarrassing her daughter found this, Mother was thinking to spare her blushes now, Nell recognised. However, there was much more to those reddened cheeks than she could ever imagine.

Stuttering, 'Oh, yes, thank you, Mother!' she reopened her purse, handed over the cash, then grabbed her gas mask and left the house, undergoing worried calculation as she hurried through the dark November mist for town.

She had not required *things* for over four months – before Billy went away. The realisation caused her to gasp aloud. Thank God her mother was no longer in earshot, for besides the sharp intake of breath, she would surely have been able to hear Nell's heart thudding as panic began to gain hold.

Forgetting all about the secret application of rouge that she would normally have made on her way, she bit her lip, her footsteps slowing as she tried to rationalise this – why, there was nothing really unusual, was there? Having only started her *whatnots* a year and a half ago, she had not yet achieved a regular cycle, and was accustomed to going two or even nearly three months without seeing a thing. What was the difference between three months and four? Exactly! Nell told herself firmly, as she began to walk at normal pace again. It was bound to happen soon. All she had to do was stay calm. Worrying over it would not make it occur any sooner. She must put any unthinkable idea out of her head.

That was rather difficult to do when one was stuck on a bus with nothing to take one's mind off it, and she concentrated on looking forward to meeting Beata. Prior to this, though, upon egress she handed her ticket back to the conductress, then made her way along the darkened streets to visit Bill's former digs. Having arranged this evening visit to town, it meant that she had had no need to call on the Preciouses directly after work, but could leave it till now. She hurried for Walmgate – the wrong side of town, as her parents would say. Well, there *were* some dreadful people here, conceded Nell, as two drunken Irishmen loomed at her out of the darkness, reeking of alcohol, and she was forced to veer around them. But there were some lovely ones too. Just the thought of what lay beyond that archway and along the alley caused her to smile.

There was an old fashioned gas lamp in the courtyard,

though now it stood redundant in the blackout. Using the wall to grope her way, incapable of seeing much but viewing it from memory, she stopped before a once noble Georgian mansion, now jammed in by slums – indeed, one itself. The spokes of its fanlight were rotten, its windows bereft of putty, centuries of paintwork eroded to bare timber. A house with psoriasis. Even her light rap of the tarnished brass knocker caused a shower of flakes.

Someone threw open the door. 'You're late!' bawled Ma Precious at the top of her voice, a sergeant-major in a floral pinafore.

Greatly familiar with this raucous behaviour, and perceiving no harm was meant, Nell smiled. 'I had to go home straight after work, so I thought I'd come now. Sorry to put you ou—'

'You're not putting us out, you daft cat! Get yourself in before the warden gives us a rollicking over the lights!' Ma waved merrily.

Nell hopped over the threshold, allowing the door to be closed behind her, though truth be told it was almost as dingy in here, there being no electric lighting, and the one gas mantle casting only a pathetic glow upon the linoleum of the hall. There was an appalling smell of fish too.

'At least you'll have time for a decent natter if you don't have to rush off home like you usually do!' Ma set off with manly strides, the soles of her tartan slippers squeaking the lino, expecting the other to follow, and calling ahead, 'Georgie, the lass is here, get that kettle on!'

'Not for me, thanks!' Nell refused hastily, remaining in the hall, the interior of the house being as neglected as the outside, with great fronds of wallpaper drooping over a once elegant staircase that wound its way up three more storeys. 'I've to meet my friend in fifteen minutes.'

Ma wheeled around, a hand placed indignantly on

each robust hip. 'Oh, so you thought you'd treat us as a convenience to save you having to wait in the cold?'

Having learned to take all insults here with a pinch of salt, Nell merely giggled at the old woman, who was at first glance intimidating, with her mannish build, her sharp brown eyes, and her gun-metal hair parted in the middle and wound into buns on each side of her head in the manner of earphones, but she was in fact a generous soul despite her bossy nature.

'Time enough to have a cup of tea and a chat with us, surely?' Ma proposed now in a more wheedling voice. 'All our lads are out at the pub. Go *on*!' And seeing Nell weaken, she dealt her a shove with one of her navvy's hands into the living room.

At once a time-traveller, Nell took delight in being plunged into bygone days, surrounded by aspidistras, Landseer prints and stuffed animals under glass domes. One exhibition of flowers and foliage, birds, field mice and squirrels was so gigantic it took up an entire corner. The furnishings were all very grand – there being much mahogany and inlay, mother-of-pearl, brocade and velvet, belonging formerly to a wealthier household – though, after fifty years with Ma, much dented, scuffed and torn – rather the same impression Nell had of the elderly man who rushed towards her now through another door.

Battered maybe, yet there was a spry delight upon the dear old face that came intimately close to hers, imbuing her with the scent of linseed oil as Georgie reached up to cup her cheeks in hands that were gnarled, the fingernails split and stained from repairing musical instruments. 'We feared you weren't coming – ooh, what cold little chops!' Dealing her cheeks an affectionate rub, he broke off in meek response to his wife's stentorian demand.

'Never mind "*your tiny hand is frozen*," Casanova – where's that tea I asked for?' said Ma.

'Sorry, dearie, the kettle's on now!' he hastened to say

with an affectionate rub of her arm. 'I was just getting rid of that pan of fish heads into the garden – I've been boiling up a little treat for our chucky hens,' he added to the visitor, explaining the stench. 'They're not laying like they used to do. We've had barely half a dozen eggs this week. yet not so long ago there was a proper glut.'

Ma lost patience. 'You know what glut rhymes with? Foot! You'll be getting mine up your khyber if you don't fetch this lass her tea – by, he can't half talk!' she declared to their visitor as her husband rushed to obey.

Nell bit her lip over this reversal of roles, as Georgie scuttled about getting teapot, cups and saucers. Never had she seen Mrs Precious lift one finger in the kitchen, or anywhere else come to that – but her husband seemed not to regard himself as henpecked, and obviously worshipped the ground she walked on. For all her bluster Ma loved him too, Nell guessed, from the way she encouraged his romantic serenades on the concertina. Hopefully there would be none tonight, though, for she was anxious to get away.

Etched against a background of dark, elaborate wallpaper with crimson roses and acanthus leaves, and varnished woodwork, Ma swivelled to address her again. 'Right, sit down!' It was more order than invitation. 'Then you can have what you *really* came for.' And with a shrewd cast of her head she went to snatch a letter from the mantel.

With every surface cluttered, Nell trod a careful path to a sofa, avoiding the black and tan rug complete with head and glassy eyes, which had been one of the Preciouses' favourite dogs. In addition to this, there was a ginger Pomeranian, also stuffed, and a live, if decrepit, black terrier with bad teeth and foul breath, which hankered to be petted as Nell finally reached the velvet sofa that had seen so many rears that it was almost bald. Perched against these fantastic surroundings, giving the dog a cursory pat, a cat on her lap and its tail snaking back and forth under her nose until she brushed the animal gently aside, Nell accepted the cup of rather stewed tea donated by Georgie, and was about to take a biscuit from the extended plate when at that same moment Ma thrust a letter at her.

'Not enough hands!' laughed Nell. Thanking them both, and trying to juggle the cup of tea, she put it aside in order to take the letter, which was then shoved straight into her gas-mask container, this being the norm.

But, 'Aren't you going to read it to us then, seeing as you've deigned to honour us by sitting down?' On the other sofa now, Ma leaned forward expectantly, her chunky legs apart to display flesh-coloured bloomers, and a hand on each knee. 'We never get to hear what he's doing, do we, Georgie?'

The old fellow gave a dejected smile, and shook his pink, bald head as he lowered his wiriness next to her bulk, the plate of biscuits on his lap.

Other than keeping them informed of Bill's wellbeing, Nell was loath to share his words with anyone else. 'Well, I'd better drink this tea, it's a crime to waste it – and I don't want to be late for my friend!'

'She's having us on – wants to keep him to herself!' Ma gave her husband a knowing wink to indicate she was joking, though Nell reddened all the same. 'Oh, never mind, lass!' she placated. 'We know what it's like to be in love, don't we, sweetheart?'

'We certainly do, dearie!' The meek old Georgie leaned towards her in adoration – though Ma had not been addressing him but Milo the stinking old terrier, which she promptly swept to her bosom and proceeded to cuddle like a baby, and to feed with titbits from the plate.

Ashamed at treating the old couple so shabbily when they obviously viewed Bill as one of their own, and were always so amenable to her, Nell gave a capitulating smile and ripped open the envelope.

And then such unexpected joy. 'He's coming up at the weekend!'

Whilst Ma and Georgie exclaimed in pleasure, exciting the dog who wriggled to be free, Nell almost collapsed from relief, her eyes filling with tears as she skimmed the rest.

'Where's he stopping?' demanded Ma, large shovels of hands casting the terrier to the floor. 'Write and tell him he must kip with us!'

'He'll surely come here of his own accord, dearie,' Georgie stated to his wife, whilst Nell continued trying to read, completely unaware of her antiquated surroundings now, more intent on the word of today as she devoured the familiar script.

'What else?' pestered Ma.

'Er, nothing much . . .' This negated the big smile on Nell's face, but she was not about to tell them of Bill's desire to spend the whole weekend as they had last time. 'He does mention coming to visit you, though.' Loud satisfaction emerged from Ma. 'They're still being trained hard, but he sounds in good spirits.' As was Nell. Bounding to her feet, she tucked the letter away and slung the gas-mask container over her shoulder. 'Sorry, but I really will have to meet my friend – so long!' And in this state of near euphoria, she left.

She was still beaming from ear to ear when, less than three minutes later, she met up with her friend outside the nearby Regal cinema, waving her most recent letter. 'Billy's coming to visit this weekend!'

'I wondered why you looked as bright as a button,' remarked Beata with a smile. 'Didn't think it could be 'cause of me.'

'Oh, I'm pleased to see you as well, Killie!' Having come to regard the latter as a favourite aunt, Nell pressed Beata's arm.

Then, in a fit of exhilaration, her hand reached up to

feel the hard little nugget beneath her clothes – the wedding ring on its neck chain which had never been removed since that last weekend with Bill. But she might need to transfer it to her finger if another trip away was on the cards! Perhaps, too, she could change his mind about marriage, get a special licence, so as to wear the ring for real.

But there might be an obstacle to meeting him at all, and in this she enlisted her friend's help. 'The trouble is, my parents still don't know about him, and I'm afraid they'll prevent me going for some reason . . .' She bit her lip. 'I know it's an enormous liberty, but would you mind if I use your company as an excuse to go out on Friday night, perhaps Saturday too?'

Beata's change of expression showed that she did mind. 'Not if it involves having to lie.'

'It needn't.' Nell tried gently to persuade her. 'If you were to call at my house, as if we were going out together –'

'Then you could ditch me before I cramp your style,' finished Beata, tongue in cheek.

'No! I'd never do that.' Although it was obvious she was only using her friend, Nell suffered barely any guilt, for she would have employed whatever desperate means to be with Billy. 'You could come out with Billy and me, perhaps for a few drinks, then . . . maybe go home a little earlier.' Her face formed an entreating smile.

'Why don't you just hang a sign saying gooseberry round my neck and have done with it?' joked her friend.

Nell showed compunction, but, 'Please, Killie! This is so important, and I just don't know what else to do! I *must* see him.'

Beata studied the urgency on that young face. 'Well . . . I suppose if I am going to tag along with you, it wouldn't really be a lie, would it?' And she had harboured such romantic yearnings herself once. Who was she to stand in love's way? 'All right,' she sighed, as Nell began to dance with excitement, 'Give me your address and I'll be your alibi – but come on now or we'll miss the picture! Not that it'll have as much bloomin' intrigue as you've got to offer.'

On Friday evening, as arranged, Beata duly turned up at Nell's house. Pleased that their daughter had such a mature, sensible-looking friend, Thelma and Wilfred made no complaint at her going out on the town yet again, not even when Nell announced that she and Beata would probably be enjoying Saturday together too.

Luckily, none of this involved Beata having to lie. 'But I'm not too keen on you misleading them like this,' she told Nell, as she hobbled alongside her to the bus stop.

'I'll make it up to you, Killie!' swore Nell. 'I promise. I hate having to do it too, but I daren't risk telling them. I've missed him so much – oh, you'll love him when you meet him!'

Beata turned impish. 'I might take a fancy to him and pinch him off you.'

But, still in high spirits, Nell merely laughed. For as lovely-natured as she was, how could plain and plump old Killie be serious competition?

It was very cold when they reached the station, which was the appointed meeting place with Bill. Buying a platform ticket for each of them, Nell and her friend hurried through the barrier.

The temperature was a good deal lower here, the icy air seeming to ricochet from the stone beneath their feet. Waiting to pounce on him the moment he stepped off the train, Nell pranced from one foot to the other, half in cold, half in excitement. 'Sorry to make you wait,' she told her friend when, after fifteen minutes, he still had not shown up. 'He's usually so punctual.'

Beata huddled into her coat, and said in her patient manner, 'Not to worry . . .' But the way she rubbed her gloved hands told otherwise.

Anxiously watching and waiting for Bill to arrive, as trains came and went, Nell made no other comment for some while. But after noticing Beata adopt different positions in the next quarter of an hour, even with her mind on other things she was forced to respond to her friend's discomfort. 'Killie, you must be freezing, I'm so sorry, I don't know where he's got to – let me buy you a cup of tea in the café. If we sit by the window we'll still be able to see him when he arrives.'

But, when the cups of tea were drained, Bill had still not come.

Nell had grown uneasy. She was trying not to be, but it showed on her face and in the drumming of her fingers on the table. 'Right, well, I can't expect you to hang around all night waiting for him, Killie. Why don't you go home?'

'I don't know if I should leave you . . .'

I'll be perfectly safe,' Nell reassured her in a level tone.

'All right then – but stay in here and keep warm,' instructed Beata, rising to leave.

'I will,' came Nell's reply. 'And I'm so sorry for dragging you on this wild goose chase. I swear I'll make it up to you – and I'll get the culprit to treat you to drinks tomorrow night, how's that?'

Accepting this, Beata wished her friend goodnight. 'And give him gyp when he does turn up.'

'Oh, I shall!' vowed Nell.

But her suspense was to continue as another half-hour ticked away. Wandering out of the refreshment room, she cast a fretful gaze around the platform, and then the one opposite. There were squads of men in khaki greatcoats about, but none of them were Bill.

By nine thirty, accepting that he wasn't going to come, and with the weather too cold to hang around any longer, a frantic Nell turned about and strode quickly towards town, intending to see if he had gone instead to the Preciouses.

But then why would he? Her stride faltered in the realisation that Bill would never have abandoned her like this unless something was wrong. And she might needlessly be disturbing Ma and Georgie, who always went to bed early. Standing still now in the middle of the pavement, a gloved hand over her mouth, Nell began to flick through a catalogue of awful things that might have befallen him, uncaring of those who occasionally stumbled against her in the darkness, her mind and heart in turmoil over Billy. Somewhere, behind a dark bank of cloud, droned a squadron of Halifax bombers. Steeped in worry, and too familiar with this harmonious sound, Nell paid it little heed either. Only a human emission caused alarm.

'Coming for a ducky with us, love?'

She jumped violently at the voice that was close to her ear, and immediately shook off the soldiers' advances.

'Oy, keep your hair on!' laughed one of them, as she fled home in distress.

How she had prevented her distress being relayed to her parents, Nell did not care, only that it was still there in the morning. A thousand thoughts had traversed her mind since then, one of them being how would she ever get through the weekend not knowing what had happened to him? Perhaps an explanation of his absence would arrive in the morning post – she must visit the Preciouses first thing.

Rising far earlier than normal, disturbing her mother who poked her head from her room and made bleary-eyed enquiry as to where Nell was going without any breakfast, she replied truthfully that she had volunteered to put in some extra hours at the Infirmary and would eat there. Then, whispering so as not to wake her father, she hissed, 'Sorry, Mother, I forgot to tell you I'd be getting up so early. Go back to bed, and I'll see you later!' And off she sped to the Preciouses, rousing them too from bed.

But Ma and Georgie had heard nothing at all.

With a quick apology for disturbing them at this ungodly hour, Nell refused the invitation to enter, and said she would return in the afternoon, following work.

But nine excruciating hours later, there was still no letter.

Distracted by her concern for Billy, baffling her parents with her strange, absent-minded behaviour, Nell was to pay these twice-daily visits to the Preciouses for the best part of a week, hope dwindling at every turn. Bill was dead. Much as she hated to contemplate it, she was certain it must be true, for he would never have been so heartless as to leave her like this. But would her fears ever be confirmed, or was she to remain in limbo for the rest of her life?

Coming over the ancient threshold again this evening, wavering bleakly in the hall to be informed that there was again no letter for her, Nell snatched at anything that might prevent her from weeping in front of witnesses. A tabby cat was winding itself around her calves. She bent quickly to stroke it. 'You're very fussy tonight, puss . . .'

'I think the dirty trollop's having kittens,' announced Ma.

Nell burst into tears.

There were exclamations of pity from the elderly couple, Georgie being the first to comfort, dealing gentle pats to the stooped figure that was racked with sobs. 'Aw, don't worry, dearie! There's probably some good excuse for Bill not coming.'

'But he would have written!' Nell's face shot up to accuse him with red and tear-filled eyes. 'Something's happened to him, I know it!'

'It doesn't mean he's *dead*!' brayed Mrs Precious with slight scorn. 'He could have been sent abroad without warning – you know what the army's like.'

'He'd still have managed to get a letter through,' sobbed Nell, fumbling for her handkerchief. 'Oh God, what am I going to do?' For she knew now, just as surely as her darling Billy was dead, that she was carrying his child.

5

Another week went by, and then another, taking Nell into December. Even now, the fear having churned her stomach into a pit of acid, she persisted in hanging on, visiting the Preciouses almost every night, and posting her letters to Billy. For, until confirmation of his death was put in writing, there remained the shred of hope that it had all been a mistake. All of it.

Being informed almost immediately that Bill was missing, Beata had been the source of comfort that Nell's parents could never be, for they remained unaware – though of course they could see that their daughter was troubled by some matter. Hence, thinking it perhaps to be something at work, they were happy for her to accept her fellow nurse's frequent invitations to the pictures, without guessing what these trips were meant to ease. Seated there in the darkened cinema, though, Nell felt anything but eased, barely concentrating on the opening film, let alone the tips on cookery and the shorts from the Ministry of Information – until the one that forewarned the audience about careless talk: 'Keep mum!'

Oh, yes, she really came awake then, and took to picking over her dilemma in such great detail that when a cheer went up over the downing of another Hun, she almost jumped out of her skin.

Then, finding herself under amused inspection from

Beata, she returned a half-hearted little smile, and momentarily attended the newsreel. But soon her mind was to wander again.

The interval brought community singing. Irritated beyond belief, Nell lit a cigarette and, whilst others sang, took puff after nervous puff of it, until the theatre eventually reverted to darkness. As if the uncomfortable seat was not bad enough, its rough moquette prickling the underneath of her legs, her bladder chose that moment to signal it required emptying again. Having purposefully gone before she came in, Nell damned her system for its current inefficiency, and tried to hold off for as long as she could.

But, constantly wriggling in discomfort, she was eventually to receive a tap on the shoulder.

'Excuse me, love, but have you got worms?' came an impatient demand from the man behind, whose view she had perpetually blocked.

Tutting with embarrassment, Nell apologised and turned back to the drama that had managed to capture her interest at last. But straight away an air-raid warning came onto the screen to interrupt a crucial moment, the slide instructing everyone who required to leave to do so in an orderly fashion.

'Get on with it!' hollered the man behind, the whole audience groaning in unison, and most people remaining in their seats.

Desperate for the lavatory by now, Nell rose quickly and made her way to the end of the row, whispering to Beata, 'Don't miss the picture, I'll be back when I've spent a penny.'

Once in the cubicle, she took the opportunity to undo the top hooks and eyes of her corset, gasping as she lowered herself onto the seat, then sitting back to savour these few moments of relief. Soon, though, the sound of someone else waiting outside the door had her hurrying to do up her corset and emerge.

But as she did so, who should she almost collide with but Sister Barber.

Both looked stunned, before Nell turned shamefully aside to wash her hands, and Sister hovered to observe: 'I heard nothing to the effect that you'd be here tonight. Nurse Spottiswood – you're meant to keep the authorities informed!'

Nell could think of no excuse, other than to stammer, 'I'm sorry, Sister, it was a last last-minute arrangement . . .'

'One that could get you dismissed!'

Nell was immediately gripped by terror: how could she support a child with no job? Her parents were going to be angry enough as it was – perhaps even kick her out – she would need every penny to maintain herself. She turned with dripping hands from the sink, about to beg for mercy, when just at that point Beata came to look for her.

'Oh, and this is your partner in crime!' came Sister's withering proclamation, giving Nell leave to dry her hands. 'I thought better of you, Kilmaster. Do neither of you grasp how important it is that we know your every whereabouts? It's imperative that we're able to muster the entire crew at a moment's notice, we can't hang around whilst the messenger visits every pub and picture house in York in the hope of finding you there! Are you masquerading as nurses?'

'No! I'm truly serious about this, Sister,' objected Nell, both she and Beata apologetic. But Sister remained waspish and obviously not satisfied. 'I'll see you both in my office tomorrow morning.' And she jerked her head for them to go.

'Oh God, I can't get the sack – not on top of everything else!' uttered a frantic Nell to Beata as they hurried for the exit. She was close to tears again, and could not understand how the other remained so calm.

'She won't get us fired,' assured her friend in that gently confident way of hers. 'She was just letting off steam.'

Nell felt like shaking her older friend for such complacency. 'Maybe not you, but she's always had it in for me!'

Beata tried to coax her, as both made the decision to abandon their night out and turn for home. 'I can promise you, you won't get the sack. Listen to your Aunty Beat.' She sighed. 'Oh, I can see you're going to spend the night fretting if I don't tell you . . .'

'Tell me what?'

'I know Sister's little secret,' disclosed Beata with a sly grin. 'She lives near me. Her husband runs a pub.'

Nell was utterly flummoxed.

'Nurses're not supposed to have a pub address,' explained Beata. 'Sister gave Matron a false one, I overheard her.'

Nell heaved a vast sigh of relief, but in that same turn she clicked her tongue. 'You could have given me this ammunition before, instead of letting her boss me around all these weeks!'

'You needed bossing around,' retorted Beata, only half-joking. 'Anyway, it wasn't my place to let on about Sister, we're all entitled to our secrets.' Then, astonished that Nell's eyes bulged with unexpected tears, she was swift to say, 'I wasn't thinking, love . . . keep your chin up, you're bound to hear from him soon. That's who you're really worried about, isn't it?'

Dabbing at her eyes and blowing into her handkerchief, Nell moved her head up and down, thinking but not saying, Oh, Killie, if only you knew the half of it. But then, *did* she know? Had she guessed? Darting teary eyes over her friend's face, Nell tried to read what was there, wondering whether to throw herself on the other's mercy . . .

But then the moment was gone. If Beata had guessed, she did not say as she delved into her pocket and handed Nell a sweet. And, knowing her friend's opinion on unmarried mothers, Nell could not bear to incur such disapproval.

* * *

Thankfully, Sister's own disapproval had mellowed by the following morning. Beata turned out to be right, neither she nor Nell were to be sacked, but received only an admonition to keep their superiors informed from now on.

Despite it being a relief, though, it was only one less thing for Nell to worry about. Awaiting news, day after day, night after night, she continued to haunt the Preciouses, and eventually those tireless visits were to bear fruit.

But it was the bitterest, most noxious of fruit. And the letter came not from Billy, but from his mother.

There was an unaccustomed delicacy to Mrs Precious's masculine features as she handed it over, that suggested she already knew what was in its pages. Inviting Nell to sit down, she and Georgie hung on the youngster's every nuance whilst the envelope was opened with trembling hands, and the reader braced herself to ingest the terrible words.

Mrs Kelly had found, amongst her dead son's belongings, a bundle of letters. '*Please forgive me for not writing to you sooner*,' she had painfully scrawled, '*but I've been so terribly upset myself, and had no way of letting you know about Billy until I gathered the courage to go through his things, and found the letters bearing your name. I recognised Mrs Precious's address at the top, because Bill occasionally dropped me a line from there whilst he was in York. And I knew, of course, that he had met a girl up there whom he thought the world of, and that he was going to marry her when the war was over. Always told me everything did my Bill, showed me your photograph, and said what lovely long letters you wrote him. Well, I could see that for myself when I came across them. I hasten to say I didn't take the liberty of reading them –*'

Nell felt sure she had, but cared nothing for this, and quickly read on, a pulse thrumming her neck. '*– they were* *private between you and my son, and must remain so. You shall have them back if you wish. Billy did say that your parents wouldn't approve of you going out with anyone, you being so young. But he was willing to wait. And he said you felt the same. That's why I thought I should let you know the circumstances of his passing . . .'*

Visualising the writer taking a deep breath in preparation of having to pen the following lines, Nell took one too, trying to fight the impulse to vomit, as the walls and all their bizarre contents seemed to press in on her, her hands trembling even more.

'*Even though it must be awfully sad for you to read, you will surely want to know why he suddenly disappeared from your life. We'd suffered a night of terrible bombing. I can't describe how bad it was to you. Billy and other soldiers were sent out to help with the rescue. There were lots of people trapped under fallen buildings, and Billy crawled in amongst the rubble trying to locate a child whom he could hear crying. The walls collapsed, and my boy was killed instantly, along with a good few of his friends. I can't tell you how my heart still breaks. I still keep expecting to see his smiling face appear round the door and saying, "Wotcher, Mum!" Life will never be the same without him. I fear I shall never get over it. But that's as it should be, I'm his mother. It's different for you, you're still a girl, and Billy wouldn't want you to be miserable. I know you'll be terribly sad on reading this, but after you've had a good cry you must try to get on with your life . . .*' Nell broke down and sobbed noisily into her lap, unable to bear any more.

The Preciouses were immediately there with words of comfort, but Nell could take comfort in nothing, and merely sat weeping in the presence of talking heads.

'She sent us a nice letter too, didn't she, Georgie?' Ma lowered her volume to fit the occasion, though it was less than gentle on the ear. 'Thanked us for looking after him

– I wrote straight back and told her we don't need thanking, he was a pleasure to have, just like a son.'

His kind old face twisted in concern for the still-weeping Nell, Georgie asked tentative permission of his wife: 'Shall I bring her it, do you think, dearie?' And at her nod, he trotted from the room.

Shocked to the core, feeling ready to faint, Nell barely noticed him go, nor return, until a wristwatch was held under her nose.

Georgie gave gentle explanation as the watch was transferred from his gnarled old fingers, their nails split and stained with oil, into Nell's young and chapped ones. 'It's Bill's. I've had it in my workshop since he went. I didn't have time to fix it then, so he left it with me. I did try, but my fingers aren't as nimble as they used to be, I'm afraid, nor my eyes as good. A watchmaker would have no trouble, though. Anyway, we thought you might like it . . .'

Touched, but even more heartbroken, the tears streaming down her face, a shuddering Nell pressed the watch between her hands, unable to thank him.

'It's not much of a legacy for a hero, is it?' submitted Ma with a heavy sigh.

And Nell sobbed again.

It was impossible, of course, to hide such deep grief from her parents.

'Eleanor, whatever's the matter?' Thelma had been sitting in the firelight with her husband, listening to the nine o'clock news, but now put down her knitting and came hurrying to comfort her daughter, who had burst into tears at the moment of entry, her face already blotched and puffy from its previous onslaught. 'Has something horrible occurred at work? We were worried when you were so late –'

Nell shook her head vigorously, spattering her coat with tears and mucus, trying to make herself stop crying in order that she might explain, but the moment she thought of Bill, she broke down again.

Wilfred Spottiswood turned off the wireless, sufficiently affected by his daughter's distress to curtail the report of British exploits in the Western Desert. But he hung back, not knowing how to handle it, and so leaving it to her mother.

Finally, Nell was able to blurt in a shaky voice, 'A very dear friend of mine was killed.' It was all she could utter before dissolving again.

'Today?' Despite trying to commiserate, Thelma could not help questioning her daughter's facts. 'But there've been no raids.'

'Not here,' Nell managed to gasp. 'London. Someone just told me.'

'Oh, how horrible for you. Oh my dear, I'm so sorry.' Issuing murmur of comfort, Thelma began to undo Nell's coat, helping the deranged girl to take it off, then drawing her to the fire. 'Come along and sit here, I've kept some cottage pie warm in the oven, you can have it on your lap just for tonight.'

The thought of this almost made Nell retch. 'Mother, I couldn't eat it!'

'No, of course not . . .' Thelma came back through the firelight to sit beside her daughter, wringing her hands and saying thoughtfully, 'She must have been a very dear friend for you to be so upset.'

Nell nodded through a blur of tears.

'How did –'

'Leave the girl alone!' Wilfred jumped in impatiently. 'You're making her worse by all these questions.'

'Yes, yes, how thoughtless of me.' Nell's mother took issue with herself. 'Maybe you'd just like to go to bed, dear?'

Nell required no further invitation to escape, and bolted for the darkness of the staircase. 'I'll fetch you a mug of

Ovaltine with some aspirin, it'll help you sleep,' came the soothing addition from her mother. 'I am very sorry, dear. We both are.'

Beneath the surface of her fitful sleep, her brain still reeling with visions good and bad, surrendering both to impulse and exhaustion, Nell chose to remain in bed the following morning. Lashing out to end the alarm clock's violent demands, she pulled the sheets and blankets up over her head, and tried to gain oblivion. But as her hand slipped beneath the pillow it encountered Bill's watch, and the tears came again. Forever seven o'clock – oh, would that it were, yearned Nell, as her mind replayed the scene that had led to this perpetuity. And to worsen her grief was the thought that poor Bill had died not knowing that he was to be a father.

A series of respectful taps came at the door. 'You're going to be late, dear.'

Nell crammed a fistful of pillow around each ear. 'I'm sick.' It was not pretence. This malaise felt as real as any bodily affliction.

But, 'Lying there moping won't take your mind off your bad news,' persisted Thelma, peering in for a moment. Not one for hugs, she tried to comfort her daughter in the only way she could: with advice. 'It might make you feel better if you throw yourself into your work – that's what I always do when I'm a bit sad. Besides, it's not very responsible to let the hospital down, is it?'

And ultimately, left alone, Nell was to see the truth in this, and to drag herself from the sparse comfort offered by the bed. After pondering one last time over Billy's watch, through eyes that contained a ton of grit under each lid, she pressed it with a tender kiss, then hid it in the same place as his photograph and letters, in a hatbox, under the boater she had worn at school. And there they must remain from now on, came Nell's miserable decision, as she donned her nurse's uniform. For only in hard work could she hope to bury such enormous grief.

Preceding this, though, she must explain her stricken countenance to Beata – although the other had guessed the moment she saw those reddened eyes.

'I do know a little bit of the way you're feeling,' Beata confided, wanting to heal the ugliness that defaced Nell's gentle features. 'I lost someone I was madly in love with – he wasn't killed,' she added swiftly, 'but he might as well have been, the way it hit me. You feel as if your own life's not worth living, don't you?' At a fresh gushing of tears from Nell, she went on softly, with a faraway look in her eye, 'We'd been courting for ages, but the only obligation he felt towards me was to let me down lightly by letter. We lived too far apart, and he'd found a girl closer to home. We'd remain good friends, he said, and me thinking we were so much more, but there you are . . .' Her glazed expression melted into one of kind concern, as she stroked Nell's arm. 'I know it can't compare with your loss, not one bit, and you won't forget about him. But believe me, it will pass.'

No it won't, howled Nell's heart. Still tearful at the mere thought, she begged her friend, 'Could you tell Sister and the others? I couldn't bear having to go through this time after time . . .'

Beata promised that of course she would.

But unnervingly, upon Sister being apprised, she insisted on having a word in person. Expecting a soulless lecture, dashing her gritty eyes for the umpteenth time, Nell approached her superior's office with dismay. And, true to form, even if the words were ones of sympathy, the sermon began in the usual terse fashion.

'First, let me say how sorry I was to hear of your bereavement, Nurse Spottiswood.'

Immediately revisited by the gargantuan lump in her throat, Nell tried to swallow it, but it refused to budge.

'I do understand the fragile state you must be in,' continued Sister. 'It's a ghastly thing that's happened to you, and there'll be times when you can't prevent yourself from bursting into tears . . .'

But you must try not to display such an unprofessional attitude, prophesied Nell, anger and resentment fermenting in her breast. And try as she might, she could not allay the scalding mist that rushed to her eyes yet again, and she bent her head so that Sister might not take this as an indication that she was too feeble to carry out her work.

'Whenever that occasion arises,' finished Sister, 'I would simply ask that you take yourself off to a cubby hole, and have your little weep in private, get completely rid of it, then clean yourself up and get on with your work. We shall all make allowances if you suddenly go absent.' As Nell's bloodshot eyes shot up to transmit surprised gratitude, Sister added, 'I'm not a complete ogre, Nurse.' And with a protracted and telling look, she ordered softly, 'Off you go now.'

Such compassionate treatment brought the tears in full flow now. Mindful of the advice, Nell dashed straight to the lavatory and spent a good few minutes racked in sobs, hoping to dislodge that choking lump in her throat in order that she might breathe, trying to wring every last drop of unshed grief from her aching body, so that it might suffer no repeat of this handicap and allow her to operate like a professional human being. Finally, she splashed her face with water, took a series of deep, steadying breaths, and emerged red-eyed, but prepared to get on with her job.

Against all determination to the contrary, that shedding of tears was not to be Nell's last. Far from it. But, with her colleagues equally sympathetic, and none of them seeking to interrogate, she was at least able to indulge in these bouts of sorrow as often as they afflicted her, everyone naturally assuming that her tears were all for Bill.

But what if they or Sister had known of her other anxiety? Would they have been so philanthropic then? The fear of being stigmatised prohibited any foray. There was no one in whom to confide, not even Beata, for Nell was well aware of her friend's views on the matter of illegitimacy.

So, Nell continued to bear her burden alone, at times consumed by terror, at others elated that her lovely, heroic Bill had left a part of him growing inside her, and though the memories of him were to endure, eventually her tears were to recede.

Following the initial concern over her daughter, and having lent her a couple of weeks in which to get over the loss of her friend, Nell's mother was finally to note one December eve, 'I'm glad to see you enjoying your food again, dear, and looking so much better too.'

Nell regarded her with eyes dulled by fatalism. How could one's body appear in such rude health, when one's soul felt close to death?

'I told you eating properly would do the trick,' said Thelma, yet she was not quite so insensitive as to believe that all was fine. 'I know you must still be feeling sad, but you've done exceptionally well in covering it up. I think you were right to go back to work straight away. There's nothing like it for taking your mind off things, especially in a job such as yours where people are worse off. Let's hope the Christmas festivities will help to put the vim back – such as they are with this blessed war on.'

Christmas. How Nell had been dreading all the manufactured gaiety that this would spell for her, having to pretend for those around her that she was enjoying it, whilst constantly arrested by this tiny being that fluttered inside.

Nevertheless, when Christmas morning arrived, for others' sakes she was to adopt the obligatory beam of gratitude over the presents that had been bought for her, and to uphold this aching rictus throughout the morning whilst helping her mother cook the dinner, indeed through the eating of it, and to carry it forward even into the late afternoon, when she and her parents made a teatime visit to their kin.

But there the invented smile was to slip. With her expanding girth under tight control from the corset, until now no one had commented on Nell's radiance, but Aunty Phyllis had not seen her niece for some time, and was quick to remark as her guests took off their coats.

'Good Lord, someone's been eating too much Christmas pudding!'

Nell flushed as everyone's eyes turned to her, and, with her jaw agape, it was left to Thelma to retort, 'Christmas pudding? Which of us has enjoyed Christmas pudding with no dried fruit to be had?'

Thankful to have the attention diverted, Nell struggled to regain her equilibrium, whilst Aunty Phyllis made a sound of disbelief. 'Thelma Spottiswood with no dried fruit? I don't think!'

Her sister-in-law laughed. 'As a matter of fact, I have been holding on to some, but it was a choice between cake or pudding, and the cake's so much more versatile and it keeps all year. So I tore a recipe out of the press for Christmas pudding using carrots – you wouldn't think they'd be an especially good substitute, but I had to tell Wilfred and Eleanor after they'd eaten it, they couldn't tell the difference. Shovelled it in, they did!'

'I can see that!' Aunty Phyllis's eyes were on Nell again, looking her up and down. Then she rubbed her niece's arms in fun. 'Mrs Roly-Poly! Well, I hope you're not going to be disappointed with what I've got for your tea, I'm not so clever as your mother.'

'I'm sure it'll be lovely!' Nell had managed to revive her smile, and hoped that her voice did not betray tension as she and her family were shown to their seats. But she was already making a premature New Year resolution to eat less, and wondered bleakly if she were the only person at that table who was thankful for wartime rationing.

Dark days ahead, His Majesty had warned in his festive speech, and for sure, the old year went out on a violent note. With an intense bombardment, the Germans had distorted the familiar outline of London into a huge inferno. Even upon viewing those cinema newsreels, it was impossible to comprehend what it must be like to endure this night after night, and this gave Nell fresh cause to worry. For, since Mrs Kelly's poignant letter, she had corresponded with the grandmother of her unborn child, as if to keep another little part of Bill alive. Hence, she was to worry over her safety, and that of Bill's brothers and sisters. She might soon need their help if her parents were to throw her out. Still, she refrained from confiding in the Kellys for now, partly through fear of rejection. She would never be able to bear it, if they too spurned Bill's child.

She would have to tell her parents soon, though. Another month was almost up, propelling her towards the inevitable. How, though? thought Nell, as she shivered through one January evening after another, nursing her secret, listening to the news with her parents. One could not just slip it in between the items from the wireless, say – 'Oh, such good news that the price of custard powder's been frozen, and by the way, I'm expecting a baby.' Equally wrong, when Father was rejoicing over those allied victories in Tobruk, and inviting his daughter to partake in a celebratory glass of sherry with him and Mother. Nell just could not bring herself to wipe away those smiles, nor to invoke the overwhelming sense of let-down that would surely follow her confession.

Hence, both that month and the next were allowed to roll by, Nell's situation worsening with every day, aided only by ingenuity. Her own corset now too small, she had rummaged through her mother's old clothes and found a replacement. There was a shop in town that specialised in nurses' uniforms, including the one she herself wore; thus was she to acquire a larger size to accommodate her growing girth, and no one would be any the wiser. For much of the day, too, she was able to disguise this under a capacious apron, and because it was winter a navy-blue cardigan provided an extra shield. Tall and large-boned, never slender at the best of times, she had managed to conceal it perhaps better than someone more delicate – though *surely* being surrounded by those with medical knowledge meant that one of them must observe it any day soon.

At least the baby did not sap its mother's strength, and she had copious amounts of energy to devote to her work, which seemed to be all that mattered to her superiors. One of her peers, though, had certainly become alert to the amount of times Nell had taken to excusing herself to the lavatory of late.

'Bloomin' heck, why don't you just set up residence in there?' sighed Joyson, as Nell broke away from her group of friends as all were on their way to lunch one day.

Though blushing deeply, Nell managed to form a sarcastic reply. 'I'm so sorry, Joy, I didn't realise you were doing a thesis on my bladder movements.' Egged on by her other colleagues' laughter, she enquired in the same whimsical tone, 'Would you care to come in with me to measure how much urine I excrete?'

'Well! You're always disappearing in there,' complained Joyson, looking her up and down. 'Anyone'd think you had a problem.'

'My only problem is you,' stated Nell, made even more uncomfortable by everyone's eyes being upon her. Had one of them finally noticed the rippling bump, and would they draw attention to it? She herself was acutely aware of it moving under her apron, so violently did the baby protest at being restricted by its mother's corset. It felt as if it were trying to kick its way to liberty, shoving its feet underneath her ribs and pressing with all its might.

'Leave the lass alone!' Beata was still chuckling over Nell's last comment. 'It's the cold weather, isn't it, love?' she prompted the one under scrutiny. 'I have the same trouble.'

'Ooh, me and all,' revealed the owlish Green.

Their grateful friend turned for the lavatory. 'Right, you all go on, I'll catch you up – I wouldn't want to keep Joy from her dinner.'

'Don't mind her, love, we'll wait,' replied the kind-hearted Beata.

Which was all very well, but it added to the pressure Nell felt herself under, as she hurried to the lavatory, unbuttoning and unhooking, then seating herself for a few moments' relief.

Granted more freedom, the one in her abdomen stretched its limbs, knees and elbows, distorting the shape of her belly. Despite the awfulness of her situation, and not for the first time, Nell felt an overwhelming wave of love for it, and placed her hand upon the mound that rippled from its subterranean movement. 'I suppose you'll want some clothes,' she told it fondly, before biting her lip so as not to cry at the thought of its poor father. Stop! Stop thinking of him, she scolded herself, biting down hard, you can't start blubbing again.

Forcing herself to concentrate on practicalities, she listed the items that she would need. One thing was certain, she would not have the outlay for many of these, perhaps a bonnet or a bib, but she would need every penny if the worst came to the worst. Well, her mother had shanks of wool from the WVS, she could filch a little of that, a tiny amount wouldn't be missed; it might mean an unsuitable colour for baby, but she could trim the items with ribbons. Nappies, she would need those too.

The word thief had never been ascribed to Nell, but desperation lured her to contemplate it now. Perhaps by volunteering to do more hours at the Infirmary she could inveigle her way onto the nursery ward, and take some nappies one by one. She was aware that every piece of linen was counted, for this had been amongst her chores, but was anyone really going to hold an inquest over the odd missing item? A feeding bottle could perhaps be spirited away from there too. But what about a pram – and a cot? She couldn't secret either of those under her clothes. Never mind, they were not necessities. The child could be carried whilst it was small. She stroked her abdomen thoughtfully, imagining its resident five years hence, all the things it would need then – indeed, where would she be herself? When would she be able to pluck up the courage to tell anyone? When would it actually arrive? What on earth was she going to do?

But as and whenever this last thought came, Nell drove it away. In any case, she was soon yanked from her ruminations by Joyson's hammering on the door.

'Come on, Spotty, I want me dinner!'

Pawing her heart, and shutting her eyes with barely contained patience, Nell shouted, 'Coming!' this begetting a hasty and awkward fastening of clothes.

But after rejoining the crew, with Joyson setting the pace and almost dragging her along, she was to acquire a dreadful stitch in her side that had her begging them to leave her behind, so that she might catch up at a more leisurely rate.

'I know what's wrong with her,' speculated Joyson, upon Nell having finally reached the restaurant where she now sat picking at her meal in absent-minded fashion. 'She thinks she's getting too fat so she's started pecking like a sparrow – it's upset all your metabolism,' she told the astounded Nell directly.

Having suffered a moment's fright that her dilemma was

about to be announced to all and sundry, Nell's relief was to emerge in an outpouring of uncharacteristic impatience. 'Honestly, Joy, are you never satisfied?' She clattered her fork onto the plate and sat back to roll her eyes. 'One minute I'm eating too much, the next too little – apparently I'm not even allowed to go to the lavatory when I want – could you please mind your own business!'

There was momentary silence, and a few sideways glances from other diners. But, though surprised by this show of temper from one so normally placid, none of her colleagues chose to ask what had caused it, for Nell's raw sense of bereavement was a good enough excuse for them. And the subject was hastily changed.

Feeling extremely foolish, Nell abandoned her meal, instead seizing advantage of the lately relaxed ruling that allowed nurses to enjoy a post-luncheon cigarette, lighting up and dragging on it as if there were no tomorrow, then blasting a stream of smoke at the ceiling. Then, trying to appear less agitated, she was to while away the rest of her break, listening half-heartedly to the others discussing the Germans' latest invasion of yet another country, and damning herself for being such a coward as not to confide.

And yet again she was left to plod on alone towards her fate, alternating the days of hard work with evenings of knitting baby clothes in the secrecy of her room.

Spring brought daffodils to enhance the medieval Bar walls, pink blossom to the trees that lined Nell's avenue, a fresh coat of paint to the Spottiswoods' front door and sills, and an increasingly murderous blitz upon London. Having maintained a sporadic correspondence with Bill's mother via the Preciouses household – though still not having told her nor them about the baby – Nell could only guess how terrible life must be in the capital, and, appreciating the safety of a York barely damaged, she had lately shelved her plan to throw herself on Mrs Kelly's mercy should her own parents disown her. It was far too dangerous.

So, too, was her recent habit of pilfering from the hospital, and it looked to Nell as if matters had finally come to a head. After a long shift, partly maintaining the casualty evacuation train and undergoing a futile exercise in which she dressed mock injuries on fellow nurses, but much of it helping out with more genuine work at the Infirmary, she had been anticipating a warm meal and a comfortable bed as she made ready to go home. Instead, just as she was due to leave on that damp spring evening, an authoritative voice accosted her in the echoing corridor: 'One moment, Nurse Spottiswood!'

Nell stopped dead, and quaked in her shoes, fearing that someone must have seen her take the baby's napkin that she was hiding under her coat, requisitioned during her opportune bout in the nursery. Her heart beat rapidly as she turned to face her superior's wrath.

But to her confusion, and not a little relief, others from the crew were being summoned as well, Matron Fosdyke announcing to all, 'I've received word that the casualty evacuation trains are required – yes, you're finally needed at last!' she said at their looks of expectation. 'So, if any of you have family who'll be concerned at your absence, those without a telephone may go home and inform them of your whereabouts, then you must immediately present yourself to Matron Lennox at Leeman Road.'

Simultaneous to that wondrous flush of reprieve, Nell could also have wept from sheer exhaustion at the thought of being robbed of her bed. Though, adhering to duty, she was to act without question, as were her friends. Yet even in the rush to obey, she saw that Beata was eyeing her in a sympathetic manner, and it drew to Nell's cheeks a crimson tinge, her instantaneous thought being that her pregnancy was finally to be unveiled.

Beata was not so candid as to mention it outright,

though. 'I'm sure they'll understand if you can't manage it,' she simply murmured to her friend. 'You really shouldn't push yourself.'

Nell bristled, immediately wishing she had not, but it was too late now, as she yelped, 'What are you talking about? I'm as fit as everybody else! We're all in the same boat – why, if there's anyone that should be resting it's you!'

In the furious hiatus, she sensed that Beata was about to say more, but just then Sister Barber happened past, took one look at the other's ankle, which was hugely inflated and spilling over its shoe, and declared in her usual brusque manner, 'Spottiswood's right! You needn't bother coming back, Kilmaster, that leg will be exploded before we reach Doncaster. Get yourself home and put it up – come along, Spottiswood, get yourself weaving and tell your parents, then hurry back!'

Observing that Beata seemed about to plead lenience for her friend, Nell suppressed her with a thunderous glance. Then, issuing a hasty goodbye, and wrapping her coat around her abdomen, already afflicted by a stitch, she lumbered off to catch a bus.

Thankfully, its arrival at the stop coincided with hers, and within ten minutes she was almost home, though the latter part of her journey was delayed by the horde of human traffic that streamed from the carriage works, both on bicycle and on foot.

Home at last, she babbled the news to her mother. Then, still wearing her coat, and under pretext of visiting the lavatory, there was only enough time for Nell to hide the stolen napkin in her room alongside the rest of the layette she had accumulated, before rushing back out again, a hastily compiled sandwich in her hand.

Once she was on the train, though, and on the way down to London, there was at least an opportunity to take the weight off her feet, and, with many jarring hours ahead, the chance to succumb to the hypnotic rackety-rack of the wheels, Sister being charitable enough to allow her nurses a nap.

Nell was to fall into a deeper sleep than most, and this was to leave her disorientated when she woke from it with a start to find that they were emerging from a tunnel to a packed platform. Suddenly she remembered where she was heading. London – maybe she'd see Billy! Maybe he wasn't – maybe it had all been a mistake – there were tales in the newspapers every day of men being presumed dead, then turning up alive, and not just isolated cases either, was it not possible that Billy could be one of them? That his mother could have been duped? It might not have been him, the witness might have been unreliable. Please, oh, please, let it be . . .

Forlorn as this hope might seem, with the train squeaking into its destination and the other nurses opening its doors, the still-hypnotised Nell found herself beset with an overwhelming mass of activity, much of it in khaki, and her immediate reaction was to scour every face on the platform. Almost at once she saw him! She called out, couldn't help herself, took a few steps onto the platform and cried out his name. 'Bill!'

A dozen men turned, then all shared a grin. 'Last thing anyone needs is a lot o' bills,' quipped one, though he and his friends moved to gather around the attractive nurse, and ply her with cigarettes and chit-chat.

Poor bewildered Nell was in the midst of a flustered explanation, when an ever-vigilant Sister bellowed from the train, 'We haven't time for canoodling, Nurse Spottiswood! Here come our patients!'

Nell's sense of outrage was immeasurable. How could anyone possibly accuse her of that after so recent a loss? Freshly bereaved, she broke through the masculine fence, wanting for all the world to shut herself away, and to heave with agony and tears.

But there was no time, for as Sister was so keen to point out, a fleet of ambulances was arriving with elderly infirm, and the logistics of getting all aboard and stacked one above the other was a nightmare in such cramped conditions – and in the middle of all this the air-raid sirens began to wail and the bombs began to fall, and people scattered. But there was no escape for Nell and her comrades, who had to don tin hats and remain courageously at their posts, and try to reassure their patients above the clanging of fire engines and the thunderous explosions, as one after another was stretchered into the pilchard tin and fitted onto the racks.

Only in the early hours did they manage to load the wagon to capacity. With their final patient handed over, the ambulance drivers slammed their doors and issued a chipper, 'That's your lot, dearies!' And made their own escape.

Though almost prostrate themselves, Nell and her colleagues were full of admiration for the London crews. 'How can you stand this night after night and stay so cheerful?' Sister called after them.

'This?' Her female informant merely laughed at the tumbling bombs. 'Why, it's not half so bad as normal!' And she jumped into her ambulance and drove away.

But it was terrifying enough to Nell, who, on top of her mauled senses, was physically bruised from the cramped conditions, and despite a swift impulsive urge to run and seek out Bill's poor mother, she deemed it a mercy when the order came for their train to vacate the station at once.

Even after the throb of the Luftwaffe could no longer be heard, its pilots' devilish games continued to trigger mayhem, the casualty evacuation train barely escaping the outer reaches of London when it ground to an abrupt halt. Everyone moaned at being forced to wait in pitch blackness. The squeaking of the wheels had completely stopped now. There was no sound at all.

'Oy!' Even through the darkness an ARP warden caught Nell's head sticking out of the wagon as she tried to ascertain what was amiss. Unable to make out her face, the white veil identified her. 'Get your tin hat on, Nurse! There's an unexploded bomb on the line.'

Having only just taken the uncomfortable thing off, Nell looked abashed and quickly redonned her tin helmet, asking politely as the man travelled past, 'How long are we likely to be?' With the leadenness of her abdomen putting a great strain on her neck and shoulders, all she yearned to do was in get home.

'I don't know!' His expression called her a bloody idiot. 'When it goes off or gets fixed, one or the other!' And he continued on his way down the track alongside their train, reminding everyone, 'Tin hats on!'

'Nurse, stop trifling!' At Sister's shout Nell jerked her head in, and hurried about tending her patients.

'Nurse, Nurse!' They all seemed to want a part of her, pulling her this way and that, and there was scarcely any room for a normal-sized person to squeeze a passage between the bunks, never mind someone of her girth. Fit to drop, Nell took a moment to flex the aching tendons of her neck and shoulders that were stretched beyond endurance by the tonnage of her belly.

'It's raining in, nurse!' warbled an elderly voice.

Pulling herself together, Nell edged her way to the complainant, and found that the patient on the uppermost bunk was incontinent, and his urine was dribbling onto the man below. Clapping her hands to her cheeks, she stood there feeling helpless, trying to concentrate on what to do, whilst overwhelmed by her own exhaustion and worry, and the heavy burden of the child.

'It's raining in, Nurse,' came the woeful cry again.

Finally coming to her senses, acting only on instinct, Nell took hold of the old fellow's hand and gripped it reassuringly. 'We'll soon get you sorted out, Mr . . .' she quickly read the old man's label, 'Mr Oak – but I'll just have to see to the chap above you first as he's copping most of the bad weather!'

With this, she summoned Avril Joyson from along the wagon. 'Joy, could you help me change these patients' sheets please?'

Joyson squeezed herself grumbling between the bunks. 'What, both of them? You should've fetched them a bottle!'

'Sorry!' whined the elderly culprit, like a little child.

'That's all right, it's certainly not your fault,' Nell reassured him in a kind voice. Then she hissed under her breath at Joyson, appalled that a nurse could show such a lack of compassion. 'It's only the poor chap on the upper bunk who's incontinent – and we wouldn't have had to change two lots of bedding if someone had thought to catheterise him! Now are you going to help me or not?'

Joy became all hoity-toity, clicking her tongue and demanding, 'What did your last slave die of?' – though partly out of conscience, and partly because Sister had come into earshot, she was forced to help her colleague struggle to exchange sodden linen for dry. At the end of this ordeal, though, she was quick to slip away, leaving Nell to dispose of the wet sheets alone.

'Are you comfortable now, Mr Oak?' Nell hoped she projected sincerity when feeling so abominable herself. 'I don't think it should rain in again now we've closed the window.' Then, having settled the two old men, it was off to tend someone else.

Hour upon hour they waited on the track for the bomb disposal team to arrive and for the detonator to be made safe, elderly patients having constantly to be nursed in the meantime, pulses to be taken, medicines to be handed out, charts to be filled in, bedpans and bottles to empty. Finally, at six o'clock in the morning, the train jerked into motion, and the exhausted crew thanked heaven to be on their way.

By now, the debilitating gravity of Nell's abdomen seemed to have crept all the way down her limbs and into her feet, making them feel as if encased in boots of lead. Her ankles were bloated to the size of Beata's, and further tortured by pins and needles. Unable to bend and get at them over her fecund dome in its iron corset, she held on to one of the poles that supported the stretchers and, amidst all the jerking of the wagon, tried to balance on one leg. Moving her other foot in a circle, she worked to improve her circulation, and whilst thus involved was to ponder on the way she had snapped at her friend. The mere thought procured a blush. She would have to eat humble pie when she saw Beata again . . . perhaps own up about the baby. The latter was unusually quiet at the moment, which was one small mercy, for even now she had no time to rest, but was at another patient's beck and call. Not to mention Sister's.

'They shouldn't *have* to call.' her superior came up to deliver in hushed tone, though this was only out of consideration for the patients, and there was reproof in her eyes for Nell. 'Forethought, Nurse Spottiswood, forethought, how many times do you have to be told? Anticipate the patient's every need . . .'

'Yes Sister, sorry Sister!' And off Nell went again, every cell of her pregnant body screaming for a bed, yet forced to endure this for many an hour to come.

It was ten thirty in the morning when she finally staggered home. She had been on her feet for well over twenty-four hours. 'Don't wake me,' she begged her mother in piteous tones, 'not even for food. I just want to sleep.' And she had only the energy to wash down a few bites of toast with a gulp of tea, and to undress for bed, before oblivion claimed her.

She was to sleep for all of that day, only rising in order to eat some supper, then it was back to bed again for the rest of the night.

'You deserve the rest,' agreed her mother.

This was quite some indulgence. Unfortunately, others were to be less so, for when Nell arrived for work a day later, it was to an impeachment. In this she was not alone, in fact all of those involved in the evacuation process had shared a similar supposition that they had given of their best and would be forgiven for catching up on their sleep. Now, they were assembled in Matron's office, to be roundly disabused of this notion by a representative of the Ministry of Health.

'Dereliction of duty! There is no other term for it,' lectured the woman, who paraded judiciously before them in her hoary tweed suit and severe bun, her tone and expression relaying that they could at any moment be taken out and shot. 'What if our soldiers should say, 'Oh, I can't be bothered to fire my gun today, I've done my bit now, I think I'll go and have a nap?' Where would the country be then?'

How unfair, thought Nell, after we slaved – though neither she nor any of the nurses dared protest that it was hardly the same, but were to stand there meekly and accept every criticism.

'What would have been the plight of those needing instant evacuation?' continued the official. 'Would they have been left to their fate whilst their dilatory so-called nurses caught up on their beauty sleep? A shambles, a complete shambles! You should be thoroughly ashamed!' Having worked herself into a froth, the tyrant then began to prowl up and down and to eye them one by one. Nell shrank expectantly, but it was Nurse Green the elder who attracted the first bullet. 'How old is this nurse, Matron?' the frowning official spun around to enquire.

Retaining her ladylike demeanour, Matron Lennox had been quietly seated at her desk throughout, and seemed hesitant to reply for the moment, for she had in fact been covering up for certain members of staff. Eventually, though, the birdlike face above the erect starched collar was to state with immense diplomacy, 'Mrs Green is perfectly competent.'

'I did not ask that!' The woman snapped her attention back to Mrs Green. 'How old are you?'

Mrs Green muttered the answer into her ample bosom.

'Speak up, woman!'

The white-haired one snatched an uneasy glance over the top of her horn-rimmed glasses, finally to admit, 'I'm sixty-seven.'

'Good grief! No wonder you failed to turn up on time. It's quite obvious you achieved this post under false pretences. Were you not aware when you applied that there is a maximum age limit? And for good reason!' The official shot a look at the others then, and in the same breath sniped, 'Though I fail to understand how the rest of you could possibly have an excuse – what is yours?' she suddenly aimed at Frenchy.

The attractive dark head was tilted in question. 'Pardon?'

The official frowned and leaned towards her. 'Are you a foreigner?'

'She's French,' Matron quickly explained before too much damage was incurred to her crew. 'Married to one of our boys.'

'Can she not reply for herself?' The official regarded Frenchy with disdain, and when nought was forthcoming, save a look of confusion, she concurred with a yap, 'I thought as much – can't even speak English! Why wasn't the Ministry informed of this?'

In the face of such rude demand, Matron was cool. 'I should have thought the Ministry to be already aware, considering that it was the body responsible for sending Mrs French here in the first place. It has always been the official assertion that, despite my having forty years' medical experience, neither I nor colleagues of equal rank are entitled to a say as to whom may be employed under the emergency measures.'

'Well, I do have a say!' clipped the interrogator, looking back at Nurse French. 'And that makes two of you whose services are no longer required!'

Matron tried to save the day. 'Despite her difficulty with our language, Mrs French is qualified in her own country – she did provide the appropriate references – and she hasn't killed anyone yet.'

'I'd prefer not to wait until she does! What else shall we find?' The official's eyes then began to examine each of the others, as shrewd and pitiless as a bird of prey. Caught in such sights, Nell's heart fluttered like a sparrow.

But, by some felicitous quirk, neither she nor anyone else was to be singled out, and the final word of caution was for the benefit of all. 'This will not happen again! I do not care that you are here on a voluntary basis, if you are to do the job then *do it properly*! Do I make myself clear?'

The nurses mumbled assurances.

'Very well! That will be all, Matron.' The raptor clamped a file under her wing, and made to leave the train. 'I'll trust you to dispense with those two. Good day!' And with three strides she was gone.

'I'm very sorry, Nurse Green, Nurse French,' murmured matron, ever the lady, not considering it a loss of prestige to apologise in front of others. 'But it seems your cover is blown, as they say. I'm unable to keep you on. Though I'm bound to add you have turned out to be far more capable than many I could mention, and it's a great shame.' She shook her neatly groomed head, and sighed at having her rank so affronted. 'Apparently I've been granted no choice in the matter.'

With the victims' pragmatic response, the rest of the nurses were instructed to go about their work, and began to file out of Matron's office.

'Nurse Spottiswood, a word if you please!' Matron signalled for her to remain behind, and when there were just the two of them there, said without preamble, 'How far along is your pregnancy?'

Thoroughly jolted, Nell immediately coloured up, the red travelling to her roots as she hung her head but did not deny it.

'There's not much you can hide from me, my dear. I've been aware of your condition for some weeks, but at Sister's instigation I decided to let it pass for a while.' She noted the sharp upturn in Nell's demeanour that indicated surprise. 'Despite what you may think,' she now revealed sagely, 'Sister Barber is very attached to you, and thinks you have the right temperament to make a good nurse. It was her opinion that your current circumstances didn't appear to interfere with your work, and so we allowed you to carry on for a month or so, as in the natural course of events you would be leaving us soon enough anyway. But now it has begun to show . . .' Matron cocked her head in sympathy, and repeated her former enquiry. 'So, tell me, how far on are you?'

'I'm not sure,' whispered Nell. 'But it was back in August that I last . . . had relations.'

'Good heavens!' Matron looked astonished. 'Why, you must be almost ready to deliver. Have you received no medical attention?'

Trying to fight back tears, Nell shook her head.

'I suppose you've been wearing a tight corset hoping it would go away,' guessed her superior, rather stern of face again, and still battling incredulity. 'Well, you've certainly managed to hide it remarkably well until now!'

But, as Nell started to weep, she clicked her tongue, adding, 'You poor creature,' and rose from her desk to lend a handkerchief and words of comfort. 'It's probably because your bump is evenly distributed around the sides that you were able to hide it – and taller girls like yourself do seem more able to carry it off. You're not the first to hide a pregnancy, and you certainly won't be the last.

At least you're not trying to deny it. I've known plenty who refused to accept they were carrying a baby even as they were giving birth! I'm just amazed that you've managed to continue with your work so uncomplainingly.'

Upon the flow of self-pity being staunched, Matron asked, 'So, what do you intend to do? Will the boy marry you?'

'He was killed last year.' Nell broke down again.

'Ah . . . it was that one. I'm so sorry.' Matron's voice was unusually soft. 'Then you'll need to be brave, my dear. Have you been concealing this from your parents too?' At the distressed nod, she told Nell rather more uncompromisingly, 'Well, you will have to tell them – in any event you cannot continue nursing at this late stage, it's unsuitable for you to even appear in the workplace, leaving aside any physical repercussions – had I guessed you were so far along I'd never have sanctioned it. It's a miracle our friendly official didn't notice. Needless to say, you shall have to be sent home.' In an untypical demonstration of hopelessness, Matron buried her head in her hands. 'Good Lord, three nurses down – let's hope there's no emergency.'

Then, with Nell still weeping, she reverted to her normal self and, in steering her nurse to the door, was to mete a crumb of benevolence. 'At least this is one instance for which we can be thankful you're not state-registered, or you would be struck off. As things stand, I'm willing for you to return after the baby is adopted.'

Ambushed from her tears, Nell wanted to shout, Why do you falsely assume that I'll give my baby up? But she did not, for it was not done and would only bring reproof, and besides, she appreciated Matron's kindness. It was a relief to have told someone at last.

'Run along home now,' ordered Matron, patting Nell's shoulder as she opened the door. 'And please do inform your mother straight away. At the very least it will allow you to claim the proper nutrition. You could have been receiving extra milk and eggs, if you'd only come clean earlier.'

Involved with the preparation of dressings, the others regarded her with curiosity as she emerged dabbing her eyes from Matron's office. She could see the question on their faces: why had Spotty been singled out to receive a more severe reprimand than the rest of them? Fending off their displays of concern with an upraised palm, Nell deterred any approach, then left without a word of explanation to any of them. Not even Beata. But a glance at her friend told Nell that she already knew.

'Goodness, you made me jump out of my skin!' accused her mother, hurriedly shoving an intended birthday gift out of sight into the cupboard, as Nell arrived home mid-morning.

Her face oozing guilt, Nell had been practising how to break her terrible news all the way home. She had finally primed herself, was on the brink of saying it, when Mother frowned and hazarded a guess:

'You've been dismissed for not going back yesterday?'

'Suspended.' The lie tripped off Nell's tongue, loaning her brief reprieve, and she thanked that horrendous shift for providing a good excuse. For now.

'Oh, how mean . . .' First came consolation, then practicality. 'Well, you needn't be bored. I'll have ample to occupy you until you're allowed to return. For a start, you can go through your clothes and put by anything that no longer fits you, particularly anything with rubber in it, such as those old galoshes you wore for school.' With their enslaved colonies no longer able to export, rubber was now having to be salvaged, which explained Thelma's manic preoccupation with the cupboard. 'I could have sworn I had an old corset in here. I was going to cut off the suspenders, but I can't find it anywhere – do you know, I swear there's a goblin in this house, the things that have gone missing lately. Either that or I'm losing my marbles. Anyway, whatever you can find, I'll take it to the WVS this afternoon. In fact, it'll be rather handy you being off for a while, because you can help by doing the cleaning up and the shopping whilst I'm on official business.'

6

So, after lunch, and indeed every day except Sunday, for the next couple of weeks Nell found herself pressganged into completing a list of housework. With her normal clothes so tight-fitting now – zips of skirts having to be left open and secured with safety pins, and emphasising her distorted shape – she chose to retain her uniform, giving lame explanation to her mother that this was simply to make her feel professional. Though in truth this was the last way she was feeling. For the previous month the passenger in her abdomen had been inflicting tremendous strain on her lower back, as well as her shoulders, and all this donkeywork did not help. But there was little chance of lying down for a rest, with Mother expecting everything to be done by the time she got home from enjoying her own freedom at the WVS. Even worse than the housework was being made to queue outside a selection of shops for the daily groceries.

Standing in line outside the greengrocer's on this Monday afternoon, after struggling to drag heavy sheets from the wringer to the washing line for much of the day, Nell constantly varied her weight from one hip to the other, trying to escape her agony. This procuring no relief, she stretched her body into an arc, pressed a hand to her lumbar region, and began to rub. Mother had heard there was a consignment of Spanish oranges arriving today, and, by the length of the queue, so had everyone else. Lord knew how long she would be standing there.

'You're entitled to go straight to the front in your condition, love.'

Nell turned to attend the woman behind her, and, to her shock, realised that her abdomen was protruding from her open coat. An immediate prickle of embarrassment sprang outwards from her breast, causing her face to turn scarlet and her heart to accelerate, as her secondary reaction was to slump and pull her coat around herself, whilst trying not to meet the curious gazes of others who were now craning to examine her.

'Oh, I'm sorry.' The speaker had noted that Nell wore no wedding ring. 'My mistake . . .'

Face burning, Nell reverted her gaze ahead, but the damage was done. She was to thank God when an angry commotion up front, over the unreliability of supplies, diverted attention from her, allowing her to break ranks and slip away.

Thelma looked crestfallen at the lack of oranges in Nell's basket when they coincidentally met up at the end of the avenue, both heading home through the late April sunshine. 'But they said!'

'Well, they said wrong.' Nell was less than apologetic, her shoulders and spirits dragged down by the heavy basket of shopping. 'Apparently the consignment was for the London area only.'

Thelma sighed. 'Oh well, I suppose that's only right, they're suffering the most.'

'I don't know about that!' snapped Nell. 'I stood for absolutely ages.'

'Well, yes, thank you for going to the trouble, dear. I shall miss not having you to help me. Did Matron not give you a specific date to return? Not that I want to lose you, but you should really go and check . . .'

'Yeah, I'll go tomorrow,' sighed Nell, changing the encumbrance to her other hand.

'*Yeah*? We didn't pay out good money for slovenly speech!'

'*Yes*, then,' Nell replied with a wince, feeling that she was about to crack in half. Notwithstanding this, when they arrived home she was to help prepare the evening meal by pulling vegetables from the back garden and washing and slicing them, whilst Mother worked beside her on the main dish. All the while Nell was teetering on the verge of blurting it out, anxious to confide in her mother before Father came in.

'I never thought I'd live to see the day when I was reduced to using this horrible stuff,' sighed Thelma, having scraped the final slick of margarine from the greaseproof paper that had held it, and folding this away for later use. 'How people can say it's a substitute for butter . . . we might as well be living on a council estate.'

Nell barely responded, though her eyes followed her mother to the cupboard, where she added the folded greaseproof to the umpteen jars and bottles, bits of string, and other useful things she had thriftily put by.

Thelma went to the stove and stirred the contents of a saucepan that were now almost ready to serve. Then she cast a sideways glance at her daughter as they waited for Father to come in. 'You're very quiet, dear.'

Nell came out of her trance with a start.

'Are you worried that they might not take you back?'

Looking into that concerned face, Nell was on the verge of saying something, then shook her head. 'No, just tired.'

And at that point her father came in. Another opportunity lost.

With her parents tucking into their meal, Nell picking at hers, there was little said until halfway through. Then, 'Next door's had one of those new Morrison shelters delivered,' Thelma informed her husband. 'The stack of girders that went in, you would've thought they were erecting the Forth Bridge. All this clanking and banging, and poor Mrs Dawson trying to stop them demolishing her house in the process. Eh, you should've seen it, shouldn't he, Eleanor? It was like Fred Karno's!'

They all chuckled, including Nell, Wilfred pausing to run his tongue underneath the pallet of his false teeth to evacuate debris, and clacking the dentures expertly around his mouth before saying, 'I hear they're saving a lot of lives. We can have one if you want.'

'Thank you, dear, but I couldn't abide one of those monstrosities cluttering up my dining room.' Thelma hated anything out of place. 'Not to mention actually having to go in it. I'd feel like a caged animal. No, we'll continue to go under the stairs, it's served us well enough up to now.' And Wilfred had gone to such trouble, fitting it out with a light and comfortable seating that could also be used as beds.

Nell was about to take another mouthful when something awful happened. She wet herself. Her knife and fork hovering over the plate, she felt a tremendous wave of panic rush over her, as she tried to control the muscles around her bladder, but the leak would not stop. With the lower half of her dress sopping wet, and her sphincter fluttering, she laid down her cutlery and, trying to appear calm, exclaimed, 'Please excuse me, I'll just have to visit the lavatory!' And, to her mother and father's bemusement, she rushed from the table.

Leaving a dripping trail, she fled first to her room, and dragged a pack of sanitary towels from the back of a cupboard. Armed with these, and still leaking, she scurried to the bathroom, where she stripped off her wet dress and underwear, the corset posing all manner of irritation, then she tried to stem the flow with a towel, but in moments it too was swamped and chafing. Giving in to panic, she began to shake. Oh my God, she should have come clean months ago! It was going to be so much more of a shock to them now. She could well imagine the intensity of their recrimination. Even the rehearsal made her break down and cry.

'What on earth are you doing?' called her mother a good twenty minutes later, making Nell jump. 'Your meal's gone cold – and your father wants to be in there!' With no response, she pounded up the stairs to mutter a warning. 'I hope you're not being extravagant with that toilet paper, else you can start buying your own.' With a roll having doubled in price, she had issued this alert before. Ignored and aggravated, she banged on the door. 'Eleanor! Answer me.'

Under this constant harassment, Nell had no option.

Thelma heard the bolt being drawn, and stood back, ready to announce, 'Oh, there you are!' But as the door opened a crack and she squinted through it, there stood her daughter, surrounded by sodden bath towels and *things*, and clutching a damp dress over her nakedness. Thelma gasped. Reflected in her mother's horrified gaze, only truly in that moment did Nell realise the enormity of this.

Lost for words, Thelma could do nothing but gape at her for many seconds. Whatever had happened to *be prepared*? Nothing could have prepared her for this! Finally, though, one of them had to speak. With Nell in tears, it was left to her mother to breathe, 'Who was it?'

Nell struggled with the lump in her throat. 'I'm so sorry, Mother . . .'

Thelma came to life then, was caught up in a paroxysm of loathing as she stabbed a finger at Nell's room. 'Get in there, and take your disgusting mess with you! And get something on!' Then, turning tail, she stamped downstairs.

Finding it hard to bend, Nell gathered the debris that lay around her, staggered with it to her room, there dropping it to grab the first thing to hand, a dressing gown, at the same time hearing her father's bilious, '*What!*'

'She's in labour *now*!' moaned Thelma, loud enough for their daughter to hear.

'And you said nothing, woman?'

The boom of his cannon fire was met by the shriek of her high explosive. 'I didn't know! If I had do you think she'd still be standing there?'

'Keep your voice down, woman, do you want the whole street to hear?'

'They won't have to hear!' screeched Thelma. 'They only have to look at her – and please stop calling me *woman*!'

Nell sobbed, and gripped the edges of the dressing gown around her enlarged form as they continued to bombard each other.

'If it's that obvious why didn't you confront her before?'

'It wasn't obvious – I had no idea! And why didn't *you*?'

'You're the blasted mother, you should know about these things – anyway, this is doing not the slightest good. Get her down here, I want to speak to her!'

'I told you, she's in labour, she's . . . *dribbling* all over the place! The bathroom's awash with – look, it's no good arguing, we'll have to fetch Doctor Greenhow!'

'She's not going to have it right this minute, is she?' snarled Wilfred. 'I want to talk to her first, find out who's responsible!' And he pushed Thelma aside and hared up to Nell's room, barging in without knocking.

'I'm sorry Fa –'

'Who was it?' he demanded. 'And why have you waited until now? Where can we get in touch with his parents?'

'He's dead!' wept a shivering Nell. 'He was killed after we –'

'Slut!' Wilfred Spottiswood brought his fingers hard across her face.

Nell reeled, but the shock of it stopped her crying and she stared at him in disbelief, her lips parting to offer soft reproach. 'We were going to be married . . .' As evidence, she offered the ring on its chain that hung from her neck.

'Well, you're not now, are you?' flung her father, trying to swipe it from her.

But Nell reared away to protect the treasured ring, tearfully begging him to comprehend that, 'We loved each other!'

'You don't know what love is!' sneered Wilfred, growing nastier by the second. 'You brazen little cat, you certainly know nothing about respect! If you'd none for yourself you could at least have had some for your parents!'

Bill's wedding ring still in her fist, tears streaking her cheeks, Nell grasped the dressing gown around her contracting trunk, and begged them both, 'Please try to understand –'

'Try as I might, I'll never understand!' interrupted her mother, her face contorted with disbelief. 'It's always been apparent you've no care for your parents' reputation, but how could you walk around for so long with . . . *that* in you, and not be cowed by shame? As if you're actually proud of being labelled a scrubber!'

'I'm not!' protested Nell in self-defence. 'We would've been married by now if Bill hadn't sacrificed his life for another.' And her face crumpled in more tears.

'Bill?' yelled Mother. 'Oh, it's all coming out now, the *lies* you must have told! Well, he's certainly left us all in the lurch, hasn't he? But he's not the only one – how could you be so completely and utterly selfish? As if there isn't enough for us to worry about with a war on!'

Nell wanted to plead again for her mother to empathise, but knew now that she never would, could never have never felt the same depth of passion that she herself felt for her man. Shaking with emotion, daring now to peer through the scalding veil of tears at her father with his glittering eyes and his sour, discontented face, she knew that even the merest attempt to explain would be useless. Besides, she was robbed of the will by another stronger pain in her lower back, as if a giant hand was gripping and squeezing it.

Seeing her wince, Thelma advised quickly, 'We've got to get her out of here before she has it!'

'Is it going to be born now?' groaned Nell.

'You stupid girl, what did you think was happening? What did you think would be the consequence of your sordid – oh, we'll argue about this later. Wilfred, I just want her out!'

Of similar mind, Wilfred let fly at his daughter. 'Don't think I've finished with you, not by a long chalk!' And, charging for the stairs, he added over his shoulder, 'I'll go and fetch the doctor!'

Disdaining coat and hat, he pedalled off to the telephone box, leaving his wife to observe the unfolding horror.

By the time the doctor had arrived in his car, Nell's labour pains had begun in earnest.

The elderly Doctor Greenhow doffed his homburg, though retained his coat and scarf, and, without examining the patient, declared in his gravelly voice, 'I'll ring for an ambulance to take her to hospital, at least we'll have her away before the baby's out.'

'Not the maternity hospital?' breathed Thelma, touching her plump breast in concern, for that was in too close a suburb. 'Oh, Doctor, the whole of Acomb will be aware of it before daybreak – can it not be somewhere else?'

The GP had treated the Spottiswoods for years, knew the parents' characters inside out. Transposing himself to their unenviable position, he spent only another few seconds watching Nell squirm, before deciding, 'I'll telephone the Infirmary, see if there's anyone qualified in midwifery on duty.'

Whilst Thelma showed deep gratitude, there came a squeal of pain and panic from Nell. Her mother immediately ran to her, but not to comfort. 'Bite on your sheet!' she commanded, and thrust a handful of bedding towards Nell's mouth. 'Bite on it, I said! At least spare us the indignity of your squawks.'

Trying to be quiet, Nell bit on the sheet and closed her eyes against the discomfort, squirming into the mattress.

'I just paid six guineas for that bed last year, and now she's completely ruined it!'

Old Doctor Greenhow drove off to the phone box, returning fifteen minutes later to say that all was in order. 'An ambulance will be arriving any minute. I've warned them not to put the bell on.'

'Thank Christ it's dark,' breathed an irascible Wilfred Spottiswood, pinching his grey temples as if to contain some volcanic eruption.

The ambulance did arrive very quickly, its two-man crew helping Nell downstairs then depositing her in a wheelchair, which was propelled down the garden path.

'Don't you cry out,' warned Thelma through clenched teeth, making sure that Nell was completed swaddled in blankets to hide that odious bump. 'Don't you dare make a sound.'

'Ooh, what's up wi' your Nell?' Geoffrey Dawson lolloped out of the darkness in an over-large boiler suit and Wellington boots, on his way out to fire-watch.

Thelma whirled in alarm at the inquisition. 'Suspected appendicitis – so we can't delay, Geoffrey!'

'Are you coming with me, Mother?' Deposited in the ambulance, the curious youth still watching, a frightened Nell raised her head from the stretcher to ask, just before the doors were closed.

Then came a rocky ride towards the city. Having heard where they were taking her, despite her pain and only wanting it to be over, Nell prayed, please don't let there be anyone on duty that knows me, please, please. Jerked from side to side in the ambulance, finally lifted out then wheeled along the familiar echoing corridors, she was relieved to be steered into a small ward that had no beds, only a trolley, and was no bigger than a cupboard really. But the relief was short-lived, for, as she was helped to clamber aboard the trolley, the contractions grew so intense that she could not help but cry out.

'Be quiet and lie down, you'll wake the patients,' came the brusque command of the midwife about to examine her.

'It hurts!' moaned Nell, beseeching sympathy.

But none was to come from the one who probed so intimately, violating her body as if gutting a chicken. 'Yes, well, your type don't think about that, do you, when you're rolling about with some soldier?' The shock of realising that a nurse could vindictively inflict pain was enough to stun Nell to silence, as more cruelty was imposed. 'I'll bet he's not on the scene any more, is he? Ran like a rabbit when you told him.'

Don't say that about him! roared Nell's mind through her adversity, he was a hero, I loved him. But, cowed by humiliation, the only insurrection she could whisper was, 'He's dead.'

'Then he's better off,' snapped her torturer, and left the room.

The spasms grew such that Nell thought she could stand them no longer. Yes, Billy was better off dead, and she with him! All she wanted to do was sleep, but the contractions were so extreme now that they kept jolting her awake, and with them came a series of involuntary shrieks. 'Please, won't you give me something to stop the pain?'

But just when Nell thought she was indeed going to die, a change came upon her, an urgent signal that her body wished to expel its unwanted lodger, and the might of this drawing forth an involuntary belch. Thankful that the pain was not quite so excruciating now, as each spasm subsided Nell took grateful advantage and closed her eyes, craving sleep.

'Don't nod off – you're supposed to be pushing!' Again her violator was there, rough and cold and unhelpful, as if Nell had disturbed her own peaceful night.

'I'm sorry,' whimpered Nell. 'I'm trying!'

'Try harder! And stop clamping your legs shut – it's a bit too late for that now!'

At three o'clock in the morning, Nell's tiny baby came slipping and slithering into an unwelcome world, the waxen face coated in its mother's blood.

'Is it all right?' Nell was wide awake now and craning forward anxiously, as the baby's face flooded red and began to bleat. 'What is it?'

The midwife was busy snipping and poking and prodding, saying without enthusiasm, 'A bit puny, but it's all right. I don't know why you're bothered what it is, seeing all the trouble he's caused.'

'A boy!' Nell felt a rush of tearful adoration for Billy's son, checking that he was whole and healthy, before falling back exhausted, but exhilarated too, at having produced another human being.

Then the midwife was jabbing her crudely again. 'Not finished yet. Give another push!'

Having little experience in maternity, Nell panicked. 'It's twins?'

'No, you clot, just the placenta.' Having delivered this, the midwife conducted another intimate examination. 'You're luckier than you deserve. You don't need any stitches.' Then she spread a sheet and blanket over Nell, and carried the baby from the room, saying, 'There'll be somebody along to see to you in a minute.'

'Can I hold him?' Nell's head shot up again.

'Later,' said the midwife, on the point of exit.

'Is my mother here?'

The midwife looked derisive. 'Do you think she wants anything to do with *you*?' And on this brutal note, she was gone.

Nell was to lie there then, subdued and tearful, clinging to Bill's wedding ring as an anchor, until someone did eventually come along to make her comfortable, not a nurse but one of the domestic staff, who had obviously been dragged from her bed. By then, though, Nell was too fidgety to sleep. Sipping the cup of tea that the woman had kindly donated after washing her and putting her into an institutional nightgown, she asked, 'Where have they taken my baby?'

The bleary face did not look at her as its owner went about the business of clearing up the gory detritus. 'He'll be in the nursery.'

Nell remained anxious. 'May I go and see him?'

'No, I'll get into trouble,' said the woman, concentrating on bundling up the soiled linen. Then, just prior to leaving, she looked into Nell's face and frowned, 'How old are you?'

'Eighteen,' confessed Nell. Then it struck her, 'No, nineteen – it's my birthday.'

The woman raised her eyebrows and offered, 'Many happy returns.'

Nell thanked her, knowing there would be few congratulations from her parents. Then, as the other made to leave, she enquired quickly, 'How long must I stay in bed?'

'Well, you'd usually be there ten days . . .' the woman was quick to deter Nell's look of horror, 'but they're letting them up more or less straight away in case of air raids, so it might not be that long.' She smiled, and left.

Intermittently dozing, the next thing Nell was aware of was being bumped by trolley to a ward that stank of kidneys, full of elderly patients who were too busy eating their breakfast to concern themselves with her. For some reason, certainly not from kindness, once she was in bed a screen was immediately pulled around it, and, shortly after this, her own breakfast was served. Brought by the intransigent midwife who had also delivered her, Nell chose not to ask her the time, but guessed it must be somewhere between six thirty and seven o'clock. Though agitated to hold her baby, she ate everything before her, then sat back and listened to the sounds of the old folk, imagining what must be going on at home, and wondering if her parents would ever forgive her.

Therefore, it was a surprise when, immediately after her empty tray was removed, her mother and father appeared around the screen, accompanied by Doctor Greenhow. Obviously not to wish her a happy birthday. Dressed in his business suit, her father was still furious, and did not trust himself to speak, all parties looking shell-shocked by the events of the last twelve hours, and grossly uncomfortable at being there.

Her mother did speak, but remained aloof. 'Doctor's arranged for you to be looked after at home.'

Flooded with relief at being accorded this token of forgiveness, Nell gushed tearfully, 'Oh, Mother, I'm so sorry I've put you and Father through –'

'What's done is done,' interrupted her mother, who had brought along Nell's coat and shoes. 'Now, let's get ourselves organised. Doctor's brought some paperwork for you to sign, then we can leave here.' Her attitude was one of distaste.

Nell shifted position to ease her throbbing genitals, propping herself up with one arm whilst taking the form with her other hand. She was immediately suspicious. 'But this says – Mother, I don't want him adopted!' Her heart had begun to race.

'Just sign it!' commanded her father, hat in hand, eager to get away.

'Please, can't I keep him?' entreated Nell.

'Stop making such a song and dance,' hissed her mother, embarrassed and tetchy as she looked over her shoulder to check that no one could overhear. 'It's going to be difficult enough getting you into the house without the neighbours prying.'

'But –'

'Don't be ridiculous, Eleanor! For heaven's sake you are eighteen years old, what possessed you to ruin your life?'

'I'm nineteen!' Nell was dismayed that her mother seemed to have forgotten. 'It's my birthday – and it doesn't have to be ruined!'

'Oh, *I'm* well aware of what day it is!' The response was brittle. 'It's you who are living in Cloud Cuckoo Land. You were stupid enough to get yourself into this, but even you can't be so dim-witted as not to realise what dire straits you'd be in should you attempt to bring it up yourself.'

'I could move away!' wept Nell, clutching at straws.

'And do what? How would you work, how would you live?'

'I could hire a nanny!'

'Who would employ you with an illegitimate child?'

'Matron said I could return after I'd had him!'

'So, let me see,' mused Thelma coldly. 'With earnings of two pounds per week you'd pay how much for this nanny? And how much for rent? How much for food, and fuel – stop being ridiculous and sign the form!'

'I can't!' Nell threw the piece of paper aside and fell upon her pillow, sobbing. 'I haven't even held him, and you want me to give him up. How can you be so cruel?'

'Because it's in everyone's best interests! It's you who are cruel – can't you see what kind of a life that poor brat will have? You've obviously no care for your parents, but for God's sake think of him!'

'I am!' sobbed Nell. 'He's already lost his poor father, he shan't lose his mother too!'

The rattle of breakfast pots along the ward accompanied Thelma's gasp of frustration. 'So you're willing to ruin your life? To end up a prostitute?'

Nell recoiled – feeling as if a cigarette had been stubbed out on her.

'Because that's what it will come to: no decent man will

marry you if he should find out your shameful secret. That's what your father and I are attempting to spare you from, trying to protect your future, in spite of you bringing such shame on us . . .'

'I'm sorry!' blubbered Nell. 'But please, oh, please . . .'

At the end of his tether, Wilfred decided to put an end to this, and, with a peevish flick of his trilby, signalled for Doctor Greenhow to take over the persuasion.

'This is doing no one any good. Please, can we all calm down.' The elderly doctor grunted as he stooped to retrieve the crumpled piece of paper from the floor, but for now he did not return it to Nell, saying quietly to her, in a voice that made her want to clear her own throat, 'Eleanor, I want you to consider this seriously, put aside your histrionics and listen to reason. If you refuse to sign this form of release for the child, then you must compel me to resort to another option.' The liver-spotted hand withdrew another article from an inner pocket. 'I had hoped, we *all* hoped, that you'd choose to do the right thing by your parents, the ones who chose to adopt you, and to give you everything you might otherwise not have had – a stable home, a good education, everything a married couple could provide. Don't throw it all back in their faces. Give your child the opportunity that was granted you. Otherwise,' he played his trump card, 'I shall have no option but to sign this.'

Her face still damp with tears, Nell could make head nor tail of the form, but guessed what it might be. 'You'd force me to give up my baby?'

'If you are so resolved, I shouldn't tear it from your arms, no.' There was a vestige of humanity on his face, and in his tone. 'But I should then surmise from your mania that you're unfit to make rational decisions, and therefore you should remain here until sanity's restored.'

Again, panic rose in Nell's breast, more violently than ever, threatening to engulf her as she thought of Cissie, who had come to the Infirmary to have her first illegitimate baby, and was still trapped here two decades later. Her heart began to sprint, pumping the blood through her veins in a deafening gush. Last night she had prayed that none of her friends would be here to witness her shame. Now, she prayed ever more ardently for dear Beata – any of them – to speed to her aid and prevent this monstrous abduction. Oh, how rash she had been not to tell anyone before!

'I can do it, Eleanor.' Doctor Greenhow saw a hint of defiance begin to arise, and assured her calmly, 'This only needs my signature and you will be detained, perhaps for good.'

Forgetting all physical pain, rent by an agony much worse, Nell cried out to her parents, 'Please, please don't let him do this!'

'You have a choice, Eleanor, which is more than you granted us when you sullied our home with your big belly.' Her father seemed to think he represented the voice of reason as he laid down the rules. 'If you sign the form you can come home immediately, and no more will ever be said, you'll never hear another recrimination. But there is no way I'll be persuaded to have that bastard in my house –'

Nell burst into heart-rending tears.

'– do the right thing by it, give it a good home.'

He's not a dog – he's a child! Nell wanted to cry, but such resistance against one's parents was unthinkable, would earn her short shrift, and so she could only sob, 'But how do I know he'll get a good home?'

Seeing her weaken, Thelma felt able to show compassion. Hurrying to grip Nell's hand, she coaxed, 'Don't you think you can trust Doctor Greenhow to find it a suitable place, and good parents? How long have you known him, hasn't he always been a pillar of strength whenever you've been ill? Look how he came to visit you every single day when you had influenza, would a man like that hand a child to any old couple?'

'I know the perfect family for him, Eleanor,' came the gravelly voice.

'Who are they? May I meet them?' Yet still Nell could not give credence to this nightmare.

'That wouldn't be wise,' he replied gently. 'Won't you take my word for it that they are a good, kind, respectable couple just like your parents, who've longed for a child of their own for many years?'

'They could have someone else's, it doesn't have to be mine!'

'Don't be so rude to the doctor,' accused Thelma.

But old Doctor Greenhow held up his hand to show it did not concern him, and continued speaking kindly to Nell. 'You'll be giving him the very best, believe me, Eleanor.' Putting away the more sinister form, to show that he would much rather do this amicably, he set the crumpled adoption paper before her again, his smile inviting her to look at it.

Against all her instincts and desires, almost blinded with tears, Nell studied it through the blur, seemingly too long for her father, who snatched an impatient look at his watch, then looked away to the ceiling.

'If I sign, do I have to give him up straight away? Couldn't I be allowed a few months . . . ?'

The sympathetic doctor glanced from one parent to another, only the mother showing any sign of compromise.

'If you're willing to stay hidden in here,' delivered Thelma. 'Which I doubt you are.'

'There must be someone I could stay with!' implored Nell.

'What decent person wants to be saddled with a girl like you?' answered Thelma. 'And I absolutely forbid that any relative of ours is ever going to find out about this.'

Still, Nell held on, clinging to the hope that she could somehow get by without them. The pen in her hand faltered.

Doctor Greenhow saw that her eyes flickered beyond

the edge of the screen, as if to gauge how fast she could make the exit. He cocked his head in a kind but stern manner.

'Don't let us involve the police, Eleanor. Haven't your parents suffered enough?'

She broke down again, sobbing, her throat raw and her tone nasal. 'At least let me hold him once! Mother, I beg you!'

Whilst Wilfred stamped the floor in frustration and despair, Thelma gripped her hand reassuringly, her own face distraught now. 'The moment you've got the formalities out of the way I'm sure it would be all right to have a cuddle, won't it, Doctor?'

At his kindly affirmation she helped Nell to hold the pen. 'There, just a little signature, then it's all over.'

How could she fight them? She was so young, and at her weakest ebb. An air of finality about her, with the look of a beast resigned to slaughter, Nell directed the nib at the form, and scrawled a signature without looking, to her parents' obvious relief and her own immense suffering. She fell back against her pillow, the only thing to prevent her from going completely berserk being the thought that this was to be the one supreme act of her life, unselfishly giving up her baby so that he might have a better life, with a proper family. Even so, she was racked with fresh sobs.

The whole atmosphere changed then. Doctor Greenhow took quick possession of the form and the pen, tucking both in his pocket. Her parents seemed visibly to relax, there was even sympathy on her mother's face as she watched Nell's eyes and nose stream.

'Let's just go home now,' she began kindly, 'it really won't do the baby good to witness your distress . . .'

'You promised!' Face blotched with anguish, Nell almost leapt at her as one possessed.

'All right, all right! Calm down.' The situation was bad enough for Thelma without attracting the curiosity of all those old people on the ward. 'Doctor will send for a nurse to fetch him.'

'I'll be late for work,' rasped Wilfred, apparently taking no further interest in this affair, as he was already ramming on his trilby.

'Yes, you go, dear,' his wife needlessly permitted. 'Doctor and I will take Eleanor home.' And by the time his grandchild was put into Nell's arms, her father had vanished.

But Nell did not care, her whole consciousness at once focused on this tiny crumpled being, her body completely overtaken by a visceral, all-encompassing wave of passion and the urge to protect, the deepest, most intense, most glorious love that superseded even the devotion she had felt for his father.

'I wanted to put him in the clothes I made.' Shaken by the immensity of her feelings, the new mother wept quietly now. 'To give him something to remember me by, but I've left them at home – they will tell him about me when he's older, won't they?' Her face was distorted by anxiety.

'I'm sure they will.' Thelma made glib reply, whilst inwardly boiling that her daughter had knitted a layette without her ever having guessed. 'Don't worry, he'll have the very best. Come on now, say goodbye to him.'

Weeping copiously, her whole body shaking with grief, Nell kissed the peach-soft cheek, inhaling deeply of his scent – she would never, *never* forget that scent – her tears dappling his face as he fixed her with confused and innocent navy blue eyes.

And then the nurse reached to take him. For one second Nell lusted to defy them all, to hold him to her breast as a mother should protect her newborn, to scream at them that they could all go to hell. But in her heart she knew that they were bound to win. Shunned by her family, she could offer him no kind of life at all, at least not one befitting a son she loved above all else.

'His name's William,' she said on a shuddering sigh, as her arms were relieved of his featherweight – oh why did he go so meekly? Why did he not cry and protest as did his mother? – and she swore that one day they would be reunited, if it took every breath of her body. *I'll come and find you one day, William*, she gave solemn oath in her head, as she watched him go.

Then, having to be helped to dress by her mother, too delirious to know which arm went where, she allowed herself to be chaperoned obediently to the doctor's car. But her submission concealed a deeper frame of mind. Nell had set her heart against her parents. Never would she allow them to make her weep like this again.

In fact, she did little but weep for the entire day. Under strict instruction from her mother not to divulge a word as she was helped along the garden path, Nell managed to contain her grief to such an extent that she had no word at all for Mrs Dawson, who came out to enquire after her health.

But Mother had hurriedly explained that, 'She's doing remarkably well after her operation! Well, enough to be at home – they need the beds, you see – sorry, must dash, we're expecting the district nurse any moment!' And in they had gone.

Once over the threshold, both were forced to drop this façade. However, with the midwife arriving soon afterwards to occupy half an hour of her time, Nell managed to hold out a little longer, not breaking down until later in the morning.

Having left her tucked up, Thelma arrived with a tray of vegetable sausages to catch her daughter out of bed and blubbering over a pile of tiny clothes. 'Oh, that's going to do you a lot of good, I'm sure!' Putting down the tray, she went to snatch the clothes, not viciously but deftly enough to excise them from Nell's reach, and to drive her back to bed. 'There's poor women who'll appreciate these, someone who's been bombed out.'

'Mother, for pity's sake, leave me those if nothing else!'

'What do you mean, *nothing else*?' demanded Thelma. 'What, may I ask, do you call all this?' She swept her arm around the room, indicating the material comforts that Nell had been privileged to resume. 'You should consider yourself very lucky, my girl – and do not speak to me in that fashion!'

'I'm sorry, I'm sorry – but I wanted him!' keened Nell.

'Eleanor, we all wants things we can't have! Your father would dearly have loved to study horticulture, but his father knew it was a waste of his abilities and steered him in the right direction. Parents know best – that's why I'm getting rid of these.' She set the baby clothes firmly aside, in order to attend Nell's bedcovers. 'Now, lie down.'

'But they're all that's left of my baby!' Face protesting, wincing in discomfort, Nell allowed herself to be tucked up again.

'And will moping over them bring him back? No!' Thelma underwent a brisk smoothing of the covers. 'So stop being so selfish, so self-pitying, and let them go to someone deserving.'

Nell reached out to implore as the clothes were spirited away. 'Mother, just one!'

'No!' Her mother's face was adamant as it turned to deliver riposte. 'One or six, it would all be the same, you'd sit there looking at them, growing more maudlin until you'll have to be locked up after all! And if I'm to run up and down these stairs for ten days, I'm damned if I'm going to put up with all this mawkish behaviour as well. So you can pull yourself together, knit some blanket squares, or I could fetch you some bandages to roll, anything to take you out of your self-indulgence.'

Nell plumbed the depths of her mother's eyes, desperate for any hint of emotion. She herself still reeled from her passionate encounter with baby William, but this woman before her had never experienced such ferocious maternity, her senses not primed by the act of giving birth. 'You don't know what it's like,' whimpered Nell, her eyes and nose stung crimson by despair.

Only the coldest of hearts could fail to be moved by a daughter's plight. A struggle took place in Thelma's eyes. Then she captured Nell's hand and shook it, trying to imbue optimism. 'There'll be other children! When you're old enough to be married.'

But this only made Nell wail all the more. 'I don't want anyone else!'

'You'll change your mind once you've got over it.'

Nell's tearful eyes condemned her with a glare.

Under such tacit accusation, Thelma could stand no more. She wheeled away, and vanished briefly, taking the layette with her. In her haste a ribbon slithered from the pile of baby clothes. Nell tossed aside the covers and, ignoring her tender flesh, pelted to seize it from the carpet, tucked it inside her nightdress, and was back in bed by the time her mother returned empty-handed.

'And the minute those ten days are up,' continued Thelma in businesslike fashion, 'you can go and ask the matron to take you back! You should think yourself jolly lucky that she'll have you, Eleanor. You've been given a clean slate, and I'd advise you to treat it with value. We'll hear no more about this – now eat your rissoles, they're going cold!'

Fiercely guarded, the ribbon was to remain beneath her clothes, tightly affixed now to Bill's wedding ring on its golden chain, the weight of these small mementoes causing almost as much agony as the breasts bound with bandages. Yet they were to be her lifeline too, in those desperate days imprisoned in her room, knitting, crying, reading, crying, along with the oft-repeated thought that she would find him one day. Oh yes indeed, she would, pined Nell.

But in darkness there were other thoughts that dragged her down to meet cruel truth. She could state as often as she liked that she would find him, but he would no longer be hers, would he?

Another question was to arise whilst she was still trapped in her bed, a question that had made little impact on her comfortable life before, but one that was truly heartfelt now: was this the situation in which her natural mother had found herself? Nell had felt no affinity before, but oh how she empathised now. Surely she must have been bullied into the same awful sacrifice, for what other reason would anyone submit to be rent of their own flesh and blood? Until this day, she had been a stranger, and Nell's threats to go and look for her had only been issued on childish whim. Now, for the first time, she regarded herself as on intimate terms with the one who had borne her, and the desire to go and find her had never been stronger.

But then, would the act of reaching out to one who had suffered the same ordeal take away this terrible pain? No, nothing would. And who was to say that Nell *had* been given away for the same reason? Her real mother might be as cold as this one, might have given her away from pure indifference – might well reject her again, should she manage even to find her. So what was the point?

Apart from the midwife, there were to be no visitors to encroach on her grief. The neighbours might have had to be fobbed off with the lie about her having appendicitis, but Mother had managed to conceal it altogether from her relatives. With their get-togethers restricted to Christmas and special occasions, it was rare for any of them to call on the off-chance – which was such a relief when one was cursed with a daughter prone to bursting into tears when someone even looked at her the wrong way. Father did not show his face at all.

Inevitably, left to deal with everything, Mother grew sick of running about after someone with self-inflicted wounds, and the instant the doctor gave permission, she had Nell on her feet and undergoing light chores around the house.

It was awful having to confront Father for the first time. He refused to speak to her, barely deigned to look at her, but when he did it was with such disappointment and accusation that Nell could not bear to meet his gaze.

Mother did her best to inject some normality, though she must have found it as big a strain as Nell, for after only three days of this awful tension, she was to announce the moment Father had gone to work, 'I think you're fit enough to leave the house now.'

A newfound cynicism told Nell that her mother did not mean just physically fit, but that her breasts no longer resembled two melons, and her flabby stomach was once more contained in a corset. Fit to rejoin society. No one would be able to tell what had happened to her, except perhaps from those haunted eyes that stared back at her from the mirror. Outwardly, it was as if William had never been born, whilst the loss of him felt like a still-smoking brand upon her soul.

'I'm sure you must be eager to get back to work.' Her mother's declaration was tart as she moved energetically between table and kitchen, still unwilling to meet Nell's eye.

At a slower pace, helping to clear the breakfast pots, Nell made a wordless gesture of acceptance. Even after being allowed downstairs, the atmosphere at home was suffocating, not least in its air of perpetual condemnation. So, taking this unsubtle hint, in the hope that she would be allowed to start straight away, she went to put on her rather baggier uniform, gathered her coat and gas-mask container, and prepared to face the outside world.

'It's nice to see you up and about, lass!' called Mrs Dawson, emerging into the spring morning at the same time as Nell to see Geoffrey off to work. 'It's a nasty thing, appendicitis. Really takes it out of you, doesn't it?' On the other side of the immaculately trimmed privet hedge that divided them, she sauntered alongside Nell towards the gate, hopeful of a chat. 'It'll be a while before you're back to your old self.'

Thinking that she would never be her old self again, Nell merely smiled and nodded, and tried to escape, but was immediately cornered by another neighbour, Mrs Tree, who blocked the gateway.

'Aw, how are you feeling, Eleanor?'

Feeling? I feel nothing. My arms are empty. With no child to hold, Nell hugged herself against the chill.

'Eh, you still look peaky, doesn't she, Mrs Dawson? Anything we can do to put the colour back in your cheeks?'

Why could they not have asked before, when I really needed someone? rankled Nell. Edging her way past, and in that same tightly smiling manner that her mother employed to fend off unwelcome attention, she replied, 'No, I'm quite well, thank you,' and walked away.

'Appendicitis,' muttered an unconvinced Mrs Tree under her breath. 'We all know what that means!'

Her companion sighed and nodded. 'Eh, the poor lass. I wonder what they've done with the bairn?' Then, feeling a rush of sympathy for Nell, she called after her, 'You don't want to be doing too much, love!'

Matron Lennox was of this opinion too, when Nell appeared before her, and warned of the physical snag of returning to work so soon. 'Have another month off, Nurse Spottiswood, you'll invite a prolapse.'

'If it's all the same to you, Matron, I'd rather run the gauntlet. I'll go mad if I have to sit around the house.' Nursing this terrible emptiness, she had really wanted to add. But just the thought of it made her face crumple in tears.

'My dear, if that's an indication of just how fit you are to return –'

'Oh, please!' Nell looked apologetic for her stridence, but begged Matron to reconsider. 'I give my word that will never happen again.' She immediately altered her demeanour, straightening her backbone to emphasise this intent. 'If I can concentrate on those more unfortunate than myself, I know I'll be able to cope.'

'Very well,' conceded Matron, who had not yet replaced her other two nurses. 'You may start tomorrow.'

'Today?' quizzed Nell hopefully.

'Today if you feel you are up to it – but on light duties. As a matter of fact we all appear to be on light duties, the train hasn't left the sidings since you were with us last. So, it will be the usual drill, a quick tidy up and make a few dressings, then you can go along with some of the others and help out at the Infirmary.' She saw the expression on Nell's face and answered her unspoken question. 'The rest of the crew have been informed that you've strained your back.'

Appendicitis, a strained back, what next? But Nell gave a silent nod of gratitude.

Then Matron Lennox thought of something more. 'Has anyone troubled themselves to line up any kind of post-natal examination for you?'

Her young nurse looked awkward. 'My doctor says I should go see him in a month or so.'

'Well, make sure you do. We can't have you collapsing on us. And I don't suppose I need remind you that your own upset must not be allowed to affect your patients.'

'No, Matron,' Nell promised quietly.

There came a satisfied nod from her ladylike superior. 'No, I'm confident that it won't. You're a good nurse. In general I'm very pleased with you. Well, run along now.'

Rejoining her colleagues, Nell felt that all were staring at her. She half-expected unkind words from Sister, but for once there were none, and, true to Matron's opinion, she was to be spared interrogation by the others too. Hence, she was to slip back into her duties quite easily. And if those duties were not performed so strenuously as usual, no one needed to ask the reason why.

Later, though, upon finding herself alone with Beata in a sluice at the Infirmary, she felt that she owed her friend an explanation. 'You guessed the real reason I've been off, didn't you?'

Having been scouring bedpans, the older nurse stopped to gaze at her for a while, as if noting the much more mature air about Nell, the one that Nell had seen for herself in the mirror; it was like viewing a completely different person. Then Beata nodded. 'Well, I had an idea . . .'

'I'm so sorry for deceiving you, Killie.' There were tears in Nell's eyes, but she fought them.

'That's all right.' Beata issued an affectionate nudge, and both got on with scouring and rinsing the bedpans.

'You're not shocked?' tendered Nell, above the splashing of water into the sink. 'I didn't dare tell you, for what you might think of me.' She could not look at the other. 'I know your views on unmarried mothers.'

'Those who have no morals, aye, but that's not the case in this instance,' murmured her friend. 'I know how much you thought about Bill . . . So, have your parents let you keep the baby?'

Nell shook her head, unable to voice this dreadful sense of loss.

Beata sighed in sympathy. 'I wish you'd told me. I didn't like to come out with it myself in case you took offence, but I'd have tried to help.'

'How?' demanded Nell. 'What could you have done?' She experienced deep upset, and a surge of rancour too, at Beata, at herself, at the thought that this might have been handled differently. But there was nothing to be done about it now. To find her son and take him back would be impossible. She swore her friend to silence. 'I just thought you had a right to know – but cross your heart you'll never tell another soul!' She saw Beata's slight hesitation, and guessed in, dull tone, 'Ah, the others twigged too, didn't they?'

'They are nurses.' Beata clanked another bedpan onto the stack of clean ones. 'But none of them condemned you – well, Joy put her few penneth in, but you'd expect that of her. The others said as I do, that you're not the first and you won't be the last – and I told them how you really thought the world of Billy.' In a gesture of compassion, she lowered the lids of her small blue eyes and shook her auburn head. 'God knows, lass, you must have gone through the mill these last few weeks . . .' At her friend's woeful nod, Beata confirmed, 'I've never breathed a word to anyone outside, not even my family, and I never will.'

'Thank you,' said Nell, quickly getting on with her work. 'We'd better not talk of it any more.'

Beata struggled for something to make her friend laugh. 'Did I ever tell you about the time my false teeth froze in the glass overnight?'

Despite herself, Nell gave a surprised chuckle. 'How long have you worn dentures?'

'Ooh, since I was your age,' came the blasé reply. 'Me and a pal had them all out on a whim – they looked far better than the ones we had – well, you obviously couldn't tell, could you? I wish I hadn't now, though, they tend to impair your freedom. Anyway . . .' Beata prepared to go on with her anecdote, unaware that Nell's mind was already drifting back to the previous subject.

The friends were not to speak of this again. But every single day, throughout the springtime and beyond, no matter how hard she worked, Nell was to mourn her baby William, unable to shed the memory of having him torn from her arms, the pain of which grew worse, not better. If only she had some news of him and were allowed to know if he thrived, wherever he was. And if only life would not keep dealing her these constant painful reminders, every day bringing another.

Today was no exception. In her recently acquired manner, never allowing herself to rest, Nell was striding purposefully along the corridor to collect a patient from surgery. Upon reaching a swing door, her way was blocked by someone approaching from the other direction, and, standing aside, she held open the door for Sister Eccles to go through first, not merely from duty, but also because her superior had a baby in her arms. Another little mite for the nursery ward. As it passed her by, as if to test herself, Nell allowed her eyes to rest upon its sleeping face, and the sight inspired a bolt of anguish – but with it came an awful thought that prompted her to catch her breath. What if they had lied to her; had fobbed her off in order to get her signature on the form. What if they hadn't sent William to a good family at all, but had dumped him in this institution thinking she would remain ignorant? Perhaps that was why she had not been required to work in the nursery ward since she had returned – not from kindness, but from expediency! After so many weeks, would she even recognise him?

Standing there, still holding the door ajar whilst she reeled over this awful possibility, Nell's heart began to hammer, and the blood to swish through her ears. Then, completely changing course, she released the door to swing on its hinges, and began to follow the one who held the baby, increasing her pace to match the sister's, pursuing her along the corridor and right into the nursery ward, where, without a word to anyone, not to Blanche on her hands and knees scrubbing the floor, not to the toddler who scampered back and forth – not even to her friend Beata on duty there, who smiled a greeting – Nell was to hurry from cot to cot, peering into each, anxiously scrutinising the wizened infants, intent on recognition.

But he was not there. Half-relieved, half-anguished, she halted in some confusion by the last cot, her hand trembling on its iron rail.

'Was there something you required, Nurse?' The baby still in her arms, the ward sister was frowning at this impertinent intruder.

Only half come to her senses, her heart still racing thirteen to the dozen, Nell showed penitence for not seeking authorisation to enter, and groped for a motive. Then her eyes fell on the simpleton Cissie, who had sneaked in to visit her five-month-old baby, Matthew. 'Sorry, Sister, I just came looking for Ciss—'

'Well, you've found her. Say what you have to, then look smart!' Sister Eccles gave a curt nod, then marched off with the baby.

Still Nell made no move to leave, at once attacked by the presence of all these infants that seemed to taunt her own loss. The toddler was dragging at a handful of her skirt, but, almost oblivious to him, she stared instead into Matthew's cot. He had rubbed a bald patch on the back of his head, a large, square-shaped area surrounded with fledgling tufts. Had William kept his dark hair? Had he grown a tooth? Had they allowed him to keep the name she had given him, or substituted one of their own? The blood still whooshed through her veins, deafening her to all reason, carrying an insane surge of jealousy and anger, anger at the people who had taken him, anger at the doctor, anger at her parents, anger with the world, anger at herself for not showing more spirit and saving him. And as for this one – Nell's glower landed on Cissie now – this imbecile, who kept popping out babies like a one-woman factory, and stood here with a gormless smile on her face . . . Never had she felt such resentment towards another human being. As much as she had told herself it was not the poor wretch's fault, that it was those who had taken advantage who were to blame, as much as it had not mattered before, it mattered now, and she could not prevent the harsh words from spilling forth.

'What are you doing here, you're meant to be cleaning!'

At this uncharacteristic treatment, Cissie's smile turned to confusion. 'I were just having a little look at me babby, Nurse.'

'Well, just make sure *he*'s your last one!' Nell stabbed a finger at Matthew's cot. 'You're a blessed disgrace, having so many!'

The unfortunate Cissie cringed and ejected a wail. 'I couldn't help it, Nurse, the man made me do it!'

'Then we'll have to get the police onto him!' retorted Nell.

'I wouldn't know him again, nurse! He was all dressed in black with his hat pulled down over his eyes and a long leather coat over his clothes.'

'Sounds like a member of the Gestapo.' Beata had wandered up to defuse the situation with a wry comment.

'You shouldn't joke!' Nell spun toward her, unamused. 'It's not right that she keeps churning out these poor little creatures who'll never have a normal life!'

Beata said nothing, but in that moment as brown eyes locked with blue, Nell caught the look of recrimination, and just as immediately felt a rush of shame for her cruel treatment of one in her care. Without either of them voicing the reason for Nell's envious rampage, both knew its cause – that this unfit mother had been privileged to keep her baby nearby, at least until it was old enough to enter an orphanage, whilst Nell, who would have loved and cosseted and treasured hers, had been forbidden even to hold him for more than thirty seconds. Not even a photograph. Just a ribbon. And the scent of a newborn forever imprinted on her senses.

Clinging to a last vestige of professionalism, Nell said nothing more, but straightened her shoulders, and strode from the ward, though she fully expected to be confronted after working hours – for how could Beata truly understand the magnitude of a mother's loss? Yet Beata never did condemn, not on that day or on any day to come – which somehow only made matters worse, for Nell would have welcomed the confrontation, the opportunity to unleash the full extent of her rage on someone other than a hapless idiot, one who could justifiably return the blows, and thus allow her to purge this terrible pent-up grief.

Instead of which, it continued to be bottled up, the level of this festering injustice bubbling higher every day, so that at times she was to feel like an unexploded bomb just waiting to go off.

7

Bombs were still going off in reality too, many of them on a devastated Hull and Sheffield, though few in York. As ever, London was to receive the worst of it, the springtime blitz relentless, and May bringing the worst raid yet. Nell had not written to Mrs Kelly since before . . . well, since before. What was the point? Under such a bombardment perhaps Billy's mother had joined the legions of those made homeless, or even killed. And even if she were alive, thought Nell, with a bitterness forged of loss, this was a different life. She wanted no reminders to drag along with her. She felt bad enough as it was.

So too did everyone else, if the glum and lean faces in the streets were anything to go by. With much of Europe under the heel of Hitler, one country falling after another, the rest of that year was a switchback ride, morale being fleetingly elevated by the sinking of the *Bismarck*, then just as quickly dunked by heavy losses in Crete. By God's mercy, their own threat of invasion had been postponed. Repelled from British shores, the Germans were to invade Russia instead.

'This is the best thing the Huns could have done!' opined a smug Wilfred Spottiswood to his wife and daughter, upon hearing the announcement on the wireless that midsummer evening. 'Mark my words, it'll be their undoing. The winters there are treacherous.' He shook his head and made an O of his mouth to express severity. 'Snow and ice up to your chin, fingers frozen to icicles! It put paid to Napoleon's reign – and the Kaiser – it'll topple Hitler too!'

Taking comfort from this, Thelma gave a nod of satisfaction at her daughter, as if to indicate that Father's word was lore.

But Nell made little response. She had long ago ceased to respect anything either of her parents said. They had told her that it was for the best in persuading her to give away her baby – how could it be for the best when she still felt such raw agony months later? That was the only reason she seated herself there alongside them every evening, not because she enjoyed their company – Mother with her irritating click of knitting needles, Father with his irritating click of teeth – no, she was there because she feared to be alone with her thoughts. As for the war, its minutiae no longer figured half so much in her consciousness, for what would be, would be.

However, as the year progressed it began to emerge that Nell's father was right in his assumptions, in a roundabout sort of way. By another December, the Germans were far too embroiled on the Eastern Front to waste their energies on Britain, and moreover, after murderous provocation by the Japs, the United States had entered the conflict.

Had she not accidentally heard it on the wireless, none of this would have been apparent to Nell, who continued to flounder through her day-to-day ministrations, regarding her patients as the only ones to matter, occasionally rewarded by a comic moment from one of the old men or ladies, in between fending off insanity with the aid of tobacco. The past year of loss had seen her relying heavily on cigarettes, even so reliant as to puff them in the street, which was still officially forbidden. Far better, thought Nell, for the smoke to be blown away in the fresh air than to impregnate her uniform and upset the patients. No one had complained so far. At least, not the patients. She no longer took the trouble to conceal the habit from her parents – for what more could they do to her – and did not mind insulting *them* with her fumes. In fact, she relished using any small way to punish them for what they had done to her. Now, though, with all smoking materials hard to acquire, she had resorted to desperate means.

'A *pipe*?' condemned her mother, upon this being brought out after tea that winter's eve, as the lights were turned off and all moved to huddle round the hearth. 'Oh, Eleanor, how uncouth!' Her whole demeanour was astounded.

'I could only manage to lay my hands on half an ounce of shag, so it was either this or roll my own, and I'm hopeless at those.' Illuminated by firelight, Nell retained an unruffled surface as she held a taper to the pipe's bowl and coaxed the tobacco to ignite with a little series of puffs.

'There's no law says you have to smoke at all!' A picture of aversion, Thelma snatched up a shawl to compensate for the poor fire – coal being in as short ration as every other commodity – and wrapped it around herself as she snuggled back into her chair. 'I've been very understanding in allowing you the odd cigarette, what with these testing times, but some of us manage to cope without turning into human chimneys. I'm glad they are in short supply if it stops you frittering fourteen shillings a week – and I draw the line at that smelly thing. Why, you look like an old tinker!'

Nell merely eyed her through the gloom. Then, having kindled her tobacco, she too sat back and made herself comfortable by tugging a blanket over her knees, puffing away on her pipe, defying further objection.

But objection there came. 'I hope you realise you're making more work for me,' reproved Wilfred, calmer than his wife as he concentrated on mending a pair of shoes, though equally disgusted at the way his daughter was choosing to behave in defiance of his own generosity. 'That patch of ceiling above your chair's begun to turn yellow.'

'After one pipeful?' scoffed Nell.

'And all the rest of the fags you've been puffing off without as much as a by your leave – and less of your lip! It isn't you who has to set to and paint it – that's considering I can even lay my hands on any flipping paint these days! As if I haven't enough to do with going out to work and the Home Guard. Put the blasted thing out.' And he turned his petulant grey features back to his task, and his ear to the wireless, obviously expecting her to comply.

Nell maintained cool insolence. 'I'll go outside and have it then.' Removing herself from the firelight, she took up her coat and trolled through the kitchen, overhearing her father's damning comment as she left:

'I don't know why we bother, she's a ruddy disgrace!'

Leaning against the outer jamb of the back door, puffing on her pipe, Nell asked herself why she continued with this charade – why any of them continued with it. What was the point in being there? Was it simply to annoy her parents? For that was all she seemed to do. It was immaterial that they had expressed no further recrimination once she had obeyed them and given her baby away, she still felt them looking at her with complete incomprehension as to how their well-brought-up daughter could do such a thing. Nothing would be the same between the three of them, so why was she still here? Out of convenience, she supposed, and for financial reasons. Perhaps some girls of nineteen could summon the wherewithal to set up on their own, but Nell had always been looked after, and had little idea how to spread the two pounds per week she earned. Still, there must be some way to reduce the hours in such stifling company . . .

With the casualty evacuation trains standing virtually redundant, she and certain members of the crew had found themselves putting in more and more hours at the Infirmary now, which was good, for this routine, however mundane, kept one busy. And Nell liked to be kept busy.

Sister Barber had apparently come to appreciate this too, and today had approached her and Beata about going on the rota for night shift. Taken aback, it had been Nell's first impulse to say that the responsibility was far too much, to be alone in the small hours with perhaps sixty patients under her care, but Sister seemed to have faith in her abilities.

'You'll rarely hear me say this,' quipped Sister, 'but you and Killie have turned out to be two of the most diligent nurses out of the original crew. That's correct: I did say nurses. I never thought to see the day when I'd suitably address you as such. You both know very well that I was totally against being lumbered with untrained staff, and certainly there are those who have fulfilled my every expectation.' Both knew that she was referring to Joyson, who had regressed from a position of keenness to one of can't-be-bothered. 'Obviously, your lack of qualifications is a great handicap. But I believe that it's only a lack of finances that prevents you from higher achievement. If devotion to duty were to be considered, then you would win hands down. You've both been on the wards for the best part of a year now, and I feel you're equipped for night duty. At any rate, I'd like you to think about it.'

And Nell did think about it seriously now, as she puffed on her pipe, thinking too of the Christmas that was imminent, and dreading having to partake in another festive meal with her parents. Out of sheer desperation she decided there and then that she would add her name to the night-shift rota. For, by choosing to work on a night, she could legitimately sleep all Christmas Day and hardly have to see her parents at all.

Christmas. Gazing up at the twinkling stars on this frosty night, she huddled into her coat and sucked on the stem of her pipe, conjuring pictures of flying reindeer and jingling bells. An effect of the blackout, the stars had never seemed so bright, each constellation perfectly defined. Did her natural mother gaze at this stellar scene and wonder over her, just as she wondered over her own baby William? At eight months old he would not yet know the excitement of dressing the fir tree, the evocative mixture of that and the scent of roast chicken, of being called from his bed to find that Santa had left a pile of toys and books. Hopefully, though, he would grow to do so. Biting hard on the pipe stem to ward off tears, his mother prayed again that he was with a good family – no, not just a good family, but a *kind* family.

Such thoughts lured her mind then to the children at the Infirmary, the ones whose mothers had died and whose fathers were in Europe, or in Malaya or Burma, at the mercy of the Japs; some with mothers like Cissie; others with parents who had abused them; some with no parent at all: and she was attacked by pangs of compassion for those wretched little mites with their scabby, purple-dotted faces. She had already taken up Matron's example and begun to make little gifts for them, and for the elderly inmates – a bed jacket here, a teddy bear there – perhaps by volunteering for night shift she could even increase her output. Unable to enjoy restful sleep since Billy had died, after catching sufficient shut-eye during the day she could go to work much earlier than was necessary. and use the time to make more dolls' clothes before her shift. Anything, thought Nell, rather than be in the claustrophobic household behind that closed door.

Holding on to this new sense of purpose, she continued to suck on her pipe for a while, no matter how bitter the weather, reluctant to go in, imbibing a sense of irony along with the sweet scent of tobacco smoke that coiled across Father's vegetable patch and away into the night. How bloody paradoxical, that she had let herself be bullied into giving up her baby so as to regain entry to their wretched little home. And how she detested the place now.

Another year was snuffed out, though not, alas, the war, its evil combatants now gaining purchase of Singapore and much of the Far East, and the threat extended to India and Ceylon, and even Australia.

At home, the casualty evacuation trains that had stood idle for months were finally disbanded, and the crew dispersed to various arenas, some like the Ashton twins going on to higher achievement, whilst Nell, Beata, Joyson and Sister Barber became fully employed at the Infirmary. Whilst her colleagues worked there by choice, Joyson would have much preferred to attend one of the military hospitals, and in the hope that her experience would hold sway she had made an application, but to her chagrin had been rejected. This being so, she managed to reap the next best thing. A ward had been set up devoted to shell-shocked soldiers and airmen, who weren't physically injured but simply needed to convalesce. Regarding this as her new vocation, Joy had almost elbowed aside the others in her rush to volunteer.

'Vocation my Aunty Fanny,' muttered Beata, drawing an infrequent chuckle from Nell, both of whom were mainly relegated to the old people's wards. 'It's because the chaps don't need much looking after, except a kind word or two.'

'They won't get those from Joy!' scoffed Nell, and decreed that, 'We must be doolally to put up with this,' as the pair of them marked the end of another night shift by transporting steaming water for one of the incontinent elderly who must be bathed.

Despite there being a bathroom at the Infirmary, there was no hot-water supply, this having to be hauled in pails down the corridor from the kitchen, and the patients manually lifted in – some of them kicking and screaming. And yes, it was exacting, having to care for sixty patients on a ward, to feed them and wash them and change their bed linen twice a week, and to be constantly familiar with their excreta. And yes, it was true, this embodied none of the heroic romanticism over which a girl might rhapsodise – yet it was somehow rewarding, thought Nell, to know that you were making someone's final years as comfortable as you possibly could. Which, for her, was the only thing that made life bearable.

'God forbid that I end up here myself,' came her wry but pertinent comment to Beata as they tipped their pails of hot water into the bath, 'but if I do, I hope I get someone like you as my nurse and not oh-be-Joyful!'

Nell arrived home several hours later, to the abrupt question:

'What time will you be getting up?'

'Do you mind if I go to bed first?' chaffed the over-taxed nurse.

'Don't be cheeky!' Mother treated her as if she were still a little girl, snatching the coat off her shoulders and hanging it up. 'This coat reeks of tobacco smoke, I hope you haven't been puffing that horrible pipe in the street – no, I only asked because I'm planning a special tea-come-breakfast for your birthday. I know it's not until tomorrow, but you work such silly hours . . .'

Nell gave a sharp laugh. 'Only my mother could talk of planning a special meal with such shortages inflicted on us! Haven't you seen the placards? No beer, no cigarettes, no whatever-it-is-you-were-going-to-ask-for!' The bitter quip concealed a host of emotions. Having dreaded tomorrow, she had been working her hardest to forget, for it also marked the anniversary of her son's birth. How she would get through it, God only knew.

'I am aware of that, but I thought it might be nice for us to eat together,' continued Thelma with manufactured patience, tweaking a strand of lint off Nell's cardigan as she spoke.'Your father and I never get to see you these days, you're always at work. I've been saving a jar of loganberries all year so's you'd have a little treat.' Her expression now intimated that she was trying to make an effort here, to show her daughter that bygones could be bygones, if only Nell would allow it.

But the worn-out nurse was unmoved as she made for bed. 'You needn't go to any trouble on my account.'

Thelma tailed her to the foot of the stairs, calling in a half-bright manner, 'Am I not supposed to celebrate my daughter's birthday any more just because she's twenty?'

Nell paused, and looked back to examine her mother. Perhaps made extra irritable by tiredness, or maybe just from stored-up bile, her self-restraint was cast aside as she stated the cruel truth. 'I'll never get to celebrate *my* child's birthday, will I?'

Then, unsympathetic with Thelma's concussed expression, she turned and uttered over her shoulder, 'Oh, just do as you like, I'm off to bed.'

She was to emerge hours later to a stiff warning from her mother.

'I hope you're in a better mood to appreciate this!'

No, I'm bloody not, thought Nell, snatching a none-too-interested look at the prettified table, and going to the sink for a glass of water. She had meant to be up and away before Father came home, but here it was almost five thirty.

'You really shouldn't be having these, after the awful thing you said to me this morning.'

Despite this opinion, Thelma placed two gifts on the linen cloth, along with a card.

Nell mumbled appeasement, though it lacked conviction as she immediately took another sip from her glass, and remained in nonchalant pose by the sink.

'Well, never mind, you can open them now if you like,' invited her mother. 'No need to wait for Father to get home

– oh, here he is!' Instantly distracted by one more eminent, she began to fuss about, pulling back her husband's chair ready for him to sit in, and beaming as he entered.

'Ah, that's right, we're celebrating early . . .' Wilfred immediately noted the best china on the table and wished his daughter, 'Many happy returns for tomorrow.' Then he pulled off his bike clips, rolled up his sleeves and washed his hands at the kitchen sink, his wife standing by with the towel. 'Twenty, eh?'

I feel like a hundred, the things I've been through, thought Nell.

'Open your things then!' prompted Thelma, as her husband dried his hands.

Not caring enough to feign interest, Nell upturned her glass on the draining board, then approached the top parcel and tore its brown paper, inside which was a plain moss-green skirt. It was hardly a surprise. Upon purchasing the utility cloth Mother had rather tellingly sought her opinion on it, and had been stitching it for weeks. But she thanked her parents anyway, adding, 'It's a nice colour.' The smaller, flatter package revealed a pair of stockings. These managed to elicit a little gasp of appreciation from Nell.

'I should think so.' Her mother wagged a finger, though smilingly. 'Two and eleven they cost me – and not even fully fashioned!' She waved aside any supposition that she had forked out too much on her daughter. 'Oh, don't worry, you were meant to receive them last birthday bu—'

But she had shoved them away in the cupboard after being presented with an illegitimate grandchild. Debunked by her own faux pas, Thelma finished quickly, 'Anyway, sit down and open your card whilst I fetch the liver casserole!'

In the shadow of this blunder, the meal was consumed mainly in silence, with intermittent compliments from Mr Spottiswood upon the quality of his wife's gravy and the fresh vegetables from his own plot.

Too immersed in thoughts about the child that was lost to her, Nell said nothing at all until laying down her spoon at the end of the meal. 'Smashing loganberries. Thank you.'

'You're welcome, dear, it was worth the wait, wasn't it? Well, I'd better pour you a cup of tea before you run off and leave us.' Thelma picked up the teapot. 'What a shame you have to work.'

No it isn't thought Nell, eager to escape this stilted conversation. I'd work every night of the week if they'd allow it.

'When do you next have a night off? Perhaps you should go out and enjoy yourself then . . .'

'With all these blasted Yanks creeping about?' exclaimed Wilfred, a cup of tea halfway to his lips. 'Swaggering round town in their slick uniforms, flashing their money about to catch daft little tarts – have you forgotten the last time we trusted her?'

'I'm sure she's learned her lesson,' cut in Thelma quickly, 'haven't you, Eleanor?'

Nell glared at them, a crescendo of fury pervading her throat and threatening to asphyxiate – as if any man could replace Bill!

'She's going nowhere,' finished her father, carelessly scooping another berry into his mouth.

'Yes, I am.' Swallowing the urge to launch an attack – for where might it stop – with great deliberation and dignity, Nell rose. 'I'm going to pack.' Leaving the birthday card behind, she picked up the skirt and stockings, and took them with her.

'And go where?' asked her mother, both parents taken aback and just a little disdainful.

'That needn't trouble you.' Nell was unsure herself; she just knew that if she did not leave there and then she would end up killing one of them, or yielding to the canker that threatened her soul.

Whilst a calm Mr Spottiswood remained at the table,

his tongue skilfully ejecting loganberry seeds from under his dentures and making that clickety-clacking that so incensed both his womenfolk, his wife followed her daughter upstairs, to observe as she packed a case. Nell stowed into it everything she might need for a lengthy self-exile, using her hatbox as an overflow. Lifting out the school boater, she put it aside, trying not to look at Bill's photograph, his watch and his letters, for even to set eyes on these priceless things opened such wounds, and immediately she crammed on top of them as much as the hatbox would take.

'Aren't you even going to leave us an address?' demanded her mother.

'When I've got one, perhaps.' Nell had almost finished packing.

'Well, if you've nowhere definite to go, why rush off so impulsively?'

'You really have to ask?' Nell turned to frown, then shook her head.

'For pity's sake!' Obviously at the end of her tether, Thelma spoke through clenched teeth, so as to keep her voice low. 'You're not even twenty-one, why do you stubbornly persist in looking backwards?'

Nell rose to the provocation. '*That's* why I'm going! Because no one here can understand what it's like to have this raw bloody hole inside me!'

'It'll be forever raw if you keep picking at it!'

'See?' retorted Nell. 'Only a *real* mother would understand – so maybe I'll go and find her!'

Thelma looked devastated – and angry. 'You stand there with your false heroics as if no one else has ever gone through the mill . . .' The look on her ashen face revealed that she had said too much, but it was too late now. 'I'll save you the trouble of searching for your *real* mother. You're looking at her. The one who sat up with you all night tending your childhood illnesses, the one who cooked and cleaned and cared for you for twenty years – *and* the one who gave birth to you. So don't you dare lecture me on what a real mother is.'

Nell felt close to fainting, her lips forming the questions that her voice was unable to utter. She flopped onto the edge of the bed, as Thelma condemned her.

'See what chain of events you've started with your bloody-minded behaviour? You've pushed me into something I'd rather have kept private, and now I'll have to relive it all. I'll be lucky if your father doesn't throw me out.' Having obviously to drag it from herself, she related the tale, nipping at the skin of her cuticles as she picked over the past. 'It *was* true about you being adopted. But your father was the only one of us to adopt. It was he who decided you should never know about me – you're not to breathe a word to him that I've told you this. I won't have him upset.'

Upset? marvelled Nell. But throttled by shock, she could only attend.

'We'd both been so desperate to have a family for a long, long time,' rushed Thelma, eager to get this over with in case her husband should intrude. 'Your father thought that I was to blame for there being no children, and things got a bit . . . overwrought. Anyway, he had to go into hospital. Whilst he was away, I made a very stupid mistake. I had a fling with a complete stranger. It was only the once and I never saw him again. And then I found out that I wasn't barren at all.' She gave a deep sigh and gazed into mid-air. 'I'll never forget your father's face when I had to tell him. He'd been in hospital for three months, so he knew you couldn't be his . . . Anyway, I don't want to go into all that. To cut a long story short, he forgave me, because he knew this was his only chance of having a family too, and we made arrangements that we should go away before anyone found out I was having you. It wasn't that difficult because we were living in rented accommodation at the time. We made up a story about your father having to convalesce, which wasn't far from the truth. We couldn't pass you off as our own because the relatives were aware how long he'd been laid up, and I'd have been ostracised – you must promise never to breathe a word to them,' she broke off to instruct Nell, who was so totally sandbagged that she could not have breathed a word if she had tried. But inside her head she was screaming, *I don't understand! How could you? Why when how?*

Thelma made a speedy return to her theme. 'They all knew how much we wanted children, of course. So, when we made up this story about discovering the perfect child in an orphanage, they accepted it without question.' She interjected a bitter laugh. 'The perfect child! Little did we know what you'd put us through . . .'

Nell remained speechless, but her mind leapt from thought to thought, like a mountain goat scaling the peaks, higher and higher, towards the zenith of hysteria. All those years of being led to believe that twaddle, having it drummed into her about how she had been chosen from hundreds of other babies, being made to feel a failure and a pariah for doing exactly the same as her mother had done – her whole life a total lie! At last she managed to gasp only one of the many things that ran amok through her brain: 'How could you force me to give up my baby after you'd contrived to keep your own?'

'You can't possibly compare the two situations!' Thelma was quick to defend herself. 'I was a mature woman with a husband willing to forgive me, and both of us with no other chance of having a family. You were barely more than a schoolgirl, even now. *I* was suitably ashamed into doing the decent thing by going away to give birth, and not bringing the whole family into disrepute. *You* left it until the last minute – it's a miracle no one found out, and only then thanks to our efforts!' Despite her strenuous justification, she looked torn. 'Perhaps if you'd come to me earlier about your condition I might have been more sympathetic, but there was no one to marry you, and you set us all into a panic, what else was I supposed to do? I'm only telling you now because I'm sick of the way you've been treating me. Sick of women looking down their noses and regarding me as a second-class mother because I couldn't have children, sick of being forced to pretend when you really were mine . . .

'Eleanor,' she sat on the bed alongside her daughter and implored her, 'try and keep a grip of what I said before, that you'll have more children one day, when you're older and with the right person. I *do* know how much it must hurt you. Having to pretend all these years that I'm not your real mother, it's been agony sometimes. But please, please believe that everything was done for the best, and not, as you seem to think, to spite you. You'll only destroy yourself with such thoughts . . .' Having laid out her case, Thelma sat back, hands in lap as if she were posing for a photograph.

In a trice, Nell rose and, with her mother tripping after her, hefted her luggage down the stairs, grabbing her gas-mask container when she reached the hall. Only then did she stop dead to glare into the dining room. Her father had not moved from the table. Nell stood for a few seconds more, to cast contempt for his share in the duplicity. Then she caught the look of terror on her mother's face; and, in a wave of sickness, moved on.

Half-relieved that her daughter was intent on going, Thelma pounced on her handbag and handed something over. 'I suppose you'll need these then . . .'

Nell barely glanced at her mother as she took possession of her ration books, just thanked her and left.

Her mother might judge it a hasty decision, but it was not really. It took only a moment's thought for Nell to gain direction, to the one place she would be assured hospitality.

It was already crammed with lodgers, most of them soldiers, but with herself on night shift much of the week, being asleep through the day whilst they were out on manoeuvres, and vice versa on a night, no one should be inconvenienced. This being so, she went now to throw herself on the mercy of Ma and Georgie Precious, in the hope that in this happily chaotic household she would find some release. But every nerve end tingled with the things she had just learned.

As expected, the Preciouses were delighted to accommodate her snap arrival that evening, and to accept her explanation that she had fallen out with her parents over something irrelevant, not minding a jot that she dumped her luggage in the hall and in the same turn prepared to rush off to work. Their only complaint was that they had not seen her for such a long time.

'We thought we'd done something wrong!' bawled Ma, legs astride. 'It must be over a year – by, how you've altered!' Brawny arms folded beneath her large flowered promontory, she turned to her husband. 'Hasn't she altered, Georgie?'

'Still as bonny as ever, though!' The smiling old man danced forth to cup Nell's face. 'In fact, even more so.' He cocked his head, trying to fathom what was so different about their young visitor.

'I don't suppose there've been any more letters from Bill's mother?' tendered Nell. Georgie shook his head, and looked momentarily sad, obviously thinking the same as Nell that perhaps Mrs Kelly had been killed too.

'Well, even if there was, she'd grow bored awaiting your reply!' declared Ma, and wanted to know, 'What made you stop away for so long?'

'Oh . . . just work really.' A smiling Nell could not tell them about her baby. 'In fact I'll have to go there now. Is it all right if I settle up with you as soon as I get my pay?' A good thing she had not yet handed this to her mother.

'You can have my food ration book now, though – I'm really sorry to inconvenience you like this.'

'Behave!' Ma used the ration book to deal Nell a vigorous thwack. 'We'll put you up as long as you like – eh up, here's our lads off out on the prowl!' A rowdy group of soldiers had appeared from the sitting room and made for the exit. 'Come and meet our new lodger, boys!'

The soldiers descended with an appreciative whoop. Though desperate to get away, Nell endured all the introductions, perking up a little when one of them said, 'Fancy a ciggy, Nurse?'

'Ooh, yes please! May I save it for later?'

''Course you can,' grinned the donor, and, ''Ere, have another for luck!'

'Thanks, you're a brick.' Nell looked on warmly as the squaddies made their boisterous exit, leaving the door wide open behind them, there being no need for precautionary measures tonight with the sun not even set. 'I must be on my way too.'

'Hang on!' Ma had seen another of her residents coming down the stairs. 'You've met Nell, haven't you, Mr Yarker? She's coming to live with us.'

'My cup runneth over,' came the well-spoken utterance from the lugubrious middle-aged man, who, with barely a glance at Nell, made splenetic enquiry as to the soldiers. 'Is that rabble gone from the sitting room?'

'Yes, it's all yours,' trumpeted Ma.

'Thank God! Perhaps before I go out fire-watching I can enjoy a page of my newspaper without the liability of being speared to death.' The soldiers had erected a dartboard, and were apparently careless with their aim. 'Allardyce!' he called up the stairs. 'You can come out now, the Zulus have gone – take some advice, my dear,' he tapped Nell with the rolled-up chronicle, 'stay well clear of this madhouse.'

'Eh, don't you be slandering my accommodation, you

cheeky monkey!' joshed Ma, threatening to hit him, then turning immediately to Nell and saying, 'There's a nice quiet room right at the top – will you come and see it now – Georgie, show her up!'

'No, I really must get to work!' pleaded Nell with a laugh, aware that Mr Yarker's testy performance was a façade, and that he was really a good man and an heroic veteran of the Great War to boot. 'I'm sure, it'll be perfect – see you tomorrow morning!' And with that she dashed off into the chilly evening.

On her way along the main corridor of the Infirmary, she was to meet a furtive-looking Cissie Flowerdew. Of too low an intellect to bear a grudge over the incident in the nursery, Cissie offered an ingratiating beam, but Nell was too intent on seeking out a more intelligent ear for her own troubles to issue anything other than a smiling word in passing.

After hearing what had happened since she and her friend had last seen each other that morning, a kindly Beata sought to lighten Nell's burden. 'And here's me thinking I was hard done by, having to wear a brassiere fashioned out of muslin.' She made wriggling adjustment of her large bust in its homemade garment, a product of the austerity controls. 'I feel as if my bosoms should be on the cheese counter at the Maypole.'

Nell could not help but utter a grateful laugh. Still, she was in turmoil, as the other could tell.

'I know it's a shock, but try putting a different skew on it,' urged Beata. 'At least you've been given a sense of identity – she's your *real* mother, that's one thing you won't have to wonder about any more.'

This did not mend things for Nell, who had always imagined her real mother as a special, rather tragic figure. Today she had been revealed as someone ordinary, and a liar. Anyway, that was secondary to Thelma's real crime.

But with insufficient time to discuss this further, she gave a nod of thanks to her friend and they broke apart. Off both went to take instructions from the day staff, before proceeding with their usual round of duties, these being quite laborious at first, and so removing Nell's mind from her tribulations. Whilst others her age might be out on the town, dancing with the glamorous GIs, she set to tending her elderly charges, all of whom must have their temperatures and pulses taken, be provided with bedpans and bottles – which must also be cleaned – a report filled out on each patient, and on top of countless other tasks to be undertaken before Nell could snatch a breather, there were churns of night-time beverage to be hauled from the kitchens. Still, work did make the hours fly, and before she knew it her watch told it was after two a.m.

All the same, she must remain vigilant towards those who slumbered. The blinds now drawn against a moonlit night, Nell moved purposefully through the dark from bed to bed with her hurricane lamp, listening for changes in her patients' breathing, making sure that those with heart and chest conditions were securely propped with pillows and had not slumped down in their beds. Lingering briefly to gaze upon one of the permanent residents, she allowed her mind to blur, to anguish over questions that were only just now arising, such as the identity of her natural father – for surely he could not be the nameless entity her mother would have her believe? Had it truly been only the once that she had gone with him? To be conceived in such a way was appalling. Had Grandma known? Dear Granny, who had always treated Nell as no different to her other grandchildren; had she seen a likeness in her and guessed the truth? Her sense of existence exposed as a sham, a legion of other questions nipped at her heels. When the dust had died down, she must go back and compel her mother to reveal more.

The patient stirred, Nell's gaze regaining instant focus,

and thereto she enjoyed a moment of tender reflection. A long-time favourite, Connie Wood was more like an angelic child than a seventy-five-year-old lady, only three foot six of her, with tiny hands and feet, slumbering peacefully in the beribboned bed-jacket that Nell had knitted her for Christmas, wisps of remarkably shiny brown hair about her pink cheeks, abandoned at two days old by her mother, who had used the workhouse as a dropping place then simply moved on. How could she? thought Nell. Then, and how could *you*?

One year old, almost to the hour.

Brushing aside the wave of guilt and agony at having given William up, with a last fond look at Connie, she moved on, and on again, to ensure that all were equally at ease. Only after ensuring that her own charges were comfortable did she take a brief diversion from her patrol, going along to the male ward to ask if her friend Beata would like a cup of tea, and in doing so answering the summons to assist with Mr Brown.

There was no brute strength involved in rolling aside the frail old man who had recently been admitted, though much care and tenderness, for he had arrived suffering from a huge pressure sore that constantly roused him from sleep and meant he had to be regularly turned. Nell winced in sympathy, her firm but sensitive hands holding the patient to one side, whilst her friend attended his sore.

'I'm sorry about having to hurt you, Mr Brown.' She murmured reassurance to the aged soul as she bent over him.

'Don't say Brown, say Hovis!' came the jaunty request.

Nell chuckled, though she had heard this many times since he had come in. 'You're very brave. It must send you through the roof, but we'll soon have it better for you.'

'I know you will, love,' came the stoical reply. 'You're grand lasses.' And he promptly emphasised his gratitude with a squeeze of Nell's conveniently placed breast.

Startled, but not unduly repelled, for she had come to accept that such gropings were part of the job, she displaced his hand with a stern rebuke. 'That is not an acceptable way to take one's mind off one's pain, Mr Brown.' And Beata was also to be censured. 'Now I see why Nurse Kilmaster wanted me to be at this end.'

To the accompaniment of Beata's wheezy chortling, the old man's ordeal was finally brought to an end, and the nurses were trying to further decrease his suffering with strategically placed pillows when there came a thud like an enormous boulder being dropped, the reverberations going right through them.

Beata looked at Nell over the fragile form, and exclaimed to both nurse and patient, 'I didn't much like the sound of that, did you?'

'Wasn't me,' negated Mr Brown.

Nell flickered a smile at him, but looked equally apprehensive too. She always looked apprehensive these days to Beata, but even more so now, as it became obvious that York was under attack – for simultaneous to the not too distant crump of high explosive came the sirens.

'They were a bit late off the mark, weren't they, Mr Brown?'

'Don't say Brown, say Hovis!' rallied the old man.

Still devoting most of her attention to the patient, Nell tried to hide her disquiet under a veil of calm, and proceeded to ensure that he was comfortable, adding a few kind words before she left the bedside. 'I don't suppose it'll be much, but if you can't sleep we'll bring you a cup of tea . . .'

But as they moved out of earshot, the hurricane lamps casting pools of light at their feet, she muttered worriedly to Beata, 'Sounds as though it's the real thing this time.' There had been several hundred air alerts to date, most of them false alarms, and it had become policy not to evacuate the patients. Just to be sure, though, 'Should one of us phone Sis – oh, good Lord, here's Matron, it must be serious!'

Having hurried there at the first thud, Matron Fosdyke had come striding along each ward and finally into this one. 'Stay where you are for the moment, Nurse,' she instructed, pre-empting Nell's query as to what to do with the patients. 'I'm going back down into the yard to keep an eye on the situation – looks like it's York's turn at last, though!' And she turned flamboyantly on her heel.

In her absence, Nell and Beata went about their usual business of settling the old folk, many of whom had been woken by the noisy vibrations, and, being so numerous, this required a great deal of the two nurses. The night sister did pop her head in briefly, but only to call, 'I'm needed at the first-aid post, can you cope on your own?'

And, told that they could, she subsequently vanished, leaving her nurses to share a look of comic unease.

It was customary for them to stay with their patients during the sirens – though both young women realised this was no ordinary alarm, for, accompanying the growl of enemy aircraft, there were shrieks of high explosives pulverising the city, and causing many of the dementia patients to quail in terror like little children. Along with her friend, Nell immediately set about reassuring them – often having to restrain the more violent – going from bed to bed, helping to insert earplugs, stroking papery old hands, as much to remind herself to stay calm as for their benefit, whilst ever conscious that this building too might soon come under attack. And she thanked God for the serene presence of her friend, for she could never have coped without such example.

One of the patients began to fit, meaning Nell must leave her favourite whom she had just been soothing. 'I'll be back as soon as I can, Connie, don't you worry now.' Gentle of word and manner, retaining that calm collectedness that was expected in the face of danger, Nell tucked the bony little arms under the covers and made sure she had sufficiently reassured the old lady. Only then did she dart off to attend the afflicted one, having to stoop over the low bed in order to control the thrashing, and suffering a wrenched back in the process.

'Can I have a pan?' came the frail request from further along the rank of beds.

'Be right with you, Mrs Turner,' reassured Nell, and as soon as she was able she supplied it.

By this time her colleagues in residence had started to pour in from the nurses' home, some to tend the casualties who had begun to appear at the first-aid station, others to assist with the patients. With Mrs Gledhill sitting bolt upright and singing at the top of her voice – 'Onward Christian So-oldiers, marching as to war!' – Nell and Beata were most glad of the help. Even gladder when Matron came back.

'With the Cross of Je-sus, going on before!'

'Shall we evacuate them now, Matron?' A young nurse prepared to move Mrs Gledhill's bed along with its singing occupant.

'Going on be-fore!'

'No, just move the beds as far away as you can from the windows. It's safer to keep them where they are, there are incendiaries dropping all over the place – Nurse Kilmaster, Nurse Spottiswood, take a bucket of sand between you and help put them out!'

Nell and Beata hurried to comply, whilst Matron, with her enviably cool and authoritative manner, remained to conduct affairs and to soothe the frightened patients, going from ward to ward and checking that her nurses were managing. Some of the bedridden quaked in terror and incomprehension, many just looked confused, whilst others seemed to revel in the entertainment. Luckily, many of the more awkward residents had already been given a sleeping draught and slumbered on throughout. Matron now decided to dose the lot of them. 'Fetch the bromide,' she told a staff nurse. 'Then perhaps we can lay a few of them under their beds for shelter – now, which of you ladies would like a nice cup of cocoa?' she asked brightly of the patients.

Meanwhile, Nell and Beata had taken hold of a bucket of sand between them – it was too heavy for one – and now clanked awkwardly down a fire escape, leaving a trail of grit as they went, for with Nell much taller than her friend the bucket was constantly tilting – occasionally barking the tender flesh of Beata's leg too, for which Nell hastily atoned.

'S'all right, love – God, we're like Wilson, Keppel and Betty,' puffed Beata at the sound of grating underfoot. 'Doing a bloody sand dance!'

Nell wondered how her friend could always summon a joke, but grimly agreed. 'By the time we get down there'll be more in my shoes than in the bucket – oh, damn that sodding Hitler and his barbarians!'

Fortunately, when they did get down to the yard, others were dealing with the incendiaries, a fire warden putting his stirrup pump to efficient use, whilst a night watchman ran about sprinkling sand. Nevertheless, the latter was glad to relieve the nurses of their bucket, for another basket of bombs had burst overhead.

'Oh, look at the candelabra!' Hitherto, the only light had been that of a benevolent moon, but now the sky over York was further illuminated by an eerie halo of magnesium. Eyes to the heavens, Nell searched beyond the bank of cloud for a glimpse of the enemy – twenty, thirty or more, judging by the noise, the throb of their engines travelling right through her body – and for a moment she and her friend were in awe of the spectacle, the beams of searchlights zigzagging from one side of the city to the other, the showers of sparks like shooting stars, the pretty chandelier flares that turned night into day, the incendiaries plummeting to earth, plop, plop, plopping onto the roofs of surrounding buildings and setting them alight.

She shivered, and not simply because of the cold, a prickle of fear causing her hair to stand on end as her imagination ran riot, for the night vibrated with Heinkels, the screech of high explosive, the shattering of glass, and the frantic clanging of fire engines. Shaken from her trance, she yelled across the yard to the watchman, 'Will you be all right on your own? We'll have to see to our patients.'

'Aye, you go, Nurse!' he threw back. 'But I'd appreciate another bucket of sand if you can manage it!'

Promising to supply one right away, she bounded back up the outer staircase nimble of foot, Beata with her swollen leg plodding heavily behind, the pair of them grabbing another bucket of sand between them and turning about. A puffy-eyed Sister Barber had also defied the bombs to come and help, but now, catching sight of her nurses about to exit, she broke away from her own orchestrations to summon them, and naturally they were forced to attend.

'It's pretty bad out there, Sister,' panted a round-eyed Nell. 'The watchman needs –'

'Yes, yes, I've no wish to hold you up, Spotty!' Sister seemed unfazed. 'But take off your white aprons in case one of those blasted Germans should see it flapping and use it as a target.' She was not being ridiculous, for now, added to the throb of Heinkels and the thuds of their highly explosive cargo, came the determined whine of a dive bomber, and the sporadic rattle of machine-gun fire.

'And remember, Nurses!' Having shed their aprons, Nell and Beata had been about to go, but the commanding voice had their heads whipping round again to meet Sister's sincere and level gaze. 'If it comes to it, look after yourselves first. These people have had their lives.'

With an appreciative nod, sand grating underfoot. Nell and Beata careered for the fire escape with their consignment.

The sky now bore flagrant reflection of ancient monuments in extremis. With a mind as to human life rather than historic loss, down the precarious outer staircase clanked Nell and Beata, to the continual rumble of bombardment, the hiss of shrapnel, the choking stench of bonfires and the deadly rat-tat-tat.

'Flippin' heck,' joked the watchman, reaching for the bucket of sand. 'I thought you'd gone to Scarborough for it!' And he relieved them of their heavy bucket then dashed away.

Turning tail herself, Beata afterwards, Nell glanced up to see a Junkers, which looked to her like some kind of evil dragonfly dipping over a pond, as it banked into another whining dive upon the old city. This was no time to stand and stare. Leaving others in charge of the yard, it was back to their patients.

The bromide had begun to work, though the scene was still hectic as nurses were summoned from one bed to another. Especially so in the nursery, everyone trying not to make the babies any more frightened than they already were by the tremendous bangs that were coming from outside. Having managed to pacify a company of wriggling infants until their own sleeping draught took hold, trying not to think too much of her own baby out there somewhere, Nell finished her lullaby and placed the latest drowsy babe into his cot, then answered the request for assistance at the first-aid post.

There, aghast at the horrific injuries she saw, she was briefly to recall her own childish wish to witness war's excitement. Having seen it now, milling around her in all its bloody insanity, she prayed never to experience war again.

Throughout those wee dangerous hours, the Luftwaffe continued to blitz the city – no air crews at close hand to fend them off, and no ack-ack – the sound and density of explosions coming perilously close to the hospital where Nell and her fellow nurses, doctors and ambulance crews worked valiantly through the busiest, longest night of their lives, as men and women with blackened faces ferried stretcher after stretcher into the first-aid post that was woefully ill-equipped to deal with them, tempers fraying, nerves jangling, weariness threatening to overwhelm all. And then at long last someone rushed in and announced excitedly: 'A Hurricane got one of them!'

And after that things began steadily to improve. Though the all-clear did not sound until dawn, by then pulses had begun to return to normal, and nurses to the nurses' home, leaving a bone-weary Nell and Beata to express their private thanks to God that the hospital had not received a hit, then to limp about the mundane business of trying to rouse the patients, to make the beds, to measure out doses of castor oil, and to lug their churns of porridge and tea from the kitchen to the wards.

In between all this, there was the night report to be written out, and checks to be made to see if there were any incendiaries left undetected that might yet send the whole building up. A tally must be done of residents too. And it was at this point that someone asked, 'Have either of you seen Cissie? We can't find her anywhere.'

Shaking her head, and rather regretting this, for its interior felt as though it contained a whole corps of drummers, Nell exchanged a worried glance with Beata, and issued genuine sentiment. 'I pray to God she didn't manage to slip out last night . . .' It still irked her that the unmarried mother of four had been granted more access to her babies than had she, but Nell's ire was redirected at those in authority, for she was able now to understand Cissie's maternal instinct to keep on replacing the babies that had been taken away. 'I'd rather she comes back pregnant than be flattened by a bomb.'

But there was no time to search with so many more to

attend. Thankfully, in this they were to be assisted, most of the day staff arriving earlier than usual, and all of a pother, telling of the devastation they had witnessed in town.

'What about the Minster?' was the first query on the night staff's lips.

'Completely missed it, thank God! They got the Guildhall, though, the swines! Completely gutted it is . . .'

Avril Joyson was amongst these informants, and though none too pleased at being relegated to the old people's section, after giving a brief report of the damage she was to roll up her sleeves and ask, 'Right, how can I help you, girls?'

Soot had settled upon the crockery, necessitating a rapid rinse before food could be dished out, the top layer of the butter too having to be skimmed. Involved in this task, Nell and Beata looked appreciative, the latter saying, 'Thanks, Joy, you can hand out the false teeth if you like.'

And though this was not what Joy might have had in mind, she went off to do their bidding, before going on to start her own shift.

Despite the bromide, most of the patients were now wide awake, and some ready to complain about their breakfast as usual.

'Nurse,' came a tremulous objection, 'somebody's stolen me butter off me bread and replaced it wi' Vaseline!'

'Never mind, it'll slip down better,' said a heavy-eyed Nell under her breath, for the amusement of Beata, this complainant being an inveterate one. But to the patient she was bright and cooperative. 'Don't worry, Mrs Bryant, I'll exchange it for you!' And the slice of bread and butter was quickly replaced.

'Bugger me,' muttered Beata as they came to another bed, 'you can tell Joy handed out the false teeth. Poor Mrs West looks like an old ewe.'

Nell heaved a sigh over such insensitivity – not to

mention the amount of extra work this would mean for themselves, for the correct teeth had now to be found. Gently prising the overlarge dentures from the old lady's jaws, she muttered her opinion on Joyson. 'The lazy devil, she must have just stood at the end of the ward and hurled them out willy-nilly, couldn't wait to rush off to her soldiers. How many are wearing the wrong ones?' But, running her experienced eye over the rest of the ward, it seemed that most did have their correct dentures, and there were only Mrs West's to find, and at last she was able to point these out. 'I think that might be them, don't you?' And both gave a chuckle, for an equally waggish Mrs Collins was trying to catch their eyes by holding up the dentures she had been given, and snapping them open and shut like castanets.

With a swift rinse of the false teeth, and much good humour, breakfast was eventually served; though the time when the exhausted nurses could go home to their beds was a long way off yet, for there were scores of helpless to spoonfeed, a painstaking process at the best of times.

Finally, though, the patients' crockery was cleared away, their care handed to others, and the night staff allowed to sit down to the meal that was normally laid on for them. Nell could never get used to having dinner when her body said she should be eating breakfast, and vice versa, but that was the way for those on night shift. After ingesting as much as she could of the lentil soup and suet pudding, she put on her coat and, with Beata hobbling alongside, processed along the corridor, where old Blanche was already on her hands and knees, scrubbing the floor, and muttering to herself as usual.

'Never did a day's work in your life, no good to anybody – morning, Nurse!' she broke off, and cocked her head up to return Nell's subdued greeting, then went straight back to her task and her persistent jabbering as the nurses went on their way.

Then, 'Oh, thank God!' Just before reaching the end of the corridor, Nell suddenly caught sight of Cissie creeping in from her nocturnal escapade, black as a chimney sweep, but otherwise unscathed. And to the recipient's consternation she was to throw her arms round her and give her a hug. 'Ciss, where have you been?' came the mild recrimination. 'We've been so worried about you – don't tell me,' she gave a sideways grin at Beata, 'there was a man in a long coat!'

Relieved at such clemency, the dirty, witless face cracked a beam. 'Aye – but you don't have to worry, Nurse, 'cause he's promised we're going to have a big white weddin', and I'm havin' this lovely dress, and a carriage, and all the trimmin's!'

'Well, I do hope that Killie and I are to be bridesmaids?' Nell was surprised to find herself genuinely moved by the safe arrival of this habitual nuisance.

'Ooh, yes, o' course!' vouched Cissie. 'I'll go and choose t'stuff for your frocks right away.' She made as if to go, then stopped dead. 'What colour would you like?'

'Mauve for me,' replied a tired but smiling Beata, limping on.

'And pink for me,' requested Nell, and with a tender rub of Cissie's arm she confirmed how glad she was to see her unhurt, before she and Beata finally went their own separate ways.

Devastation, the day staff had said. But no words could aptly describe the havoc that Nell was to encounter for herself as she moved towards town. The entire city of York was girdled in a haze of smoke, mingled with the sickly sweet odour of burning sugar from a ravaged warehouse. Yet even through this ghostly veil could still be seen the horrors. At every place she was to encounter blackened faces, streaked with the same exhaustion that she herself had accumulated over those last dreadful hours – and their work was not yet over, for thick fire hoses still enlaced the flooded roads, toilworn firemen still balanced precariously atop long ladders, fighting to douse the glowing roof timbers of ancient buildings, whilst wardens restored order to the streets below.

Nell's pace faltered. In the normal course of events, she would only have to travel a short distance to reach Walmgate, at the far end of which lay her digs. On this smoky, throat-scouring morn, however, a growing unease forced her upon a different route, to check first that her parents were safe. Thelma's exposure had only served to make things worse between the three, but they were still her mother and father, and it was only respectful to ensure they were unharmed.

So, fatigued or not, Nell was to plod instead towards the centre of town, in the hope of catching a bus. Crunching her way through broken glass, splinters and shrapnel, past schoolboys rummaging for trophies amongst the spent cartridge cases and burnt-out fins of incendiaries, she could feel the heat from the smouldering hulks of once gracious buildings. Centuries of history reduced in one malicious act to skeletal ruins. Only by some miracle had the Minster remained untouched, thrusting its way through that pall of smoke towards the heavens, to Nell a symbol of all that was noble and defiant. But oh, the damage to ordinary folk . . . the homes completely demolished.

However shocking, however apoplectic it made her, Nell had been prepared for the wrecked buildings, even for the bodies, for she had dealt with plenty of them over the past twenty months. But until this morning bodies had always come neatly laid in hospital beds, not mangled beyond recognition, not indistinguishable from rubble, not skewered with metal rods, not one piece here and another there to be quickly concealed under red blankets. At one such shambles, half a dozen starlings were busy gobbling tiny remnants of flesh from the pavement. Sickened, and weary beyond words, she groped in her pocket for the last of the two cigarettes given to her the previous night by the soldier.

'Oy, don't light that up here, you clot!' Face crusted with dirt, the female warden who had yelled at her was quick to recant, upon gauging a similar exhaustion to her own. 'Sorry, Nurse, but there's a bit of gas still hanging around, I wouldn't like you to go up in flames.'

Nell apologised too, and finding there were only dead matches in the box anyway, she wandered off to buy some – though it was probably not safe to light up anywhere.

Remarkably, between the burnt-out shells of offices and stores, there were shops open, their proprietors having swept the debris from the pavement before erecting a defiant placard 'Business As Usual'. Nell selected one of them and entered to the comforting sound of the wireless. The girl who had been listening to it, aged about fifteen, came forth to serve her, her attitude surprisingly cheerful. 'Well, we can't let them beat us, can we?' she chirped upon handing over the matches.

'Indeed, we can't – do you mind if I light my fag here?' Given the go-ahead, Nell put one of the matches to it, then inhaled deeply and gratefully. The smoke from the tobacco hit the back of her throat like a blowtorch, rushing to fill the pit of each lung, before emerging with her next question. 'Do you know if many have been killed?'

'Dunno. I'm just waiting for the news to come on – but someone told me the Bar Convent really copped a bramah, and some of the nuns got killed rescuing others. Someone else came in and said the station's completely flattened – and all the goods yards – trains and wagons thrown about everywhere, just like toys!'

Nell suffered a jolt, as she pictured herself only a short time ago working in that vicinity. Had the casualty evacuation trains been a success, she might not be standing there now. 'I wonder if the buses are still running,' she murmured, with an absent drag of her cigarette.

'Mine was!' chirruped the girl. 'Had to take a few diversions, though.'

Nell thanked her and turned to go, but at that moment the BBC news came on, and so she paused to listen to the reader's dulcet tones for a moment, only to hear what she already knew, that contrary to everything else the Minister was undamaged.

'Oh that's right,' quipped the girl. 'Let Hitler know, so he can come and finish the job!'

It was obvious to Nell that, with such blithe spirit, the other had not lost a loved one, nor had her own home flattened, nor been up all night treating the wounded. But keeping this thought to herself, she quietly imbibed the rest of her cigarette, eyes narrowed against its rasping smoke, as she listened to one or two more items of news, before moving on her way.

Wandering further through town, she could see by the vaporous pile of black timbers that it was true, the Guildhall had been completely gutted, only its stone walls left standing. Much of the neighbouring church too, shards of its stained glass embedded in the melted tarmac – though its clock was still attached to its bracket, as was the little admiral who stood atop it, proud if a little charred. The broken hands of its timepiece had frozen at the moment of impact.

Driving away the thought of Bill's watch, forever stuck at seven, Nell continued to the bus stop. Well, she announced to herself upon arrival, there was a queue at any rate. The British and their queues; amidst all this gross destruction, it was comforting, somehow, to know that there were certain things the Germans couldn't take away. Tagging on to the end of the line, she hovered there with languid eyes, watching others clear away wreckage, not knowing if the bus would even turn up; nor was there anyone who could enlighten her.

It did eventually come, and Nell hoisted her stiff limbs

aboard. On quite a few occasions, though, it was forced to divert around a crater in the road, and with each scene of havoc her concern was to grow, to weigh upon her already burdened mind like a millstone, alongside the pounding headache and the thoughts of her heroic young lover and his son. She was finally to alight at the carriage works, and the nearer she drew to home, the worse her premonition. The railway yards had received a terrific trouncing – obviously the Germans' main target, for it was true what the shop girl had said, it was a scene of annihilation, with sheds demolished and lines ripped up and twisted like coils from a burst mattress, and locomotives tossed hither and thither, just like children's playthings.

Hurrying now, Nell approached the avenue in which she had once lived – but already she could see that the street was roped off, with a sign that gave the reason: UXB. Furthermore, an elderly special constable was keen to limit sightseers, a great deal of whom were already gathered. Brought to an abrupt halt, Nell craned her neck to see beyond the barrier yet another scene of wreckage.

'Are you a resident?' asked the special.

In dazed response, she shook her head, for her house was no longer to be seen, just a huge mound of rubble, and water spouting from a broken pipe, forming a puddle in what had once been her garden. 'Not any more,' she somehow managed to murmur through her state of shock, her eyes averting briefly to the Morrison table shelter that marked the Dawsons' front room, its protective cage buckled but resolute in the ruins of its former abode; and the neighbouring houses, which bore lesser signs of violation – tiles ripped from roofs, curtains billowing gently through jags of glass, furniture outside some of them, salvaged by the owners and piled in neat stacks on the grass verge. Nell paid these only the briefest glance, before once again focusing her bleak confusion on the debris of her own home, as if mentally trying to piece it back together.

'Then you'd better go, it's not safe,' issued the constable. 'And you lot can move on as well, unless you've a valid reason for being here!' With outstretched arms he began to herd the onlookers away.

Jerked from her state of inertia, desperate to know the entirety of it, Nell took this opportunity and ducked underneath the barrier, and began to hurry towards the ruins of her home, picking her way through a layer of bricks and shattered glass, occasionally cockling over and wrenching her ankle, until finally reaching the place. There she was to sway in uncertainty, to look on as the Civil Defence teams and soldiers clambered back and forth across the rubble, attempting to make things safe, whilst simultaneously checking for casualties.

What had become of her mother and father? Revisited by that painful cannonball which had clogged her gullet so many times, Nell glanced around her, but there seemed no one to ask. Lower down the street, a man with bloodied bandages sat on the kerb with his head in his hands. His face was unfamiliar, and, not wanting to intrude on his travail, she finally swallowed, and called to one of the workers instead.

'Excuse me . . . have you any idea where I might find the residents of this house?'

The face beneath the helmet was caked in sweat and brick dust; its owner broke off his labours to regard her at first in botheration, then in sympathy. 'Related, are they?' At her quick nod, he explained that he had just started duty, but, 'I'll ask my friend, he's been here all night.'

Thanking him, Nell cut a lonely figure as she stood awaiting an answer, pursuing him with forlorn brown eyes as he loped over to his colleague. The latter wore his pyjamas under his coat – Nell could see the cuffs protruding – but she was more intent on his face. Closely observing his lips as they formed an answer, her ears were to learn what her heart already feared: 'Butter Market,' came the barely audible reply.

And as the first man stumbled back towards her, she knew without even looking at him the reason for his mask of pity, for the Butter Market had lately been designated a more macabre purpose, of housing the dead.

Standing in that queue of equally hollow-eyed relatives outside the emergency mortuary, in the shadow of the city abattoir, Nell was to ask herself what on earth was the point in waiting here, shuffling along the pavement an inch at a time, when she knew for certain that her parents were deceased? But to leave now, as if grown fed-up of waiting, would seem disrespectful somehow, would attract the opprobrium of those who still retained that glimmer of hope; that asinine, optimistic glimmer that she herself had sponsored long ago, and knew to be a fallacy . . . and so she remained there, to shuffle along like a penguin with the rest, attacked by a series of what-ifs? What if William should be in that charnel house? What if the people to whom she had entrusted him had failed to keep him safe, and his corpse was amongst those arrayed?

This was more than Nell could bear. She yanked her mind from the image, channelled it into a happier outcome, envisioned her son being carried to safety by loving parents, whisked away in a nice fast car into the country – perhaps he had already been evacuated long before last night . . .

But all the while that she queued and shuffled, these worries were relentlessly to nag at her, peck, peck, pecking like the starlings at their gobbets of flesh. And no amount of reassurance from a kind-hearted trooper, who travelled down the line to certify that everything was under control, could dispel these monstrous what-ifs, until eventually it was her turn to enter the mortuary.

Then, of course, all flights of fantasy were dispersed, as she was bludgeoned with the facts: invited to peer at one corpse after another, before finally identifying her mother and father, both relatively unmarked, save for a few cuts and grazes from the rubble, and apart from being very dead. Erect and dignified, acutely conscious to the weeping of others who patrolled the ranks of cadavers, she herself found it almost impossible to give vent to her distress, choked as she was by the guilt of walking out on them only the night before, her voice emotionless as it confirmed identity, delivered a few further details to the officer in charge, then emerged into the still-smoky morning.

Unable to cry, with only a few hundred yards to travel from there to her digs, Nell made her silent way under the medieval Fishergate Bar, and into a blackened slum district, where a milkwoman on a horse-drawn cart was handing out her late delivery; past a pub and a Roman Catholic church; then along the insalubrious Walmgate, her face still wrought with shock upon finally arriving in the Preciouses' dingy hallway.

'Thank God!' boomed a relieved Ma, blundering from the sitting room at the first sound of the door being opened. 'We've been right worried! Haven't we, Georgie – eh, the racket last night – our poor Milo hasn't stopped trembling, have you, my honey?' She was already hugging the whining terrier to her breast, and now added a series of reassuring kisses to his quivering black muzzle.

'I'm sincerely glad to find you're unharmed.' Nell slipped off her coat, asking herself how she could sound so normal?

'Well . . . not all of us.' Ma had turned grave, and immediately Georgie's eyes oozed brine, which he dabbed away with a hastily produced handkerchief.

Glancing into the living room as she hung up her coat, Nell saw that it was obviously not Mr Yarker who had perished, for he sat in his usual place amidst a fog of cigarette smoke, looking even more haggard than usual. Still without mentioning her own loss, she turned questioning eyes on the Preciouses.

'Mr Allardyce,' whispered Ma, in as quiet a tone as was possible for her. 'Hanged himself from the middle landing.' She waited for this to sink in, but Nell was too stunned and too spent to offer anything more energetic than a parting of lips. 'Georgie and me were under the stairs,' went on Ma, 'we didn't know a thing till this morning when Mr Yarker came back from firewatching and found him on his way up to bed. Ooh, real upset he was – had to cut him down, you see. Eh, what a to-do. The police have only just taken the poor lad away. He certainly knew which banister to use: it's the only decent stretch of timber in the house. Anybody my size would have brought the whole staircase down, but he was only a lightweight, poor chap.'

Dull of eye, Nell moved her head in recognition. That accounted for Mr Yarker's stark demeanour, Mr Allardyce having been his batman in the Great War, and a close friend ever since. Even after two decades Allardyce had still been afflicted by the psychological effects of that terrible shelling.

'The noise drove him to it?' she murmured a supposition.

Still cradling the terrier, Ma gave a wordless nod, before adding quickly in her more characteristic tone, 'Right, better get the kettle on, Georgie, and do this girl some breakfast, she looks worn out! Gas is off,' she explained loudly to Nell, 'but we're managing to cook all right over the fire – come in, sit down!'

'Nothing to eat, thank you, but a cup of tea would be appreciated.' Only now realising that her throat was parched, Nell wandered after the couple into the acrid haze of the sitting room, where her first act was to deal Mr Yarker a little gesture of condolence. Receiving his dull nod in return, she sank gratefully onto a sofa, allowing a cat to jump onto her lap and taking comfort from its silken coat, feeling as if she were in another dimension. Her head was still pounding, and her mind spinning too with all manner of images.

Georgie lifted the teapot lid to examine leaves that had been brewed so long ago they were swelled to the size of cabbage, then added more boiling water.

'A piece of toast, mebbe?' coaxed Ma.

Nell refused, then took a deep breath, to reveal, 'My parents were killed in the raid.'

'Aw!'

With Ma expressing such loud condolence, and old Georgie looking set to weep again, Nell closed her eyes and begged them tiredly, 'Don't, please, don't say any more. I feel bad enough that I walked out on them, last night of all nights . . .'

'Well, good job, I say!' exulted Ma, as an ashen-faced Mr Yarker rose without a word and, like a wraith, drifted from the room. 'Or you'd have been flattened too – aren't you going to wait for a cup of tea, Mr Yarker?'

'I'm drowning in fucking tea,' came the typically blunt reply from the hall, before the outer door clicked shut.

'I shouldn't have mentioned it in his presence,' droned Nell, her expression glazed. 'He'll feel bad enough.'

'Stop bothering about what others are feeling,' urged Ma. 'You've had your own terrible shock. Eh, I'm that sorry, lass – but what a miracle you weren't with them.'

A depressed sigh came from her young friend. 'I don't know . . . it might have been as well.'

'Eh, don't be saying that!' Ma levelled a finger in a gesture of reproof.

'Why not?' murmured Nell, her hand absently stroking the cat, who purred contentedly on her lap. 'I let them down, and now I can never tell them how sorry I am, nor make it up to them. I'm no good to anyone.'

'You are to us,' soothed old Georgie, and he placed a cup of reheated tea on the table at her side. 'Isn't she, dearie?'

'And what are you talking about, let them down?' demanded Ma, still ignorant over Nell's fall from grace.

'All parents and children have squabbles, I'll bet they were proud of you really.'

Listening to their platitudes, Nell tried hard to believe them as she ran her hand over that silken fur, stroking, stroking, stroking – until inexplicably the cat took umbrage and jumped off her lap, leaving her to sit and stare, and the tears to trickle down her face.

8

An estimate of a hundred dead, an equivalent figure seriously injured, and many more with minor wounds. The toll might have seemed insignificant compared to other cities harder hit, but it was all too momentous for those who had lost loved ones, and for the multitude turned homeless. Within ninety savage minutes some nine and a half thousand houses had been destroyed or damaged; and many, like Nell, faced a lengthy wait for financial redress.

Not that monetary inheritance was the first thing on her mind, or even on it at all. Despite being shocked, and burdened with guilt at having walked out on her parents, Nell had not the luxury to wallow, but, after snatching a few hours of fitful sleep, was compelled to perform the onerous task of informing her father's kin. Her way there was painfully slow that late afternoon, not solely due to the potholes at every turn, but because the police had set up barriers at all entry points to the city, and were halting cars and turning back those who had come merely to gawp. A constable boarded the bus she was on and examined everyone's identity card to check they had a legitimate reason to be there, giving Nell a good fifteen minutes in which to stew, before being allowed to go on her way.

And after all that, it transpired that Uncle Cliff and Aunty Phyllis already knew.

'I thought perhaps you would,' murmured Nell, extending a comforting hand to her aunt, who had crumpled in tears upon seeing her, 'but I thought I'd better come . . .'

However, it emerged that the tears were not just from sorrow, but partly from relief.

'We've been praying you were on night shift,' said a gaunt Uncle Cliff, steering Nell through the wood-panelled hall into his equally brown sitting room, along with his wife. 'But we just didn't know . . .' Whilst Nell's aunty dabbed at her eyes, he explained that they had gone to check on his brother's family as soon as it got light. 'We've been asking around all day, trying to find out what shift you were on, but no one seemed to know – well, thank God at least one of you is safe.' On the last word his voice cracked, and his eyes misted over.

With the others staring dully at the carpet, Nell shelved her own anguish and sprang to fill the void, selfishly relieved that they were unaware of her quarrel with her parents, and mentioning nothing of her permanent departure. 'It looks like poor Mrs Dawson and Geoff got it too.'

'Oh no,' after clearing his throat, her uncle rushed to assure her, 'we saw them down at the church hall when we went to look for our Wilf and Thelma. They'd barely a scratch on them – we had a word, to see if they knew where you were, but they didn't even know what day it was. Seems the Morrison shelter saved them.'

Nell heaved a sigh. 'That's good to know anyway . . .'

'Well,' sighed her uncle, 'York's certainly had its share now, hasn't it?' And they spoke for a little while on the tragedy.

Aunty Phyllis blew her nose and managed to speak. 'Eh, fancy this happening on your birthday. I intended to post your card this morn—'

'It's bad enough happening any day!' Raw over his

brother's loss, Cliff beheld his wife with a look of impatience.

'Well, yes, I didn't mean it that way! I just didn't want her to think I'd forgotten . . .'

Tearful eyes beheld Nell, who had in fact forgotten her own birthday, but said now to avert further torment: 'I knew what you meant, Aunty Phyl, and thank you for the thought.'

'You must've been so shocked when you got home,' breathed her aunty picking at her damp handkerchief, and receiving a plaintive nod from Nell, who answered:

'I hoped that perhaps one of them might not . . . that they might have gone out to help when the bombs started to drop.'

Aunty Phyllis cocked her head. 'You poor lass – where on earth have you been since this morning? You should have come straight here.'

Nell hedged her reply, looking at the worn carpet as she spoke. 'Well, I had to go back into town to identify . . . and then I called in on friends. They're letting me stay for a few days.'

'Well, you must move in with us of course,' said her aunty this invitation seconded by Uncle Cliff.

'No, really, thank you, but I'm nearer to work where I am – I'm sorry, that sounds terribly churlish.' Nell looked up swiftly to display amends.

'Of course not.' Her aunty took no offence. 'Your Uncle Cliff and I understand, you live where you want, dear. We just want to make sure you're being looked after. But whatever you do, you mustn't lose touch with the rest of your family.'

Nell came upright. 'Yes, I was going to ask if you have everyone's address, for the funeral . . .'

'You don't have to bother yourself with any of that, Eleanor,' put in Cliff. 'We'll let them all know, and make all the arrangements, to spare you the trauma.'

Obviously he and Aunty Phyllis adjudged their niece too young to cope. Did they really not understand what the job of a nurse entailed, thought Nell. But she merely dealt them a nod of appreciation, content enough to let them get on with it if they so wished. She had forfeited any rights to have a say in the proceedings by walking out on her parents on the very night she might have been able to save them. And for that she would never forgive herself.

'I hate to raise the subject of finances, and the only reason I'm saying this is because I don't want you worrying about any of that either,' Uncle Cliff was saying. 'About having to pay the mortgage on a wrecked house, I mean.' Noting the bafflement on her face he explained, 'I know there's a bit of a one outstanding, but we'll get that sorted out for you, and you'll get help to rebuild from the War Damage Commission . . . though it might be a year or two before you can move back in.'

'I don't want to move back,' said Nell hurriedly, totally confused by all this talk of mortgages. 'I couldn't bear it.'

Her uncle raised a gentle palm. 'It's all right, lass, you don't have to concern yourself with any of that. We'll take care of it all – now then, how you are you off for cash for your everyday needs?' His hand thrust deep into his pocket.

'No, I'm fine, thank you, Uncle Cliff, yes, yes, I'm positive,' she affirmed, before hurrying to change the subject, seeking to ask after the couple's daughters, one of whom was in the Land Army and living away from home, the other making munitions at Rowntrees' factory. 'I'm sorry, I should have asked before, how are Daphne and Margaret?'

'Both safe, thank goodness,' Aunty Phyllis was quick to reply. 'Daphne's nerves have been much better since she went to live in the country – I think it's the manual work, takes her mind off it, you know. She pedalled over first thing to check on us. And Margaret's gone to work as usual. We must let them know you've turned up.' She gave a tearful sniff. 'I'm not looking forward to telling our Ron. He was very fond of your mother and father.'

Smarting over this application of salt to her wounds, Nell enquired over her cousin's wellbeing. Uncle Cliff, who had been battling tears by honking into a handkerchief, seemed glad of the opportunity to regale her with tales of his son's exploits.

The young man's mother had other concerns, though. 'You can't help worrying,' murmured Aunty Phyllis. 'He writes to us, of course, but we've only seen him once since he joined up, when he came home on leave prior to being sent overseas. It's bad enough imagining what he must be going through, but – and this might sound silly – it almost seemed worse for having him here in the flesh, because in a way you're losing him all over again, having to go through those awful goodbyes . . .'

Stop, please, stop, Nell wanted to yell.

'And you know, he's lost so many good pals. You remember that going-away party we held for him? Well, I believe Ron's the only one of those boys still alive . . .'

Whilst her aunty's eyes betrayed the dread of losing her son, Nell found herself assailed by memories of Billy, even more so when a spontaneous change of expression took over Aunty Phyllis.

'Oh, but I'm forgetting, you knew one of them quite well, didn't you?' She turned to her husband. 'Cliff, remember that photograph we saw of Eleanor and – what was his name? Bill, that's right – the photo of the pair of you on the front of the press – oh, your mother was mortified when I mentioned we'd seen it! You'd have thought from the way she went on that you were Lady Godiva . . .' Noting her niece's stricken expression, Phyllis changed tack with a sympathetic smile. 'Well, it was all quite innocent, we realised that, and it's all such a long time ago. I'm sure Thelma forgave you. Poor Bill, he was such a handsome, lovely young chap – did you ever see him again?'

Stiff as a board, wondering what was to come next, Nell shook her head. Under attack by demons, she rose abruptly and went towards the kitchen. 'Shall I make us a pot of tea?'

But, after drinking only half a cup of this, and listening to her aunty and uncle's painful reminiscences, she declared that with another evening shift ahead she must regretfully depart.

Her prime reason for leaving so soon, though, was the agitation she still felt at the thought that her son might have been one of those killed in the raid. It was a futile pursuit, Nell knew it, when she was totally unaware of what name William went under now, but, in her demented state, that did not stop her alighting from the bus in town and going to scour the lists of dead and injured that had been posted, looking for a child of a similar age. Superfluous to say, she was to come away none the wiser, and no less demented.

Undergoing the last stage of her journey on foot, she was to witness a queue of blood donors at the County Hospital. It had occurred to Nell to contribute too – though not at this minute, with a twelve-hour shift ahead of her. However, upon mentioning it to Beata when she arrived on the ward, her friend, who was a regular donor, said that they ought not to inundate the already overstrained doctors and nurses there. 'They'll ask if they need us,' she assured Nell.

The latter was quite thankful, for she felt drained enough already, and was to feel sucked completely dry after spending much of that night terrorised by her imagination. Thankfully, the German bombers did not strike again, the only disturbance during those small hours being Mrs Gledhill's hymn-singing, and this easily remedied by a measure of bromide.

It was with deep gratitude that Nell handed over to the day staff and went home, to be greeted by Ma with a different little dog in her arms. Poor Milo's wiry black coat had turned white overnight.

In the aftermath of the Baedeker raid, those houses that were not totally demolished were patched up and their owners allowed to return, the city appearing like a mouth that had suffered much dental work, some teeth completely missing, others snapped and jagged, with a great amount of emergency bridge work yet to be done.

Excluding the death toll and the calamitous depredation of housing, the main target of the German raid was miraculously easy to fix, for against initial fears the railway signalling system was virtually unscathed, and within days the trains were once again running as normal, albeit from a skeleton of a building.

But Nell wasn't going anywhere, apart from to her parents' funeral, this being just one in a massive round of burials during that week following the raid. Friends and relatives turned up from far and wide, to converge first on the church, and then on Uncle Cliff's for the funeral tea; some she hardly knew, but all were totally benevolent towards their orphaned member. It was obvious that none of them were acquainted with the parental rift created by her illegitimate baby, not even Uncle Cliff and Aunty Phyllis, for they would have treated her very differently had they known. Despite everyone's niceness, though, Nell felt out of place amongst them, as if she had no right to be there. Which was strange, really, when she had just found out that her mother really was her mother . . . even if her father was not. None of which she could reveal to these nice people. Nice people, who said silly things.

'Did you see her, Eleanor?'

'Sorry, what?' Nell turned her dazed expression on the aunt seated beside her.

'The Princess Royal, did you see her when she paid her respects to York?'

As if I'd be out flag-waving at a time like this, thought Nell, but simply shook her head as the mourners discussed similar trivialities.

'We were just saying, your hair looks nice, worn up like that,' offered Aunty Vera.

'Thank you . . . it's only because I never seem to have time to get it cut.' Feeling awkward under their sympathetic examination, once again Nell used the excuse of her very important vocation to depart. 'And I'm afraid time's in short supply, even today. I must be away to my patients.'

Yet there was to be one last ordeal.

'Before you go . . .' Her uncle rose and withdrew, returning with a brooch and a pearl necklace displayed athwart his palms: her mother's jewellery. 'Just a few things we managed to sift from the wreckage before the looters got in – did you read in the press about that wretch pinching from his neighbours?' He broke off to ramble on to the gathering about the prosecution, before finally returning to his tack.

'We didn't salvage much else, I'm afraid, apart from one or two documents that we handed to your father's solicitor. The furniture and pictures were all splintered, the car wrecked, and there was nothing that belonged exclusively to you –'

No, well, there wouldn't be, thought a frozen Nell, who had taken all cherished items with her.

'– but at least this is something personal for you to keep,' finished Cliff. 'And as I told you before, there'll probably be a decent amount of cash from the War Damage Commission once this is all sorted out –'

I don't want it! came Nell's inner scream. None of it.

'– I know for definite that your dad took out an endowment for when you're twenty-one, him being a big one for insurance. That's only another year off. Must seem a long time to a youngster like you, but I'm going to apply on your behalf to the Air Raid Distress Fund, too. I'm sure you must be entitled to something to tide you over.'

Feeling utterly wretched, Nell thanked him for rescuing the tokens she now held in her hand. But she did not look at them for long before shoving them into her bag and proceeding to leave.

'Don't regard yourself as completely alone in the world.'

An anguished Nell wrenched her gaze from the door to blink at Aunty Phyllis, who appeared to have read her mind.

'I know what it feels like when your parents go,' came her aunty's kind addition. 'And it was a much greater shock for you, with it being so premature. But there are lots of us you can turn to if you're ever in need – not that you have to be in need, we'd love to see you whenever you feel like it,' added Phyllis, with a touch of her niece's arm.

Intent on escape, Nell gave an appreciative nod.

'Try not to picture your mum and dad as you last saw them in that awful place.' counselled Uncle Cliff, as, to a host of sympathetic murmurs, his niece finally managed to open the door. 'Remember them on the day before, going about their everyday affairs, happy and smiling, and content with their lot . . .'

How was he to know that his words made her feel a hundred times worse?

Throughout all this heartrending upheaval, and in its chaotic after-effects, Nurse Spottiswood was to remain at her post. There were millions in her position who had no option but to go on; why should she be any different? But just because

Nell carried on her valiant work, did not mean she coped on an emotional plane. Had she not felt responsible for so many less fortunate, she would perhaps have been unable to hold herself together at all.

Thank God that others seemed able to function in this awful aftermath, if purely on a mundane level, for Nell did not know what she would have done without the Preciouses' hospitality. The gas was off for five days, requiring them to fall back on even more out-dated oil lamps for their lighting. Whilst it might be little hardship to sit in half-darkness, the lack of cooking facilities was another matter. The situation had already been testing enough, the meagre allowance of coal failing to throw out enough heat, and much of it going to waste in the high-ceilinged rooms, and even though it was late spring the residents were forced to wrap themselves in blankets to ward off the night-time draughts. But now with the gas oven redundant, the coal would have to be used for cooking too. None of this appeared to faze old Georgie, and, somehow, there was always a nourishing meal for the soldiers and the resident nurse, who might otherwise have neglected herself.

All this fine fare was at personal cost, though. 'Me last little chucky hen, Nell,' mourned Georgie, as he carried in another lifeless creature from the back garden that ran down to the river. 'Those bloomin' Germans have done for every one.'

'Thank God!' heaved his unappreciative wife. 'We might get summat else to eat now.'

'But there'll be no more eggs, dearie,' he warned.

'Ruddy things'd stopped laying anyway!' stated Ma. 'Bung it in the pot – and make it taste like summat different tonight. We're sick to death of blasted chicken – aren't we, Milo?'

The poor old man looked so comical in his balaclava, being kept on his toes by Ma, who, typically, only exerted herself with the odd reassuring cuddle to a blanched and trembling Milo, whom she perpetually nursed like a baby. At any other time Nell would have laughed; but not now.

Following the shock and the guilt came anger. Anger that, much too late, York had received its protective battery of ack-ack guns and barrage balloons; anger at her parents for dying and leaving her with no idea where in the world her son was; anger, too, that they had forced her to give him away to save their reputations, and now they were dead and united in heaven, whilst she was left with no one. Sometimes the fury and loneliness made life feel unbearable; certainly too unbearable to sleep, whether on night shift or day. The scrap of ribbon attached to Bill's wedding ring had received such punishment from her twitching fingers that it was frayed almost to nought. In danger of being left with nothing at all to mark William's existence, and not daring to risk unpicking its knot for fear of the silk disintegrating completely, she had been forced to remove the chain and its pendants from around her neck and consign them to the hat box. Yet another thing, the one last comforting thing, that the Germans had taken from her.

Kept awake by these bitter feelings, further stirred by the drone of British bombers as squadron after squadron winged over her roof, Nell tried to gain comfort from the knowledge that they were intent on wreaking vengeance, felt glad at the havoc that would be visited on the German people, and wondered how her counterparts would fare under such ruination as she had suffered. She knew it was wrong for a nurse to want revenge, knew that many others had lost loved ones, too, for that was what happened in war. But she just could not help it. It all felt so overwhelmingly personal. First they had taken Bill, and now Mother and Father. God forbid they had taken William too.

Added to this emotional unrest, the summer of '42 was turning out to be exceptionally hot. In contrast to those earlier months and their paucity of coal, the Preciouses' high-ceilinged sitting room was now a much more pleasant venue than Nell's attic. Finding it nigh impossible to sleep at the best of times, but even more so with the sun beating down on its roof and creating a furnace, more often than not she was to rise long before work demanded it, to seek out the cool tranquillity of downstairs – at least, tranquil for so long as the soldiers were out on their daily exercise. Once those khaki-clad terrors were unleashed and came home to run berserk, there was no scrap of peace to be had. Many a stuffed animal had fallen prey to a mis-aimed dart, and some had been rearranged in the most lewd positions. None of which seemed to bother the rough and ready Ma, though Nell found such disorderly behaviour grating, particularly when one was faced with a twelve hour shift after snatching only a quarter of this in sleep.

It was therefore quite a relief when the soldiers moved on to different climes, some of them possibly to their deaths. It was solely due to this latter prospect that Nell withheld any malice towards them for what were, after all, quite petty disruptions, instead sending them on their way with a kiss. That last exchange with her mother reverberating through her mind, she was to remain ever conscious of the importance of one's parting words.

Soldiers came and went, bricklayers too, bussed in to help rebuild the city. Another Christmas converged, made merrier for some by the glorious victory at El Alamein that followed so many disasters. But not for Nell, she citing heavy workload as an excuse not to linger over the festive dinner laid on by Ma, and to duck out altogether of the amateur concert that came after. And another year was gone.

With the threat of invasion lifted, the Minster bells rang out the following Easter. This transitory joy fooled nobody. The war had become a way of life now, no one able to foresee an end to it, children being born who considered it the norm to have no father on the scene, or to have their vision obscured by an ugly network of brown tape; who didn't know the taste of a banana, a grape, or a tinned peach – or even what these looked like – to queue half an hour for scraps that one might normally feed to a dog; to undergo a scrum at every issue of new ration books, to have coils of barbed wire impede one's route, and sandbags at every turn, and large, inviting tanks of water in the middle of a city street into which an unsupervised toddler might tumble and drown.

Nell had shuddered to read of too many such accidents during the last twelve months, and more prevalently during a summer that augured to be as hot as the last. Each little death was another crack in her heart, and she wondered angrily which of these children could be judged the less fortunate: those with the so-called respectable parents who allowed them to drown, or those relegated to an institution like Cissie's twins. It was such thoughts as this that tormented her as she bustled about the wards, trying to keep sane – ten times harder when she was at home and trying to sleep in her claustrophobic attic. For then her hands would inevitably be drawn to the irritating patch of dermatitis this had developed on her trunk, the one that would not go away even when lathered in cream, that prompted her fingernails to rake deep, to scratch and to claw until they drew blood, the relentless pain of it making her want to scream for the hour to arrive when she could go back to work, for only devotion to others could lure her mind away . . . Hence the reason she was never to complain when asked to sacrifice her day off for the benefit of a married colleague.

'Surely they'd give you the time off to enjoy a birthday

party,' Aunt Phyllis had written, sounding rather aggrieved that her offer to organise this for Nell had been summarily dismissed with such a lame excuse. 'I know it might seem insensitive of me, when your parents were killed on that date, but I just meant to give you a quiet celebration with me and your uncle, and the girls. After all, you're only twenty-one once . . .'

Twenty-one. The key of the door. *What door?* asked a bitter Nell, who felt as if she had died two years ago. What magic key could unlock this misery, and give me back my future? And she had despatched Phyllis's letter to the waste-paper bin.

Be that as it may, a card had arrived on her birthday. Enclosed was another letter explaining that her father's estate had still not been through probate, because of the backlog due to the war. Showing no interest, Nell disposed of this letter. But she was extremely grateful for the cheque for ten pounds, being the proceeds of the endowment policy, and an extra two pound notes from Phyllis and Cliff; grateful, too, that she had managed to intercept this and the other relatives' cards from the doormat before Ma Precious got wind that it was her twenty-first, or she too would have organised some event. As it was, her land-lady was forever making the same objection as Aunt Phyllis.

'Eh, you're always working!' Ma would grumble, finally to make a stand one summer's evening. 'Always running round, never eating a thing – come on, honey, just have a bit of oxtail – tell her, Georgie!'

'I do get fed at work, you know,' Nell laughed this off, as Ma blocked her exit and signalled at Georgie to help corral their lodger into the dining room.

'Well it doesn't look like it!' Cradling Milo, Ma reluctantly moved aside, but one hand shot out to squeeze the nurse's arm as she came by. 'Eh, what happened to the big strapping lass we used to know?'

'Thanks, you make me sound like King Kong.' Nell's eyes flickered over the brooch and pearls that graced Ma's large bosom, the ones belonging to Mother that she had given away in a fit of incomprehensible dudgeon. How she longed to have them back now. But Ma had been so good to her . . .

'You'll fade away, you will!' Counter to this opinion, the big hand released her.

'No danger of that with Queenie, is there, puss?' Nell tried to sound flippant as she crouched to stroke the plump feline who rubbed against her ankles, tenderly ruffling the fur of its belly.

'No, and we all know why!' Ma spoke accusingly to the cat. 'She's been tomming – *again*!'

Suffering a pang, Nell turned deeply thoughtful as she murmured acknowledgement of the kittens that distended Queenie's abdomen. Then, with William on her mind, she dealt the animal a final pat, and left for work.

With other things to consider, not the least of them the arrival of a new batch of soldiers, and American ones at that, the pregnant cat was to fade into the background over the next month. To Nell's relief, her new housemates turned out to be much less rowdy than the last, meaning that she and Mr Yarker could eat their meals in peace, which in turn induced Mr Yarker to revert to his former habit of taking up the most comfortable chair in the sitting room afterwards.

At Ma's resolution that she stay and get to know their new guests better – 'They're ever so interesting, and you've hardly even spoken to them!' – she agreed to take a cup of tea amongst the GIs before the night's shift.

Still fairly new, they were on their best behaviour, fresh out of the box in their expertly tailored uniforms, well-mannered too, though they were beginning to relax under Ma's noisy influence. Nell found them especially agreeable as they were free with their cigarettes – obviously earning them points from Mr Yarker too, for he was less rude than usual. Whilst desultory chat took place between others, Nell merely listened, smiling politely and answering any questions that were put to her, whilst she enjoyed one cigarette, and then another.

'Hey, sister,' chimed one of the Americans, eyeing her legs. 'I can't help noticing you ain't wearing nylons –'

Nell gave a shrug. 'Me and most of the girls in York.' Gone were the days when this was frowned on by employers, for stockings of any variety were in dearth. 'Thankfully, Matron's being very understanding.'

'I can get you some! Come out with me tomorrow.'

Keen as she was to have this luxury, Nell felt there might be a high price to pay. 'Thank you, but I'll be working.' Throughout the conversation, she had been more intent on something else. Now, after grinding a short stub into an ashtray, she reached down and hooked a hand beneath the mewing cat, dragging it onto her lap and attempting to stroke it. But Queenie was restless and refused to sit there for long, jumping off her to prowl the room with a piteous cry, a weird unnatural sound.

Never having heard anything like it, Nell became tense and now consulted the collection of faces, none of which seemed to be as anxious as hers. 'Do you think she's trying to tell us something? Perhaps there's going to be a raid!' Ever since that dreadful night, she had lived in suspense of a repeat, and indeed there had been other bombings since then, though none so severe. Despite this, the threat itself was almost as bad. Her brown eyes held a gleam of edginess as they followed the distressed cat around the smoky room. 'They say animals can sense these things long before humans –'

'Eh, will you stop worritting!' blared Ma, feeding a titbit to the little dog in her arms, before propounding matter-of-factly, 'It'll be her kittens that's making her act like that.'

‘Oh, she’s had them?’ Feeling foolish in the presence of the American strangers, Nell allowed herself a bashful smile, then began to crane her neck around the furniture and aspidistras, in search of babies.

‘Yes, this afternoon,’ announced Ma over Milo’s wiry head, the dog reaching up to lick her face, she kissing him back. ‘I had to get Georgie to drown them in the water barrel – she keeps going around crying for them. I think she misses them, you know.’

Temporarily concussed by this insensitivity, Nell soon recovered to issue a hot reply: ‘I should think she does!’

Afraid that her spleen might explode, blind to her astonished audience, she shot to her feet and fled the room.

‘Eh, she’s as soft as I am,’ sighed Ma to the GIs.

Without pausing even to visit the lavatory, Nell rushed straight from the house and marched briskly to the Infirmary, hoping to work off some of this all-consuming fury by the time she got there. But all this did was to make her heart race twice as fast, and she was still wrought up when she arrived, spilling it all out to Beata the moment she set eyes on her fellow nurse.

‘I can’t stay there, Killie! I feel so let down – how could she be so cruel? And for Georgie to do her bidding . . .’ Such a crime was unthinkable from this lovely old man. ‘I just can’t stay there!’

Beata could give no reason, but, looking into those moist, angry eyes, she guessed this whole episode went much deeper than the death of a few kittens, and told Nell shortly, ‘I’ve been thinking of moving out of our Gussie’s and looking for digs of my own, though it wouldn’t be up to much on the money we’re paid. But if we were to pool our funds we could maybe get something more decent.’

Nell’s reply was hurried, and her eyes still red with acrimony as she fidgeted over the tying of her apron.

'Thanks, Killie, but I'm not fit to live with anyone these days. No, I shall have to find a place of my own, so that I can lock myself in and not be forced to speak to anyone if I don't feel like it.' She hoisted her palms in defensive mode, as if trying to keep the world at bay. 'But how I'll continue to live with Ma till I find somewhere . . .' She shook her head in utter despondency and alienation. 'I'll never regard her in the same light again. I feel like throttling the woman.'

Beata thought she might have an answer. 'Just to tide you over, I could ask our Gussie if she can squeeze you in for a week or two. Well, it's not a case of asking, I know she'll make you welcome, so you can just bring your bags round tomorrow if you like.'

'Why, you must be bursting at the seams!' exclaimed Nell, who had heard many interesting tales from the large household. It was the second marriage for Gussie's husband, and his grown-up children were also to be found in residence, alongside his new family and in-laws.

But Beata said, 'You can share my bed as long as it's only for a few weeks – that's if you don't kick, mind.'

And so, after only a few moments' thought on Nell's part, she being still so rattled and there being nowhere else for her to go, the deal was struck.

Upon arriving home from work the next morning, having calmed down, though still intent on her plan, Nell managed to slink up to her room without encountering anyone, and was able to snatch three or four hours' sleep before having to face the uncomfortable task of informing Ma and Georgie. Without reference to the cat incident, and feeling slightly guilty that she had eaten Georgie's lovingly prepared Spam fritters first, she let them know that she would be moving out that same afternoon.

Both were upset, though Ma obviously had no idea that she was to blame. 'I thought you liked being with us!' The sergeant-major was reduced to a lamb, her big face riven with bafflement. 'What's changed?'

'Nothing,' lied Nell, trying to appear unruffled and friendly, when this was far removed from her inner turmoil. 'I'll always be grateful for the way you've both looked after me – but it's just that I've been offered a room that's almost next door to the hospital –' another lie, it was further away, '– and what with the long hours and everything – you do understand, don't you?'

And of course, the Preciouses replied that they did, though their moans of disenchantment were to ring in Nell's ears as she went upstairs to collect her luggage. But with the pitiful sound of the cat still resounding in them too, she knew she was doing the right thing.

There was perhaps a mile or more to walk, along a straight linkage of roads, from grimy Walmgate with its run-down shops and slums, under its medieval limestone bar, and along a dusty highway that was heavy with horse-drawn traffic and army vehicles, before she eventually turned into a quiet Victorian terrace. As Beata had told, the house was about halfway down, small but handsome, with a bay window to the lower storey, and a walled forecourt with a foot-wide patch of garden enclosed. Some of the other householders had not yet donated their ornate cast-iron railings to the war effort. The only evidence of such former glory here was the sawn-off stumps on the low front wall, which Nell glimpsed as she came through the gate, towards a door that was wide open to admit the summer, and anyone else who cared to enter. She tapped politely and waited.

Beata had instructed her eldest sister to wake her up the moment her friend arrived, and within seconds of seeing Nell there, Gussie was already heading back along the passageway to call up the stairs.

Nell swiftly prevented this as she came over the threshold

with her hat box and case. 'Let her sleep, I can sit and wait. It'll be a long enough night for her as it is.'

Gussie stopped short, and turned to address her guest. 'You look tired, love. Shouldn't you be in bed as well, if you're on nights?'

Upon first sight, Nell had thought Gussie quite dissimilar to Beata, for she was slightly taller, and her hair was a darker, richer auburn. Both had blue eyes, but where Beata's were small and twinkly, Gussie's were large and clear, and brimming with an almost unearthly virtue. Excepting the gingham overall and the shabby dress beneath, this woman could still have been judged quite beautiful, had her physical attributes not been wrecked by overwork. She was not yet forty, but looked a decade older. However, upon probing more deeply, Nell could detect a greater, more intrinsic similarity between the sisters: both harboured a deep compassion within their ample breasts. She responded to this show of concern with a smile, and told Gussie that she had managed to catch sufficient rest.

'Right, well, just leave your luggage there, love, and we'll have a cup of tea.'

Depositing her burden in the dim hallway with its brown varnished dado, Nell followed Gussie into the back living room, which had an old-fashioned Yorkshire range, and was plainly furnished yet clean and comfortable. There were already two other occupants: one, a little girl who was playing with her dolls on the hearth rug; the other an elderly man wearing a collarless shirt under a waistcoat, and seated in a fireside chair smoking a pipe. Both gave only slight acknowledgement of her entrance. There, in exchange for a cup of fresh tea and the promise of an evening meal, Nell was to sit and help her hostess peel vegetables. During this, she also sought assurance that her presence was not an intrusion. 'It's awfully decent of you to put me up at such short notice – do tell me if I'll be in the way.'

'Nay, one more won't make a difference,' came the blasé response.

'How many do you accommodate at the moment?' enquired Nell.

Gussie totted them up on her potato peeler. 'There's me and Mick . . .' Nell glanced at the portly man in his fireside chair. Michael Melody had lovely smiling blue eyes; she could see how anyone would have fallen for him in his youth. But the silver hair and stubble implied that he was much too old for Gussie – perhaps thirty years older – and Nell had heard from Beata how huge a responsibility her sister had taken upon herself, with Mick's large family plus the two they had had together.

Gussie was still tallying those who relied on her boundless generosity. 'Our two little ones, three of Mick's bigger lasses, and one daughter-in-law; then Beat, of course, and our Mims, who's a widow – they're all out at work, though some of them'll soon be in for their tea, so I'd better get cracking.' She resumed her peeling as she continued to list the inhabitants. 'Let me see, who have I missed? Oh, our Mim's little lad, he's around somewhere . . .'

Nell had already counted eleven. It was a four-bedroom house, but with the married couple requiring privacy there would be little free space. 'Are you sure –'

Gussie stopped her, adopting a bossy tone. 'Be told! If the lads weren't away at war it might be different, but you and Beata are on nights, so you'll only be using the beds through the day – you can have one of your own, by the way. She said you were willing to share, but you nurses need your rest.'

Nell praised the other's charity. 'You're an angel.' It was no platitude: Gussie could rightly be termed one of life's true saints – and not a wishy-washy one either, for even prior to this, Nell had guessed that any sister of Beata's must be equally down-to-earth. 'I won't be in your hair for long,' she added, then hesitated a while, pondering on something that appeared to concern her, before asking, 'Did Killie, I mean Beata, tell you anything about my situation?'

'She tells me nowt, love,' chuckled Gussie, thereby shaming Nell. How could she have thought her friend would break her promise to keep baby William a secret? 'None of them do, I'm just the landlady.' But Nell sensed she was much, much more. Whilst they were chatting and drinking their tea, there was the sound of a heavy footfall coming along the passage, and, shortly, a middle-aged woman in an overall and turban entered the room. Actually, she passed *through* the room, merely nodding to Gussie on her way to the back door, and leaving by the rear gate.

'Mrs Crow,' explained Gussie to Nell, as if it were all perfectly logical. 'She cuts through to the shop in the next street, well, it saves her going right round on the top road, you see – right, that's that lot done!' With great dexterity, she scooped the vegetables into two receptacles, one a saucepan, the other a steamer, then went to check on the meat in the oven.

'That smells gorgeous,' murmured Nell, wearing a look of enquiry.

'Aye, a couple of bunnies,' divulged Gussie.

'Your own?'

'Ooh, no – our Mick's too soft-hearted to kill 'em.' Gussie looked on her husband with love. 'One of his pals got them for us – I'm not sure where from and I don't want to know. Would you mind putting those few bits in the swill bin for us, love? It's in the back lane.'

Nell jumped up and began to gather the inedible stalks. 'Certainly, anything to make myself useful.'

Immediately upon exit from the back door, she saw that there was a pram in the yard, and a baby fast asleep in it, his little limbs bared to the warm day. Aching, Nell moved quickly past. But a couple of steps further on, she was alerted by the sound of weeping, and turned to see a little boy, of perhaps three or four, crouched in a gap between the lavatory and a shed. The sight and sound of him made her falter, but when he uptilted a face wet with tears she did not quite know what to do, and so she hurried onwards to the bin.

But once the handful of waste was deposited, she must travel past him again, and the sight broke her heart, conjuring immediately to mind her own son who would be only a little younger than this one. Unable to trust herself to speak to the woebegone child, she blurted uncertainly, 'I'll fetch your aunty!' Then she hurried inside.

But with Gussie vanished, she was obliged to consult the old man by the fire.

With what seemed like great effort, Mick removed his pipe to issue in a faintly Irish brogue, 'Oh, that'll be Mim's lad . . .' then he promptly stuck it back in his mouth, and went back to staring into the fire.

'What should I do?' Nell wrung her hands.

At his unhelpful shrug, she wandered reluctantly back into the yard, where the child still wept. With no other option, she crouched towards him and forced herself to ask softly, 'What's up, old chap?'

His shoulders juddered and he turned his face to her, his eyes swimming tears. 'Me dad's gone to a watery grave.'

It was more than Nell could bear. For years she had been trying to contain this overwhelming grief, but now the floodgates ruptured. Her face contorted, and on noting the little boy's expression turn from misery to terror at the sight of it, she reeled away from him, out into the back lane, where she sobbed and sobbed, her whole body racked as she slid down the brick wall to her hunkers, and wrapped her head in her arms, wailing uncontrollably.

Having just been woken by her sister, a puffy-eyed Beata came clumping down the stairs, tugging on her clothes as she came, for even if Gussie had not roused her, the noise would have. Moreover, by the time she reached its source, it had drawn curious neighbours from their daily treadmill.

'Eh, get poor lass inside,' advised a turbaned member of the audience, not asking what was wrong with Nell, for each of those gathered knew well enough what was amiss. 'This bloody buggering war . . .'

Still racked with sobs, Nell was shivering too now, and feeling hemmed in by all these pinafores. A bolt of panic sent her smashing through their ranks and running up the back lane, heading she knew not where. Neither overworked Gussie, nor Beata with her dropsical leg, could hope to keep up with the fleeing figure. But that did not prevent the latter sallying forth on her trail, explaining to the worried neighbours as she went that: 'She lost her sweetheart three years ago and it's just caught up with her!'

Nell would surely forgive this indiscretion. Rather that than have them learn the truth about her baby, which was where the real problem lay. With everyone still watching her, the little boy now quiet and solemn in his Aunt Gussie's arms, Beata limped away.

Out of sight by now, unable to gain a moment's privacy, Nell was heading away from town, though the busy main road did nought to heal her mood. Driven by panic, she veered away from the traffic, into a different lane. This one backed the houses on the far side of the street, and was verged on its other flank by grass and mature trees, the quiet shade of which was to deliver momentary respite from the world. Hidden behind one of the large chestnut trees, she fell against its trunk and released heart-rending sobs.

Arriving at the lane, Beata did not see her, and might have hurried straight past had not the pitiful sound alerted her. Wandering to within a few yards of the tree that shaded her sobbing friend, she stood quietly by, allowing Nell this leeway to purge herself of grief.

A good ten minutes she stood and waited, her senses keyed for any interference from passers-by, ready to ward them off, until at last the noisy tears were quelled. But as she made her wary approach through the grass, she saw that her friend seemed confused, as if not knowing where she was, nor even what had caused her to break down like this. Her face puffy and mottled, breast still rising and falling from the effort, Nell wheeled around and flung herself backwards against the trunk, pressing her whole length against it as if for support.

'I can't breathe!' Her eyes were open wide, and her mouth sucking in air like a fish out of water.

Calm as ever, Beata stepped up and grasped her with a steadying hand. 'Just try not to inhale so quickly –'

'I'm choking!'

'No,' came the firm reply, 'you only think you are. Just try and breathe normally and your heart'll eventually stop beating – I mean thudding! We don't want it to do that, do we?' Her friend tried to make a joke of it, and gave that throaty chuckle which Nell knew so well. But it had little impact today.

Trying distraction, Beata lifted her eyes to the green canopy, and murmured in a casual matter-of-fact way, 'Look at this chestnut tree, it's laden. There'll be a bumper crop of conkers in autumn . . .'

'I don't think I'll see autumn,' blurted Nell. 'I think I'm losing my mind.'

'No, you're not.' The ever calm Beata gripped her wrist. 'You've just been through a lot.'

'So has everybody – there's a war on!'

'But not everybody has lost their lover, their parents and their child,' instructed her friend in, deliberate and soothing manner. 'Not in such a short space of time.'

'I'll bet all your neighbours think I'm mad!' gasped Nell.

'Do you care?' Beata maintained her even pitch.

'No.' Nell shook her head, still miserable, but beginning to feel slightly calmer herself now.

'No, then that's one less thing to worry about, isn't it?'

'I can't stop thinking about him, Beat.' Tears came again, but quieter ones this time.

Her friend was unsure whether she meant Billy or the baby, but by allowing Nell to speak, duly she found out.

'Especially during the raid . . . I just kept wondering if . . . praying, please keep him safe, *please* don't let him be killed. I thought I was doing the best for him by giving him to a couple so he'd have a father as well as a mother, but they wouldn't tell me where they'd taken him, so he could have been killed for all I know!' Her utterance without pause, Nell was inviting hysteria again.

Beata tightened her grip, steadying her, as Nell continued in, disbelieving tone, 'How could they do it to me, Killie? I know, I *know* what shame I must have caused them, but they could have sent me away somewhere, lent me money until I was able to get on my feet – they were hardly paupers – how could Mother go to such lengths to keep her own daughter, yet force me to give away her grandchild? How could they trick me into believing all these years that I was adopted, then go and die on me before I'd a chance to find out more – I mean, what about my natural father? He might as well be dead too, for all I know of him.' Fists clenched, she threw at her friend all the things she would have liked to have hurled at her parents, were that possible.

At the end of her outburst, during which she had been had allowed free flow, Beata posed a question: 'Did they thrash you?'

'No!' Nell was quick to dispel this. 'Well, only a slap in the heat of the moment. I probably deserved it.'

'Did they starve you?'

Nell was angry that Beata had no idea what it was like

to be deprived of one's child. 'There are more ways of being cruel!'

'Oh, I know all about mental cruelty,' her friend was swift to concede, 'and I'm not making light of your loss, it must have been absolutely terrible to have your baby taken away. But truly cruel? I don't think so. They were just doing what they thought was right – yes, they might have been thinking of themselves, wanting to protect their reputation, but they were thinking of you too, and your little boy. Would you have wanted people to call him names just because he was born without his mother being wed? It might not seem much to you, but it's unpleasant for an adult to carry that stigma, let alone for a little boy. People can be so cruel to children, and I mean *really* cruel. My stepmother being one of them. Your mother would have a long way to go before she could compete with her . . .'

Winkled out of her own troubles, Nell saw the vacant expression that had taken over her friend's face. She knew then that Beata had her own ghosts, but not caring to summon these, she asked instead, 'How did you end up so kind and considerate and patient yourself, with her for an example?'

'Because I had a proper mother till I was nine.' Beata remained nostalgic, absently swatting a fly that buzzed around her face. 'She was lovely, she'd do anything for her kids. She even died because she'd rather have been at home looking after us than be in hospital . . .' Shaking herself from this painful episode, she saw by Nell's face that her friend had taken this as an accusation that she was not a good mother, was selfish for putting her needs first, and said quickly, 'I often wish she hadn't been quite so perfect, then we might have had her a bit longer. You did the right thing by giving your baby a good chance in life. I'd have done the same . . .'

Nell felt certain that she had not done the right thing, nor had her parents. But she did admit now, 'Well, it's true, my mother wasn't intentionally cruel, she could be very thoughtful sometimes, but she just seemed to find it impossible to empathise. That's what makes it so hard to understand, that she *was* my real mother, and must know how it felt, yet she made me give him up. She could try and explain till the cows came home, but . . .' Nell shook her head, totally bewildered. All at once aware that her throat was clogged and tangy with salt, she experienced virulent need of a cigarette to mask the taste, but with none to hand she tried to focus on Beata, and tendered with vague curiosity, 'Did you never think of marrying, Killie? After the one who let you down, I mean.'

'Nobody ever asked me.' Beata's face cracked into a rueful grin, but somehow it made Nell feel incredibly sad.

'Then there are a lot of idiotic men walking about,' she announced loyally. 'You'd make a perfect wife.'

'Nay, I'm too old now, love,' sighed Beata, far too wearily for her thirty-three years. 'But there's still a chance for you to find someone and start a family.'

A puffy-eyed Nell was adamant. 'No, I'll never marry either. Because I'll never ever love anyone as much as I adored Billy. At least I thought so, until I held William . . .' Tears threatened again. She took a deep breath that filled her head with an overpowering scent of greenery, shifted her aching back against the rough bark, and sighed. 'I don't know if I can stay with you, Beat, the sight of that little boy . . .' She shook her head as if to rid herself of the image.

'You seem to cope well enough with the kids at work, and they're not exactly happy little souls,' mooted Beata.

Nell shook her head. 'If I seem to cope it's only because they're mostly asleep whilst I'm looking after them.'

Enlightened by retrospect, Beata saw now that Nell did often make excuses when it came to a day shift on the nursery ward; and had worked there only a handful of times during the last few years.

'Besides,' went on Nell, 'they're in a totally different

environment, but seeing him there in a normal home, I would just keep thinking of what I've lost. I don't know if I could bear it.'

'You shouldn't be on your own,' warned Beata.

'I'm not going to kill myself.' Nell found the energy to smile, but it was an insipid effort. 'I'm too much of a coward.' Still, she felt shaky and uncertain. 'I do feel all at sea, though . . . perhaps you're right about me staying for a few days.' If she was sleeping most of the day, or at least attempting to, she would not have to manufacture polite conversation for any of the other occupants.

'You'll be all right.' Her companion delivered a bolstering tap. 'We'll try and keep Johnny out of your way.'

'You shouldn't have to do that,' protested Nell. 'Poor little chap, I feel rather ashamed now, thinking only of myself. After all, his mother's managing to carry on, what have I to grumble about?' She looked around the shady lane, her expression abstracted, as if only now seeing where she was. 'Shall we wander back? Here's me keeping you standing around on your poor leg . . .'

Both of them glanced down at it. Then Beata declared: 'I've only gone and trodden in blasted dog muck! I should kill you for dragging me round here!' But she was chuckling as she scraped her foot back and forth through the long grass.

Trying her best to smile at the comic moment, though still quite distrait, Nell made a promise. 'I'll clean it off properly for you when we get home. I feel guilty enough about disturbing your sleep – God, I could murder a fag.'

Arm in arm, they made their way to the top of the lane, were briefly exposed to the noise and dust of the traffic, then re-entered the quieter street, chatting of lesser topics along the way.

Before they reached the door, though, Beata was to give last-minute advice. 'You should see the doctor, he might be able to give you something for your nerves.'

'And have him think I'm crazy, and ban me from treating patients? Everybody's got nerves, Killie, it's this blessed war.' Her head still banging from its tearful onslaught and her face puffy, Nell braced her shoulders to enter. 'No, I'll be all right, I promise. I feel much better for having let it all out. I'm sorry to have burdened you with my problems. It's just the not knowing that's worst. If I could just be sure that I did the right thing, that William's safe . . .'

'You did,' vouched Beata. 'And he is.' Her friend nodded, wanting desperately to believe it, yet retaining her look of uncertainty. For whilst this war continued, she could never feel sure about anything.

It was embarrassing to say the least, having to face those who had witnessed her emotional collapse. But with Gussie being as altruistic as her sister, Nell came to the decision that it would be wiser to remain here for a while. Swallowing a couple of aspirins for her headache, she retired to the upper room that had been temporarily allocated to her, there to wash the signs of tears from her blotchy face – though, alas, not the grief, which was to remain etched, perhaps forever. She accepted that now, in whatever way possible, she must cope with it, must steel herself to face the curiosity of others again. Gussie's lodgers would doubtless be home from work by the time she went down.

Hands pressed to her cheeks, struggling to pull strength from anywhere and desperate for a smoke, Nell went to rummage in her pocket, with no cigarettes having to fall back on her pipe. It was perhaps impolite to light up here, but the scent of Mick's tobacco could be smelled all over the house, so she guessed no one would mind. Puffing on this substitute, she rested her buttocks on the edge of the creaking bedstead and allowed her bleak gaze to roam the bedroom. Someone had brought her luggage up. Whilst an aromatic twirl of pipe smoke drifted to the ceiling, her eyes became fixed on the hat box, which contained Bill's letters and other heart-wrenching things; things that had not been looked upon for a long time. Since depositing the ring and ribbon, she had not been able to bring herself even to open the lid. Pipe still in mouth, she arose and wandered over to the box, staring down at it, daring herself to be Pandora. If she could only do that, could lift them out one by one, touch those precious objects without breaking down, then she knew she would be able to face all else . . .

But for now, she remained a coward.

However, there were certain other demons that could, and should, be tackled, if she was not to become a total weakling. That same night, on her way to work, Nell made a decision that she would no longer contrive to avoid the nursery ward, and that when her assistance was required she would place herself in the firing line, come what may.

If it was difficult to contemplate then, it took even more valour when put to the test. A fortnight later, swapped to day shift and enlisted to work in the nursery to fill in for a colleague who was ill, she found herself trembling like a leaf, and hoped the sister could not detect this as she attended the morning handover. If only Killie were here to assist her. But no, this was something she must do by herself.

One by one the patients' notes were gone through, and Nurse Spottiswood was guided around the rows of cots.

'You're already familiar with Gordon, I assume,' commented her middle-aged informant, Nurse Mullen, as they passed the cot in which he was dozing, even though the rest were awake.

'I certainly am.' Nell was wholly familiar with Gordon Flowerdew, the only one of Cissie's twins to survive, who had now almost reached the age when he would be moved to an orphanage. 'The last time we met, he stood and rattled the bars of his cot all night long.' And no wonder, she thought now disapprovingly, if they were allowing him to sleep through the day.

'Yes, he's such a blessed nuisance when he's awake,' came the other's explanation. 'We tend to leave him as long as we can, or we'd never get anything done.'

'No, you leave him for us on nights!' Though junior in age and also in status. Nell could not help objecting.

But the other only laughed. 'Aye, well, you've more time on your hands than we have.' Ignoring Nell's splutter, Nurse Mullen added, 'He's big enough to clamber over the top, so just keep your eyes peeled . . .'

Nell determined to wake Gordon as soon as was feasible, and that for the duration of her stay on this ward she would try to adjust him to being awake at the correct hour.

They came then to a recent addition. 'This is Angela Smith.' Her colleague paused by a cot whose occupant had an arm and leg in plaster, the latter suspended by a pulley over the bed. She also had the most beautiful violet eyes that Nell had ever seen. 'You'll see she's got a double row of teeth. Her adult ones have come through but her milk teeth haven't fallen out yet, so she has difficulty taking food. She needs her bread dipping in milk.' Nurse Mullen lowered her voice to give confidential advice. 'But you can dip it in tea if you're too busy and Sister's not about.'

Nell felt her dander rise, and it was a good job the other had already turned her back and did not see the contempt levelled at her. Please God, thought Nell, that her own child was with a family who might show him more regard than this.

She was taken past one cot after another, about two dozen in all, and upon the final one received a caution. 'And, last but not least, this is Arthur. Don't leave anything in his reach, or he'll have it down his throat whether it be a piece of soap or an elephant.' The elder nurse spent a moment explaining the child's fascinating disorder, which compelled him to devour everything in sight, including his bedding if it wasn't properly secured, before ending brightly, 'Right then! The night staff have already made the poorly ones comfy, so we'd better start on top and tails – there'll be a few who need a bath, though, can you just see to that whilst I go and fetch the pots?'

Whilst the other proceeded to deposit those infants who were not bedridden on a row of potties, Nell donned a flannel pinafore and went to fetch jug after jug of water, and to fill a succession of baths, into which was dunked one tiny body, and then another. By now Nurse Mullen had begun to top and tail, not refreshing her bowl of water between each child, a disapproving Nell noticed, as she rapidly dealt with each of her charges as if trying to break some record. She herself decided to confront this personal issue once and for all by taking her time over it. For only by over-exposure could Nell perhaps inure her senses to the touch and feel of infant skin, and the physical feeling of loss this still evoked. For this reason she was deliberately to handle each child as much as time allowed, and instead of rushing through the ablutions was to extend her attention to petting and talking to each individual, so that she might come to know them better.

Even Cissie's Gordon was to receive this personal treatment, for though he was a terror, that was explicable by his deprived beginnings and the loss of his twin, and after waking him she sought to show him some affection whilst giving him a bath.

The little game they played with the boats and ducks seemed to be appreciated by the child, who splashed about to his heart's content, but was viewed with some obliquity by Nell's colleague.

'You're making a rod for your own back.' Whizzing through a score of tasks to Nell's half-dozen, Nurse Mullen wore a look that said she knew better. 'He'll have you forever at his beck and call.'

'Isn't that what we're here for?' demanded Nell reasonably. 'To look after them.'

'Pff! You'll change your tune after a day with that little demon. But don't mind me, you do as you like!'

And Nell did do as she liked, proceeding to treat Gordon as she would have done her own son – not as a substitute, for he could never be that, nor could any child – but to try to give the poor little mite some form of normality, before the water grew too cool and she was forced to lift him out. Then she was to see the wisdom of the other's words, for Gordon showed his displeasure by kicking and lashing out with his limbs as she tried to shove them back into his institutional clothing, and even when she managed to install him in the playpen with the others, upon seeing his nurse devote her special treatment to another infant, he became lost in a tantrum, rattling the bars like an enraged monkey at the zoo.

To others this was a nuisance, to Nell quite distressing, though she managed to shut her ears to his noise and concentrate on the task of bathing Arthur, to make sure that he did not bite a chunk out of the soap, or, even worse, the sponge, for that might warrant a surgical operation.

It took a great feat of resilience, due to Gordon perpetually rattling and shaking the bars of the playpen and calling for her, but somehow she managed get Arthur bathed and dressed, then ensconced in the playpen too, checking there were no soft toys for him to eat, before reaching for the next in line.

Though hardly enjoying this, Nell was proud of herself for not breaking into fits of tears under such emotional pressure, for it came to the point when the last child had been bathed and put in the playpen, and she had managed to achieve this without panic. It was with a sense of victory that she untied her flannel pinafore and set about damp dusting the windowsills and cot rails.

But this was premature. Ignored by the nurses, Gordon

had begun to take his frustration out on one of the other toddlers, and now hit him over the head with a wooden lorry, drawing forth howls.

'You'll have to see to him!' called Nell's colleague. 'My hands are full, and it's your fault he's like it.'

So, draping her pinafore over the bars of a cot, Nell rushed to pick up the screaming toddler and to comfort him, before turning to reprehend Gordon – only to see Arthur sneaking up on her pinny. Before she could stop him he was ramming it for all he was worth into his mouth. With an exclamation of concern, she set the yelling toddler down and rushed to prevent Arthur from choking, which was like trying to extract a goat from a python that had already swallowed half of it. With screams in the background from the injured toddler, and this setting off others too, Nell fought to keep her head whilst maintaining tight hold of one end of the pinafore, and inch by inch managing to extricate it from teeth that were clamped as tight as a bulldog's, though she needed the help of the other nurse before eventually both succeeded in pulling it from Arthur's jaws.

Even then there was no time to relax, for it was immediately pointed out to her that Gordon had taken this opportunity to escape from the playpen and was nowhere in sight. With an exasperated gasp, Nell rushed from the ward and looked both ways along the corridor, before hearing a commotion. Following the sound into one of the adult wards, there she caught sight of the tiny absconder, running between one elderly patient and another, and dealing each a hefty thump or a kick, which obviously gave him deep enjoyment, for he gave a maniacal laugh before cantering off to inflict the next bruise.

Apologising profusely to Gordon's victims, and to the ward sister, Nell managed to grab the infant thug before he had done too much damage, and with his flailing limbs pinioned beneath her arm, carted him to his rightful place.

On her way back there, though, who should she see hurrying up to greet her but the culprit's mother. Before that beaming face could utter even a greeting, Nell threw her a not entirely jocular warning. 'If you so much as mention that man in the black hat, Cissie Flowerdew, I'll swing for you both – the trouble I've had with this child of his!'

'It's all right, Nurse, he's going to marry me this time!' proffered the gormless one.

Nell stopped dead and gasped as the truth hit her, and her joke was transformed to a nightmare. 'Oh, surely, Ciss, not another?' Then, clicking her tongue in despair and shaking her head, with the noisy, wriggling child under her arm, she strode on.

'I warned you you'd regret it!' Nurse Mullen smirked, as her perspiring colleague dumped Gordon back in the playpen and tried to distract him with a game.

'So you did,' Nell had to concede, soon to be glad that her attempt to calm Gordon was successful, for at that moment Matron Fosdyke made an appearance, and she was wearing her stern face.

Both nurses came to attention, Nell praying that Gordon wouldn't kick up another fuss, whilst Matron cast an experienced eye about her, checking that all children were safe and well-tended, that their cots were all neatly made, the castors turned in, the ward scrupulously clean, the floor polished, and nothing out of place.

Apparently satisfied with what she saw, Matron seemed about to leave, then in afterthought turned back. 'You look as though you're in dire need of a cup of tea, Nurse Spottiswood.'

At the terse observation, Nell flushed, and her hands went up to check that her hair was not poking from her headdress. Was this a precursor to a more severe reprimand?

'I'm pleased to see that Gordon seems to have settled

down a little now,' noted Matron, who had quite obviously heard the commotion.

'I'm very sorry he got out, Matron.' Nell was instantly contrite. 'It won't happen again.'

'I'm very glad to hear it. A shame that can't be applied to his mother,' replied Matron, remaining stiff, but with a jovial glint in her eye. 'Go and get yourselves a cup of tea – and whilst you're about it, bring me one too. I think we all need it after hearing Cissie's news.'

'Oh, she isn't?' groaned Nurse Mullen to Nell, after Matron departed.

''Fraid she is – baby number seven!' But despite everything, Nell found that she could raise a genuine smile as she sailed off to aid her recovery with a cup of tea, before the rest of the morning's duties must be resumed.

As expected, these turned out to be equally taxing, from having to hold the infants still whilst medicines and painful treatment were administered, to the time-consuming feeding of those who lay helpless, added to an endless round of nappy changing and potty emptying.

But at the end of the day, when it was time to hand over to the night sister, and Nell went from cot to cot wishing her little charges goodnight – and even reading them a short story before she went home – she was left with a feeling that she had succeeded in jumping the first hurdle. No matter how arduous the test, she had managed to keep her head. The weight of a baby in her arms had not engendered the insanity she so feared. True, it had only been one day. But it was a start.

One step forward, two steps back, was how Nell's life was to go from there. Gaining confidence in her ability to manage the nursery ward, often alone, she was eventually to progress in finding a home for herself. At least it was a home of sorts: an upstairs room in a Victorian terraced house in the Groves, a shabby but respectable enough area that was a stone's throw from the Infirmary and also from town. Lacking just about every mod con, it had a two-ringed gas stove and a fire, and a washstand that served both for personal ablutions and to sluice the pots. Of the latter there were few, this also applying to furniture, for Nell was only able to afford the very basics, and all of them utility items – a bed, a small table, an upright chair, a few utensils and some crockery – and had only acquired these due to her inheritance and the generous twenty-first gift from her aunty and uncle. This expenditure had left her with five pounds, which she had decided to retain as a contingency, for she was not yet sure how she would manage to run a household, even one so modest as this.

If life had been austere before, then it was even more so now, baths being restricted to one a week and costing a shilling, the landlady seeming to think herself most generous in providing the soap. For all that, its lack of comforts did not really matter that much when its tenant was hardly in residence, except to sleep. As ever, Nell was most often to be found at the Infirmary, where, after so many years, she had formed a close working bond with her colleagues – as close as she would ever allow herself to feel towards anyone, in case they too should be snatched away like others she had loved. After their rocky start, Sister Barber had come to be included in her favourites. Having long ago renounced the opinion that these untrained girls had been foisted upon her, and the notion that their intelligence was nil, Sister had also relinquished much of the hierarchical nonsense that had marked their earlier years. Recalling her own surprise at first being invited to share a pot of tea with her superior, nowadays Nell took it for granted that they would drink together whilst going over the patients' notes. And though each retained a professional air towards the other, it was no rarity to hear them sharing a chuckle with the residents – unthinkable in the old days – Sister having the same particular favourites as herself. Having cut herself off from her true relations through fear of pain, and taken diversionary measures to avoid them in public, one might say that Nell had her own little family at the Infirmary: with Sister, Cissie, and Blanche who scrubbed the corridors, and pretty little Connie Wood who had been written off at birth, but would have been an entertainer if ever she could have escaped the institution, with a repertoire of dirty jokes picked up from lord knew where. In a way Nell was similarly trapped, not by authority, but by affection for all these dear folk – though none so dear as Beata.

Her friend, too, had become independent now, renting a single room in a house quite nearby. Strangely, though, Nell had chosen not to be a regular visitor there, nor to the Melody household – however many times she had been invited – preferring the stillness and quietude of her own room in the hours when she was not at work. Though, of course, she had promised her friend that, 'If any of you should ever need my help, just say the word and I'll be there in a flash.' For she had become well-acquainted with Beata's sisters via all the snippets of news about them, which she loved to hear, and she had come to regard them, too, as second kin of sorts.

But, like all families, its members had their differences. That morning, Nell's mind was consumed with the latest development as she made her way home from night shift through autumn fog and smoke. The youngest sister, Mims, was about to remarry: an act she herself found hard even to contemplate. But then, Nell did not have a child to care for, like Beata's widowed sister. As a mother, one must put one's own needs aside.

Ruminating over the position she herself might be in now, had she been allowed to keep William, Nell found herself tormented by dire need of a cigarette, and she changed direction to seek out a tobacconist – but in doing so, she almost bumped into one of her cousins, and had to jump into a doorway in order not to be seen, and to hide there like the Scarlet Pimpernel until the danger had passed.

Her visit to the tobacconist was to attract rude reception, for, on the threshold, she was tumbled to the ground by two labourers engaged in bitter struggle. Apparently one had bought the last packet of cigarettes in the shop, and the other was determined to get it, not caring that he trampled a nurse in the process. Shocked, and with the oafs' boots still scuffling about her, she rolled out of their way whilst the shopkeeper helped her up and set about berating them. 'Ruddy hooligans! As if it isn't bad enough the Germans trying to kill us. I'm sorry about that, nurse . . .'

Wearing a disgusted frown, Nell brushed herself off. Why do, I bother to help folk, she asked herself bitterly, if this is what the world has come to, Even more desperate for a smoke, she headed into town in the hope of finding a packet. But the situation was no better there. She would just have to hope that there was tobacco left in her pipe when she got home. Even a stale smoke would do, the way she felt at this moment. Empty-handed, and depressed at being so unappreciated, she resumed her trail home.

However, as she was passing a shop that sold furniture and carpets – at least it had before the war, its window displays were much reduced nowadays – the salesman who was leaning against the jamb, without anything to do, made an exclamation of delight at seeing her nurse's badge. 'Just the person I've been waiting for!' And he summoned her in clandestine fashion, and from behind a cupped hand whispered: 'I've got a lovely bit of coconut matting just arrived!'

'I've no wish to sound churlish, but can one smoke it?' said Nell, tongue in cheek. But she followed him anyway, for such commodities were as scarce as tobacco. 'Anyway, I've no permit –'

'If you don't let on then neither will I! We have to look after the ones who are looking after us!'

Tell that to the two who just smashed me to the ground, Nell wanted to grumble, but her upset over that incident was gradually being dispelled by the eager generosity of this man, who, having unfurled the small but very pleasing rug, declared: 'There! What do you think of that?'

One would have thought he was displaying a Persian carpet. Rubbing her mouth, Nell pondered on whether it was wise to break into that precious five pound note that was meant for a rainy day. In fact she vacillated so long that he thought she was trying to negotiate a discount, and he was quick to reduce the price even more. 'I swear that's no more than I paid for it!'

Still, she found it a wrench to part with the cash, but then it was so very difficult to get one's hands on anything decent these days, and her room was so very bare, that she eventually relinquished her fiver.

'Blinking 'eck, if I'd known nurses were paid that much I would've protected my own profit! Put your moniker on the back, will you, Nurse – not for me, you understand, just regulations.'

'Look, no printing ink on my hands, honestly!' Displaying her palms, she laughingly explained that the money had been a birthday gift, and scribbled her name on the fiver. Then, pocketing her change, and feeling rather pleased with herself, she humped her roll of coconut matting from the shop – though thereafter, her progress was to be retarded. For all the way home through dingy old streets with boarded-up windows and peppered with bombsites, she was to meet eager interrogation, every man and his dog delaying her to ask where on earth she had managed to acquire such a gem.

Half-amused, half-irritated, as she shifted the heavy roll from one arm to the other, by the time she did arrive home, Nell was glad to throw it upon the floor, and also felt like collapsing into bed. But, being even more eager to see if the bowl of her pipe held enough for a smoke, which, thank God, it did, she put the kettle on first, made a cup of tea, then lit up and sat on the bed with her feet up, to admire her recent purchase.

But then her drowsy gaze was to stray to the hat box, neglected in a corner. It was all very well feeling pleased with oneself over a bit of coconut matting when there were things that must still be confronted. Was now the ideal time, though, argued the weaker side of her character, when she was worn out from her shift, and her mind perhaps not able to cope? You've managed to look after those babies without crumbling, she told herself forcefully, now do this. *Do* it.

Drawing a last disquieted puff, she set her feet to the new rug and laid her pipe on the hearth. Even then, it took much effort to push herself from the bed, and to finally confront the box. Still, she simply looked at it for a while, her fingers abstractedly picking at the skin at the edges of her thumbnails. Her hands seemed glued to her sides. She fought the cowardly urge to leave them there, and directed them at the lid, her whole body trembling as they hovered just above it. This was ridiculous! With a self-scolding gesture, the lid came off and was set aside. And there was Billy's photograph grinning up at her. Placing the box on the bed, Nell delved in quickly and took firm hold of the snapshot, looked masochistically into that beloved face, those eyes . . .

His voice, she thought to her sudden horror, I can't remember his voice. And though she strained to recall that southern twang, she could not; would have to be satisfied in remembering it in essence, the effects of its laughter upon her, the intense happiness it had sired, the murmured endearments . . .

Her heart aching, Nell allowed her eyes to fill with tears. Tears were all right. It was the suppression of them that caused all the problems. The man in the photograph became a blur. She wiped away the veil of moisture and allowed him back into focus, gazing at Billy for long moments, just to ensure that she could, before laying his portrait aside on the red counterpane. Then came his watch, its time forever at seven; this too she gripped with quiet determination, studying it for long moments before setting it on the bed. The gold chain that held her wedding ring came next, Nell placing a tender kiss on the grubby little scrap of baby ribbon, before hanging the chain once more around her neck. Finally, the letters. Repositioning herself on the bed, her back supported by the wall, Nell undid the ribbon that bound them, then proceeded to take each from its envelope and to read every single line, though she knew most of them off by heart. It hurt. And she cried. And at the bottom of the box was a gaping maw of emptiness, which was how she herself felt – as if someone had taken a large pair of shears and hacked her heart from her breast.

Did she feel better for putting herself through this? Not better, no. Nor had she gained any form of comfort, nor would she whilst her son remained lost. But at least she *had* been able to face them, and to remember that only because of the blackout could one truly appreciate the stars.

Eventually re-tying the ribbon around the letters, she began to return everything to the box, including the chain and its ring. But on picking up the watch she noticed that the metal was not cold, but warm, as if it had come straight from Billy's wrist. Overwhelmed by loss, she clutched the timepiece in her fist, gripped it fervently to her breast and closed her eyes, spilling more tears, wondering what kind of a God would take a young father before he had held his son – or even known of his presence – praying with all her might that there truly was a heaven, and that all this hideous violence was for a greater cause – begging for a sign that she would be reunited with her son some day, no matter how long her wait. Please, *please*, yearned Nell with every cell of her being, if I could just know that William was safe, that he'll live a happy life, to be an old man with grandchildren, that I'll get to see him again someday, then I could carry on. I promise I would. It's just this uncertainty, this bloody awful feeling of hopelessness that I can't bear . . .

With a final, shuddering sigh, she opened her eyes, still gripping the watch. Then, unfurling her palm, she was to catch her breath. The hard metal had left an imprint, but she felt no pain, and her eyes were not on this but on the round white face. The hand that measured the seconds had begun to mark time.

PART 2

9

'Come to the window, Nurse!' commanded Sister, just after twelve on VJ night. 'And listen to the bells!'

And admittedly, it had been uplifting to witness that glorious clamour from the Minster, and from churches all over the city – as indeed it had following Victory in Europe, the patriotic celebration that went on for days, and the relief that there would be no more bombs, no more killing, that this hellish time was finally over.

But what now? The enemy's defeat brought no superabundance of food to a famished nation; the city was no less drab and demolished under its swathes of Union Jacks. A year down the line, and there was no tangible evidence of improvement, other than the victorious hordes of warriors returning home in their demob suits; the lucky ones, that was. On the contrary, things had become a good deal worse, for they were now having to ration that most staple of food: their daily bread. Some days Nell would not get to taste it at all, her entire diet seeming to consist of lentils, herrings, oatmeal and suet. Added to which there was still no butter, no meat, no sugar, no Billy, no William . . . just a painful sense of waiting for a life that would not return.

But Nell had vowed that never again would she allow herself to surrender to depression. She would strive to live a useful life, and be content with the sign that had been channelled via Billy's watch: that she would hold their son again one day. She held this to be true. The watch had ticked for only eight seconds, no matter how excitedly she might have shaken it, but it was enough to ignite the spark of hope that would light a path through the rest of her life.

And when all was said and done, what had been her own suffering when compared to others? Those poor skeletal wretches in the concentration camps, the ones she had been reading about for years in the newspapers. Only upon liberation had she seen the true evil of the Nazi doctrine exposed through cinema newsreels. Unable to fathom such depravity, Nell had found it too unbearable to watch, might have dismissed it as sensationalism had she not witnessed the evidence of such wickedness pass through her own neat rows of beds – not that of the Germans this time, but of the Japanese. To see one's own brave soldiers reduced to bags of bones, jaundiced of skin, sunken of eye, to hear and read the tales of torture, beheadings, atrocities – Nell's fury was of such atomic proportions as the bombs that had done for the Japs. No matter how ghastly the suffering to innocent children, to whom her heart cried out, those devils had had to be stopped. And now they were, leaving Nell and others like her to try and pick up the pieces.

Elsewhere, women in other walks of service exchanged their uniforms for aprons, some forced to relinquish jobs they had come to cherish, in order that men might work. A lot were disgruntled, others quite glad of the chance to be housewives again, at least those lucky enough to have a roof over their head – still, on that score, the urgent need of housing in York was rapidly being addressed, asbestos prefabs erected at record speed in every available space.

For Nell, though, little would change, nor for her friend Beata, except perhaps in titular regard, their experience accrued during the war, plus their valuable contribution, entitling them to be listed on an official roll. Though pleased to be so recognised, both held the wry belief that this would make not one iota of difference, either to their state-registered colleagues, who would always view them as poor relations, or to their own technique. In whatever regard, Nell was content to remain here at the Infirmary, for what other purpose did life hold than to devote herself to the care of others? She would never marry. Many colleagues did, however, and she was happy for them, even the lazy Avril Joyson, who was set to wed an RAF chap she had previously nursed on her ward. Obviously he was fitter now, and able to provide for her, hence she would be resigning her post.

There had been another marriage in the Melody household too – now back to its full complement since the men had come home from the war – and Nell had lately been introduced to Beata's brother Joe, finding him a similarly warm and down-to-earth character as his sisters. Yet the meeting had not been without tension, primarily due to his choice of wife. Having fallen in love with the flaxen-haired Grette, Corporal Joe Kilmaster had been permitted to marry her and bring her to England. The young frau had earned a cool reception from some neighbours, and Nell too felt the hairs of her scalp bristle upon being obliged to shake the hand of a former enemy. But with Grette receiving the seal of approval from Beata and her sisters, what right did Nell have to say who they could or could not have in their home, and she kept her true feelings locked in her breast. Besides, there were others to get to know, with whom she would have closer contact.

A new staff nurse was due to arrive on her ward – not new to the Infirmary, for she had started on day shifts three weeks ago, but new to Nell, who had not yet encountered her personally. However, she had heard the newcomer's reputation, which had been doing the rounds within days of her arrival. Word had it that nurses were now refusing to work with her.

'That's why I've put her on nights,' explained Sister Barber one evening as their paths coincided at handover. 'So she can do less harm.'

Nell looked incommoded. 'Is she really that bad?'

Even though the two of them were alone, Sister Barber attempted to be diplomatic in describing the newcomer, as she herself prepared to go home. 'She's a bit . . . how can I put this? Oh well, you'll be able to form an opinion for yourself shortly. At least you will if she remembers what time she's meant to start.' Here the sister stole a quick look at her watch, then gave firm instruction to Nell. 'When she does arrive, you must allow her to think she's in charge, without letting her poison anybody. Make her give you the keys to the medicine cabinet.'

'Sister, how can I do that when she's above me in rank?' protested Nell, her brown eyes wide.

Sister Barber shook her head with a look of resignation as she made to depart. 'You'll just have to somehow. You're one of my best nurses, Spotty, I'm trusting you not to let her kill anyone.' And she left her youngest member of staff to mull over this dubious honour.

Half flattered, half in awe of this responsibility, Nell sighed to herself. Then, after liaising with the night sister, who afterwards decamped to the other end of the hospital and would not expect to be bothered for the rest of the shift, she strode purposely back along the corridor, to see if Staff Nurse Cloughton had arrived yet. Finally, she was to come upon her, at least Nell presumed it was she, for though the figure in Sister Barber's office had her back turned, she was wearing the relevant uniform. Disallowing others' judgement to cloud hers, Nell put on a smile and approached from behind, to politely introduce herself. But when the face turned around, her heart sank. The dull expression could have belonged not to a professional, but to one of the inmates – why, there was more intelligence to be read on Cissie Flowerdew's face. Vacuous or no, it smiled at Nell, who sought to retain her friendly persona and to take an interest in the one she would be working with.

'So, which hospital did you work at before, Staff?' she asked brightly, collecting all that would be necessary for their rounds.

'Oh, you wouldn't know it,' came the vague reply. 'It was in Malta.'

Nell maintained her look of interest, but the other's mind had apparently wandered.

'Is there a clock on the ward?'

Nell was nonplussed. 'Er, no, there isn't actually . . .'

'Best take this then,' decided Staff Nurse Cloughton, and reached for the clock on Sister's desk. 'It's got a minute hand on it.'

Noting that her superior wore no watch, and seemed intent on using the cumbersome clock to take pulses, Nell realised to her horror what she was up against. And only minutes into their twelve-hour shift, as the pair embarked on the ward to take temperatures and blood pressures, she decided that whatever rumour had been put about, it had surely been understatement: the staff nurse could justly be described as retarded.

How on earth had she passed written exams? Nell asked herself, watching Cloughton hawk the clock from bed to bed, and frown over each patient's notes as she struggled to decipher them. How had she passed any form of exam, come to that? Surely she must have friends in high places for her to be on the register – and certainly it was an aberration on Matron's part for hiring her. But Nell reminded herself that this was none of her affair. Her task was to prevent any of her charges coming to harm – which seemed highly likely if she did not take precautionary measures.

So, recalling Sister's instruction, she asked respectfully, 'Would you like me to read out the notes to you, Staff, so that you're free to get on with the more important business?'

The lacklustre eyes were slow to come up from the page, the lips silently mouthing the words like an infant in class. C-a-t, thought Nell, itching to get her hands on not just the notes, but the keys to the medicine cupboard. Staff's face had barely altered, but it was clear she was pleased, for she handed over the records without quibble.

It was a mean feat on Nell's part, affecting to follow the other's orders whilst remaining close enough to keep watch, and lending helpful pointers along the way. Even so, progress was incredibly slow, much slower in fact than if Nell had been there by herself, and, fearing they would never get the patients settled down for the night, she sought to bolster the other's ego. 'With all you've done, you must be ready for a cup of tea by now, Staff. Shall I make you one? Then perhaps you'd like me to attend the medicines, so you can get on with your reports . . .'

The latter suggestion was issued in the full expectation of being rebuffed. But with barely a trace of animation, Staff Nurse Cloughton muttered, 'Go on then, thanks. I'll carry on till you get back . . .'

Hoping that staff would not cause too much damage in the short while it would take to fetch a cup of tea, Nell hared off.

And, thankfully, when she returned, the exceedingly slow nurse had only got round another few beds.

'I've put your tea in the office, Staff,' Nell informed her with an ingratiating smile. 'I'll finish off here for you – if you tell me what to do.' Let her think she's boss, Sister had said.

Instructing Nell on which patient to handle next, and what measures needed to be taken, Staff Nurse Cloughton ended with the information that, 'I've just given Constance Ward her mistalber.'

Alarmed for her personal favourite, Nell turned away and discreetly dipped into the notes to check, and saw to her relief that this was the correct instruction, by which time her senior was already making for the office.

'Er, I'll need the keys, Staff!' Forced to remind the other of her offer to do the medicines, Nell took possession of them with a great sense of relief. And, checking periodically on Staff's whereabouts, she was to continue on her rounds. At any other time she would have been furious upon noticing that the only other nurse on the ward was already drowsing, and barely two hours into her shift. But upon catching sight of Staff's mouth agape, Nell's mood was considerably lifted at being allowed to attend her patients without having to watch her too – might even be able to snatch a cup of tea herself if her senior were to remain comatose – but for now there was much more to do.

In the course of doing the rounds of the three-score beds, the need arose for another patient to receive an aperient, and with the staff nurse preoccupied, Nell went along to the cupboard to fetch this. Seeing no mistalber on the shelf, she was about to go and find a new batch, but at that point her eyes fell on the bottles of diluted Dettol, and her heart missed a beat. They looked exactly the same as mistalber – but, surely, *surely* a registered nurse could not have been so careless? Hand over mouth, she dithered between waking Staff and so ruining the rest of the night for herself, or taking the gamble that Connie had been purged with disinfectant.

A moment's quick thought told her there was another way to find out. Hurrying now to seek out the empty medicine glasses that staff might have used, and which were yet to be washed, Nell sniffed each of them, and on the last her fears were confirmed. It had contained Dettol.

Hovering by Connie's bedside, Nell anguished over what to do. The poor little dear looked so peaceful, it would be cruel to wake her, and even more cruel to cart her away on a trolley to have her stomach pumped. Concerned as she was, she decided to wait and see. To her knowledge, no one had ever imbibed Dettol before; and if it were poisonous, they would know soon enough anyway.

Shaking her head in despair, as much for her own laxity in allowing one of her charges to be harmed as for the staff nurse's error, she was to return many times to Connie's bedside throughout the night, checking her breathing, her colour, her pulse. In the meantime she felt herself become a nervous wreck, unable to decide whether the nonarrival of vomiting was a good sign or bad, her ordeal made worse when Staff Nurse Cloughton suddenly jerked awake and proceeded to travel the ward, making adjustments to certain beds.

In shadowing her, Nell saw to her horror that those who had been propped up on pillows, for very good reason, had now been laid flat. She hurried to intervene. 'These are all coronary patients, Staff,' she murmured hastily.

'Yes, they should be made more comfortable,' said the dolt.

'But they have to sit up – Doctor's instructions,' added Nell as a precaution, and only by this means did she persuade the staff nurse to her point of view, and haul the elderly patients back into position.

Even with this disaster avoided, Staff Nurse Cloughton remained at large, compelling her so-called underling to follow her about for the rest of the very long shift.

The tension of this displaying itself in her aching shoulders, Nell would have loved to have massaged them, but dared not take her eyes off Staff for a moment, in total quandary as to how to transmit all this to Sister, who had invested deep trust in her. But most worrying of all was that poor Connie might have suffered damage.

She was therefore much relieved at five a.m. when she was able to rouse the victim to imbibe a dose of castor oil, either this or the Dettol having the required laxative effect, and leaving her otherwise unscathed by the events of the night.

'If only I could say the same!' she pronounced to Sister Barber, upon encountering her prior to going home. 'I feel as if I've done forty nights instead of one – I'm a shambling wreck – crikey, my back, my head! Oh, you can't inflict her on me again, Sister, I beg you. The only time she's safe is when she's asleep!'

'Well, that's easy to fix then! Stick some bromide in her tea,' advised Sister in her breezy manner, dealing Nell a kind but less than helpful pat. 'And I'll do some digging on her.'

'Well, dig deep!' pleaded Nell, as she went off home. 'Or else we'll be digging graves for all the patients she kills – that's if I don't kill her first!'

That Staff Nurse Cloughton did not kill anyone during the following nights was solely due to Nell's assiduity. But this could not go on. It was a physical impossibility to follow her about for the whole twelve hours. Complaints to Sister Barber achieved nothing, nor had her investigations yet produced any sort of result.

'You and Killie are the only ones good-natured enough to handle her,' she said, flattering Nell into maintaining her role for as long as it might take to get rid of the woman. 'If I put her back on days I'll lose all my nurses.'

'You'll lose me too,' Nell was finally to state, in a fit of despair.

And at that point Sister did give way, though only as much as to advise Nell, 'Take a holiday. A week off should help you rejuvenate, give you the energy to deal with her again. Though how the rest of us will cope with her whilst you're gone I can't begin to imagine . . .'

Nell could safely say that she did not care. Rarely having taken any time that was due to her, on this occasion she was to grab the opportunity with both hands. Driven near insane by the dilatory staff nurse, for once she was looking forward to her time away.

It was many years since she had had a proper holiday – since before the war, in fact, when her parents had taken her to Wales. She would not have been enjoying one now, but for the generosity of Beata's aunt and uncle. Having deliberately avoided her own relatives since that terrible time, for fear that any contact would disrupt her carefully maintained temperament, she could hardly impinge on their hospitality now. But the thought of being cooped up in her bare little room for a week provoked nightmares, and so she had dropped a hint to her friend, who had in turn dropped a line to an aunt and uncle in Lancashire, asking if they would consider it a cheek if Nell were to call. Far from it, they had been delighted to accommodate her, and so off she had gone. The weather turned out to be lovely, and there were places galore to walk and to climb or to splash, and with Beata's relations being such good company, before she knew it the vacation was over, and she was back at work to be greeted by an outbreak of dysentery.

Whether Staff Nurse Cloughton had anything to do with its spread was impossible to prove. Suffice to say that a whole children's ward with incontinent bowels was not the kind of welcome to raise one's spirits. Still, Nell declared, she would rather an entire fortnight of being up to her neck in diarrhoea than one hour in Staff's company, and she was very much relieved when she was paired with Beata to transport the afflicted children by ambulance to the isolation hospital up the road.

Actually, it was not the best part, for the ultimate joy was to find themselves far removed from the austere workhouse building, if not in distance then in ambience, their little patients to be housed in one of the open-fronted pavilions that were set in verdant grounds. In fact, apart from the obvious effects of the dysentery, the whole atmosphere was an extremely pleasant one.

There was little chance to enjoy it at first, with their charges so poorly, but even so, it was nice to be able to feel the fresh air whilst one was working, and to see the sky. And by the miraculous aid of antibiotics, plus diligent nursing, the children were soon well on their way to recovery, and the nurses able to chat with them.

'I remember coming to visit my mother in that bed you're in,' Nell overheard Beata tell a little boy, in an effort to coax him into accepting the drink she had brought.

'Did you, Nurse?' In spite of his debility, he showed interest. Nell, too, as she handed out drinks to others.

'Yes, and I brought her a bottle of stout, and sat here and watched her drink it, so just pretend this is stout.'

'And did it make her better, Nurse?' came the wan little voice.

'It certainly did. So, come on now, there's a good lad . . .'

'Was that true about your mother?' asked Nell hours later, when they had laboured to make all their charges comfortable, and all were settled down for what she hoped would be a peaceful night.

'Well, I made it up about it being the very bed she was in,' admitted Beata, her voice low so as not to disturb the children. 'But yes, they used to put the TB patients in here before Fairfield opened, and I did come to visit her. My God, what we would have given for penicillin in those days . . .'

Nell was eager to hear more, but there was sadness in her friend's eyes. So, much as she would have loved to sate her curiosity, she chose not to pry, and murmured agreement about this phenomenal drug, as she glanced around at those who had benefited from its influence. 'Yes, it's so wonderful to see them all so quickly recovered – though for once I'm glad we're not allowed to give injections.' It was bad enough having to hold down the screaming beneficiary, the viscosity of penicillin making it extremely painful to transfuse.

Then, after a moment, she asked, 'Did you mean what you said before, about wanting to swap places?'

'And work here?' mused Beata. 'Aye, I wouldn't mind it.'

'Mm, me too,' agreed Nell. 'Although, I'm not saying I'm unhappy where I am. Matron was right when she said the old people can be very rewarding.'

'Yes, I just love scraping somebody else's shite from under my fingernails,' agreed Beata, but her smile conveyed that she knew what her friend meant.

'It's just that after being here in these lovely working conditions,' added Nell, after she had ceased chuckling, 'seeing how the other half live, I can't say I'm looking forward to going back to those dreary wards – and I'm absolutely dreading the thought of being stuck with that ruddy Cloughton!'

But, upon their return to the Infirmary after the outbreak of dysentery had been stemmed, Nell was ecstatic to find that a stroke of luck had removed the staff nurse from her life – or at least an ambulance had, to a mental institution – following belated intervention by Matron. It transpired that the glowing references which Cloughton had brought with her from other hospitals had been granted as a means of getting rid of her. Thereto, all thoughts of leaving were banished from Nell's mind. Pleasant as her stint at the fever hospital had been, after six years she felt too much at ease here, trusted and liked by her peers and, more importantly, the patients. The only home she had, it would be imprudent to abandon it.

So contentment was restored, at least for a few weeks. Then she was to receive a devastating blow. It was not so much the series of deaths that had taken place recently that affected her, for, sad as these were, Nell had learned to switch off her emotions where the old folk were concerned, considering that she had done her utmost to make their last days restful. It was not so much the inconvenience of being dealt another surprise departure at the end of her shift either. Death was no respecter of how tired a nurse might be after caring all night for her slumbering flock, nor how problematic his visitation might be to her. But Nell could not help give a sigh as, just as she was about to snatch a much-needed cup of tea in the lull before the bedpan rush would start, she noticed that another of her old ladies had passed away, clutching a large section of dung in her fist.

Abandoning any idea of tea, Nell dealt with this in philosophical fashion, before going along to the office. The usual night sister was off sick, and others were taking it in relay to stand in. It was currently Sister Barber's turn, hence Nell allowed a little flicker of humour to play about her lips as she popped her head in to enquire:

'What have you put in your report about Mrs Casey?'

Somewhat engrossed, Sister Barber looked up from her desk. 'I've written "comfortable".'

Nell gave a straight-faced nod. 'She is comfortable. She's dead.' Laughingly informing Sister as to the circumstances, she concluded, 'I don't know how long she'd been holding it, but it took the very devil to prise it out.'

Sister Barber shared her weary amusement, then said they had better organise the old lady's removal. 'But whilst I've got you here, I'd better tell you . . .' The way she bit her lip told Nell that she had been putting this off. 'I'll be leaving at the end of the month.'

'Oh no! You can't mean it . . .' Nell's dismay was genuine. After so many years together, she would miss her. Plus, this was the kind of job where one needed to like and trust one's colleagues. 'Gosh, I will be sorry to lose you.'

Sister Barber showed equal regret. 'I'll be sad to go too. But I don't care for the sound of this new National Health Service they're proposing, I think there'll be a lot of rigmarole once it's set in motion –'

'But surely it's marvellous for everyone to have free treatment and medicine?' Nell could not help contradicting, having known Sister long enough to risk such a liberty.

'We'll get all sorts of improvements to the hospital, not just to benefit us, of course, but primarily our patients.'

'That part of it is extremely good, yes,' agreed Sister Barber, her tone firm, whilst her face retained a look of caution. 'But I think there'll be far too much interference from the bureaucrats. Plus, my husband's fed up of us hardly ever seeing each other, so we decided this is as good an opportunity as any to make our little ambition a reality. We're going to give up the pub and set up our own nursing home.'

In spite of her own disappointment, Nell saluted her. 'It's a brave step.'

Sister conceded as much. 'That's why I'll need competent nurses such as yourself and Killie, ones I can trust to leave in charge. It's shameful to poach you from Matron, but if you should feel like a change . . .' She cocked her head.

Nell's lips parted, half of her flattered at being considered suitable for such a responsible role, but the other half of her feeling it would be a wrench to leave. It was certainly tempting from one aspect, for Sister's departure would mean having to acclimatise herself to the idiosyncrasies of a new superior. Had Staff Nurse Cloughton still been a menace, she might have jumped at this chance to get away, but things were working smoothly again now, and Nell had grown too fond of many of the residents not to include them in her decision. 'Thank you very much for the offer, Sister. I'll certainly consider it –'

'– And then forget all about me.' The pretty freckled face was roguish.

'The one who taught me all I know? Certainly not!' Nell grinned back at her.

'I haven't even broken the news to Matron yet,' admitted the other. 'So don't say a word.'

Nell was honoured to have been forewarned. 'Of course not. But we'll certainly miss you anyway,' she added warmly. 'I mean it – and good luck.'

'I haven't gone yet! And neither have you.' With a tart expression, but fondness in her sharp blue eyes, Sister rose as if meaning business. 'So, as there's no one else here, we'd better go and sort out Mrs Casey, the poor old girl. Then you can fetch us both a cup of tea, and we can go through these reports together – so's you can advise me of any other calamity that needs to go in them.'

The wards were to feel rather empty after Sister Barber had gone. Her replacement was quite pleasant, but totally lacking a sense of humour, which in this line of work was cardinal. Before the leaves had even begun to turn, both Nell and Beata were regretting their decision to remain, and so took to discussing their options. As good as it would be to work for Sister Barber, both agreed that there would be better prospects of a pension elsewhere. Consequently, both were to acquire positions at the fever hospital, and then to hand in their notice.

Ever the lady, Matron Fosdyke spoke of her regret in accepting their resignations, especially after sharing with them so many crises during those war years. But she also voiced understanding of their desire for a fresh start, and wished them all best wishes in their new role. 'And there will always be a place here, should ever you feel the need to return.'

Taking leave of Matron was one thing; explaining to Connie and Cissie was another matter, but Nell promised to come and visit both whenever she had a day off. Then, bearing gifts, and the hard part behind them, Nell and her friend ventured forth to their new workplace.

10

'Welcome to the home for overworked nurses,' was the greeting, upon them entering the doors of the City Fever Hospital. But Nell and Beata laughed, and said their colleagues did not know what work was.

This was true, for though there were acute and geriatric cases there, there were not nearly so many, and apart from the times when there was a polio epidemic, or other seasonal outbreaks, the work on the fever wards was much less gruelling, with no lengthy medicine rounds to put up with. And best of all was the chance to vary shifts in the main building with ones in the open-fronted pavilions in the grounds. Of course, there were difficult aspects to face, one being the hostility of parents when arriving in an ambulance to take their child away – Nell knew well enough how harrowing such a parting was – but somehow she was able to placate them by vowing to do all that she could to make their child well, and, with her gentle smile, to convince them to trust her. In addition, there was the fear that she herself could fall prey to contagion. But one was willing to tempt fortune in return for a happier workplace, and to put up with the regulation of changing gowns whenever one left the infectious wards, for the great reward of seeing a child recover after one had properly nursed them.

And when a child did not recover, well, it was all extremely sad, of course, but over the years Nell had learned not to hijack the next-of-kins' grief, and how to manage her own emotions. Ever in mind was the fact that this was not her child, and any tears she might shed were in the privacy of home.

Both night and day sisters were lovely to work with, the elderly Sister Fawdington being exceptionally polite, and never abusing her authority by treating them as personal servants, always begging a cup of tea rather than demanding it. It was a pleasure to serve her. She was very kind to the patients too, and Nell knew she must have stayed up for hours knitting all the little gifts for those who were forced to spend Christmas in hospital. The festive season was particularly touching in there, the nurses coming round with lanterns and singing carols, and the wards gaily decorated. From the top to the bottom, everyone was good to work with, the only downside being the terrible cook. But, to be fair, ingredients were still few.

Other than this, life was brighter than it had been for some time. At least, inside the hospital. In the outside world things were to remain extremely dire: on top of severe frost, the New Year swept in with a transport strike, an upshot of this being more shortage of coal and food than ever, and the additional hardship of a reduction in the meat ration.

But Nell had resolved never again to be cowed by such trivia. 'How can you reduce nothing?' she roared with laughter at those colleagues who grumbled. 'I haven't had meat in years! When it's a choice between Dobbin or Moby Dick, I think I'll stick to lentils.'

'Fine chance of anything else with this cook of ours,' snorted Jean Wintringham, to whom Nell had taken very quickly, and who was wading her way through another unpalatable bowl of such broth that January morning. 'I wonder if there'll be any improvement when they nationalise us?' A moment was given over to discussing the nationalisation programme, which the government seemed so set on, and the medical profession so against.

But again Nell countered with humour. 'I doubt it'll make a ha'porth of difference to us nurses, they'll still work us like donkeys. We should be issued with nosebags instead of this crockery.' She wrapped her hands around her cup, pleased for once to be in the main block instead of those frost-encrusted pavilions outside.

Jean recalled something then. 'Eh, Spotty, did I tell you about that lovely wooden farmyard set I got for our Tony?'

'Ooh no!' Nell showed immediate interest, for toys were in very short supply. 'Where on earth did you get that?'

'There was a knock on the door the other day,' told Jean, 'and there's this German POW standing there with this lovely thing he'd carved – beautiful it is, all the little animals with moving legs and what-not. A bit steep at six bob, mindst –'

'You mean to say you *bought* it?' Nell could hardly believe her ears. 'After those thugs killed your husband?'

Jean blushed a little, but explained, 'Well, where else would I get such a thing? I mean, you wouldn't see my lad go without on his birthday, would you? He's suffered as much as the rest of us – you'd do the same if you were a mother.'

Would I? thought Nell, who thought it appalling that former enemies were still in the country and allowed to pedal their wares. Before she could issue an answer, though, Beata gave warning that Sister was coming, and all began to rise.

But Sister Fawdington bade them to remain seated. 'Do excuse me from barging in on you like this, my dears, but I just thought I should let you know that a replacement has at last been found.' She had been overdue to retire for some weeks. 'So I shall probably be leaving tomorrow evening.'

They voiced their sorrow at seeing her go, and waited for her to tell them about the new appointment.

'Her name is Sister Pike, and she'll be starting tomorrow

morning. I'm not acquainted with her myself, but she is by all accounts a very good nurse, and was highly decorated for her services during the war in India.'

'I wish I was in India,' sighed Nell, tossing a worried glance from the window at a sky that held threat.

'You're joking, dear, surely?' enquired Sister, prompting a chuckle from Nell at the silliness of her remark, and brief conversation on the bloodletting that was going on there – and in numerous other countries for that matter.

'No, I only meant on the weather front. There looks to be a ton of snow up there, just waiting to drop on me the moment I set foot outside.'

'I reckon it's too cold to snow,' said Wintringham.

'Well, I don't think I'll hang around to find out.' Nell took decisive action, and, excusing herself to the sister, jumped up and went to put on her coat. 'See you tonight, ladies!'

The blast was icy as she exited the outer door of the main building, and sliced her to the bone as she galloped home through the dark morning. As predicted, snow had already begun to flutter down, and she was glad to be almost there – though it was small comfort to arrive, for her room was not much warmer than outside.

A thick layer of frost had formed an exquisite pattern on her window, making it impossible to see out, and her breath remained white on the air. Meagre warmth though her clothes might afford, she was reluctant to exchange them for an even thinner nightdress, nor even to take off her coat for now, as she hurried to ignite the two gas rings. Shaking the kettle to check its contents, she heard the chinking of ice. Deciding this would melt, she placed it on one of the rings, then went to light a fire, and afterwards hovered about whilst waiting for these sources to deliver warmth. Last night she had tipped her last bit of milk powder into a jug and mixed it with water in readiness for the morn. The sharp particles of ice that were now encrusting its surface were hardly commensurate to a hot beverage, and so when the kettle boiled Nell took her tea black, then crouched over the hearth, where the house brick that she used to warm her bed had already been put by – though at this rate both she and the brick would take a long time to heat through.

When it was hot, though not nearly hot enough, she wrapped it in newspaper and set it between the freezing cold sheets. Then it was back to the fire for Nell, where she pulled the grips from her hair and let it tumble around her ears and neck for extra warmth. The frost took an age before its feathers and ferns even began to melt around the edges. Once it had, with quick, jerky movements she stripped off her coat, and much of the rest, apart from underwear and socks, which were to stay under her nightdress. She moved the brick to the foot of the mattress, spread her coat over the bed, which was already piled with blankets, and laid her shivering carcass upon the small patch of warmth. With the rest of the sheets still icy, she scrunched her body into a ball, occasionally pumping her legs up and down in an effort to generate more heat. And, somehow, she managed to sleep.

By the time she awoke five hours later the fire was almost out, though just how wintry it was, she had yet to discover. Upon opening the outer door she was at once lashed by a blizzard that had, whilst she slept, already piled three foot of snow upon the pavements. One thing for sure, she could not endure such terrible conditions in these flimsy shoes. Slamming the door against the flurry of flakes, and leaving some to melt in the hall, she hared along it to knock on the landlady's door.

'I'm so sorry to bother you, Mrs Connell, but have you such a thing as a spare pair of wellies – or anything, actually, so's I can get to work?'

The middle-aged woman was clad in several layers,

besides clutching a heavy shawl around her, and was obviously feeling the nip herself, hence her spontaneous offer. 'Aye! You can borrow our Rodney's. I never threw anything away after he died. You've got big feet, haven't you . . .'

Nell overlooked the insult with a smile. 'Oh, are you sure?'

'Well, he's not going to want them, is he?' sighed Mrs Connell, looking freshly bereaved over her fallen son as she turned away. 'Hang on, I'll get 'em.'

The wellingtons were duly handed to Nell, along with some thick socks to go underneath, and a khaki scarf.

'We're not allowed to wear scarves with uniform,' began Nell, removing her shoes to hop into the socks. Then she snatched the item gratefully. 'Oh blow it! I'd rather get a rocketing than freeze to death.'

And once her wellingtons were on, she wound the scarf around her head and neck, replaced her brimmed felt hat on top, put her shoes in a bag, and thanked Mrs Connell profusely before hurrying back to the outer door.

Here, though, her rush was to end, for with the thick layer of snow and the continuing blizzard totally obscuring many landmarks, it was difficult to tell even where the kerb was in this swirling, dizzying world. Her workplace was set at a farther distance from her residence now, perhaps a mile or so, which had not caused much effort in the summer. Today, it might have been five hundred miles, as she trudged her way through that pristine nightmare, ironically to arrive dripping with perspiration at having so struggled.

'Too cold to snow!' With mockery in her eyes, she berated Jean Wintringham, who was already in the nurses' room, trying to warm herself through as Nell entered in a trail of melting flakes. 'Don't ever apply to be a weather forecaster, Wince.'

She was not to arrive last by any means, for it was another fifteen minutes before Beata stumbled in to join those who hugged the radiators. Now almost warmed up – though her soles felt a great deal thinner having removed the socks – Nell chuckled affectionately at the sight of her friend coated from head to foot in snow, and went to cup her cheeks. 'If it isn't Nanook of the North! You poor thing, how's your frozen undercarriage – oh, lucky you, wearing trousers!'

Too frozen to laugh in return, a stiff-necked Beata allowed her young friend to help in the disrobement of her outer gear. 'I don't know about wearing them, they've nearly been round me ankles three times! They're our Joe's old ones, he lent me them to keep warm. Blasted things, they're more trouble than they're worth. I've worked up a lather just trying to hang on to them.' With Nell's help, having now managed to peel off the trousers, she threw them aside.

Nell acted as retriever. 'You're going to need them when it's time to leave.'

'Nay I won't,' answered Beata, pressing her stocky frame against a radiator. 'We'll all need a snow plough. They say there's plenty more to come. Have 'em if you want. They're too long for my little legs.'

'Cut them down, then,' advocated Nell, reluctant to deprive her friend, though coveting them really, which Beata was quick to spot.

'I'm not the right shape for breeches,' she insisted to her friend. 'Go on, you have 'em.'

And so Nell gladly accepted, folding the trousers into her locker for the journey home.

Preceding this, though, there was a twelve-hour shift for Nell, throughout its entirety the snow continuing to swirl outside. Then, in the morning, dinner-cum-breakfast to be shared with nurses Kilmaster and Wintringham, during which they were to talk about the new sister, asking if anyone had seen her. No one had.

However, it transpired that there was another new face

to greet, when a young man bounced into the dining room, his effervescent smile a beacon of light. 'Hell's bells, it's a lot warmer in here than out there!' He swept off his hat to reveal floppy dark hair, and loosened his scarf before addressing the nurses. 'Good morning all! I'm Doctor Barker.' But with the reception less than enthusiastic, he faltered slightly. 'I'm here to liaise with Doctor Parrish . . . it's my first day, got a bit lost.'

'You're keen,' Nell observed to the rather bumptious individual, with only half an eye on her as she picked at her unpalatable meal of herring and oatmeal. 'He won't be here for a good hour.' Then, not wanting to give the impression that she and the others were hostile, she tilted her gentle smile up at him and explained, 'You'll have to forgive us, we're just off night shift. You must be nervous enough about meeting your superior without our grumpy mugs.'

But Doctor Barker did not seem unduly nervous, in fact he seemed full of himself as he threw his hat on a table and rubbed his hands upon viewing the nurses' full bowls. 'My, you live like fighting cocks!'

Worn out, but still managing to conjure a jocund retort, Beata begged to differ. 'You what? I've had enough fish to give me the brains to do your job, and enough lentils to blow the top off the Minster.' Nell and the other nurse added their voices, whilst the young doctor merely laughed.

'I suppose it must seem funny having dinner when you should be having breakfast,' he conceded, obviously happy to hang around the young women.

'What I'd give for a thick slice of white bread, plastered with butter,' complained Nurse Wintringham. 'Any bread at all, come to that.'

'Me too,' agreed Doctor Barker. Then he focused his interested gaze on the plate that sat on a counter. 'Is that a suet pudding? Wouldn't mind a helping of that to warm me up, if there's one going.'

'If you can find yourself a machete and hack through it, you're welcome to a slice,' invited Nell, hiding a glimmer as the young doctor advanced eagerly upon it with a knife.

'Ye gods – it's like the Rock of Gibraltar!' Thwarted in his attempt to cut through the pudding, he turned to view them in amazement.

The nurses guffawed. 'Why do you think it's sitting all forlorn down there?' demanded a crinkly-eyed Beata. 'If I ate that I'd never be able to walk home.'

Still smiling, she then proceeded to relay a series of cautionary tales about the hopeless cook, during which Nell assumed a look of impishness and momentarily disappeared.

'What's she up to?' Nurse Wintringham wondered laughingly to the others.

They were to chat for a while until Nell scuttled back in, her hands crammed full and her face the incarnation of glee. Proceeding to drape cotton wool around the edges of the pudding to resemble waves, she then inserted a series of matchsticks all over it, so that now it looked like a mine bobbing out of the sea. But her *pìece de résistance* came in the handwritten label propped against it: *We Dive at Dawn*.

Doctor and nurses fell about cackling, others overhearing and coming to see what all the fun was about, which was most inopportune, for one of them happened to be the new sister.

For a second they did not see her, all still poking fun at the object, until one by one they became aware of an icy emanation. Then, as each turned to meet the robust figure in the dark blue uniform, whose attitude was as brittle as her starched white apron, and whose face was like a speckled egg – and a hard-boiled egg at that – their eyes quickly lowered in respect, and they fell away to expose the three who were still tittering.

Finally, Nell, Beata and the young doctor twirled around

too, immediately losing their grins, for Sister Pike's dark eyes held not the least spangle of fun, as she glared at the vandalised pudding and enquired:

'Who is the architect of this?'

'I'm sorry, Sister, it was me.' The traces of a smile upon her gentle face, Nell was quick to assume blame, as others around her expediently withdrew.

'I fail to see the hilarity of such behaviour! Not only do you insult the cook, who has gone to extreme lengths to cater for you in these dire times, but you show not the slightest regard for the fact that your childish antics have made it inedible for anyone else.'

The gallant Doctor Barker stepped in. 'With respect, Sister, it was inedible befo—'

'And *with respect*, Doctor!' interrupted the sister. 'I would be obliged if you would leave the discipline of the nursing staff to me. You must have patients to see, let us not delay you.'

With an apologetic look, both for the sister and the nurses, he backed from the room, hat in hand.

Sister hardly noticed him leave, concentrating on those at the centre of the disturbance. 'What are your names?' When the subdued trio provided them, the speaker gave hers. 'I am Sister Pike. Not the most auspicious of introductions, is it?'

'No, Sister,' they mumbled.

'As for you, Nurse Spottiswood!' The Pike regarded Nell as if she were a fluffy duckling to be devoured. 'I should have assumed the last eight years of privation would have taught you the evils of wasting food, but it seems this is not so. Report yourself to Matron, immediately! The rest of you, get out!'

Made to look silly and inexperienced, as if her devotion to duty counted for nought, a jaded Nell consigned herself to Matron's office, to be given a rare dressing-down. Feeling that it had all been blown out of proportion, she was afterwards on her way to put on her outdoor clothes, when she was to encounter the young doctor again in one of the corridors.

This time he was wearing a white coat and a stethoscope round his neck, though in the absence of any superior he did not stand on ceremony, and exclaimed impulsively to the nurse, 'I'm so sorry for my part in your downfall! Were you hauled over the coals? If I hadn't drawn attention to the pudding . . .'

'Oh, don't give it another thought.' Nell's eyes and voice forgave him, though more through a weariness to have this over and done with than due to any of the sexual attraction she saw in his own eyes.

'So how long have you had to put up with that?'

'The cooking? Since I came here last autumn.'

He laughed and leaned an elbow against the wall, his mood flirtatious. 'You deserve the Victoria Cross! Actually, I meant how long have you had to put up with Sister. Gosh, she's a tartar, isn't she?'

'Oh, she only started this morning,' said Nell.

'Good grief, if that's what she's like on her first day . . .' breathed the doctor, shaking his head, and adding that he found her most intimidating too, whilst his eyes examined the attractive dark-haired nurse.

Nell smiled, but looked about to move on, saying she must lay her head down.

'Hang on!' He put out a hand to delay her. 'I'm afraid I can't invest you with the Victoria Cross, but could I reward you instead with a night out dancing?'

She turned him down with a flat, 'No, thank you. Nothing personal. It's just that I lost someone very dear in the war.'

Her meaning was unmistakable. The doctor's amiable nod of acknowledgement told her she had no need to explain, though Nell thought she might have been a little too blunt in her rebuff. 'Besides, I'm feeling decidedly shabby,' she added, looking down at her nursing shoes, which were beyond redemption. She had managed to mend them until now, but the uppers had begun to split. With a decent pair costing more than three weeks' wages, and most of the latter being taken in rent and coal, this meant there was no food on the shelf at home, and when she went to bed shortly it would be to remain there all day, no food to pass her lips until she returned here this evening.

She did not tell the doctor this, though, as, with a cordial goodbye, she went on her way.

Whether she told him or no, he would obviously not have been concerned, for when she glanced over her shoulder he was already flirting with another. Content for him to do so, Nell formed a quirk of her lips, then gave him not another thought as she went to don her armour against the freezing waste outside.

Joe's trousers were much darned and patched on the buttocks, and she fancied she must depict herself as an old tramp, what with these, along with her muffled throat and mouth, the long woollen socks and the over-large Wellingtons. But she was very glad of anything to keep out the cold, as she lurched through the even thicker layer of snow – so deep now that in parts it came over the top of her boots – and was even gladder when Mrs Connell shouted upon hearing her climb the stairs:

'I've lit a fire for you!'

'Oh, God bless you, how thoughtful,' smiled Nell.

But no. 'Well, I didn't want you stoking it halfway up the chimney,' confessed her landlady. 'You never know how long it'll have to last with this strike business.'

Replying glumly that this was true, a frozen Nell finally stumped up the rest of the stairs and into her room.

The contents of the grate turned out to be more than adequate to warm this small space. Still panting, Nell peeled off her garments one by one, hung her coat on a hook, with a newspaper underneath to catch the melting snow, then stood her wellingtons on this same piece of paper, before making a cup of tea and parking herself by the fire. Having worked up quite a lather in ploughing her furrow, it was only her extremities that were really cold, these throbbing as they thawed too swiftly, and her nose beginning to stream. She was to remain there for a while with her cup of tea, staring into the flames whilst awaiting the pre-heated brick to warm her bed. Then, in a split second she was elevated to another place, for the heat of the fire, and of her own body, had begun to entice a familiar scent from the trousers she wore. The scent of a man. Allowing herself a moment of nostalgia over Bill, Nell hunched over and stroked the warm fabric that clothed her calf, her face adopting a sad little smile as she recalled their brief and lovely time together. Still thinking of him, she tossed back her tea and went to check on her bed. Then she pulled out her hairgrips, rapidly undressed, and jumped between the sheets, shivering and huddling up until she felt warm.

Briefly, before she fell asleep, Nell hoped that this fall of snow would quickly thaw, as had the last. Little was she or any of her countrymen to guess that they faced the coldest winter of the century.

11

Once that first blizzard had ceased, even with such difficulty in getting to work, the terrible weather was merely a talking point at first, the dirty old city looking rather beautiful in its pristine cloak, its rivers frozen solid for people to lark upon, and sledges launched down the banks of the city walls. But with more violent storms on its tail, and snow continuing to pile up day after day, the foot-long icicles quickly began to lose their novelty. Power cuts were to follow. No coal, no industry. Within a week, the whole country had ground to a halt.

Nell was almost at her wits' end as to how to maintain warmth, the poverty of her room being eminently noticeable after coming from the centrally heated hospital.

'If only I could get rid of that bloody draught that whistles under my door,' she complained to Beata, as both rugged up at the end of another shift, yet again to brave the icy world. 'At least I could keep some of the warmth in. I've tried rolled-up newspaper, but it's not pliable enough. I'd make a sausage out of old rags, *if* I wasn't reduced to wearing them.' Every single item of clothing was already being utilised, and still this was inadequate.

'See me tomorrow,' murmured Beata intriguingly. 'I might have something for you.'

'Something else? Why, you've been generous enough

already . . .' But Nell was fascinated enough to see what it might be.

Until then, there was another glissade to endure.

But on the following shift, Beata was to sidle up to her and hand over the promised item, wrapped in brown paper. 'There you are! Don't say I never give you owt.'

Upon unwrapping the present, Nell's eyes glistened with irony. 'Thank you very much. I'm sure a green elephant will prove invaluable.' Grinning widely, she examined the large stuffed toy.

Beata clicked her tongue at the sarcasm, then explained, 'If you unpick it, and jiggle it about a bit, it'll make a nice door rug to keep out that draught. Don't tell our Johnny, though. It came in an aid parcel from America.'

Nell made an exclamation of reluctance. 'Oh, I couldn't take a toy meant for him . . .'

'I'll have it back then,' Beata reached out.

'You bloody well won't!' Nell laughed, and hastily rewrapped the elephant, lest some one else should purloin it. 'Oh, thanks, Killie, you're so good to me – and it won't be wasted on any draught-stopper. I'll get a lovely thick pair of mittens out of that.' She sized up the elephant and exclaimed again, 'I might even get a pair for both of us! You've only got little hands.'

'Aye, and I'll bet you'll give me the pair that has the trunk attached,' joked Beata, seemingly content to have made her friend happy, as both went off to their wards.

It was good that they could laugh, for Nell doubted there would be much opportunity under Sister Pike if that first encounter was anything to go by. As yet, their working patterns had not concurred, but now, as the shifts were rotated, as was the norm, it was inevitable that they came under her regime.

Whatever the sacrifices, it would be some weeks yet before Nell could purchase those new shoes for which she had been saving. Having changed from her wellingtons into her tattered footwear, she was set to begin a new day shift when her shabby demeanour was pounced upon by Sister Pike.

'A tramp, an absolute tramp!' she lashed Nell, who was forced to hang her head and take the abuse. 'Immediately you've done backs and prepared the trolley for Doctor's rounds, you can go home and change them!'

Released to begin her duties, Nell hurried away to fetch a bowl of water with which to sponge down the first of twenty or more bedridden patients, being her usual gentle and cheerful self as she checked for pressure sores, trying to hide her underlying worry about the shoes. Perhaps Sister would have forgotten about it by the time this was done, thought Nell, powdering the patient's skin, then just as quickly she mocked herself, for Pike had obviously not forgotten their first encounter. Never having given way to the temptation of using one bowl for all – not out of fear, but conscientiousness – all the tipping out and refilling seemed to take a lot longer today, as she wondered how to tell Sister that she had no shoes to change into.

After finishing backs, she rushed off to set a trolley with all the instruments that the doctor might need for his rounds. It was then that she was pulled up and reminded of the order.

Faced with the prospect of being exposed to that inclement weather, Nell gave an apologetic but helpless shrug. 'I'm sorry, Sister, I've nothing to change into. These are my only pair. I've been saving for new ones, but –'

'I will not hear excuses! The rest of us manage to look presentable; so can you! And I refuse to have such a raga-muffin on my ward. Now go and buy some if you have to, but do not return until you are suitably attired!'

'And be quick about it!' Sister bayed in afterthought as Nell fled.

Thanking heaven that she was not working on a fever

ward, or then she would have had to change out of her uniform too, Nell put on her coat and boots, thinking better of donning her trousers, for that would surely spell trouble – but oh how the tops of her legs were to perish in that icy wind.

First she slithered home along impacted snow, all the way along Huntington Road, onwards to Monkgate, off which branched the Groves, there to collect what money and coupons she had saved, before tottering and skidding to the nearest shoe shop, which was thankfully not too much further on. It was a poor little shop, its meagre display of footwear lit by candlelight. But with her body stiff with cold, Nell was grateful of any harbour, and strung out her visit for as long as she dared in an effort to thaw her frozen marrow. When all was said and done, though, with insufficient funds, she was only able to afford a very basic pair made of stiff leather, which she knew from experience was false economy, and would render her almost crippled by the end of the day. But purchase them she must, then she began her trek along the frozen mile or more back to the hospital.

Naturally there was rebuke for the amount of time it had taken, and the threat of her wages being docked. Then, a cursory flick of the wrist from Sister Pike signified that the properly clad nurse was fit to continue with her work – though on no account was that an end to the haranguing, for within half an hour the enemy was strafing her again, this time for having the temerity to voice an opinion on one of the patients who had been admitted with enteritis.

'Sister, I'm beginning to think Mr Callow might have an intestinal blockage . . .'

'Are you a doctor?' demanded the imperious Pike. 'No! You are not even a qualified nurse. It is not your place to make diagnoses! Kindly do not overstep your limitations again!'

And Nell was forced to withdraw. But she was to remain

worried about Mr Callow, and thereafter, even with so much else to do, she was to keep a close watch on him during the following hours.

Within those hours, alas, she was to be castigated yet again by the sister, for overtaking her at speed.

'I do apologise, Sister,' said Nell, not in any way panicked, yet eager to be away with her bowl of water. 'But we've an emergenc—'

'It will be an emergency if anyone should slip on that water you are so keen to spill! Now calm down and try to adopt some degree of professionalism!'

Nell had remained calm, but it was hard not to lose her temper. 'It's Mr Callow –'

'Not him again! How many times do I have to tell you?'

Intimidated though she felt, Nell was determined her patient would receive help. 'I strongly urge you to come and see him, please, Sister.'

Sister Pike uttered a gasp. 'If you are so incompetent as to be unable to handle it. I suppose I must!' And, pacing ahead of Nell, she went along to the ward, where, when the screen was pulled aside, it was plain to see that Mr Callow was in dire straits, for he was vomiting what appeared to be excrement.

Giving a little 'Oh . . .', Sister went immediately to the telephone and informed the doctor. Alas, by the time Mr Callow was prepared to be taken to the operating theatre, he was in extremis.

'The time that was wasted in trying to convince her!' moaned Nell to her friends upon meeting them at lunchtime, though unable to stomach much food herself. 'Too busy telling me I'm not qualified – I know very well I'm not qualified, people have been throwing that at me for years, but I thought I'd served enough time by now not to be taken for an idiot!'

'You've got instinct,' said Jean Wintringham, who was state-registered herself but never a snob. 'That's something we don't all possess, and no amount of exams can supply. Just remember that when she's treating you like muck.'

'Thanks, Wince.' Nell showed deep gratitude, then her face suddenly puckered and she went off at a tangent. 'God, these shoes are absolutely killing me!' She took one off to examine her blistered heel, then twisted the leather this way and that in an attempt to soften it. 'They're so stiff, I'm sure they're made of rhinoceros hide – but shoes are one thing, patients are another! That poor man.' Her eyes brimmed with angry tears. 'I tried to tell her it was more serious than she made out. Perhaps she'll take *me* a little more seriously from now on.'

But if Nell had been expecting some sort of apology, some acknowledgement that she had been right all along, it was not to be granted. The best she received was slight lenience from Sister Pike, who chose not to pick so much fault with her during the rest of the afternoon. However, Pike was to maintain her starchy attitude, and it was a very difficult shift, without any form of camaraderie to rely on.

Limping home through yet another cascade of snow some twelve hours later, her blisters rubbed away to expose raw flesh and made even more painful by the overlarge wellingtons, and the heels of her stockings caked in dried blood, Nell tried to rally her spirits by reminding herself that Sister Barber had been similarly voracious at first. Admittedly, it was dispiriting to be treated again like a junior after so many years of experience, and yes, much of the criticism was unjust – for apart from the shoes the rest of her appearance was scrupulously clean and neat – but she must give this newcomer the benefit of the doubt. For at least Sister Pike had acted upon Mr Callow's situation once she had been apprised of the emergency. She would probably mellow in time, and besides, they would not always work together. But oh dear, Nell could not help sighing to herself, as she sank her injured feet into a bowl of hot water by the fire, the hours on day shift would seem very long indeed with no laughter to lighten them.

The next day turned out to be equally horrendous. Despite her heels being padded with sticking plasters, it was still painful to hobble about, and on top of all her normal duties – bathing patients, filling in charts, sluicing soiled linen, taking temperatures, pulses and throat swabs, testing urine, changing dressings – there was again much disparagement to bear too.

Still four hours away from the end of her shift, Nell found herself hungry for home, something she had not felt for many years, for she had always been happiest at work. She still could be, if Sister Pike were not so harsh. But then, mulled Nell, it was understandable that she would want to stamp her own mark. Whatever the reason, Nell accepted that they were going to have to work together. Seeking to motivate a better relationship, in preparation of days to follow, she limped to her superior's office, knocked, and waited for permission before entering.

'Sister, I was just going to make Nurse Kilmaster and myself a cup of tea, would you like to join us?'

But the hard-boiled face was unmoved by Nell's friendly smile, as it glanced up from the notes and announced haughtily, 'Sisters don't drink tea with nurses. Besides, if you're trying to get into my good books you're going the wrong way about it. You should try being a little more efficient for a start. You're far too keen on making cups of tea instead of looking after your patients.'

Flushing with offence, Nell dared not argue, and started to back away.

'Now you're here, what's the latest on Mr Wren?'

Nell gave a progress report on the cancer patient. 'Nurse Kilmaster's sitting with him now, sister.'

'He doesn't require *sitting* with –'

'I didn't actually mean sitting,' Nell quickly informed the pedant. 'I meant –'

‘You meant gossiping,’ said the infuriating woman.

‘No, I mean we’re rather worried about hi—’

Sister cut her off. ‘If the patient wants to chat he’s got no amount of neighbours who’ll entertain him. Your job is to attend to his physical needs. So long as all are comfortable there’s no need for any nurse to dally around the beds. I’ve also noticed that the tiles in the sluice have been neglected –’

Not by me, simmered Nell.

‘Before you even think of making yourself tea, you can both go and scour them,’ ordered Sister. And she lowered her unforgiving eyes back to her notes: an act of dismissal.

Lips compressed, Nell marched off to deliver the edict, complaining vehemently to her fellow nurse, ‘Too keen on drinking tea and gossiping indeed! I’ve been run off my feet since she arrived.’

Beata responded with her usual pragmatism, as both limped to comply with the order. ‘We got spoiled under Sister Barber. It was always that way in the big houses, too, parlour maids didn’t drink with Cook . . .’

‘I’m unconcerned at not being allowed to drink with the bloody woman,’ hissed Nell from the side of her mouth. ‘I just don’t know how I’m going to get through this set of day shifts with such a lack of respect. Why, she’s treating us worse than prisoners of war!’

Still much aggrieved over the insult, even days later, and on top of all the others that had been hurled at her since, Nell began to doubt herself, and to think that perhaps there was some truth in what Sister Pike said. As much to seek verification as to initiate dialogue, she was to enquire of the elderly resident whose leg ulcer she was attending, ‘Do you think I’m neglectful, Mrs O’Hara?’

The owner of the liver-coloured ankle cocked her moustachioed face as if she had misheard, and said in a hoarse voice, ‘Who?’

'Me. Sister says I drink too much tea and I neglect my patients.' With firm but gentle ministrations, Nell applied the compression bandage.

'You? Never! You're a lot nicer to us than her ladyship. She's not going to drive you away, is she?' The croaky old voice sounded pessimistic.

'I love being here,' said Nell, finally elevating Mrs O'Hara's leg with a pillow. 'But she's making my life a misery.'

'Here, have one of my goodies, love.' With great deliberation, the old lady shifted her buttocks and produced a fiercely guarded bag.

'No, you shall have one of mine.' Nell was always swift to share her own ration with the patients, though not wholly out of kindness, being aware that many of the incontinent ones stashed their sweets under the bedclothes all night. 'But just wait till I've disposed of your old dressing or I'll get another telling off.'

After going to the incinerator and washing her hands, she returned with the promised bag. 'Hurry and take one before Pikey catches us.' Then, with Mrs O'Hara sucking on a pastille, she quickly handed them out to those nearby, the ones who could appreciate them anyway, all having a good moan about Sister Pike in the meantime as they dipped into Nell's bag.

'Shouldn't I get one?'

Nell swirled at the accusation from Sister Pike. 'Just going, Sis—'

'Not before you've given me a sweetie!' It was as if someone had had a word in Sister Pike's ear – as if she were a totally different person, in fact – for she was actually cheerful as she came to delve into the bag. 'Hope there's a black one – oh, good! May I have that?' And to Nell's astonished nod, she popped it into her mouth and made much of it as she went around beaming at everyone. 'Is Nurse Spottiswood treating you all well?'

Everyone sang Nell's praises, except for Mrs Dolan who uttered demented howls, but only because she had lost the power of speech.

'Good!' said Sister Pike. 'Then I can safely leave you in her competent hands.' And away she sailed, leaving Nell to gape.

Scarcely able to believe the change in her, Nell spent the rest of the day waiting for Pike to find fault. But no, she was as nice as pie. As indeed she turned out to be the day after that too.

Then, lo and behold, she was back to her sarcastic self again, finding fault with something that had been to her completely satisfaction only the day before, telling Nell off for doing things that were beyond an enrolled nurse, even though she had previously stood and watched her do it, and generally making everyone's life a misery.

'I just can't fathom her!' fumed Nell to other colleagues, after yet another example of this strange behaviour.

'Nor me,' agreed all of them, Beata adding, 'but I feel a bit sorry for her –'

'You would, Mrs Goodheart!' she was told.

'No, I think it must have been the heat out in India or some bad experience there that's made her so odd,' explained Beata.

'Potty, you mean,' said a grim-faced Wintringham. 'You never know where you are with her. Well, I'm not putting up with it, I'm off.'

And this seemed to goad others into action, staff resigning in droves, which only exacerbated the problem for Nell and Beata, for it left them with more work to do. Even with probationers replacing those who had left, this was of no assistance, in fact it made more work for they had frequently to be surpervised. And all the time there was Sister's voice accosting her.

'Nurse Spottiswood!'

Nell flinched, and, though it turned out to be Matron

who had summoned her today, as she was hurrying to the sluice with a bedpan, she remained on tenterhooks, for that official savaging over the *Dive at Dawn* episode had been quite enough.

'I don't wish to interrupt your duties,' said Matron, in the no-nonsense manner that Nell had come to expect. 'But I'd be obliged if you'd answer a question for me.'

Only slightly less tense, Nell replied that of course she would.

'Why do you think so many staff are leaving us lately?'

Taken completely by surprise, Nell's first instinct was to tell the truth. But remembering Beata's opinion that something awful must have happened to Pike to make her like this, and considering that Beata was usually right, she thought it better left unsaid. For if Matron knew how disruptive the new sister had been, she would not hesitate to throw her out. As much as she abominated Pike herself, Nell would not want to be responsible for putting someone on the dole. Rather she be the one to leave than descend to such tactics. And so, as much as she would have liked to grasp this chance to rid herself of her bête noire, her reply now was innocent. 'I've really no idea, Matron.'

Matron missed nothing. 'It seems to me that prior to Sister Pike's arrival, all you nurses got along like a house on fire. Is that not the case now?'

'Oh yes, we still get along,' said Nell, hoping this half-truth would suffice.

Matron could see she would receive no tales here. 'Very well, Nurse Spottiswood, thank you for your time.' And with that she directed Nell on her way.

'You bloody clot,' complained a less generous colleague, when later an astonished Nell divulged this exchange over refreshments. 'One word from you and we could have been shot of her!'

And indeed, Nell was rather inclined to regret her own

reticence after enduring more weeks of being verbally abused.

'I'm all for showing someone understanding, Killie,' she muttered through tight lips, as she caught Beata up in the corridor, having barely spoken to her for days and grabbing this chance to pace alongside her. 'But we can't go on letting her trample all over us.'

'She's par for the course, love,' said Beata, narrowly escaping injury from a swing door that had been let go by the person in front. 'Like that one.'

'Who does he think he bloody well is, lord of the manor?' Nell glowered at Doctor Barker, who had become too full of his own self-importance to heed the two nurses behind him. It hadn't taken him long to go the way of the other medical staff, one minute asking her on a date, the next ignoring her. 'Treating us like serfs – God, what a day I've had!' she declared, marching alongside her friend again. 'I hope the plumbing's fixed by the time I get home, the last thing I need is having to lug pails of water over the glaciers after all the horse-work I have to put up with in here.' As at countless other households, Mrs Connell's pipes had burst under the Alaskan temperatures, and Nell had felt obligated to tote water from a neighbouring house, in return for the kindly donation of the wellingtons. 'Actually, can you do me a –'

'Nurse Spottiswood!'

Yet again, Nell was to close her eyes in exasperation as Sister Pike accosted her for the umpteenth time that day. 'You are supposed to be taking Mr Marshall for his x-ray!'

Nell gritted her teeth, then set forth a deferential response. 'I was just asking Nurse Kilmaster to help me lift him into the wheelchair, Sister, he's such a large chap. I can't lift him on my own.'

Her superior tutted. 'Nurse Kilmaster has her own duties! A big lump like you ought to be able to do it in your stride – were you never taught how to lift? Come along, I'll show you!' And, without waiting, she set off.

Rolling her eyes at Beata, Nell followed, but did so resentfully, seething over the insults to her physique and her competence.

'Now look! You stand at the foot of the bed, and get him underneath, like this!' Sister began to manhandle the very large fellow, but was interrupted by Nell.

'I'm *sorry*, Sister,' she sounded firm, and not sorry at all, 'but I refuse to treat human beings like sacks of coal. It requires two of us.'

For a moment, it appeared that Sister was about to pack her insubordinate nurse off to Matron. But then emerged a gasp of contempt. 'Oh very well, if you're so useless I'll have to help you! I don't know what nurses are coming to these days!' And between them they managed to shift the hundredweight of Mr Marshall's flesh into the wheelchair. Then, whilst Sister Pike dusted her hands and went away to harry another, Nell wheeled the unfortunate man off to the x-ray department, apologising to him for the rough treatment meted out.

'I can't take much more of this,' she was later to object to Beata. 'Things had better change, or I'll apply to go on permanent nights.'

Condemned to limp about in cheap footwear, insult heaped upon insult, with only the patients and fellow drudges to heed her woes, Nell was much relieved finally to return to night duty, even though the weather was still making it terribly difficult to get to and fro. Weeks turned into months, and still there was to be no let-up – not in Pike's discipline, nor in the sporadic power cuts that were meant to save the nation's coal amidst the most extensive chaos since the General Strike, nor in the weather. By March the situation had become very grave indeed. Nell had never thought to hear the word avalanche associated with the English landscape, but fear of this there was, with thirty-foot drifts on the higher ground. Far from being hard done by, she began to regard herself as lucky to live in this austere little room, for with rail and road impassable to the hillside villages, there were many who were completely isolated. At least she had no need to call on the RAF mountain rescue squad to deliver her food.

Even so, it was taxing enough. Around York, snow ploughs were a daily necessity, creating large ramparts to either side of the highways, white turned to black by exhaust fumes, and then to white again as another cascade was piled on top. Yet still those interminable blizzards continued to lay siege, tier upon tier being frozen to ice, daily life as hazardous as in wartime, and food being more difficult to acquire than ever before.

But worse was to come. For when the tons of snow that had transformed the landscape for the past three months finally began to thaw, it was under an assault of heavy rain. Packed hard by weeks of frost, the ground was unable to cope with the ensuing torrent, which teemed from every conceivable aspect to overfill rivers and becks, every water-course bursting its banks to envelop the city, and sending a dirty brown flume complete with rainbow oil slicks pouring into cellars and living rooms, and sewage back up the drains.

'As if we don't see enough shite in here,' proclaimed Beata, with her usual droll observation, 'without having to wade home through it an' all.' For although their wards, and thankfully their houses, were on sufficiently high ground to escape the morass, to travel back and forth was a feat in itself.

In fact, even to wade became impossible at points, the roads in parts too deeply submerged under that effluent tide that swirled and eddied into shop and public house and church alike. Not for the first time was York transformed into Venice – though deeper by far was the resultant level, the expanse of water quickly become so vast that it was nigh impossible to recognise the waterways' previous course – and in place of gondolas were doughty little rowing boats, into which Nell and others must clamber and be ferried from one stretch of duckboard to another, in order to reach work.

Where streets turned to rivers, the rivers themselves were unnavigable, their swollen levels creeping up and up to record heights, until almost obscuring the archways of the bridges that spanned them. Not to be subjugated, Nell and her friends took a trip to the cinema, thinking it awful jolly still to be able to watch a film, with the organ elevated to its full extent by automatic lift, and light from the screen illuminating the floodwater in roped-off stalls.

But really it was no joking matter, for along with the tangled branches, dead dogs and other flotsam, the perilous current was to sweep away livelihoods, to cause death and destruction across the country, and to leave millions of farm animals to rot, before eventually trickling backwards down the drains.

The floods might have receded, but in their horrible sludge-ridden wake came grave financial crisis for a nation still destitute from war. Nell might joke that she herself was in perpetual financial crisis, and were she to pull in her belt any tighter she would have a waist like a wasp. But truly it was hard to retain one's optimism with such disaster stacked upon disaster, and if she was grown thin, there were many grown fat via the boom in pregnancy that had come with the soldiers' return. How were these poor things to manage, faced with such a state of bankruptcy? thought the tender-hearted Nell. Her worries were not solely confined to the abstract, for she knew Joe Kilmaster's wife to be expecting too, and while Beata was delighted to anticipate the arrival of a half-German nephew or niece at the end of the year, she too had voiced worry over its welfare.

Inevitably, whenever she laid down her head, Nell's thoughts went to her own son, also vulnerable in this parlous national dilemma. William would be six years and three months old by now. As with countless times before, she tried to picture him – with dark hair, certainly, for both his parents were so. But did he have Bill's blue eyes, or her brown ones? Was he tall for his age? Was he a serious little chap, like most of those in her care; or was he blessed with his father's happy-go-lucky smile? Hopefully the latter, for, armed with such charming ammunition, no one could ever bring themselves to hurt him. Somehow, over the years, the wound of loss had turned from being raw to that of an amputated limb. In the same way that amputees survived their ghost pain, Nell had learned to cope with hers too. Before drifting off, in customary mode she offered a short prayer that her child would not suffer in these grave, dark days . . .

She was not to know if her personal prayers had been answered, though perhaps they were. For as Nell and her fellow nurses began to wonder just how much more hardship could be thrown at them, the crises of that summer began to abate, day by day, the tension continuing to unwind, this terrible year drawing to a close with a royal wedding.

Perhaps that was the signal of better times ahead, for as the year turned, changes came thick and fast: a different name for the hospital; an even bigger change in the way things were run, no longer a two-tier system for those who could pay and those who could not, and everyone receiving an equally excellent service. But to those who had hoped otherwise, these improvements were solely due to the inauguration of the National Health Service, and nothing whatsoever to do with Sister Pike, who remained as inflexible as ever.

'What are we going to do?' bewailed Nell as she and her friend performed the twice-weekly gutting of beds. 'I can't face another year like the last.'

'I don't know about you, but I'm going to get meself some new teeth,' announced Beata.

'To savage her with?' volleyed Nell.

'Well, it's all free,' grinned Beata, depositing another bundle of laundry in the bin. 'Why shouldn't we take advantage of it, after what we have to put up with?'

'I'm going to get myself some specs,' butted in the elderly man on the walking frame who had been supervising their work.

'You don't need them, Mr Simpson!' Nell laughingly pointed out to this regular curmudgeon.

'I'm entitled, same as everybody else! They're free. And I want them – you haven't tucked that corner in, Nurse.'

'As I said, you don't need them.' Nell gave a helpless laugh at Beata as she hurriedly tucked in the sheet. 'I haven't finished it yet, *thank* you for pointing it out! You're as bad as Sister Pike.'

'You have a complaint, Nurse Spottiswood?' Yet again Pike was there, making the nurses jump.

'No, Sister.' A dutiful Nell increased her already efficient speed in stripping the beds.

'Well, I have,' snapped her constant detractor. 'Mr Simpson is meant to be taking exercise, and you are meant to be working, not fooling around with patients. Any further warning and you shall find yourself in Matron's office again.' And she led Mr Simpson away.

'I'll be going to Matron's office off my own bat!' stated Nell, who had come to the sudden decision that the only way she could bring change to her own life was to enact her earlier threat. 'And applying for permanent nights.'

Primarily, Matron was to show reluctance to grant this request, saying that it would be no good at all for the nurse's health nor her spirits. But when Nell insisted on this arrangement, otherwise she would have to leave, consent was finally granted.

Going to work and coming home in darkness might indeed be an unnatural existence, but with sufficient time off between shifts in which to recover, Nell found her life to be a lot more contented than it had been for some time. How wonderful was the peace of the night ward, without that carping voice in one's ear. There were downsides, of course, such as the fact that she saw little of her friend now, unless Beata happened to be working nights too, and even then they would be in different areas. It could be a lonely existence, if one let it. But with Pike off her back, Nell was grateful to make do with the snippets of news that came her way, and could still share her friend's delight over the baby niece who arrived later than expected on New Year's Day.

12

With her nocturnal role continuing over the next four years, Nell was to treasure any news of this child, Nina, for even though they had never met, she had seen many photographs, and Beata had described her character so well that Nell felt she knew her inside out, and especially welcomed hearing all the comical things she said. Joe and Grette were expecting a second child to be born any day. They wanted a son this time, Beata had said, though the little girl wanted a sister, and had vowed she would take it back to the shop if the wrong variety arrived.

Nell was pondering these fond thoughts as she enjoyed the last few hours of quietude before her rounds started on that wintry morn, and thinking of her own son, who had been born at such an early hour.

But her reveries were shortly to be interrupted by a student nurse, who had been put on nights to gain experience. How Sister Pike would hate it, thought Nell with a smile, to see this girl defer to me.

'I'm not sure what to do,' posed the student, as she presented a shrivelled object on a wad of lint. 'Mr Kettlewell's penis has just dropped off.'

Nell gave a murmur of recognition. Rampaged by cancer, the poor man was not long for this world. She gave kindly instruction. 'Just make him as comfortable as you can.'

'But what shall I do with this?' The youngster held up the detached part.

Nell gave an impish instruction. 'Put it on Sister Pike's desk for morning. I'm sure it'll make her day.'

It'll certainly make mine, thought Nell. And later, when the day staff arrived, she was to hover outside the sister's office, waiting for her to come upon the 'gift', and to listen out for her utterance of disgust.

Later still, in the afternoon, after catching up on sleep, she was to use this humorous episode to entertain some of her old colleagues at the Infirmary. It made good listening, too, for Connie Wood, the one to whom she still made regular visits and bestowed small gifts. Connie's face lit up at Nell's arrival, and so did other familiar faces too, Cissie Flowerdew rushing to tell her excitedly all about her coming wedding, to the father of her latest child. Yet, pleasant as this meeting was to one with such a poor social life, Nell felt glad she had decided to leave there, for despite being renamed the Grange, it was still the old workhouse building with those same drab wards.

After spending an hour or so amongst old friends, she went on her way, to the hospital that was further along the same road. Tonight she was to be on the isolation wards. A look at her watch told she was far too early, but this would give her legitimate time to chat to the patients. Nell felt so sorry for them, not being allowed visitors – especially the little ones – but most of all those in the iron lungs. There was only one in at the moment, thank God. She was fourteen, at least able to understand what was being done to her, but that made it no less frightening. Nell was frightened too. She had nursed Annette on the first day she had entered hospital, and watched the paralysis set in. Would she still be there tonight?

To Nell's relief, she was. And though she could not move a muscle, not even her head, which was the only thing sticking out of that metal crate that acted as lungs, she appeared to recognise Nell behind her barrier gown, and to be pleased to see her.

'I'm early, so I've plenty of time to gossip.' Nell leaned over to sponge the patient's face with cool water, her eyes smiling into Annette's. 'Sister can't tell me off if it's my own time! Nurse Potts was just coming to see to you but I said I'd sort you out whilst we're gabbing.'

Acting casually, so as not to create great ceremony out of it, she began to chat at the same time as sticking her hands through the rubber cuffs of the portholes, attending the toilet requirements of the naked body inside, and trying to minimise the embarrassment. 'I went to town on Saturday, tried on all these lovely coats in Marks and Spencer's – of course I can't afford them, I was just having fun – but there was also this cerise jumper – that's my favourite colour. I hope they're not all sold before I can save up for one. Maybe I should have tucked it under my coat and run out of the shop!' She rambled on about clothes and make-up and other fripperies, of what she would buy if she did have the cash, her arms still gripped by the rubber cuffs of the iron lung, her hands working inside the box, until she thought perhaps she had gone on too long. At which juncture she suddenly apologised for this one-sided conversation. 'I'm sorry, I'm very boring, aren't I?' But Annette, who found it difficult to talk, conveyed with her eyes that she enjoyed listening to anything Nell had to tell her.

So Nell went on. 'Oh, I don't know if you've seen Nurse Kilmaster lately? I expect she's told you about her niece. I haven't met her, but by all accounts she's a canny little thing. Killie comes in and tells me all the funny things she's said. Anyway, they're having another any day soon. Hoping for a boy this time.' As usual when discussing children, her mind went to William, and her face was animated as she spoke of Baby Kilmaster.

This good mood was to last throughout her twelve-hour shift, enhanced by the fact that her patients had all come safely through the night. With a fond farewell to each, saying she would see them that evening, she took off her barrier gown, scrubbed up, then went to the main dining block. Only there was her weariness to hit her, due to a sombre announcement on the wireless. The King was dead.

After oozing tears with her night-time colleagues, Nell was making to leave for home when she came across Beata in the corridor, her friend being abnormally glum. 'Oh, Killie, you look like I feel. You've obviously heard the news . . . isn't it sad?'

Beata agreed. 'But it's not just the King. Grette died in labour, the baby too. A little boy . . .'

Nell jumped in shock, and gave only mute attendance as her friend explained that it had been due to, 'Eclampsia. The ambulance came straight away, but it was too late to save either of them. Our Joe's inconsolable.'

'I'll bet he is . . .' Nell's fingers played with her lips, such memories being dredged up for her, creating nausea in her stomach and a trembling of her limbs. But then she was to rebuke herself. This was not her grief but someone else's. 'That poor, poor man, and his little girl.'

'Funeral's on Thursday,' murmured Beata, beginning to move away. 'I'll have to ask Pike for time off. What a pleasure that'll be.'

Nell caught her sleeve. 'Well, I'll be off work too then. Is there anything I can do to help?'

Beata nodded appreciation. 'Could you sit with our Nina? Joe doesn't want her standing round an open grave, we had enough of that when we were kids. Our Gussie said she'd have her, but if you could do it instead it would leave her free to come to the funeral. I know she'd like to go. Though, you'd have the other kids to keep an eye on as well as Nina, and it might be a long do, us being Catholics . . .'

Nell was in the process of saying, 'Think nothing of it,' that she would do this, of course, when someone interrupted.

'Do you two do *nothing* but gossip?' demanded Sister Pike, coming suddenly upon the pair. 'Please show some respect for His Majesty. Nurse Kilmaster, get about your business.' Beata went. 'Nurse Spottiswood, if you're going home then go!'

Nell sought to explain quietly before Pike did any more damage, 'Nurse Kilmaster's sister-in-law's just died –'

'Is that any reason for you to get involved too?'

Nell would gladly have strangled her. 'I just thought you should know, Sister.'

'And now I do – clear off!'

Clear off yourself, you old bat, seethed Nell, but quickly walked away.

Knowing it did not pay to get too close to the children she was nursing, despite her devotion to them, over the years Nell had somehow managed to draw a protective shield across her heart. But against all wishes, at the first sight of that solemn four-year-old with the skin so pale, the sad blue eyes and the reddish-blonde hair, she felt her defences snap. The father looked dazed, his grief somehow appearing twice as acute in that he had made such an effort to smarten his demob suit with a starched white collar, and Nell felt immense pity for him too. But her main sympathy was for the child, who was soon to capture her eye again. How she itched to embrace that fragile little thing; to fill her own empty arms.

With the hearse arrived and everyone departed, Nell allowed the older children to play in the street. 'But not too rowdily, eh?' And finally she was left alone with the bewildered girl.

From her shopping basket she drew an oval box, and enticed Nina to peep in. 'Look what I've brought. Do you like dates?' At the wan nod, she said gently, 'Let me cut the stones out for you then – come on, you show me where the knives are kept.'

Small soft fingers curled themselves around the proffered hand, their owner leading Nell into the scullery where she indicated the cutlery drawer. Then the little girl in the Fair Isle jumper and tartan kilt stood to observe. 'Don't cut yourself,' came her sober warning.

'I'll try not to.' Nell looked down at her and smiled.

'You will if you don't watch what you're doing,' instructed Nina.

'Sorry, you're absolutely right,' agreed Nell, and concentrated on the sticky dates.

Having sliced enough of them open and removed the stones, she put them in a bowl and handed this over, steering the infant back to the sitting room. 'There, you can sit and eat them whilst I read you a story.'

The box of dates had been a Christmas gift from a patient, but aside from bringing this, on her way there she had purchased a book, having vetted it carefully to make sure it contained nothing sad. Lifting the little girl gently onto her lap, she made them both comfortable and sat back to read. But as her lips formed the words, her senses were all over the place, the warmth of the child's body seeping through her clothes to her heart.

Even when the tale was over, the dates eaten and sticky hands wiped, she was reluctant to let Nina go, and chatted for a while to her about one thing or another, enquiring about likes and dislikes, unconsciously caressing a skinny arm or thigh. Notwithstanding today's solemnity, she was obviously a bright little thing, and able to hold a conversation with an adult. And the woman whose arms enveloped her never wanted to give her up.

All too soon for Nell, though, the crowd of mourners was to return, and Nina immediately slipped off the woman's lap to scramble onto her father's. Feeling strangely bereft herself, with the absent child's body heat quickly evaporating into a cool patch, Nell took consolation in the sandwiches and cakes that Gussie had laid on.

Joe partook of little, either of food or conversation. Although he was to share a few courtesies with Nell as she left sometime later, following her to the door and thanking her for looking after his daughter, whom he now carried on one arm.

Nell merely dealt him a little smile. What could one say in response – it had been a pleasure? Not very apt when he had just buried his wife. 'She was good as gold,' was all she said in the end, taking Nina's stubby fingers and giving them a gentle squeeze.

Joe nodded, obviously thinking himself obliged to say more. 'It's unbelievable: I came through six years of war without a scratch, and now I lose everything . . .' Apparently unnerved at being lured into voicing his innermost feelings, he suddenly shook hands with Nell. 'Well, thank you very much again, Nurse, for taking care of this one – say goodbye, Neen.'

The little girl's solemn farewell was met with another caress, before the father took her back inside, and the visitor set off home. Nell would always remember the day of that funeral as the strangest of times to fall in love.

It was to be fifteen months before she saw Nina again, and this time in much happier circumstances. The last year had been one of mourning, for Grette, and for the King. But, as with each monarch's passing, the nation's remembrance must give way to celebration, this time with a new queen, and a bright Elizabethan age.

It was only by luck that Nell found herself able to enjoy the coronation, as it was to fall between shifts. Poor Beata would be on duty, but had told her friend, 'Go and watch it on our Gussie's new telly. Get there early, though, or you'll be watching it from the street.' And of course Nell had jumped at the chance.

Some hours of overtime had allowed her to purchase a flowery shirtwaister dress and summer cardigan for the occasion, though the overcast weather made it necessary to spoil the effect with a mac. When she arrived there was already a houseful, the furniture being rearranged so that everyone could have a view of the television set on a high corner shelf. This had been turned on to warm up, everyone's eyes fixed to it, and though there wasn't actually anything to see yet, they seemed fascinated. Knowing Joe and his daughter would be there – for after Grette's death they had moved in for convenience – Nell's eyes immediately sought Nina out, and, upon seeing her, lit up in pleasure, whilst her voice offered a general hello to the others.

Joe rose at her entry, and pushed back his hair in an act of self-consciousness. 'Hello there, Nurse, come in if you can get in.'

'Thanks, Mr Kilmaster, call me Nell.'

'I'm Joe, then.' He too looked happier of late, this mood displayed in the same kind of way as his sister Beata's, never gushing but rather composed, apart from the blue eyes that sparkled, and the obstinate mouth that twitched in a smile that was dry as a bone. Whereas Beata was the round russet apple, Joe was more the tree, his limbs slender branches, pliant but tough, with an outer coating of bark to represent strength, yet at its core a pithy warmth. There was evidence that his hair had once been auburn, for it bore the odd streak of this, though now its hue was mostly silver. Despite this, the hawkish nose and angular cheeks, there was still much youthfulness in his appearance and behaviour.

Nell attended politely to what he was saying, glad to see him looking much better than last time, but she was dying to pay more heed to Joe's little daughter, who was kneeling on the mat and running a miniature coach and horses along the hearth. Nina was still the same dainty, strawberry-blonde cherub, in a red, white and blue frock today; less forlorn than she had been a year ago, though still bearing the heavy load of her bereavement inside, suspected Nell.

'Grab yourself a good chair,' the little girl made casual invitation. At which both Nell and Joe laughed, the latter saying, 'Aye, before they all start pouring in.'

Smoothing her new dress, Nell edged her way through those already seated on the ranks of dining chairs, bypassing the few empty ones and choosing to squeeze onto the sofa beside Joe, so as to be within touching distance of Nina. 'There's more to come?'

'The whole damned street,' old Mr Melody removed his pipe to grumble, his armchair pushed right back into a corner.

And this seemed only slight exaggeration, for all the time people kept arriving, some to sit on the wooden chairs they carried, others to stand, until the room was crammed and the audience began to spill over into the passage.

Music emerged from the television, and a grainy picture. Amidst the buzz of anticipation, Gussie sent her ten-year-old boy to alert stragglers that the excitement was about to start.

'Tell them to fetch their binoculars,' teased Joe, at which Nell grinned, for the picture that had them all glued was so tiny that it was difficult to see even in this room. Still, it was miraculous.

Young Nick went pelting off to knock on several doors and summon the latecomers. By the time he returned, the passageway was so crammed with viewers that he was trapped outside, and had to keep bouncing up and down in order to catch any glimpse of the screen.

Then the celebrations began. 'She's here! She's here!' yelled Mr Crow, shooting to his feet and signalling furiously for everyone to do likewise. Which they did for a moment, but then Joe observed in his laconic fashion, 'We can't stand up for hours!'

'Do you think she can see us?' came an anxious enquiry from the genteel and elderly Mrs Grey, who had dressed in her own finest attire, a grey artificial silk dress, and a hat with a veil. 'Will she know we're insulting her if we sit down? Only my bunions . . .'

Assured that Her Majesty would be unaware of such disrespect, everyone who had a chair lowered their buttocks again. Then the room fell silent except for whispers of awe, eyes glistening with emotion as the golden coach carrying the Queen made its way past cheering crowds to the abbey.

'It's like mine!' Nina piped up to display her miniature version of the coronation coach.

'Shush!' accused everyone, including her father, all except Nell, who, feeling immensely sorry for the crest-fallen child, scooped Nina onto her lap – which she had been dying to do since she entered – smiling encouragement but laying a finger over her lips to show that she must be quiet.

The twenty or more adults remained captivated, especially when the coach arrived at the abbey and the Queen emerged in all her splendour, clad in ermine robe and jewels.

'Hasn't Her Majesty got a lovely bust,' observed Mrs Crow in admiration.

Her neighbour was less impressed, arms folded across his suited chest and the look of the curmudgeon about him. 'I can't see a blasted thing. What size is it?' he turned to demand of his host.

'What, the Queen's bust?' asked Joe.

'No, the set, man!' Accompanying gasps were issued for Joe's disrespect.

'It's a nine-inch Bush,' provided Mick.

The killjoy donated a curt nod to those around him. 'I knew we should have gone to Eric Chapman's – he's got a fourteen-inch.'

'So he tells the girls,' murmured Joe, too quietly for most to hear, but causing Nell to grin at his smut.

'They all look like blasted midgets on that,' declared the killjoy. 'If this is television, you can keep it.'

'Why doesn't he bugger off now, then?' grumbled another of the squashed neighbours, hoping for a better view, but this was not to be, for the large square head remained steadfastly in place.

Nina burst into song. '*Cigareets and whisky and wahld wahld women* –!'

'Can we please have a bit of hush?' demanded Gussie, and the room fell silent again.

Whilst as rapt as the other adults in this momentous occasion, Nell could not help be more preoccupied with the child on her lap. Enfolding her in her arms, as might a lover, she rested her chin on the golden head, letting her hand caress the bare leg, whilst imagining herself in paradise . . .

But even paradise had its drawbacks, especially after a couple of hours, when Nell's lap had grown numb from the restless wriggling of the child – and when Nina heaved yet another sigh of boredom, this seemed the right moment to give her the comic she had brought along.

'Will you read it to me?' pleaded Nina. But again she was urged to be quiet, and to read it for herself.

With the pages of *Sunny Stories* soon riffled through, she began once more to wriggle in boredom.

'Look there's Prince Charles!' whispered Nell, drawing the little girl's attention to the screen. 'He was born the same year as you.'

Though Nina watched for a second, she did not appear too impressed, and was now fidgeting with the buckles on her sandals. Nell wanted to offer to take her out for a walk, but the ceremony was reaching its pinnacle. Disrobed of her ermine and jewels, the Queen was anointed with oil, then adorned with the golden ceremonial robes, finally to be crowned.

'God Save the Queen!' resounded the choir. Trumpets fanfared and bells rang out, taking everyone's spirits to glorious heights – how could one interrupt at such an emotional and historic moment, with old ladies wiping the tears from their cheeks? But if Nell didn't speak now, she might be stuck here the entire day.

'I need to widdle,' announced Nina in a loud whisper, lending Nell the opportunity she desired.

'I'll take her,' she murmured hastily to Joe.

'How are you reckoning on getting out?' With dry enquiry, he indicated the full house, not a space between chairs. 'Up t'chimney?'

'Well, I'll have to get out somehow, I don't fancy having my lap drenched.' Nell gave a light-hearted laugh, and began to extricate herself from those seated alongside her. 'To save us spoiling everyone's enjoyment, once we are out, should I take her for a walk? It's a bit much expecting one so young to sit still for so long.'

Rising with her, Joe agreed, telling his child, 'Be good for Nurse.'

Then Nell began to squeeze her way between the chairs and bodies, and with a series of ungainly strides eventually made it to the back door. The child was somewhat easier, being swung overhead from hand to hand, and deposited into Nell's arms. By this manner, also, was her mackintosh despatched from the hallway, plus one for Nina.

At last there was only the two of them. It was quieter even than a Sunday, the traffic being drastically reduced, and barely another soul to be seen. At leisurely pace, treading carefully between the puddles, Nell and Nina paused on a bench at the top of the street to eat their sandwiches, then made towards town, chatting about one thing or another, and buying a tub of ice-cream along the way.

'Is it okay if I sing now?' asked Nina, her mouth caked in white.

'You can sing your head off,' permitted Nell with a smile.

And thus was launched a favourite, complete with American accent. '*Cigareets and whisky, and wahld, wahld women! They drive you crazy, they drive you insay-ne!*' Nina broke off suddenly. 'They're the only words I know – do you know any more?'

'Afraid not,' said Nell, and between avoiding the puddles tried to steer her towards something less raucous. 'I like the one that goes, "little red monkey, monkey, monkey, deeh-dah, deeh-dah, diddley-diddley" – sorry I don't know the words either! Oh, hang on, you'll like this one.' She began to swing Nina's hand in time to her chanting: '"Here comes the nurse with the red-hot poultice, slaps it on, and takes no notice! Oh, said the patient, that's too hot! Oh, said the nurse, I'm sure it's not"'

Nina laughed aloud through the drizzle. 'Sing it again!'

And Nell complied, feeling that she was walking on air, and that she would do anything for her small companion. Which is why upon reaching Walmgate Bar she agreed to Nina's demand, and scampered like a child herself up the stone steps and onto the battlements, to embark on a round tour.

'But you must hold my hand!' she called to Nina, who had broken away and was galloping too close to the unprotected perimeter. 'We don't want you tumbling off the edge.'

The golden sprite was not keen to be so mollycoddled, and set her foot right to the limits to peer down at the scene of demolition below, at the flattened street and the piles of soot-encrusted bricks where urchins romped. 'Is that what you call a bombsite?'

Nell hurried up to snatch her from danger. How did one explain that the slum clearance, which had been postponed by the war, had now been resumed? 'I think they're knocking all the old houses down to build new ones,' she said, more intent on her young charge than on her surroundings. 'Come away now and finish your ice-cream, before it's completely melted.'

But Nina dodged her and ran to launch the upper part of her body over the ramparts, to gaze down on the cattle pens now. 'Why are there no cows in them?'

'Because it's not cattle-market day,' said Nell, taking a grip on the child's blue plastic mac. Then, at Nina's sound of disappointment, she said, 'I must bring you back when it is.'

At this point, Nina tilted her tub of ice-cream slightly too far, and the contents slid to the ground, leaving her with only an empty carton. 'Never mind!' Nell forestalled tears. 'We'll buy you another when we get to the end of the walls.' And finally she managed to coax the wayward one into holding her hand again.

For a while, as they squelched along the ancient walls, the child appeared to drift off into some faraway world. Noting that her baggy cotton ankle socks had worked themselves underneath her heels and must surely be causing discomfort, Nell took the time to unbuckle each sandal and tug the hosiery back into position, smoothing them around the thin ankles.

Whilst she was doing this, Nina suddenly asked, 'Nurse, have you got any children?'

'No, I'm not married.' Feeling the child's breath against her ear, she turned to smile into Nina's face.

'Ooh good. You could marry my dad, then you'd be my mother.'

And though Nell was extremely careful with her answer, her heart could not help but swell with joy as they continued on their way.

When they returned, most of the visitors were gone, and Nell said it was time for her to depart too.

'Thanks for all your help,' said Joe. 'I'm sorry you had to miss everything, what with seeing to madam here.'

Nell disagreed. 'I saw the important parts, and I had a better time with Nina. I thoroughly enjoyed it.'

The little girl had looked slightly downcast at being blamed by her father, but Nell's words perked her up, and she asked, 'Will you come to my party?'

Joe corrected her. 'It's not just your party, it's for the whole street.' Then he informed Nell, 'We had to postpone it because of the weather, so we decided to take no more chances and hold it at the Co-op Hall next Saturday. I doubt it'll be up to much, but come if you fancy it.'

'I'd love to, but I can't.' Nell spoke directly to the little girl, gazing into her eyes and thoroughly apologetic as she gave her reason. 'I'll be back at work.' She lifted her face to address the taller figure. 'I'm only here today because I'm between shifts.'

'Might you be off a week on Sunday?' asked Joe, apparently wanting to buck his daughter's spirits, for he had laid his hand on her reddish-gold head. 'We've hired a bus to take us to Scarborough for the day. I think there's a few seats going spare.' He quickly interpreted the expression on Nell's face. 'You won't have to cough up, it's already been paid for – if you'd like to go, that is.'

'Yes, thank you, I would!' Looking down at Nina's eager smile, Nell took no time at all to respond.

And, after that day, her life began to take on a wholly different outlook.

The instant Nell turned up on the day of the outing, Nina raced to show her the souvenirs of the Coronation party. One was a paint box in the shape of a crown, the other a mug bearing a portrait of the Queen. 'I got this from school, full of sweets! I've been saving it for you!'

Nell was touched, and bent to receive the mug. 'How kind!' Then she found that it was empty.

'I ate all the goodies,' explained Nina. 'But I thought you could have that, 'cause I don't really like the picture of the lady.'

'I think that might be high treason,' observed her father.

The laughing recipient gave thanks, and said she would leave the mug here for later, as an equally amused Joe directed his hand towards the bottom of the terrace, where there stood a red double-decker bus.

Amongst the other residents of the street, there were quite a few members of the Melody and Kilmaster families here to enjoy the excursion. Nina asked Nell if they could ride on the upper deck. Though pleased to be asked, Nell said the child must ask her father; and with Joe's permission, to the upper one they were to clamber. Nell had had second thoughts about going to Scarborough, and not because she was straight off night shift and had had no sleep. The last time she had gone there it had been with Bill. But one could not keep avoiding places and people that reminded her of what she had lost. And besides, she was so very happy in her present company.

The bus seemed barely to have set off when it arrived at its destination. This was because, Joe explained with a laugh, that she had slept for most of the way. Blinking away her confusion, Nell apologised profusely to him and his daughter, and swore to give them her full attention from now on.

Thankfully, Beata had also managed to be there, helping her sister Gussie to look after the other children, as soon as they got off the bus, doling out pennies to insert in the slot machines, and generally spoiling each and every one, so allowing Nell to devote herself to the one who had stolen her heart. In spite of the inclement weather, which required that they kept their coats on, Nina wanted to go on the sands straight away, so with Joe collecting deckchairs, not just for him and Nell, but for Mick and Gussie too, this was where they went.

Whilst her own canvas chair flapped in the wind, and the rest of the group looked on, a happy Nell dropped to her knees on the sand and set to helping the little girl make castles, tipping out a dozen or more from the bucket, and placing them at Nina's instruction in a semi-circle to hem the deckchairs in. Then came a paddle, and screams as the icy waves rippled over blue toes, the woman and child scurrying away, then back for more; then they searched for shells, finally to head back with pink, gleeful faces to those in the deckchairs.

Gussie had taken out her knitting, the wool disappearing into a bag at her side, and the pattern about to blow away across the sand. Nell made a grab for it at the same time as Joe, the latter showing amusement over the male model on the front. 'Who's the jumper for, Gus?'

'You,' she told him.

'Very nice. But do I have to stand like the bloke on the front?' He struck up an exaggerated pose, hoisting one foot onto the deckchair, one hand on his hip, the other shading his eyes, and his narrowed gaze fixed on the horizon.

Nell gave a laugh as, at last, she flopped into her deckchair. Though in the main her attention was for the little girl who was once again playing amongst her sandcastles, this time studding them with the shells she and Nell had collected.

Joe was saying something. Nell allowed him a moment's consideration, in between helping the child. 'Sorry, what was that, Joe?'

'I was just asking if you come from York originally,'

She dealt him a smiling nod, though was instantly draw back to Nina.

'I wasn't sure,' said Joe. 'You sound too posh.' When she laughed, he told her, 'We're West Riding wallahs – at least most of us. Gussie was born in Dover – me father was an RSM in the York and Lancs, you see, and we moved around all over the place.'

Nell said, 'That must have been interesting,' then was diverted yet again by the arrival of Beata and the other children, come to steal Nina away, though she continued watching her fondly during the rest of the day.

And such a lovely day it was: fish and chips for dinner, laughter with the one she loved, donkey rides and ice-cream in the afternoon – why did Nell have to go and ruin it with tears?

At first Joe did not see them, and maintained a string of wisecracks with which to entertain her, until he realised she was abnormally quiet, and craned his neck to see what was wrong.

In the absence of Nina, who had gone off to the amusements with her cousins, Nell had been granted space to think. Feeling her eyes suddenly well up, she had averted them, but not in time.

His smile froze as he saw the moisture in her eyes. 'I know they're not the funniest jokes but—'

'It's not you!' Nell was quick to say, with a half-laugh. 'I feel so stupid – it was just that I was having such a lovely time and it brought back memories. I last came here during the war, with Bill, the boy I was to marry. I never saw him again.'

'Killed, was he?' asked Joe softly. To which he received a nod.

'Not in the fighting.' She quickly dashed her eyes with a handkerchief and blew her nose. 'He went into a bombed house to rescue a child and it fell on him. He wasn't even twenty-one. But then there were thousands like him. Sorry for being so wet.'

'No, no, you're not.' It was obvious Joe was thinking of Grette, his face thoughtful and grave as he leaned forward in his deckchair. 'I suppose I should count myself lucky. At least I had a few years with the one I loved, and got a child out of it. A lot more than you were left with.'

Nell flinched at the thought of William, but he did not

see it, his mind far away as he sifted a handful of cool sand from one fist to the other. 'Sometimes I've felt like giving up this past year. I would've done if it hadn't been for Neen. She deserves better than I can give her. Thank God for our Beat and Gussie, who look after her while I'm at work.'

He seemed to regret discussing such deep things, then, in the middle of a crowded beach, for he broke off with a self-conscious laugh, and would have reverted to flippancy had not Nell pressed the issue.

'I'd like to help with Nina too, if you'd allow it.'

'Oh, there's no need to put yourself out.' He glanced at his eldest sister, who sat a few yards away alongside her husband, both snoozing in their deckchairs. 'Gussie doesn't mind . . .'

'I'm sure not, but it would mean she had one less to think about,' pressed Nell. 'And, truth be known, it's you who'd be helping me, not the other way around. I'm at such a loose end on my days off.'

'Haven't you any nieces and nephews of your own – not that I'm saying you should be taking them out. I'm very grateful you've shown such kindness to my lass.'

'It's my pleasure. She's a joy. And no, I'm an only child.' Here Nell gave a little laugh, and revealed, 'Actually, I believed I was adopted until I was twenty, because that's what I'd always been told.' At his keen look of interest, she went further. 'I don't suppose I'm breaking any confidence now, with my parents being dead. As a matter of fact they were killed only hours after Mother revealed her secret. I won't go into her personal reasons –' nor mine either, thought Nell, 'but it certainly came as a shock. So, I'm the only one left of my family – direct family, that is.'

Watching her intently, Joe gave a compassionate nod. Then he lightened the mood with another quip. 'I sometimes wish I was, when it comes to buying Christmas presents.' But immediately he smiled and contradicted himself. 'No, not really. They're grand sisters for any man to have.'

'Do you see your brothers at all?' From Beata, Nell knew there were two more.

Joe's face altered, and she glimpsed a much harder side of him as he shook his head. 'Once in a blue moon. Only the girls kept in contact when the family split up. If it wasn't for their efforts I'd be cast adrift God knows where. Men are like that.' He forced himself to grin at her, then looked away across the grey North Sea.

Nell was used to examining patients closely, to check for signs of change, and her intellect soon detected an unspoken pain. She was curious to know what had rent the family apart, and guessed it was something to do with the cruel stepmother Beata had mentioned, but she was more hesitant over poking her nose into other people's business than she would have been in her youth. It must have been something in her attitude that alerted Joe, for he said, 'I might tell you about it one day . . .'

'Oh, I'm sure it's none of my affair,' rushed Nell with a smile, upon realising she had been peering too intimately at him. 'But to get back to what I was saying before, I'd really count it an honour to look after Nina on my days off.'

At that point the child in question came rushing back with a prize she had won, managing to draw Nell's attention straight away, though having quite a job to distract her father and in the end throwing herself into the sand at his feet.

'Ow! Behave yourself – I'm talking to Nurse!' With a frown, he saw that his trouser leg had ridden up to expose the suspender that held up his sock, but he was laughing as he rebuked Nina for twanging it. 'An honour, you say?' he portrayed disbelief at Nell. She laughed, and her repeated offer appeared so genuine that Joe decided, 'Well, it would be a help, with the school holidays coming up.'

'That's settled then.' She made the sunny announcement, both to him and the more important one. 'I shall be Aunty Nell from now on!'

Taking Joe at his word, during the school holidays Nell wasted no time in calling again at the Melody house, to divest Gussie of at least one of her young burdens and take her into town. There was no danger of the other children being put out. Being older, they were allowed to stray further from home, and had left Nina behind to play with friends of their own age. Nell thanked providence that they had, for she had been looking forward to this, and had no desire to share her companion with anyone else.

Elated, she set off into the dazzling sunshine, planning to spend a few hours looking around the toy shops, then take Nina for lunch at a café. But come twelve o'clock, they were still amongst the toys, a particular one seeming to hold Nina's gaze.

'Come on now, let's go have some fish and chips,' said Nell, feeling hungry herself.

The child peered up from beneath the floppy rim of her sun bonnet. 'Can we have pickled onions as well?'

'If you want,' came the gay reply.

'I love 'em, but me dad won't let me have 'em.'

Nell looked dubious. 'Oh, in that case –'

'It's only 'cause they make me trump,' explained Nina quickly. 'Me Aunty Beat buys me them when I go out with her. She doesn't mind trumping. So if you don't mind either, it'll be all right for you to buy me 'em.'

Nell broke into giggles. 'As long as you try not to do it whilst we're in the café.'

The child was pleased at having her wish answered, though still reluctant to leave the shop, staring intently at that one particular toy, a ray gun.

With a patient smile, Nell waited a while longer, then

tried to lead her little charge towards the exit. 'Come on, let's go get those pickles, then.'

Dragging her feet, Nina gave a long backwards glance as she went obediently. But when her hint failed to register, she looked up at Nell to proffer an even heavier one, jabbing her finger at the coveted gun. 'I'm not being cheeky, but if I'd been with me Aunty Beat she would've bought me that.'

Nell bubbled with laughter. How could one win against such charming cajolery? So, even though it would take the money that was earmarked for household necessities, she heaved a sigh of surrender. 'Go on then! Let me see if I can afford it . . .'

A radiant Nina darted back to claim the ray gun from the low shelf, and handed it to her benefactress. But the moment Nell turned it over, she found that it was made in Japan.

Instantly her mind was altered, and she replaced it on the shelf. 'I'm sorry, love, but I can't buy you that. I don't buy anything made in that country, because of what the Japs did to our lads in the war.'

Thoroughly confused and disappointed, Nina hung her head and began to sulk. Unable to bear that crestfallen face, Nell quickly began to pick over the countless other toys displayed. 'But let's see if we can find something similar . . .'

Nina stood on tiptoe to examine them too, turning each over, just as Nell was doing. She eventually pounced on a small chariot, with a detachable Roman in charge of its two black horses. 'Am I allowed this'n?'

Nell winced at the price. It was half a crown. 'Would you not rather have something more feminine?' she asked, forgetting that the little girl might not understand the word.

But Nina clung to her desire. 'It says . . .' she tried to display her prowess at reading, and mouthed the letters, 'E-m-p-'

'Empire made,' Nell provided. 'Oh well, that one's fine – if you really want it?' At Nina's pleased nod, she took it around to the till, intending to have it wrapped, but Nina requested to carry it as it was. Glad to have made her so happy, Nell asked as they were leaving the shop, 'What are you going to call the horses?'

Nina gave this some thought. 'Blackie and Rex.' She disengaged the Roman soldier's foot from its loop of plastic. 'And he's called Dave.'

'Very fitting,' approved Nell, smiling down at the one whose hand slipped so naturally into hers, and thinking her heart would burst with happiness. 'Right, I think we'd better go and have dinner before you wangle anything else out of me, you little monkey.'

The little girl's father was slightly reproving of the purchase. 'I hope she didn't con you into spending too much money on it?' he quizzed Nell, upon his return home from the factory.

'I was allowed it 'cause it's Empire made,' Nina butted in to tell him. Then, after a pause, she asked, 'What *is* Empire made?'

'It refers to one of the countries that make up our British Empire,' began Nell, but was interrupted by Joe's bitter laugh.

'What ruddy Empire? This mob are falling over themselves to give it all away. Centuries we took to build it up, me dad'd turn in his grave . . .' Then he gave a more genuine chuckle. 'Sorry, I was ranting, wasn't I? *And* getting off the subject. Thank you very much for buying it for her, Aunty Nell, but it must have left you out of pocket?' He immediately fished into his own, but Nell was swift to refuse.

'No, honestly, I came out with the full intention of buying her a little gift. She's such good company.'

'Oh, well, if that's the case, you can take her out

whenever you want!' offered Joe, with a nod at his eldest sister who was preparing tea in the scullery. 'I'm sure Aunty Gus'd be glad to get rid, and I know I would!'

'And me,' donated old Mick from his fireside chair. But a sly wink at Nina showed he was only teasing.

However, Nell was quick to accept the offer. 'You might be sorry you said that, I could be round every week.'

'You come as often as you like,' invited Gussie.

Joe agreed. 'But, if you insist on making a habit of it, make sure it's not an expensive trip. Instead of taking her to town, why not the Castle Museum, she loves that, or a walk round Heslington . . .'

'Sounds good to me,' beamed Nell, delighted to be given such access to the one she loved. 'I'll come as often as work allows.'

13

Thus were the following months some of the happiest Nell had known, she and Nina getting together almost every week, at least until the school holidays came to an end. Even in the autumn there was conkering to enjoy, and if the outings happened to fall on a Sunday they would be joined by Joe, who seemed to enjoy Nell's company as much as his daughter, and made great effort to entertain her with his down-to-earth wit.

By the time winter came, though, and the days were short, their outings were inevitably curtailed. Not only that, but things had become busier at the hospital, and with other staff falling prey to coughs and colds, Nell had been forced to stand in for them on her days off. Because of this, she had not dared to make regular appointments with Nina. Treasuring her, as Nell did, the separation was awful.

But once the pressures of work had eased, after catching up on her sleep, her first act was to make an impromptu visit. She had come through town, and was hurrying along Lawrence Street on this dark and damp early evening, with her head lowered against the drizzle, and still half a mile to the Melody residence. Taking up where Walmgate left off Lawrence Street was an extension of the main road that continued all the way to Hull. It was made up of pubs and warehouses, a tannery, shops, narrow lanes and dingy archways, an ancient graveyard and a Norman church tower, almshouses, an ice-cream factory and a convent. In between were many categories of dwelling, including asbestos prefabs erected since the war. To each side, between pavement and road, was a strand of cobblestones, which, on certain days of the week, would be invaded by herds of cattle being driven to the nearby market – though not on this horrible night. Intimate with all its landmarks, Nell forged on with her head down, when who should she almost bump into but Nina and her father.

'Fancy meeting you here!' Both she and Joe made the same exclamation, then laughed aloud, Nina too.

Replacing the hat he had doffed to her, Joe asked, 'What finds you over this side of town?'

'Were you coming to see us?' Clad in, tweed coat with, velvet collar, and, knitted bonnet against the damp cold, Nina was jumping up and down more from excitement than from chill. ''Cause we've moved house.'

'You weren't meant to tell her!' Joe gave a hiss of rebuke, then grinned at Nell to show he was joking.

'Oh, charming!' laughed Nell. 'A subtle hint that I've been visiting too much, was it?'

Both Joe and Nina lost no time in saying they had missed her. 'Our Beat said she'd let you know.'

'I haven't seen hide nor hair of her for a couple of weeks,' admitted Nell, as the traffic droned past along this main highway. 'We've both been flat out.'

'Well, as a matter of fact we only moved last week,' revealed Joe. 'Thought it was about time I got back into a place of my own. Beata offered to share the rent and, as I'd have a live-in babysitter, it seemed like a good idea.' He saw a look of disappointment cloud Nell's face, and hurried to assure her, 'We'd still be glad of your help, though, when you can manage it.'

'Will you come with us now?' pleaded Nina.

Nell's gloved hand reached out to stroke the sweet little face. 'But you're obviously on your way out . . .'

'Nowt to stop you coming with us,' invited Joe. 'If you fancy going to see a dead whale?'

When Nell laughed, he cracked a droll smile. 'You've noticed, I have this scintillating line in seduction. Some men do diamonds, others serenade, I do dead whales.' Explaining that it was the main attraction of a travelling show on St George's Field, which she knew to be only ten minutes away, he offered keenly, 'You're welcome to come along . . .'

'All right, I will!' grinned Nell, immediately turning about and moving to Nina's left-hand side in order to take her free hand. 'I might never have another chance to see a genuine whale.'

It turned out she was not really to see anything resembling a noble leviathan, for the object displayed on the back of the flatbed lorry seemed no more than a mountainous pile of frayed blubber, several tons of it in fact, and with a thousand gallons of embalming fluid vying with putrefaction, it reeked like nothing on earth.

Nina let go of her father's hand in order to pinch her nose. Nell and Joe pretended to balk, each grimacing laughingly at the other as they joined the crowd that was gathered on the dank beak of land between Ouse and Foss, beside the dogs' home and the public baths, which had become the traditional fairgound. Shielding Nina from clumsy rubber-neckers, they led her through the darkness, to study those large jars arrayed along the edge of the lorry, in which were displayed various parts of the unfortunate creature's anatomy, including a huge tooth, baleen, and bristles from its jaws.

'What do you reckon to pickled whale then, Neen?' her father stooped to ask.

'Stinks,' she replied, through gloved fingers.

Her eyes beginning to water at the stench, Nell wheezed agreement. 'And I dread to think what that formaldehyde's doing to us!' Clamping her own mouth again, she craned to see what was in the row of cages some yards away, and spoke through wool. 'Shall we go and have a look at what's over there instead?'

But, after working their way through the crowd to see what other delights the enterprising individual had brought with his travelling show, they were to view a series of deformed animals – a goat with an extra leg dangling from its side and suchlike – and, noticing that the little girl seemed afraid, Nell suggested to Joe that they take her into town for a milkshake instead.

Though this interlude was enjoyable, it was not to last long. Being a weekday, Nina must be up for school the next morning.

But, 'Can Aunty Nell come and put me to bed?' requested Joe's daughter as they made to leave the café. 'Then she can see our new house.'

'Hardly new,' smiled Joe, and told Nell, 'It's an old corner shop that's been turned into a house. But it'll do us for now – come if you like, it's only where you bumped into us in Lawrence Street. Our Beat might not have set out for work yet, so you'll have chance of a natter with her.'

'And we've got a telly now, so we can watch Billy Bean and everything!' enticed Nina.

Needing no further incentive than the honour of putting Nina to bed, Nell accompanied the delightful little companion and her father home.

She found it a quaint abode. A dark little vestibule preceded a front room that had obviously been the shop, but was now lacking in content, save for a rough square of carpet atop some lino, a trunk of toys and a tricycle – in essence an indoor playground for Nina. As further indication that it had been a grocer's, there was a hatch that gave vent to the rear quarters, with the retailer's name etched into its glass. Divested of her coat, Nell was taken straight through to Joe's living room. This was more comfortably rugged and furnished, with a brown imitation-leather suite, a table and chairs, and a bureau. A short flight of varnished banisters intruded upon the room, the rest of the staircase hidden behind a wall and closed off by a door five steps up. There were cupboards, painted light green, to either side of the beige-tiled fireplace, and a kitchen and scullery tacked on behind.

Beata had in fact left for work, but Nell was more than happy to get the child ready for bed, standing guard outside the lavatory in the dark back yard, then taking her to the scullery for a wash, and finally to read her a book prior to bed. Having chosen to recite for her *The Night Before Christmas*, at the end of this Nell declared:

'It won't be long before Father Christmas pays us a visit – have you written yet, to tell him what you'd like?'

Nina was keen to do so, scrawling her message in crayon, then being led to the fireplace to release the note and watch it be sucked up the chimney. Then, without shenanigans, she allowed Nell to tuck her into bed.

'She never goes down for me like that,' said Joe, rising out of courtesy when Nell came back downstairs. 'If Beat isn't here to do it I always have a fight.'

'Ah well, you have to know how to handle them.' She gave an arch smile as she closed the door on the staircase and descended the last five steps. 'Any more trouble, you just send for Nurse Spottiswood, she'll come and sort you out.'

'I'll bear that in mind.' Joe went to turn off the television, which he had been watching in his visitor's absence.

'Don't turn it off on my account,' bade Nell, upon noticing that a war film was about to begin. 'I've got to be away now, you sit down and watch your picture.'

'No, I was going to turn it off anyway. I never watch that kind of thing.' Joe switched the set off. 'Did you happen to see what she'd asked Father Christmas for?'

'A biro,' smiled Nell. 'May I buy her that?'

Joe said she could. 'I'm sure there'll be plenty more on her list by the time he comes – can I get you something to drink?'

'No, really, I'd better go,' said Nell with a smile. 'I've to walk across town.'

He apologised at being unable to walk her home, but, 'I'll pay your bus fare – there's a stop across the road.'

Nell laughingly refused, but thanked him.

'I'm taking our Neen to a Civil Defence demo on Bull Lane tip on Saturday, if you fancy coming along?'

'Sorry, work again,' said Nell.

'When's your next night off then?' he asked, as he fetched her coat and held it open for her to put on.

'Not until next Tuesday,' replied Nell, slipping her arms into the sleeves. 'That's if they don't ask me to work it. The married staff seem to get preference when it comes to time off.' She smiled at him, expectant of an invitation to look after Nina again.

'Well, I think our Beat's on holiday next week.' He knew very well she was, for he had already asked her. 'If she'll look after the bairn, would you come and keep me company at the pictures? That's if you've nothing better to do, of course. I don't get out much, and when I do I have to go on my own. It gets a bit boring just sitting in a pub.'

'Of course I would,' came her kind reply. 'Though if you'd rather go with your sister, I could look after –'

'Don't you think I see enough of our Beat?' demanded Joe, then chuckled. 'Good job she isn't here and can't hear me – she'd clip my ear'ole! No, I just thought it'd be a break for you as well, if you don't get out much . . .'

'Oh, well, if you're sure, it'd be lovely.' Nell buttoned her coat. 'Can I come and meet you here? I don't want to leave you standing outside the cinema if I can't manage to get away.'

Joe gave a happy shrug. 'I don't feel very chivalrous,

you having to come and pick me up, instead of the other way round, but if you think it's best . . .'

And Nell did consider it best, because that way she would get to see Nina into the bargain.

Luckily, she was able to get away the following week, and a very pleasant night out it turned out to be too, the easy-going Joe allowing her to choose what picture they would see, and Nell receiving a goodnight cuddle from Nina before she left.

It was also to mark the beginning of a new phase, of Nell calling in at the house in Lawrence Street any time she felt like it, sometimes lucky enough to be allowed exclusive access to Nina, sometimes having to share her with Joe or Beata. By now, she had come to regard Joe as much of a pal as she did his sister, and this was obviously reciprocated, for he had lately given her a spare key, so that she would never find herself locked out after trailing so far to see them. Evidently, he had realised that her offers to collect Nina from school when he was working were not made out of charity, but because Nell genuinely enjoyed doing so, and he had stopped regarding her as a benefactor, and more as another sister.

It was all extremely endearing, the only trouble being that, working permanent nights, one's body clock was not in tune with that of normal folk, making it very difficult to socialise. Her days off were irregular, and often she would find herself having to use a greater part of this time to catch up on sleep. Hence, there were all sorts of things she was forced to miss. She had promised to take Nina to see Santa at a store in town, and had moved heaven and earth to fulfil this, but, due to work, the invitation to Christmas dinner with Joe and Beata had perforce been refused, the New Year also passing without ceremony.

Making her way home through a thick blanket of fog, mixed with smoke from factory chimneys on yet another dark winter's morning, Nell made the sudden decision that she was tired of living like a bat, and regardless of whether Sister Pike was difficult to work with or not, she would arrange to be included on the day rota. This might not allow her to see any more of Nina, but she could at least coordinate her movements with that of normal folk, so that when opportunities did arise there was more chance of her being able to respond to them.

For today, though, it was the usual routine, and once she got home she was soon in bed. But at least tomorrow was her night off. That being so, she had pre-arranged to collect Nina from school later on in the day. Drifting towards sleep, she smiled now as she looked forward to their meeting.

Upon answering her alarm, Nell had some buttered toast and tea, got washed and dressed, then caught a bus across the city to Nina's school.

As ever, the little girl showed delight as she ran from the playground to meet Nell, and, after giving her a kiss, skipped all the way home ahead of her – not that there was far to go, just a stretch of narrow lane between an ancient graveyard and a row of prefabs before they crossed the main road to Joe's house.

First attending the banked-up fire and bringing it to life, Nell then gave Nina a drink of lemonade and switched on the television for her, finally tearing herself away to make a start on cooking Joe's tea, as she had lately taken to doing. It was the least she could do to repay the trust he had invested, allowing her such free access to his daughter.

But before she had taken the meat from the pantry, a little voice moaned: 'Aw! Not bloody Andy Pandy . . .'

'Oy! You're not supposed to say words like that!' Nell sounded stern, but could not help covering a smile as a dejected Nina trailed in to join her.

'I hate him,' she grumbled, both hands gripping the edge

of the worktop and standing on tiptoe to see what Nell was doing. 'He's got a twisted gob.'

'Poor thing! He can't help looking the way he does.' Then Nell's face turned mischievous to confide, 'But I can't stand him either, he should be called Namby-Pamby.' After undergoing a few moments chatter about which children's programme was best, Nell said, 'I'd better turn the television off then, and save on electric. Come on, you can help me make tea.' And, rather more slowly than she had anticipated, with the constant interruptions of her small helper, she managed to prepare a casserole.

Once it was simmering in the oven, she had time to relax, informing Nina as she cleared away the peelings, 'I've brought some old ration books for you to play with. They're in my handbag. You can go and get them if you like, and we'll play shops for a while.'

Upon joining Nina some moments later, Nell was instructed to open the hatch window between the two rooms. Then, 'You go round into t'front room!' ordered Nina, clambering onto the arm of an easy chair, and waiting for the other to do so.

As Nell approached the hatch from the other side, the small grocer took one of the redundant ration books from a pile, licked her pencil and enquired: 'What can I get for you this morning, Mrs – what's your last name?'

'Spottiswood.'

'Mrs Spottiswood.' Leaning on her counter, Nina opened the ration book and licked her pencil again, about to write.

'Don't do that,' warned Nell. 'You'll get lead poisoning.'

'Doesn't matter. You're a nurse, you can make it better.'

'I'm glad you have such faith in me.' Nell arched her brow and smiled, and, for a time, pretended to be the customer. Then she noted that one of the ration books was the wrong colour. 'Hang on! You didn't get that from my bag . . .' She frowned and reached for the one that Nina was about to write in.

'No, I got it from up there.' A finger was pointed at a shelf.

'Good heavens, Neen, it's your daddy's meat ration book!' Drawing in her breath, Nell quickly examined it for signs of damage. 'We mustn't deface that or you'll have nothing for next week's dinner.'

Taking this as castigation, Nina said, 'I'm fed-up of this game. Shall we play summat else?'

'You're easily bored, aren't you? Let's see . . .' said Nell, then went to look through cupboards and drawers, forgetting for a moment that she did not actually live there, and behaving as she would in her own home – which was why she was pulled up so sharply by what came next.

In her search for a game, she came across a tin holding buttons, needles, other odds and ends, and a wooden darning mushroom that was obviously a souvenir, for it was emblazoned with the crest of some German town. This had been Grette's sewing box. There came a pang – as if someone had stabbed her in the breast – not of shame for snooping amongst another woman's belongings, but of jealousy that she had not been the one to give birth to this child she so adored.

'What we gonna do?'

Glancing at Nina, she underwent a moment of poignancy, and also guilt, that she was pretending to lay claim to her, when somewhere out there was the son she had given away. William would be thirteen soon, and on the way to being a man. Had he been in the room now, there would have been no contest as to which child she would pick. But this one was here, not just a memory, and looking up at her in expectation of something to play with. Who would have foreseen that Nell would play mother to a German's child?

Gazing back into those blue eyes, and overcome with love for Nell, she broke into a smile, and shook such thoughts from her head.

'I'm going to teach you how to do French knitting!'

Finding an empty cotton reel, she went to the shed and collected four panel pins, which she hammered on the top of the reel around the hole in its centre. A short stub of broken knitting needle made the ideal tool. 'Right, Neen, this is what you do . . .' She revelled in the hot sweet breath against her ear, as the child draped herself over a shoulder to watch, and to copy.

But soon, the growl of a motorcycle alerted them both. 'Ooh, look out!' warned Nell. 'It's Billy Bean and his funny machine. I hope he won't tell me off for using his hammer and nails.'

'He won't,' replied Nina with a smile of surety. 'He likes you.' Then a thought struck her as she ran from the sitting room to open the back door. 'Do you like him? 'Cause if you do, you could get married instead of being all on your own.'

Joe entered the kitchen to see Nell looking flustered.

'I was just asking Aunty Nell if she wants to marry you,' Nina informed her father, dragging at his leg in greeting.

There was embarrassed laughter all round. 'Bloomin' hangment, an ancient codger like me?' guffawed Joe, his cheeks all pink from the cold as he took off his gauntlets and raked his silvery hair. 'I'm old enough to be Aunty Nell's father!'

'You're not *that* old,' soothed Nell, trying to make herself look busy by lifting the casserole from the oven, then setting out warm plates. 'At least, you don't look it.'

Joe affected to swank. 'Well, 1907 was a decent vintage.' He scooped a handful of toffees from his pocket and dropped them on the sideboard. 'For after tea.'

'Look!' His daughter showed him the short length of French knitting she had created. 'Aunty Nell taught me how to do it.'

'Did she? By, she's a clever woman – you're doing a good job and all! Right, let me blow me nose, it's streaming.' After a quick ruffle of her hair, he tugged out a handkerchief, trumpeted into it, then took off his motorcycle jacket and travelled through the sitting room to hang it up in the lobby.

'Fetch your daddy his slippers,' suggested Nell whilst he was absent. 'Then you can help me lay the table.' Nina scurried to comply.

Joe came back to sit down and change his footwear, sounding most appreciative as he called out to Nell, who was still in the kitchen, 'That smells grand, whatever it is.'

'Thank you. It's amazing what you can do with some old boot leather and an Oxo.'

Joe smiled to himself, then looked thoughtful, and called out again. 'Getting back to the subject of vintage . . . I don't suppose you fancy going out for a ducky later, do you?'

She paused in doling out the casserole. 'Who'll look after Nina?'

'Our Beat'll be in by then,' Joe called back. 'I've already asked her, she doesn't mind.'

'Well, if it's all right with her, then why not?' Nell sounded cheerful. 'Now, is that table all ready, Neen? Then we'll eat!'

Even after his hunger had been slaked, Joe continued to gorge on the casserole, for the years of near famine had conditioned him into snaffling every morsel. 'Eh, look at me, fond brussen!' Projecting satiety, he patted his belly.

'What's that mean?' enquired his daughter.

'It means I'm as full as a butcher's dog – thanks, Aunty Nell, that were lush.' Joe rose and, instructing his daughter to do likewise, carried his empty plate to the kitchen – though Nell was the one who rolled up her sleeves to wash them.

'Eh, has somebody been knocking you about?' Joe was instantly alert, and came up to frown at the circular bruises that disfigured both her arms.

Baffled at first, she looked down at herself, then laughed,

and continued washing the pots. 'Only the iron lung. It has these rubber collars for one to stick one's hands through in order to tend the patient. Naturally they have to be very tight for the machine to work effectively.'

Joe relaxed with a slight sound of relief. 'Our Beat must get them too, though I've never noticed.'

'It's an occupational hazard, I'm afraid,' smiled Nell, 'along with many other things I won't mention.'

'What's an iron lung?' asked Nina, who had now resumed her French knitting.

Nell gave an honest description as she raced through the small amount of washing-up.

Then she said, 'Right, that's my bit done! Why don't we get you into your nightdress, Neen – no, don't worry, you don't have to go to sleep yet! I just meant that if you're all ready for bed, I could read you a few stories before I have to go – that's if your daddy doesn't want to read for you?' She spun towards Joe with an apology. 'Sorry, I'm forgetting my place again!'

'Nay, be my guest,' invited Joe, going to switch on the television. 'Better use the lavvy before you get your clothes off, though.'

Nell helped the little one into her coat in order to brave the cold dark yard, and left the kitchen door ajar to allow a stream of light to aid her passage.

Nina soon returned. 'I meant to ask the other day, Dad, what does Government Property mean?' And she presented a shiny square of toilet paper upon which this damning phrase was stamped.

'You little snitch!' Joe gave an embarrassed laugh and explained to Nell, 'I have friends in high places.'

But she could not have cared less about such pilfering, her smiling eyes intent on the little girl as she rinsed a flannel in the sink and wiped it quickly around Nina's face, neck and hands. Then they all went to sit round the hearth.

'Fancy a ciggy?' Joe was in the act of lighting one for himself.

'Thank – oh, you've only two left.' Nell withdrew her hand upon observing the extended packet.

'Our Neen's given up.' Winking through the smoke, he pressed her to take one, holding his lighter carefully as she bent her head over it.

'Can I have the cat, Dad?'

'Aye, go on.' Joe exhaled a chestful of smoke at the same time as Nell. 'But get your nightie on while I cut it out for you.'

'I'll do it, you watch your telly.' Setting her lighted cigarette in an ashtray, Nell reached for some nail scissors off the mantel, and proceeded to trim around the outline of the black cat, and to detach it from the red background, half-listening to the programme as she did so. The little cut-out was handed to Nina when she was down to her liberty bodice.

Having helped the skinny little figure into her nightdress and brushed her hair, Nell then sat back with the child on her lap, smoking contentedly and going on to spend a lovely hour reading stories.

Nina would have let her read all night, and Nell would probably have complied, had not Joe announced at the end of the current story, 'Right, bed!' And the two girls were forced to relinquish their happy interlude with a goodnight kiss.

When Beata came home an hour or so later, Nell went to fetch what was left of the casserole, then, after spending a few moments chatting with her, she and Joe went along to the Tam O' Shanter, which was only a couple of doors away.

Along with the drinks came light-hearted conversation. 'You know, I'd never have believed you were so ancient if you hadn't told me,' joked Nell, sipping the stout he had just placed before her.

'I think there was a compliment in there somewhere.' Joe took a smiling gulp of his own pint, before asking, 'What vintage are you then?' Though he had already been supplied this information by his sister.

'Nineteen twenty-two,' said Nell.

'And you don't mind being seen out with such a crock?' His eyes twinkled at her over the rim of his glass.

'You're a very handsome companion.' Out of kindness Nell exaggerated, though he was nice-looking.

'Even with this grey hair?'

'It's not grey! It's a very distinguished silver.'

He looked pleased at being so described. Until Nell went on to point out:

'You've got a dew-drop ready to fall into your pint.'

With a quick laugh, he pulled out his handkerchief and brushed the droplet away. 'That's what I like, a woman who says what she sees.'

'You'd have to, with Nina for a daughter. She doesn't pull her punches, does she?'

Smiling back at her, Joe shook his head. 'I don't know – what must you think of us, having knocked-off lavatory paper!'

'Ah well, hard times require desperate measures. Where do you think I get my supply of cotton wool from?' There came another shared laugh at the little girl's comic faux pas.

'She's great company,' effused Nell. 'I love her. I really do.'

'Don't we all,' came Joe's warm agreement, and he took another deep pull of his pint, imbibing almost half of it at once, before lowering the glass back to the table and gazing down into the froth for a while. 'And she does have some bright ideas.' He did not enlarge for the moment, but spent a while in deep thought before eventually saying, 'Would you ever consider marrying someone fifteen years older than yourself?'

Astonished, Nell's glass of stout paused in mid-air as

she was about to take a drink. Only after a few false starts did she eventually manage to stutter, 'Well, that was a bit of a surprise! I don't know what to – are you saying – I mean, I like your company very much, but –'

'No, no, 'course you wouldn't!' Joe shook his head rapidly, as if to decry his own foolishness in proposing. 'I don't know what I was thinking of even mentioning it – *me*, who played hell when our Gus wanted to marry Mick, going on about him being too decrepit for her and whatnot, how bloody arrogant is that? Sorry –'

Infected by his embarrassment, yet touched too, Nell rushed to placate him. 'It's just, you know, I don't think I'll ever feel the same about anyone after losing Bill . . .' Even after so long his shadow still accompanied her.

'I feel the same way about Grette,' Joe hurried to agree. 'I still miss her as if it were only yesterday she died.' He paused a moment, as if on the edge. 'What really made me blurt it out was that, well, I've watched you with our Nina. I can see how much you like her – I'm not saying I only want a mother for her, I'm thinking of meself as well.' Looking at him more carefully now, at his eyes that roamed about her as he spoke, a stunned Nell bewailed her own stupidity in mistaking his interest for brotherly love. It was all too obvious the physical attraction he felt, as he added, 'I really enjoy our times together. I even find meself thinking about you after you've gone home, wondering what you're doing and that. You're a lovely lass to have around.' Unconsciously he picked up a spare beer mat, and tapped the edge of it against the table. 'I'd like you to be there all the time . . .'

Nell's eyes were now on the blue coal scars on his hands, a relic of his mining days, as she sought a fitting response. 'I think about you as well,' she said, careful not to hurt him. 'In the same way I think of your sister, as a good friend who makes me laugh, and who I know I can rely on.'

Joe looked slightly deflated, but gave a shrug and

continued to press suit. 'That's a decent enough basis for a partnership. I wouldn't expect mad passion –'

'Oh Joe.' Nell leaned forward to prevent this getting out of hand. 'I really enjoy being with you and Nina, but with the job I have, I couldn't be a proper mother or a proper wife –'

'I wouldn't ask you to give it up, I know it's a vocation, like it is for our Beat –' Seeing the anguish on her face, he quickly changed tack, at once detached, yet friendly and blasé. 'Anyway, I can see I've put you in an awkward position, so you don't have to say any more! I just thought I'd let you know how it is with me – I hope I haven't put the kibosh on things between us? Neen'd kill me if my blunder drove you away. Can we just go on as we were?'

'Of course!' Nell smiled and laid a comforting hand on his arm, then quickly withdrew it.

'Right, will you have another drink?' Cheerful again, he lifted his glass suddenly and tilted his head back to drain it, and, as the froth ran slowly back down the sides, added, 'Sorry for being daft.'

'You're not daft! I'm very flattered, and if things were different . . .' Her voice trailed away, for she had no wish to lead him on. The only passion involved in this relationship was that between herself and Nina. But how could one say to a man, 'I absolutely adore your daughter' then tell him, 'You're okay too, I suppose'? It wouldn't be fair. Besides, there was the question of disloyalty. She had sworn she would never marry. All right, it was thirteen and a half years since dear Bill, and she knew he had not been the type to hold her to this for the rest of her life, but she could not help feeling it would slur his memory . . . Still, it was very flattering to be asked, and very tempting, in the sense that it would mean she could be with Nina all the time.

Her head was still fizzing with the surprise of it all, as Joe ambled off to the bar.

* * *

A vocation, Joe had said, and yes, Nell supposed, after a somewhat inauspicious start, it had accidentally become such over the years. In spite of that, he had given her cause to think about what was more important to her, during the hours that followed. And even days later, she was still mulling over his proposal in her mind – though only because of the fact that it would bring legitimate access to her surrogate child.

This being so, it was not something she felt able to discuss with Beata. For what would she think to her brother being so used? And anyway, Nell was soon to put it out of her head in favour of her patients. Having spoken to Matron about the matter, she was no longer working permanent nights, but alternating them with day shifts. Her old adversary, Sister Pike, had greeted this with one of her sarcasms, of course, and said what an honour it would be to have Nurse Spottiswood working alongside her again. But other than this, Pike had not been able to cause much unpleasantness so far, for she had gone on leave.

In her absence, Nell was making the most of things in the place she loved best: the children's section. How wonderful it was to see them cured of a deadly disease, knowing you had been part of that. Of course, this must be balanced with deep sadness too: the sight of parents attempting to be brave as they peered through the window for a glimpse of the child who was beyond help. Nell felt dreadful at not being able to ease their grief, but she always reminded herself that it was their grief, not hers, and she must not be so egotistical as to steal it. At such times she would cope by lowering a portcullis on her emotions, and though this might not prevent her howling with sorrow upon reaching home, she could draw solace from the majority who recovered, the letters of gratitude from indebted parents, or from patients themselves, expressing thanks to dear Spotty for making them feel as if they were the only one she had had to care for.

Thankfully, there was no death on the wards today, and Nell was cheerful as she prepared a five-year-old boy to be reunited with his parents in the grounds, having to disinfect him and his essential belongings before he could be discharged. 'No, I'm sorry, darling, you can't take that with you!' He was trying to hide a toy that had become a favourite during the time he had been in with scarlet fever, and Nell was tender in removing it from him. 'You'll have to leave it for the poorly boys and girls.' Whilst most were content to accept this rule, this one began to kick up a fuss. 'Well,' declared his nurse in blithe manner, 'if I let you keep it, then you'd have to live here with me all the time – and I'd *love* a little boy to keep.' And this, of course, did the trick.

And upon being given back to his parents, he gladly forgot all about the toy, and about the nurse who waved him off, who watched him skip away before turning back to the wards to succour another in distress.

The rest of that day turned out to be equally satisfying, as Nell tended her charges in the airy pavilions. Yet, at the end of it she must bring her mind back to the question raised by Joe. She had promised that it would make no difference, that they could still be friends. But now she felt awkward at the thought of seeing him again, and if she could have avoided him she would. But she had arranged to pick Nina up from school again on her day off, and so there was no choice.

Their first meeting since the proposal turned out to be as awkward as she had feared, though both of them attempted to hide it, Nell trying not to display inhibition when her little playmate's father came home to interrupt their game, Joe being as friendly and jocular as usual as he consumed the tea Nell had made for them all. Yet once Nina was put to bed, she seemed eager not to hang around.

'I won't bite you, you know.' Joe threw her a casual

laugh from his easy chair. 'Sit down and watch a bit of telly till Beata comes in.'

'I really oughtn't . . .' began Nell.

'I've not suddenly changed into Jack the Ripper. I thought you said we could still be friends?'

And of course, she had said that, and so she must sit down and smile, and chat, and act as if nothing had changed.

But things had changed for others. 'Old Mick's died,' Joe suddenly announced, between programmes.

Nell gave instant condolence, her velvety eyes on his face. 'Oh, I'm so sorry – when?'

'Yesterday. Didn't quite manage to reach eighty.'

'Poor Gus . . .'

'Aye, she's broken-hearted,' sighed Joe, reaching for his cigarettes and offering one to Nell, then lighting it for her. 'I feel really guilty after the way I went on at her when she first married him, pointing out how much older he was – as if she didn't already know – saying she just wanted to look after his kids. She really loved him, you know.'

'I know.' Nell's voice was soft, her heart fluttering as she guessed where this was leading.

And it was a great relief to her when Beata came in.

14

Nell was not to see Joe for a while after that, for after her few days off she was once again on nights. As usual, she arrived early for her shift, this allowing her to a spend little time chatting with the occupants of the iron lungs, and thus hopefully ease their miserable existence.

To her dismay, Sister Pike was back from her leave and had been in command that day, but at least, Nell thought, would be going home soon. Praying for this to come quickly, Nell gathered with other oncoming night staff as the sister went over each patient's notes. There was only one new arrival: a six-year-old boy with polio. After the handover, Nell was quick to remove herself from Pike's company, and went to make her acquaintance with the small patient. All gowned up again, she entered his cubicle to find him steeped in misery, and spoke kindly to allay his fears.

'Hello, old chap . . .' She smiled into the wan face with its thick mop of dark hair. 'My name's Spotty. I haven't come to hurt you. See, I've brought my friend with me – his name's Fred.' She had concealed a miniature teddy bear under her arm, and now made him peep out as if acting independently, bobbing quickly out of sight when he saw the boy, then gingerly peeping over her arm again. There was the flicker of a smile, but the patient's face soon crumpled in nausea.

Nell quickly put aside the teddy in favour of a bowl,

into which the boy suddenly vomited. Issuing reassurance, she remained calmly at his side whilst he retched. 'That's right, you just get rid of it, dear, and we'll soon have you better.' And she stroked his thick fringe away from his brow as he continued to heave over the bowl, though his reflex was to veer away. 'Sorry, old chap, is it your headache? Well, we'll do something about that too, don't you worry.'

Even with his stomach relieved of its discomfort, the boy was quite irritable and, atypically, did not appreciate his nurse's attempts to lower his fever with an icy sponge, but jerked his limbs about all over the place and kicked her. As she continued to nurse him according to his illness, Nell gradually became suspicious. She had been tending polio victims for some years now, and even though the diagnosis complied with his symptoms of severe headache and vomiting, there was something about his intermittent grizzling and peculiar behaviour that made her have qualms.

Remembering the last occasion she had questioned her superior, she deemed it best to keep her own counsel for a while, at least until Sister Pike had gone home. But she resolved to watch him closely, and the more she watched, the more concerned she became.

Eventually, there seemed no choice but to go and offer her opinion to the night sister, and to ask her to come and check that this really was polio, for, 'He certainly isn't acting as if he has it, he's playing me up for all he's worth.'

When she and the night sister entered his cubicle, it was to find he had become lacklustre again, and was obviously on the verge of being sick. Nell's superior was none too pleased at being dragged here on a whim. Being comparatively new, and unfamiliar with the nurse's experience, she saw only the state-enrolled uniform, and relayed in condescending manner, 'You'd better get some wool on your back before you start trying to tell others their job. He's a classic case if ever I saw one.'

And Nell was forced to submit to this view, for she had not the medical expertise to prove otherwise. Yet her hunch was difficult to shift, and though she had others equally sick to care for, during the following hours it was constantly to lure her back to the boy's side, to check that she was not deluded. Whether she be right or wrong, Nell did not care, her anxiety being that his behaviour had grown progressively odd. And, unable to do anything to appease him, nor to ease his pain, it was a very long night.

With her suspicions pooh-poohed by others, Nell was to lean on her trusted friend Beata. The latter was enjoying a few days off, before the rotation of shifts took her back on to nights, and at first she laughed when Nell turned up unexpectedly at the house in Lawrence Street that morning, joking that she could not stay away and guessing whom she had come to see. But upon hearing that Nell had actually come to speak to her about a serious matter, she paid careful heed, before promising to give her own opinion on the boy once she was back at work.

Thirty-six hours later there came confirmation of Nell's fears. 'He's never polio,' stated Beata, as the two kept their appointed rendezvous outside the cubicle that evening.

'That's what I think!' appealed a worried Nell, as both peered in at him. 'So why can no one else see it?' Reminding Beata about her visit to the night sister, she had more news to give. 'The day staff ignored me too when I mentioned it.'

At this point the small patient let out a wail, causing Nell's face to collapse in despair. 'This is what he's been like all the time. The poor little mite's in agony. What can we do for him, Killie?' Then, after an anxious moment, she decided, 'They're more likely to listen if there are two of us pestering them. Will you come with me tomorrow morning, then we'll both tackle Pike and the others together?'

With Beata's agreement, they parted, the friend scrubbing up and returning to the main building, Nell going back into the cubicle to try to pacify her fretful charge.

'Poor old chap,' she murmured tenderly, and stroked his head – but to her alarm that made him scream all the louder.

And it suddenly dawned on her what this might be. Trying instead to soothe with her voice, she told the sobbing child how sorry she was for hurting him, but, determined to verify what she had just accidentally stumbled upon, she held him down so as to examine his head again. And that was when she found the swelling. Sick at the discovery, and the frustration of having to watch a child in agony, she scrubbed up then went straight away to find Beata again.

'Oh, Killie, I think he's got a tumour or something.' She looked deeply concerned. 'It's not that obvious, but it's definitely there – why didn't I find it before this?'

Beata tried to remove her look of guilt. 'He's got that much hair, it'd be hard to tell just from looking.'

'Oh God, listen to him . . .' breathed Nell. The cries were ones of agony and could be heard from afar. She wanted to cover her ears, but that would not help him. 'I'll have to fetch Sister – but I know she'll refuse to listen to me.'

The stockier figure had already set off with determination in her eye. 'She won't have to listen to you, she must be deaf not to hear that. I'll go and tell her he's keeping everyone awake, and needs to be given something.'

Mercifully, she was to succeed where Nell had previously failed, the child being given an injection that at last allowed him to sleep. But only for a time, and Nell was to sit with him for the rest of the very long night, stroking his hand and singing to him softly, anything that might help to reduce his agonised writhing.

* * *

At handover the next day, joining forces with Beata, Nell made it her a priority to inform the day sister about the swelling she had found on the boy's head, she acting as spokesman. 'I think it might be a tumour.'

Sister Pike was in one of her better moods this morning, though her attempt at wit was just as derogatory. 'Oh, Doctor Spottiswood, is it? How many times have I told you not to get above yourself? The paediatrician examined him when he came in, and there was no sign of a swelling.'

'Well, there is now!' Nell's voice began to rise. 'He screams whenever his head's touched.'

'But he cries at us too!' the day nurse jumped in, fearing she too would bear the brunt of Pike's temper, her attitude as flippant as sister's. 'He's just being naughty.'

'It's *not* naughtiness!' Nell spluttered at her detractors. 'He's in agony – and if you don't do something about it he might die within hours!'

Beata, who had been quiet until then, spoke up and confirmed Nell's view. 'His head is distorted, sister. I've seen it.'

'But have you felt it?' demanded Pike.

'I didn't want to add to his pai –'

'No, you haven't then!' Sister cut her off. 'So, it's probably a knot, with all that hair of his!'

Whilst Nell looked about to explode, Beata remained calm, but there was an angry glint in her eye. 'You don't scream like that from knotted hair.'

But still she and Nell were both met with derision. 'He was quiet enough when I looked in on him,' declared Sister Pike, and turned her back to do something else.

'Only because he's too weak to cry any more!' Livid at being ignored, Nell pattered after her. 'Sister, I'm begging you . . .' She felt her eyes burn, not for her own humiliation, but at the thought of not being able to save the child. 'Won't you please at least let the doctor know what we've found, so he can come and have a look?'

'Go home, Nurse Spottiswood,' laughed Sister Pike. 'If that child isn't here when you get back this evening, I myself will pin a medal on your chest.'

They discussed going over Sister Pike's head, and taking the matter up with Matron, but that was a dangerous game, and with everyone against them, would she believe them either? As a stop-gap, and a measure of desperation, they decided to consult a friendly staff nurse, and, assuaged by her promise to take it up with the doctor if she got the chance, Nell and Beata were finally to go home.

But the sense of helplessness and worry was to accompany them on their separate ways. Nell was to sleep little that day, and doubted that her friend could either.

Long before she was due to begin her shift, she was back at the hospital and entering the child's cubicle. There was little joy in seeing that he was no longer crying in agony, for in the hush Nell detected another sound, and she went to inform the day nurse who had mocked her this morning.

'He's formed a lot of mucus in his throat. Do you want me to fetch the . . .' she flapped her arm in search of the word, the frustration of it all affecting her memory for even the commonplace, '. . . sucky thing?'

The other poked fun. 'Sucky thing? Is that a technical term?' Then she added, 'No, you'll break his teeth.'

'He'll grow new teeth, but he won't grow a new brain,' accused Nell, more furious than ever, but trying her best to contain it. 'Has the doctor been to see him?'

There came a shake of the head.

A stocky little figure had wandered up quietly, and now made contribution. 'He needs to be told,' said Beata.

'What can I do if Sister says no?' the day nurse enquired of both. 'I can't stride over her and drag him down by his scruff.'

Nell moaned in despair, then lunged her face close to

the other's to make an indictment of neglect. 'I'm telling you! If nothing's done that child will be gone by morning – and it'll be your fault, and Sister Pike's too!'

Such was her frustration and anger on the child's behalf, that Nell felt like banging her head against the wall. However, with others to be nursed, she and Beata were forced to go about their everyday affairs. But once the rest of the patients were asleep, they were to take it in turns to sit and hold his hand, and to watch him slip into a coma, to share the burden between them, for it was too harrowing for one to bear.

When he died in the early hours, both were beside themselves from the effort of having to contain such rage and grief. Nell confessed to hating Pike more than she had ever hated anyone, even the Germans and all that they had done to her. How that detestable pig of a woman could call herself a nurse, could sneer at them for their lack of qualifications, when she had not one ounce of humility nor compassion . . . Had she been before them now, Nell would have gladly smashed her fist into that condescending face, imagined the act of doing so again and again.

Alas, their only outlet for this fury was to clean the dead boy's cubicle from top to bottom, scrubbing like maniacs until the job was done. By the time the day staff came on, she and Beata were almost too choked to speak.

'Good morning!' sang Sister Pike, in that self-important fashion that told she was in a good mood as she bustled around the wards on her rounds. 'Oh – where's our little brain tumour this morning?' She turned in surprise to Nell, who launched herself.

'He's in the mortuary – where *I* said he'd be!'

Somewhat shocked by the distraught attack, Sister looked from Nell's angry face to that of Beata, then immediately withdrew, obviously to investigate, for when she returned a few moments later she had with her the other nurse who had doubted Nell, and neither of them could do enough for her, nor Beata. 'Come into the office, my dears, and have a cup of –'

'We don't want your bloody tea!' Beata looked ready to throw it in that patronising face.

'What we want to know is *why*?' demanded Nell, almost in tears. 'Why wouldn't you take a blind bit of notice of our warning? Did you think we were just saying it to bull ourselves up? We're not idiots!'

'Of course you're not, nobody said –'

'Well, that's what was implied!' retorted Beata, equally emotional.

'Not at all!' Sister tried to mitigate. 'It was extremely hard even for a physician to differentiate between the boy's symptoms and that of polio. Nurse Spottiswood did very well to spot it.'

Nell contorted her face. 'You think I want praise? A monkey could have detected there was something amiss! Both Killie and I have worked here long enough to know how polio presents itself, and we both said that poor little chap didn't have it – I *begged* you to do something, and you mocked me!'

Sister Pike fidgeted over this criticism, but maintained her repentant tone whilst managing to hang on to her authority. 'Well, I'm very sorry if it appeared that way.' Grim of face, she folded her hands as if to end the matter. 'You were right, and the rest of us were wrong.'

'At that child's cost!' A bileful Nell refused to be fobbed off.

And nor would Beata, all caution thrown to the wind as she spat, 'You can thank your lucky stars he isn't a member of my family, because I'd kick up such a bloody stink!'

'You'll say nothing of this outside the hospital!' Pike warned them.

'No, because I'm ashamed to be associated with it!'

Too furious and tearful to say more, her heart pumping dangerously fast, Nell wheeled away, and, with a last recriminatory look at Pike, Beata followed.

Sister called after them, eager to make amends. 'Would you like to stay behind and attend the post mortem? Just to see what it really –'

'I don't need to see!' Nell spun back and came charging at her again. 'I can tell you what killed him – a brain tumour, or an abscess. But it doesn't matter which, because that poor child still died in agony, and I'll never bloody forgive you!'

Knowing they would both be unable to sleep, let alone eat, Nell shunned the canteen and invited Beata to accompany her to her austere abode to share a dram of whisky. Seated side by side on the bed, their backs against the wall, neither really wanted an inquest over what had just occurred – for what more was there to add – but simply to try and drown their sorrows as best they might. Amongst the many gifts received from grateful patients was a bottle that Nell had not yet opened. It was certainly put to good use now.

But, if anything, the firewater made them even angrier, Nell's tongue soon loosened enough to declare, 'I feel like packing it all in! For all Pike's fine words I *know* she still won't pay any more heed to what I say. If I thought my staying would make a difference, then I would, but I just keep thinking, what if it had been William? Or Nina? Honestly, I do, Killie, I feel like packing it all in . . .'

'Then do,' said her friend, her own eyes similarly grave as she sipped from her glass.

'And abandon more poor souls to those incompetent butchers? I know it's harsh, I know everybody makes mistakes, but really . . .' Nell took an angry swig. 'And who'd stand up for them if I were to go?'

'I would,' vowed Beata, slightly less free with her intake than Nell, for she had yet to walk a straight trail home.

'Pff, why should you have to stand alone?' demanded Nell.

'Just because I've made nursing my life, doesn't mean you have to do the same. You're still a young woman –'

Nell cut in with a groggy laugh. 'I seem to recall that when you were my age you regarded yourself as an old maid!'

'Maybe that's because everybody's treated me as an old maid from the day I was born,' murmured Beata. 'And we're not talking about me. You've been in this job for fifteen years –'

'So've you!'

'Aye, and often I've felt like chucking it all in as well, no more so than now. But there's no point, because I know that this is what I was put on this earth to do. I'm married to the job, but you, with your good looks, could escape.'

'Are you saying I'm a useless nurse, so I might as well get married?' slurred Nell.

'Oh, I can see there's no talking to you when you're kali-ed,' scolded Beata, though with a fond look in her eye as she took a slurp of her own drink.

'I know what you're saying, Killie.' Nell bumped shoulders with her in gratitude. 'As a matter of fact, I received a proposal of marriage not very long ago.' Her inebriated expression bore an additional look of smugness.

But Beata didn't seem surprised. 'Joe, was it?'

Nell sat bolt upright. 'He told you?'

The other shook her head. 'I've been expecting it, from the way he talks about you. Been asking a lot of questions –'

Even in her glassy-eyed state, Nell looked nervous. 'You didn't tell him about William?'

'No, you clot, just normal stuff, mostly to do with work.'

Nell showed uncertainty. 'Do you think I should tell him?

Beata replied in her usually understated manner. 'That

depends on whether or not you intend to accept his proposal.'

Nell slumped back against the wall, eyelids droopy, head lolling, both from drunkenness and exhaustion. 'Well, actually, I didn't like to tell you before, but I turned him down. I felt terrible at hurting his feelings, but it was just such a shock and I reacted on impulse. I always said I wouldn't marry.'

'No law to say you can't change your mind,' said Beata, sensing a hint of regret.

'I'll never change my mind about Bill,' replied Nell softly. 'I know Joe's your brother, Killie, and he's a lovely chap, but I could never feel the same way about him . . .'

'No, but you do like him?'

'Oh, yes! He's smashing company, we have lots of laughs. And Nina . . .' Nell's face lit up totally now, her thoughts obviously consumed by the little girl. 'She's just the gorgeousest little thing! Sorry, I'm making words up now, aren't I? But it would be no hardship being her mother, I feel as if she's mine already. But would it be fair?'

'To marry him when you still love Bill?' questioned Beata. 'I'm sure he feels the same way about Grette.'

'Oh yes, he told me that.' Swaying, Nell tipped back her glass again.

'Well then. So long as you're both aware what you're getting into . . .'

'But Joe's not aware, is he? Not aware of William. And if I do the right thing and tell him I have a son, he might change his mind.'

'Would it concern you if he did?'

'Why yes, it would concern me greatly!' revealed Nell. 'I value his respect. I'd hate it if he looked at me in a different light.'

'Then that says to me that you feel strongly enough to marry him. Knowing Joe, I don't think he'd look at you the slightest bit differently. But by the same token, I can't see the point in upskelling the applecart over something that happened all that time ago. So, you won't find me sticking my oar in, it's up to you whether you tell him or not. If William were on the scene it would be a different matter –'

'But he isn't.' Nell looked set to weep again.

'No, and I know you'll never be able to replace him, but you could have more children. So, why don't you take this chance, Spotty? It might not come again.'

Nell gazed into mid-air, rubbing her midriff, for the whisky had scoured her empty stomach. 'I suppose there is no point in staying to bang my head against a brick wall . . .' she belched. 'Pardon me.'

'No point at all,' agreed Beata. 'Go and get married, have a family, whatever you bloody need, but don't stay in nursing just to torture yourself, or for promises you made long ago.'

After just two tots of whisky to Nell's five, Beata went home to her own bed. But Nell, even with a great deal more alcohol to fuzz her brain, and having sobbed her guts up over the dead boy, did not immediately sleep, remaining just below the surface, and picturing herself answering all the demands that marriage to Joe would put on her. Could she have sex with him? Yes, probably. He was not physically unattractive, and even if he had been, she doubted it would matter all that much, for he was an amusing and likeable companion, and laughter had always been an aphrodisiac to her. And she was fond of him.

Then there was Nina. Nell's lips formed a wide, involuntary smile upon picturing herself cuddling that dear little body. Feeling guilty then, in her head she told William that it would not make the slightest difference to the way she felt about her son. He was her flesh, and she would always love him best, and yes, she would find him again one day. But whilst she was waiting . . .

* * *

Sobriety brought more thought, but no change of mind. It didn't really matter that Pike could not do enough for her and Beata, in the confirmation that the boy had died from an abscess on his brain. That poor child's death had precipitated the realisation for Nell that she would never be truly appreciated by her superiors. But she would by Joe and his daughter.

First, just to make sure that he had not changed his mind, she needed to discuss it with him again, wanting to make sure he knew the situation, that although she would never stop loving Billy, she did think a great deal of Joe.

And so, on the next afternoon that she picked Nina up from school and made them tea, the moment they were alone, she sought to broach it. 'I've been reconsidering what you said . . .'

Helping her by drying the pots, Joe cocked his head, trying to think what that might be.

'About us getting married,' she reminded him.

He immediately perked up. 'Oh, that!'

'It's obviously been on your mind too,' Nell joked, he sharing her amusement. Then, he was to suspend his activities and listen with curious expression, as she tendered her question. 'Is your proposal still on offer?'

Joe looked astonished, but his face had turned even brighter. 'You want to marry me?'

Nell gave a keen nod and bit her lip. She should really tell him about William. Married couples should have no secrets. But it was all she could do not to cry just from thinking about her lost baby . . .

Joe remained happily thunderstruck. 'By, you really like to spring surprises, don't you? Well, blow me . . . what made you change your mind? Not that I'm complaining!'

Nell had no wish to relive that awful catalyst, saying cheerfully, 'I know when I'm on to a good thing – I might never get asked again! I'm going to give in my notice at work, but I thought I'd better check that you haven't changed your mind about wanting to marry me.'

'Have I billy-oh!' he laughed, as if unable to believe his luck.

'Are you going to marry me dad?' Both of them swivelled, and there stood Nina, back from the lavatory, with a look of sheer delight spread upon her face.

Sharing laughter with his bride-to-be, her father asked, with a rascally sparkle in his blue eyes, 'Why, would that make you happy?'

And, shouting affirmation, Nina jumped up and down in glee. 'Can I call you Mam now? Is it all right to tell people?'

'I suppose –'

Joe only managed to get two words out before Nina ran to the front door, threw it open and shouted excitedly to the first passer-by, 'Me mam and dad are getting married!'

Collapsing against his soon-to-be wife in despairing laughter, Joe called her back in. Upon which, Nina came racing straight to Nell, who picked her up and squeezed her, the two of them hugging and grinning for all they were worth.

And Joe stood smiling on, then only in afterthought did Nell hug him with such enthusiasm.

15

There seemed no point in delaying things. So, the moment her notice expired, Nell left the hospital to set up home with Joe. To be married she must first purchase a copy of her birth certificate. Therein lay another shock, seeing not only her mother's name writ large, but her father's too. Wilfred Spottiswood. Had it been male pride or pity that occasioned the lie? What a tangled web, thought Nell, her upstanding parents doing the lawful thing in having her registered, whilst for the sake of morality pretending to others that she had been adopted. Such farce!

It was a quiet ceremony at a register office – very quiet, with no one to represent her side of the family, and only a discreet get-together afterwards out of respect for Gussie's recent bereavement. Joe did not invite his brothers, a fact that neither surprised nor bothered Nell, who presented a happy face throughout.

No one had suggested that Beata move out, but the instant she had learned of their plans she had chosen to set up residence with her sister Maddie, who was also a nurse, therefore granting Nell and Joe the privacy they would need to get to know each other.

With this in mind, only in hindsight did Joe admit, 'I've been a bit thoughtless. You might have liked a honeymoon, this being your first time around, so to speak, and to make up for not having a big flash do. Fancy a trip to Scotland?'

But, 'Too far on a motorbike,' claimed Nell, paying more heed to the reflection of her glossy brown hair, which had been cut and styled for her wedding, and made her look younger and happier – though perhaps truer reason lay in the Mothering Sunday card crayoned at school. The ecstasy of receiving it was with her still.

'You nit, I meant on the train! What sort of a cheapskate would I be, expecting you to get all dressed up for the bike?'

Nell laughingly apologised, but asked, 'But how will Nina travel?'

He looked nonplussed, then, 'Well, I was just thinking it'd be thee and me, seeing as it's a honeymoon, like!'

Having not attached any romantic significance to their union, Nell reacted on impulse. 'Oh, we can't leave her behind! Why don't we just wait till summer and have a family holiday then?'

Joe hid any disappointment, to say with munificence, 'Well, if that's what you want, that's what you'll have!' So setting the mould for the rest of their marriage. 'And let's hope there'll be an extra member on the way by then.'

Aware of his dearest wish to have a son to replace the one he had lost, despite her qualms and her feelings of disloyalty to William, Nell was looking forward to presenting him with one. 'At least we've got the room.'

'Aye, but we won't be staying here,' came Joe's happy announcement. 'I thought I'd mentioned that I put my name down for a council house a while back.'

Nell appeared thoughtful. Having found it difficult to get a job after leaving the army, Joe had taken what had been meant to be temporary work at Craven's sweet factory, but had found that he actually enjoyed it, and so was still there almost eight years later. Even having worked his way up, it did not provide the highest of incomes. But he was to repudiate her supposition that he was unable to afford to buy, asserting that if the state was prepared to give them a house, he couldn't see the point in investing all his savings in bricks and mortar to then have to scrimp on food. Bodily succour had always held great importance after the deprivation he had suffered as a child. 'I'd much rather have that, and a seaside holiday every year – maybe a car like our Beat's got her eye on!' They shared a laugh here, for poor Beata had so far not managed to pass her driving test. 'There'd be no rates, and no repairs. Just one thing: I haven't notified the council we've moved out of Gussie's, so if they should want to check, you might have to pretend we're living there.' Nell said she didn't mind if he preferred to stay here, as she rather liked this quaint old place. But, 'I can't have my wife living in a mucky old house with a back yard!' declared Joe with an affectionate chuck of her chin. 'You want to see a bit of sky and greenery – first chance we get, we'll be off.'

For now, though, they were to remain in their decrepit ex-grocery shop, with its worn-down steps and centuries of grime, and the cattle being driven past to market every week. Nell threw herself wholeheartedly into being a mother and housewife. Devoted to her new vocation, she hardly missed nursing at all, and even her visits to her old friends at the infirmary tailed off. Despite her fastidiousness at work, though, she was not the tidiest of people at home, but Joe didn't seem to mind that. A wholesome cuddle and a nourishing meal was all he desired of his wife. Which was just as well, for the housework was often neglected if Nina was off school, Nell rushing through the essentials so as to be with her, to share a meringue and enjoy giggling competition to see who could lick off the biggest dollop of mock cream, or who was the better at remembering the words of the latest hit.

Besotted as Nell was, there was inevitably a slight sense of abandonment when Joe came in, and Nina went running to greet the one she loved best, though she would never dream of voicing complaint.

In fact there was to be no grumble from any of them, for theirs was a happy little family, with outings to be enjoyed every weekend – to a park, or the races, a walking match at Whitsun, or a stroll in the countryside – plus a week's holiday at the coast in summer. To date there had been no offer of a council house, and with thousands more waiting it could be some time yet, especially since Joe had expressed a preference to live on one of the new estates being built on the southerly outskirts of York. It would be worth the wait.

'But we'll have to get cracking with this lad you keep promising me,' he joked one morning at breakfast. 'I thought you might have something to tell me by now, you've been a bit dreamy since our holiday.'

Nell had not wanted any celebration to be premature, but now looked coquettish. 'Well, as you ask . . .' Seeing his face immediately light up, she rushed to add, 'I might – only *might* be.' There had been a lengthy gap in her cycle, and she had been feeling slightly off-colour.

'Might be what?' Nina had appeared and was watching and listening intently.

'Bloody hell!' her father looked apologetic for his inadvertent swear word. 'You're always creeping up on folk!' But, in lifted mood, he grinned at her, before turning back to his wife for elucidation. Nell cautioned him not to raise his hopes until she had been to see the doctor – following which there had to be swift reassurance to a worried Nina that she was not ill. Understanding his child's fear, Joe quickly dealt the truth. 'Your mam's just going to see him about having a baby brother for you.'

'Or a sister,' prompted Nell.

'No, it's got to be a lad,' smiled Joe, grabbing a slice of toast. 'We don't need another lass, do we, Neen?' And he reached out an arm to hook her into a cuddle, before taking a bite.

* * *

With an excited Joe unwilling to wait, Nell was cajoled into making a visit to the surgery that very same morning. Joe instructed her to come to the factory the minute she had any news, for he would not be able to last until evening. Being a senior employee, no one would object if he nipped out to see his wife. Nell would have preferred not to include Nina in her assignment, but with school being closed for July, she was forced to take her along.

It was all academic, though, for after a series of questions and an examination, the practitioner said he didn't think she was pregnant. Nell made a sound of disappointment, and admitted as she dressed, 'I'm sorry to waste your time, Doctor. My cycle's always been irregular, but I just thought after four months that I might be . . .'

'You still might be, Mrs Kilmaster,' he said, trying to cheer her up as he scribbled on a hitherto blank record sheet. 'If nothing's happened in another month come back and we'll examine you again.'

It was a very deflated Nell who went to collect Nina from the waiting room. She could already imagine Joe's face collapsing in disappointment.

'Am I getting a brother?'

With that earnest little face gazing up at her, Nell was instantly cheered. 'Not yet, love – but that doesn't matter when I've got you.' And she confirmed this with a happy squeeze of her hand.

Nina looked decidedly glad, as they headed for the centre of town, and by the time they got to crooked old Coppergate, with its higgledy-piggledy skyline of ancient buildings alongside the sweet factory, with such an entertaining companion Nell was over her setback and laughing at something Nina had just said. Partaking of a nervous cigarette as he awaited their arrival, Joe became alert at the light-hearted approach of his wife, and his own expression began to mirror hers. Which made it even more difficult for Nell to inflict the crushing news.

But, 'All's not lost yet,' she comforted, trying to be discreet with Nina attending so carefully to their exchange. 'Maybe in a few more months you'll have your dream.'

However, in only a few weeks, without revisiting the doctor, Nell was to be informed by her own body. There would be no baby that year. Speaking for herself, she was immensely happy as things stood, and thus her mood was to rub off on Joe, who managed to remain optimistic that he would have his son in the new year.

This was all well and good, but Nell wished that he wouldn't watch her so closely for signs of its arrival.

Meanwhile, she was to be dealt another concern. Nina's habit of drifting off seemed to be getting worse. Fearing the glazed expression might signify petit mal, Nell was to relate her worry to Beata. But with her reassuring chuckle, Beata said that was the trouble with being a nurse, it turned you into a hypochondriac. And she seemed less concerned about her niece, as about the failure of yet another recent driving test – her fourth. 'I'm sure the tester's got a down on pupils from my driving school. I'm going to Harrogate next time!'

But Nell's qualms remained such that only a doctor's opinion would do, even if it was to bring ridicule. 'You have what is medically known as a daydreamer,' she was informed to her great relief, after tests came up negative.

However, just as this fear was discarded, another arose, when Nina came home from school covered in bruises. 'What on earth's happened to you?' Nell said, horrified, upon first seeing them, and presented the skinny thighs for Joe, who was equally concerned.

'Bloomin' hangment, you're black and blue! Has somebody been bashing you, Neen?'

The little girl seemed so chirpy in denying this that there could be no doubt she was telling the truth. But this in itself was to provide greater worry for Nell, that there was some physiological cause for the bruising – perhaps anaemia.

But again this was to be assuaged by the physician, which was scant relief to Nell, for it meant her prime instinct had been right: Nina's bruises were as a result of being bullied. With anger surging to her fingertips, on her way to spy on the playground, she imagined throttling her daughter's assailants . . .

Yet all that transpired was a rough-and-tumble game with some boys, Nina obviously great friends with them and enjoying every minute. Much relieved to have discovered this harmless source of the bruising, and that her beloved child was happy, a smiling Nell went home, vowing to curb her own paranoia.

Happy or no, over the coming months, having also to deal with Joe's hankering after a son, Nell felt that Nina must be taken in hand, for by the time another summer came round she had become a proper little tomboy, and was pestering for some jeans. Nell cautioned that Dad might not approve, but with Joe's opinion that they were very serviceable, Nina was to receive her fashionable attire. Unfortunately her waist was so thin that the jeans had to be kept up with one of Nell's white belts off a summer frock, and the latter did not know whether to laugh or cry at the pathetic sight, the surplus denim gathered into an uncomfortable bunch at the back.

Nina seemed not overjoyed either, observing that, 'The zip's in the wrong place.'

'It's meant to be on the side, you're a girl!' Nell giggled, this for some reason causing a look of hurt. Mindful of this, she sought to alert Joe over his own reaction when he came home that night.

Perhaps he had overcompensated, for in the morning Nina donned the jeans for school. With this set to be the hottest day of the year so far, Nell tried to persuade her otherwise, but, unable to deny the child anything, the wish was reluctantly granted. When Nina came home, of course she was cross and perspiring, though adamant she would keep the jeans on – until Nell's clever purchase brought an about-turn.

Then the tomboy's stubbornness collapsed, her jeans being quickly cast aside in favour of the pink dress with blue polka dots, in which she twirled, and flourished its three-tiered skirt. 'It's like a Spanish lady's!'

'Yes! You only need the castanets.' Nell grabbed two shells from the mantel, mementoes of their summer holiday, and tapped them in time to Nina's attempts at flamenco.

And at her father's homecoming, the delighted child was to twirl for him as she had done for Nell, but alas to a different reception. 'Hang on, I think they've sent the wrong bairn home from school!' he jokingly exclaimed. 'Where's that lad who was here yesterday? By, doesn't she look bonny?'

Looking on, Nell smiled fondly over this pretence, until she noted a slight clouding of their daughter's face. And she could not help the suspicion that her husband's longing for a son had resonated with Nina. For it seemed too much of a coincidence that, within minutes, she had changed out of her dress in favour of jeans and shirt.

Unequipped to deal with such a sensitive issue, for any word to Joe would be seen as accusation, Nell could only encourage Nina by demonstrating her own love, and pray that when his longed-for son did arrive, Joe would not set such great store on the matter, as he was doing now.

Still, Nell was perhaps as bad in laying importance on this too. The fact that after fifteen months of marriage she remained barren continued to worry her, even when she was meant to be enjoying a second summer holiday at the coast. Waiting alongside Joe for Nina to return from her donkey ride, her eyes strayed to a group of young teddy boys, strutting like peacocks in their colourful shirts, brocade waistcoats and drape jackets, their legs encased in drainpipe trousers and terminating in thick crepe-soled shoes. They were hardly old enough to shave, bless them, their upper lips downy with bum-fluff, causing Nell to wonder wistfully over her son's development – if he dressed in such outlandish fashion, and how it was that she could have produced him so easily, yet was unable to give Joe the one for whom he yearned.

'What a bunch of clowns – all brocade and brothel creepers.'

Pulled from her reverie by Joe's amused observation, and unable to tell him what she had really been thinking, she could only chuckle agreement, that their son would never be allowed such eccentricity – when they were lucky enough to have one.

'Well, I'm doing me best on that score,' teased Joe with a wicked glint in his eye. 'So get your job done, woman, and gimme that lad!' But he made sure Nell knew he was only joking, as, with a kindly grin, he stepped forth to lift their little girl from the donkey.

If Joe had hoped the holiday would help in that quarter, this was not to be. Another year turned – was almost through – and still there were just the three of them. As a matter of fact, there *had* been an addition to the family, but this was inanimate. More inanimate than Joe had anticipated when making his purchase.

'Thank you, bloody Nasser!' he declared, upon news that petrol would have to be rationed due to the hostilities in Suez. 'I just get me van and now I can't drive it!'

An authority on the news, being always transfixed to the television, Nina asked if there was to be another war, but Nell was quick to stave her worry. Still, Joe muttered under his breath, 'Bloody Yanks, putting the stranglers on us . . .'

'Are Yanks the same as Russians?' For many evenings, Nina had watched the Hungarian uprising on the screen, seen the terrible things done, and heard her father's comments on the matter. To curry favour, she said proudly, 'Do you know what I wrote in my notebook at school today? "All Russians are pigs."'

Joe's head did swivel then, to gasp along with his wife, 'Ooh, you can't say things like that – it'll get you shot! Has your teacher seen it?' Flattened by such a reception, Nina hung her head and replied in the negative. 'Then make sure you rub it out,' ordered her father with a shake of his head. 'Good heavens, what are we rearing . . .'

And at that, feeling pity, Nell drew Nina onto her lap and kissed her. 'I'd leave all the fighting talk to the men, Neen,' she advised.

Whilst the dream of a male child was not to come to fruition that year, lesser dreams were. For, one Saturday morning shortly before Christmas, Beata pulled up outside their window in a shiny black Austin. Her response to their cheers of congratulation was the chuckling admission that she had still not passed her test, but was taking advantage of the Suez crisis that allowed learners to drive unaccompanied.

'You must be the only one to be better off!' claimed Joe, acting aggrieved.

'Well, I do essential work, you see,' grinned Beata. 'Not like you, just making goodies.'

'Oh, get the sherry out, Joe!' His wife prevented more jousting, and drew her sister-in-law in to be seated amongst paper chains and a fragrant Christmas tree, upon which Nina was in the process of dangling a plaster image of Field Marshal Montgomery, and other home-made decorations.

Beata interrupted her. 'I hope you've totted up my diddlum money, missus. I want to do my Christmas shopping.'

Nina balked at having to surrender the tinful of silver she had been banking for others. But she dragged herself off to fetch the notebook ledger, and to tot up the amount owed. Only slightly appeased by the half-crown that was handed back as dividend, she tested it with her teeth.

Joe had been handing round his cigarettes, and whilst they smoked and drank sherry, Beata discussed her acquisition 'You should have heard the porter when I drew up for work. "Look at the night nurse in her posh car, when the night sister has to pedal to work on her bike!" I said, aye, but the night nurse doesn't squander her money on fags and booze –'

'No, she just comes and bloody pinches ours!' scoffed Joe.

Beat gave her chesty chuckle, warning, 'Shurrup, or you won't get this letter I've brought you.' Saying she had fetched it from Gussie's, she handed over the envelope.

Joe put down his glass to open it, having to hold the sheet of paper at arm's length.

'He's going to have extensions to his arms if his eyes get any worse,' ribbed Nell.

'You wait!' retorted Joe. 'I shall remind you of your mockery in ten or fifteen years' time.' But, with spectacles allowing him to focus, his tartness was quickly replaced with a delighted beam. 'It's from the council – they've reserved a brand-new house for us and it'll be ready in the new year!'

Thrilled to bits over the letter, Joe had been spurred into dashing out for some last-minute purchases, returning to give Nell a private showing of the magnificent six-shooter he had bought for Nina. 'Not only that! The holster, *and* the hat.' With boastful expression, he demonstrated his prowess with the miniature firearm.

Nell remained amused. 'I hate to question its suitability for a little girl . . .'

'It's what she asked for!' retorted the father with a laugh.

And, when Christmas Day came, Nina was, as he predicted, cock-a-hoop over the gun and accoutrements, though she was equally thrilled by the books her mother had bought for her too. For Nell there was a lovely little garnet and pearl ring from Joe. She, knowing how he liked to look smart, had bought him a pullover, shirt and tie, in which he dressed for dinner. However, Nina was to provide the surprise of the day, by bestowing her stepmother with a glass ashtray, this taking much of the proceedings from her diddlum.

Nell was immensely touched – rather guilty at receiving it too, for Nina had given Joe only a bag of liquorice. Still, he didn't appear to mind at all, with stacks of roast chicken, Christmas pudding, drink and cigarettes to pacify him. Plus the big get-together at Gussie's later, for another slap-up meal. In all it was a lovely festive interval.

And even if they were still without the son that would make this family complete, by February, when it came time to move into their new abode, both agreed that there was plenty to do at the moment without having a baby to look after.

After parsimonious use due to the petrol crisis, Joe's van was finally to come into its own, with so many belongings to be transferred from the east side of town to its southern limits. Approximately three miles from where they had abided, this residence would be even further removed in style from their antiquated dwelling – on a council estate, maybe, but situated in one of the modern suburbs that had been hailed as the Mayfair of York. Being not far from Knavesmire racecourse, this was a much greener enclave, with no industry in sight. All right, they had just crossed a railway bridge, over which bulged a cloud of smoke as a train passed beneath, but as far as Nell could see, this was the only source of noise or dirt. Soon they were turning away from it, with Nina kneeling up in the back and peering out between their shoulders, eager to be first to spot the name of their avenue.

Steering past those houses still under construction, Joe finally pulled up outside their own at the end of a block of four, this particular quartet being set back from the street, and thus granting them a long front garden – full of weeds at the moment. Although a kerb had been installed, as yet there was only a bed of cinders along which to crunch their way to the gate. After a quick recap of the exterior, they entered to be met by a smell of newness. Off a narrow hallway, the living room had a window at each end, and combined both sitting and dining area. The kitchen was small, though it did have a pantry and plenty of cupboards. Upstairs were two good-sized bedrooms. Joe had really wanted three, but the council had been prepared to grant only as many rooms as his present family required. Still, it was of little consequence at present with such an agreeable situation as this. Although, looking from the back bedroom window, they were alerted that the railway line ran only a hundred feet away.

'I'm sure we'll get used to that,' smiled Nell, as a steam express clattered by the thicket of brambles, vibrating the house and the people within.

Joe pointed out that because their house preceded a corner it had an extra triangular plot of garden on the side, more than enough on which to grow produce. He was even more enthralled with the bathroom. 'No more chamber music in the night – thank you, Lord!'

Whilst awaiting the removal men, who were bringing the larger items, they discovered an attached outhouse containing a gas boiler to do their washing, the other half of it providing an open porch. All were thrilled with their new home – though agreed the huge garden was daunting, for, apart from a bright patch of celandines, it was choked with weeds and briars.

Joe surveyed the jungle that came over Nina's head, and

proclaimed it fortunate that he had added a few days' leave onto the weekend in order to attack it. 'And here's me relieved I never got sent to Malaya. God knows what we'll find in there. Could be the Mau Mau, the lost treasures of the Incas, or any bloomin' thing.'

At the mention of treasure, Nina immediately began to forage, whilst her smiling parents rolled up their sleeves and left her to play. But with the house newly painted, both inside and out, in a pleasant mushroom colour, all that was required was to swab a few stray blobs of cement and builders' dust from the dark brown floor tiles, and polish the windows, before erecting the new living-room curtains Nell had brought with her. By which time the removal van had begun to install the furniture.

By early afternoon, with everything in situ, Nell provided lunch, a happy Joe plonking heavily onto one end of their new red studio couch – and promptly launching Nina into the air.

'Flaming hangment!' After checking she was unhurt, he picked her up from the floor and reseated her beside him with an affectionate rub and a chuckle. 'I think I've bought a trampoline instead of a couch!' Nell laughingly agreed as, settling himself more gingerly, he partook of a sandwich. 'Have you found any gold yet, Neen?' At her shake of head, he promised, 'I'll try to get the scythe on it before I go back to work.' He had bought one for this purpose.

Keen to get her hands on that big curved blade, Nina volunteered, but her assistance was to go only so far as to hack herself a tunnel to the far corner of the wilderness. Once a campsite had been cleared, she remained there, only the twitching movement of the vegetation showing her parents she was still around.

The densely rooted couch grass and ground elder took strenuous effort, and once Joe had returned to work, and with Nina playing in her camp – the school being on half-term holiday – it was Nell who was left to dig and turn the earth during the week, in between washing and shopping and cooking. But she appeared to thrive on it, Joe noticed, for there was always a smile on her face when he came in, making him feel welcome, and appreciated, just as he felt about her.

With another week at the factory behind him, Joe gave a sigh of happiness as he flopped into his armchair after tea and looked around at their collection of ornaments, particularly the frames on the sideboard: containing one of his father, a beefy-looking man wearing a waxed moustache and the uniform of a regimental sergeant-major; his mother, all gentle and pretty with angelic eyes; and a group shot of himself with his army pals. 'I know I keep saying it, but isn't it grand to think we're the first people ever to have lived in this house? We don't have to put up with any old battle scars on the woodwork, nor six layers of paper to scrape off. Nobody else's memories in the walls . . .'

Their child seated on the fireside mat, playing with the zip of her blue corduroy windcheater and listening to her parents' conversation, Nell smiled down at her as she handed out bars of chocolate, and agreed, 'There's enough to be done in the garden. I've been on the front all day.'

Joe shared a joke with his daughter. 'Your mam makes it sound like a battlefield.'

'Well that's what it felt like!' chuckled Nell, inspecting her blisters.

'You won't spoil my camp, will you?' Over the week, suitably dressed against the cold, Nina had carried extra bits and pieces to the clearing amongst the brambles.

'You don't think I'll get that far, do you?' laughed Nell. 'It'll take years. A pity there's no one to play in it with you yet.' Although the few neighbours they had met were very pleasant, none of them had children Nina's age. 'That's why it'll be good to start your new school on Monday – you might make friends with someone who lives nearby.'

'Don't go skiving off just yet, though,' said Dad. 'There's plenty of gardening to be done.'

But it was he and Nell who were to undertake most of the digging, and by Saturday night they were completely worn out. Therefore, Sunday brought a leisurely sleep in, and a marital cuddle, before they rose to devour bacon and eggs. Church was a thing of the past for both, though rather more of a departure for Joe, he coming from a devout family of Catholics. But, somewhere over the years, what with all the widowhood and other upheaval, only Gussie retained her piety. Joe had not attended Mass since boyhood, and was more devoted to his fried breakfast, the grease dripping down his chin as he wiped out a decade of austerity.

A mischievous Nell offered him the pan, laughing when he accepted the last dregs of fat, and loving it that he appreciated her attempts to make a good home for him. Once the pots were cleared, she joined her husband in reading the newspapers for a while, though soon had the Sunday lunch to prepare.

After which, Joe said to his bored little girl, 'Tell you what, I might give gardening a miss this afternoon and treat us to an hour's fishing at that pond across yonder.' Beyond their wild garden lay an even wilder stretch of land. Thereafter, he and his daughter climbed over the fence and went off, looking for all the world, thought Nell, like father and son.

By Monday the fun was over. With her first morning at her new school being so daunting, Nina's mother accompanied her on the school bus, to guard her as best she could from the jostling crowd of other youngsters who piled on board.

The parting such a wrench, Nell went off to town to take her mind off it. It was whilst she was at the toy counter in Woolworth's, selecting threepenny cowboys on horseback, that a voice exclaimed: 'Eleanor! Where on earth have you been hiding?'

Nell blushed deeply. Whenever spotting any relative, she had gone out of her way to avoid them – but the years had made her careless, and now here stood Aunty Phyllis and Uncle Cliff. How could she explain to these kindest of people, who would never understand her reasoning?

In the event it was Aunty Phyllis who spoke again. 'We've been searching for you high and low!'

'Well, here I am!' Nell gave a lame laugh. 'How good to see you both.'

'You too, love,' nodded a reserved Uncle Cliff, much greyer than at their last meeting.

'But why didn't you give us your new address when you moved on?' demanded his wife, cornering Nell, who was attempting to slip away. 'We sent letter after letter to Walmgate, till back they finally came, with "unable to deliver" on.'

Nell fabricated confusion. 'I could have sworn I informed everyone – I do apologise, I was always so busy at work, time seems to go so quickly.'

'But it's *fifteen years* since we've seen you!'

'Is that really how long it is?' Nell pretended to be flabbergasted – and it was as she raised a hand to her mouth that Aunty Phyllis noticed the wedding ring.

'You're married!'

The blush, which had just begun to fade, resumed its glow. 'Oh, yes – it was a very quiet affair! Just myself and Joe really. It's his second marriage – he has a little girl – and he didn't want any fuss.'

But her aunt was deeply offended, and her voice cool. 'Still, it would have been nice to be informed. If you knew the trouble your uncle has gone to in looking for you. Didn't you see all the notices in the press?'

'No, I'm afraid not – miss!' To escape those looks of accusation, Nell quickly hailed the shop girl at the other end of the counter, and, cheeks blazing, made her purchase. But once the brown paper bag was in her hand, she was compelled to face them and explain. 'I'm really sorry, I did intend to write, but I moved to several different places in quick succession, and the longer I left it, the more difficult it became . . .'

'Anyway, you're here now,' said Uncle Cliff, bringing the condemnation to a halt with a kind smile, though his wife remained hurt. 'The reason we've been trying to contact you was about your father's estate.' He saw Nell's demeanour take a plunge, and asked, 'Why don't you come home with us, and we'll talk in private?'

His niece looked wrenched, glancing at Aunty Phyllis as she said, 'I have to be home to meet my daughter from school . . .'

'Never mind then.' Cliff's tone displayed understanding. 'Let me just give you the gist. I think I probably told you before that our Wilf left most of it to your mother, because of course he wasn't expecting her to go at the same time as him.' Gauging Nell's pain, he moved on quickly. 'As executor, I thought it best to put the house up for sale, once it had been rebuilt. We didn't think you'd want to live there – I hope we did the right thing?'

Her hand gripping the paper bag of cowboys, every muscle tensed, Nell assured him with a firm nod.

'We've done something right then,' sniped Aunt Phyllis.

Uncle Cliff went on, 'The money's been sitting in the bank for the past ten years or so – since just after the war, anyway, so it'll have accured a good bit of interest – don't expect thousands,' he hastened to tell her, 'once the mortgage was paid off – and the solicitor and other fees – it took quite a hefty chunk –'

'I wasn't expecting anything at all,' said Nell quickly.

'– I just don't want you to think we've fleeced you.'

'Uncle Cliff, I wouldn't dream of it! If it hadn't been for you and Aunt Phyl it would still be a pile of rubble. I told you all those years ago, I don't want anything. You should keep it for all your hard work and inconvenience.'

Cliff was startled. 'Eleanor, it's over eight hundred

pounds! If this has something to do with you being adopted, then I can tell you right now that your parents looked upon you as their real child.'

Nell looked at him sadly. If only they knew. 'No, it's nothing to do with that,' she replied, masking her complicated feelings with a half-truth. 'I just wouldn't feel right spending their money when they're dead.' Especially after the way we parted, came her dismal afterthought.

'Well, it's yours,' shrugged Cliff. 'We've already had a decent bequest for my being executor. It's a thankless task, you know, but better me than you.' Here he showed concern for her wellbeing. 'How are you coping these days? I suppose you still miss them?'

'She's got her own family now,' put in Aunty Phyllis, still quite huffy. 'And it's been a long time.'

Nell was swift to contradict this. 'I do still miss them terribly. That's why I've never been able to come and see any of you – it would be such an awful reminder, and so would their money.'

'Well, leave it in the bank until you're inclined to use it,' pleaded Cliff. 'It'll come in useful, now you've got a family. If you give me your address . . . or if you just want to call round at our house, you can have the bank book.'

'I will call round one day, I promise,' said Nell. 'I am really sorry about neglecting you.'

'Well, it was a terrible loss you suffered,' acceded Cliff.

More terrible than you know, thought his niece.

'Our Ronald came through it unscathed – if you're interested, of course,' added Aunty Phyllis.

'I'm genuinely glad to hear that,' murmured Nell. 'I'd love it if he and Margaret and Daphne could be there when I come round.'

This managed to sedate her aunt, to the extent that she said, as Nell finally took her leave, 'Please don't leave it too long – we're not getting any younger, you know.'

* * *

Shaken by the incident, Nell was to relate it to Joe when he got home from work, and also told him of the amount of money that had been left to her. Delighted for her, he was to say the same as Uncle Cliff, that she was entitled to it.

Nell said she supposed he was right. But then Joe was still unaware of the turmoil behind her reluctance to take it. Whilst he had confided in his wife about his cruel stepmother since their marriage, and his feelings on the matter, she felt unable to reciprocate on such a deep level, because that would involve having to tell him about William.

Then he had surprised her by saying, 'It might be as well to make this visit soon, mind, otherwise you'll never do it. I'll go with you – we'll take Neen if you like. Have a walk to Acomb next Sunday after dinner. That'll give you a chance to drop them a line to prepare them.'

She was to appreciate Joe's support, both then and on the day of the visit. For it turned out to be quite a stilted affair, after being out of touch for so many years. Even though it was nice to see Ron, Margaret and Daphne with their families, they were all strangers really. Thank heavens for the children, who played together whilst the adults chatted, and provided a source of amusement when the conversation petered out – especially Nina. Though, as usual, where she was involved there was a little embarrassment towards the end of the afternoon, when Uncle Cliff made great ceremony of handing over the bank book to Nell, and Nina asked: 'Are we off now you've got your money?'

Thankfully everyone had laughed about it, and upon them parting, Aunty Phyllis had insisted that Nell and Joe maintain contact. Happy that it had gone so well, Nell promised she would, though doubted it would extend to much more than a card at Christmas.

On the way home, Joe asked what she would be spending the money on, she giving a shrug and saying, 'I think I'll put it away for a rainy day.'

'Well, whatever you do, don't go frittering it all on that one,' warned Joe, cocking his head at their small companion, who was galloping her plastic cowboys on horseback along a wall.

His wife smiled, and said there was no one on whom she would rather spend it. After fearing Nina might be in need of a little treat after her first day at her new school, she had been much relieved to hear that her stepdaughter had made friends quickly, two of them even calling round the day before to take her to the Saturday matinee.

But whilst playmates for Nina might have been found, the child that Joe longed for was not yet destined to be. 'Perhaps you shouldn't be working so hard on the garden,' he advised his wife, after another month or so of such activity. 'If you were to catch on – I mean, you might already be expecting – well, it wouldn't do the bairn any good, all that digging.'

Nell understood this concern after Joe had lost his wife and baby son, but, 'I'd think I'd know if I was,' she told him smilingly. 'Be patient. It'll happen.'

And, until then, Joe had to content himself with Nina, who seemed happy enough to be surrogate boy, to accompany him fishing, and hand him tools as he worked on his van. Nell, however, had grown worried about this. One needed no experience in psychiatry to reason that it must dent a little girl's self-esteem. She had not done enough to remedy this so far, but upon going to meet Nina from school one afternoon, she realised that something would have to be done.

Travelling along the main thoroughfare on the other side of the road, her view blocked by a rag and bone cart, Nina had not yet seen her stepmother. But Nell had seen her – and the boy who had tight grip of her arm. At the thought of her child being hurt, she immediately increased her pace and, once the cart had passed, dashed across the road.

Nina saw her then, and dealt her a happy wave. The

boy, too, released his grip with a cheery, 'See you!' And hopped away down a snicket.

'See you!' echoed Nina, and bounced to meet her mother, adopting an attitude of bravado as she came. But Nell knew her child, and though Nina might have succeeded in hiding her pain from the boy, she had seen that wince. 'Was he hurting you?'

'Nah! We were just playing torture. I had to resist his Chinese burn.'

'Charming!' Nell laid a hand across the skinny shoulders as she turned to walk alongside. 'And what did you give him?'

'Oh, nowt, I always let the lads try and torture me,' said Nina in blasé fashion, kicking a stone out of her path. 'They like to see if they can make me cry – but they can't.'

Nell wanted to kill them. 'It doesn't sound like a very nice game to me,' she murmured, and tried to take her stepdaughter's hand, but had her own rebuffed until Nina was sure the boy was out of sight. Nell cursed herself for not doing more about this earlier. 'There must be some girls you could play with.'

'They're all daft,' came the blank statement. 'They only want to play fairies and witches.'

'They can't all be that way inclined,' argued Nell. 'It is possible to play Cowboys and Indians but be a girl at the same time, you know.'

The child said nothing, but had turned introspective. Nell watched the cogs whirr in that golden head, and, to ram the idea home, added brightly, 'I like being a girl.'

'You're a lady,' Nina tittered.

'All right then, clever clogs! A lady – and ladies can do all sorts of things that men can't. Such as wear lipstick, and pretty clothes and high heels, and have –' she had been about to say have babies, but changed her mind to, 'their hair permed. You like getting dressed up, don't you? Then I've got a lipstick that's nearly finished – it's yours!'

Nina looked up at her then, the blue eyes quizzical, but it took a while before she could spit out her question. 'Will Dad –' She broke off.

Nell knew what she had been about to say: Will Dad still like me? But, brushing this under the carpet for fear of causing her child more pain, she issued in gay tone, 'Your dad won't mind, I'm sure. So long as you don't wear it for going out with him – people might think you're his girlfriend.' And they both laughed at the thought as they walked on.

But, hurting for her loved one, Nell resolved to nurture the child's sense of femininity, and prayed there would be a female playmate for her soon.

At present quite isolated on this unfinished estate, Nell was glad of Beata's regular visits, to keep her up-to-date with what was happening at the hospital, or with the rest of the in-laws, few of whom had had the time to come so far. The Suez crisis over, her friend had lately brought more good news. 'I told you they had a down on my driving school – I passed first time at Harrogate!'

Nell smiled to herself, and chose not to bring up all those other failed tests – though she was rather apprehensive when Beata announced to Nina, 'I'll be able to take you out for trips to the seaside now!' And throughout the school summer vacation, she was to fret that both would be killed in a crash.

But if it prevented Nina from loneliness it was worth the worry, and towards the end of another year, both were still in one piece, by which time the situation had changed. One by one, the rest of the houses in the street were completed, so the occupants moved in. Nell had already made acquaintance with the elderly couple who lived to one side of her, Mr and Mrs Potter – very genteel, and obviously fallen on hard times – and on the other side of her lived Mr and Mrs Stewart, who were not so genteel, and in fact rather whiffy, but very friendly neighbours all the same. Now came plenty more to feed Nell's inquisitive nature: war widows with children; the odd divorcee; but, in the main, just normal working-class couples, the wife staying at home to keep house, the husband going out to earn a living and mowing the grass on a weekend. Nell made a habit of stopping to chat with them all if she happened to be passing.

Other than this she had no special friends, though she was to retain her abiding curiosity of all that went on around her. Thus, had she discovered, to her utter relief and joy, that several of these families had girls the same age as hers. One in particular was to catch her daughter's fancy, and, almost instantly, Nell was to witness a rebirth, Nina breaking contact with the boys and tagging along with Shirley as if they were Siamese twins. They were totally different in looks and in character – one small and slender and golden, the other tall and dark, and quite mature in build for a ten-year-old – but this seemed the attraction for both. At one stroke, the mixed-up period of Nina's life had been cured – for even if the tomboy jeans were still worn, it was along with lipstick and ponytail.

'Looks like I've lost my sidekick,' observed Joe in forlorn tone as he was set to go fishing one weekend, watching Nina laughing and skipping on the path with her friend.

'There's nothing to stop you taking them both along,' mooted Nell, a lot happier. 'I'm sure they'd enjoy the ride.'

'Aye, and I'm sure they'd enjoy giggling and scaring all the fish away,' came the blunt rejoinder. 'No thanks, I'll go on me own.' He thanked her for the sandwiches, picked up his fishing tackle and departed.

Standing by the window, Nell watched him lope up the path with his fishing basket and rod, saw Nina turn with a hopeful smile, drop the skipping rope, and hurriedly open the gate for him. But she saw, too, the envy on Nina's face as her father enjoyed an unscheduled kickabout with a group of boys in the road, before driving away on his own. And her heart ached for her little girl.

Nell wondered if her husband would think she had engineered it: the close relationship she and Nina continued to enjoy that left Joe somewhat out in the cold. Of course she hadn't. Not consciously, anyway. It was just that she hated to think of her child feeling so rejected, simply for being a girl. He didn't know he was doing it, of course. Just as Nell didn't deliberately poach his daughter from him. But, by accident or design, that was what had occurred.

No one mentioned a thing about this. Well, one wouldn't. But one stewed over it, and tried to make amends. And because so much effort was put in, hence there was still to be plenty of laughter in the marriage, good holidays, and lovely Christmases. But that did not completely mend the fissures that had started to appear.

Where Joe might have pandered to his wife's frailty before, in her obsession with their daughter's health, he came down hard against her latest fad. 'Have her stuffed with dope?' he retorted, to Nell's information that she would be taking Nina to be immunised against polio. 'Not on your nelly, Nelly!'

'It's not dope – it's a wonderful, marvellous discovery!'

'Nell, it killed people in America!'

'But they've made it safer now! Just ask Beata. It's a different vaccine.'

'I don't care. You're not taking her.'

'Oh, I am, Joe!' The gentle stepmother temporarily vanished, replaced by one who was determined to have her own way. 'You haven't seen what polio can do. It's a terrible, disgusting disease – imagine yourself being slowly paralysed until you're no longer able to breathe – and even worse to watch your own child suffer a lingering death! And all it takes to prevent it is a needle in the arm. She's having it.'

How could he argue against that? He wasn't pleased, though, and with thousands as militant as himself, Joe had support for his claim that Nell had inflicted his child with needless pain, and himself with needless worry. It took a well-known footballer to die of polio before queues began to form outside the vaccination clinics, Nell's husband finally admitting that perhaps she had been right all along.

And Nell had been kind, not taking the moral ground, but saying that she understood his fears. For their daughter was the most precious thing in the world to her too.

As regards to Nina, Nell continued to be indescribably happy watching her grow. She was a voracious reader, constantly visiting the library and returning with armfuls of books, and in no time having them read and exchanged for a new batch. However, this hunger for knowledge was to prove inefficient in terms of formal education, and to Joe's dismay the letter he so confidently opened one morning was to announce that his daughter had failed her eleven plus.

Nina was shaken too, upon not being one of those selected for praise during class, and having it confirmed when she came home from school. But by then she had had several hours in which to recover. 'Oh well, it's good in a way, 'cause Shirley didn't pass either, so we won't get split up – we've decided we want to go to an all-girls school.'

'Is that all you're bothered about?' her father exploded. 'What about letting your parents down?'

Nell saw the devastation that crossed Nina's face, and rushed to explain. 'Your dad didn't really mean that, he's just a bit surprised – you could never let us down, could she, Dad?' Seeing those teary eyes, outwardly Joe agreed, though it was obvious he was still disappointed and cross with his daughter. 'But what about letting yourself down, eh? I know you were capable of passing if you really tried

– oh well, not to worry,' he tried his best to be kind about this, 'you might get another chance next year.'

'Of course!' Nell tried to lighten the mood. 'Right, Neen, you run and change, then have a game with Shirley – but only for half an hour, I've got some steak for tea!'

But, after waiting until Nina had donned red tartan trews and left the house, Nell was to reprove her husband. 'You were a bit hard on her, Joe.'

'Because I know she had it in her to pass! She's been too busy daydreaming, that's her trouble.'

'But some people are just born to be dreamers,' said Nell. 'And really, does it matter in the long run, as long as she's happy? I mean, look at me,' she invited. 'I went to a grammar school and had plenty of opportunities, but where have I ended up?'

'Thank you!' Joe was uncharacteristically bullish. 'Now I know what I'm worth.'

'I didn't mean to disparage, I love being where I am!' protested Nell. 'I couldn't be happier, looking after you and Neen, but my point is, I could still be doing this whether I had an education or not. She's a bright girl –'

'Yes, she is!' retorted Joe. 'And I would've liked her to capitalise on that.'

'So instead you punish her for what you see as failure!' accused his wife.

'What are you talking about, punishing her? You'd think I'd beaten her within an inch of her life. I'm allowed to voice my disappointment, aren't I?'

'You could have done it privately,' reproved Nell, more accomplished in retaining a calm, persuasive manner. 'How do you think it makes her feel, that she hasn't lived up to your expectations?'

'I didn't say that at all – oh, look, it's done now! We'll be sending her to a secondary modern and that's that.'

'Then do it with good heart,' pleaded Nell. 'So's she doesn't think you love her any the less.'

‘Oh for God’s sake!’ Joe shook his head in exasperation at his wife, then went out, lighting a cigarette on the way.

Left on her own, Nell lit one too, her hands trembling from his stormy reaction.

Listening from behind the kitchen door, Nina pressed herself against the wall as her father went up to the bathroom. When he had passed, she slipped quietly away, and escaped to the camp at the far corner of the garden, where she took a packet of cigarettes from a secret cache amongst the brambles. Then she sat lost in thought, leaned on her tartan knees, and watched the smoke curl away over the nettles.

In the hope that Nina would have a second chance of a scholarship the following year, Joe drove her hard to complete her homework, and was always there to assist with any subject she did not understand. But the latter were manifold, and it soon became obvious that no such opportunity would arise. Hence, he resigned himself to the fact that his daughter was not cut out for academia, and, as his wife had suggested, tried to show that it did not make him love her any the less.

It bothered him, all the same, perhaps feeling it more acutely because of other things that brought him down that year. For, after a lifetime of toiling for the good of others, Gussie’s huge heart had finally given its all.

It was an unspeakably sad funeral. Relatives and friends came from far and wide, including Joe’s brothers, whom Nell got to meet at last, and enjoyed listening to their reminiscences afterwards – though this was abruptly ended when her husband could bear no more and drove her home.

Joe was distraught at losing his beloved eldest sister. ‘Fifty-six,’ he breathed in total disbelief, once able to voice his sorrow at all. ‘There’s all manner of evil bastards walking the earth, what kind of a God takes a woman like our Gus?'

'I've never been able to make sense of that,' replied Nell softly, their daughter at her friend's, and so just the two of them in the house to share the doleful atmosphere. 'I can only suppose it's because she was so very good that she was taken prematurely.' Her mind went to Bill, who had died a hero.

'The good die young,' said a bitter Joe, ripping off his funereal coat. 'I've always thought that was a bloody stupid saying.'

Feeling personally belittled, Nell murmured a postscript. 'Well, I'm very sorry all the same. She was lovely to me.'

'She was lovely to all of us,' said a red-eyed Joe. 'There'll never be anybody to live up to Gus.'

Least of all me, thought Nell. In some ways, the past six years since her marriage had been some of the happiest she had known, with good living, and an abundance of laughter with her husband and daughter. Yet those years had also been marred by the sporadic visits to the doctors, to be treated like a nuisance, or even worse pitied and told, 'Better luck next time.' It was as if her body were saying, *You might try to forget about William, but I haven't.*

So embarrassing had these appointments become, that Nell had decided some time ago not to make any more. If a baby did happen, she would feel him moving, without needing this confirmed by a doctor. Perhaps the devout Gussie would put in a good word for her with the Creator. It was a selfish thought, with the entire Kilmaster family so bereft. But it was for Joe's sake she prayed, as her eyes turned to him now in his deep despair. He was never more in need of uplifting news.

Sadly, although Nell's body grew plumper by the month, as if playing host, it was obviously due to the profusion of good food and confectionery, and she was never to feel that movement from within. The only thing she did experience was a sense of failure. Her monthly cycle, which had always been irregular, was now giving even more cause for concern, for upon calculation Nell found that a whole year had gone by with nothing in that department, without her realising it. Hence, she was finally to cave in and visit the doctor again, just to put her own mind at rest that there was nothing seriously wrong.

Fearing cancer, she was quickly disabused of this notion by the GP, who said she was as healthy and robust a specimen as he had seen. 'I suspect it's the menopause,' he told her.

Nell jumped visibly – she had not even considered this. 'But I'm only thirty-eight!'

He gave a sympathetic shrug. 'It happens, Mrs Kilmaster, particularly if a woman begins menstruating late.'

Her eyes had begun to mist over at the blow he had delivered. 'I was almost seventeen.'

'That might be it then.' He scribbled it down on her record sheet. 'Or else it could be some trauma. I've known a woman's periods to stop dead after a particular shock. Have you suffered any traumatic event?'

Nell remained dazed, through a tunnel hearing herself say, 'Only the same one that millions of others went through.'

The doctor guessed she referred to the war, and could offer no explanation. 'Well, I'm very sorry, but I doubt that after a year your cycle will restart . . .'

And with that, Nell found herself on the way home to give Joe the bad news.

Staring at herself in the mirror, as she waited to convey the awful verdict, she began to make partings in her dark brown hair, searching for a hint of grey. But there was none. No wrinkles either, save for a few laughter lines around her eyes, eyes that were bright and clear, and her complexion as fresh as a girl's. How could this large healthy specimen, seemingly built for motherhood, be such a useless vessel? Her sense of emptiness at the thought of never bearing another child was eclipsed by concern for Joe. For that was the main reason he had married her. It was awful enough having to wipe that look of eager expectancy from one's husband's face yet again; but when on this occasion it would be forever . . . Nell turned away from the mirror, a complete failure.

But, *oh well, never mind*, was all Joe conveyed with his silent shrug when he came in from work, after she had given him that familiar shake of her head. Such nonchalance, though, was before he knew it was final. What would his reaction be when he knew? Dreading the moment, she was happy for Nina to deter it, at the moment trying to persuade her father to buy a newer television set.

'See, if we had ITV, Dad, you'd have so much extra to watch.'

'You mean you wouldn't have to traipse round to Shirley's to watch *Oh Boy!* and we'd be inflicted with that bloody Cliff Richard and his sneery lip round here.'

'No! There's *Rawhide* and all sorts what you'd like.'

'Neen, it isn't just the set! I'd have to pay for an extra aerial as well . . .'

And on it went, until Nell pointed out it was bedtime, and their daughter bounded off.

Joe chuckled at his wife, and picked up the *Radio Times* to consult the schedule. 'I think she might be right for once, we could do with more choice . . . so, no luck at the doctor's then?'

Nell braced herself to give him the worst. 'Apparently I'm in the change.'

Joe looked up sharply, a gamut of emotions taking turns on his face – those same emotions that had assaulted Nell. He even voiced the same words. 'But you're only thirty-eight!'

Nell gave a despairing nod to the man who was fifteen years her senior, but now, all of a sudden, it was she who had become the elder: old and useless. 'It happens to some women. They start late and finish early. Just our luck for me to be one of them. I'm really sorry, Joe.' Her eyes filled with tears, not for herself, but for him.

He rose then, and came to put his arm round her, and said cheerfully, 'It's not your fault.'

She laid her head on his shoulder for a while, murmuring into his warm hard flesh. 'No, but you must feel dreadful. You thought you were marrying this nubile young creature, and instead you've bought a pig in a poke.'

'You daft twillock, I never regarded you as some . . . brood mare!' With a ripple of sympathy, and compassion in his eyes, his arm tightened around her, trying to rally her spirits. 'What do I want with another bairn anyway? We're happy enough with the one we've got, aren't we?'

'I am,' said Nell, not lifting her face. 'But I know how much you wanted a son . . .'

He shrugged. 'Well, if it's not to be, there's no good moaning over it. It's nobody's fault, it's just one o' them things.' With a last reassuring clasp, he released her. 'And think of it this way, we'd only have had to move for the extra bedroom if we did have a lad, and we wouldn't really want that after all the hard work we've put in.' He fell into his chair and resumed his scrutiny of the *Radio Times*. 'Now, let's see if there's anything good on . . .'

But Nell guessed he was not really concentrating on the lists of programmes – even though he was scanning the page as if he were – but was peering into the darkness of his mind, in search of the son he would never have.

16

Not one word of blame had been cast, but it was as if a page had been turned in their marriage. Whether or not it was in Nell's imagination, their lovemaking seemed less hearty after her announcement. It was as if, thought Nell, Joe no longer regarded her as a woman, and so not worthy of the effort, even though he still went through the motions from time to time; it would have been too blatant not to. But she had no right to accuse him of neglect, of putting all his energy into garden beds, and tending lawns, and building a shed in which to hide away, for she was the one who had brought this about, the one who had failed him. Besides, speaking for herself, now that the pressure to bear a son had been irrevocably lifted, Nell was otherwise generally happy. And so was Nina, that was the main thing. For, having come to terms with the fact that she would remain his only child, Joe seemed to accept her for what she was: a girl.

Despite the fatherly teasing and little gifts and chats, though, Nell could sense a gap between them, whereas the lack of blood relationship between Nina and herself was proving no handicap at all. They could not have been closer.

'We're just like twins,' joked thirteen-year-old Nina as they sat side by side on the couch with their frizzy home perms, yellow dirndl skirts and white blouses.

'Apart from the Billy Stampers.' Joe smiled at the artificial tattoos on his daughter's thin wrists.

'And the stink.' Nina raised an armpit to sniff suspiciously beneath. 'Pooh, I smell just like Mrs Stewart.'

'Well, you're growing up,' her mother said kindly, both parents sharing a fond chuckle, for although she might be growing upwards, Nina remained as sticklike as before. 'Remember, I said you'll have to pay more heed to your hygiene now. Have a good wash before bed, then rub some of my Odo-Ro-No under your arms.'

With Nina inserting one last stitch into the length of fabric with enormous gingham squares of russet, Joe tried to show an interest. 'What's that you're making, a tablecloth?'

'A *skirt*!' She regarded her dinosaur of a father with mild contempt.

'It's the fashion, Joe,' explained Nell.

'Oh, pardon me.'

'Right, I'm off to bed!' Nina bounced off the couch, then adjusted her stockings, which had bagged at the knee.

'Er, do you mind?' asked her father, at the glimpse of suspenders.

'It's only you and Mam,' laughed the girl, smoothing down her paper nylon petticoat. Then, as if remembering, she wheeled to make a request. 'Er, Mam, can I wear your high heels when I go into town tomorrow?' Up to now, she had only been allowed the most modest of elevation. 'Shirley's mam's lending her hers.'

Nell consulted Joe. 'I don't see why not, do you, Dad?'

'I don't know why you're asking me.' He gave an amused sigh. 'You women always have your own way.'

But it had been said with affection, and when, the next day, he watched his daughter mince down the path alongside her more well-developed friend, he was to laugh until he cried, for Nina's legs were like twigs, and the mushroom suede high heels only served to exaggerate their thinness. 'There's Shirley looking like a young Sophia

Loren, and our Neen like Minnie Mouse!' Pulling out a handkerchief, he was hardly able to speak from mirth. 'Eh, God love the poor little bugger . . . Should she be that thin at her age? Maybe she needs a tonic.'

From the inference that she was not a good enough mother, Nell's own amusement paled. 'I feed her well enough! She's just slender like you.'

Joe patted his belly, the top button of his trousers undone after a heavy lunch. 'Not so slender these days, I'm afraid.' Then he gazed again at his daughter's willowy figure as she went through the gate, and his voice was wistful. 'She's not really like her mother at all, is she? Apart from her blonde hair.'

Nell looked startled. Her husband rarely said anything like this. Personally, she was glad to have few reminders that someone else had given birth to this dear child. But, 'Even that's got a little bit of you in it,' she said, of its reddish tinge.

Joe nodded thoughtfully, then said on impulse, 'Take her to town next week and get her some shoes more befitting her legs – get yourself an outfit as well.' Here he turned to smile at Nell. 'She'll probably have your heels wrecked by the time she's tottered over them cobblestones in town.'

The donor was not too bothered about that, but she was to buy her daughter some high heels of her own the following Saturday, taking advantage of Shirley being away on holiday. Such outings had become a rare treat, for these days Nina seemed to prefer the company of her close pal to her mother. Lately, too, Nina had become more secretive, retiring to her room on an evening. Nell had offered mild complaint to her husband about this, saying, 'I can't think what she finds to do up there.' But Joe, of course, had not cared less, so long as his belly was attended, and told her not to take it personally. For, as she had said herself, Nina was growing up. Nell had tried, but could not help taking it to heart, which was why she intended to make the most of this outing by spending the whole day in town, with lunch in a restaurant, and girlish chat throughout.

It was a changed York from the one of her youth, at least on the surface. Whilst it retained the same identity it had had for a century or more – a military city, a railway city, a chocolate city – the amount of traffic had increased, and was now restricted to one-way along some of the narrower streets, a policeman on point duty at the busy junctions. A programme of sandblasting had been set in motion, and the blackened walls of historic monuments had begun to regain their original splendour. Such improvement, though, was in some part obliterated by the department stores that had sprung up everywhere, their concrete edifices much less appealing than their luscious contents.

With never such choice before her, Nell drew similar pleasure as her daughter in treating Nina not only to shoes, but a blouse and skirt, a can-can petticoat to go beneath, and American Tan stockings. Although Joe had instructed her to buy herself a dress too, with her happiness gaining momentum at each purchase, she said on a whim to Nina, 'Let's buy you one instead!'

Nina was not one to turn down an extra treat, but felt it was only polite to show hesitation. 'You're meant to be finding something for yourself – and Dad might be annoyed when all your money's been spent on me.'

'Pff!' came her mother's gay reply. 'You leave Potato Pete to me.' This was the nickname she had given Joe, him being so keen on gardening. 'Anyway I can't find anything I like.' Secretly, though, there was a deeper reason for this, Nell having no wish to make herself more attractive to a husband whose half-hearted attentions were tiresome enough, without encouraging him by dolling herself up. 'He probably won't even notice.'

* * *

However, she was surprised when Joe took her to task. 'I told you to get a dress for yourself – I was going to take you out.'

'Sorry, you should have said . . .' Nell looked apologetic.

'Never mind,' conceded Joe with a sigh. 'It was only the pub.'

'Oh well, nothing spoiled then – and it's a good night on telly,' she reminded him.

He gave a half-hearted shrug. 'Well, if you're not bothered . . .'

'No, I'm so much happier having spent it on Neen. She's getting to be a young woman, with an eye to impress.'

'And it would've been a wasted effort for you to try and impress me,' came Joe's perspicacious remark as he turned away.

Nell looked hurt, and opened her mouth to deny it, but then instead gave an awkward little laugh, and turned away as well.

The purchase of that dress seemed to have meagre significance at the time, but now, a year later, Nell wished she had never bought it. Not just because she had only seen her daughter parade it the once, before relegating it to a drawer. No, it was not just this waste, but the fact that it had only served to drive a wedge into the crack that had appeared in her marriage. There was no animosity, not in the least, but once Nina had gone to bed on an evening there was little conversation at all between Joe and his wife.

And nor would there be, thought Nell, with me stuck in the house all day. So, with Nina being out at school from seven thirty in the morning till four in the afternoon, to broaden her own horizons, and because she had begun to miss it, she decided to return to nursing.

Joe put up no objection to his wife working part-time. 'So long as you're here when we get in – I wouldn't half miss that smiling face of yours.' And he gave her his blessing with a pat on the cheek.

Though it had been lovely to work at the fever hospital, the bad memory of her final days there still festered – no matter that Nell might try to lock this away with all her other painful thoughts, she could not help but relive it from time to time, and she had no desire to encounter her old adversary again. Being informed by Beata that Sister Pike was still in residence was enough to make her turn to older haunts. The Infirmary that had become the Grange was now renamed St Mary's, though no cosmetic remedy could prevent it from being easily identified as an old Union workhouse. Inside, though, it had changed for the better, the wards being brighter, and smaller, and, amazingly, one or two of the residents were still there.

'Why, Cissie Flowerdew! Do you remember me?'

Blank eyes perused her for a moment, then the elderly cleaner broke into a smile. 'Hello, Nurse, did you hear I'm getting married?' At which Nell had a good old chat with her before going along to Matron's office – a different matron, of course, for Miss Fosdyke had long been retired. Blanche who'd scrubbed the floors was long dead too, but to Nell's delight on that first day back on the ward, she found that little Connie Wood, her favourite, was there, aged ninety-five, but still possessed of that bright little face which had so endeared her to Nell and others, though completely bedridden now.

Nursing had changed a lot in the eight years Nell had been away, and it took a while to ease herself back into the swing of things. But the job itself was still the same one she had loved, with all its sadness and humour, and there was the added bonus of being able to share this with Joe at the end of the day, giving husband and wife something serious to discuss, or to laugh about, rather than sitting in silence before the TV.

Yet it was always Nina who was privy to these tales

first, upon coming home from school. For there was nothing Nell loved more than to hear her fourteen-year-old daughter's hearty laughter when she related what had been said that day; the excuses the old folk came up with for their unsanitary habits.

'There's one old girl wraps all her business in sweet papers.' Nell put on a frail little voice to mimic the culprit. 'She said, "it's the bread and jam that makes me do it, Nurse!" I told her, "It's very odd that no one else's comes ready wrapped!"'

Nina fell about giggling. 'Oh, you'll have to tell Dad that one!'

And indeed, Nell was to do so much later, after Nina had gone upstairs following tea, as was a teenager's wont. The crinkles of laughter were still around the parents' eyes when there came the sound of their daughter's passage down the stairs, the clomp of high heels, and the swish of her coat. 'Right, I'm off,' she eventually popped in to tell those seated by the fire.

'Where's Dan Dare?' A startled Joe beheld her hairdo, stacked six inches high into a dome. 'Well, you look like the ruddy Mikon, I thought Dan couldn't be far behind.'

'Da-ad!' reproved Nina.

Her mother too. 'Don't be mean, Joe.' Nell admired the grey swagger coat with white flecks, the smart black court shoes with a strap over the instep. 'She looks very elegant.'

'Thanks, Mam – oh, bugger!' Nina let out a sudden wail.

'Oh yes, extremely elegant. We'll have less of that,' warned her father, to no avail as Nina hurried to apply an unsightly blob of pink nail varnish to her snagged stocking. 'Where is it you're off to anyway?'

Nina showed exasperation. 'Speech Day, of course!'

'Looking like *that*?' Joe observed her bouffant hair and shocking-pink lipstick. 'And I don't remember being told. Aren't parents usually invited?'

'I *did* tell you! You never listen – anyway, I'd better go.' Nina shot for the door.

'Wait on!' yelled Joe, only to hear a slam. Then he rolled his eyes at Nell.

'Well, I suppose she thought we wouldn't want to go, you being so bored the last time,' shrugged Nell, who held the firm suspicion that their daughter was lying, for she had overheard her and Shirley discussing a pop concert, and both had clammed up when she arrived. But, wanting Nina to be happy, she made no mention of that to Joe.

However, someone else was to blab. With both parents working, the morning post had remained unopened all day, and not until tea had been consumed did Joe finally put on his glasses and sift through the collection of envelopes. One in particular drew a frown.

'What's all this? *Dear Mr and Mrs Kilmaster, it was very disappointing to see neither of you at our Speech Day on Wednesday evening. Perhaps you had prior commitments. However, I should have been obliged if your daughter had attended . . .*'

Nina had carried the wireless into the kitchen, so as to listen to Radio Luxembourg, and could be heard singing along to it. Joe's face darkened as he shouted for her.

A head appeared round the door, adorned with metal rollers. 'Was that you bawling?' At the black summons that was thrown at her, Nina came fully into the room, accidentally tripping over the wire that snaked under the door from the radio to a point on the wall by the window.

'Speech Day, was it?' he announced tartly, showing her the damning letter. 'Where did you really go?'

After a flush of guilt, his daughter came clean. 'To see Joe Brown.'

'Right! Where does he live?' Joe put his glasses aside, meaning business. 'I'm off round to speak to his father!'

Nina poured scorn on his ignorance, and jabbed at the

radio that was still playing 'A Picture of You'. 'I mean *him* – at the Rialto.'

'That lanky, spiky-haired lout?' spluttered Joe.

'And the Tornadoes.'

'Ooh, are they the ones who play "Telstar"?' cut in Nell.

'Yeah!' Nina lit up for her mother. 'And Johnny Ki—'

'I don't want to hear the full blasted programme! I want to know what you were doing there – and where you got the cash.' Then immediately Joe's eyes turned to his wife. 'Or do I need to ask?'

'It wasn't me!' Nell looked injured.

'Well you're always funding her for some bloody thing!'

'Not this time – I had no idea!' She turned more disapprovingly now to Nina, but her tone was not so much recriminatory as disappointed. 'You should have told us where you were going, Neen –'

'Asked!' barked Joe. 'I think you mean *asked*.'

'We wouldn't have known where to find you if anything had happened.' Nell continued to handle this with tact. 'We're only angry because we're worried about you being hurt –'

'Aye, and she will be hurt if she lies to me again!' cut in Joe. 'Do you think your teachers want to go to Speech Day either, to sit through somebody droning on for hours – and take that smirk off your face!' He had seen Nina's lips twitch over his admittance that the event was boring. 'Right, well, if you're going to lie about where you're going, then you won't be going anywhere for a month.'

'Can't lock me up,' muttered a sulky Nina under her breath.

'You *what*?' Joe overheard – and in one swift movement he had grabbed the teapot from a tray and emptied its contents over her head. 'You cheeky little sod!'

Her head dripping lukewarm tealeaves, the victim cried out. 'You could have scalded me to death!' And with a frustrated gasp for her newly washed hair, Nina stormed upstairs, from whence came the sound of running water, much banging about, then the growl of a hairdryer.

The parents sat in silence after she had gone, staring at the television screen, though digesting little of the programme. Joe was still fuming, Nell pursing her lips.

'I suppose you think I've been too hard on her again,' he said eventually.

Nell lifted one shoulder, trying hard to sound diplomatic. 'Well, I agree she shouldn't have gone without asking, but locking her away for so long won't help.'

'I might have known I'd be the villain.'

She clicked her tongue. 'I'm not saying that! I'm trying to find some middle ground. A month is aeons to someone so young, all you'll achieve is resentment. Can't you remember being her age? The curses I piled on my parents . . .' She broke off to regard him slyly. 'I'll bet you didn't always do as you were told either.'

Joe was calming down, but his denial was strenuous. 'I bloody did! Eliza used to clatter us for splashing water on the windows when we washed our hands – even for looking at her the wrong way . . .'

'And you don't want Nina to feel that way about you, do you?' asked Nell softly. 'Things are different today, Joe, people aren't so strict with their children . . .' Seeing him rear, she quickly adopted a subordinate role. 'I'm not arguing with you! She has to learn she can't get away with it . . . but a month is a bit steep.' Ending with a look of entreaty, she went to make a pot of tea for supper. And when this arrived with a plate of assorted cakes and biscuits, he was in a more lenient frame of mind.

'A week then,' he allowed grudgingly, and dunked a gingernut.

Nell beamed and thanked him. 'I'll just go up and tell her, to save her stewing about it.'

Hair back in rollers, Nina was leaning over the open

windowsill when her mother appeared, and underwent a moment of panic trying to disperse the cigarette smoke.

'Now then, Fag-ash Lil,' said Nell. 'Don't bother trying to waft it out of the window, I could smell it miles away.'

Caught out again, Nina's sulk turned to expectancy as her smiling mother handed over the cup of coffee she had made. 'Did you talk him round?'

'What do you think?' Nell chuckled as her daughter's face broke into a relieved grin. 'I managed to get your sentence reduced to a week.'

'Better than nowt. Thanks, Mam. I knew you'd talk sense into him.'

Nell cocked her head in slight disapproval. 'I don't think Dad'll be so lenient if he smells the fags.'

'Well, he wouldn't, him being such a bloody hypocrite – I had to wash my hair all over again!'

Nell turned cross then. 'Now, I won't have you speak about your father like that! He thinks the world of you.'

There came a genuinely repentant mumble, after which an indulgent Nell sat on the bed to ask, 'So, was Joe Brown worth it then?'

'Oh yeah, he was fab!' Nina flopped on the bed beside her mother. 'Tornadoes were great as well. Me, Shirley and Bridget can play, "Telstar" on our combs. We performed it for the RE teacher the other day – we do a Shadows walk to it – she thought it were right good.'

'Your teachers sound nice,' Nell said, at which Nina agreed, but added with a heavy sigh that it was just school that was crap. Nell tried to sound optimistic. 'Well, it's not really that long until you're sixteen.'

'*Sixteen?*' Nina's head shot up. 'I was reckoning on fifteen – and that's bad enough!'

'Oh, Neen, I don't think your dad'll swallow that. He's expecting you to take your GCEs.'

'That'd be another year and a half! It'll nearly be time to get married. Can't you persuade him to let me leave next spring?' Nina cuddled up to her, using the well-worn ploy.

And, despite knowing full well she was being played for a mug, Nell uttered a growl of submission and declared, 'I'll see what I can do – but you'll have to act your part in keeping him sweet!'

So, in the following months, Nina did try her best not to upset her father, for this being rewarded with a record player at Christmas. Nell too paved the way by making this festive season the best yet – a white one too – with stacks of Joe's favourites to eat and drink. Though Nina's cause was not helped by a school report in February, which informed Joe that despite his daughter's abilities being of a high standard, she rarely exerted herself and was occasionally insolent. As much as Nell might try to smooth things over with rump steak for tea, this was not a good time to put in one's request. Nevertheless, with her fifteenth birthday well under her belt, Nina was itching to be free. Hoping Shirley's presence would prevent her father from going completely berserk, she had invited her to be there.

Entering without knocking, her collection of rollers veiled with a headscarf and an aura of frost, Shirley rushed straight to the roaring fire and presented her mauve fingers. Nell enquired if it was still as bad out there. Since Christmas there had been snow and ice of catastrophic proportions. They were saying it was even colder than 1947, but Nell found that hard to believe. 'Let's hope we don't have to travel by rowing boat again when it melts!' She sought to compliment the teenager's attire. 'Love your jumper, Shirl. It shows off your smashing figure.'

'Thanks, Mrs K.' Shirley removed her headscarf, so as to allow her hair to dry.

Nell continued to chat to her woman to woman, and asked, had she done her hair a different colour? The other said she had: Black Tulip.

'I should have mine done – look at all these grey hairs.' Nell bent her head for Shirley to see.

'If you want to buy a colour I can run it through for you if you like.' The small mound of snow on the toe of each of Shirley's white ankle boots had begun to melt, and above the cuff of fake leopard-skin her legs were blue, as the dark-haired siren lowered her hips onto the hearth rug.

Joe had abandoned the *Radio Times* and was now, over his reading glasses, eyeing the tight jersey fabric of Shirley's skirt. 'By, that's a snug fit. Are them suspenders I can see, or have you got a couple of fruit gums shoved down your stocking-tops?'

Having been teased like this from childhood, the voluptuous one merely grinned.

'He's an impudent devil,' scolded Nell, then remembered her daughter's promise. 'Oh, Neen, you were going to play Telstar for us! Come on, here's a comb, Shirley!' And with Nell's encouragement, Nina and her friend took a moment to wrap some toilet paper around their combs, then, with fancy footwork, performed the massive hit.

It was a hit with her father too. Though, 'I can't help the feeling I'm being buttered up for summat,' said Joe with a knowing smile, upon being served a cup of tea and a slice of cake by his daughter after the performance.

Momentarily diverted, Nina said brightly, 'Well, as it happens, I'd love to go and see Chris Montez . . .'

'How much?' Joe gave a sigh of resignation, but was in a kindly mood tonight, and dipped into his pocket to count out four and sixpence.

'By, you are nice, Mr Kilmaster.' Chewing on gum, Shirley sought to provide an opening for Nina. 'I have to pay for meself now I'm at work.'

Then Nina said, 'See, I wouldn't need to tap you and Mam up, Dad, if I had me own job . . .'

It took a second to register, then Joe exclaimed, 'So that's the reason behind all this lubrication! Well, you can forget it, you're staying on to do your GCEs.' And no amount of argument could shift him.

'Shirley's parents let her leave! And Mam says it's all right with her.'

'Well, it's not with me – isn't it about time you were going home, Shirley?'

Dropping her sultry mien, the friend was quick to pluck up her headscarf and depart.

'That one's leading you astray!' asserted Joe. 'Just because she's in a dead-end job –'

'I *can* think for meself, you know, Dad!'

'Nobody wants to undermine you, Joe,' said Nell, trying to dismantle the hurdles that Nina kept erecting. 'Just hear me out a minute before you decide.'

'Go on, then, know-all!' He granted her the floor, obviously not expecting to be persuaded in any way, judging by his attitude.

'Just what are you expecting her to do once she passes all her exams?'

'Well, get a decent job for a start – maybe even go to university. She wouldn't even have to leave home with one right on our doorstep at Heslington –' His daughter interjected a puff of complaint, for all she could see was the destruction of her old countryside haunts to make way for this seat of learning. '– she's lucky enough to still have that opportunity, even if she did fail her eleven plus!'

'Oh, you'll never let me forget that, will you? I don't *want* to go to university! I'd hate being hemmed in by people so brainy they can't even manage to fasten their buttons in the right hole – anyway, I wouldn't be seen dead in a duffle coat. I just want to earn some cash and enjoy myself whilst I'm at it, get married when I'm seventeen, then have two kids.'

Nell's outspread palms told Joe that he could not really argue with that.

'I just want more for her than I've got!' he exploded.

'But I'd be happy with that, Dad!'

'And I thought you were happy with it too, Joe?' proffered his wife. 'You never showed any inclination to buy your own house –'

'That's an entirely different matter! I daresay I would've if I'd had loads of cash, but I didn't want to be skimping on food and clothes and – hang on a minute! This isn't about me, it's about her education . . .' But under Nell's gentle look of persuasion, and his daughter's resolute glare, he let out a curse. 'Why do I flaming bother? It's a bloody conspiracy!'

But Nina's gleam of triumph was short-lived, as her father declared, 'Well, *maybe* if you convince me you can get a decent job without those exams, then I might let you leave.'

She erupted in frustration. 'How can I prove that until I've actually left bloody school?'

'Well, for a start you can drop that bolshy attitude! My father would've knocked my head off for backchat like that!'

Nina became instantly submissive, lowering her eyes. 'Sorry, Dad – I just really hate school, that's all, and staying on to do exams won't alter that. Is it so bad not to want the earth? You only work in a factory, yet you like your job and the people you work with, don't you?'

'It's true I prefer it to clerical work, like I was forced into by Aunt Eth—'

'See!' she butted in sweetly. 'You didn't like being forced into something you didn't like, so why should I?'

'I might not have liked it, but it was a thousand times better than hewing coal like my stepmother made me do! I had to do as I was told or I'd be out on my ear. Young uns today don't know they're born. Look, Neen,' trying to calm down, he used fiscal persuasion, 'I'm not trying to force you down the mines, I just want you to get some qualifications so's you can earn more money . . . Tell you what, you write a letter stating your intentions and asking for an interview, make some copies, then post it off to different firms. Then we'll at least have an idea of what we're up against.'

Nina obviously did not consider this much of a compromise.

But, 'I think you should be grateful,' advised Nell.

Joe had not really expected his daughter to receive any serious offer, so when a letter came inviting her for interview, he was thrown off guard. Even more so when she was offered the post of junior clerk in a department store.

Backed into a corner by both his daughter and his wife, he was forced to give way. But he warned, 'There'll be no favours. You'll pay for your keep – how much is your wage, by the way?'

'Three pounds, seven and six.'

'That's before your stamp's taken off, I suppose?'

'Stamp?' Nina looked baffled.

'And you reckon you've had enough schooling?' replied a sarcastic father, explaining about national contributions.

Nina looked annoyed upon learning that over five shillings would be deducted. But Joe snorted there would be even less of it when she'd handed it over to her mother, adding to Nell, 'And you're to give her back only as much as she needs for her bus fares and dinners – there'll be no buying records, nor going to the pictures every night, nor spending it on fags – don't think I'm daft, I know you've been puffing them off since you were twelve!' His face held a momentary glimmer of fun, then was serious again. 'So, are you going to take up this crummy offer, or stay on at school and give yourself a better chance?'

'How much of my wages will I be allowed to keep?' asked Nina.

Joe threw up his hands in a gesture of despair. 'Good

God, what hope is there for this country – you can have a pound a week. Like it or lump it.'

Nina reworked her budget, totting up her requirements under her breath. 'Cigs'll take about half a quid if I can keep to less than ten a day, same again to get me into a bop for five nights, and maybe the flicks on Sunday – okay, I'll tell 'em I'll take it then!'

17

Nina's inauguration to the workplace coincided with the massive thaw, although the floodwaters came nowhere near the Kilmaster house, thus providing only mild inconvenience on her daily travels to the city.

After only a matter of weeks, Nell was dismayed to learn that her stepdaughter did not really enjoy her work at the department store. However, her fear that Nina would be forever hopping from job to job was soon dispelled. It was better than school, admitted Nina, as she handed over her wage packet to her mother. The snobbery between departments made for a good laugh, and – the main thing in Nina's book – it kept the money coming in. If only her allowance would stretch a bit further . . .

And, naturally, the soft-hearted Nell fell prey to this lament, and was to slip much of it back into Nina's hand during the week. So far as Joe was concerned, though, he was quite satisfied with the way his daughter had been contributing.

So much so, that tonight he was polishing her shoes for her, prior to a concert. 'I'll bet Shirley doesn't get this done for her,' he told Nina, who was in the kitchen alongside him, sharing the washing-up with his wife.

'I know – you're such a good dad.' She grinned back at him as she dried the last cup.

'By the way, there's the hair lacquer you asked me to

get off the market.' Nell indicated the clear plastic tube on the windowsill as she wiped down the draining board.

'Thanks, Mam.' Nina hung up her tea towel, then, for her father's benefit, opened her purse and handed over sixpence, which an equally dutiful Nell accepted, both knowing it would probably be slipped back to her later.

'A *tanner*?' Joe raised his eyebrows at the plastic tube. 'Are you sure it's for your hair? Looks more like lighter fuel to me.' Then, with an amused shake of his head, he broke off his polishing to fish a coin from his own pocket. 'Here, have it on me.'

'Aw, thanks!' Nina patted him tenderly, then decanted the lacquer into a plastic puffer spray. 'Is it okay if I wash me hair now, Mam?' She reached for a packet of washing powder.

'Daz?' exclaimed Joe in wonderment. 'You'll end up like Yul Brynner!'

'S'only thing that gets the lacquer out.' Bending over the kitchen sink, she stuck her head neath running water. With his wife chuckling, a flabbergasted Joe watched his daughter's strawberry blonde hair being scoured of the crust of lacquer it had accrued and asked couldn't she get some decent stuff like her mother used. 'At half a crown a can?' came her reply, through the splashing of water.

'Here!' Joe added a florin to the sixpence already on the worktop. 'Rather I be skint than you be bald.'

Later, though, when his daughter was set to go out, he had to admit that the Daz had generated admirable results. 'A pity you've sprayed it with that bloody lacquer again.' He rose to give her hairdo an experimental tap with his knuckles. 'Bloody Nora, it's like cardboard.'

'You cheeky bugger.' His daughter hit him with a laugh. 'I think I'll go and live at Shirl's.'

'Pff! You know when you're well off.' Joe sank back into his chair. 'I hate to tell you, but you've put your cardigan on back to front.' At the teenager's sigh, Nell explained that this was the fashion; making it double as a jumper. 'What do I know – eh up!' The click of a door-knob interrupted Joe's banter. 'Here's your mate come for you.'

But no, it was Beata, come to visit. 'You're too late, we've had our teas.' Her brother's joke was negated by courteous ascent from his chair.

Beata clicked her tongue as if thwarted, then smiled and received Nell's kiss, the latter telling her to take no notice of him, it was lovely to see her. As a child Nina would have run to greet her aunty with a kiss, though now she was too busy with last-minute touches to her hairdo. Informed she was off to a concert, Aunty Beata cautioned her niece. 'I hope you're not like them screaming lasses I've seen on the telly, are you?' Nina denied it with a grin, and received one in return.

Beata had just been settled with a cup of tea, when Shirley entered the living room, another girl hanging back behind her. Joe urged them all to come in. 'Now then, Shirley, how's work going?'

'All right, thanks, Mr K.'

'Must be – looks like a new coat you've got on.' He eyed the emerald-green jacket over the black polo-neck sweater. 'Very nice – Oi'll give it foive.'

Attracting scorn for his rather passe catch phrase, Joe turned to the bespectacled one in amber corduroy. 'Who's this then?'

Nina heaved a sigh at his interrogation. 'Bridget.'

'Bridget Bardot, eh? Where do you work, love?'

'Freeman, Hardy and Willis.' She raised a grubby finger that had chipped nail varnish, and shoved her spectacles back on to the bridge of her pug nose.

'Ah, I shall have to come and see you. I'm after some pointed-toed wellingtons – I like to keep up with fashion, you know. Can you get me discount?' A wink was to douse her look of uncertainty, before Joe turned his attention to her chestnut coiffure. 'Is your hair as rock-hard as it looks an' all?'

'Da-ad!' chastised Nina, as she donned a red belted mac.

Nell shook her head at Beata, who sat there issuing her throaty chuckle throughout.

Joe continued to tease as he surveyed the trio, each in a coat of brilliant hue. 'Blimey, red, green and amber – don't all stand together like that, folk'll think you're a set of traffic lights.' Warned laughingly by Nell, he too smiled, 'Aye, I'm only kidding, you look fab. That's the word, isn't it?'

His daughter sagged with embarrassment and began to rifle through her handbag. 'I had a doff in here somewhere – ah, here it is!' Having unearthed the squashed and discoloured stub from a pit of other rubbish, Nina put it to her lips. 'Giz a light, Dad.'

'Good God! The Castle Museum'd be interested in that.' But he held out his lighter for her, and also the other girls, who extended whole cigarettes towards the flame.

Nina pulled a face at the acrid contents of her throat. 'Tastes like hair lacquer – but it'll have to do.'

Joe saw Beata's hand go to her pocket, and stopped her with a look. 'Er, she's been indulged enough tonight!'

His sister disobeyed, shoving her fist at Nina and pretending it held only rubbish. 'Here, put that in the bin on your way out.'

'Thanks, Aunty Beat – see you!'

As the girls turned to leave, Joe bade them, 'Enjoy your concert then – who is it you're off to see?'

'Roy Orbison,' the sultry dark-haired one turned to tell him.

'Is that the blind fella?' Joe winked at Nell and Beata.

'Shurrup, he's great!'

'And t'Beatles,' added Bridget.

'Aw, not them blokes with hair down to their backsides? Take a can of DDT with you. In at ten then.'

'Drop off,' bantered Nina, and left with her friends.

Joe chuckled to his wife and sister, spending the next half an hour chatting with them until Beata went home.

Alone with his wife again, he had a bright idea, saying eagerly, 'I don't see why them lasses should have all the fun. Nat King Cole's coming to Leeds soon – do you fancy going? I wouldn't mind seeing him meself.'

Nell was directing her concentration on stitching a hole in the toe of her stocking, and did not match his zeal. 'Oh, if he was in York maybe, but Leeds always gives me a headache.'

'We can't have that,' ribbed Joe. 'You have enough of them. Just thought I'd offer, that's all.' And, throwing her a smile, he retreated behind the *Radio Times*.

Joe's good mood over his daughter was not to last, though. A few months down the line and Nina had begun to take days off work, pretending she had a sore throat. 'I don't know what you're moaning about,' she said when he confronted her. 'I still get paid.'

Joe gasped at such audacity. 'So the firm's got an excellent system – is that a decent reason to take advantage of it? It's meant for people who are genuinely ill! Not little skiving buggers who want to lozzock in bed all day.' Nell supported him in this, saying Nina didn't see either of them taking a day off for no good reason.

'Well you *have* to turn up in your job,' Nina pointed out to her mother, 'it's a matter of life or death. But nobody's gonna die just 'cause I don't turn up to scribble a few numbers down.'

Joe had had enough of this. 'Aye, well, you're getting your arse there whether I have to drive you there meself!'

And, more out of fear of being humiliated than from duty, for a time Nina was to do as her father ordered. But her obstinate attitude was never far from the surface.

'What's she doing here?' Joe demanded of his wife, upon

coming home from on early shift one sunny afternoon in August to find his daughter there too.

'Er, it's Wednesday, dopey.' Legs slung over a chair arm to display stocking-tops, and a magazine in hand, Nina barely tore her eyes away except to issue retort. 'Half-day closing.'

'I'll give you dopey.' Joe slapped her feet off the chair.

'Stop being so cheeky,' added Nell, who had herself not long ago finished work. 'Come on, get the kettle on for your dad. Then I might let you have one of my cigs.'

Nina prised herself from the chair. 'I've given up, they've started tasting funny.'

'I'm not surprised,' laughed Nell, 'if they've been sitting at the bottom of your bag for months covered in hair spray.'

Joe chuckled too, more amenable now that Nina had gone to make him a cup of tea. 'By, it's mafting!' He took off his jacket and loosened his tie before flopping into the chair she had vacated. 'What's this you're reading?'

'*Ousebeat*,' came the response from the kitchen.

'Very intellectual.' Flicking through the magazine, he found it crammed with, 'Long-haired nancy boys – that un's like bloody Rapunzel. I'll give you good warning, don't be fetching one of them home.'

'Behave, you were young once,' scolded an amused Nell. Picking up the magazine from where he had thrown it, she too had a quick perusal, at one point holding it at arm's length. 'What does it say they call this group?'

'I warned you it'd eventually come to thee!' Joe mocked her failing eyesight. 'Get yourself some specs, you decrepit old bugger.'

Nell used the magazine first to swipe him, then to fan her face, as their daughter returned carrying two cups of tea. Over the striped sleeveless dress, Nina wore a royal-blue mohair cardigan, for which her mother gave an affectionate laugh. 'You girls and your fashion – you'll be breeding maggots in this heat.'

Nina replied quickly, 'It's to cover my skinny arms.'

But her blush, and the look she had darted towards her father, caused Nell to have other suspicions. Very grave suspicions, which were to gnaw at her all the while she was sipping her tea, and beyond.

It was shocking to contemplate, with Nina only fifteen. But, remembering her own trauma, Nell was determined not to react so hysterically as her parents, and to meet this with calmness and common sense. There was obviously something on Nina's mind, so even if the misgiving turned out to be fallacy – and she hoped to God it would – it needed to be dealt with at once.

Alas, it was not as simple a matter to broach as those other teenage vicissitudes, the prudery of Nell's background causing her to shy away at every turn, and to use Joe's presence as an excuse to shirk her duty. Deeming it vital that he not be there when she did finally confront Nina's problem, she was to delay it for another week, waiting for his shift pattern to change, this also lending her time to watch Nina more closely.

And the more she watched, and was to witness that faraway expression, the more concerned she grew. Yes, Nina had always had a habit of drifting off, but this was different. Different, but familiar – for Nell had seen that worried glaze in her own reflection many years ago.

A hoar frost crept over the mother's thoughts, her heart soon encased by crystals of ice. Wandering up to Nina's empty room, she looked around as if seeking answer. Such a conflict of styles here: the three pale blue walls of childhood almost obliterated by pin-ups, the fourth side clad in Beatles wallpaper; the dressing table with tubes and pots of make-up, amongst which grazed favourite horses from her cowboy days; shelves stacked with encyclopaedias, a dictionary, fairytales and the lurid tomes of Harold Robbins and Frank Yerby; library books on the bedside table, which used to be a miniature kitchen dresser, made for her as a child. Moving thoughtfully across the blue carpet, picking up stockings along the way, Nell untangled the ball of clothes left on the floor, throwing some on the landing to wash, hanging the rest up, and using this opportunity to cast a troubled eye over the jumbled contents of the wardrobe.

Was that a diary peeking from the top shelf? Nell fought her inclination to pry. Then, balancing her curiosity against the thought that it was for Nina's own good, she took down the handmade volume, lifted the cover and read the first page:

It was a dark and stormy night, when the stranger rode into town . . .

With a sigh, she put Nina's secret novel back where she had found it, and closed the wardrobe door; though not on her problem.

It was Joe's complaint that finally prompted action.

'Aw, who's eaten all the sodding aspirins?' came his loud exclamation from the bathroom, prior to departure for work. 'There was half a bottle there the last time I looked, and now it's empty. I've got a splitting headache . . .'

Downstairs, Nell's eyes flew to their daughter – and saw her guilt. My God, had she left it too late? Had desperation pushed her to attempt suicide?

Then, 'Sorry!' Nina called back to her father, as she too made ready for work. 'I've been using them to holding me stockings up. One of me suspenders is bust . . .'

Almost tearful with relief, Nell scolded her. 'You could have reused the same tablet, you didn't have to be so extravagant!'

'God, you'd think I was a Great Train Robber,' muttered the culprit, as her angry Mum sprang up to provide Dad with aspirin from her own handbag.

Even as Nell apologised for the over-reaction, it served

to make her see how imperative it was that she put aside her modesty and challenge the problem. Today.

Confrontation not being her style, Nell chose to be slicing greens on the worktop, a pan of potatoes already simmering on the hob for tea, and chatting about work to Nina, who stood beside her, as she summoned the courage to act. The other was meant to be helping on her afternoon off, but her mind was obviously on other things, as her listless gaze pierced the kitchen window.

Today, this well-noted habit was to provide Nell with an inlet. 'Wool-gathering again?' She gave a warm sideways smile.

'What?' Nina looked dazed, then shook her head as if to clear the fog. 'Oh, sorry, I didn't catch what you were saying, a train went past.'

'Ten minutes ago, maybe – you were miles away.' But Nell's voice remained gentle. 'I was just on about old Mr Coffey grumbling about the man in the next bed.' She put on her doddery voice to relate the occurrence. 'Nurse, he keeps throwing Maltesers at me, and he knows I don't like 'em!'

The fresh face cracked into a grin, though Nina did not split her sides as she normally might.

Her knife faltering over the cabbage, Nell hoped with all her heart that she was mistaken, and that her daughter would scoff in embarrassment when she broached the question. But much rather a few seconds' embarrassment than what Nell feared. For all that, it was hard to come right out with her suspicions. 'Neen . . . all these big jumpers you're wearing, well, your arms don't look that skinny to me . . .' They did, pathetically so in this situation. 'Is it something else you're trying to cover up? You can tell me anything, you know,' she added with sincerity.

Nina's face had turned white. 'Has Dad noticed?' came her hasty question.

Nell shook her head, looking directly into her daughter's eyes. 'Not yet, but he's bound to sometime. So am I right, you're expecting?'

With a great outpouring of relief, Nina nodded and burst into tears. 'He'll be that ashamed of me!'

'Aw, I'm sure he won't!' Nell dropped the knife to grip the weeping figure, offering encouragement with her tone. 'Your father's a good, kind man.' And, drawing the other into her arms, she held her for a while as the tears flowed, finally to take out her handkerchief and dab her own moist eyes, before handing it to Nina.

'I'm really sorry!'

'It's all right, it's all right! I'm not angry.' How could Nell explain that she was not upset for herself, but for the torment her daughter would have to suffer? She hated to think of that slender body racked by labour.

After blowing into the square of linen, the distraught girl wiped her face, hardly able to meet Nell's eye, but at last doing so as she begged, 'Will you tell him, Mam? I can't bear to see his face.'

Nell sagged at the thought, but, presented with such woe, and knowing all too well what Nina was going though, she eventually heaved a sigh. 'All right . . . I'll do it after tea.'

'Not while I'm here.' Nina sniffed and looked anxious. 'He'll go mad at me.'

Nell considered when *was* the time to break such news? There'd never be a good time. No man would react well upon hearing his teenage daughter was pregnant.

'Have you been to the doctor?'

'No, but I'm certain I'm expecting.'

'We'll have to take you. How far on do you think you are?'

'Four or five months.' Nina waited for an outburst, but her mother remained calm.

'At least it gives us a bit of leeway then . . .' Thoughtful of face, Nell pictured another young girl in a maelstrom of panic, in labour on the bathroom floor.

Escaping this awful scene, she was to make a suggestion to Nina. 'After tea, you go over to Shirley's – I suppose she knows?'

Nina shook her head. 'I didn't want to tell anybody before you.'

Nell moaned at this pathetic show of loyalty. 'You poor thing, keeping this all to yourself. Well, maybe you can confide when you go over tonight. I'll let your dad watch the news first, then tell him.'

'I can't believe how understanding you're being.' Nina gulped. Her cheeks were mottled and her eyes red, but there was also an air of relief. 'I thought you'd be raving too.'

'Well, I can't say I'm happy about it.' More serious than her daughter had ever seen her, Nell shook her head. 'But what's done is done, and as your mother I'm bound to help.'

The girl took a deep breath and nodded. Then she asked, 'Do you think he'll have calmed down in time for *Coronation Street*?'

'Oh, Neen . . .' Her mother did sound recriminatory now.

'No, I wasn't being –!' Nina's eyes were instantly flooded once more. 'I just meant, will it be safe for me to come home by then?'

'I doubt he'll have calmed down even by the Epilogue!' declared Nell. 'And if I were you, I'd be ready to face him well before *Coro*. The minute he hears, he'll want to come banging on Shirley's door – oh, don't worry, I won't let him,' she appeased quickly, to Nina's look of terror. 'I'll fetch you when it's safe. But, you're going to have to face him sometime, so you might as well get it over with.'

'I'm really sorry!' Nina broke down and wept again at

the thought of all the trouble she had caused this lovely woman.

Hugging her close, Nell patted her and spoke with compassion. 'These things happen, Neen.'

'Not if you're careful. I've been so stupid, Mam. I'm really, really sorry.'

With a last comforting pat, Nell released her. 'I think I need a cig.' Having lit one for herself, out of habit she extended the packet to Nina. 'Oh, I forgot, you've given up. Now we know why they tasted queer.'

Her daughter was quick to recant. 'Queer or not, I will have one if you don't mind. I need it.'

'We both do,' agreed Nell, and they were to draw deeply on these lifelines for a while, before discussing the matter again.

'It must have been just after you started work, was it?' she asked in due course.

Her daughter gave a nod.

'I wasn't even aware you had a boyfriend.' Nell sounded a little hurt. 'Will he marry you?'

Nina shook her head and sniffed. 'He doesn't know I'm expecting. I haven't been out with him since . . .'

Nell was instantly suspicious, her cigarette pausing in mid-air. 'He didn't force you?'

'No! No, honestly, he didn't.' Nina squinted, her scrawny chest exhaling one blast of smoke after another.

'Then maybe it's not too late to fix this,' mulled Nell, gradually become fog-bound. 'If we can talk your father round, we might be able to get you and this boy back together. Once he knows –'

'Mam,' Nina's eyes brimmed with tears again, as she was forced to confess, 'we never were "together". We just sort of bumped into each other one night. I was tanked up and got carried away . . .'

Nell started. 'So you'd never been out with him before? Don't you even know his name?'

A tearful shake of the head from Nina caused Nell to exclaim to the heavens, 'Oh, good grief!'

Nina was sobbing now. 'That's what I meant! That's why I daren't tell you before – me dad'll go nuts!'

For all her shock, Nell threw the cigarette into the fireplace and sought to comfort her girl, knowing how alone Nina must be feeling, especially so as she was an even more tender age than Nell herself had been upon giving birth to William. She thought of her own mother too, having sex with a stranger. But she managed to remain calm, and said now, 'Don't worry, love, we'll fix it somehow. I promise I'll do all I can to help.' Then she frowned and shook her head in disbelief at how she had not noticed her own daughter's inebriation. 'But how did you get in such a state – the drink, I mean?'

This batch of tears exhausted. Nina gave another huge sniff and wiped her eyes, which were now red and sore. 'You know that bottle of Emva Cream somebody got you for Christmas?'

Nell recalled with a sigh that it had been shoved in a cupboard and forgotten, but obviously not by some.

'Remember when me and Shirley went to stay that night at Bridget's? Well, I took it with me. Sorry.'

'But her parents must have noticed you all drinking,' objected Nell. 'What were they thinking about?'

Nina shook her head. 'We swigged it down by t'river, sneaked back in later without them noticing.'

'Staggered, more like,' said an annoyed Nell. Exhibiting despair, she listened as Nina gave further brief details.

'Anyway, some lads came by, and he was among them. I've always fancied him.' Nina looked vulnerable, her face wan and her voice hollow. 'He's really good-looking. I thought he was a nice lad as well – he seemed it, really funny, and good company and that – till I went up to talk to him a few days later.'

'I thought you said you hadn't seen him again,' frowned Nell.

'I said I hadn't been out with him! I've *seen* him. I see him every bloody week at Empire bop, but he made it plain he didn't want to go out with me again after he'd had his leg over.' She broke down, choked by tears of self-pity.

Nell was furious now. 'Well, he might not care to go out with you, but he's got a responsibility!'

'But I don't want anything to do with *him*!' roared the tearful face. 'He's a scumbag, and I bloody hate him!'

Minding that her own sensibility was assaulted by the disgustingly modern term, Nell fought this reaction, and put an arm around the speaker, trying to staunch her misery. After a long interval, during which she was constantly to assuage Nina's distress, she was finally to get around to the baby itself. 'What are we going to do about this then? Would you like to keep it?'

Nina blew her nose and wiped her eyes again. 'I've thought about it a lot . . . I don't know what's best. I didn't want it at first – 'cause I hated *him*. I would've taken something to get rid of it if I'd known where to turn –'

'It wasn't a fib about those aspirins, was it?' Nell burst in. 'Please say you didn't take them!'

Nina assured her that she had indeed used them to replace a suspender. 'No, there's a shop down Church Street that's supposed to sell pills or whatnot, but I daren't go in.'

Her mother exclaimed aloud. 'Thank God you didn't! It would've been useless, if not downright dangerous.'

'I thought it'd probably be adopted,' continued Nina. ''Cause I've never been really interested in babies. But then I felt it move inside me, and the more it moves, the more I love it.' She placed a protective hand over her abdomen, her face momentarily lighting up at the child inside her. 'You know when it –' She broke off with a look of awkwardness. 'Oh no, sorry, I forgot you haven't had one of your own . . .'

'Yes, I do know what it feels like.' Overwhelmed by the situation, Nell made an impulsive announcement. 'I was once in the same position as you are now, and I was forced to give my baby away, and there isn't a day goes by that I don't think about him, so if you want to keep this one, then I'll do everything in my power to help you, because if you let it be taken from you, you'll regret it for the rest of your life.' Her rushed delivery cracked with emotion, and, to Nina's further astonishment, she broke down sobbing.

It was the daughter's turn to comfort then, to hug and to hold and to dab away the tears. And, after the painful episode receded, she breathed incredulously, 'Mam, you've really floored me – I never knew!'

'No one did,' sniffed Nell, wiping her eyes quickly, as if regretting this lapse. 'At least, I didn't tell anyone, though your Aunty Beat guessed. I swore her to secrecy, and she's kept her word ever since.'

'So Dad –?'

'Has no idea,' Nell responded swiftly, at the same time realising that the time might be nigh to speak up. 'But I might have to tell him when I plead your case. He can't possibly understand what you're going through, and I want him to know before he makes any rash judgement. If that's the only way, then so be it. I have to make him understand, so's he'll allow you to keep it.'

Nina gazed into her mother's face for a moment, as if trying to read all that had happened in her past. Then, with nothing volunteered, she was compelled to ask, 'Did you say it was a boy or a girl?'

'A boy,' replied Nell, adding quickly that, 'I can't bear to speak about him any more.' Then, looking deeply into her daughter's eyes, each obviously as stunned as the other, she reached for her packet of cigarettes. 'God, what a day . . .'

* * *

The news had been over for ten minutes, yet Nell had still not plucked up the courage to tell Joe. It was not merely out of support for Nina – wanting to get this right, so that her father would be persuaded to show mercy – no, it was that all this turmoil had picked Nell up like a hurricane and carried her back to her own desperate situation. She was eighteen again, bereft of her darling Billy and terrified beyond words. Her heart was beating twenty to the dozen, and her breath coming in irregular little gasps as she relived every minute. She heard herself pleading to be allowed to keep her baby, experienced again the weeks of agonised silence that led to that point when all hell had erupted. Was this the way to go, to tell Joe first all about her own personal nightmare, hopefully to gain his sympathy, before dropping the real bombshell? For only that way might he be made to see just why Nina must be allowed to keep her baby . . .

'Come on, out with it, then!' came a dry interjection.

Nell jumped back into the present, and turned to stare at him.

'Well, you've obviously done summat.' Joe inserted a cigarette into his lopsided smile. 'You've been sat there looking guilty as hell since teatime. What is it?'

His wife took a breath. 'Neen's having a baby.' Oh no, it had come out all wrong!

Joe gave a sharp little laugh. 'I hope to Christ you're joking.' But he could tell from the look on her face that she was not.

A second of astonishment, then: 'I'll kill her!' Throwing his just-lit cigarette onto the fire, he shot for the door, but Nell got to it first and barred his way.

'Wait, wait!' Her busty figure grappled with his lean one. Unwilling to use his greater strength, Joe ordered her to get out of his way, but Nell stood firm, pressing with all her might against the door whilst he attempted to get round her. 'Let's just discuss it between ourselves first as to what's to be done!'

'What's to discuss? I'll clatter the bloody pair of them!'

'There is no pair! Only Neen, and she's already devastated without you laying into her!'

This served to delay Joe, whose scowl was both angry and anxious. 'She wasn't . . .' He could not bear to say raped.

But Nell quickly assured him. 'No, but the boy's no longer on the scene, and she doesn't know where he lives.'

'We could soon find out! She must know his name!'

Nell shook her head. 'It was just the one time, a meeting of strangers . . .'

This damning statement proved sufficient to deter him from charging after Nina. Shocked to the core that his child could have descended to such immorality, Joe stayed to listen, putting his hands to his head as his wife relayed the basic details. Then another blast of gunpowder. 'I knew that bloody Shirley'd be involved! Little tart, with her skirt up to her arse –'

'Joe, it's nothing to do with Shirley. Nina was the one who took our bottle of sherry, she admits she was idiotic to drink too much, but it doesn't have to ruin her entire life, only if we let it.'

Joe continued to rant for a while about the irresponsibility of others. Then he let out a moan. 'Jesus Christ, what the hell are we going to do? That bastard! She's fifteen, for God's sake!' Only now did this gain double importance, and he responded with alacrity.

'We could have him done for it!'

'And drag her through the courts?' Nell shook her head.

'The stupid little bitch!' Joe thumped both arms of the chair in frustration. 'Ruining her life . . .'

'Oh Joe.' Nell came to perch on the arm beside him, rubbing his back whilst he kneaded his own injured hands. 'Don't go heaping blame on her, she was worried enough about what you'd think.'

His head snapped round and his face flared red. 'She

was right to be! As if it wasn't bad enough her chucking away her education just to earn a swift quid – do they know about this at work?' he added quickly.

Nell shook her head. 'They can't do or they would have sent her home. No wonder the poor little devil's been wearing sloppy sweaters – to hide her bump.'

'How many months is she?' When told, Joe looked sick. 'It makes my flesh crawl to think of my little lass and that . . . pervert! How could she let him, Nell? We didn't bring her up to behave like a slut.'

'Don't you ever call her that!' Nell shot to her feet, tortured by the memory of having this insult hurled at her. 'It's not fair –'

'Fair? What's fair about her family being sniggered at because she couldn't keep her bloody knickers on? You're a nurse, for God's sake, you of all people should have been able to warn her about this happening!'

Nell blushed. Yes, she of all people should have ensured her child avoided pregnancy. But no, she had been too busy dictating rules of housekeeping: wash glass and cutlery first, iron collars and cuffs. It was ridiculous, considering the intimate tasks she performed for patients. But that was not half so embarrassing as discussing sex with one's child. The subject taboo in her own youth, she had not even been able to tell Nina about periods, but had fobbed her off with a pamphlet – more than her own mother had ever given her.

'You've always let her think she could behave as she liked, haven't you? That whatever she might do we'd forgive her –'

'Well *I* will!' vouched Nell, her anger growing.

'Oh yes, and don't we know it – you're worse than our Beat for letting her have her own way! At least she only ever spoiled her with toys and whatnot, she made sure the lass knew right from wrong!'

Nell showed offence that he scoffed at her morals. 'You're

one to talk! Has it never crossed your mind that you could be a little bit responsible here for making her feel she should've been born a boy?'

Joe was momentarily poleaxed, but soon recovered to counter angrily, 'What sort of logic is that? It's not boys who get pregnant – so even if I did do as you're suggesting, I didn't make a very good job of it, did I?'

Nell was in danger of losing her own temper. 'What I mean is, you might have created some kind of hang-up in making her think she wasn't good enough in some way, and – oh, I don't know! I'm not a psychiatrist. I just know that you've never been satisfied with anything she's achieved.'

'And what exactly has she achieved?' he threw at her. 'How to get up the spout – that's what you've taught her.'

He remained ignorant of William, but his attack could not have been more hurtful – and how much more hurtful he might be if she were to reveal the truth. Well, she was damned if she would tell him now. Nell bit her tongue and glared at him.

'Anyway, shut up and let me think!' Joe turned away dismissively. 'Maybe it's not too late: she doesn't show – I had no idea, so neither should anyone else – we can get her into one of them mother and baby homes before any of them notice. A private one, not one of them religious ones, I had enough of bloody nuns preaching at me when I was growing up . . .'

'Joe, she wants to keep the ba—'

'No bloody chance!' He cut her off with a bitter laugh. 'She might have twisted me round her finger before, but she's certainly put paid to that now. She can think herself bloody lucky I don't sling her out.'

'You wouldn't do that,' Nell said with certainty.

'Wouldn't I? I will if she continues to play silly buggers. The minute I find out where to send her, she'll be away, and she'll not come back until it's dealt with

– and you'll back me up on this! None of your ganging up on me . . .'

'Of course I'll back you,' said Nell, playing for time. 'But first things first, we'll have to get her to the doctor's and have it confirmed. But it's pretty certain. I think,' she added, dashing his look of hope. 'Do you promise not to go berserk if I fetch her in?'

With a snort of derision, Joe guaranteed not to resort to violence. 'But, like it or not, she'll hear what I have to say!'

Nina was compelled to hear her father's piece, and in no uncertain terms. Learning that he planned to send her off to a mother and baby home was hard enough to take, but when it became obvious he expected the child to be adopted, she immediately spun to Nell for assistance.

'Your mother isn't going to help sweet-talk me this time!' Joe told her. 'It's being adopted, and that's that!'

'I could go and stay with Aunty Bea—'

'And bring shame on her? You will not! You're not even going to tell her about this, neither of you!'

'But Dad –'

'Leave it, Neen!' Fearing the girl might inadvertently let out her own secret, Nell bundled her daughter from the room and towards the stairs, whispering into her ear as they went, 'Let me do it, love. Don't worry, I'll talk him round.'

But, turning to look at Joe's angry face, she was not at all sure that she could.

In the hours that followed, Nell was to relive her own nightmare, the scenes she had once been part of being replayed again, only with different players taking the roles. It was small mercy that Nina had been spared from having to carry her deception right to the point of labour, for otherwise their ordeals were the same. Joe was still as furious the next day – just as her own father had been – and, as Wilfred had laid down the law, so it was Joe who instructed them on what would be done.

First on his list was for Nina to go to the doctor, and for Nell to go with her. Secondly, Nina must give in her notice. 'And you can work it! I don't see why your employer should be let down as well as us. You've managed to hide it for this long, another week won't make much difference, and you'll need a reference to get you another job when you come back.'

There were no tears now, just a resigned nod, for Nina had invested her trust in Nell, and had agreed to leave any persuasion to her.

And, by the end of that week, when Joe had also organised a place for Nina at a home for unmarried mothers, where she would stay until after the baby was born, she was to depart without argument. It was Nell who was the one who shed tears, as she watched her daughter's forlorn journey to the car with her suitcase. The one she had sworn not to let down.

18

Once the problem had been shoved from sight, Nell began in earnest to try to talk Joe round, though to little avail. He remained adamant on the topic of adoption. Cleaved of her daughter, even if that loss was temporary and had only been for a week so far, Nell coped by throwing herself into nursing during the day. But, coming home to another evening of argument with Joe, she could barely sleep for worry, picturing that fifteen-year-old girl, no more than a child herself, crying over the fate of her baby. Don't go bothering our Beat with this, Joe had warned. But Nell had to confide in someone, even if her sister-in-law felt unable to help.

Though times had changed, attitudes had not, and it was still an awful confession to have to make. When she had at last unburdened her heart to Beata in a letter, she was still unsure of the response.

But how could she have doubted her friend? Within an hour of receiving the cry for help, there was the faithful Beata come to offer her shoulder.

Seated beside her in the latest two-tone green Wolsey, having been spirited twenty miles out of town, and now at the top of a hill that overlooked the most breathtaking scene, Nell's face remained woebegone. 'I don't know what to do, Killie.' Her fingers traced the grain of the walnut dashboard, her eyes gazing out over the Vale of York. Beyond the hawthorn hedgerows entwined with convolvulus, a thousand white trumpets to herald the fall, on this clear blue breezy day one could see fifty, sixty miles across the flat plain, to a purple ridge, and, in between, a checkerboard: a shorn barley field, a clutch of terracotta roofs, a coven of cooling towers that belched forth smoke into the blue yonder, a hamlet, a farm, a village spire, a glittering puddle, a dark splodge of woodland, an historic cathedral, from here a mere chess piece . . . 'I vowed not to let her down, but Joe's so rigid.'

'Well, you can stop blaming yourself for a start. She's the one who's let *you* down. Little bugger, after all you've done for her . . .'

'Oh no, don't say that,' groaned Nell. 'That's exactly what they said of me. I am disappointed, yes, but I'm sad for her, not me. I just want to do the best for her, and if that means helping her to keep her baby then so be it.'

'It'll be hard, you know,' warned Beata, reaching for a bag of boiled sweets, taking two out and offering one to Nell.

'I'm prepared for that. And believe me, it won't be as hard as having to give the baby up.' Nell did not unwrap the sweet, just fingered the twists of its cellophane wrapper and stared across the vista.

'You're sure you're doing this for her sake?'

Nell's chin tilted slightly, but her eyes remained on distant hills. 'You think I'm trying to make up for having my own baby taken away.' Her voice was dull, in the knowledge that this childless one could never appreciate how traumatic that had been. 'I'm not. If that's what Nina wanted then I'd support her – even though it would break my heart to see the baby go.' Her voice caught and her eyes filled with tears over the awful memory. 'But she's its mother, she should be the one to make the choice, not be bullied into it like I was.'

Beata nodded. 'Whatever I can do to help, I will. Did you want me to have a word with Potato Pete?'

Nell shook her head, still toying with the wrapped sweet. 'He's forbidden me to tell anyone, so he'll go mad if he finds out you know. Besides, you can't say anything to him that hasn't already been said. I just needed somebody to talk to – thanks for listening, Killie. And thanks for bringing me out here. What a marvellous view.'

Beata gave a nod, then asked for the address of the mother and baby home, and murmured, 'I'll drop the lass a line. She must be feeling terrible.'

More than terrible, Nell suspected, which was why, against Joe's wishes, she was to journey down south at her first opportunity. Whilst visitors were not discouraged in this private home, there were few apart from her. Her fears that Nina would be badly treated were unfounded, for her daughter said the people in charge were not at all preachy, though she and the other girls were made to do a lot more housework than at home, her chapped hands indication of this. By a stroke of luck, amongst the little treats Nell had brought was a tin of cream. If only there were good news to accompany her gifts.

But, 'Don't worry.' Nell forced her voice to be bright, as along with some books she handed over a bag of half-melted cream eggs. 'There's still plenty of time for us to work on him.'

'You keep telling me not to worry – I *am* bloody worried!' Paying the chocolate short shrift, Nina's hands moved to protect her abdomen, lately draped in a maternity smock.

'I know, I know!' Nell immediately reached out to her. 'But believe me, I'm wearing away at your father whenever I can. He'll come round in the end.'

Not yet, though. For whilst Nell continued to visit their daughter on a regular basis, and to worry over her emotional state, Joe remained cold, refusing even to listen to news of her.

Fortnight after fortnight, month after month, Nell travelled to see Nina, despite the inclement weather, the expense, the embarrassment, and the inconvenience of reaching this remote place. Even with late November fog swirling under her skirts to freeze the bare tops of her thighs, Nell rolled up to lend support. Despite the austerity of the communal sitting room, and the presence of others in the same unfortunate position as Nina, her face was pink and cheerful as she kissed her daughter, then sat down in the cottage armchair beside her, and straight away began to take gifts from her bag.

'You're looking well!' The poor little thing looked ready to burst, even the maternity smock unable to conceal her enormous bulge.

'I feel like a Bumblie,' lamented Nina.

It was so unbearably poignant that Nell could have wept, but instead offered a sympathetic laugh and a cigarette, lighting one herself, then continuing to bestow gifts. 'I've brought you some batteries for your transistor, forty cigs – they should keep you going – and here's a couple of Taylor Caldwells and a Leon Uris. And Shirley thought you might like this programme from the Beatles concert.' In fact, Nell had asked her to buy an extra one, guessing she would not want to part with hers, Beatlemania having gripped the entire nation. 'She said you could hardly hear for all the screaming – she nearly got mown down as well, when the Beatles car roared towards her down that lane at the side of the Rialto with all these hysterical girls in tow!'

Dragging on her cigarette, Nina inspected the programme briefly, along with the paperbacks. 'She wrote and told me about it.'

'Did she? Oh, that's nice of her.'

'Yes, I enjoyed reading about all the fun she's had whilst I'm stuck in here.'

Nell tutted. 'Don't take it out on your friend. It's not her fault . . .'

Rebuked, obviously feeling abandoned, her daughter looked away. Nell wished she could sweep her up and kiss all the troubles better, but Nina had barricaded herself in, and she feared she would never be able to reach her lovely child again.

Still, she tried. 'Hey, did you hear about President Kennedy being assassinated – wasn't it dreadful?' This was obviously not the ideal thing to remove the look of disdain, so she began to hand over a range of baby clothes, a blanket, and a shawl, one after another. 'Anyway, these might cheer you up a bit!'

And indeed, Nina did gain enjoyment from them, holding up each pretty dress in turn, and seeing them as representing her mother's belief that all would be well.

'You're getting close now, aren't you?' Nell struggled with her inhibitions, wanting Nina to be prepared for her ordeal. 'Has anyone explained what's going to happen?'

Her daughter gave a nod of trepidation. 'They've given us all a book – with pictures.' She formed a look of distaste.

'It'll be all right,' said her mother kindly, hoping not to infect the other with her own apprehension, and relieved that she had been tutored.

Then, 'Have you told him about your son yet?' Nina asked, as she played with the arms of a tiny cardigan, a haze of tobacco smoke curling around them.

Nell shook her head, already regretting disclosing this to her daughter. 'I'll only use that as a final remedy.'

'But what if you leave it to the last minute and it doesn't make any difference?' protested Nina. 'I need to know if he'll let us both live with you, because if he won't then I'll have to make other arrangements – and I will, Mam,' she added forcefully. 'He might think he's frightening me into giving it up, but –'

'He's not trying to frighten you! He's your father, he cares about what happens to you, that's the only reason he's being like this. He just doesn't want to think of you ruining your life – you and I both know that isn't the case, but it's all your dad can see!'

'But you keep saying you'll talk him round. I can't go on not knowing one way or the other. If you were to explain to him the way you felt about having to give your baby awa—'

'Neen, I hope you realise what you're asking me to do,' her mother butted in. 'I'll only keep that as a last resort, because it could ruin our marriage.'

The youngster had obviously not considered this. After a brief pause, she murmured on an exhalation of smoke, 'Well, I don't want to ruin your life . . . I'd rather live in some hostel.'

'It won't come to that,' promised Nell, with a look of purpose, grinding her stub of cigarette into an ashtray. 'I've got money, we could arrange somewhere better – but I don't want you to live somewhere else, I want you with us!' After a moment of anguish, she made a suggestion. 'There is a way he might consent. I haven't put it to him, so don't get your hopes up, but what if we were to pretend I'm its moth—?'

'No.' The firmness of that reply put an end to any speculation. 'I'm its mother.'

Nell lowered her eyes and gave a little nod of acceptance, knowing too well the ferocity of maternal possession. 'Then why don't you write your dad a letter?' she said, with nothing else to suggest. 'Pour out your heart to him. It might be easier on paper. Tell him absolutely everything, so's he'll understand.'

And, despite her lack of optimism, Nina was to agree as she lit up again. 'Can't make things any worse, I suppose . . .'

* * *

But instead of being touched by her three-page missive, after an angry perusal, Joe blamed his wife for conniving against him. 'I don't know what rubbish you've been putting into her head on these visits of yours! But she seems to think I'm going to change my mind, and I'm getting pretty fed up of being manipulated. Instead of spending your time giving her false hope, why don't you persuade her not to ruin her life?' And he folded the letter back into its envelope and shoved it behind the wooden mantel clock. 'Now, I'm telling you, I don't want to hear any more about it!'

For hours afterwards they were to pussyfoot around each other and tolerate the other's presence. But, determined that Nina would not suffer the same ordeal as herself, Nell was merely rehearsing what she was going to say, and what seemed like placid acceptance to her husband was to end in outburst.

'I don't think you understand what a terrible thing you're about to do, depriving a mother of her child!' she blurted, in the middle of a favourite television programme that would normally have held her. 'All right, I accept it's impossible for you to empathise, but I want you to think, really *think*, what it'll mean to hand your grandchild to strangers –'

'I have.' Joe never took his eyes off the screen.

'No, you haven't! Would you have given Nina away when she was little?'

'It's not the same thing and you know it.'

'Maybe not the same situation, but in essence it is – you're throwing away a member of your family, another human being, to God knows what end – you of all people, with the kind of childhood you had!'

Joe was incensed at being compared to his violent stepmother, of being made to face memories he would rather block out. 'She was just like that because she didn't want us, because she'd been lumbered! Somebody who goes to the bother of adoption isn't going to act like her.'

'How can you be sure? There are all sorts of evil people out there with motives of their own – and what happens if nobody wants it and it ends up in an orphanage?'

Joe's face told her she was being overdramatic. 'It'll be looked after.'

'If it's lucky! If it gets somebody like me or Beata to take care of it – but that's not always the case. I should know, I saw enough of the poor little devils pass through the Infirmary, and plenty of them neglected by their nurses too!' Having captured his imagination now, she implored him not to do anything reckless. 'I know, I *know* you're furious with her, Joe – you've a right to be – but don't let your anger make you do something downright cruel.'

'You can never bloody accuse me of that!' he retaliated.

'I'm not saying you *are* – but you will be if you carry this out! Believe me, I know, I've been on the receiving end of such treatment, people thinking they're being cruel to be kind – well, it's not kind, it's just bloody cruel!'

Joe looked at her strangely then. 'When you say you've been on the receiving end, do you mean to tell me that you've been in the same position as our lass?'

Hard as it was to face that narrowed gaze, Nell was to do so honestly. 'I had my baby taken away, yes.' Then she looked at the floor, and went on, 'I didn't see any need to tell you be—'

'Didn't see the *need*?' Joe sounded amazed and shot to his feet.

'It was a very long time before I met you!'

'You told me everything else about your family; didn't you think I might be just that little bit interested to hear that the woman I was marrying had a secret baby an' all?'

'It hurt too much to speak of him, Joe! And he's gone – to God knows where!' Her eyes filled with tears, and as she lowered them to the floor they spilled over. 'And I was afraid it might make you feel differently about me if you'd known.'

'Just a bit!' came his acid response.

'Well, there you are!' cried Nell. 'What was I meant to do, spend the rest of my life a spinster?'

'It might have been nice if you'd allowed me to make the decision for myself! All these years I've been thinking . . .' A nasty shrewdness came to his eye. 'Well, well, not such a hero, after all, our Billy – I'm presuming it was *his*?' Nell gave outraged affirmation, but it was to put no brake on her husband's sarcasm. 'Run off and leave you, did he?'

'No he did not! I spoke the truth! He was killed, before he could save me from others who professed to love me while they were tearing our precious son from my arms!' And she broke down sobbing in anguish.

But whilst Nell was facing her demons, Joe left the arena.

However, he had only gone upstairs to spend a while in the bathroom, obviously hoping to by the time he came down the whole episode would be over, for he sat down and began to watch the television as if nothing had occurred. Though the heavy smell of tobacco that clung to his clothes and the twitch in his jaw told otherwise.

It was excruciating for Nell, but she must force him to listen. 'We have to talk about this, Joe.' She sounded determined.

'I thought we just had,' he muttered.

'But it didn't solve anything!'

'By solving, you mean you didn't manage to get me to change my mind.' Still his eyes were fixed to the screen.

'Joe, I'll talk till I'm blue in the face if it stops you making a huge mistake with –'

'Have you any bloody idea what it's like to be second best?' he turned in his chair and demanded of her.

Nell became instantly contrite, and her voice was at once gentle again. 'Joe, if you're saying that I make you feel like that, then I never, ever intended to, and I'm deeply sorry if you felt you were being compared to Bill. You weren't. You're a good man, and no more second best than anyone else – we all feel second best at some point in our lives, whether it be in our career or –'

'I've always been second best at *everything*!' shot Joe, his attack catching Nell off guard, for he had always shied away from confronting anything of an emotional nature, but now the festering pustules burst. 'In Dad's eyes it was always our Clem who was golden boy! It was obvious to everybody – none of them ever said to me, "You'll be following in your father's footsteps," they just treated it like a joke when I mentioned wanting to be a soldier, as if I wasn't regarded as good enough to fill his boots – that's the only reason I joined the blasted army, so's to prove to everybody that I *was* good enough!'

'Of course you are!' Nell tried to staunch his wounds.

But the bad blood continued to flow. 'Stop being so bloody patronising! I wasn't even good enough to make sergeant! Fourteen years, and I still didn't make the grade!'

Nell was horrified. 'Honestly, I wasn't meaning to patronise! I was trying to say that I know what it's like, because I've never been regarded as a proper nurse. Just because I couldn't afford to take the exams or pay for the uniform. I know how it rankles, but –'

'I'm not just on about the army, nor your blessed career!' yelled Joe. 'Can't you see? Nobody, not one single person, has held me in their heart above all, prized me for what I am, told me, "You're the best"! Not even Grette – truth be known I think she only saw me as a way of getting out of Germany – do you know how much that hurts, even from people who don't really matter, but from the one you're married to? For God's sake, it's not too much for a man to expect of his wife, is it?'

Disconcerted by his angst, Nell pondered long and hard, her heart going out to him.

'Your silence speaks volumes!' spat Joe in disgust.

She shook herself from the momentary stupor to object, 'Of course you're the best!'

'Aye, the best *you* can hope for,' responded Joe with bitterness, and lit a cigarette.

'No!' Nell spread her hands, her face brimming with compassion. 'I'm just searching for the right words to let you know how I feel!' But she wasn't even sure herself.

'Well, don't bother to think too hard about it.' Joe's voice cut into her thoughts. 'I'll make the choice for you. I've had enough of playing second fiddle. I'm off to see about a divorce.'

Nell could not have been more shocked if he had hit her. When she found voice, all it could utter was, 'But what will Nina –'

'Nina, Nina, Nina!' He employed the name like a weapon. 'It was always bloody Nina, wasn't it?'

And now she was stunned to realise that he had not been referring to Bill when he declared himself second best – but must have always been aware that she had based her decision to marry not out of love for him, but for his child. Still, she managed an accusing stutter, 'But, Joe, she's your daughter!'

'You're damned right she is! I'm glad you've finally acknowledged that, in between making decisions about her future. She's *my* daughter, *I* say what happens to her, what's best for her – not based on anything that might have happened to you twenty-odd years ago, nor whether or not you're hankering after a grandchild, but on what's best for *her*.'

'But you *are* basing it on old grievances! Grievances of your own, that you've had since boyhood. Please don't take it out on her because of the way you feel about me or anyone else. I'm sorry I didn't tell you, but I just couldn't.'

'No, but I bet you told her, though, didn't you?' His narrowed eyes caught the wince of guilt. 'I bloody knew it – before your own bloody husband! Who else?'

'No one!' To protect Beata, Nell wove truth into the lie. 'Not one member of my family – please, you mustn't mention it to Aunty Phyl!'

'Too right I won't! I'm already hanging on to what's left of my reputation.'

'But things are different these days, more relaxed – it needn't be the same for Nina as it was for me – no woman should have to go through that!'

'Enough! I'm sorry for what you went through, Nell, and I'm sorry if what I've said about it has upset you, about Bill and everything, I didn't mean it and I'm sure he was a good bloke – but things haven't changed that much – and people haven't changed. So, she'll be having it adopted – and you were right about something: just because yours was an awful experience doesn't mean the same thing'll happen to Nina. I'll make sure she's well treated, and that the b— blasted thing goes to a good home!'

Nell moaned, on the point of collapse, for it was obvious nothing she could say or do would change his mind.

Faced with the threat of divorce, tears of defeat rolled down Nell's face when she was finally compelled to announce to Nina, ten days before Christmas: 'I'm sorry, love, I really tried . . .'

But, perversely, the tearful response she had expected was never to come, just a silent look of resolve.

Not until some weeks later was she to find out why.

Having continued to lend her support with an extra visit just before Christmas, however futile that might be, Nell was banking on the fact that a letter would surely arrive any day now to say that Nina had given birth. On the strength of this she had postponed her latest Saturday afternoon visit, in the high hopes of receiving the information that there would be two people to visit instead of one. Thoroughly disappointed that nothing had come in the post, she resigned herself to spending the afternoon with the man who was responsible for this state of affairs.

It was an odd time: lovely in one way, at the thought of having a grandchild, yet distressing too, in knowing that it might be taken from her before she ever saw it, if Joe did not have last-minute qualms. The relationship between herself and Nina's father had calmed down over the Christmas and New Year period, though only because she had stopped trying to whittle away at his resolve. Divorce might have been averted, but the joking and laughter that accompanied the festive get-togethers with relatives soon dispersed upon Nell and Joe coming home. It was not a happy state to bc in.

'I'm going to make a cup of tea, would you like one?' This was the only kind of exchange they seemed to have these days. Receiving her husband's nod, Nell rose, and before going to make the tea, bent to pick up one of the flimsy cards that had contorted from the heat of the coals and fallen into the hearth. 'Thank heavens it's Twelfth Night.'

'I don't know why you bothered leaving them up till now.' Joe's eyes remained on the television screen. 'It's not as if it'd bring us any more bad luck than we've already had.'

Ignoring this sarcasm, his wife began to collect the cards from the mantel, then an outside movement caught her eye. 'Oh, who's this coming down the pa—?' She broke off upon seeing the caller's identity.

Immediately suspicious, Joe tore himself away from the televised rugby match, and rose to see Nina, babe in arms. First, he spluttered, 'The litt— what does she think she's at, coming here carrying that, bold as brass?'

'I don't think bold's the word,' said Nell, for Nina had faltered the moment she saw him.

Joe's face turned red then, and he took out his ire on Nell. 'Oh, you're really scraping the bottom of the barrel now, aren't you? Cooking this up between you, thinking to play on my sympathy –'

'I had no idea she'd even had it!' cried Nell, still as astonished as he, before rushing off to the door.

'Don't open it!' ordered Joe.

'I'm not making them stand outside!' Disobeying him, she hurried to summon their daughter in, briefly smiling a welcome, but at the same time displaying worry. 'Love, I thought you were going to write? Come in, come in –' Fearing Nina would think she was more concerned about the neighbours, she added, 'You must be freezing in that mac – and you shouldn't be exerting yourself so soon, come and sit down!'

'I had her a fortnight ago, just after you left,' a shivering Nina informed her as she came over the threshold.

'A girl!' Besides her astonishment, Nell clasped her hands in pleasure, and peered amongst the thick folds of blanket, from the midst of which poked a tiny nose.

'Six pounds three ounces.'

'What a lovely birthday present – did you get the card and money by the way?' At the recipient's nod of thanks, Nell breathed a happy sigh that was mixed with anguish on recalling her own son's birth. 'But a fortnight ago, and you never said a word!'

'Sorry, I've been taken up with this one.' Arms laden, Nina smiled adoringly at the face within the swaddle of lambs' wool.

'I can see why!' Nell gazed delightedly for a moment. Then, remembering that Joe stood waiting, she became more serious and drew their visitor into the heat of the living room.

'She's had a little girl, Joe,' his wife informed him softly.

'I heard.' Even now, he remained unmoved. Though the television was off, his eyes remained on the blank screen as he smoked a cigarette. 'So how come they let you out then?'

'You're talking as if it were prison!' Nina glanced at Nell, who had touched her arm, a mixture of sympathy and warning. 'As it happens, I did have a job persuading them to let us leave. Lucky somebody there told me my rights.'

'Good for you – so why have you bothered coming here?'

Nina stepped forward, emotion glistening in the eyes that beseeched him. 'Just look at her, Dad. You can't want to abandon her, surely?'

'Save it! I've just been telling your mother, your tricks won't wash.'

'Mam had nowt to do with me coming here.' Eyes still fixed to his, Nina rocked her cumbersome bundle, within which the baby had begun to stir. 'I made the decision alone. Just as I've made the decision that I am going to keep her. If you won't let us live here, there's others who'll help us.'

'If you dare try and inflict yourself on our Beat—'

'She's been good enough to say she'd have us.'

Again, automatically, Joe vented his odium on Nell. 'I told you not to tell anybody!'

'I had to have someone to talk to, Joe!'

'I don't see you rushing to tell your Aunty bloody Phyllis – why show me up with my relatives?'

'Because there's nobody as good as Beata.' Nell splayed her hands, denying that there had been any collaboration. 'I knew she'd want to help . . .'

'See, some people believe in helping family, Dad.' Nina remained quietly defiant as she held his gaze. 'Anyway, don't get into a frenzy about it, I'm not going to embarrass her any further, nor you. I just came to let you see what you'd be missing.' Then, all at once, she could no longer withhold a sniff, and groped at her pocket for a handkerchief.

'Oh, love . . .' Nell reached out.

'I'm not crying! It's the bloody fire that's making me nose run.' This half true, Nina held the baby with one arm, dragged a hankie from her mac pocket and nipped her nose with it, blinking away moisture before glaring at her father, so that he could see he had failed to cow her. 'Go on, have a good look at her, Dad,' she said, as she put the hankie away and once more presented her daughter. 'If you won't let us live here, then we'll find somebody who will have us – but I won't be giving up anything, you will.'

Nell's breast throbbed with admiration for the way one so young was making a stance – envy too. If only she had possessed such courage to go against those in authority. She watched Joe's eyes flicker with indecision.

Yet still came blustery resistance. 'And if I were to let you back, how do you think you'd pay your way without a job? You'd expect me to cough up, as usual!' He spun on Nell. 'See, if you'd made her do her exams she would've got a good job and could have got a house of her own, and paid somebody to look after it – in fact, if you'd made her do her exams none of this would have happened, because she'd have been too bloody busy to mess with lads!'

Nell had hardly dared breathe for fear of ruining the progress her daughter had made – for Joe seemed to blame her for this much more than Nina – but, in as respectful a tone as possible, she proposed, 'I could look after her to allow Nina to work –'

'So you have to give up your nursing to look after her daughter!'

'Our granddaughter!' Nell tried to imbue with her eyes just how wonderful this would be if he'd let it. 'How could nursing compare to that? I've no real need to work, have I?' Even though she had grown used to having her own money, it would not mean financial hardship, for there was still her inheritance sitting in the bank. 'We managed all right when Nina was growing up –'

'She's *still* growing up – and she's got a great deal more growing up to do, if she expects other people to look after the child she created!'

'Joe, you can't have it all ways! You say you expect her to pay for her keep; how can she do that if she doesn't work? You wouldn't want her applying for benefits.'

'I would not!'

'Then let me look after her – it would be a joy.'

'Oh, I'll bet it would! I wouldn't be surprised if you hadn't engineered that as well during those visits you've been paying her! All this is really about you, isn't it? Because you can't wait to get your hands on a bairn to replace the one you had taken away.'

Nell stared at him for a second, then, with an expression of defeat, left the room.

'You cruel bugger,' came the muttered accusation from Nina.

'And you can sodding-well shut up!' Joe yelled at her, before barging out himself.

Having calmed the baby and rocked her off to sleep, Nina laid her on the sofa, then took off her mac and went to put the kettle on. She gave her mother fifteen minutes or so, then went to tap on the bedroom door. 'I've made a pot of tea, Mam. Do you want to come down or shall I fetch it up here?'

There came the sound of rustling, then the door slowly opened and Nell's tear-stained face appeared.

Nina's own expression collapsed upon seeing it. 'I'm really sorry for causing all this.'

But her mother simply shook her head. Then, after giving a final rattle into her handkerchief, she put it away, brushed her hair, then indicated for them both to go down. Preceding her, Nina went to pour out two cups of tea, handing one over.

'I should be the one looking after you,' sniffed Nell, reaching for her cigarettes and offering the packet.

Nina shook her head. 'Don't tempt me, I've given up, can't afford them now – doesn't mean you can't have one, though.' Her mother had put them aside.

'No, we must have solidarity,' murmured Nell. 'I'll give up too.' Then she asked, 'Where is he?'

'In his shed, I think,' replied her daughter, taking a sip of tea. 'Should I take one out to him?'

Nell moved her head in negation, then went to gaze at the babe on the sofa, whose eyes were closed, though her lips emitted little squeaks and grunts. 'May I hold her?'

'You don't have to ask, you're her granny.' Nina formed a smile as her baby was picked up and cradled in Nell's arms. Then she glanced at the clock. 'But she'll want feeding in a minute . . .'

Nell looked at the clothes Nina wore, the bulging belly in the too-tight skirt, and the blue crimplene cardigan that had never been so well-filled before. 'Are you feeding her yourself?' At the ensuing nod, she suggested, 'Well then, get your cup of tea in first. I'll try and keep her quiet for as long as I can.' And oh, how wonderful it felt to rock this tiny creature.

But the new mother had not taken three sips before her baby started to bawl.

'Me dad's going to love that.' Nina looked agitated.

'Better take her upstairs then.' Reluctant to part, Nell gave a last fond smile at the crumpled face, then transferred the bundle into her mother's arms.

'He's going to love that an' all,' murmured Nina. 'He'll think we're conspiring to let her stay here.'

'She will, if I have my way,' promised Nell, with a newfound mettle. Then, left secluded, she sat thoughtfully to drink her tea.

After only a while, Joe came in to lean on the jamb. 'Where is she then?'

'Upstairs – and before you ask, it's only so she can feed

the baby in private, seeing as the sight of her is so loathsome to you.'

Joe closed his eyes, mumbling weary apology. 'I'm sorry for saying them cruel things to you. I suppose some might say I'm jealous . . .'

'Because I have a son I'm never going to see?' Nell sounded bitter.

'Partly. But also because of the way you regard his father. Your first love, that never had time to go rotten, because you never had chance to discover his faults – who knows, he might have driven you mad with the way he filled the house with his farts, or kept leaving the seat up like you moan about me doing – but no, there our Billy'll stand for eternity on his pedestal, whilst you're left in the real world having to make do with this inferior model.'

'What are you talking about?' demanded Nell with a twisted face. 'You're the one who won a blinking medal!'

'Only by default! Because I couldn't stand the incessant bloody noise of the gunners and went to shut them up – and for that they gave me a bloody gong! What's a scrap of metal on a ribbon, compared with a golden youth who sacrificed his life to save another?' Joe shook his head in a gesture of utter helplessness. 'I've tried to get over it, but I can't see the point in us going on when you'll never let me forget that Bill gave his life for his country and I didn't!'

Nell was defiant. 'I have never *ever* thrown that at you!'

'You didn't have to.' Joe was quieter now, and sadder. 'I always knew what I was in for, from the way you told me you could never love anyone else like him.'

'But you felt the same way about Grette!' she reasoned, with slight exasperation.

He swiped his hand to dismiss this. 'I only said that so's you'd feel better, because that's what you expected me to say. I feel as much for you as I ever felt for her.'

Nell gaped at him in shock – she, who prided herself on her intuition, how could she have been so blind to his genuine love? 'Joe . . . I'd no idea, you should have said . . .'

'Well, I'm saying now. Anyway, it would have made no difference, and I'm not the sort to go spouting romantic tripe. But if you knew how you've hurt me . . .' He allowed her to witness those tears of suppressed fury before he turned away.

Nell sped to him then, and tried to convey with a grip of his arm, 'I'm sorry, I wouldn't hurt you for the world. You mean as much to me as Nina does, I *swear* it, Joe.' She tried to instil this by an even firmer grip and an earnest expression in her eyes – and suddenly she found that it was not just to make him feel better, but because she meant every word. Somewhere, over the years, she had come to love this man in his own right. There was deep emotion in her voice as she entreated her husband, 'I couldn't bear to lose you. Please don't leave me.'

Joe turned to look at her, to check that this was genuine, and probed deep into her eyes before making his gruff reply. 'You silly bugger, where would I go? It's all been a bit of a bluff, hasn't it?' Then he heaved a huge sigh, pushed back his hair, and made a gesture of surrender. 'All right, they can both stay – I don't like it, and I could still throttle the little sod for doing this to us, but she can keep the baby.'

The little breath she uttered could not suitably convey the overwhelming depth of Nell's relief. Tears shimmered, and her voice caught as she reached out to thank him.

Then, at the last moment, she faltered. 'But you'll do it with good heart, won't you? Not let her back in then cut her off emotionally, as my parents did to me, because that would almost be as bad as throwing her out. Believe me.'

'It won't be all nicey-nicey forgive and forget,' warned Joe. 'I'm still mad as hell with her –'

'But that baby girl's done nothing.'

'No, and that's why I'll do me best to reach some sort

of normality, because the insults that poor little devil's going to face, with her mother not being married, well, she'll need all the support she can get.' With a last sigh, he tilted his head at the stairs. 'Feeding time at the zoo must've finished by now, she must be frightened to come down and interrupt us. You'd better go fetch her – that's if everything's been said between us?'

Nell wanted to add all manner of things, but they sounded too trite, and they had both been sufficiently candid to achieve a new understanding of each other. Immensely grateful, and fluttering with excitement, she gave Joe her best smile and moved to obey.

Shortly, she reappeared carrying their granddaughter, and accompanied by Nina. The latter opened her mouth to thank her father, but Joe held up his palm and gave her a look that conveyed she was still on probation.

Considering herself lucky, Nina sat down and remained silent, until her mother asked: 'So what've you decided to call her then?'

'Romy.'

Joe puffed out his cheeks and shook his head in despair.

But Nell retained her smile as she cradled the sleeping baby. 'That's nice – unusual. Any particular reason?'

Nina reached out a finger to smooth the golden fluff on her daughter's head. 'No, it was just a film I saw with this actress called Romy Schneider – I liked it.'

The smile frozen on her lips, Nell dared not look at her husband for fear of seeing a glint of comeuppance. She had no right to feel jealous, for was it not natural that Nina would recall her German mother; her *real* mother. But oh, how painful was the sting, after she had wrung herself inside out these past months for the one she called daughter.

19

It was as difficult as they had expected, and more besides, to venture out that first time and present this illegitimate offspring to the world.

Joe displayed bravado, and said, 'Well, if we're going to do this, we'll do it in style!' and he had forked out for a Silver Cross pram.

Nell spent a great deal too, on pretty clothes for the baby, its mother, and herself. But all this did was attract criticism from people who might otherwise have sympathised, and there were audible whispers at the brazen nature of that first parade.

'I'd want to keep her well out of sight if it were my daughter, wouldn't you?' sniped one woman to another as the entourage passed them by in the street, both of whom Nell had formerly liked and had chatted with before.

'Take no notice,' warned a stiff-necked Joe. 'Just let them dare say it to my face . . .'

None of them did, of course, and some of the neighbours were in fact very sweet about it, Shirley's parents amongst them, coming forth with knitted gifts – though this in itself did not please Joe, for to him it smacked of condescension. And, perhaps for this reason, having made his point, he was not to accompany his women after that.

Nell continued to run the gauntlet, though, for it must be hard for one so young as Nina to bear such denunciation.

Concerned not to serve any of the latter at home, guessing how strange she must feel in her new role, for those first few weeks Nell devoted herself to the care of mother and baby, making sure the former was well-nourished, taking charge of the little one – when Nina would let her – to ensure her mother caught up on lost sleep. Anxious, too, not to be accused of taking over, Nell had managed to withhold any criticism over the way the teenager handled routine tasks, such as nappy-changing and bathing – in fact, Nina had given her little cause, for she had adapted to motherhood remarkably well. Even so, in the hostile world outside, when the grandmother asked, 'May I push the pram for a bit?' Nina seemed relieved to let her. At least until they were away from dagger looks.

As weeks went by, though, and the insulting behaviour continued, Nina appeared to harden against her detractors, and began to stride out with her nose in the air as she wheeled her glossy, deep-bellied vehicle, even seemed to take delight when some old lady paused to admire the baby and ask in all innocence, was this her little sister? At which she would retort with a slightly hostile smile, 'No, she's mine!' – and seem to enjoy their embarrassment as they backed away.

Nell shared that embarrassment, made painfully aware now why her own mother had not wanted to go through such humiliation. With maturity too, she had come to understand why her adoptive father had been so cruel: he had been punishing her for his wife's infidelity, had been unable to throw words like slut at the woman he adored, so, with no other outlet for his sense of betrayal, he had vented it on Nell. She understood both their vulnerabilities much better now, and could forgive them. For she was in no rush to broadcast Romy's birth to her own relatives, even by letter, only her closest confidants attending the christening.

But really, were all these misgivings so bad when

compared to the joy of having a grandchild? And when all was said and done, she could tell Nina was putting on an act, pretending she didn't care when in fact it hurt like mad that she was so looked down upon. Nell, too, felt hurt for all her loved ones: Nina, Joe, and that dear little baby. What worried her most of all, though, was that Nina had forfeited the opportunity to go out and be a normal teenager.

'She's not a teenager now.' Joe was blunt. 'She's a mother, she's got responsibilities.'

'And she knows that! She's a smashing little mother, so calm and patient – there aren't many ten-week old babies who sleep through the night, and that's all down to the way Nina handles her.'

Joe grudgingly agreed. 'Aye, well, I did expect to have a lot more broken nights than we've had.' Whilst still tiny enough, the baby slept in her pram downstairs. 'I just wish she wasn't up and about when I have to do early shift – speaking of which, isn't it about time me lass was looking for a job? That was the deal. I agreed to her keeping Romy, but she has to support her.'

'And she will!' objected Nell. 'But even those with legitimate children are allowed to have a bit of enjoyment from time to time. I'm only suggesting one night out a week. Once she starts back at work she'll probably be too tired to go anywhere.'

Joe shook his head, looking beaten as usual. 'What if she gets into trouble again?'

'Are you really so bloody insensitive?' Nell held his eye.

Joe's expression admitted this was unlikely. 'I just worry about her.'

'And I don't?'

'Not in the way I do. You don't know blokes. Once they think she's loose –'

'I know well enough! But she has to learn to look after herself, and she deserves a bit of light-heartedness after all she's been through.' Conversant with the way their daughter must be feeling, Nell urged him to allow her some leeway. 'She accepts she's made a mistake. She won't make the same one twice.'

'Well, I suppose you'd know . . .' He saw Nell's eyes sharpen. 'I didn't mean *that*, you dateless bugger. I were just meaning you seem to understand what lasses want.'

'And what would that be?' Silently, Nina had reappeared from feeding Romy, carrying the baby with her, and laying her in the pram that took up most of the dining area.

'Bloody hell, I'm going to buy you some hobnailed boots so I can enjoy a private conversation. Your mother was just saying you could do with a night out – before you get a job, like.'

Nina's hackles rose. 'I have been looking.'

'It wasn't a jibe, keep your wig on!'

Nell jumped in, assuring Nina that the offer was genuine, making sure she knew how much they trusted her not to do anything stupid again. 'You haven't seen Shirley for ages . . .'

'No, well, she's not interested in babies.' Although the first to come and inspect the child, her friend's visits had tailed off.

'Well, why don't you see if she's going to a dance or something,' urged Nell. 'Now Romy's on a bottle and sleeping through, she won't get us up even if you're late in.'

'Hang on,' Joe frowned. 'I didn't agree to her stopping out all night.'

'She won't be, will you?'

More cheerful now, Nina gave a firm shake of her head. 'Can I just nip and see if Shirley's off to t'Boulevard on Saturday?'

'If you can be home by eleven,' said her father. And, when she looked thwarted. 'It's that or nowt.'

* * *

Eager to help Nina recapture some of her youth, on Saturday morning whilst Joe was in his shed, Nell slipped three pound notes into her daughter's hand and whispered for her to nip into town. 'I'll look after Romy, go and buy that dress with the chiffon sleeves you saw in Bradmore's! The blue one not the black one, we don't want you looking as if you're going to a funeral.'

Nevertheless, there was to be a slightly funereal air about Nina when she arrived home almost an hour earlier than the eleven o'clock deadline, upon entrance going straight to the pram to inspect Romy. Looking generally fed up, she told her parents, 'Shirley met up with her boyfriend, so I left them to it.'

Nell sympathised. 'Did you have a good time until then?'

'So-so. Has she been good?' Her glum expression slowly taken over by adoration, she dipped her hands into the pram.

'Oh, don't, love! I've just got her off after her ten o'clock bottle.'

Slightly peeved, Nina glanced at the clock. 'I rushed home to give her it.'

'We said not to!' Nell was bright as she rose to her feet. 'You should have made the most of it. Come on, I'll make you a cup of something – ooh, you do look nice in that dress!'

Nina allowed herself to be torn away from the pram. Leaving Joe watching the TV, she and her mother went into the kitchen, where, masked by the sound of the boiling kettle, Nina confided, 'That was only half the tale. I got stuck with Shirley's boyfriend's mate – a right drip he was. I left him to it.'

Nell bit her lip as she spooned Horlicks into mugs. 'What did Shirley have to say?'

'Nowt, she was too busy with Mr Wonderful,' came the sullen reply.

'I think I've seen her with him,' said her mother. 'Is he the one with Clark Gable looks?'

'If you mean big lugs and a rubbery face, then yes. I can't think what she sees in him – and his friend was even more gruesome.'

'Oh, don't say that, the poor lad . . .' Sounding reproachful, Nell thought of her own son, adding, 'Beauty is in the eye of the beholder.'

'Well, put it this way, there's ugly attractive and there's just plain bloody ugly. I'll let you guess which one he was. Anyway, that looks like the end of my nights out,' her statement concluded in a heavy sigh.

'Not necessarily!' Nell tried to inject encouragement. 'There'll be somebody else you can go with – what about Bridget?'

'Mm, I could see if she's going to New Earswick Bop on Tuesday, I suppose.' Nina sounded bored, the fingers of her right hand absently stroking her left arm in its blue chiffon sleeve.

Nell risked a question. 'Do you ever see Romy's father on your travels?'

Immediately her daughter's hackles rose. 'No, and I don't want to.'

'He might like to know about her. I wish I'd told Bill . . .' By now, having shared so much, Nell had divulged the rest of her own story to Nina.

'He does know! Mam, stop being so innocent. Your baby's father might have really loved you, but that bugger isn't bothered!' The tears of rejection were not for herself but for her daughter. 'Anyway, I'm fagged. I'll take that up to bed with me.' Hooking her fingers through the mug, she made for the stairs. ''Night.'

''Night, love,' murmured Nell, watching her go.

With Shirley totally occupied with her boyfriend, Nina was to have little luck with her second-best friend either. In fact, Bridget turned out to be not much of a friend at all.

'She's so childish,' complained Nina, arriving home

prematurely again, in the dress that seemed to bring bad luck. 'I don't know what I ever saw in her. Giggling and carrying on . . .' But she did not immediately elaborate, for the giggles had been at her expense, and had accompanied some unpalatable truths about the way others regarded her. 'I don't think I'll bother going out again – least, not with any of them. There's no point spending good money to be in the company of prats.'

'I'll agree with you there,' said her father. 'What about this job then, have you made a start on looking?'

'Yep.' As ever, Nina's first instinct had been to go to the pram. Finding Romy awake, she beamed and picked her up to cuddle and coo to her. Watching such devotion, Nell felt a wave of envy, but fought it. She would soon have Romy to herself all day long.

'Well, just let me know when to hand in my notice.' Nell sounded bright at the prospect, and asked, 'Have you applied for anything interesting?'

'Only ones that pay good money.'

Joe sought to warn his daughter. 'Beggars can't be choosers, you know. Expect a few rejections once a prospective employer knows you've got a bairn.'

'What business is it of theirs?' Nina shot back at him immediately, her eyes resentful as she pressed a kiss to the baby's head, and her arms protective.

'See!' said her father. 'You're jumping to conclusions already, assuming I meant about you being unwed! What I meant was, as soon as they know you've got a bairn to look after, who might fall ill, or take you away from your job, they won't want to hire you. All I'm saying is be prepared for that.'

Nell suffered a flashback to her mother, who had always been prepared for any emergency, apart from an illegitimate grandson. What was William doing with his life now? At twenty-three, he would surely have a girlfriend, or a wife. Maybe even a child.

Nina was still arguing with her father. 'I am prepared! I've got ten lined up, or at least I've got the letters ready to post. If I don't get the one I'm really after at Rowntrees offices –'

'Ah, you might be in with a chance there!' Joe's outlook changed. 'They're very good to their employees – as long as you don't go in with that bolshy attitude of yours.'

'They can take me or leave me,' retorted Nina, to his groan of dismay.

Nell cut in again. 'Well, as I said, let me know in good time when to hand in my notice. In fact I think I might do it tomorrow, I can't wait to get my hands on that little choochy face!' She reached out to tickle Romy. 'We'll have to get you some new clothes for work, Neen – come to town on Saturday and I'll treat you!'

It was good to see her daughter enjoying herself after so much trial. The pram laden up with carrier-bags of clothes, Nell was happy as they made their way home from town, especially as Nina's prime application had resulted in interview. On the way, they popped into a newsagent's to buy sweets and magazines. Whilst selecting the latter, Nell noticed a youth wander up to Nina and start chatting. He was a good-looking boy with a warm smile. Lingering over the row of magazines, Nell smiled, feeling pleased that a young man was taking interest, and admiring the way he leaned against the window and flirted with Nina. Was William able to converse so easily with girls?

She watched for a while longer, fearing the youth might be unaware that he was chatting up a young mother – for Romy's pram was several feet away – and hoping he would not run off when he learned the truth. There came a time, though, when it would look suspicious if she continued to linger, and she was forced to make her purchases and exit. Nina was facing away from her, though she appeared to be chatting quite amicably. Regretting that she was about to spoil this happy interlude for her, Nell made hesitant approach, then heard her say:

'You really fancy yourself, don't you?'

'Not as much as I fancy you,' flirted the boy.

'Has anyone ever told you, you've got a face like Paul McCartney's?'

'Do you reckon?' He sounded pleased.

'Yeah – Paul McCartney's arse.'

Nell heard the youth mutter something derogatory as he launched himself away, and she herself came forth. 'That was a bit cruel, Neen.'

Her mother's soft reproof took Nina by surprise. She turned and reddened. 'He was asking for it,' she muttered, and went to snap the brake off the pram, Nell catching up to walk alongside her.

'You won't get many boyfriends if you speak to them like that.' She wondered bleakly whether a female had broken William's heart in such cavalier manner, and was still cogitating when Nina turned on her:

'You didn't hear what he was saying to me!'

Nell's lips parted in surprise. 'Why, what –'

'Too crude for your ears!'

'But he looked so nice . . .' Nell appeared confused, then remembering how Nina could overreact to her father, said, 'Are you sure you didn't misinterpret –?'

'All right! I wasn't going to tell you, but if you really want to know – they all think I'm a scrubber! Every lad on earth seems to think I'm free game, that they've got a right to grope me, or to say what they like – satisfied?' Nina's pace alternated, one minute practically come to a halt, the next her high heels performing a tattoo along the pavement.

'No!' Nell was disbelieving, also aghast.

'They do! Shirley's boyfriend's mate, the lads Bridget knocks around with, all of 'em.'

Totally shocked, Nell's heart bled for her. 'Is that why you came home early those times?'

'Yes! I'm sick of being treated like dirt, Mam. I only did it the once – once in my entire life – and now I'm apparently Christine Keeler!'

'Oh, Neen, I'm so sorry . . .' breathed Nell, prior to displaying anger. 'If I'd known I would have come out and knocked the little swine's block off – and the others as well!'

Nina was cooling down now. 'I can handle them.'

'You shouldn't have to!' objected Nell. 'Disgusting creatures.'

'Don't worry about it. That's me finished with blokes.'

'Give it a few years,' tendered her mother. 'There might be a nice man who wants to marry you.'

'I'm not getting married. Lads, men, they only want you for one thing.'

Her words made Nell reflect on her own past; and the memory of what Joe had said about putting her dead lover on a pedestal. Had Bill only wanted one thing? Would he really have married her had he not been killed? Yes, of course he would . . .

'There's Romy to consider,' she hypothesised now. 'She might like a father.'

The snort that emerged was like that of a rebellious horse, and that angry glint warned Nell to say no more.

Then Nina thought to add, in a little voice, 'You won't tell me dad, will you – about the morons, I mean. I don't want him thinking I'm a slag as well.'

'He'd never think that!' How much more heartbreak could there be, thought Nell. 'I'm sorry you've had your afternoon spoiled. It was intended to cheer you up . . .'

'It has.' Nina donned a smile, and indicated the carrier-bags. 'Away, I can't wait to go and try them clothes on again.'

But, pleasing as the new outfits might be, there was nowhere for the owner to parade them, Saturday night being spent watching the wrestling on TV with her parents and visiting aunt. After the sordid afternoon, Nell was quite relieved that the poor girl was amused by the boos, cheers and loud objections that emerged from those glued to the screen – though she was unaware that Nina gleaned as much entertainment from listening to the comments from the viewers.

'What do you think that is down his trunks?' pondered Nell.

Joe looked at her and raised an eyebrow.

'Down the back, I mean!' sighed his wife, and shared nursely interest with Beata. 'It looks like some kind of support, Killie, doesn't it? He must have spinal trouble.'

'I'm not surprised,' said Joe, wincing out loud as the competitor in question was thrown onto the floor of the ring and stamped on with gusto. 'By, he's a mucky bugger that Jackie Pallo, you know, he really is. Never fights fair . . .'

The women agreed. 'And he thinks he's it,' said Nell.

'Don't they all,' muttered her daughter, and went to tend her baby who had been woken by the howls.

If life on the social front was to remain non-existent, then Nina could at least take pride in acquiring the job at the top of her list. Even so, Nell could see what a wrench it was for the young mother on that first day away from her child.

'Don't leave her outside any shops!' warned Nina, tearing herself reluctantly from the cherub in the pram.

And that heartfelt plea served to illuminate the differences between them. Nell might have been robbed of her newborn, but, in a strange kind of irony, had been spared that visceral, ever-present dread she saw in Nina's eyes, the trepidation of parting with her baby in case she might never see her again. Nell would never share that particular fear, for the worst had already happened.

Yet there could be recompense now for William's lost babyhood, and, once permitted, she wasted no time before indulging herself in a blissful session of bathing and cuddling and murmuring sweet nothings into Romy's fragrant shell of an ear – all the things she had so longed to do with her son – playing with tiny fingers and toes, brushing and coaxing the fine blonde wisps into little curls. 'To make you nice for when Mummy comes home . . .'

And how soon that time came round. But whilst the day was to flash by for Nell, she suspected it had been much too long for Nina, who, the instant she returned, went directly to her child and fiercely reclaimed her. Whereupon Nell had to suffice in the knowledge that this had been only the first of many wonderful days, and not feel resentful at coming second in line for attention.

Anxious for her to do well, both mother and father were pleased when Nina displayed a willingness to retire early, in order, she said, to be up the next day and do it all over again – though Nell guessed it was more that she wanted to spend time alone with Romy, who now had a cot in her mother's room. For, when asked if she enjoyed being a messenger, Nina confided in rueful manner to Nell:

'I'd never have gone to work there if I'd known Rowntrees make you go to their school if you're under eighteen! Don't tell me dad, he'll laugh his socks off.'

Hence, to Joe's surprise, in contrast to Nina's former way of thinking, she was to turn up to work every day, no matter the weather or the way she might be feeling. On top of which, once she had gained experience and fulfilled the required hours in the firm's school room, she was to grab every scrap of overtime that was on offer. Nobody, least of all her father, was going to accuse her of being a sponger.

Nevertheless, there was little she could do to counter the guilt and deprivation she felt, being at work instead of with her baby – another aspect Nell would never know first hand – and, whilst the grandmother was in seventh heaven in at last being able to shower all her attention on a tiny individual, now it was Nina's turn to feel resentful at the loss. She hated being away from Romy, and was jealous of her mother at having the luxury of being with her all day. Divining this, Nell tried not to make too much of it, when, against her wishes, Nina came in from work and picked her baby up straight away, whether asleep or awake. But there were times when each had to bite their tongue, and Nina would spirit her daughter up to her room, so as to have her all to herself. Never could Nell have guessed such jealousy would exist between them.

Eight months into Romy's first year, and Nell still wasn't really sure how Joe felt about the situation. He smiled at the baby as any grandfather might – if he happened to look in her direction, that was – but Nell had an inkling that if someone could wave a magic wand and make that child disappear, he would not be so heartbroken.

At that moment, Joe was enjoying a week's holiday – at least a week away from the factory. With the weather being too miserable for an excursion, he had decided to wallpaper the living room instead. He had moved the furniture to one end, had set up his trestle in the other half, and cleared a space all round the walls, when Nell wheeled in the pram.

'There, you can sit and watch Grandad whilst Nana bakes her buns!'

Paste brush in hand, Joe beheld her with amazement. 'You can't leave her sitting there!'

'She's strapped in,' Nell said of the baby, who was now able to sit unaided, and had been made comfortable with lacy pillows. 'And she's got her rattles to play with. Look at her little face!' Her hands reached out to fondle the blonde cherub. 'She looks just like Charlie Drake.'

'I'm wallpapering, woman!'

'Well, she can sit and watch you!' chided Nell. 'I can't put her out in the porch, it's too cold, and you always complain if the pram blocks the hallway, so there's nowhere else. She won't bother you, she's a good baby, aren't you, chicken?' she patted Romy's bright red cheeks and received a happy smile, and a flourish of the baby's rattle.

Joe continued to object, but his wife told him not to make such a song and dance, and went to do her baking. For a time there was only the sound of a paste brush, slopping from one end of the table to the other, the crisp clip of scissors through paper, and a lot of grunting and muttering as Nell mixed her cakes and buns.

'Thank you, Edmundo Ros, that's enough!' she heard Joe exclaim at the baby's persistence in bashing her rattle about, but it did not the slightest good. Then, 'Oh, she's only gone and thrown her rattle in me paste bucket!'

'Don't make such a fuss! She's still got the one fixed to her pram.' Nell shook her head for his impatience. Then, after dividing the mixture into tins, and putting these in the oven, she washed up all the mixing implements, and went to perform several more tasks, by which time the oven was emitting a mouth-watering smell. Setting some of the buns to cool, she made a pot of tea.

When she went in, to tell Joe it was time for a break, she could hear him still chuntering to himself – but no, not to himself, she realised, he was talking quite amicably to the baby. Creeping nearer to peep around the jamb, Nell held her breath, not wanting to disturb the exchange.

'What do you think to that then?' Joe was asking of Romy, and displaying his handiwork on the wall. 'Can't spot the joins, can you?'

Happy to be addressed, the baby gave her toothy, slavering smile, and twanged the row of rattles that were strung on elastic across her pram.

'See, you've got to butt the edges up to each other without overlapping.' Joe wiped a blob of paste from the finished section. 'You have to dangle your plumb like this,' he demonstrated for the baby's benefit, 'and mark a dead straight line, so's once your first bit is on straight, the rest'll follow. Easy, in't it?' He turned again to see that Romy was rubbing her eyes. 'That fascinating, eh? Right then, off you go to bobies and let Grandad get on with his craftsmanship.' And he hummed a happy little tune under his breath.

Smiling to herself, Nell left a suitable gap before going in to lie the drowsy infant down, telling her husband, 'I'll just settle her, then I'll bring you a cup of tea.'

'Aye, it's busy work papering, just ask my apprentice, Montmorency.'

Nell chuckled and, with loving eyes, she stood and watched as the baby's eyelids closed and her face grew pale in sleep. 'I'll bet you'd miss her if she wasn't here, wouldn't you?' Raising a cynical eyebrow, Joe continued to paper the wall. Nevertheless, his wife saw that little smile of concession, and considered how lucky she was that everything had turned out so well.

That Christmas was the best ever, everyone agreed, with this dear little one-year-old to buy toys for. It was even more fun in that Romy had developed an infectious belly laugh, and needed no excuse to use it, sending everyone else into hysterics. Perhaps it would work on those outside the family too. So inured had Nell become to Romy's illegitimacy, and Joe's side of the family being so well-disposed too, that she had finally gathered the courage to write and inform her aunty and uncle of her granddaughter's existence, mentioning it quite casually in a note enclosed with the festive card. Fully expecting not to hear again from the elderly pair, she was touched to receive a quite understanding reply, and a pound note enclosed to buy something for the little girl. Added to which was the invitation to bring her granddaughter to visit whenever she liked. Thus was her aunty and uncle's residence to be included in the festive itinerary, and though there was a little awkwardness at first, Aunty Phyl was soon as taken with Romy as was her grandmother, she and Uncle Cliff almost wetting themselves over that infectious laugh.

Nell was beginning to feel she had never been happier, which made the blow all the more felt when Nina announced one night, as she cuddled Romy on her lap before bed, 'I've decided to put me name down for a council flat. So she can have her own room.'

Her parents had been watching a rerun of Sir Winston's state funeral on the evening news, but now any sign of reverence vanished. Nell was first to sound the alarm at being robbed. 'But she won't need one for years!'

Joe, meanwhile, masked his own apprehension with a joke. 'I was still kipping with me three brothers till I was twenty-one!'

'And could you afford it, love?' asked her concerned mother.

'I'd be eligible to get it rent-free – don't fuss, I won't need to. So I'll be a lot better off when I start working in the punch room.'

'Is that where they give you a smack in the gob?' tendered Joe. 'Tell them I'll volunteer.'

'Yeah, hilarious. It's attached to the computer department.'

Nell said, 'That sounds complicated.'

'No, you just tap the keys and the machine cuts little holes in these cards.'

'And what's that in aid of?' asked Joe, who was well-informed and just testing.

This his daughter guessed, and her reply was befitting. 'To make oblong confetti – well, ask a silly question,' she riposted. 'Anyway, all I care about is it's piecework. Once you get your speed up you can earn maybe eight or nine quid.'

Nell expressed amazement. 'Still, it would all go on bills. We don't mind having you here . . .'

But Nina remained unwavering. 'No, I need a room to meself. She burbles to herself in the middle of the night and wakes me up.'

'That's what babies do,' Joe pointed out, adding with sarcasm, 'Why not shove the poor little bugger out in the garden and have done with it?'

Even after all these months there was rawness. Nell watched their daughter's nostrils flare as she took Joe's comment as reproof for her unplanned pregnancy. But all she said was, '*Anyway*, it probably won't be for a while yet. I just wanted to ask, Mam, if you'd be able to continue looking after her through the day while I'm at work?'

Flooded with relief, Nell exclaimed, 'Of course I will!'

But she hoped it would be a good while yet before their daughter's name reached the top of the housing list.

20

What a painful extraction when the time finally came. Watching the car being loaded with boxes of Nina's belongings, Nell could not prevent a whimper.

'You daft twillock, you'll be seeing them in a few hours when she brings the bairn round!' Joe had scoffed. Which was perfectly true, and it was only five minutes away to the block of council flats on the far side of the estate, but still the grandmother felt her heart enclosed in blackout.

Once she became used to them not being around on a night, though, and adjusted to the new routine of Romy being dropped off after breakfast, and picked up again after tea, Nell came to rather enjoy the status quo – even if Joe did still voice his resentment as though their daughter were still in residence.

'No wonder milady can afford to run her own place!' he would jeer, whenever his wife came home from town with another dress or pair of shoes for Romy. 'We're still bloody feeding and clothing her bairn!' Not to mention that after letting Nina take her bed, his wife had promptly gone out and bought another so that Romy could stay overnight if need be.

Contrary to his habitual grumbling, though, Nell knew he secretly loved having the little girl there. But, 'You'll have to curb your swearing,' she warned him, the child being nearly three now, and an excellent talker. 'We don't want her picking up your bad language to take to Aunty Phyllis's.' Apparently, though, her warning had come too late, for when Nina had just arrived from working overtime to pick Romy up, they heard a small voice say, 'I can't get this bloody paper off, Nana.'

'Eh! You shouldn't say words like that!' Nell chuckled at an equally amused Joe, as she went to help their granddaughter remove the chocolate wafer from its wrapping.

'Mammy says it,' replied the child with the curly blonde hair, quite logically.

'Well, she's a naughty girl!' Nell turned on Nina and pretended to administer a whack.

At the sight of her mother under threat, Romy burst into tears, which mortified the perpetrator, who tried to take her onto her knee, but Nina was to grab possession, giving her daughter a fiercely maternal hug, and drawing forth that rattling belly laugh by tickling her ribs.

'What a soft-hearted soul your daughter is,' smiled Nell. 'I can't think who she gets it from.'

'It's me,' came Joe's dry utterance. 'I'm a very emotional type.'

'Oh, yes,' Nell showed cynicism, 'well both of you make sure you're not teaching her anything else for when she starts school.'

Luckily, by the time Nina and her daughter left on this occasion, she had managed to coax Romy back to her arms, and extended this togetherness by accompanying them to the gate. As ever, she was loath to part with this dear little thing, who was quick to cry but equally quick to laugh, open in her feelings and quite different from her mother. Comparing them now, hand in hand, Nell felt sad over how much more different Nina had become since her child had been born. Yes, she laughed at the same things that had always sparked merriment, and in the same abandoned way when solely in Nell's company. But amongst strangers, especially men, there was a guardedness about her, a hard, sometimes brutal, edge for those who had done nothing to deserve it, apart from being young and male. There was evidence of that now, for just as Nina prepared to take leave, two of their neighbours, Mrs Garbutt and her thirty-year-old son Brian, swooped on them.

Appearing not to notice the mask that had come down, the woman paid polite fuss over Romy, before mentioning that she had heard Nina had a flat of her own these days. 'Well, people talk, don't they? We were just saying, you won't be able to get out so much . . .'

Nell was quick to dispel this. 'We'd still have her if Nina gets an invita—!'

'My Brian's free tonight!' jumped in an excited Mrs Garbutt, almost stealing Nell's breath.

But Nina curled her lip at the one who would court her, sending a disappointed mother and son on their way. 'He's free every night, and no bloody wonder, a face like a doily.'

'Neen, shush, they might hear you! All right, he's not the best looking, and he's older than you, but you're not doing yourself any favours by being rude to all these young men who ask you out.' Nell felt compelled to speak out, envisioning the queue of suitors dwindling to nil. 'There might just be one amongst them who really likes you, who isn't just interested in one thing.'

'Hang on!' Nina raised her free hand, the other holding her daughter's. 'Is this the same woman who did all she could to talk me out of playing with lads, and now she's trying to talk me back into it?'

'I can understand why you're cautious,' conceded Nell. 'But if you keep being nasty –'

'I don't want to get married, Mam – ever. So I don't need to impress, do I? Say ta-ta, Romy!'

And with a last kiss, Nell was forced to wave goodbye to her little granddaughter.

* * *

Two more glorious years Nell was to spend with Romy, feeling even closer than she had to Nina, if that were at all possible, during their trips to the park, or a coffee bar, or the seaside. But all that had to end when the time came to start school. Romy objected, upon the news being broken, saying that she would rather stay with Nana and eat grapes and cakes and read comics. But, against her own feelings, Nell was to give an encouraging pat of a small knee, saying they would still see each other every day, and at school there would be all sorts of lovely things, like drawing and reading, and playing with other little boys and girls. And, so ably did she lyricise, that by the time the dreaded day arrived, the child was raring to begin her education, and it was she herself who shed the tears.

Actually, she was not alone in this, for Nina admitted to shedding them too, when she and her mother shared a private moment after tea in the kitchen. 'Yes, I realised why you rushed away so quickly.' Nell conveyed a smile of understanding as she herself snipped a dividend stamp from a packet of tea and stuck it on a card. 'I'll bet you cried buckets, didn't you?'

Nina laughed at herself. 'I know I leave her every day, but that's with you. You just think of them in the big wide world, don't you?'

'Well, put your mind at rest,' smiled Nell. 'She almost wrenched my hand off in her haste to be there. Still, the house is really empty here without her – oh, sorry, I didn't mean to upset you! You'll set me off now!' Changing the subject, she remarked over the inappropriate comments that percolated from the lounge, and asked what on earth Joe was watching.

'Ooh, that's right, give him some stick!' With a questioning grin at her mother, Nina went to poke her head in. 'I hope you're not teaching my child violence!'

Romy on his knee, and derision on his face, Joe indicated the TV, on which university students could be seen battling with police. 'Look at this long-haired rabble – ooh, that's right, get stuck into him. Mr Policeman!' cackled Joe, bouncing Romy up and down.

'Surely this can't be the echelon of society you were so desperate for me to be part of?' Nina gave an impish wink at her mother. 'See, that's where university gets you, Dad.'

But, with Joe resisting the bait, she was to offer her own scornful opinion of the rioters. 'These are your so-called intelligent people, are they? Behaving like pampered bloody toddlers . . .' Then, saying it was time to go home, she summoned Romy, who as usual took her time in dragging herself from Grandad.

Tutting, the young mother withdrew to the kitchen. 'Didn't miss me very much, did she?'

Nell felt sorry for her, and, wanting to cheer her up, said, 'You were the first person she asked after when she came home from school.' Then, 'Listen, Neen, your dad's planning to give you twenty-one pounds to celebrate your twenty-first – I know it's not for a couple of months, but let's you and I go to town at the weekend and spend it early.'

For once Nina was unresponsive, though not impolite, and her ears did prick up at the amount of cash. 'Oh, thanks, Mam, but there's not much point in wasting it on clothes, seeing as I hardly ever go anywhere – yes, I *know* you'd look after Romy –' she inserted a laugh that had a slight edge of annoyance, 'you've told me a thousand times.'

'I'm not trying to fix you up! Honestly. But there must be girls at work you can pal up with, maybe go to one of those discotheques, or wherever . . .'

'After a hard day's slog I've not the slightest interest in trailing round pubs chucking seventeen vodka and limes down me neck in the hope of picking up some bloke, which is all the lasses at work talk about. You don't have to worry about me, if I need a friend I've got one who lives in the flat below, she's in the same boat as me with a little kid.

I'm perfectly happy watching telly – although having said that, I wouldn't mind a decent one, so if you want to give me that twenty-one quid early it'd do as a deposit.'

Nell studied her daughter's eager grin, looking for signs of pretence, for surely one who had always enjoyed being out every night of the week could not really settle for such a middle-aged existence? Maybe Nina cared more than she let on about the lack of a partner, but she was never going to tell her mother.

Nell could sigh all she liked about this, but it was obvious that with such close commitment to Romy, Nina would remain true to her word about never wanting a man to encroach. Only once did Nell suspect she might have weakened, when there was a different perkiness about her, and she requested a babysitter in the middle of the week. Obviously, the person that had invoked this radiance was trustworthy enough, and Nina fond enough, for her to have broken her own rule – which was all the more of a pity that, for reasons only to be guessed at, it ended as abruptly as it began.

Nell had learned to keep out of it now. And, single or no, Nina did seem content enough with the life that she led with her little offspring, and otherwise involved in earning a living and working her way up. Admired by her superiors for making such smooth transition from the old-fashioned punch machines to magnetic tape, she had lately been chosen to supervise a number of other operators. Typically, she divulged none of this to Joe, who was only made aware via Nell, the one who constantly tried to bolster their daughter's image.

Since the old factory in town had been closed and a new one built on the outskirts, Joe too had worked his way into a managerial position, though in contrast was approaching the end of his career. The succession of second-hand vehicles that had taken them on many a family holiday had been replaced by a brand-new saloon. Nell's husband, who had always been one for trappings, had become much more so since Romy's birth, filling his house with modern devices, as if to cock a snook at those who looked down on him for his illegitimate grandchild. His current acquisition was a telephone, though Joe stated his reason for this as being practical, rather than ostentatious, so that he could be contacted at any time by the factory.

And it would be handy for Nell, too, he was to tell her, after several months of listening to her complain about the lonely hours between taking Romy to and from school. 'Once she's gone, you'll be able to chat to your friends all morning if you like.'

'Who else do we know with a telephone?' Nell had to giggle with Nina, who had just turned up with Romy as this was being discussed.

Joe spread his palms. 'Well, sit and listen to the talking clock – I don't know! You've only got a couple of weeks and it'll be the flipping school holidays.'

Nell shook her head in amusement, and thereafter involved herself in taking Romy to school. Upon return, though, she thought about what Joe had said, deeming it not such a silly idea. Making a cup of tea, she sat down with the telephone directory, rippling backwards through its pages. Well, she certainly didn't know anyone with their first initial Z, Y, X or even W – then, oh yes! Jean Wintringham, whom she had worked alongside at the fever hospital. She ran her forefinger down the list of Wintringhams, but sadly there were none with the address she had in her own book for Jean.

Back to flicking idly through the pages, she came to the G section, and became deeply thoughtful. There were only a couple of Greenhows. Her old family doctor was one of them, still living at the same address. She had deliberately shoved the memory of him to the back of her mind for years, so what possessed her to act on such rash impulse,

Nell could not say, as she lifted the beige receiver from its cradle and dialled the number. Her blood curdled, and her heartbeat increased with each circuit of the disc, especially upon hearing that responding burr from the other end. Gripped by a spurt of panic, she was about to put down the receiver when her call was answered at once, and she was forced to stutter, 'Oh, hello . . . is it possible to speak to Doctor Greenhow?'

'Speaking,' said the voice at the other end.

Nell was struck momentarily dumb.

'Hello?'

'Sorry,' blurted Nell, 'I think I must have the wrong number.' Apart from the speaker, she could hear more cheery voices in the background. 'You sound much too young . . .'

'It's I who should apologise,' replied the other with a laugh. 'I was passing the phone when it rang, and automatically answered thinking I was at home! It must be my grandfather you want – but are you aware he's no longer in practice?'

'Oh yes, yes!' replied Nell, feeling stupid. 'It's purely a personal matter, not urgent at all really . . .'

'Then would you mind if I get him to ring you back? We're celebrating his eighty-fifth birthday, and he's rather involved with cutting the cake –'

'Certainly!' said Nell quickly. 'I'll give you – oh no, wait a minute . . .' How could she explain this to Joe, if the doctor rang back whilst he was there? 'Would it be possible for me to call and see Doctor personally one morning this week?'

'Come tomorrow, if you like!' invited the voice. 'He'll be rather flat I'd imagine, after his guests have gone, and he does enjoy company. What name did you say?'

'Sorry, I didn't.' Nell quickly provided it. 'It's Eleanor Kilmaster. Mrs. I'll call at ten, if that's not too early?'

'I'm sure it won't be. He's usually up at five – and he rarely goes out. Right, do excuse me, I'll get back to the shindig!'

Nell gave a polite goodbye and laid down the receiver, her hand trembling.

When the voice had said that Doctor Greenhow rarely went out, Nell had been expecting perhaps to find him in a wheelchair. But the man who opened the door to her was neither physically nor mentally frail. In fact, he looked not a year older than the last time she had encountered him. She had thought him extremely old then, but to her nineteen-year-old eyes he would have been.

'Why, Eleanor! I've been racking my brain as to who Mrs Kilmaster could be . . .' Shaking both her hands, he drew her into a hallway that was panelled in dark wood, and cluttered with coats, footwear, and an old-fashioned hallstand.

'I didn't expect you'd recognise me after so many years – and so much extra weight.'

'I can still tell it's you! Eleanor Spottiswood, well, well. Do come into the kitchen and have some tea, my dear!'

With a composed smile, Nell followed him into an equally cluttered but welcoming kitchen, a large pine table at its centre, which had obviously been laid in expectation of a guest, with scones and three varieties of cake, and a white china teapot and crockery. But she balked at the presence of another individual.

'This is Marjorie,' said Doctor Greenhow, in that gravelly voice that took Nell back decades, and even now made her want to clear her throat. 'She comes in to help me since my wife died.'

Nell smiled, said she was sorry to hear about his wife, and thanked them both for going to so much trouble.

'No trouble,' chuckled the old doctor. 'It's all left over from yesterday's party – did my grandson tell you?'

'Yes, he did. Many happy returns.'

'I hope not, my dear, I sincerely hope not.' Doctor Greenhow was smiling, but his eyes told that despite his good health he was slightly tired of life. 'Anyway, you don't want to hear my troubles, nor do we want to keep Marjorie dangling.' He turned to his helper. 'Thank you very much, my dear, I'm sure I can manage to wash up these few things . . .'

Much relieved that she was to be allowed private access to him, Nell was cheery as she too wished Marjorie a safe journey home.

'Now, let's have a cup of tea.' Doctor Greenhow poured this himself, and got straight to the point as his liver-spotted hand gave Nell her cup. 'It was nineteen forty-one, when last we met.'

She looked impressed.

'It's not such a blessing as it might seem, to still have one's mental faculties. It just allows one to see how badly the rest of one has decomposed. Still, I should be grateful to have come through two world wars unscathed. I was very sad to hear that your parents were victims of the Baedeker raid.'

Painful though it was, Nell could not have asked for a better opening for her enquiries. 'There were many good people who died.'

'Yes . . . it makes one wonder why some are chosen to survive and others not.' Doctor Greenhow looked moved, then pushed a plate towards her. 'Come along now, try a piece of this cake.'

To hurry things along, Nell obliged by taking a bite and saying it was delicious, but was soon to lay it back on her plate. 'This is very difficult for me, Doctor.' More difficult than she had envisaged. She might have thought that telling Joe had been the hardest part, but Joe hadn't really been involved in it, had he? Not like this man here, who had been present on the night William was born. 'You must guess why I'm here.' One so sharp as this old man must surely deduce her reason for coming.

He paused in the eating of his scone, and queried gently,

'It's about the child?' At her nod, he too moved his head. 'Yes . . . it's something that's always been on my conscience.'

'I don't wish to cause any trouble for anyone involved,' Nell assured him swiftly. 'I promise you, I won't turn up unannounced on his adoptive parents' doorstep, demanding to see him –'

'You wouldn't be able to do that even were you so inclined, dear,' sighed Doctor Greenhow, looking troubled. 'That's what I was referring to, when I said it had been on my conscience. There is no doorstep, no house. Not the same one, at any rate. The poor devils were flattened on the same night as your parents.'

Nell could not prevent an involuntary whimper as her whole world collapsed.

'Oh, no, no, no!' he assured her post-haste. 'The boy wasn't with them! No, he was fit and well by all accounts. No, poor Mr and Mrs Jackson were enjoying a rare night out at a dance hall –'

Jackson. My son is called Jackson, thought Nell, her heart soaring in relief at him being alive.

'– and they had left the child at its grandmother's house as they intended to be late home. If only they had all stayed there. Tragic, just tragic.'

'How dreadful . . .' Nell hoped her words of agreement would sound sincere, but all she was desperate to know was, 'What happened to William after that?'

'William?' The doctor's age finally caught up with him, his eye holding hers in bewilderment. But only for a few seconds. 'Ah, was that the name you gave him? I think they changed it, but I'm afraid it escapes me for a moment.' He finished off his scone.

'Maybe it'll come back to you,' said Nell, wanting to hear the more important information, which she was now forced to repeat. 'What happened to him when his adoptive parents were killed? Did he stay with the grandmother?'

The doctor was more positive on that score. 'Oh no,

she was far too advanced in years to cope with a one-year-old. As he was so young it was decided that he be put into an orphanage, so that someone else might soon come along to adopt him.'

Initially stunned, Nell soon found her voice – and it was a furious one. 'He wasn't an orphan! He had a mother who loved and wanted him, and he should have been given back to me!'

The doctor was genuinely sympathetic. 'But how could you possibly –'

'My parents were dead!' Nell interrupted. 'There was no longer anyone for me to bring shame on!'

'I understand you must be ang—'

'Yes, I am!' Anger did not begin to describe her emotions. She could have killed the old man who sat there as if butter wouldn't melt, acting as her judge. 'Why did no one deem it fit to inform me? You were aware I'd lost everyone close to me!'

'Those were less liberal days, Eleanor. Perhaps in these Swinging Sixties you might have been able to make a life for him, but then . . .' He ended with a shrug and a sigh.

Nell thought of her own daughter's humiliating treatment, and for once could see his argument. 'People are not really so different, still ready to point the finger.'

'Did you have more children?'

'I've a stepdaughter, none of my own.'

'And does your husband know of the other one?'

'Yes, though not that I'm here.' Tired of being distracted, she sought to speed matters up, asking tersely, 'To which orphanage was he sent?'

'I believe it was a privately run organisation – Eleanor, do you really want to disrupt his life?'

Nell was back in that room, being bullied by this very reasonable man and her parents; tugged this way and that. 'I just want to know he's all right,' she said, trying desperately not to cry. 'If you could just remember which orphanage it was, and the name they gave him.'

'I doubt they'd tell you one way or the other,' said Doctor Greenhow gently. 'These matters remain confidential.'

'A doctor could find out.' Nell levelled her gaze at him, conveying that he had a responsibility for this.

'Supposing I could acquire this information, what good would it possibly do – if, as you say, you have no intention of seeing the young man – for that is what he'll be now. Why, he'd be . . . twenty-seven, twenty-eight.'

'I know that,' said Nell through gritted teeth. Twenty-eight years, two months, and fifteen days . . .

'Perhaps with a family, a wife and child of his own,' rambled the old man. 'You'd be strangers to each other.'

'Please,' insisted Nell. 'If there's anything you can remember, any way you can help me, I'm begging you, Doctor . . .'

At length, he nodded. 'Well, I can see if that particular orphanage still exists, and give them a ring. I'm not sure they'll tell me any more than they'll tell you. Still,' he dabbed up crumbs from his plate, 'I could say it was due to a matter of medical emergency concerning a relative that we must contact him.'

'Thank you.' Nell closed her eyes in gratitude.

Then, as they drank their tea, she sought another answer, of not quite such monumental importance, but to sate her curiosity nevertheless. Fanciful though it might be, she had imagined various possibilities over the years as to the identity of her real father, this man amongst them. Might his collusion over William indicate some closer link with her mother than simply that of family doctor?

'On a similar subject,' she tendered with caution. 'The belief that I myself was adopted was somewhat shattered when my mother revealed I was her natural child. You wouldn't happen to know anything about that, would you?'

'My dear, I had absolutely no inkling.' Indeed, the elderly face did look thoroughly surprised. 'You were already with your parents when first they consulted me. I too was led to assume you were adopted.'

Adroit at reading faces, Nell would have known had he been lying. This man was not her father. Resigned to leave this as something she would never know, she finished her tea, and shortly departed.

Nell had refused to give Doctor Greenhow her address and telephone number, this in itself causing him to point out her error in wanting to keep the matter from her husband. Nevertheless, she insisted, and said she would call again in person in a week's time. If that was not long enough for him to discover the information, then he could have another week. As many weeks as it might take.

It was a stressful wait, made even more so in having to pretend to Joe that she was as excited as he, as they watched hour after hour of the televised moon landings over the weekend, when all she could ponder was the old man's detective work: would it all end in failure?

However, when she did finally call round again, he was in possession of the basic facts. Accepting his offer of tea and cake, for it would have been churlish not to spend an hour keeping an old man company, Nell's excitement rose, as he proclaimed success in finding out what she had wanted to know.

'The boy was adopted within months of his arrival at The Willows orphanage –'

Well, that was some slight relief, that he wasn't like those poor unwanted souls dumped in the old Infirmary.

'His name at the time was Robert Jackson. I recalled it the moment you'd gone.'

Nell's eyes followed his to the photograph on the refrigerator, obviously taken at the birthday party. She fought the impulse to be angry that this contented old man had his entire family grouped around him. All she wanted was to be allowed to share her own son's life.

'He was adopted by a couple named Morgan. As he was still under two years and not wholly conversant with his name, they decided they would like to change it – to William, strangely enough.'

Nell's heart soared, and she gave a little laugh.

'They were able to tell me little else,' said Doctor Greenhow.

Nell said, 'That's better than I could have hoped for. Thank you.' Her misty eyes were drawn again to the photograph on the fridge.

'You must be very proud that your grandson followed your profession.'

'Yes, my granddaughter's a doctor too. Though neither of my sons were.'

'Adoption severs all those links,' stated Nell, meeting his eye once more. 'That's why, if there's anything else, good or bad, I must insist you tell me.'

'Well, there is . . .' But the doctor seemed hesitant to convey this, having to be prompted by a sharp look from his guest. 'It just so happened that the particular person I spoke to at the orphanage had worked there for a very long time. Since the early fifties, in fact . . .'

Nell's pose stiffened.

'William Morgan re-entered the orphanage at the age of ten or eleven, after his adoptive parents were also killed –'

She emitted a haunting moan.

'– in a crash this time,' relayed Doctor Greenhow. 'The unfortunate boy then continued to reside there until he reached his teens. My informant assures me that he was a perfectly level-headed individual, a pleasant and exceptionally popular boy, that's how come she remembers him. There was some kind of migration scheme at the time for disadvantaged youngsters, and it appears he was one of those selected to take part. Your son is, so far as I am aware, in Australia. Now, I beg you, my dear,' he reached across the table and clasped her arm, 'just go home and forget about him, and be sure that he is gone to a better life.'

Gone to a better life. That's what they said of the departed, at funerals. But William wasn't dead. He might be ten thousand miles away. But she was sure in her heart that he wasn't dead. And he was still William.

PART 3

21

Well-rehearsed at shouldering her burden, Nell had gone home and got on with her life, for there was nothing else to be done. But never a day was to pass that she did not think of William.

Nell had become a lot closer to Joe since he had laid his cards on the table; had at last said goodbye to Bill in her head and her heart. In appreciation of this, her husband had presented her with a diamond eternity ring, plus the additional surprise of a foreign holiday. More jaunts were to follow, to Italy, then to Spain – they had better make the most of it, said Joe, before retirement put a halt to such luxuries, because they'd still have milady to look after even when he was a pensioner. Grumble though he might over the child's continual presence, his wife could tell it was all manufactured, and so could Romy, a bond having sprung up between them, much tighter than the one he enjoyed with his own daughter, Nell was glad to see – glad too that he did not treat this one as a boy. Instructed on the error of his ways, Joe steered well clear of guns and cowboy hats these days, in favour of dolls and prams. Though more often than not, Romy was to prefer a board game with her grandad.

One evening, anxious to start cooking tea, Nell had let Romy and her new friend Tash scamper off to the back bedroom, whilst Joe went to pass an hour in his shed. She got out her electric mixer, but within no time at all the girls' shrill squeals were to be heard even above it. She called from the bottom of the stairs – 'Simmer down please!' – but the resulting giggles were soon on the crescendo again, and her tolerance eventually snapped. Barging in, she found them parading about in her clothes – which was not such a liberty, for they were old ones she had given Romy long ago – but a viler trespass had her swooping on the other eight-year-old, from whose neck dangled a gold chain, a wedding ring and a dirty strip of baby ribbon.

'Who gave you permission to wear that?' Whipping the boater from Tasha's head, she threw it aside in order to be at the more precious item. 'Haven't I given you enough to play with? Take it off at once!' And it appeared she was trying to strangle the wearer in her haste to remove the chain and its contents from the scrawny neck. 'Go home now, Natasha – and you're a very naughty girl to let her do it!' she scolded Romy, as the other fled.

Then, whilst Romy bawled, a furious grandmother was to collect strewn letters. 'Did you read any of these?' She brandished them under her granddaughter's nose. There came teary denial, mucus spluttering out all over the place. 'You'd better not! You shouldn't have touched anything in this box.' Nell grabbed the hat box, replacing everything inside and banging on the dusty lid. 'These are my private things – that's why they were on top of the wardrobe! Were you the one to climb up?'

Tears coursing down her face, Romy shook her head and squeaked. 'No, it was Tash!'

'That nosy little madam – well, she won't be coming in again!' Hoisting herself onto the same chair that the culprit had used, Nell replaced the hat box on top of the wardrobe, and descended heavily. 'And you can tidy all these clothes away and sit and read a book until I call you down for tea!' Then she went down, leaving Romy to blubber.

Using her fury as momentum, Nell had the meal concocted long before it was ready to be eaten, and, with Joe still in his lair, this gave her plenty of latitude in which to explain to Tasha's mother why her daughter had gone home so distressed. Though unwavering in her indignation over the raid on her intimate belongings, after pacifying her neighbour, she calmed down sufficiently to reconsider her granddaughter's participation, and went up to see if she was all right.

'I'm sorry I was so angry with you,' she murmured, upon peeping in, 'but those things were so precious to me, and you had no right to snoop . . .'

Her face already mottled, Romy began to cry again. 'I'm sorry, Nana!'

'Oh . . . never mind,' said Nell softly, then approached her granddaughter.

Romy wiped her eyes and nose on the sleeve of her cardigan, but looked guilty as she admitted, 'I found this under my quilt when you'd gone, but I daren't put it back because you said not to touch that box . . .'

From the child's hand, Nell received the photograph that had escaped her frenzied clearance. Injured though she was, Romy was intrigued by the heartfelt sigh as her grandmother went to get the hat box down again and took off its lid. 'Who's that man, Nana?'

'Nobod—' Nell bit her tongue and decided to be honest for once. Otherwise, how would the child realise the extent of her infringement? Instead of hiding the photo, she put aside the lid and brought out the chain and its intimate treasures, then sat down beside her granddaughter on the bed. 'His name was Bill,' she explained slowly and in murmured tone. 'He was the one who gave me this chain, and this wedding ring. That's why I was angry, because it's something private. Only Grandad and your mummy know about it, so I don't want you to tell anyone else. Do you understand?'

‘Cross my heart and hope to die . . . but I thought you were married to Grandad?’

‘I am now. But a long time ago I was married to Bill,’ the white lie could be explained when the listener was much older, ‘but he died. Anyway, we had a baby, and this little ribbon was meant to be for him, but he was taken away from me too . . .’

‘Did he die?’

Nell shook her head. ‘No, but some people said I was too young to keep him, and they gave him to someone else.’

Romy looked as if about to cry at the thought of her grandmother so treated. ‘But then you had the little girl that was my mummy?’ It had been explained to her before that Nana was her mother’s mother. ‘It was a good job you had her to make you feel better.’

‘It certainly was.’ Nell curled an arm round her then, and hugged her. ‘Though I’m not her real mother – she was born to another lady who sadly died.’

A look of shock appeared on Romy’s face, and she clapped the back of her hand to her brow. ‘This is the worst day of my life!’ And she collapsed backwards on the bed.

Smiling as much for the histrionics as to reassure the drama queen, Nell was quick to console with hugs and kisses. ‘What I meant to say was, I’m not her *first* mummy. I came along afterwards to look after her and her daddy – that’s your grandad. But I still look on your mum as my real daughter, and I hope she feels the same, we couldn’t be closer than if we were flesh. And I *certainly* look upon you as my very real granddaughter. I couldn’t wish for a better one – even if you are a nosey little monkey.’ She finished with a squeeze and a grin.

Then she saw that the discussion had provoked even more curiosity on her granddaughter’s tear-stained face. Fearing that it might precursor a query about the child’s own beginnings, which was not in her remit, she said, 'Now, I think I can hear Grandad in from his shed, so we'd better go and make sure his tea's ready.' And, making great play of blowing on the hat box to create a great cloud of dust – which made Romy sneeze and laugh – Nell put it away, then took her downstairs.

When Nina came to collect her daughter at the usual time, Nell revealed that they had had a bit of an altercation, which had forced her to explain about her secret son.

'Why the hell did you do that?' Nina looked dark. 'A clout would have done.'

Nell realised that Nina's anger did not just stem from her child's meddling, and said, 'You're thinking I was paving the way for you to tell her about her father – but you're wrong, it occurred on impulse. Still, she's bound to question her own background. And there are some precocious children about . . . you'd be wise to tell her sooner rather than later.'

Nina performed a complete change of subject. 'I think death is a big enough topic for one day – did she tell you her budgie's conked out?' Nell touched her lips, and said no, she must have been too upset to mention it. 'I meant to bring it this morning so she could bury it in your garden, but I forgot. Hope it doesn't stink when we get home. Anyway, Mam, I'll be off the rest of the week, so you won't have her to look after – Romy, time to go!'

Her child came dashing, then at the last minute remembered her hard-boiled egg which was to be decorated for school.

'I hope it wins a prize!' the doting grandmother told Romy, who spun to ask if she would come and see the exhibition? Nell said she would love to, at which Romy clapped her hands, then ran to ask if Grandad would come too.

Joe threw her a look of ambivalence, before ruffling the

blonde head, with a smile and a yes. Though he was to complain to his wife after Romy had gone. 'Did you volunteer me for that? I'd better not miss my *Tomorrow's World . . .*'

The following evening, Joe and Nell drove round to Nina's flat, where a sigh was heaved that they had to tramp to the top floor. 'I thought you said she's been off work all day? She could at least be ready and save us from walking up all these steps . . .'

'It won't be Nina,' puffed Nell, 'it's probably Romy.' And, sure enough, when they entered the flat with its orange and brown decor, Nina was scolding her daughter for keeping her grandparents waiting.

'Aye, away Greased Lightnin'.' It was a derogatory term, conjured by Joe for his granddaughter's leisurely movements. 'I bet you'd come running if I was offering a pound.' And, to demonstrate, he presented one.

Romy accepted with glee. 'Can I buy them hotpants out of your catalogue, Mum?'

'You can not!' Rifling her bag for her keys, Nina's freshly made-up face came up to object between two curtains of hair, the strawberry-blonde tresses grown almost to waist length these days. 'I can't stand the tarty things.'

This drew the others' attention to her own attire. 'They're pretty knickers you're wearing,' said Nell, catching a glimpse of flowery nylon beneath the shortest of dresses. 'I don't know how you can bear to wear your pantyhose underneath, though, they must chafe.'

'I wear a pair of pants under them as well,' informed Nina.

'You'd need two pairs of drawers in that draughty thing,' sniped her father, then led the way out.

The school hall was filled with proud parents, their children dragging them around the trestles that formed the exhibition, when Nell and Joe began their tour. It did not take long to spot their granddaughter's contribution, for it stood out from all, adorned as it was in green budgie feathers, complete with wings and a tail. Nell did not know how she or Joe managed to control their laughter, as both complimented Romy on her innovation.

Not until their delighted granddaughter had raced off to seek out her classmates was Joe's restrained hysteria to escape with a hiss, a swiftly drawn handkerchief covering his grin in the process. 'I think it's safe to say she won't become a vet.'

Blue eyes watering with hilarity Nina refuted that she had in any way influenced the violation of a dead creature. 'After we got home last night, she sneaked Joey out of his coffin and had his wings snipped off and glued onto the egg before I had a clue! She insisted he was being put to good use – "Nana said, you haven't got to waste anything!" The rest of him's waiting to be buried in your garden – not that there's much. It was all I could do to stop her sawing his head and feet off.'

Still merry, they were to mill around for twenty minutes or so, looking at the amazing display, until Joe felt they had sufficiently done their duty. Tutting at their daughter, Nell said he was never in a place more than five minutes before he wanted to be off. Nina replied that she would just skip to the loo, if her mother would go and find Romy amongst this lot. So, leaving Joe standing, Nell made her way through the throng of parents, and emerged into a corridor. There were several children there, but no Romy. Then, wandering beside a cloakroom, she heard a childish voice declare, 'Your mam and dad are old, aren't they?' Which made her smile. 'Is that your aunty with them?'

Romy's scornful giggle drew her nearer. 'No! That's my mum. The others are Nana and Grandad.'

'Oh, is your dad at work then?'

'Haven't got one.'

Nell bit her lip and continued to eavesdrop.

'You must have. Was he killed in Aden, like my uncle?'

'No.' Then Romy sounded less sure. 'I don't think so, anyway. I just haven't got one. My mum isn't married.'

'She must have had a boyfriend then.' It was issued with certainty.

'She hasn't, then,' came the rebuttal, 'because I'd know if she had – she doesn't even like boys.'

'Well, she must do, cause you can't have a baby without a husband or boyfriend.'

And at that point Nell intervened. 'Ready to go, love!'

'She's a twit,' Romy told her grandmother, upon walking away from the cloakroom with her. 'D'you know what she just said?'

Nell was forced to hear it all again, but instead of commenting, made some excuse, and was relieved that Romy spotted her mother and ran to meet her. But as she herself rejoined Joe, she was hurriedly to repeat the exchange as they followed the others to the car. 'She'll have to be told the truth now.'

'What, that her father was a scumbag out for what he could get?'

'Please don't use that revolting term!' Nell reared in disgust. 'I don't know who thought it up – probably the Americans – I remember the exact time I first heard it, and I hoped never to hear it again. And see, that's what I'm worried about,' came her added undertone, 'that Nina will put it as discreetly as you. I don't want Romy influenced against all men – come on, we'd better catch them up, I want to alert Nina if I can.'

But it was too late, for by the time they caught Nina and Romy up, the latter had already begun: 'Mum, were you ever married? Because this girl said . . .'

Having hoped to delay the story of Romy's conception for another few years, Nina was obviously dismayed at having to convey this in front of an audience. Joe whistled discreetly as he unlocked the car for his family to get in, Nell pretending to look out of the window at the lamplit streets, as Nina tried to avoid answering – though being trapped in the car there seemed no escape. Waiting for her to begin, Nell pondered the thought that she would have had to do this herself had they not taken William. And oh, what a more uplifting tale she could have told him about his father. No, she did not envy Nina one bit. However, as she listened to them murmuring in the back seat as the car negotiated twists and turns, there was relief in that Nina had decided to temper the truth.

'Well, that girl was right in a way,' came the mother's matter-of-fact explanation to her child. 'You either have to be married or have a boyfriend to have a baby. It is best if you're married, but I just had a boyfriend. When I found out you were going to be born, well, I wasn't really old enough to marry him, and we didn't really know each other well enough. So we didn't see each other any more.'

'Didn't he want me?' The plaintive query went straight to Nell's heart, and, she suspected, Nina's too, from the way her voice caught as she delivered a kiss to the cheek.

'I'm sure he would've! But he had no idea you were even born.'

'We could tell him now.' The voice from the back seat sounded hopeful.

But the manner in which her mother replied told Romy that this was impossible. 'Sometimes, things don't always go how you want them to, love. I wish you could have a dad who lives with us, but you just don't. And you never will.'

'Not bothered,' Nell heard Romy declare, as if she meant it. 'I've got Grandad instead.'

And with this she leaned forward to throw her arms around the driver's neck, instigating sudden laughter as he fought to maintain control of the car.

* * *

'My, that was a relief,' breathed Nell to her husband later, when they had dropped Nina and Romy off and were on their way home. 'All's well that ends well.'

'Apart from missing my telly!' But Joe was not really cross, that is until they were settled down for the evening. Then, 'Sod and damn it!' he howled, at being plunged into darkness halfway through the current TV programme. 'Bloody miners, they earn a king's ransom compared to what we had, and still they're not happy – how many more of these power cuts – remind me again, who was it said "what a good idea it'd be to get an electric fire"?'

Nell objected with a laugh as she fumbled for matches. 'I wasn't to know!' Thank goodness that Beata turned up at just the right moment to lighten the atmosphere. 'I don't know what he's complaining about,' Nell told her sister-in-law as they huddled in candlelight. 'We've had such a giggle at school . . .' and she proceeded to related the comical scene with the budgie, she and Joe chortling all over again, and Beata being similarly tickled. 'My God, the colour of Joe's face – I thought he was going to have a stroke!'

And for a time they maintained their light-heartedness, but soon Joe was grumbling again about the unions and all the strikes and the shortages these inevitably brought. 'Yes, nothing much changes,' sighed Nell. 'It's like living through the war all over again.'

'Worse!' screeched Joe. 'At least then it was only foreigners trying to kill you. You can't go to a football match any more without hooligans spoiling it for you – they should hang the buggers just for wearing them stupid loon pants and girly haircuts.'

His sister agreed. 'Along with them IRA sods. That's all you see these days, violence.'

'That's when you're allowed to watch the blasted telly!' rounded Joe. 'And even when you are, it's full of poofs in white satin – and we thought the Beatles were bad! And as for being in the Common bloody Market – ooh, don't get me started. It makes you wonder what you fought for, it really does.'

Beata said she was glad to be retired, the way nursing was going. Joe said he couldn't wait either. 'I'm as good as retired now, what with these three-day weeks – hang on,' he held up the conversation with a note of finality, 'I think I'll just go cut me throat.' Then they all laughed, and as if by magic the electricity came back on.

Nell jumped up to silence the television. 'Like a spring chicken,' joked Beata. 'By, you wouldn't think she's got a fiftieth birthday coming up! What's he going to buy you, Spotty?'

Nell said she wouldn't mind a colour telly, but was shouted down by Joe who denounced them as too garish: people with faces the colour of tomatoes, and the turf on the racecourse looked like summat out of *The Wizard of Oz*.

'Does he never stop?' With a laugh at Beata, Nell went to make a pot of tea, returning with this and a plate stacked with chocolate cake. Then, taking a piece for herself, she sat and watched brother and sister with fondness as they put the world to rights.

After two pieces of cakc, Beata said she would have to get weaving. 'Send me a photo of Romy's egg if you can – I could do with a laugh.'

But, when she had gone, Nell chuckled to her husband, 'I don't know if I should. It was bad enough thinking you were going to have a stroke, I should hate to be responsible for Killie having one too.'

Joe seemed amused for a while, but as he prepared to watch the television again, and the laughter slowly faded, he announced in more sober fashion, 'I pray to God I don't, Nell.'

Collecting the empty cups, she tried to jolly him. 'You, who never ails a thing? You'll outlive me.'

But Joe had turned deadly serious, and he shook his head. 'No, joking aside now, that's what got me dad.'

There was a deep-seated fear in his eyes that Nell had never seen before. In a surge of compassion, she put down the cups and reached out to him. 'But remember, your father died fifty years ago. With modern treatment –'

'I don't want to be hooked up to a bloody machine. It's bad enough being paralysed, but the thought of not being able to tell people how you feel . . .' A coat of moisture slicked his eyes, though it did not wash away the dread. 'I saw that look on me dad's face – a big strong sergeant-major reduced to a baby – I don't want the people I love seeing me like that. By God I don't.'

'It won't happen, love,' swore Nell, clutching his hand for all she was worth. 'But if – *if* it did, I'd be here to look after you.'

'I don't want my wife forced to look after me! For who knows how long . . .'

Nell understood his protest, but, 'I wouldn't have to *be* forced! I'd do it because I love you –'

'What I'm saying *is* . . .' Joe took a deep breath. 'If I'm going to go I want it to be quick. I want you to give me something so I don't linger.'

Nell was shocked. 'For heaven's sake! You're only sixty-four . . .'

'Me dad wasn't even fifty.'

Nell saw him reach for his cigarettes. 'Well, it might help if you gave those up!'

Joe studied the packet for a moment; there was only one left. Then he lit it and said, 'Right, this is my very last one.'

'I'll believe that when I see it,' said a somewhat disquieted Nell, and escaped to the kitchen.

Surprisingly, Joe remained true to his word: when that last cigarette was gone he was never to buy another. But that night's exchange had left Nell concerned about being married to one so senior in years, and she began to envisage a time ten years hence when she might find herself living alone.

Added to this, it was obvious that Nina entertained similar worries – oh, not to do with her parents, but in picturing herself alone once Romy had grown up, which was happening so very fast – and it was all so premature, for Nina herself was only in her twenties. What must it be like for her, thought Nell, with no one else to care for, to see her daughter blossoming, and to know that in five years she could be a mother herself, if fate dealt her the same blow.

Romy had begun to assert her independence, as if being equipped with the information on her parentage somehow made her more adult. Nell feared there was a difficult time ahead for Nina, who had managed to keep a tight rein for now on the child with glitter on her cheeks and adventure in her eye, but as another year flew by, things could only get harder.

Having witnessed the battles for liberty – which Romy ostensibly won, little knowing that when she celebrated freedom with her friend, she was actually being stalked by her mother, who ducked behind cars and privet hedges so as to keep an eye on her precious child – Nell was impelled to speak on her granddaughter's behalf.

'Love, you'll have to let her go sometime, or she won't be able to relate to people her own age. It won't be that long before she takes her eleven plus. She'll want to go places once she's at big school.'

But, 'That's a good while off yet,' said Nina. 'We'll face that when it comes.'

And then, in the blink of an eye, it did come, Romy sailing through her eleven plus with aplomb.

Amidst all the celebration that preceded her entry to grammar school, Nell wondered what Nina must think and feel, as she watched her father shower his grandchild with the praise he had never accorded her. Obviously, she was immensely glad for her child, though surely, thought Nell, this must be tinged by the singular lack of acknowledgement from Joe. Thus, anxious to alleviate any resentment, or sense of failure, Nell was to lay the congratulations firmly at her door.

'What a great job you've done in bringing her up on your own,' she was to remark.

And then, as usual, Joe went and spoiled it with derisory laughter. 'On her own? That's a good un, all the cash we've shelled out over the years . . .'

Although with Romy present, he did appear to have second thoughts, and, concerned that she might think he was grumbling about the money she had cost him, he patted his granddaughter and said, 'But she's worth every penny we spent on her, indeed she is, what a brainbox!' And as usual displayed his love in pecuniary mode.

And, as ever, Romy treated the donation with glee, and asked could she go into town with her friend on Saturday. And, as ever, came Nina's flat reply, that she was too young to go on her own.

'Aw, but that's ridiculous! Tasha's been allowed to go on her own since she was ten! You treat me like a baby!' Romy's eyes turned in protest to her grandmother, who secretly felt that Nina was overprotective, but knew better than to interfere.

However, within a few months of being at grammar school, Romy began to object more and more about these unfair restrictions, especially when prevented from accompanying a group of friends to the cinema one Saturday afternoon, in order to take an excursion with her mother and grandparents. Told not to grumble, Romy had 'accidentally' let it slip, and at this point Nell decided she must risk Nina's wrath by offering a timely reminder:

'You didn't want to sit with old fogies when you were her age. Let her go, Neen – what harm will she come to in the pictures? We can drop her off at her friend's house on our way, pick her up on the way back . . .'

And, with Romy looking up so beseechingly, and after much angst, Nina had caved in – though she was none too pleased with either of them. The youngster danced up and down then, and, eyes bright, ran off to phone her friends so they did not leave without her. But whilst she was delighted, her mother remained concerned.

'Stop worrying,' Nell instructed quietly. 'She's a mature girl –'

'That's what I'm worried about!' cut in Nina. 'There are all kinds of creeps waiting to take advantage.'

'But there's a whole group of them, and she's quite sensible – you *have* to trust her, Neen, or she'll resent you for it.' Finally receiving a nod of surrender, she felt glad to have assisted her granddaughter. Romy's school friends, too, were equally thrilled that she was to accompany them, gathering round the car to enfold her as she was dropped off by her grandparents and mother.

'We'll be home around seven,' instructed Nina through the window, her face anxious as the car pulled away. 'Make sure you're there.'

Though obviously embarrassed at being babied, Romy promised that she would be. And, with some misgiving, Nina turned her eyes ahead, though Nell could sense her worry, and gave a little squeeze of her hand to show she knew how it felt to reach such a milestone.

Nell did not feel so confident several hours later, though, upon arriving to pick Romy up.

'She's not here!' A frantic Nina came hurrying back to the car, her face heaping accusation on Nell, who was tweaked by panic herself, until Mandy's mother approached, clutching her sweater in apologetic mode, to say they had chaperoned Romy onto the bus.

'Well, then, she'll be safe enough,' said Nell, trying to

calm the situation, but Nina slammed the car door and urged her father to: 'Drive!'

Fumbling over the gears, an equally worried Joe earned his daughter's wrath. 'Put your bloody foot down!'

'I'm not getting done for speeding!' His tone was annoyed, but the reflection of his eyes in the rear-view mirror was as anxious as his daughter's – though neither of them suffered the additional guilt of Nell, who had been the one to validate Romy's need for freedom. Sick with foreboding, her fingers were tight around the strap of her handbag as the car went much too slowly across town, and though her voice might offer words of reassurance, they were for herself as much as her daughter. 'She'll be there, I know she will . . .'

But she was wrong, for when they came to a halt outside the block of flats, and Nina leaped out and tore up the stairs, the landing was bare. By the time her parents were even halfway up, Nina was thundering back down, her face deathly pale.

'Perhaps she's at our house!' Nell quickly provided the answer.

In her haste to return to the car, Nina almost shoved her father back down the stairs to the car, angry at his dallying. Finally they were in motion again, though not quickly enough for Nina's liking, Nell having to offer words of solace to try to calm her down.

And then they turned the corner and suddenly everything was all right! There was Romy, sitting on the gate and waving as their car approached – though her smile did not prevent a near hysterical outpouring from her mother.

'You told me to come home!' objected Romy, taken aback.

'No, I said, make sure you're *there* – I meant at Mandy's, where we left you!'

'I thought you meant here, sorry!' Though actually it

was a streak of stubbornness and independence that had caused Romy deliberately to misunderstand.

Stung even further, that her daughter naturally regarded her grandparents' house as home, Nina gave short shrift to any apology. 'You will be sorry! Because that's the last time I let you out alone – come on, let's be having you!'

'Well, everything's all right now we know she's safe.' Nell tried to mediate, adding to an outraged Romy, 'Your mum was just worried because she thought you'd got lost . . .'

But, 'Honestly, I can never do anything right!' said her granddaughter, and stomped off down the avenue.

'Now you know what we had to put up with,' came Joe's sour contribution, before turning indoors. 'Fun being a parent, isn't it?'

Nina looked as if she was about to bellow, though with her daughter so far ahead she simply shared a glower with Nell, before departing.

'Just comfort yourself with the thought that you're preparing her for the wider world.' Nell called after her, in the hope that this might soothe, but Nina gave no hint that she had heard as she charged for home.

Despite that clash, and the shock of thinking her child had come to harm, having finally calmed down and seen that Romy was capable of navigating herself from A to B, Nina did eventually permit her to branch out. Nell was glad of this landmark, though could not help feeling a little sad that it marked the end of childhood for her granddaughter. But if she had feared that this would be an end to their close relationship, this was not to happen. For, now that liberty had been conferred, Romy seemed to have no need to assert her independence, and was quite happy to be seen with her grandparents, and to accompany them on trips to the coast every now and then.

There was certainly plenty of opportunity for this in the

heat wave that had been suddenly visited upon them. It was turning out to be a very strange summer, thought Nell. The beginning of June had been icy cold – colder, possibly, than December, and with a flurry of what had looked very much like snow, as she and Joe braved the promenade at Scarborough. Then, on their way back, as if by magic the sun had come out, and continued to shine for weeks on end. With no change predicted to the drought that had turned his lawn brown, Joe had put away the spade that had been donated by his colleagues on his retirement, and spent almost every day taking his wife to the beach. And here they were yet again at the weekend, with Nina and Romy and several thousand others.

Unlike the younger generation of men, in whom the heat wave seemed to have awoken a very unBritish penchant for shorts, Joe's only concession was to remove his tie and roll up his trouser legs, as he basked alongside his wife in his deckchair. Loving the sun, though not its effect on her shoulders, Nell was most careful to apply lotion, though with so much regular exposure even she had begun to turn golden. Desperate to catch every ray, Nina sat up only to baste herself with a homemade concoction, before turning over.

Sweat glistening from his brow, Joe squinted through his sunglasses, and asked, 'What's that she's putting on? It stinks like vinegar.'

'It is,' informed Nell. 'With olive oil.'

'I thought I could hear sizzling – you'll end up looking like battered haddock,' he told his daughter, who as usual ignored him, and gave herself up to the sun god.

Nell smiled, but enjoyable though it was to be all together with Nina and Romy – who was having a whale of a time digging a hole with her friend – she was growing bored with these endless days of sun, and was not sure she was suited to the indolent life. Upon her granddaughter's entry to grammar school, she would dearly have loved to return to nursing, but with Joe retired by then, and not wanting him to feel neglected, she had sacrificed this desire. Though, at fifty-four, something felt missing. But then, she supposed it always would . . .

Half child, half woman, her granddaughter was busy digging her way to Australia. Stung to remembrance, Nell tried to be happy – it was wrong *not* to be happy on such a cloudless day as this, in such wonderful company, but somehow the relentless sunshine only served to highlight that which was absent from her life. She looked away, and tried to concentrate on others who inhabited the wide stretch of sand, the happy squeals of children, the swish of the sea . . . Her eyes fell on an attractive dark-haired girl, aged about twenty, who was throwing a beach ball back and forth between two friends and the young man who was obviously her husband. She wore a black one-piece swimsuit, distorted by six months of pregnancy. Nell thought of herself, desperate not to let hers show, cramming, squeezing, constricting her baby into a corset, not like this girl, showing it off . . .

'Are you thinking what I'm thinking?'

Eyes still vague, she turned to see that from behind the screen of his sunglasses Joe was regarding the girl too. 'Come again, love?'

'That brazen madam,' he commented. 'They don't seem to have any decorum these days, belly out to here . . .'

'True enough.' Trying to escape from her past, Nell sighed, and in the same breath, as she rose from her deckchair, asked, 'who fancies another ice-cream?'

The melancholy just would not go away, though she managed to put on a brave face until after dark. But lying there with the sheets thrown back, trying to gain some relief from the open window, she could not help silently screaming for William. At the foot of the garden, a train went past. Oppressed by heat and misery, Nell barely noticed as its thundering passage trembled the mattress. But then she suddenly became aware of a constant hissing, and began to shake the bed with her soft laughter, breaking out of her mood to say to her husband:

'Listen . . .'

Joe attended the sound of running water.

Nell chuckled. 'Mr Lazenby's sneaked out to beat the hosepipe ban.'

'Thank God,' breathed Joe. 'I thought it was you pissing the bed.'

Lured away from her maudlin, his wife elbowed him. 'Stop making me laugh!'

'You started it!' reasoned Joe.

'It's bad enough trying to sleep in this heat without you making me all hot and bothered,' said Nell.

'Christ, you're right there.' Joe heaved in discomfort, sweat trickling along each rumple of his naked, ageing torso. 'Are you sure there isn't a single fan left in the shops?'

'I told you, not one. I asked everywhere, they've all sold out.'

Joe wiped his brow with the one sheet that covered them. 'It makes you wonder how people cope in Australia.'

Nell was so quiet for a while that he began to think she had gone to sleep. Then he heard the faintest of sniffs. 'Are you all right?' he enquired immediately, turning his head.

'Yes, my nose is just so stuffed up. There must be tons of pollen about.'

Joe hoisted himself onto his elbow, and extended a careful hand through the semi-darkness to touch her face. 'You're crying,' he accused.

'No, I'm not.' She tried not to let him feel the tears.

'Lazenby's hosepipe must have sprayed a bloody long way, then! Come on, what's up?'

'Nothing really, it's just not being able to sleep, I get to thinking . . .'

'What about?' Joe laid down again.

Nell despaired that she had to tell him – why could he not guess? She took a deep breath.

'My son.'

'Ah . . .' He turned his head away to gaze through darkness at the ceiling, wondering what he could possibly have said that had instigated such thought.

'It was just when you mentioned Australia,' sighed Nell, the tears gone now. 'That's where he was sent.'

Joe made a soft exclamation of discovery. 'Have you always known that?'

'No . . .' she hesitated, then admitted, 'I only found out about seven or eight years ago. I'm sorry, I should have told you, but I didn't want to stir things up. Do you mind me talking about it now?'

'No, don't be daft.' Joe stretched out a clammy hand to her.

She confessed then about her visit to Doctor Greenhow. 'I don't know what spurred me to do it. It was just on impulse – don't think I plotted behind your ba—'

'I don't,' emitted Joe's soft growl. 'I know you, you're not a plotter.'

'Anyway, it was all rather a waste of time and emotion,' continued Nell. 'It would have been hard enough to find William if he still lived in York, but to locate him on the other side of the world would be impossible.' She was weeping again, quietly.

'And would you like to?'

There was a flash of anger that Nell only just managed to rein in. *Of course I would, you fool,* she felt like screaming. But the one who lay alongside her was so kind and attentive, passing her his own handkerchief from the bedside table, that she merely said, 'I always promised myself I would. That was the one thing that kept me going through those terrible war years, that I'd see him again one day . . . but there's not much hope of that now.'

Joe crooned sympathy. 'You know if I had the money, I'd pay for you to go there?'

'Oh I know you would, dear.' She gripped his hand firmly now, thinking she did not deserve so generous a man, after her selfish thoughts.

After a slight gap, he began to hoist himself up. 'Sorry, I'll have to go for a slash. It's that bloody hosepipe . . .'

He was away a long time. Finally stumbling back, he apologised for disturbing her. She said he hadn't, she was wide awake. Joe emitted a grunt as he lay down beside her again.

'Feeling no better?'

'Oh, take no notice of me harping on about it – I've been so lucky to have Nina, I love her as if I'd given birth to her, truly I do. Most times I can cope, it's just some days . . .'

'I hate to think of you hurting.'

'No, I'm fine,' she assured Joe, and briefly laid her head on his bony shoulder. 'So long as I'm able to hold that picture of him in my mind, under the Australian sun, rounding up sheep, or boxing a kangaroo,' she gave a little laugh for this silliness, 'then I'll be satisfied. I'll have to be, there's nothing anyone can do.' She withdrew her head, for this night was much too sticky for contact.

'You never know, we might win the pools,' murmured Joe.

'You don't do the pools!' He had her chuckling again.

'Well, I'll make a point. And the moment my draws come up, you'll be on a plane.'

Nell gave sincere thanks, even though it would remain only a dream. Then, with a peck of each other's lips, they both settled down and tried their best to sleep.

22

Inasmuch as she had prophesied that, as an eight-year-old, Romy would forget about William, Nina had been right. At least, she had forgotten the details. But, obviously recalling the gist of that poignant saga, it being germane to her own situation, Romy had continued to raise the topic time and again over the years of her childhood, forcing Nell to repeat that painful episode of her life, until her granddaughter was old enough to retain it. By that time, Nell adjudged her old enough to be told every element of the tale, so that Romy might know how lucky she was not to have been removed from her natural mother. It was not her intention that the tale should break her heart.

'I promise, when I'm an adult, I'll do all I can to help you find him, Nana,' the thirteen-year-old vouched through her tears. 'Even if he is in Australia, I swear I'll find him.'

And Nell had blessed her, and said, 'I know you will,' when both of them knew that there was no earthly way that would ever be.

That year's Jubilee party in honour of the Queen was probably one of the last occasions in which her granddaughter would be content to participate, thought Nell, watching Romy and her friend trying to make out they were too adult to indulge in jelly and ice-cream, in their silvery shoes performing the latest gyration to the radio that someone had turned up full blast, so the partygoers could dance in the sunshine. How different it all was to the Coronation, and how those seated around her had changed. A wave of nostalgia washed aside the woman with the long blonde hair, allowing Nell briefly to see again the infant with whom she had fallen in love – still loved more than life, as well as feeling desperately sorry for the lone mother. If only Nina could find a good companion, like she herself had in Joe . . .

The face of the estate was much changed too. Over the years tenants had come and gone, various newcomers arriving to share a path with Nell and Joe, lasting for only a spell before moving on too. And then had come Mary.

Mary McCullough was of indeterminate age, though her wrinkles, and the fact that she had an adult daughter, would connote she was of a similar vintage to Joe. Whether she had ever been married was hard to say, for she wore a wedding ring though never mentioned a husband. If she had had any intentions on Joe by addressing him as Snakehips then it came to nothing, for he treated it as a joke and responded with nicknames of his own, most of them uncomplimentary. So Mary was forced to look elsewhere. She certainly went out a lot, dressed to the nines, always in beautifully applied make-up, and her legs still good enough to carry off those stiletto heels – though she was not one for keeping up with fashion, as portrayed in the tight silver perm, the bouffant skirts, and many layered net petticoats.

Despite her flamboyance there was an air of misery and loneliness about Mary McCullough. On a jaunt to the theatre, and to a pub afterwards to celebrate their silver wedding, Nell and Joe had caught sight of their elderly neighbour sitting on her own on a tall stool at the bar, hoping for a man to throw her a line, which none did in the whole time they were there. Touched by this incredibly pathetic sight, Nell thought of asking Joe to buy her a drink, which was very generous, for then she herself would have the indignity of Mary purloining her husband's attention for the rest of the night. In the end she and Joe had crept away before Mary saw them, so as not to embarrass her. But that pathetic sight was the reason Nell chose to put up with all manner of annoyance from Mary after that – the regular unannounced visits for early-morning tea, the scarlet lipstick she left on Nell's cups, her habit of revealing all her intimate complaints in front of Joe. This kind of behaviour had obviously been a great embarrassment to her daughter, who, in Nell's opinion, thought herself a cut above, and at her first opportunity had moved out to get married, and never were they or Mary to see her again.

They were certainly to hear of her, though: Mary never tired of boasting how well she had done for herself in America. But, blessed as she was with her own daughter, Nell felt it her duty to be kind, even though this only attracted more unwanted intimacy. But at least there was slight dividend, for one could always rely on Mary to report on the state of the supermarkets, the cheapest places to buy, or who had supplies of a certain commodity – which was vital in this awful decade of endless strikes and political unrest that stripped food from the shelves and imbued Nell with a sense of déjà vu, and of hopelessness, the feeling that life just kept picking her up and throwing her back to that same awful spot.

The strikes and shortages, and human nature, might always remain the same, but the face of society had changed out of all proportion to the way it had been in Nell's youth – and was even a stark contrast to Nina's. The eyebrows that had been raised in the sixties would surely lift off completely at today's sexual shenanigans: young women living quite openly with their boyfriends to make sure they were suited to each other before marriage. How Nina must fear for Romy, thought Nell, who shared this unspoken worry with Joe, now that their granddaughter was of a similar age to when her mother had given birth to her. There was little comparison – apart from in looks, both often mistaken for sisters rather than mother and daughter, with their willowy figures, long blonde hair and blue eyes – for the level-headed Romy appeared to be excelling at college, ploughing methodically through her heavy workload, no inducement required. And it was encouraging that she remained close to her grandparents, always finding time to drop in on them whilst still managing to gain As and Bs in most of her subjects, according to her proud mother.

Though with her A Levels in progress, Nina was taking no chances. 'We'll have to leave a bit earlier than usual, if you don't mind,' she told her parents, when she and Romy came on their regular Sunday visit. 'She's got a lot of revising to do.'

'She'll have no trouble, this brainbox,' said Joe, with a confident smile at Romy. 'But I'm glad to hear you're concentrating on school work, and not wasting your time with lads – you're not are you?' he said in afterthought.

Romy shook her head, but confided with a laugh, when she, her mother and her grandmother were in the kitchen making tea, 'I am, actually, but Mum said I hadn't to say anything to Grandad, he'd only worry.'

'Oh, and you're not concerned with worrying your nana?' Nell demanded of them both jokingly. 'What's his name then?'

'John.' To Nell's pleasure, Romy was to tell her all about him. Though, judging by the gleam in her eye, her granddaughter was besotted, and, when she had finished eulogising, Nell sought to issue a caution.

'You won't do anything silly, will you?' She saw the look that passed between Romy and her mother, and for a second had qualms, until Nina murmured:

'She's on the pill.'

'Oh . . .' Nell tried not to look shocked. 'Well, good for you, being sensible . . . still, I don't think we'll tell your grandad,' she uttered confidentially. 'He's a bit old-fashioned like that.'

Ignorant of female secrets, a happy Joe continued to boast of his granddaughter's prowess to anyone who would listen – more so than ever when, as he had forecast, Romy attained good results in her A levels and won a place at the university of her choice. But, 'What the hell are you going all the way up to haggis land for?' he demanded to know.

Nina put in a shrewd guess. 'To get as far away as possible from me.'

Romy laughed, and, by a slip of the tongue, informed her grandfather, 'That's where my boyfriend's applied for.'

The old face showed disbelief. 'I don't know! You shouldn't be bothering with boyfriends at your age – where did you meet him then?'

'When I did that stint on the Viking Dig.'

This fired her grandfather's memory, for the archaeological discovery had come via the demolition of the factory in Coppergate where he used to work, and he spoke for a few minutes about the sensational treasures unearthed. Then he made a joke. 'Tell him if he found that two bob I dropped under a machine in 1955 I won't ask for it back, so long as he's treating my granddaughter right.'

'Yes, he's lovely, Grandad.' The shining blue eyes told this was true.

'Well, don't be letting him take your mind off your studies, we need new blood to put this country right.' Then Joe glowed with pride. 'The first of our family to go to university! I don't know where you get your brains from – certainly none of us.'

'Speak for yourself!' objected Nina and Nell alike, though the latter voiced great faith in their granddaughter too.

Joe then handed over a twenty-pound note. 'Reward for your hard work.'

Romy thanked him. 'It'll go towards my car fund. Mum's bought me driving lessons.'

'It's for her eighteenth as well,' Nina joked quickly. 'She needn't think she'll be getting anything else.'

'I don't know! We had to wait till we were twenty-one, didn't we, Nell? And even then all we got was an apple, an orange and a lump of coal. Now they get two special birthdays.' With smiling face, Joe left the room.

With the old man gone, Nell displayed a more personal interest in her granddaughter. 'Couldn't bear to be without your boyfriend, eh? Aw, how romantic! What's his name again?'

'Steve.'

Nell filed this away, then said, 'Well, don't forget to take your pill whilst you're away. Much as I look forward to being a great-grandmother, I wouldn't like it to arrive too soon.'

Romy seemed not at all awkward, not like her mother, who wore a rather prudish expression, thought Nell. 'Don't worry, Nan, it'll be a long time yet,' she said with a laugh.

Later, when Joe had come back and was keeping Romy occupied, Nell whispered laughingly to her daughter, 'I nearly put my foot in it before, I thought his name was John.'

'It was.' muttered Nina. 'He was kicked into touch ages ago. There've been a few since him.'

Nell saw the disapproving look, but did not comment on it in case the subject, or Joe, should overhear. Instead, she spent a moment in fond reflection, listening to Romy and her grandfather tease each other, and finally said during a gap, 'We're certainly going to miss your little face popping in to see us – especially me. I don't know how I shall keep your grandfather fed without all those recipes you bring me.' Sharing Nell's love of cooking, over the years Romy had introduced some adventurous new meals to her grandparents' menu.

'If I come across anything nice I'll send it along with my letters,' Romy vouched.

'You what?' teased her mother. 'From what I know of students it'll be takeaway curries from now on.'

'For you, you mean,' retorted her daughter with a laugh, before adding to her grandparents, 'I'm counting on you two to look after this one. I shall expect regular reports of what she's getting up to whilest I'm away.'

But when all the joshing was over, there was the indisputable fact that the removal of Romy's cheery presence would leave a big hole in the lives of those who remained behind.

After all the excitement of Romy getting her place at university, in transporting their granddaughter there – Joe being the only one of them who could drive – Nell was feeling at a loose end on the Saturday following her granddaughter's departure, and suggested she and Joe visit Nina.

Joe threw back his head as if to sob. 'Please, can't I have one blasted Saturday in peace to watch a bit of sport?' Every day I have to get up an hour earlier than I'd like to, just to attend me lavatory requirements before that bloody Mary comes pestering. We've just got shot of our Romy – much as I love her – you've got Nina coming round for dinner tomorrow, can't you wait till then?'

'I just keep thinking of her sitting there all by herself and lonely . . .' But Nell showed sensitivity to her husband's needs too, saying as she packed a macrame bag, 'I'll go on my own.'

Though pacified, Joe thought he should ask. 'Do you want a lift?'

'No, the walk'll do me good.' Nell packed a macramé shopping bag with all her requirements. 'I won't bother ringing, she's bound to be in. Won't be long.'

'Take your time – and lock the door! I don't want Mary bloody McCullough creeping in unannounced . . .'

Nell did as he asked, then set off. Having a key to her daughter's flat in case of emergencies, just as Nina had one for her parents' house, she tapped politely as she entered. 'Only me, Neen!'

There was the scuffling of paper and the sound of rapid movement and a certain amount of clattering. Nina was coming out of her bedroom when her mother entered, slightly breathless and red-faced, but wearing a friendly smile. 'Now then! I wasn't expecting you.'

Nell hesitated before coming further into the room that, over a decade, had changed from the garish orange to a more subtle hue. 'Sorry, have I disturbed you?'

'No! I was just tidying up – the place is a tip, you'd think Romy was still here.' She began to clear notepads and library books from the sofa. 'Sit down, if you can find anywhere – do you want a cup of coffee or tea?'

Noting that her daughter had very deliberately shut the bedroom door behind her, Nell tried to listen for any sign of movement within. But, doubting very much that she had stumbled on a romantic assignation, she made a joke of it. 'You haven't got a man in there, have you?'

'Pur-lease!' Nina gave a slightly disgusted laugh, and went to the kitchenette.

Whilst she was gone, an inquisitive Nell snatched a look at the titles on the spines of the library books, but not wearing her glasses had difficulty. Hearing the rustle of clothing as Nina came back, and not wanting to be caught snooping, she was in the act of removing a paper bag from the macramé one.

'So, to what do I owe the honour?' asked her daughter.

'Oh, no particular purpose! I just thought you might be feeling a bit jittery now Greased Lightning's gone.'

'I am,' confessed Nina. 'That's why I'm keeping busy.'

'You'll soon get used to her not being here,' soothed Nell. 'You want to get yourself a little hobby.'

Nina glossed over this somewhat. 'I've enough to do

with work, thank you very much – what have you got in there?'

'These!' Nell finally managed to unwrap some china mementoes that commemorated the wedding of the Prince and Princess of Wales. 'They were reduced, I thought you might like one.'

Nina smiled in exasperation. 'Haven't you got enough Charles and Di souvenirs?' Her mother's sideboard was littered with china bells, plates, mugs and thimbles.

'I know, but they're such good quality I couldn't resist them – take your pick.'

Without much thought, Nina pointed to a little round pot, then said the tea should be brewed, and went to fetch it.

'Let it stand for a bit,' said Nell. 'Don't jiggle the teabag for five seconds in a mug like your daughter does and call it tea. I don't suppose you've made it in a pot? That's so idle.' Suddenly hit by how like her own mother she had begun to sound, she saw Nina's slight irritation and said, 'Sorry, but I get the distinct feeling I've interrupted something . . .'

'No, honestly.' Trying to be more amenable, Nina served up a couple of slices of Swiss roll. 'I was just cleaning up.' And to emphasise how relaxed her attitude, she went to add some biscuits to the plate.

Nell wasn't fooled, though, and was quite excited when she arrived home. 'I think Neen's doing an Open University course!' she told Joe, who was trying to watch the racing. 'She had all these obscure text books strewn about, and as soon as I came in she looked flustered and started clearing them up. I tried to see what subjects they were but I'd left my glasses behind –'

'What have I told you? Keep a special pair in your bag! You'll be going to the supermarket and serving me rat poison by mistake.'

'What makes you think it'll be a mistake?' Then Nell hunched her plump shoulders with anticipation. 'No, I think she's going for a degree, Joe!'

'How can you get a degree without GCEs, or whatever they call them these days?'

'I don't know – but she's definitely doing some course or other, I think one of the books was about psychology or psychiatry –'

'It could have been psittacosis. You didn't have your specs on.'

'Oh, there's no use telling you anything!'

He stopped hectoring then, seeing Nell had been pushed to her limits, and took his eyes off the TV to say genuinely, 'No, I'll be pleased for the lass if she gets it. Romy going off to university must have made her think – maybe she's jealous.'

'Why would you be jealous of your own child?' Nell despaired that he could have so little insight. 'Envious maybe . . .'

'Well that's what I meant. We'll just have to wait and see. I don't know why she was acting so guilty about it, though. Maybe she's scared of failing.'

Nell's mood darkened. 'Why would she fail? She's got the ability. It's more likely that she dreads being reminded of her decision not to stay on at school, made to look a fool for changing her mind.'

'I wouldn't do that!' Failing eyesight or no, Joe saw the way she was looking at him.

'Well, make sure you don't. And when she finally does get around to telling us she's passed, act surprised!'

Unsure how long an Open University degree course would take, but using Romy's progress as their yardstick, neither Nell nor Joe was to make any mention of their suspicions to Nina, content to bide their time until she voiced it herself.

Long before this, though, came a more personal milestone for Nell, who was about to draw her old-age pension.

'I can't believe I'm sleeping with a blasted pensioner,' teased Joe. 'There was me thinking I'd got meself some young dollybird.'

Nell smiled to herself. 'They didn't have dollybirds thirty years ago. Even if they had, I shouldn't have numbered amongst them.' And the years of cooking for her family, nibbling on anything they might leave, had stacked on more pounds – though gladly she still resembled an hourglass rather than a dumpling.

'Is that how long we've been wed, thirty years?'

'Well, twenty-eight, but what's two years between friends?'

But there were more sombre events going on that year, one of them being the dreadful clash in the Falklands. Having followed the triumphant battle every night from the safety of their armchairs. Nell thought she caught a glimpse of tears in her husband's eyes, and had to assume it had brought back memories of wartime, just as it had for her. He was never to openly shed them, though, for like most of his kind he kept all his experiences shut tightly away. Nell wondered what a man of his generation must really feel at the way the world was going, when God knew it was hard enough for her to cope with all the terrible savagery that occurred not just on the battlefield, but that was committed by the IRA on the streets of England. Not to mention all the casual violence one read about in the daily newspaper. It frightened him, she knew, that he might not be able to protect her, for he had fitted locks on all the windows, and never went out after dark now. No amount of locks, however, kept some people out.

'Here she is, Mary McCullough with an arse like a bullock.' Joe didn't look up from his newspaper as their neighbour came to plonk herself down amongst them.

'Have you seen it?' asked an animated Mary.

Nell deduced 'it' to be the latest outrage by the IRA, for Mary was never happier than when speaking of an atrocity. Nell herself had no desire to wallow. 'It's appalling, but no amount of discussion from us is going to help, so we just have to focus on the good things like little Prince William.' What a coincidence that the royal heir had been named after her son.

But Mary had short shrift for the monarchy, nor for dwelling on happy events. 'It's all right for you, Nell, looking on the bright side. You haven't had the kind of life I've had.'

'We've all had our trials, Mary.'

'Why, you've nowt to complain about,' scoffed Mary. 'You've got your family all round you.'

Well, that was partly true, admitted Nell, Mary's child might have been dead for the number of occasions she had contacted her mother. In contrast, over the time that Romy had been away at university, she had sent her grandmother half a dozen informative letters, whilst Mary had received nary the one, apart from a cursory scribble in a Christmas card.

'Anyway, as it happens I *do* have some good news.' Mary arranged her full skirts before making her important announcement. 'Rosemary and her husband are going to buy my house for me!'

'Good for them.' Joe sounded unimpressed as he studied racing form in his newspaper.

'I might have known Snakehips would crib,' she told Nell. 'Bet he'd jump at the opportunity to buy his.'

'With the neighbours I've got? You must be joking.'

Mary advised that the government was offering hundred per cent mortgages if he couldn't afford it. 'My Rosemary says anybody who doesn't buy must be mad. She says it'll be an investment.'

Joe eyed her cynically. 'Aye, for *her*. That's if she bothers to keep it in good repair. She's not likely to dash over from

America just to slap some putty on the windows. Nell and me'll have to sit and watch it crumbling – it'd bring the value of ours right down, and you wonder why I'm not bothering to waste my money?'

Mary started going on about America then, and how much better than England it was, further getting Joe's back up. Tired of listening to their sparring, Nell allowed her mind to drift to the faraway land that was home to her son, wondering too how Romy was progressing at university, and Nina with her Open University course . . .

Convinced that the latter was what occupied Nina these days, Nell allowed her to get on with it, and during the intervening years busied herself with daily chores, plus local bits of excitement. Struck by lightning, part of the Minster had been destroyed by fire. Mary had been stricken too, immobilised by two frozen shoulders and unable to even get herself to the lavatory – wasn't it a boon to have a nurse right next door? Nell, had previously suffered a very painful frozen shoulder of her own, and had gained no sympathy from Mary. Yet she harkened to her neighbour's beck and call for as long as she was needed, because that was the role life had carved for her.

If reward was not to come from Mary, then it eventually arrived in a different form. Cheered by the news that their granddaughter had won her degree, it was even better for Nell and Joe when she came round in person, along with her proud mother, that Saturday after tea. First comment, though, was for her hair, which had been fashioned into spikes and dyed bright cerise. 'Good God!' cackled Joe. 'What planet are you from?'

'That's my favourite colour,' put in Nell, replacing shock with diplomacy.

But Joe had no such tact. 'What do you want to go hacking at your lovely mane for?' he asked his granddaughter, but his manner was affectionate, and Romy gave an indulgent laugh as they exchanged hugs, especially as he so applauded her too. 'Never mind, you're a genius – by, we're that proud of you!'

'Oh yes, love, we are – congratulations!' An equally delighted Nell hugged her too, before Joe handed their granddaughter fifty pounds. Then she asked, 'What job do you have in mind, Rome?'

'She can be anything she wants with that under her belt,' grinned Joe, hoisting his trousers in that triumphant way old men had of emphasising a statement.

Romy gave a self-effacing laugh and said that everybody had a degree nowadays. All of a sudden she seemed to have lost the self-assured air of a woman, and to take the spotlight off herself, she put in, 'Did Mum tell you her fantastic news?'

'Er, thank you!' Nina held up her palm, as if to prevent more indiscretion; but too late, for her mother was keenly awaiting an answer. 'It's nothing much, I was going to tell you, if milady hadn't stuck her oar in.'

Nell looked at Joe, the glint in her eyes saying this was the degree she had prophesied. Ready to bellow congratulations, her jaw dropped as their daughter added: 'I'm having a book published, that's all.'

Nell and Joe looked at each other again, their expressions pleased but confused. 'What kind of a book?'

'Oh, just a novel.'

Romy bent over and chortled in glee at her grandparents' shock. 'Isn't it intergalactic – my mother, the author!'

'But . . . well, I never did!' an astonished Nell finally managed to blurt, Joe similarly inarticulate. 'We were expecting you to say you'd been studying for a degree too!'

It was Nina's turn to be nonplussed. 'What would I want with a bloody degree – no offence to you, love,' she was swift to tell Romy, so as not to bedim the occasion.

'But what about all those books I've been seeing in your

flat?' asked a flabbergasted Nell. 'I thought you were studying for an Open University course . . .'

All became clear now. 'Ah, bloody nosey parker!' Nina threw back her head and laughed at her parents' total surprise. 'You've been biting your tongue for all these years, dying to know, but not daring to ask – well, now you do!' Throwing a loaded smile at the graduate, she explained to the others, 'I was keeping this as Romy's day, but never mind, it's her fault for letting the cat out of the bag.'

'Well, goodness me, congratulations!' enthused Nell, launching forth to plant a smacking kiss on her daughter's cheek, just as she had done for Romy. It seemed to her that Nina was eleven years old again, instead of in her thirties, bashful under this approval from her mother, yet awaiting that more important word from her father's chair.

'Aye, well done!' Joe rose again, and, with stiff movements and an awkward smile, came to pat her shoulder. 'So, what kind of book is it?'

'As I said, a novel.'

'But what's it about?' pestered Nell, and in the same breath, 'Have you read it, Romy?'

'No, she's kept it well hidden!' The daughter's laughing eyes accused her mother, whilst Nell remained flummoxed.

'But why did you keep it a secret, even when you knew it was going to be published?'

'I just wanted to see your expressions when I presented you with a copy.' Nina chuckled at the ones her parents wore now.

'Blow me . . .' said Joe, shaking his head. 'When did you manage to write it then?'

'On an evening, and weekends.'

'So *that*'s what you were up to when you said you had work to do!' Nell was beside herself with excitement, and hugged the fledgling author to her bosom, shaking her about. 'Oh, well done you – am I allowed to tell Aunty Beat?' Permitted to reveal the closely guarded secret, she asked excitedly, 'When do we get to read it?'

'When it's printed.' Nina retained her nonchalant carapace, though it was obvious she was elated, for her eyes shone. 'It's not out till next year. You'll all just have to wait.'

'Oh, just give a little hint of what it's about!' Nell was greedy for details, until Joe gave her a playful shove and warned:

'She's told you to wait and see!'

'Well, I'm just so excited and proud!'

'You can see the lass doesn't want us mithering her,' scolded Joe. 'Let her enjoy it in her own quiet way.' And he turned his attention once more on Romy, asking all manner of questions about her degree, and her life at university, finally saying how good it was to have her back.

'Sorry, I'm only here for the weekend, Grandad.' Romy looked deeply apologetic.

'I thought you'd be moving back in with your mam . . .' Joe looked in turn deflated then concerned. 'You're not staying in Scotland?'

'No, I'm getting a flat with a friend in Leeds – so I won't be too far away.'

Nell was disappointed too, but had seen the way Romy had hesitated over the word friend, and guessed she must be moving in with Steve, so did not ask why Leeds.

'A Leeds Loiner, is she, your friend?' said Joe, only the women noticing Romy's little smirk, as she gave a nod. 'Well, make sure you find a decent area. I don't want to be getting roughed up when I come to visit.'

'We will – and once I get a job I can afford a car, so I'll be able to get over and see you.'

'It'll never be often enough for me, though. Eh, we had some lovely times when you used to live with us . . .' Rather flattened, he sought to make himself feel better by focusing on the good news. 'Well, never mind, let's have a drink to celebrate your achievement,' he told his granddaughter, and rose to get a bottle of sherry from the sideboard.

'And Nina's,' his wife had to remind him as she set out the glasses.

'Ooh, aye, Neen too!' said Joe, hoisting his glass at their daughter. 'Here's wishing you success.'

'In all you do,' added Nell, joining the toast.

Once emptied, the glasses were topped up a few times during the course of the evening, Romy and Nina remaining till nine.

As they left, with Joe heaping more congratulations on his granddaughter, Nell diverted Nina's attention and whispered, 'So, she's moving in with Steve then?'

'Hayden,' muttered Nina, and rolled her eyes, as if to say, *another*.

'You don't approve,' deduced Nell.

'Well, do you?' retorted her daughter.

'It's what they do these days.' Age had taught Nell to be philosophical, though with all those dreadful television adverts about Aids with which they were bombarded, she could not help but worry. She had played it down in front of Joe, who would have been even more concerned had he known of all these sexual partners. 'As long as she's happy . . .'

'He'd have a lot more to say.' Nina referred to her father, who was showing Romy around his large, well-kept garden.

'Yes, well, your father's old-fashioned.'

'You always take things in your stride, don't you?' It was said in the way of an insult.

'You have to, with your children,' said Nell.

'You don't! I was as mad as hell when she told me. She's only known him five minutes.'

'Well, let's give them the benefit of the doubt,' was the grandmother's suggestion.

'Don't tell me dad, I'll never hear the last of it.'

Nell said she would discourage Joe from visiting. Then she sought to deliver the same amount of praise her husband was, again, heaping on their granddaughter. 'Oh, and I'm so thrilled about your book! It's such a splendid accomplishment, love, many, many congratulations – and to you, too, Romy,' she called as both left.

But once inside, Nell was to rebuke Joe for his unsentimental treatment of Nina. 'You should have made more of it, Joe.'

He looked taken aback. 'You performed enough song and dance for both of us! She made it plain she doesn't want attention . . .'

'There's none so blind as those who will not see,' Nell quoted at him.

'How does that refer to me?'

'Think about it,' sighed Nell.

23

Apparently Joe did think about it, during the months that were to pass, because he put a cross on the calendar to mark the publication date of their daughter's novel, and was also to make an expedient request to the author. 'About your book – will you be able to get it at cost price?'

Her chair being near the phone, Nell was able to hear the voice at the other end of the receiver, and thought it sounded peeved: 'You don't need to pay, you'll be getting one free!'

'Aye, but I'm thinking of the relatives,' Joe said into the phone. 'If you can get it at cost, order me seventeen copies. So it'll give you a good start.' And he glanced at Nell as if to say, Look, I'm doing what you said.

As much as she could not fathom Joe's reluctance to praise outright, Nell was even more perplexed by Nina's embarrassment upon finally handing over a personal copy to each of her parents.

That is, until she read it. After only a couple of pages her heart was to sink – not because it was bad, on the contrary it was exceedingly moving – yet the autobiographical element left her dismayed at how Joe would react.

Stealing a look between turning her own pages, she saw him fully immersed in his copy. Did he recognise himself, as the father who craved a son instead of the daughter he had?

No more than a hundred and fifty pages, the book was to be devoured by both in a single day. The first to complete it, Nell crept off to make a start on tea, leaving her husband still engrossed. Not until her re-entry some time later was she to break the silence.

'Ah, I didn't want to disturb you . . . tea's almost ready.' She studied her husband, who had been very quiet since turning the final page a moment ago, and, not knowing what to say, she jabbered, 'I feel awful reading it so quickly when it took such a long time and so much effort went into it! It was just so gripping . . .'

'Yes, very, very interesting,' affirmed Joe, without the rancour she had expected, just a deeply pensive expression on his face.

She was not to get anything more out of him than that, nor was she to request it, nor even to discuss it with their daughter, the subject being far too sensitive – and Nell did wonder what must be going through Nina's mind, now that publication day was finally upon them. What would she say if anyone asked outright if the characters were based on someone she knew?

That there had been not the slightest recrimination from Joe made Nell wonder if, in fact, he had even seen himself as the inspiration for Nina's book. But that was Joe, he'd bumble on about all manner of political frippery, but he'd rarely let out about anything deeper. At any rate, his manners were impeccable at the book launch, which was held in one of the best hotels in York, the author's father saying how big an honour it was to be invited, convincing everyone he was enjoying himself, chatting to those from the strange world of publishing, even though Nell knew it was not his cup of tea, nor hers either. Perhaps best for her and Joe was that, on top of witnessing Nina's success, they got to see their granddaughter again, Romy bringing along Hayden, whom neither of them had met before. He was very good looking in a roguish kind of way, and charming too. Perhaps a little too charming, thought Nell, watching him trying to impress the star author, but kept her thoughts to herself, lest she mar Nina's day.

Joe didn't have a very high opinion of him either, Nell was to find out afterwards when he drove her home – though not until after they had exhausted talk about Romy herself.

'Well, I'm glad to see she's got rid of that puce haircut! I was dreading her showing us up in front of them London folks. So . . . is she living with fella me lad then?'

Nell turned to him in slight surprise.

'Aye, I thought so,' nodded Joe. 'You all think I'm a silly old bugger.'

'No we don't, love,' she rushed to mollify. 'The reason we didn't tell you was because we didn't want you to be upset.'

'They told you, though.' He sounded hurt.

'Well . . .' Not knowing what to say, for anything would be insulting, Nell shrugged it off, to ask, 'What did you think to him?'

'Bit of a wide-boy if you ask me,' growled Joe.

His wife offered a nod of agreement, and turned her eyes to the traffic. 'He'd better not hurt her . . .'

For now, though, the spotlight was to remain on Nina, Joe maintaining the effort he had shown on the afternoon of the launch, and phoning the author a day later to exclaim, 'Your book's in the Press!'

'Don't sound so surprised,' came the faint reply. 'It's not exactly *Time* magazine, is it? If you can't expect support from your local newspaper there's not much hope for anybody.'

'No, but it has a good write-up,' complimented Joe.

'That's not bad for somebody who never got to grammar school. You should be proud of yourself.'

Tell her *you're* proud, Nell wanted to urge.

Though this he failed to do – even after a great deal of publicity and favourable critique had seen Nina's book ascend the bestseller charts. And Nell felt their daughter was in some part to blame, for to any praise that was offered, Nina made out she could not have cared less, responding in her usual unenthusiastic tone:

'I suppose I'll have everybody tapping me up for cash now, thinking I'm worth millions.'

Nell, who was thoroughly delighted for her, asked, 'And would it be cheeky to ask, have you made a lot of money?'

'I've seen nothing yet. Only a thousand advance.'

'A thousand?' Joe shrieked. 'For *that*?'

'Joe!' Nell was almost as offended as Nina.

The rheumy eyes looked momentarily blank, then Joe realised how he had come across. 'No, I didn't mean it that way! I meant, well, it's only a thin book, isn't it. It's very good, though. You've really surprised us.'

'Not me,' said Nell. 'I always knew she had it in her.' Then she rose with dignity. 'I'll put the kettle on.'

'I'll do it, Mam.' Even though Nell said it was all right, Nina followed her into the kitchen as Joe shambled off upstairs.

'I don't think he ever really expected it to sell more than the seventeen copies he handed round to relatives,' she muttered with a fake laugh.

Nell tried to make light of it too. 'I know it doesn't sound like it, but he is really proud of you. And on top of that, it lets him get one up on Mary when she's wittering about how wonderful her daughter has it in America. We were in the paper shop the other day, looking to see if they had your book – which they did, I'm glad to say, and you should have heard your father: "My daughter wrote that!" It's ingenious how he manages to wangle it into the most unlikely conversation – I think if somebody was talking to him about quantum physics he could even slip it in.' Nell shook her head in amusement as she sluiced hot water around the teapot. 'You ought to hear him going round telling everyone . . .'

Everyone except me, Nina's expression said. But her lips said something completely different. 'I want to ask you something, Mam, but I don't want you to be sad.'

Nell turned anxious then, and put down the teapot to devote all her attention to what Nina had to say. But when her daughter appeared reluctant to impart her question, she prompted, 'Well, we won't know unless you spit it out.'

'All right, here goes.' Nina took a deep breath and looked her in the eye. 'Would you like to go to Australia and look for your son?'

It took only a second for Nell to burst into tears.

Nina swore. 'I knew I should have kept me gob shut!'

Her mother waved aside any apology, hardly able to speak. 'No,' she finally managed to say, sniffing and wiping her eyes, 'I'm just so touched that you've thought of me above everything else.'

'Of course I have, you're my mam.'

'Oh, let me give you a hug!' Nell enveloped Nina in an embrace, totally overwhelmed by her gesture. 'Most people in your position would treat themselves first –'

'Well, I did buy a pair of earrings,' admitted Nina.

'– but your first thought was to do this for me,' wept Nell, her dark head pressed to the blonde one. 'I can't tell you what that means.'

'You don't have to.' Still trapped in her arms, Nina gave an affectionate series of pats to the much plumper frame. 'If somebody'd forced me to give up Romy, I'd move heaven and earth to get her back.'

'But I can't,' said Nell, all of a sudden pulling away, and her eyes pouring regret into the other's face. 'It might hurt your father. I know he wouldn't stop me, but I couldn't leave him on his own . . .'

'Well, I was going to pay for both of you,' chuckled Nina.

'Ooh, I can't let you blow your hard-earned money!' Nell looked horrified. 'No, no, I won't hear of it!' She gripped her daughter's arms and looked right into her face. 'God bless you, darling, for thinking of me. Please don't think I'm being ungrateful, but it would be a total waste of time. Australia's a massive country, and I haven't the slightest idea to which part of it he went. So, you spend that money on yourself, or your daughter – help her buy that car so we can see more of her. Thank you a thousand times for the offer, but we'll say no more about it – and not a word of this to your father.'

No matter how her would-be benefactress might reason, Nell stubbornly refused to accept, and so Nina put the money to other use. By the time that year was out she had begun to earn royalties – enough for a deposit on a house. Joe nagged at her, of course, for putting it to this purpose, repeating his adage that she would be out on her car if she couldn't keep up the mortgage repayments. Nell schooled him into being more civil when they received an invitation to come to tea at their daughter's new abode – which he could not fail to compliment, for both house and garden had been impeccably kept by the previous owner. The peaceful district was conducive to artistic talent too, as Nell was to point out.

'So, do you think you'll write another book, Neen?'

Nina showed more patience than if her father had asked this question. 'I already have – at least I'm halfway through. I'm hoping after the next lot of royalties I'll be able to hand my notice in and write full time.'

Joe looked worried. 'Jack it in? You've just got a mortgage!'

'Which I'll be able to pay off much quicker if I concentrate on my writing.'

Joe remained sceptical. 'You never know what's around the corner . . .'

'Listen to him,' sighed Nell, and wished Nina good luck with her chosen path. 'And how's Romy doing with her career?' Their granddaughter had decided to go in for accountancy.

'Great,' said Nina. 'So you don't have to worry about me money, Dad, I'll have my own personal accountant.'

'Eh, I don't know, who would have thought it . . .' Joe noticed then that the house had a granny flat, and joked to his wife, 'Is that for us when we get infirm?'

'It bloody is not,' parried Nina in similar vein, before supplying the true reason she had bought this particular house. 'I hoped Romy might want to come home if she had separate accommodation, but it's not to be . . .'

'Still with me laddo, is she?' enquired Joe, receiving a less than enthusiastic nod, before Nina summoned them to view the interior.

Whilst Nell proceeded to comment on the décor, Joe made a beeline for something else.

'Is this one of them personal computers?' He had donned his glasses to peruse it more closely.

Nina moved to stand beside him at the desk. 'Yes – I can't tell you how much easier it is than a typewriter.'

'How much did it cost?' asked Joe. And when she told him, he screamed in disbelief.

'Well, look at it this way: I'm saving on about fifteen gallons of Tippex a week, so I'll soon recoup the layout. I can't type to save my life,' added Nina.

'But you worked on a keyboard for years at Rowntrees!' said Joe.

'Those machines were mainly numerical, though – look, I'll show you what I mean about this.' She turned on the Amstrad, pulled out a chair and sat down, then proceeded to demonstrate, inserting discs, her fingers going clickety-click over the keys and writing appearing on the screen.

It was all beyond Nell, but Joe was fascinated. 'Fancy! If you could do that in real life, correct all your mistakes with the click of a button . . .' Looking over her shoulder, Nina saw that her elderly father was dying to touch the keys, and bade him take her place.

'At least I know what to buy him for his birthday,' she muttered to Nell, as they left him to it.

Joe could hardly believe it when he unwrapped the large box that had come from his daughter.

'Well, you're always bloody moaning that you can't get in the garden at this time of year,' said Nina, in her usual offhand manner. 'So I thought this might spare our lugs – makes a change from socks, anyway.'

Her father was like a child then in his eagerness to remove it from its packing, a mountain of cardboard and polystyrene growing on the sitting-room carpet, and once Nina had helped him to set it up, it was impossible to tear him away. In fact, he was to spend not just his birthday, but the entire winter playing on it, only emerging to mow his lawn in the spring, and doing the minimum amount of pruning and weeding before hurrying back to his desk in the spare bedroom.

'I don't know what on earth he finds to type on it,' Nell was to say to Nina, the two of them enjoying one of their regular weekly trips to town, made possible by Joe's addiction. 'It certainly takes something to get him away from his garden. He's never off the blessed thing – not that I'm complaining if it means he doesn't want to come into town with us. I hate going with your father, he always races round the shops, gets what he wants, then goes home. He refuses to browse.' That's what she and Nina were doing at the moment. 'Ooh, there's a display of your new book!' Her face lit up at the window display, and her voice was proud as she recited from the placard: 'Exclusive, Nina Kilmaster will be signing copies of her latest book on –'

'All right, Mam, keep it down.' With a gentle nudge, Nina moved her on.

Nell gave a disappointed laugh. 'It's a good thing you've got others to sing your praises.'

Then, at her daughter's self-deprecating shrug, she looked closer, to perceive an underlying concern. 'You don't seem very excited . . .'

'No, well,' Nina puffed out her cheeks, 'I wasn't going to tell you, but I've nobody else to unload it on . . . That bastard our Romy lives with, he's been seeing somebody else.'

'I *knew* he was that type the minute I laid eyes on him!' Nell felt a stab of pain, everything else around her disappearing as she asked anxiously of Nina, 'Will she be coming home, then?'

The other shook her head. 'She says they're working it out – I'd work it out all right, I'd plunge a bloody screwdriver into his chest. I've begged her to move into the granny flat, I've told her it doesn't have to be permanent, just a bolthole till she finds another place of her own. But she says she loves him – and she says he loves her and doesn't want to finish.'

Nell felt sad and angry. 'I can't understand how anybody can say they love a person then betray them like that.'

'Well, that's just it, Mam, he doesn't love her! I told her, he'll do it again, but she won't have it.'

'Should I write to her?' asked the concerned grandmother. 'I don't mean to interfere, I just mean to let her know we're here if she wants us.'

Nina shrugged, and said she was at liberty to try.

In the end, though, Nell decided to stay out of it, and to hope Romy would come to the right decision by herself – though she did confide in Joe, which was a huge mistake, for he immediately resolved to smash Hayden's face in, just the threat causing his blood pressure to soar. That the matter was eventually resolved by the young couple was of no comfort to either of them, or Nina, for Romy was subsequently to present them with an even bigger worry.

'They're only trying for a baby!' Nina announced to her mother, who had demanded regular postings. 'Now then, how bloody stupid is that? No mention of marriage – it's only a piece of paper! That's his words, of course.'

Unfazed by the eccentricities of the modern world, Nell was dismayed for reasons other than her future great-grandchild being born out of wedlock, but said she supposed they should be thankful there was no stigma attached any more.

Nina delivered an outburst. 'Sod stigma! I'm bothered about my grandchild having *that* for a father!' A look at her mother's face told her that Nell harboured this fear too. 'The daft little bugger, thinking this'll make him mend his ways. When I think of what you and me both went through – you most of all, Mam, treated like vermin, and there's her on about giving birth on purpose without a care in the world!'

'We mustn't be hard on her,' advised Nell. 'You and me least of all. Romy'll need our support, and we'll love it when it comes.'

Nina was grim. 'Aye, well, she isn't having one yet, thank God, and let's hope she doesn't – with him at any rate!'

Recalling the time of Romy's birth, the angry scenes, the tears and recriminations, both agreed that it was better not to worry Joe until there was something to worry about, for it mattered not that times had changed when parts of society remained stuck in the past. There would be hell on, said Nina, if Dad heard. But Nina was to be regularly buttonholed by a worried Nell about the state of Romy's health, both of them relieved and thankful when there was no pregnancy to report.

'There must be a guardian angel looking after us,' opined Nell, after a year had gone by, and then another.

‘Or else Hayden’s firing blanks,’ said Nina, which indeed would have been her mother’s preferred option too.

But there was nothing either of them could do by worrying. They would all have to get on with their lives. Conversely, though, after more years had taken them into a new decade, the pair began to worry for Romy’s sake, that there might be some gynaecological reason why she had not yet conceived – though medical opinion said not, and, after all, she was only twenty-six.

‘You hurt for them, though, don’t you?’ murmured Nell, with an expression of deep feeling, her daughter’s nod conveying empathy. ‘I’m certainly glad I’m not her age again. Not just because of the awful world we live in now, all the violence and drugs and whatnot, but I shouldn’t like to be faced with all these choices they have today.’ She gazed into mid-air and hesitated for a moment. ‘I never asked you at the time, Neen, it was all still a bit raw . . . but did you ever consider what you’d have done if she’d been conceived just a few years later when the abortion law was relaxed?’

The one at her side shuddered. ‘I’m glad I didn’t have the choice, Mam, really I am. I know back then I said if there’d been a magic pill I would have taken it, but that was early on, when I was terrified . . .’ She shook her head firmly. ‘I’ve every sympathy with a woman who finds out she’s carrying a deformed baby, it would be an horrendous decision – even then, I don’t know if I could live with myself. But it’s impossible to hypothesise once you’ve actually met the baby who might have been destroyed, if you see what I mean. What I do know is,’ she said with certainty, and not a little condemnation, ‘I can’t stand the way some of them go about it today, as if they’re just cleaning out their cupboards.’

‘Me neither,’ agreed Nell. ‘But I can’t help thinking what I would have done about William if the choice had been open to me. When you’re so alone and frightened, you’re not right in the head, you might snatch at any way out that's offered . . .'

'Not you,' said Nina with great conviction.

Nell shook her head. 'No, you're probably right. Whatever the case, I don't know which would be less difficult to bear, having a baby ripped from one's uterus or one's arms.'

Nina closed her eyes against the image, and when she opened them again a look of compassion had taken over her face. She said nothing more, and soon she was to depart, but there was a thoughtfulness about her attitude as she went.

A short time after this conversation, Joe was to say to his wife, when they were settled in for the night, the doors and windows all locked against an increasingly hostile world, 'Why don't you go and find him?'

Slightly absent-minded, Nell had been unravelling a length of knitting, having just discovered a mistake, and was picking up stitches with her needle. 'Who?'

'The one you're always thinking about.'

The knitting was dropped to her lap, his wife looking at him sharply to demand, 'Has Nina been talking to you?'

A few more wrinkles appeared in Joe's brow, his milky eyes projecting confusion. 'Should she have?'

Nell shook her greying head, and got on with her knitting, mumbling, 'Just wondered.'

Joe turned back to the screen, ostensibly watching the colourful underwater display on the Great Barrier Reef. 'If you mean, did she tell me she offered to pay for your trip all them years ago, and you turned her down, then yes.'

Nell's head shot up again, her voice annoyed. 'I asked her not to say anything!'

'Because you thought it'd inconvenience me,' divined Joe, turning to look at her, his eyes asking, am I not right?

She became less obdurate, her gentle brown eyes

searching his face as she asked, 'If I were to take her up on it, would you come with me?'

'At nigh on eighty-three? Oh, I don't think I could manage it.' He looked downcast.

'That's what I thought, so I'm not going either,' said Nell, looking down again.

Then he uttered a chesty laugh. 'You silly bugger! If you'd bothered to ask we could have gone years ago!' And, rising, he pulled two airline tickets from his trouser pocket and presented them.

'That little tinker!' Nell shot to her feet, looking cross. 'Has she bought those?' But her complaint petered out in a smile of gratitude as she clutched Joe's arthritic fingers and gushed with emotion, 'Oh, isn't she the best daughter . . .'

'Aye, she is that.' He chuckled with her, wrapping his arms round his wife and holding her for a while, before Nell put him aside and said:

'Just wait till I see her!'

But, of course, after jocular rebuke there was to be only gratitude for the daughter who had made this possible, and excited conversation about their expedition to the other side of the world. Although Nell confessed to being so nervous she had hardly been able to sleep since she had found out, not just because of the enormous implications, but also because of the flight. 'We've never flown in our lives, and here we are on one of the longest trips one can make! And what's going to happen if bills arrive whilst we're away, we've never been gone longer than a fortnight – and the garden'll revert to jungle. Why, I don't even know what clothes to take . . .'

'That's why I bought the tickets well in advance,' a smiling Nina indulged the catalogue of worries, 'so you've plenty of time to plan for all eventualities – you'll need visas, by the way.'

'We'll need to renew our passports too,' Nell warned Joe. 'We haven't used them for years.'

'It'll be coming into autumn over there,' informed Nina. 'I thought I'd better book it for then, we don't want to kill me dad off with the heat.'

'Check them tickets, Nell,' kidded Joe. 'I'll bet the little bugger hasn't booked a return flight for me.'

'Damn!' Nina thumped the air as if foiled. 'I knew he'd twig.' But she cracked a grin.

'It's all very well, and I'm so grateful, Neen, for this chance of finding William – but I've no idea where to start.' Nell's hands were now clasped to her breast, her eyes worried. 'It could turn out to be a wild goose chase, I don't even know where to begin looking – you shouldn't have spent all this money, it could all be wasted.'

'Will you shut up about the bloody money! I've got more than I know what to do with.'

'Ooh, get her!' laughed Joe. 'Haven't you heard the saying pride comes before a fall?'

'She's a right to be proud with all those books under her belt,' defended Nell. 'It's only by reason of her success that we can go.'

With a chastened Joe falling quiet, Nina said, 'Right, I thought about hiring a researcher over there, but he'd need something to go on, so we'll have to do some digging over here first. I've got this neighbour who keeps boring me to death with her family tree, in which I've not the slightest interest, but she does seem to know how to go about tracing people. She says there have to be immigration records, or whatever, they wouldn't just let people in willy-nilly –'

'You mean like they do here?' mocked her father.

A mordant nod summed up Nina's own feelings on this matter, but she was soon back on track. 'You know all William's different names, Mam, let's poke around a bit, see what we can find.'

'But where?' Nell dared not allow herself to become over confident. 'It's too late now for Doctor Greenhow to be of help, I saw his obituary in the paper. That big house that used to be the orphanage was turned into offices years ago. Although I suppose it's good that there's less need of such institutions these days . . .' finished Nell, thinking of those unfortunate waifs.

'Yes, but that doesn't do you any good,' said Nina. 'Can't you think of anywhere else we can start?'

'Would his birth certificate be any good?' helped Joe.

'No, how could it?' returned Nina.

Dismissed so cavalierly, Joe shrugged and, with a curt tug of his fawn trousers, lowered himself into his armchair. 'Ah well, you're more up on these things. Maybe you should be going on this trip with your mother, you'd be more help, and you are the one who's paying . . .'

'She wants you to go,' pointed out Nina, then turned to see that Nell's face had turned ashen. 'What is it, Mam? Do you feel ill? Shall I get you a glass of water?'

'Why haven't I thought about it before in all these years?' breathed Nell, her eyes staring at them both in dismay. 'I don't even know if his birth was registered under his proper name!' She felt sick at the thought that there might be no record of her being his mother. Yes, it would be illegal, but the way she had been treated by the doctor and her parents, people she had trusted, they could be guilty of anything. Her voice and eyes portrayed how unbearably awful this would be.

'Well, there's only one way to find out,' said her daughter. 'The register office.'

Nell became visibly afraid then. 'I'm not saying it's going to help with the search – and we might need an appointment . . .'

'Mam, nobody's going to arrest you for wanting to find what's rightfully yours. All you have to do is go up to the counter, say you'd like a copy of your son's birth certificate, and give them the date. Don't worry, I'll be there with you to sort them out if there's any quibble.'

It was no coincidence that Romy turned up for the visit to the register office too, having been in on the surprise, and telling Nell that she had taken a week's holiday to devote to this search. 'I always promised I'd help you find him, Nan!' Though it was more in the hope that this involvement would take her mind off her own fixation over the lack of a baby.

'I know you did, love,' said Nell, allowing herself to be guided between them along the splendid Georgian parade of Bootham. 'But I don't think any of us took it seriously – I can't believe I'm actually going to Australia to look for him!'

'And the search starts here!' came Nina's melodramatic utterance upon reaching the register office, and she led the way inside.

'Take that worried look off your face, Nan,' said Romy, linking arms. 'Everything's going to be all right.'

And it was. After the tiniest interrogation, armed with the details Nell had given her, the superintendent registrar went off to search the indices, soon to return with a copy of the red certificate. All as simple as that. With shaking hands, Nell held the document before her, with an immediate sense of victory. William exists. I exist, as his mother.

Watching that expression of joy, and sharing it, Nina saw her mother's mood turn in an instant to dejection, and wondered what had caused the metamorphosis. Having paid the fee, she and her daughter each took one of Nell's arms, steering her through the foyer and back to the main road and its fumes.

'They've left the father's name blank.' An angry mutter joined the noise of traffic. 'He *did* have a father! His name was William too. William Kelly.'

'I know, Mam.' Nina tried to give comfort, Romy too.

'But *he* won't!' objected Nell. 'What if he has a copy of this, what will he think of me?'

Nina could not immediately answer, but Romy could. 'You're his mum, Nan, he'll just be glad to have you.'

Nell felt this was too simplistic. 'Just because you're well-adjusted doesn't mean he will be. He was born at a time when to have no father was unthinkable –'

'Well, it wasn't exactly a picnic for me having no dad,' laughed Romy, with an apologetic glance at her mother. 'But I never once blamed Mum. I love her. And your son'll love you.'

'Have you ever thought of looking for your father?' Nell saw Nina's lips purse, but she made no apology for asking.

Romy shook her head, and spoke truthfully. 'I felt curious, yes, but I never felt the need to pursue it, given we'd be strangers.'

'That's what I'm worried about,' agreed her grandmother, a disturbed look in her eye.

Then they went home to discuss where they could go from here.

After the Christmas intervention, their search resumed. Bent on solving the mystery, Nina wondered whether there would be any embarkation records at the Public Record Office in London, and, having found out that there were, proposed this as their next port of call.

Again, Joe was to remain behind. 'You've got Cagney and Lacey to help,' he said to his wife. 'I'll only get in the way.'

Feeling slightly piqued at this show of martyrdom, Nell had become so caught up in her investigations that she had no intention of allowing this to stop her. Though she did make a great fuss of him prior to departure, and left a home-cooked meal that only required a few microwaves, and plenty of his favourite cakes, and made a point of responding merrily to Joe, who waved from the bottom of his garden as the train carrying his wife sped past.

Alas, it turned out to be a wasted journey, for the records did not cover the right dates, and any others that might have helped them were not open for public scrutiny.

Nina apologised for this, but said there had been no real way of knowing for such amateurs. 'It's the orphanage that'll provide the key,' she decided as they were on the train home, all rather despondent. 'Yes, I know we can't get at their records, either,' she forestalled her mother's interruption. 'But that's not to say we can't find out from one of the other orphans who was there at the same time as William. I should have thought of this before. We'll put an ad in the press, asking for anyone who was at The Willows orphanage in the 1950s to contact you – no, better still! Put, "*anyone who knows the whereabouts of William Morgan, who was at The Willows orphanage between blah de blah, and so on – REWARD.*"'

'Hang on a minute,' said Nell. 'Who'll provide this reward – not you, you've spent enough.'

'It doesn't have to be a fortune,' put in Romy, who was seated on the other side of the table, travelling backwards. 'Just the mention of cash should do the trick.'

'Even so . . .'

'Mam, I'd be willing to pay anything if it got your lad back for you,' vouched Nina.

'Lad?' Nell smiled fondly at this description. 'He's nearly fifty – not that I think of him like that, he'll always be a baby in my mind.' Then she saw a wistful expression spring to Romy's face, and she leaned over to grasp her arm, all of them knowing what she meant as she said encouragingly, 'Don't you worry, love, it'll happen in time.'

As the train raced on, Nell was to adopt an air of reminiscence, and stared out of the dirty window as if seeing her own lifetime streak past, the good bits and the terrible. 'Gosh, haven't we had interesting lives,' she murmured. And how different things could have been for all of them, the others were to murmur in response. Whilst not wanting to vilify Joe, Nell pointed out that it might well have been Romy whom they were looking for now.

'I'd go to the ends of the earth to find her as well.' Nina made no move to touch her daughter, but sent a caress across the table with the warmth of her voice and her eyes.

But she had never allowed her child to be taken in the first place, Nell pointed out, in a tone that held self-blame. 'I wish I'd fought more . . .'

Nina said briskly then, 'Anyway, back to this reward thing. We'll get all sorts of nutters, I suppose, but there's bound to be someone who can give us a lead.'

And Nell agreed that this was the way to go.

Joe seemed awfully glad to see her when she got back, but his first words were not to ask how she had gone on but to show her the renewed passports that had arrived whilst she had been gone.

'Look at these bloody little red things they've sent us!' He brandished the offending items at her. 'What happened to our blue ones?'

'Can't he even wait till I've got in the house?' Nell sighed to Romy and Nina, who had brought her home. Too tired and disappointed from her wasted journey to display similar agitation, she gave him short shrift. 'We're a part of Europe now.'

'I'm not, I'm British, and I want a passport that says so exclusively, not with European Community printed first!'

'Well, we'll have to lump it, Joe.' She wished he would shut up.

Romy read her face, and announced cheerily, 'You won't even need a passport soon, Grandad – think how great that'll be, we can go anywhere we like!'

'Aye, that works both ways! You won't think it's so great when we're overrun – as if we're not crowded enough already!'

But Romy only chuckled at him, and nudged her mother

as he continued with his grievances. 'Six bloody years of my life I gave to defending this island – not that it's an island any more with that damn tunnel – and it wasn't so very long ago we were inundated with that Buy British campaign –'

'A lot's changed in fifteen years.' Nell's sighs grew heavier.

'– and now we're not even allowed to have it at the top of our passports!'

'Yes, well, I share your disillusion!' declared his wife. 'But as long as they take us where we want to go, I'll be satisfied – now, if you don't mind, we'd like a cup of tea.'

'Oh, sorry, love, here's me going on in me usual pisspotical fashion . . . didn't you have any luck?' At his daughter's shake of head, he too showed disappointment. 'Ah dear, sit down, all of you, I'll make your tea.'

In serving them with this, Joe was to learn of Nina's idea about the advertisement, and, like his daughter, he projected faith that a reward would do the trick.

Leaving its execution to Nina, Nell was to watch out every night for the advert to appear in print. And, finally, there it was, giving her phone number as the one to contact, for either she or Joe were always there to answer it.

Optimistic though Joe might be, not even he had expected it to reap such quick harvest. Within a few hours of the press coming through his door, he was pouncing on the phone that was next to his chair, saying – 'Hang on, it's my wife you want!' – then handing it to Nell with a look of anticipation. And within another few moments, she had learned to which part of Australia her son had gone.

'Well?' demanded Joe, when she had put the receiver down and was just sitting there looking bowled over.

Nell took a deep breath. 'She can't be absolutely certain, and she doesn't know the exact town, so she refused the reward in case she's wrong – but she's certain we were talking about the same William. She thinks he went to Queensland.'

'To Queensland we go then!' declared Joe.

Nell felt exhilarated, but there was a problem. 'Those tickets are for Melbourne.'

'That doesn't matter! If we can't get them changed we'll just get on another plane once we get there.'

Whilst they were still talking, Nell voicing her happiness and inability to believe such a piece of luck, they saw Mary tottering down their shared path and Joe supposed they would have to tell her. They had not done so yet for fear she would spoil it for them by comparisons with America. It would be 'Ugh, what do you want to go there for? Why don't you go to America . . .'

But no. After only a moment of surprise over their announcement, Mary said, 'I've a sister who lives there!'

'I might have known you would have,' retorted Joe. 'Can't even have exclusive rights to a blasted holiday without you muscling in.'

'I'll get her some presents for you to take for me!'

'You cheeky bugger,' said Joe. 'It's not just like nipping to Scarborough, you know!'

'I'll cut your grass for you,' came her swift bribe.

'I know you! You'll be sat painting your talons whilst my garden looks like summat out of Sleeping Beauty.' However, he grudgingly said that they would take a few things. 'But don't go buying her anything heavy, we've enough to carry.'

However, Mary was to return a few hours later with a carrier laden with all manner of gifts.

'The brass neck of her,' Joe grumbled to his wife, as he pretended to stagger under the burden. 'Pop in on our Millie, she says – and you say yes like a meek little lamb!'

'Well, I know she's a nuisance,' acceded Nell, 'but it's not just to save money she's doing it, it's that she wants to feel a bit closer to her sister, and by using us in proxy she will.'

Joe shook his head. 'Women and their intuition – it's all

right for you volunteering, you're not the one who'll be doing the lumping about – nor driving miles out of our way.'

'Are you sure you'll be up to it?' cautioned Nell. 'In a strange country . . .'

'As long as they drive on the proper side, I'll be fine,' said Joe, who was still physically and mentally fit enough to drive quite regularly. 'I'm quite looking forward to it, you know.'

'Oh, me too!' Nell clutched her heart, which had become quite jittery at the adventure of it all. Then she said in a little voice, 'I just hope we find him, Joe. It's a big country.'

'Don't worry, lass,' said her kind champion. 'We will.'

Due to fly out from Manchester on a Thursday morning in March, the night before they were to travel, whilst his wife went about the room re-checking visas and worrying over things she might have forgotten to pack, Joe was viewing the progress of their troops in the Gulf. 'I wonder if those lads have got the sweets you sent them yet.'

'Probably – have you set the alarm for five?' she suddenly remembered to ask during her restless peregrinations.

'I will when we go to bed,' Joe was replying in calm manner, when Nell, in stepping backwards, suddenly tripped over the bag of gifts left by Mary, and landed hard on her bottom. 'You dozy bugger.' He turned to eye her on the floor. 'What are you doing down there?'

Laughing at herself, but half annoyed with him as she rubbed her painful buttock, she reached out her hand. 'Don't just sit there! Get a crane . . .' And, using the arm of a chair, along with belated assistance from her husband, both of them grunting and groaning, she managed to haul herself from the carpet to a chair.

'And they call me the silly old fool,' teased Joe with a glint in his eye as he flopped back in his chair and resumed his viewing. 'Come and watch this with me. Stop rushing about and pretending you're twenty again.'

'You'd be the first to cop it if I was!' she threatened. 'One of us has to pack, and it won't be you.'

'I laid me stuff out on the bed, what more do you want?'

'You could at least make me a cup of tea whilst I'm doing all the donkey work,' accused Nell, but despite being harassed she was tingling with excitement at the prospect of going to look for William. 'Now then, what the devil was I going to do before I tripped over Mary's things?' As much as she racked her brain, she could not remember. 'Oh, isn't it infuriating getting old?'

'You? You'll never be old,' flattered Joe. 'But sit down for a while, it'll come to you.'

'I haven't got time to be sitting down!' She was far too preoccupied with the thought that she might finally be going to meet her son.

'I think I'll have a drop of brandy,' Joe suddenly decided. 'I'm feeling a bit queasy. Why don't you have one?'

Nell refused, saying she was silly enough without alcohol, and carried on with what she had been doing, leaving her husband to pour his own drink.

Eventually, it was time to go to bed. Knowing there was no way she would sleep, Nell followed his advice and downed the milk and whisky he had poured for her.

This must have worked, for the next thing she knew was that the alarm clock was beeping frantically.

'Joe!' With a start, Nell elbowed him, for the alarm was on his side of the bed. 'Joe!' she bawled at him this time, and, when it continued to beep, with a grunt of annoyance she launched herself over his immobile form to make a grab for it.

But, in doing so, she felt that his shoulder was stone cold, and so was the rest of him. No amount of shaking would help.

Her own heart pounding, whilst Joe's stood still, she fell on him and wept.

24

Mary, too, had wept over the death of her sparring partner, though Nell suspected she was crying as much from the disappointment at being handed back the carrier of gifts for her sister. Romy was heartbroken, of course, and Beata devastated to be the last one of the Kilmaster children left. And what must poor Nina be feeling with her father gone and nothing resolved?

None of them, though, could match Nell's guilt. And if any of them had heard her on that last night, refusing to sit down with him because she didn't have the time, not even caring to pour him a last drink, not even waking when he had died beside her . . . they would have despised her as much as she despised herself. Well, she had plenty of time to do whatever she needed to now. But no Joe to share it with.

Between bouts of grief, as they helped her organise the funeral, Nell issued wan regret for the loss of all that money on the unused tickets. Nina could have told her not to be so bloody stupid, what did cash matter compared to the loss of her father? But she didn't, she just hugged her, crying her poor little eyes out.

The worst part was not the funeral, though. Nor was it the manner of Joe's death, for it had been a blessing that he had not lingered as he had so dreaded, but had gone in a flash. No, it was after they had first taken him away, and Nell had entered the bathroom and seen all his little things spread out on the windowsill: toothbrush, shaver, comb, all ready to use . . . How could anyone find poignancy in a tube of pile cream? Nell did. The grief flowed in a volcanic rush that spluttered all over the basin, her body racked with sobs as she thought of the way she had treated him.

And her culpability was for so many reasons, not just because she had no time for him on his final night, but that she had made little time for him during their early years; had married him out of selfishness, neither knowing nor caring how deeply this good, kind, often infuriating man had loved her. It didn't seem to count how much she had grown to love him. The fact that she had treated him so abominably overrode anything that had followed.

Nina had invited her to move in, or at least to stay a few nights until she felt able to cope, but Nell said no, it was best to get on with it, for she would have to get used to living alone. Unable even to touch that cold and empty stretch of mattress, she took to sleeping in the back room. Yet here were more reminders. It had been Joe's little office, housing his computer. Even though she covered it with a sheet, pretending to herself that it was to keep out the dust, it was still there to haunt her.

Hence, when Nina bypassed her own terrible grief to issue tender sentiment, saying, 'I just wish there was something I could do for you, Mam . . .'

Nell was quickly to reply: 'There is. I've been sorting your father's things out for the charity shop – best to get it over with I thought. I hate thinking of anybody else going round wearing his clothes, but if it does some poor devil a bit of good . . . But I don't know what to do with his computer, it's just sitting there, doing nothing.' Except keeping her awake, with thoughts of its owner. 'Would Romy like it?'

'She's got one, Mam,' said Nina gently, her eyes still glazed with tears. 'But thanks for the thought – I'll put it out in the shed till I can arrange to have it taken away for you.'

Immediately going to do this, she added that she would check there was nothing important on the floppy disks first. Her mother settled back in listless fashion, thanking God for daytime television, but though she sat and watched, her brain hardly registered what was on.

Nina was to be upstairs for quite a time. Nell heard the dreadful racket of the printer, and finally the sound of tearing paper, but could not be bothered to shout and ask what she was doing. Her daughter was to make several trips up and down the stairs, before finally going into the kitchen to make an umpteenth pot of tea. Above the rumble of boiling water, Nell heard the sound of a nose being blown. Then Nina reappeared at the living-room doorway.

Her eyes appeared to have shed fresh tears, for they were bloodshot. She was holding a wad of paper. 'You know you were always wondering what Dad was doing up there?'

Without saying more, she came to lay the sheaf gently on her mother's lap.

A dazed Nell put on her glasses, then gave a little sound as she looked down at the title page – *My Life, by Joseph Fitzroy Kilmaster* – and she looked up to murmur, 'Have you read it, Neen?'

Her daughter nodded and turned about, appearing that she might burst into tears if she stayed. 'I'll pour you some tea, then leave you in peace.' And, after placing the mug within her mother's reach, she gave her a kiss and left, saying she would ring later.

Joe's life gripped between her hands, Nell wondered if it were right for her to invade his innermost thoughts. He had never mentioned to his wife what he was doing. But why, then, had he written them down? Perhaps because they were too painful, too emotional to voice, even to her. Joe had been one of the old school.

Tentatively lifting the first page, she saw that he had set his memoirs out in chapters – a proper book. Had he secretly yearned to have it published, to bolster a sense of self-worth? The account of his childhood was brief, but emotive, his mother's death taking just one line. She had delivered a goodnight kiss, and in the morning was gone. He had hardly been given a chance to know her, yet it was obvious to Nell that this maternal influence had been so strong that it coloured his whole life – this, and the resentment Joe had felt over his brother Clem's preferential treatment, his father's remarriage, and the cruelty of his stepmother. What had been touched on only briefly during Nell and Joe's years of marriage was laid out in much more depth here, for her to weep over, to see why Joe was the way he was. Or, had been.

Perhaps the most moving confession of all was his account of being a soldier, not simply the way he felt about being unable to live up to his father's reputation, about which she already knew, but his experience of battle. Now she was to learn why he rarely watched a war film. It was because, wrote Joe, they could not possibly depict it as it really was. How could they translate a man's horror at seeing a child being crushed under a tank? Not just seeing it, but reliving it all his life. How could the finest actor portray the love Joe had felt for his comrades, and the dreadfulness of seeing them blown apart? The guilt he felt at being alive when they were dead?

Sad and aghast at what this ordinary man had gone through, Nell was compelled to read on to the end, including the bits about Grette, and then Nina – who was, said Joe, the best daughter a man could have, and he was very, *very* proud of her achievements. Yes, perhaps it was a little contrived, but he had said it, which made Nell so thankful, she wished Joe was there so she could wrap her arms round his bony frame and kiss him.

But he wasn't there.

Even when the initial shock and the grief had eased, and she was able to speak of him without crying, it did not mean that Nell's period of mourning was over, nor that her guilt was any the less. With the long days that followed Joe's demise, Nell was quite thankful for Mary, whose grumbles helped to break up the hours, though she could not help being cross that her neighbour would persist in harping on about the aborted trip to Australia.

'All those presents for our Millie,' she wailed. 'I keep seeing them there on the sideboard and I just keep thinking of Snakehips . . .'

'You could always post them!' Nell was finally to snap one day, when Nina had popped in at the same time, and Mary was dropping heavy hints about another trip down under. 'I won't be going, so get over it. Now for God's sake change the record.'

Then, after Mary had slunk home, Nina had started on her, saying, 'I could always come with you, you know, when you feel up to going . . .'

'I've told you, I don't want to go!' Asked to explain her change of heart, Nell had a hard time putting it into words, finally blurting the fear that even if she were to travel all those thousands of miles, there was no guarantee of success. 'I've come to think I'm not destined to find him, Neen.' Her face was anguished, but resigned. 'That's my only explanation – your father dying, William being transported to Australia – I make him sound like a convict, don't I? But you know what I mean, it all seems to be a conspiracy to keep us apart. Perhaps I have to accept that that's why he was taken away from me, because it wasn't meant to be, because I wasn't a suitable mother . . .'

'Don't talk bloody daft!' spat Nina, but was too choked

with emotion to say that Nell had been a wonderful mother to her.

'No, please, don't keep on about it! I don't even want to think of it.' Because it made her think of her final night with Joe, and how she had been too busy fantasising over her son even to pour her husband a drink. She didn't deserve to find him. 'You put your money to better use. If I do decide to go I've still got cash in the bank.' But she couldn't see herself going in the foreseeable future. Not with this pall of guilt hanging over her.

Nina yielded with a teary sigh. 'All right, I'll say no more.'

Nell made a grab for her hand then. 'I'm sorry for throwing your kindness back in your face.'

Nina said she did not think that at all, and rushed to give her mother a little hug. After which they sat and cogitated for a while, till Nell sought to ask, had she found a good home for her father's computer, to be told that it had gone to the skip. She was appalled at the waste.

'Well, it's obsolete, Mam.' Nina gave an apologetic shrug. 'Technology's moving so quickly, things get left behind.'

'I know the feeling.' Nell had become very disillusioned with modern Britain.

Nina cocked her face in sympathy and said, 'Won't you reconsider about moving in with me? To the granny flat, I mean, then you could still have your independence.'

'I'm sixty-eight, not a crone!' But for a second it appeared that her mother might accept, until Nell decided with gratitude in her voice, 'No . . . I don't think so, thanks, love. I'll stay in my own little house.'

'You won't be saying that when you have to mow the lawn every week!' warned Nina, but was not going to argue with the one who had suddenly become so emotionally fragile.

As if that first Christmas without Joe wasn't bad enough, they had to put up with Hayden, whom Nina suspected was still giving Romy the run-around, but as Romy would not hear a bad word against him, they all had to be polite at the dinner table, for her sake. Somehow, Nell managed to get through it, and once the echo of other people's 'Auld Lang Syne' had died away, she resolved to try and make a life for herself without her dear companion. They all missed Joe like mad, of course – including Beata, who felt very susceptible these days at being the last one in the slot – but they were able to reminisce about him on the anniversary of his death without causing too much hurt to each other. And, one way or another, Nell was to carry on down the years, though she doubted she would have been able to do so without Nina and Romy to give her life meaning. If only she could wave a magic wand for them, for as much as Nina's career remained on a high, she could not be truly contented whilst her daughter was unfulfilled.

Then, one memorable day, just as Nell had grown used to having Hayden around, rogue that he might be, an excited Nina phoned up to say that Romy was leaving him! He had cheated on her for the last time. She sounded triumphant and relieved that her daughter was rid of the man who had hurt her, as was Nell, yet on the other hand, 'It's awful, the poor little bugger's heartbroken.'

'She must be . . .' Nell's eyes welled up. 'Wasting the best part of her youth on that sod, when she could have been with someone who made her happy . . .' She pondered for a moment, before emitting brightly, 'Well, at least she can get on with her life. What now, then, for our golden girl?'

'She's packing up and moving in with a friend – a girl friend, I hasten to say. I asked her to come and live with me, but she likes it where she works and doesn't want to have to commute.'

'But, she'll still be coming at Christmas?'

'Ooh yes.' Nina was obviously looking forward to it. 'She's got to, she promised to cook dinner for us!'

Nell had a thought. 'Would it be all right if I invite Mary too?'

'If you must. Romy'll have to come and cook for us at your place, though, I can't be doing with moaning Mary round here, I might need to make a quick getaway if she gets on my wick – oh God, it's going to be such a great Christmas without Hayden!'

Not so good for Romy, though, who seemed to be working on automatic pilot as she went about her grandmother's small kitchen concocting the festive dinner. Try as everyone might, it was all a little underwhelming, but hopefully the next one would be better.

It took quite a few months, but Romy was eventually to regain her natural *joie de vivre*, and to bring it with her when she came to stay for a week with her grandmother in the summer – which Nell enjoyed immensely, stating it was like the old days again, with the two of them side by side in the kitchen.

She was, then, all the more shocked when another end-of-year birthday get-together in honour of Romy brought an extraordinary setback in her appearance. It looked as if she had not eaten for months. Her face smiled as she opened the gifts Nell had bought her, but there was a worrying gauntness about it. Not daring to ask directly, for fear of learning that Hayden might be once more on the scene, Nell waited until the subject was out of the way, before murmuring to Nina, 'Romy's looking awfully thin – don't tell me she's been on a diet?'

The reply was rather shirty, but then Nina often was. 'Don't ask me. She's got a life of her own, as she's quick to tell me. I don't know what the hell she gets up to these days – there's nothing medically wrong with her, if that's what you're worried about.'

Nell had left it alone at the time, not wanting to spoil the get-together – especially when Romy was putting such a brave face on whatever it was – and hoping she would have put the weight back on when next they met.

This was to be several weeks into the new year. Catching sight of her granddaughter's car pulling up, Nell rose expectantly and moved closer to the window to receive the usual merry wave, but there was no merriness today, just a malnourished, sad-looking wraith coming down the path.

Her heart sank, but she did her best to hide it, making the usual fuss of Romy when she came through the door, immediately switching on the electric kettle, and setting out mugs and plates.

But, 'Don't cut into that cake for me, Nana.' Romy's hand shot out, her face tense.

Nell put down the cake-tin lid abruptly, and demanded, 'What's wrong, love?'

'Nothing!'

'Yes there is, you're so thin . . .'

'I'm always thin.'

'Not that thin! I can see your bones through that jumper.' Through the cream lamb's wool sweater, Romy's shoulder blades jutted like wings, her brown slim-flitting trousers hanging like a bag. 'Come on, whatever it is I'd like to know.' Gentle of face, Nell went back to making the tea.

A look of resignation displaced the one of innocence, and Romy sighed. 'I'm in a bit of a quandary, Nan.' She rubbed her hands over her emaciated face, and stared out of the rear window as an express train thundered past.

'You're not back with Hayden?'

'As if.' Romy gave a little laugh, then turned serious again. 'No, I've fallen in love with somebody, but he's married.'

'Oh dear . . .' Nell tapped her spoon on the side of the teapot, then replaced the lid, her expression vague. 'That would be a quandary. Do you want a Kit Kat with your tea?'

'No thanks.' Romy helped her carry the cups into a

living room that was much changed from her childhood, the boxed-in fireplace having been completely removed now, and a gas fire fitted to the wall. She and her grandmother sat together on a new red sofa.

Romy found it difficult to begin. Nell remained patient, then gave her a helping hand. 'What's his name?'

'Patrick.'

'And where did you meet him?'

'Work. I haven't just met him. We've worked in the same building for years, but we've just been talking a lot more recently. I don't know why I told him about Hayden, it just seemed to slip out naturally.' She saw a cloud pass over her grandmother's face. 'That's what my mother thinks.'

Nell looked at her. 'What?'

'The same as you: that he's taking advantage of me, sees me as vulnerable. But he's not like that.'

Nell relaxed her look of concern. 'Well, you know him, love, I don't.'

Romy looked at her feet. 'I feel dreadful, knowing what it's like to be cheated on, I'd never do that to somebody else – we haven't done anything, we haven't even kissed, nor been out together. But I know he feels the same as I do. He's told me. He's not happy in his marriage, but he doesn't want to start anything with me until he sorts things out with his wife. He wants to do the right thing by everybody.'

'When you say everybody, do you mean he has children?'

Romy nodded, her lank curtain of hair trembling and her face steeped in guilt. 'One – a little boy. I just can't get my head around this – I never dreamed I'd be in such a situation. I keep trying to fight it, but I can't think of anyone but Patrick, and how he'd feel if I were to reject him. He's so unhappy, and so am I.' Quietly, she wept.

Nell allowed her to, pulling a handful of tissues from a

box and handing them over. Romy used one after the other to blot up the smears of mascara, constantly blowing her nose and sniffing.

'Mum isn't talking to me. Well, she is, but only just.'

'How old is the boy?'

'Five. Mum went mad when I told her. "Why did he have a child with her if he was so bloody miserable!"' After mimicking Nina, she directed watery eyes at her grandmother. 'But it's like when I was with Hayden. I knew in my heart he wasn't right for me – I mean, I loved him, and Patrick loves his wife, but not in the same way – and, of course, you're not miserable all the time because you wouldn't be able to endure such an existence. Of course you enjoy a joke and a laugh with them, and have sex, and generally get on with the life you've made yourself. But then somebody comes along to show you what it could be like . . .'

Nell gave a sage nod.

And immediately Romy said, 'See, I knew you'd understand, Nana.'

Nell did not really understand at all, but she was willing to listen.

'Mum's never been madly, totally in love – oh, I'm not blaming her for the way I was conceived.' She forestalled any reproach. 'As you'd say yourself, these things happen – boy, do they happen – but because she's never been in love, she doesn't know what it's capable of doing to you. I didn't purposely set out to wreck a family! I hate anyone who has affairs behind their partner's back, I know what it feels like to be betrayed. I'd never deliberately inflict that on another woman, let alone a child.' Fresh tears washed away the last trace of mascara, and she reached for more tissues. 'I just don't know what to do. I feel I can't live without him. When I said that to Mum she went up in the air – *don't be so bloody melodramatic!* But you must know what it's like, Nana?'

Yes, I know what it's like. Nell too had tears in her eyes, but contained them. Age tended to stultify passion of all types; one didn't sob and rant like one had as a girl.

But in Romy it was still aflame. 'You can't eat, you can't sleep . . .'

Nell acted as go-between. 'Your mum's only mad because she's worried about you. She's made you the centre of her life. You have to see it from her point of view.'

'I do! I hate upsetting her, but it's as if somebody else is pulling the strings: the more I try to go on the right path, the more something hauls me back. I've thought about handing in my notice so we don't see each other, but it wouldn't solve anything . . . and I can't bring myself to do it. Mum thinks I'm lying about not sleeping with him –'

'Oh, I don't think she would . . .'

'I can sort of understand her being suspicious. I mean, it sounds so daft. When you think "love affair" you imagine Scarlet O'Hara and Rhett Butler. We've done no more than hold hands . . . But I've never felt closer to anyone. I've told him just about everything about myself, and he's told me all about his life, right from being a baby. We've been spending our lunch hour together for the past four months. But it's not long enough – it goes just like that.' She clicked her fingers, except they did not click, but skidded off each other with a sound that was as dull as her next comment. 'I hate going home. I just live for nine o' clock, when I'll see him again – and when I do see him, every time feels like the first time. He's got this lovely smiley face that wraps you up – oh shit, Mum's here!' She shrank in her seat like a child caught out as Nina came striding up the path.

Apprehension reigned, as they both waited for her to enter.

'I knew I'd find you here!' Nina looked furious.

'Hello to you too,' said a calmer Nell.

'Hello, Mam – I warned you not to go bothering your

nana,' she scolded Romy, from whose bloated face oozed more tears. 'But no, you won't be bloody told!'

'Neen, sit down and take the weight off your mouth,' sighed Nell. 'Let me get you a cup of tea . . .'

'I can get it!' An annoyed Nina swivelled and went to the kitchen, returning with a mug, though she hardly took a sip before laying into her daughter again. 'All you've done is upset yet another person, your nana'll be worried sick now – won't you, Mam?'

'I'm concerned, naturally,' said Nell in reasonable tone, 'but she hasn't done it deliberately to hurt anybod—'

'She wouldn't have done it if her grandad was alive!'

Nell felt the same, a little let down. But, 'There's no good us going off about it, we can't make her fall out of love.'

Nina snorted. 'Bloody men!'

Romy stood up to her then. 'Before you say any more, it is not Patrick's fault. It's nobody's fault. I don't need you bending my ear, I want somebody to give me advice on what to do, that's why I came here because I know I'll get sense out Nana. I'm trying to do the right thing.'

'I know . . .' Nina quietened down at last. 'I just get so mad when I think you're being taken advantage of.'

The trio were silent for a few moments. Nina looked at the end of her tether, as she gulped from her mug and stared into space. Then her whole demeanour swerved, and she directed a look of genuine compassion at her child. 'Will you come on holiday with me?'

'To get me away, you mean?'

'To lend you the breathing space to get your act together,' pleaded Nina. 'You can't think clearly while you're still in the middle of it all, we need to get you right away – and God knows, I can't write a word while I'm worrying about you. You know in your heart it's not right, love. But . . .' She took a breath, and her tone changed to one that was half-beaten, 'if you still feel the same way when you come back, then I'll support your decision, whatever it is.'

Romy looked grateful, but sick at the same time. 'All right then. I don't know how I'll bear to be parted from him, but I'll try and explain to him . . .'

'Good.' Nina looked relieved, and a little bit guilty. 'Because I've done a very silly thing. I rang your boss.' She quickly poured oil on her daughter's look of outrage. 'Not about the affair. I just told him you were on the verge of a breakdown and you needed to get away for as long as he'd allow.'

'Aw, no – Mam, I could kill you!'

'Well, what was I meant to do? You're driving me loony – as if I'm not worried enough about this one!' She indicated her elderly mother, turning to Nell and adding in businesslike fashion, 'So while we're at it, you can pack your bags and all!'

'Why, where am I going?'

'Australia – we all are. I'm going to sort you buggers out once and for all. Romy's going to mull over the drastic step of breaking up a family, and you're going to look for that son of yours.'

Nell looked startled. 'I've –'

'Mam, you're going!' Nina jabbed an authoritative finger. 'I'm not hearing any arguments. I'll be paying for everything and doing all the arrangements – give me your passport now, I'll need it to get you another visa.' She rose herself and went to grab it from the bureau. 'If I pay for special delivery we should be able to do it within a few days, before either of you can chicken out.'

The pair of them bamboozled, all Nell and Romy could do was give a despairing laugh at each other.

'Well, as Aunty Beat would say,' quoted Nell, 'that's us told!'

There was not so much excitement as last time, for Nell could not bring herself to believe that the trip would actually happen. And as for Romy's affair, try as she might to be modern and liberal thinking, Nell could not so lightly dismiss her granddaughter's contribution to the break-up of a marriage. After the others had gone home, the first thing she did was to ring her sister-in-law, ostensibly to let her know about the coming trip, but also to speak of her disappointment at Romy's fall from grace.

'I don't know, Killie,' her voice was sad, 'they seem to do whatever they like these days, and blow the consequences. Joe would be horrified.'

There was barely a pause from the other end. 'Well, people don't always do what you want them to do,' murmured Beata. 'Maybe it's better to live your life the way you see fit, instead of always pleasing others.'

'Well that's good, coming from you!' Nell laughed into the receiver. 'You who'd run to somebody's aid at the drop of a hat, who'd put everybody else's comfort above your own.' She leaned back in her chair with a knowing grin. 'I bet you'd do exactly the same again, if you had your life over.'

'Nay, I wouldn't.' Beata's voice was resolute. 'I wouldn't stand aside and let somebody else marry the man I loved. My word no, I'd fight for him. Today's generation might have their failings, but they certainly know what they want, and they do their damnedest to get it.'

Nell exhaled in wholehearted agreement. 'If only I'd been more like Nina, determined to keep her baby . . .'

Beata was quick to change tack. 'They were different times. Spotty. Nobody went against their parents.'

Nell murmured endorsement. 'I suppose so . . . I didn't mean to sound resentful about the young ones doing as they pleased, Beat. Romy didn't choose to break up a family, and it breaks my heart to see her fretting like this . . .'

'Well, I'm sure it'll work its way out, one way or another,' decreed the sensible voice at the other end. 'So, Australia, eh? Are you all packed?'

Ten minutes were spent in trivial discussion about what

to take and how it would be autumn over there. Then Beata said, 'Well, I don't think I'll manage to get and see you before you go, but I'll say a little prayer that you find that lad of yours . . .'

'Bless you, Killie – and we'll get together when I come back.'

'I hope everything goes well, and you all enjoy your holiday. Give my love to Neen and Romy . . .'

At this juncture, Nell became aware of Mary's curly bleached head poking around her door, which made her a little annoyed. Issuing warm thanks to Beata, and saying they would come and see her when they got back, she hung up.

'You're going to Australia again?'

Nell sighed at the look of bright anticipation, and held out her hand. 'Yes – go and fetch your blasted bag of presents, Mary!' But she was smiling when she said it.

25

The few foreign trips Nell had taken had been by ferry, and even that was when she had been much younger. Thank God for a trusty companion on either side to protect her. Just the airport was a nightmare, with all the trundling of luggage, the policemen with guns, the snaking queues, and all the rigmarole of passport control, finally to emerge the other side feeling utterly bewildered and with a twenty-four-hour flight still ahead.

'What a blasted bun-fight,' grumbled Nell, manipulating her ample hips around all the human obstacles in her way, as they looked for their seats. 'It's a good job we like each other, isn't it? Does it matter if we swap round? I'll need to get to the loo more often than you two, so I'd better have the aisle seat.' There was an awkward reshuffle, following which she continued to grouse about being elbowed in the head by those who were cramming belongings into the overhead locker. 'My God, what's he stuffing in there, a three-piece suite?'

'I thought I was meant to be the intolerant one?' jibed Nina. 'What happened to your sunny nature – did me dad bequeath his grumpiness in his will?'

'Is there any wonder I'm bad-tempered?' demanded her mother. 'What idiot expects a woman in her seventies to contort herself into a seat for a five-year-old?'

'Maybe the idiot who paid for the flights.' Nina gave a

sideways laugh at Romy – who was trying to put on a brave face, though was obviously torn at having to leave her sweetheart.

Nell grabbed her daughter's wrist in a gesture of pacification then, said 'Oh, I'm sorry, Neen, I wasn't being ungrateful . . .' But Nina only smiled, and agreed that for three thousand pounds one might expect a more comfortable ride than on a hopper bus.

Settling back, Nell experimented with buttons, trying to gain a more comfortable position from her seat, until the steward came hurrying up and returned it to the correct position for take-off. She gripped the arms of her seat in preparation, as the plane inched away from the departure gate and was to continue at this tortoise pace along a runway. 'Is he going to wheel it all the way to Brisbane? I thought this thing had wings?' Then the sudden roar of the jet engines had her grappling for Nina's hand. Despite her daughter's reassurance, she was to remain queasy as the aircraft raced down the tarmac and lifted them into the air.

Even when the plane levelled out, Nell took a good look around to check on the condition of the other passengers, and, more importantly, the crew. Then, with no one seeming perturbed, she began to relax and even enjoy herself – especially when the trolley came round with drinks. Nina saw her rooting about in her purse and told her to put it away. But Nell insisted, 'No, I'll get these! You've paid for everything else.' Informed that the food and drink was free, she exclaimed, 'Is it really? Oh, if your father were here he'd be in his element.' She was pretty happy herself, and was to tuck into everything that was put before her during the following hours.

There were films too, though not really up an elderly lady's street, and Nell took to studying her fellow travellers, wondering at their backgrounds. The man across the aisle was even porkier than herself; she didn't know how they'd managed to squeeze him into his seat, and she was relieved she wasn't sitting next to him. It was barely possible to catch sight of his wife on the far side of him, but when Nell did, she diagnosed a thyroid problem. When the man in front scratched his head she noticed he had a ganglion on the back on his hand. There was a baby right at the front. The poor little thing had screamed blue murder on take-off, obviously annoying certain people – including Nina. It was crying again now. She smiled in sympathy at its mother, who wandered up and down the aisle, rocking it in an attempt to keep it quiet. In fact, she studied everyone who came down the aisle. There was one particular stewardess who interested Nell, a beautiful girl in immaculate make-up, who beamed widely as she came along the rows offering in a bright voice, 'Tea or coffee! Tea or coffee!' But her friendliness was rather mechanical, and when she looked at you her gaze rested on your forehead. Nell was determined to engage her eye before the flight was out.

In an attempt to cheer up Romy, whose mind was somewhere beyond the clouds, she leaned over Nina to ask had she bought anything new for her trip. Romy gave half-hearted reply, but thought enough of her grandmother to return the compliment.

'Ooh yes, I got quite a few nice things,' replied Nell brightly, 'I saw these nice little cardies in Marks –'

'*Little?*' blurted Nina, and eyed Nell's large bust with great exaggeration in the hope of making her daughter laugh, which she did.

Nell grinned too, pleased to be the butt of their jokes if it helped lift the mood. 'Be quiet, you, or I shall buy myself a swimming cossie in Brisbane and show you up.'

The conversation eventually petering out, Nell sat back for a while, before breaking in again to voice puzzlement over how quickly it had become dark. Nina explained that it was because they were travelling forward in time. Then there was another meal, and another film, and a procession back and forth to the toilets. Nell complained how little space there was inside the latter. 'And when you go for a widdle nothing comes out. It must be the pressure in the cabin.'

Even with the aid of earplugs, masks, and herbal tranquillisers it was difficult to get any decent sleep. The passenger across the aisle began to snore. With a sigh, Nell pulled up her mask and glared at him, though little good this did. Allowing him to rumble for about five minutes, she could stand it no more and leaned across to jab him awake. But it only worked for a while before his head began to loll, and he set off snoring again. 'Have you heard him?' she prodded Nina to ask. 'It's because his neck's so fat. How do they expect you to sleep with that going on?'

'Here, have my Walkman for a while,' sighed Nina.

'Have you got any golden oldies on it?' Nell squinted over the tiny earphones, trying to make out which was left and which right.

'Mostly old ones, yes. Beach Boys –'

'Oh I like them! Has it got that one that goes *bob-bob-bob-bob-bobaround?*'

'*Barbara Ann*, you daft bugger!'

'Is that what it is? All these years I've been singing the wrong words.' Nell shook with laughter.

Nina turned to her equally amused daughter. 'What's she bloody like?'

Catching their indulgent smiles, Nell wondered, When did I become a silly old fool? But instead of annoying her, the thought caused her to twinkle, as she sat back to enjoy the music.

For a time she continued to listen, spending the rest of the boring hours plodding up and down the fuselage, finally to return to her seat and plonk herself down, shaking the whole row and causing eyes to open. Eventually the lights came back on and there was activity from the stewards in preparation of breakfast.

'Good morning, ladies and gentlemen,' announced the captain. 'We trust you managed to get a decent night's sleep –'

'No we bloody didn't,' said Nell, loud enough for others to overhear and smile at her.

Face all creased, Nina arched her aching back, then waited for someone to unblock the aisle before clambering over her mother and heading for the bulkhead. 'The toilets are in a dreadful state again, aren't they?' she remarked when she came back, wafting of toothpaste and perfume, and generally spruced up.

'They're even worse since I broke the seat,' admitted Nell from the side of her mouth, setting them all chuckling.

Previously enjoyed, the food had begun to smell nauseating, every meal tasting identical, whether meat or pastry. Nell just had a roll for breakfast. The marmalade came in dinky pots, and a knife was not a suitable implement to remove it all. Watching her corpulent neighbour across the aisle trying to figure out a way to get that elusive blob of jam out of its pot, Nell took bets. 'You watch, he won't be able to resist leaving something uneaten,' and, sure enough, he eventually worked out a way, upturning his teaspoon and using its tapered end to scrape out that last skerrick.

The plane touched down, allowing them to dodder off, though their horrendous journey had eleven more hours to go. Nell clung on to Nina and Romy's arms, and, after checking on their wellbeing, exclaimed, 'My God! I feel as if I'm walking on a bed of nails, my feet are that dead I'll be surprised if none of us get a thrombosis.'

Back on board the tidied-up aircraft, there was more food served, more films to watch. Hour after boring hour.

Until finally, 'Ladies and gentlemen . . .' the captain's voice announced. 'We have now entered Australia.'

A ripple of applause went through the cabin, everyone craning their eyes through the portholes to espy through the vapour a magnificent swirling pattern of salt pans thousands of feet below, shimmering like opals under the brilliant red of a dying sun. Not long after this, though, night fell, leaving nothing to see but miles of inky void.

Hours were to follow the announcement, making them aware of just how vast this country was. How am I going to find him in all this? thought Nell, suddenly engulfed by a wave of futility. And after that she retreated into herself.

Towards the end of that final haul, everyone was stiff and tired and short-tempered, their ankles inflated from being squeezed into economy seating. Another delivery of drinks was performed. Nell knew the routine by heart now, idly watching as the beautifully made-up girls worked their way along – how could they look so pristine after being crammed in all these hours? Having failed to get that particular stewardess to look her directly in the eye, and still determined to do so, Nell reached out to take a plastic container of orange juice from her, both their hands colliding and the orange being spilled down her white blouse. And even then, she didn't meet Nell's eye.

'Never mind, love.' Nell smiled at her profuse apology, and took the offered tissue to wipe away the stain. Then, after the stewardess had passed, she grumbled to her neighbours, 'Clumsy berk. What a sight I'm going to look with a big orange stain down my front. I feel grimy enough as it is – but at least I don't stink as bad as that man in front.'

Nina and Romy shook with laughter, both agreeing, 'You can't take her anywhere.'

'I don't care! He should know to have a wash!' Nell squirted perfume over the seat in front.

A head craned round to investigate. 'I think he gets the drift, Nana.'

'Ladies and gentlemen, in a moment the crew will be coming round with immigration forms, if you'd kindly fill those in . . .'

'We've already got ours,' interrupted Nell, her pen poised

over the leaflet. Then she accosted Nina. 'It says you're not permitted to bring food in. Do you think Polos count as food?' When no answer was forthcoming, she tucked the tube of mints in the pocket of the seat in front. 'Better safe than sorry. Drugs – does that mean medication? I've got my painkillers.' They were for her joints and back, a legacy of all the heavy patients she had lifted.

'I think it just means illegal stuff,' explained Nina.

'Yes, but if I don't tick the box and they search my bag they'll think I'm lying and not let me in – I couldn't stand to turn around and go straight home. It would kill me.'

'You and me both,' agreed Nina, with an edge to her voice. 'Look, just ask the bloody steward if you won't take my word about your blasted pills.'

'Currently, the temperature in Brisbane is a very comfortable nineteen degrees. For those who have not yet adjusted their watches, the local time is twenty twenty-two.'

'Just get us there!' sighed an exasperated Nell.

Then she remembered that only by reason of another's kindness was she here now. Nina could have spent the fruits of her success on other things; instead, she had chosen to allow the woman who was not even her real mother to realise her lifelong dream. Feeling churlish, she reached out suddenly and laid a hand over Nina's, gripping it in a gesture of deep affection and gratitude.

'What was that for?'

'Just to show you I'm not really an ungrateful old so-and-so, grumbling about everything. I totally appreciate what you're doing for me, Neen, I promise I'll stop complaining from now on, or they'll be calling me a whingeing Pom.' And the rattiness that had characterised those final hours now lifted as the landing gear came down and the lights of Brisbane spread out below them, like dew on a spider's web.

At last the plane touched down. If their feet had been painful earlier, it was nothing compared to how they felt now. 'It's like Elephant Walk, isn't it?' said Nell, looking down at three pairs of swollen ankles as they waited at the carousel for their baggage to come around, and forgetting her promise not to whinge. 'The minute we arrive at the hotel, you must get your feet up,' she ordered Nina, whose were by far the most swollen.

'Here comes ours – excuse me!' A short-tempered Romy edged her way through the cram of Asians to haul a case off the conveyor. After a brief skirmish, enduring security and passport control, Nell could hardly believe they were free to go.

Automatic doors opened onto a balmy night. It was evident they had arrived in a completely different land; the air that hit their faces was like being stroked very pleasantly with a warm velvet glove, and, once untainted by aviation fuel, was sweet and fresh.

Romy screamed as a huge insect came bumbling out of the night to land on her T-shirt.

'Christ! You nearly gave me a heart attack,' gasped Nina, as the cicada was dashed away, leaving them all prickling with nerves. 'Come on, let's get in one of those bloody taxis.' She aimed the trolley towards them, this taking only a few more painful steps, then they were ensconced in a cab and on their way towards the lights of the city.

Their ankles still bore signs of oedema the next morning, though were not quite so inflated, and that awful pins and needles had gone. After a luxurious bath, Nell tapped on the adjoining door, which was opened by a bleary-eyed Nina, and, after waiting for Romy, they all went down to the dining room. Here they were to stack their plates and bowls with several types of melon, yoghurt and muesli, anything remotely fresh, in an effort to remove the memory of the airline food from their tubes. There was a strange contraption, a sort of conveyor belt on which to toast bread to one's personal taste. Not realising the etiquette involved, Nell took the first slice that came off.

Nina laughed and, unusually polite this morning, said of the victim, 'Mam, this gentleman's been waiting ages for that.'

Under Nell's profuse apology, the businessman smiled and said, 'No worries.' Though he did take possession of his toast, whilst telling her how to use the machine. Notwithstanding that he was the wrong age to be her son, Nell continued to show interest in him, and afterwards stood and chatted to those others who congregated around the toaster, waiting for the slices of bread to turn brown at a painfully slow rate of knots.

'You've finished interrogating everybody, have you?' asked Nina, when Nell finally joined the others.

'Well, you never know what you might learn,' said Nell, then eyed Romy's plate, which held a sweet pastry. 'I don't know how you can eat cakes first thing on a morning!' But then she noticed that her granddaughter's expression was not in keeping with the excitement of her surroundings, and remembered that she must be pining for Patrick. So, 'You eat what you like, love,' she instructed warmly.

During breakfast, they discussed what to do first. Romy had found out prior to their trip that there were two main repositories: the State Archives and the State Library. Looking at their little map, provided by reception, the library was in walking distance, so it made sense to consult this source first.

'I don't feel like doing it this morning, though,' said Nell. 'I won't be able to get my head round anything.' They had arranged to stop three nights in Brisbane, then take things from there. So, 'Let's just have a wander round the shops for today, and get our bearings.'

'If we ever get our cup of tea!' Nina looked around at the busy dining room. 'Where the hell has that waiter got to? He said he was bringing it ages ago. Oh there he is, look at him, trying to pretend he hasn't seen me.' She rose and marched to a counter upon which were pots of tea and coffee, and an altercation occurred. Nina came back somewhat ruffled, muttering, 'Little shit . . .'

Following breakfast, taking the map with them and wearing comfortable sandals, they made their way down towards the main business district. The tranquillity of the hotel foyer soon gave way to a steady stream of human traffic, commuters in lightweight business attire, tourists in vest and shorts, and Nell clung on to her daughter's arm to avoid getting in anyone's way – though at least there was plenty of space, the streets not cramped as they were at home. Gradually descending, they came to a busy intersection, the traffic going only one way but this making it seem like a racetrack. On the map it looked simple, the streets and roads laid out in parallel and perpendicular lines, but with noisy vehicles thrown into the equation, it was all totally confusing for Nell.

Intimidated by so many high-rise buildings, commuters gathering around her at the kerb, the steady blip of the traffic signals warning them not to cross, she tried to study the male faces of those around her, looking for a hint that one might be her son. But it was all too overwhelming, and her eyes were now on those gathering on the other side of the road, which seemed such a distance way, 'Isn't it busy?' The stream of one-way traffic flashed past them, the thunder of motorbikes and enormous chromed trucks with smoke stacks.

'You want to try London,' said Nina. 'It's a madhouse. This place is really laid-back.'

'I did go to London once in the war, but only to Kings Cross. The ambulance train just turned straight round and went back.' Which was what Nell wished she could do now. 'Can we find a shop to go into?'

'That's what we're looking for, Nana,' said Romy, who

consulted the map. 'There's meant to be a shopping mall just a bit further on.'

Nell was wondering if she had bitten off more than she could chew, when the flow of traffic suddenly halted, and a rapid blip-blip-blip-blip indicated that it was safe to cross. She held on tight to her daughter's arm as they encountered the throng of people who came from the other side, a moment of confusion occurring. The intersection seemed even wider now that the green signal had suddenly expired, and there were yards yet to go. Nell was flustered and out of breath when she finally reached the other kerb.

The snarl of traffic behind them, another busy stretch of pavement, then, at last, Nell found herself steered into a pedestrianised street, here able to relax a little and pause and look about her at the architecture without being mown down. It was indeed a beautiful city, clean, and youthful – between the amazons of concrete and glass with their sleek flanks of black or turquoise glass reflecting the sunlight were grand and sedate colonial buildings, such as one with an ornate clock tower, or tranquil oases of palm-studded lawns in which to catch one's breath.

Meandering about the broad-paved mall, they found it composed of ultra-modern department stores, souvenir shops, restaurants and arcades. The area was partly canopied, both by artificial awnings and by the trees that were dotted about, though there seemed little danger of rain on this bright blue day.

'I could live here,' said Nina, giving a nod of approval for the salubrious ambience.

To Nell, her daughter had never seemed so carefree, laughing at her companions, who had failed to bring any sunglasses and were being intermittently dazzled. But there was no shortage of places to buy these, and in fact at bargain price, for there were sales at every turn, this being the end of the season.

'Can we go in here?' Though an air of misery lay behind the smile, Romy was doing her best not to spoil anyone's holiday, and indicated a glitzy hall of glass and chrome, about which they were to browse before taking an escalator down to where they had come in. At least, they assumed this to be the case, but they did not recognise any of the landmarks. After much confusion they realised they had emerged on a different street level.

'I don't think I can face going back in,' said Nell. 'Can we just mosey over and see what the Grecian-looking building is?'

It turned out to be the Shrine of Remembrance, a haven of chequered stone amidst lawns and trees with bottle-shaped trunks and exotic palms. Atop a flight of granite was a circular colonnade of sandstone pillars. Making their way up the steps, the three women stood for a while in reverence of the eternal flame, and ran their gaze around the sphere, reading the names of battles.

'I'll stay here for a while if you want to go back to your shopping,' said Nell eventually, and whilst they were gone she was to enjoy the aura of calmness, wandering back down the steps and into the crypt beneath to peruse a roll of honour.

There were two more elderly women here. Nell cast a smile at them as she drifted around, and later she was to see them again when she had moved back to stand in daylight, the sun glinting on the bronze statue of a soldier on horseback. How beautifully this land venerated its fallen heroes. Nell turned to murmur this to the women, and, as usual, engaged these strangers in conversation for a moment or two, asking if any of their menfolk were commemorated here. No, they said, but one of them had lost a son in Vietnam. They might have physically abused her, such was Nell's shock.

In her ignorance, she had always presumed it to be an American war, but here was an Australian mother who had lost her son, along with a good many besides, so she was informed now. Had William been amongst those who died?

Nina and Romy were to find her looking dazed when they finally came back. Nell pretended it was the heat of the sun, and tried to jolly herself for another bout of shopping. By the time they had toured more shops, bought some T-shirts with an Aboriginal design, and examined the architecture old and new, it was almost midday, and then it really was the sun that was responsible.

Whilst Nina still looked pristine in her linen top and trousers, Romy too as fresh, Nell had taken to wafting her perspiring face. 'I'd hate to be here in summer.'

'Well, you would put that jacket on,' they both told her.

'I know, but I couldn't believe autumn could be so hot.'

'I absolutely love it. Nina scrunched her shoulders in happiness, Romy offering total accord.

Over her shock about Vietnam, Nell was happy too that they were having such a good time, and not there merely for her sake.

After a leisurely lunch in a restaurant, they continued their explorations, looking for the State Library, and stumbling across some botanical gardens in the process. Adjacent to a river that glittered in the sunshine with a flotilla of pristine yachts, were sweeping lawns, palms, clumps of bamboo, and giant fig trees with trunks so massive that a dozen people could have stood shoulder to shoulder around their circumference. Above the tree line could still be glimpsed the high-rise offices and hotels, yet they failed to intrude.

Whilst other individuals were to be seen dotted around the lawns, reading a book or eating a sandwich, Nell professed she would never get up. So she and her companions wandered through the gardens until they came to a bench overlooking a stretch of lake, where ducks sat on an island beneath a palm, and leggy moorhens strode upon the blanket of water lilies. Sitting to enjoy the view, Nell wondered if her son could be sitting in this same park . . .

Eventually leaving by a different route, they found the State Library, though Nell declared it unnecessary to go all the way there. 'As long as we know where to come tomorrow, I think I've had enough,' she said, arching her back. 'I feel as if I've suddenly hit a brick wall.'

'I'm buggered as well,' confessed Nina. 'Must be jetlag.'

'What a couple of old crocks,' mocked Romy, but led the way back to the hotel, consulting her map as they went.

Relieved at last to see the clock tower resembling a pineapple, which told they were almost back to their hotel, there was a final slope up which to battle before they reached the air-conditioned foyer.

Before anything else, Nell switched on the kettle, whilst Nina removed her sandals from blistered feet, and Romy collapsed on a bed. 'I'm gasping for this.' Nell sat on the sofa and had a cup of tea with them, before going to her own room. 'Just to shut my eyes for five minutes. I can't keep them open.'

The next time she lifted her lashes it was dark. She came round fully clothed, and the clock said it was ten. No, it couldn't be! A strip of light shone under the door of the adjoining room. Dragging herself from the bed, Nell tottered and groped her way to join the others, who had not been long awake themselves if their bleary eyes were anything to go by. Too late to acquire an evening meal, Romy suggested they ordered a pizza. But, looking distinctly unappetised, her grandmother said she would make do with biscuits and tea, and withdrew to her room. Whilst she drank her tea. Nell stood and gazed out at the nocturnal panorama, wondering if her son was somewhere down amongst those glittering lights. Then, she ran a bath, tipping in some deliciously perfumed bubble bath and luxuriating in the thick towels, before going to bed.

With the next day being similarly ruined by jetlag, Nell said, 'I don't know whether it's worth going to this library, my brain feels as if it belongs to Cissie Flowerdew. But anyway, we might as well go and have a gander.'

So back they went, braving the Grand Prix traffic and taking one of the streets down toward the river and the vast library. After finding the correct department, and making further enquiry at the desk, they were given instruction by a librarian.

Nell made a tentative approach. 'I don't know if we're in the right place, even, but maybe you'll be able to help us.'

The amiable girl flicked back her blonde hair, and said, 'I'll try.'

'My son . . .' Nell broke off, and looked to her daughter for assistance.

Nina stepped in. 'My mother's trying to trace her son, who emigrated from England in the nineteen fifties. We're not sure when exactly.' She explained he had been adopted and put into an orphanage, giving the girl what information she could. 'I'm sorry, that's all we know.'

The librarian tapped her lips and said a lot of records were restricted. Walking ahead of them and gathering leaflets along her way, she took them to a public search room. She indicated a large card index and said perhaps they might find a William Morgan in there, though on second thoughts it wouldn't go up to the date they wanted – but there were electoral rolls, and also birth, marriage and death indexes.

'That's for the whole of Australia, not just Queensland, so if you're not sure if he entered the country in this state then you might just get a lead there.' There were more obscure sources, too, she pointed out, such as an index of people called before government committees. 'It's a long shot, but you never know.'

Nell, who had been looking confused, now appeared to buck up as the girl handed over the wad of leaflets she had collected. 'Thank you very much for all your help,' she told the librarian, though in truth, with far too much information to take in, she felt totally out of her depth.

'Not a problem,' replied the very pleasant girl, adding as she left them to it, 'If there's anything you need, just ask.'

The three set about their daunting task. Everyone else in the search room seemed to know what they were doing, marching purposely back and forth between shelves of files – and even tapping away at computers – whilst Nell and her co-searchers just dithered for now.

Once they began, it became clear that without a specific date it was obviously futile. After going through ream after ream of microfiche, studying electoral rolls, death and marriage, and the more obscure indexes, all they acquired was sore eyes and splitting headaches.

They broke for lunch, then went back in the afternoon. To no avail. It was all a mass of meaningless statistics.

'We can come back for another look tomorrow,' said Nina to her disappointed mother at the end of a very testing day. 'I'm willing if you are. After a good night's kip you'll feel more up to it.'

'It's hopeless.' Nell put her head in her hands, then rubbed her eyes and looked over the tips of her fingers in despair at the banks of extraneous information that surrounded them. 'We could spend a month of Sundays trawling through that blasted lot and still never find him.'

Romy stretched, and tried to sound cheerful, though it was obvious to Nell her mind was elsewhere. 'What about the archive place then? It's mad to come thousands of miles then give up after just one day.'

A blank expression in her eyes, Nell had begun to toy with her diamond eternity ring, when she heard Joe commanding her to pull herself together, and so she did. 'All right, we'll ask that girl if there's anything we might not have looked at.' And all three of them approached the desk.

This being the end of the day, the librarian had been asked countless questions and could not think what to suggest. 'Other than the insanity files, but you'd need permission to look in those, as it would be under seventy-five years old.'

'If he is in them I'd rather not know,' said Nell with an air of finality. And, thanking the girl, they went back to their hotel.

On the way, Nina tried to coax her mother from despondency. 'You never know, we might have missed something. He could have gone back to that other name you said. We can extend our stay –'

'No, I can't face another day of squinting into one of those bloody machines,' said her mother. 'We should be out enjoying the lovely weather.' She could not bear the idea that Nina, having spent a fortune, would gain no benefit herself. 'I might have another go when we've got Mary's sister out of the way.'

So, back to the hotel they trudged, to have a cup of tea, and to sit three on a bed with their feet up, like schoolgirls in a dorm, as they discussed their trip to the small coastal town where Mary's sister lived.

Nell told them, 'It might be an idea to arrange somewhere to stay before we set off. From the sound of it it's in the middle of nowhere, and we might find ourselves stranded. There's nothing much there, Mary said – well, only a few hundred inhabitants. No police station, no doctor, no dentist, no shops other than a general store and post office – what possesses somebody to go and live in the middle of nowhere with thousands of acres of wilderness between them and the nearest town?' It fascinated Nell. 'Anyway, I don't know how much room Millie's got, but we can't expect her to put us all up.'

Romy grabbed the RAC road book from the pile on the table, and began to thumb through it. 'There seems to be heaps of motels and caravan parks, even in the tiniest places.'

'I suppose it's in their culture,' said Nina. 'The place being so big. See if you can find us somewhere cheap, Rome.' It had been costly enough for the three of them at the hotel for three days. 'I don't mean a backpacker hotel,' she laughed. 'Just a nice self-catering cottage or something.'

Romy continued searching. 'But what about food, washing powder, all that crap? It's only a little car I've hired, you know.'

'We won't be carting food all the way up there,' said her mother. 'There's bound to be a supermarket nearer to where we'll be, or how would Millie cope? I think I'll nip out later and buy a cool box, though, to put some drinks in.'

Romy suggested, 'It might be an idea to get a phone card as well.'

'All this expense because of Mary,' grumbled Nell.

'It's only a few dollars, Mam.'

'I don't mean the phone card, I mean the car and everything!'

'There's a limit to where you can go on public transport,' said Nina. 'We'll be able to take diversions if we have a car.'

'Yes, I suppose so,' agreed Nell. 'And it means we can buy all our food so we'll save on eating out.'

'This sounds good.' Romy read out a description of a holiday villa.

Nina agreed. 'Let's give them a ring now and book it.'

This being their final evening at the hotel, they decided to eat in the restaurant. Spirits were pretty low over the total lack of information. To exacerbate this, they were served by the waiter who had taken a dislike to Nina on that very first morning, and she to him.

The meal of salmon with a caper sauce was good, though a little rich for Nell, who finished eating first.

Nina took a few more mouthfuls, then set down her

cutlery, dabbed her lips, and reached over the linen cloth to take her mother's hand. 'It'll be all right, Mam,' she vowed softly. 'We've got over a fortnight left to find him. We don't have to waste all that time at Millie's, we can stay here and go to the library every day till we do find something.'

'Ooh no, I couldn't let Mary down!' Nell sounded aghast at the very idea.

'We haven't come for her benefit, we came here for yours. For Christ's sake, we can post the bloody knickers.'

'It's not just a case of knickers! Don't you see? I'm the only human link she has with her sister. Apart from her daughter, who never ever comes to see her, it's the only other relative I've heard Mary mention. No, I can empathise with having someone you love being out of reach – anyway, we've booked that holiday apartment now,' finished Nell.

'We can unbook it. Your son's more important . . .' Concentrated though she was on this intimate exchange, Nina felt someone hovering, and turned in annoyance to find the waiter looking decidedly peeved.

'Are you going to eat that?'

'What are you, the bloody dinner lady?' Nina gave him a waspish glare and he gave her one back, then she turned her back on him and focused on her mother. The disgruntled waiter tossed his mane of black hair and minced off.

Nell was laughing now, saying to Romy, 'She talks about not being able to take me anywhere!'

'Well! He's an annoying little shit.' But Nina was smiling too as she tried a last attempt at persuasion. 'Are you absolutely certain you want to check out?'

'Well, we could stay here till you've insulted *all* the staff, I suppose,' mused Nell with a twinkle in her eye for Romy. 'I hope he isn't on at breakfast tomorrow. He'll probably spit in it.' Then she patted her daughter's hand. 'No, thanks, love, but I need a break from the city as much as anybody. I'm looking forward to it actually.'

So, in the morning, straight after breakfast, they packed up and went by taxi to pick up the hire car: then, with Nina giving directions, headed north. Leaving behind the sprawling suburbs and finally open countryside, they followed the motorway, across a wide, brown river, past open fields. There came splendid views of a far-off mountain range, one of which took on the shape of a colossal gorilla. There were to be more enormous specimens along the roadside, though manmade ones this time, which Nell delighted in pointing out en route – a giant pineapple, and a huge black and white cow – and further incongruity in the swathes of densely planted pine trees, more fitted to Grimm's Fairytales than this land of sunshine. At times cut through rock, the road was ever undulating, the views often spectacular, the hillsides so densely wooded they seemed as if clad in velour and always in the background another purple range.

Having eaten quite early, after a few hundred kilometres they were ready for a snack, and pulled into a remote petrol station, to which was attached a café called Smiley's. It was a tiny place with basic facilities and four tables, two of them occupied by truckers. They gave their order, and sat down. But within minutes of being seated close to the water heater, sweat was dripping from their brows.

Nell fanned herself, and said she would have to move, calling to the young man who was making their sandwiches, 'We'll just move to that table by the door, love!'

But, 'Now we're by the bloody dustbins!' complained Nina.

All chuckling at the irony of this, her mother said, 'Well, there's nowhere else to move to. Behave now, the boy's here with our lunch.'

Each sandwich bore a perfect imprint of the young man's

fingers, where he had pressed down in order to dissect them into daintier blocks. The tea was served in industrial-sized mugs, but had been placed on saucers with a paper doily to add a touch of finesse.

Taking in these, and the odorous dustbins, Nina muttered, 'I don't know about Smiley's – more like Slimey's.'

This set her mother laughing, and in doing so she was to inhale a crumb, so that the tears ran down her cheeks and a period of coughing was to ensue before she recovered.

Obviously related to the boy, if looks were to go by, a woman appeared from the kitchen behind the counter and eyed them. 'Everything okay?'

Nell wiped her eyes and forced herself to stop laughing. 'Oh, they're lovely, thank you very much! We're just laughing at a film we saw last night.' Then her watery eyes turned to scold the others, as she murmured, 'The poor lad's done his best.'

The sandwiches being so huge, none of the women were able to eat more than one, obliging Nell to apologise yet again as they made their exit. Also, just on the off-chance, she asked if the woman knew anyone around here with the name of Morgan. That was too much to hope for, but the woman was sympathetic to Nell's dilemma.

'Isn't everyone lovely and friendly over here?' she opined later, as they made for the car.

Jumping in first, so as to turn on the air-conditioning for the older women, Romy yelped as the hot seat burned the back of her thighs, and jumped out again, to wait for the interior to cool down. Then their journey resumed.

There was another hour of driving, a quick lavatory stop, a fruitless query over William Morgan, and then on again.

The terrain suddenly became monotonous, the view hidden by trees. But after being flat for countless miles, the highway began to incline again, lending the passengers the opportunity to comment on more spectacular views. Already there was a hint of richness in the ochreous verge to either side, but now, beyond the fences were sanguine undulations, acre after acre of orchards and vineyards.

'It's absolutely beautiful – look, Romy!'

'I can't, I'm driving! And I've got one of those gigantic trucks up my arse – oh, and now the one in front is blocking the road sign! Christ, it's like Smokey and the Bandit . . .' Whilst she glared straight uphill, her passengers continued to gasp over the vista, and shortly they reached the top of the incline, the road levelling out again as they entered another small country town.

'Did you see the name of this place?' asked a flustered Romy, having to concentrate on the traffic signs ahead. 'I couldn't see a thing because of that lorry.'

'No, but isn't it pretty?' Their car now approaching an avenue of trees, Nell and Nina were admiring the finest examples of Queensland architecture they had seen thus far, an elegant high-set hotel with ornate balconies adorned with iron lacework, and shady verandahs.

But in less than two minutes they had left the town behind them and were once again passing through farmland and cane fields, with signs that advertised paw-paw, mango, avocado, lychee, macadamia.

Romy was becoming dubious about proceeding further, should they be travelling out of their way. As soon as she was able, she turned the car around.

Once back in the town, her grandmother begged, with a look at her watch, 'Can we get out here and stretch our legs and ask for directions? It's been over five hours since we set off!'

'You want to be driving!' Unusually short-tempered, Romy cruised along, looking for a place to pull in. This township had the same laid-back feel that they had come to expect of Queensland, though on a much smaller scale than Brisbane, not a high-rise building in sight, apart from a water tower. From a cable strung across the road was suspended a fruit bat. Remarking on this, they continued to glide slowly along for a while, admiring the old buildings, graceful arches, awnings and verandahs, Some constructed of timber, others of painted masonry, with parapet frontages, classical pediments and urns – all beautiful. Yet this architectural elegance did not extend to society; most of the inhabitants seemed quite countrified.

There seemed to be few traffic restrictions here, the ranks of cars and utility vehicles parked directly outside the front of the shops, nose to kerb.

'Go there under that lovely tree!' instructed Nell.

There were many lovely trees with smooth mottled bark, though Romy steered under the dense shade of the one her grandmother had indicated. Upon getting out and stretching limbs, she tried to make sense of the parking sign, to see how long they would have, whilst Nell and Nina stood to admire their canopy of bright green feathery leaves and scarlet blooms. Now standing still, Nell was better able to survey the faces of male passers-by, some deeply tanned and clad in work shorts and broad-brimmed hats, others with faces almost as pale as those at home, in business shirt and trousers. It was a stretch of the imagination that any of them might be her son, but one could dream . . .

Having found out the name of the town, Romy made quick consultation of the map, and to everyone's great relief, said that their turn-off was just a few hundred yards away.

Nina advised, 'We'd better stock up with food then, at that supermarket across the road – milk, bread, bacon – in case there's nowhere nearer to Millie's.'

They approached a pedestrian crossing and waited for the signals to change, all three jaws dropping as an elderly woman, wearing a flowered dress and a German war helmet, pedalled by on a three-wheeled cycle.

'My God, what the hell have we struck?' asked Nina.

Romy started to giggle, Nell too, then the lights changed, and, still laughing, they crossed the highway to a canopied walkway. Nina spotted a butcher's and led the way. They had only gone in for bacon, but her mother admired the lamb cutlets on display and insisted on having them.

'I'm not like you two,' reproached Nell, in reality wanting to put some nourishment into her granddaughter. 'I can't live on plankton, I need a decent meal – don't worry, I don't mind cooking.'

'Good, I'll be happy to let you.' A weary Nina asked for four. Whilst the butcher was weighing these, she narrowed her eyes at the heavy whiff of smoke and suspected the bacon was of this variety, to which she had an aversion. 'Is that bacon smoked?'

'Yes, got my own smokehouse out the back,' said the butcher proudly.

'Hmm, have you got any that doesn't reek of bonfire?' requested Nina.

The butcher looked put out, and informed her, 'All bacon's smoked.'

'Well, no, actually, we ate some unsmoked down in Bris—'

'All bacon's smoked,' he repeated like an automaton.

'Really? Even in Outer Mongolia?' Nina gave a caustic mutter from the side of her mouth, Romy disassociating herself to chortle in the background, and Nell feeling unable to ask if the butcher knew of anyone called Morgan.

Paying for the cutlets, they left without the bacon.

'Honestly, they make these sweeping statements,' objected Nina. 'All bacon's smoked – my arse. I'll bet he's never been ten miles down the road, let alone outside Queensland . . .'

Their visit to the supermarket was brief, the few items they purchased being packed into the cool box. Nell did enquire about William Morgan in there, but all she got was a blank stare at her accent, then they were back en route.

And in only minutes they were to come across the signpost that they had missed earlier. Taking the turn-off, it seemed they were on their final leg at last – until Romy stopped the car, got out and ran to a fence.

'Where's she off now?' bayed Nina.

'I think she just wants to get a photo of that view.' Nell craned her neck to see it too.

It certainly was fantastic, stretching into the distance, the rolling red soil with its verdant ranks against the vivid blue of the sky . . .

Then it was onward, past more fields of fruit trees, with signs that warned, Dingo traps – Do Not Enter', the sun sparkling on a dam, a secluded farmstead, a distant windmill across a cane field, a herd of Brahman cattle, mile after flat mile of grazing, eucalypts with leaves that wilted in the afternoon heat, and ochre turrets, home to termites.

Finally they arrived at the town where Millie lived. Well, Mary had called it a town, but in England it would be termed a village, and a very unprespossessing one at that. The road that had been long and straight now began to snake between a welter of tall but spindly gum trees, and an open area of what looked like a swamp. Shortly, a cluster of unattractive bungalows appeared, and some kind of mast.

Relieved to have finally arrived, Nell could not help but shake her head at the odd places people turned up in. 'What on earth possessed Mary's sister to move ten thousand miles to live here? Apart from to get away from Mary that is.'

'I think that might be the reason,' observed their driver a few seconds later, as the main road suddenly terminated in a T junction, and thereupon appeared a breathtaking view of the Coral Sea.

Both Nell and her daughter let out a gasp of incredulity, Nell craning forward to gaze over Romy's shoulder through the windscreen. 'It's paradise . . .'

Her granddaughter agreed, and asked, 'Which way do I turn?'

'Any way you like,' breathed Nina, feasting her eyes on the turquoise sea and pristine sands.

Romy steered to the right, only able to snatch the occasional glance at the stunning view as she kept her eyes on the road. To the other side of it were houses, none of them very prepossessing, a mixture of fibro-cement shacks with corrugated tin roofs, plus brick and tile bungalows. On the ocean side the foreshore was dappled in shade from the graceful tassels of casuarina trees, the ground beneath covered in succulent foliage, pink flowers, and hummocks of spiky grass. Whilst her passengers strained their eyes between the dangling branches, uttering gasps at the gem-coloured sea, Romy drove slowly along an esplanade.

After only a short way, she was to steer off the road under a group of pine trees – not the Christmas tree variety, but a more exotic type. 'There's the general store. You two stay here, I'll just nip in and get directions for this apartment, and they might know Millie too.'

A blast of heat accompanied the opening of the door. 'I'll leave the air-con on for you,' said Romy.

She left Nell and Nina to exchange amazed comments, but they had only a few moments to feast their eyes on the panorama, for Romy ran back over the road and got back into the driving seat. 'They do know her!' She waited for a car to pass by, then pulled out.

This was no surprise to Nina, who supposed, 'If she's anything like Mary they'll know her for miles around.' She had noticed that Nell was flagging. 'But we'll go to our digs first, chuck our bags in, then have a dip and relax. Mrs Kerfupps can wait till tomorrow.'

As they motored slowly along the esplanade, Nell tore her eyes from the sea to examine the township, able to see now that it was complemented by more decorous houses than those they had initially seen: picturesque chalets of timber and weatherboard; nautical colour combinations of blue and white, others of cream, maroon and dark green;

colonial-style palaces set on stilts, with a grand frontal staircase and a balustrade all the way round, their ornamental pediments, and finials and lattice inherited from a more elegant age; ultra-modern dwellings too – the whole strung like limpets along the breathtaking length of coast.

'I couldn't give a bugger if Mary's sister lives here or not. This is where I'll be spending the rest of my holiday . . .' Pulled up in her thoughts, Nina glanced at her mother. 'Sorry, Mam, I was only kidding, we'll go anywhere you want to look for William – but isn't this just fantastic?'

Nell happily agreed. 'Look there's not a soul on the beach . . .'

With Romy keeping her eye out for the appropriate avenue, alas the car was soon to turn away from the sea. This was a slight disappointment to its occupants, but not for long, for the brick villa they came upon was eminently suitable. Part of a small complex, each was set amongst trees and shrubs and had its own private area of garden partitioned by trellis. The interior was quite cool with, tiled floor, and was to become even cooler by evening, though they left the patio doors open so as to let in fresh air and hear the crickets, the insects kept out by fly-wire screens. To the rear of the complex lay a sandy firebreak, then dense bush that gave the impression that one might get lost within moments of entry. Discovering a swimming pool, Nina was glad that there were no noisy children in it – in fact, there seemed no other people at all staying here, and they had the entire pool area to themselves. Once ensconced, all three went for a dip, but were initially disconcerted by the large hornet-like insects that hovered over the water – until they saw what appeared to be little ballet pumps at the end of those pendulous legs, this reducing their scariness. After a long wallow, too tired to visit the sea that afternoon, they were happy just to relax on sun loungers and imbibe cool drinks, no longer bothered by the hornets, which were in fact harmless, as were the skinks that sunbathed on the walls.

Around five, Romy said she felt rejuvenated enough to go for a walk to the general store.

'What can you possibly want?' demanded her mother. 'We've got all this stuff . . .'

'I forgot a magazine,' replied her daughter. 'I'll only be fifteen minutes.'

But as ever, she was widely off the mark, taking twice as long as this before rejoining them to partake in a tea of lamb cutlets – which turned out to taste of smoke too, much to Nina's disgust. Anxious to put some meat on her granddaughter's bones, Nell tried to cosset with a great wedge of apple pie and ice-cream, and was pleasantly surprised when, for once, Romy seemed hungry enough to clear her plate. Then for a while they were to remain al fresco, watching a whole variety of birds – colourful parrots, honeyeaters with moss-green wings and bright blue eyes, others like clowns who fought and squabbled amongst themselves, musical magpies – but soon the mosquitoes were to drive them indoors. As the sun began to go down, and the parakeets grew more vociferous, kangaroos emerged from the bush, one of them hopping over to crop the lawn right outside the patio doors.

'Hey, did you know male kangaroos had their tackle on upside down?' blurted Romy.

'Trust you to notice that,' said Nina, but was interested to take a look for herself.

'I wonder if the men do,' said Nell with a sly grin, causing the others to exclaim over her audacity, Romy delivering that infectious rumbling belly laugh that they had not heard in months.

The noise from the parakeets had grown into a cacophony, when night suddenly descended like the throw of a cloak and the birds fell silent, making way for the chorus of crickets and frogs. The kangaroo was still in the garden; they couldn't see where, but could hear his tail dragging along the concrete and the occasional grunt.

Attracted by the light from the kitchen, a cicada bashed against the fly-wire screen, making the occupants jump. It bumbled about for a while, until a big green frog that had been patiently sitting on the sill jumped up and devoured it.

'Oh my God!' Halfway through a biscuit, Romy clutched her chest. 'What's that on the wall?'

Her grandmother peered at it and made a soft murmur of delight. 'I think it's a gecko. It won't hurt you. Oh, look at its little feet . . .'

'I'll never sleep with that in the room,' declared Nina, rising to have a closer look.

'What happened to paradise?' scoffed Nell.

'No! I like the rest, it's just the wildlife that gives me the creeps. I shall have to get rid.' Nina took a glass from a cupboard, and one of the postcards she had bought.

'It's not the same as a spider,' warned her mother, she and Romy splitting their sides as Nina proceeded to chase the gecko up and down the walls and floor, finally managing to capture it in the glass.

'Aw no, the poor little thing's gone blue!' She immediately freed it outside – though within minutes was to report another atrocity.

'There's a frog down the loo!' And, sure enough, the small green inhabitant was clinging to the underside of the rim, and no amount of flushing would dislodge it.

Deciding to grin and bear it – as must the frog – they finally settled down for the evening.

'Shall we see what's on the telly?' Nina turned it on.

'Ah yes, I'll have to check what day *Home and Away*'s on,' said Romy. 'I've had instructions from the girls at home to find out what's going to happen.'

'How sad is she?' said Nina to her mother.

There were some dreadfully tacky adverts, with strident voice-overs, then a documentary. The title had not alerted Nell at first, but within a few moments' viewing, she realised its pertinence. She was to sit anaesthetised as the narrator related the fate of many child migrants who had come from the orphanages of England, to be beaten, worked like slaves, and worst of all sexually abused. All at once, this heaven on earth became hell.

Watching her mother shrink visibly before her, Nina reached out a supportive hand. 'It doesn't mean William went through that, Mam, they always beat these horror stories up. it was probably only a small percentage of the hundreds who came.'

'No, I realise that . . .' Nell tried to shake off her mantle of horror, to convince herself he was not amongst them. 'But those poor little devils, how they must have suffered.'

'He was a teenager when he came over,' chipped in Romy. 'And a big strong lad, probably, from what you've told me about his dad. Bullies normally pick on smaller kids.'

Nell acknowledged all of this with a movement of her head, but she was very contemplative. 'Even so, it doesn't stop the fear. All these years, these decades, when children went missing or were murdered, my heart would stop, thinking, What if it's him? Then I'd realise how silly I was being, because William would be years older than those poor kids. It couldn't possibly be him. But they were somebody's babies all the same . . .'

'Turn it off now, Rome.' ordered her mother.

'Watch it if you like,' said Nell, as cheerfully as she could. 'I think I'll go to bed and read.'

Nell didn't sleep much, owing in some part to the humidity, but also the programme which preyed on her mind throughout the night. Nina had apparently slept little too, though due to an entirely different cause.

'Bloody birds woke me up at the crack of dawn! Sounded just like a herd of zebras – heehaw, heehaw!'

'Zebras don't go heehaw!' laughed Romy.

'Well, that was the that was the noise they made, smart-arse.'

'Grumpy!' came the rejoinder.

'And look at these bites!' Nina displayed a collection of large swellings on her arms and legs, one so distended with lymph that it swung from her elbow like a watery bag. 'I look like the bloody elephant man!'

Nell showed concern. 'That looks nasty, we'll have to get you some antihistamine – try to leave it alone.'

With Nina still raking her arms, they sat down to breakfast.

More talkative this morning, Romy asked, 'Are we going to see Millie today?'

'We are not!' retorted her mother. 'The minute I've had this I'll be off to that beach – if that's all right with you, Mam?'

'Yes, I'll go with you,' said Nell. 'It's no good visiting Millie so early, she might not be up.'

'If she's like every other bugger here, she will,' contradicted Nina, scratching her arm again. 'That was another thing! Somebody was mowing their grass at six.'

'Well, I expect they have to because of the heat,' said Nell.

'Don't mention heat –'

'For heaven's sake, Neen,' laughed her mother. 'You've done nothing but moan.'

'You can talk!' parried Nina. But it was all good-natured banter.

'You look a lot happier, I'm glad to see,' smiled Nell to her granddaughter as breakfast progressed.

'Yes . . . well, yes and no.' Romy reverted to being quite anguished, as she finally managed to blurt, 'Patrick's left his wife.'

Her mother looked startled, and so did Nell. 'When did you find this out?' the former demanded to know.

'I phoned his friend last night,' admitted Romy, 'to see how he was. Patrick had just called to tell him.'

'How do you know he's telling the truth?'

'Because he said so, and I trust him.'

'So did his wife once,' said her mother.

'We haven't been deceiving her. I told you, nothing, happened.'

'Not much! There doesn't have to be sex involved to constitute betrayal. What was it the pope said, about adultery of the heart?'

'Well then, I'm guilty of it,' came Romy's flat reply. 'I can't help loving him – and I'm ready for all the heartache that'll involve.'

'It's not your heartache, though! It's his little boy who'll suffer most – do you really intend to ruin his childhood?'

'We'll try to minimise the hurt.'

'You're fooling yourself!'

'It's easy for you to pontificate!' Romy accused her mother. 'You've never felt passionate about anybody.'

Nina's jaw dropped in outrage. 'How come you're here then?'

'That was an accident. You didn't love my father.'

'I'm talking about you, not him! I'll never feel so passionately for anyone – I fought tooth and nail so's my dad would allow me to keep you! Talk about raw need – you go on about all these romantic yearnings – well, let me tell you, they could never equal the way a mother feels for her child! I know just how Patrick's wife will be feeling!'

Everybody got upset then. 'Oh, please don't fight,' begged Nell, as close to tears as they were.

'I'd give my life for you.' Nina glared at her daughter. 'That's why I cringe to see you heading for this weakling –'

'Well I've made up my mind,' said Romy. 'And you said you'd support me!'

'And I will,' said Nina. 'But I don't have to like it.'

'Shall we just listen to a bit of music?' suggested Nell, and left the table to switch on a bedside radio.

And within half an hour the animosity had evaporated,

as they shared laughter over the country music that seemed to be all they played in Queensland.

Then, after Nell had washed up, and all had showered, Nina said, 'Right, come on, you little bootscooters, wagons roll!' And they headed for the beach.

Whilst they were lounging for a while on the sands, a jet-ski came tearing along the coast, filling their lungs with the tang of fuel and assaulting their ears.

'These people are completely mad,' accused Nina. 'A beautiful place like this, and still they can't resist buggering it up with their toys! They don't deserve it. Anybody normal would just sit and appreciate the space, gaze out at that view, listen to classical music on the Walkman, not bash about on machines. That's what I'd do, anyway.'

'You, live here?' laughed her mother. 'You wouldn't last five minutes.'

'I would!' Nina looked slightly cross.

'Who are you trying to kid? Nobody around to argue with? You'd be bored to tears in paradise.'

Nina conceded this with a laugh, then both peered up the beach to see how far Romy had gone.

When she returned, they went home to a cold lunch, and in the afternoon finally did what they had gone there to do. Using one of the phone boxes next to the general store, Nell dialled Millie's number, and, whilst waiting for it to be answered, she warned Nina and Romy, 'Don't say a word about William in case it gets back to Mary.' Illegitimacy might mean nothing to the young ones, though to Nell it was still her shameful secret. 'But I'm going to pick Millie's brains about the farms around here that might have taken anybody from Eng— oh, is that Millie?' Suddenly breaking off, she attended the phone. 'I hope you don't mind me using your first name, but I'm your sister Mary's neighbour – yes! She's sent –' Nell fought to get a word in, as the woman gabbled excitedly about having been waiting for their visit. '– that's right. Well, we've arrived, and apparently we're just around the corner from you . . . are you sure? Right, see you then!'

Hanging up, she said, 'We've been invited to tea, but she says give her till four.'

Nina groaned. 'Probably rolling the carpets up for a spot of line dancing – shall we have a wander along the front till it's time?'

The harsh lines of Millie's brick bungalow were lost behind a small jungle of lush greenery, palms of different varieties, shrubs, elkhorn ferns and bougainvillea that tumbled in a vermillion curtain over the picket fence. There was a scent of tropical blooms in the air. For a moment, Nell thought they were at the wrong house, for Millie looked nothing like her sibling, but was short and whippet thin, with not a lick of make-up, her face like a walnut, and her hair a natural silver. Just give me time to get back from my bowling session, she had said, and she was still in her whites, her leathery face looking even more tanned against the clothing.

Nell did the introductions. The wiry little woman had a vigorous handshake, her Yorkshire accent all but gone except for the odd word. She had been here since after the war, when she had married an Anzac. Spotting her late husband's photograph as a young man in uniform, Nell mentioned that her own had also passed away, then spent a few minutes commenting on how beautifully kept the military memorials were over here.

'Even the tiniest places we've come through seem to give them great prominence. Quite right too, it was a marvellous thing they did, helping the mother country. It wasn't really their fight, but they came . . .'

'Well, don't forget they were under threat themselves,' said Millie. 'They were in real danger of invasion from the Japs – not many Poms realise that, this being the arse end of the world – pardon my French, as my father used to say!'

'Oh, so did my friend,' laughed Nell, thinking of Beata back home. Then, 'Don't let's mention the Japanese! It makes me boil that we're helping their economy – after what they did to our lads I vowed to boycott their products forever, but nowadays you're never really sure what firm owns what, and as for being lumped with Europe – oh, listen to me! I'm at it again.' Even though Millie had been agreeing with every word, Nell changed the subject and, referring to the wilderness behind the town, she asked, 'Is this what they call the outback, Millie?'

The other smiled. 'Suppose it would seem that way to some, but there's many more remote towns than this, believe me – right, sit yourselves down, my dears, and I'll get us some tea!' Less annoying than her sister, Millie had adopted the minimal lifestyle of the locals, sauntering about as she catered for them. Her home held none of the brass knick-knacks of Mary's living room.

'I did have a lot when I first came here.' Millie explained the lack, as she made sandwiches in the open-plan kitchen and spoke to them over a breakfast bar. 'But the sea air and the humidity corroded them. I've tried to wrap up a few of my precious ones, but there doesn't seem a lot of point if you can't have them on display – here now, tuck into these!' She handed over plates of sandwiches, pastries and muffins, and a bowl of huge tomatoes.

'That's a lovely big fridge, Millie.'

'Well you have to be able to get everything in or it goes off so quick in this climate.' She saw that Nina was raking her swollen flesh. 'Sand flies been troubling you?' Asked if she had any antihistamine tablets, she went off to fetch a packet. 'Don't take any till tonight, though, they'll knock you right out.'

She sat down again. 'So, let me get this right, you're Romy's mum?' She was directing her question at Nina. A nod was to verify this. 'You've no husband either?' chanced Millie, seeing no wedding ring – but it was not an accusation, just a commentary on their shared situation. 'Four of us with no man between us – oh, sorry, Romy, you might be attached?'

Nell quickly enlarged on her granddaughter's shake of head, as she saw the look that passed between her and Nina. 'She's got plenty of time for that, eh, Romy? I must say, Millie, this all looks smashing, I think we must have put you to a great deal of trouble.'

'Get away! It's the least I could do with my sister dragging you hundreds of miles out of your way – well now, what's Mary up to these days?'

Presented with such hospitality, Nina and her daughter had to politely endure listening to Nell relate the minutiae of her neighbour's life.

'It must be lonely for you now your husband's gone,' mused Nell. 'Would you ever consider going home?'

'Never,' said Millie, who, in spite of her desiccation, obviously thrived on such conditions. 'Our Mary would drive me crackers within an hour of her company. If the weather didn't kill me off first. Besides, my family's here.' She spoke of her two sons and one daughter, their spouses and children.

'Six grandchildren, how lovely! Speaking of children . . .' Nell hoped in subtle fashion to find out which local places had been involved in the Child Migrant Scheme. 'Did you watch that documentary last night, Millie?'

'Oh, about the CMS? No, that's been on before.'

'Wasn't it dreadful,' said Nell quickly, before Millie could talk about something else. 'It broke my heart. You've been here a long time now –'

'Almost fifty years – not here, Brisbane originally, then a few other places before we retired. Been here nearly twenty.'

'You must know anybody who's anybody,' flattered Nell. 'Are there many from England?'

'Quite a few in Brisbane.' And Nell was forced to listen to a lot of useless chit-chat before being allowed to ask:

'But what about here?'

'Oh, not many Poms here. A lot of German stock, and Scandinavians for some reason.'

'I thought maybe with there being a lot of farms,' Nell steered her back, 'they might have taken a few of those migrants.'

'Well, they might,' said Millie. 'But I don't know any of the farmers, they're stuck out in the back of beyond – I think historically they captured a load of black fellows from the islands to cut the cane . . .'

And here we go again, thought Nell, as Millie droned on about totally the wrong subject. During a break in the dialogue she managed to say, 'Don't think I'm not fascinated, Millie, but I'll have to use your loo . . .'

'Oh I'm the same, dear – wait till you get to my age, you'll never want to be more than twenty yards from a dunny.'

Whilst Nell was gone, Nina risked her mother's wrath by divulging the reason for her questions. 'Please don't mention I told you, but Mum's looking for somebody in particular. She gave a son up for adoption fifty-odd years ago, and we're here to try and find him.'

Millie touched her cheek. 'Oh s'truth, he wasn't a child migrant, was he? And me rattling away like a tram – the poor woman.'

'Please don't tell Mary either,' Nina begged quickly.

'I wouldn't dream of it, love.'

Faced with so little time, Nina cut her off. 'His name was William Morgan, at least that's the name we think he had when he emigrated. We're not at all sure that it was Queensland, it's just on hearsay.'

'It'd be looking for a needle in a haystack, dear.'

Nina agreed. 'We must have looked at every scrap of paper and reel of microfilm in the State Library.'

'If they couldn't help you, I doubt I'll be of use.'

'Never mind, I just thought I'd let you know, so's you could maybe ask around your friends – someone might know someone. Mum's address is the same as your sister's, but number sixty-six instead of sixty-four.' Watching Millie scribble this down, she added, 'It's a long shot, but I'd give anything in the world to find him for her – best shut up now, she's coming.'

'Will you have another cup of tea before you go?' Millie was asking, as Nell returned.

'Ooh yes, always ready for a cuppa,' smiled Nell, though she had the sense that they had been talking about her.

'Looks like another of my friends has come to see me.' Copying Millie's example, everyone craned their necks.

A utility vehicle had pulled into the drive. The three women looked out to see a very powerful-looking man in the driving seat.

'Should we be going, Millie?'

'No! It's only the ranger, Shane – lovely bloke.'

Nell observed with an admiring eye. 'He looks a big fine chap.' Though, as he climbed out, she and the others were surprised to see that his body was somewhat out of proportion. Whilst still chunky, his legs seemed a little too short for his trunk.

Millie caught the younger women's smirk. 'Yes, you were expecting him to be a lot taller, weren't you, him being built like the proverbial outhouse?'

Nell passed the others a look that told them to watch their manners, then made ready to greet the visitor as his tap was heard on the fly-wire screen.

'G'day, Mill—' his drawl broke off as he caught sight of others. 'Ah sorry, you've got visitors . . .'

'That's all right, Shane.' Millie summoned him in and introduced them.

He had removed his hat to greet Millie. One of the old school. Nell liked that in a man. As ever, she calculated his age straight away. But even guessing that he was too young to be her son, in his late forties rather than his fifties, she knew he could not be related, for he was the antithesis of Billy, not as tall but twice as broad, padded with a little fat as well as muscle, and his hair was fine and light brown, and slightly thinning.

Invited to sit down for a cup of tea, Shane selected a chair that was set apart from the others. Watching his movements, Nell saw now that there was a slight similarity with Bill, in that his limbs were quite hirsute, the hair of his shins and forearms bleached to a golden fuzz by the sun. She couldn't tell if he had a hairy chest, all she could see was a small vee of smooth tanned skin, his khaki shirt being buttoned almost to the throat – and freshly donned that morning, judging by its crisp pleats and his neutral smell. Realising she was staring, she smiled and looked away, but not before she had noticed that Shane's hazel eyes seemed to linger on Nina. Not that it would do him any good. What a shame. He did seem a lovely chap, and his voice a far cry from the excitable rattle of that television commentator, a quiet, steady drawl, but soothing rather than monotonous.

During the conversation she was to discover why. Shane had been a lecturer at university but had given it all up to come and work as a ranger for the National Parks department. As usual it was Nell who asked and replied to any questions, Nina being very unreceptive to anything he might ask of her – not that he did after the first time. Despite being big and brawny and tanned with a friendly smile, he was quite reserved, and, Nell suspected, rather shy too.

Whilst they had been speaking, a row of black and white birds had assembled on Millie's window ledge, looking like robbers with their black hoods. Then, one of them emitted a haunting note, as if the leader of a barber's choir setting the tune – and what a beautiful tune it was, each bird performing his own individual note in turn – in the way that tapping wine glasses filled to different levels with water might create a melody – each little beak extended to the sky, then the head swooping down in a bow as he delivered. The watchers found it enchanting.

'Australian magpies are a lot more musical than ours.' Romy smiled at Shane.

'Yes, it's a bit like a Gregorian chant, isn't it – but they're butcherbirds. That one's a magpie over there.' Touching her shoulder, he steered her to look through another window, then said, 'Listen . . .' And they were to hear a totally different, but equally beautiful, cadenza. 'They're asking for their dinner,' smiled Millie.

'What have I told you about upsetting the balance of nature?' Shane wagged a finger, but seemed quite relaxed as Millie fed the birds with a few scraps of mince. And whilst this amused the visitors, he was to relate to Romy some of the comical things he had seen the birds do. 'Watched them play all kinds of games – would you believe they were surfing the other night after a rainfall! Jumping onto a stream of water, surfing along it, then jumping off again just before they would've been swept down the drain!' Enacting all the movements for the benefit of a smiling Romy, he seemed all at once aware that he might be making a fool of himself in front of her mother, who was altogether less receptive. And he withdrew with a sheepish look to finish his tea.

It wasn't long afterwards that he was on his way – another one escaped, Nell silently accused her middle-aged daughter. Silly girl.

'Divorced,' Millie leaned forward to whisper, even though he had gone. 'No children.'

Nell wondered how she had managed to draw such personal information from this buttoned-up fellow. 'Is that what made him throw up his career? I thought it was an odd move to have made.'

'I get the idea he had some sort of road to Damascus

experience. I know he was wounded in Vietnam, might be something to do with that . . .'

'I noticed he had a nasty scar on his leg.' Nell spoke of her ignorance over this war, though did not divulge the fear that her son might have been involved. 'So, your sons must have been in it too, Millie?'

'No, luckily their birthdays never came up.' She quickly explained that selection had been on a lottery system.

Hearing that not every young man had gone to war, Nell relaxed a little, and, noting that her daughter was getting restless, said, 'Well, it's time we were going too. Thank you very much for your hospitality, Millie.'

'And thank you for coming all this way to bring me this rubbish from Mary. Dear me, what a long way –'

'Hopefully your sister might be able to come and see you herself one day.'

'I hope to God not! I can't bear to be in the same room as her for more than two minutes.'

Laughing about this as they went on their way, Nina said to her mother, 'Whilst I've got you in a good mood . . . I told Millie about William.'

'Oh, Neen!'

'Well, I thought she might be more inclined to help if she knew the reason.'

'I suppose you're right.' Nell appeared to be reconciled to her secret being leaked. 'What does it matter in this day and age? I'm just a silly old fool.'

'No, you're not.'

At the same time as Nina made this declaration, Romy took her grandmother's hand and patted it. 'And didn't I always promise I'm going to find him, Nana?'

Whilst not pertinent to their search, there was plenty to investigate during their time here: the sulphurous mangroves at the northern end of town, where the creek opened her mouth in a passionate kiss of the sea, to the mournful cry of the curlew; the breathtaking estuary across which they roamed when the tide went out, to marvel over the prehistoric sand dollars, and the big red starfish marooned amongst the swirling patterns of its watery flats; and the sanctuary beyond, where turtles came to lay.

And, like the turtles on their mission, under cover of darkness, at the same time every evening Romy would tiptoe off to make contact with her lover.

Nell was relieved to see the anxious wraith gradually dispelled, and in its place a happier glow, which was partly enhanced by the sun-bleached hair, and the limbs turned golden brown, but in the main stemmed from a decision being reached. Romy could now see her future, and was eager to be home to it. And though she was still quite emaciated, Nell was doing her best to remedy this with liberal servings from the barbecue. None the less disapproving, but resigned to her daughter's intentions, Nina had begun to relax too. The insect bites dealt with, her body had taken on a similar healthy glow, as had Nell's.

After a few more days at this glorious oasis, all three felt refreshed enough to return to Brisbane and start trawling through records again.

'Though much good it'll do,' came Nell's pessimism.

'Ah well, you've got Millie to help now,' said Nina. 'She might unearth something after we've gone.'

Having packed up and paid the bill the night before, they set off in the early morning. Before turning off the esplanade, Romy paused the car and gave a forlorn little wave to the sea, 'Farewell lovely place . . .' Though barely up, already the sun was glittering the waves, the ocean sighing answer, as if sad to see them go.

Despite the sentiment, Nell sensed a new purpose as her granddaughter steered them away from the view, and, before long, home to Patrick. It was sad to think that another family would be rent, but she was glad all the same that Romy had been delivered from the slough of despond.

Driving slowly whilst they were amongst the houses, the young woman put her foot down once they reached the open road. Birds of prey hovered over the verges, the sun behind the gum trees casting their shadows across the road like stripes on a long straight snake. Romy put on some music, and was about to sing along, when from one of the shadows on the tarmac a grey kangaroo popped up, looking straight at them as the car slammed into it with a sickening crump of flesh and metal.

There were yells and screams, the screech of brakes, the tinkling of glass, then silence.

'Romy!' Nina instinctively turned to check on the driver.

'I'm all right, Mam!' Her daughter's pale face emerged from a curtain of hair, shaken but uninjured, then immediately they both turned to Nell in the back.

'Yes, I'm all right,' a dazed Nell hurried to tell them, though the seatbelt had wrenched her shoulder and the pain went right across her breast.

Romy staggered out then, and went around to the passenger side. 'Help your nana,' ordered Nina, exerting herself from her seat, and between them they assisted Nell from the back.

First examining each other for signs of injury, ascertaining that none of them needed to go to hospital, then came the car. It was a mess, one of its wings completely dished in, its driver having only managed the slightest of veers before the impact had sent the kangaroo into the air, glancing off the bonnet – which had also received a dent – and over the roof. A bloody carcass lay several yards behind the skid marks on the road. Romy clasped her hands to her face, squashing her cheeks as she saw the extent of the damage.

Nell tried to limit her concern. 'Ah well, it can't be helped . . .'

'It could be if the fucking kangaroo hadn't been lying in the middle of the road – sorry, Mam, but really, what a stupid place!' Nina was furious at the thought of any harm coming to her daughter or her mother.

'It could have been worse had it come through the windscreen.' Nell rubbed her upper chest, which had begun to throb.

'I'm really sorry, this is going to cost a bomb to fix,' said Romy, to her mother in particular. 'I'll have to ring the hire firm and get a replacement. I wonder where their nearest depot is . . .'

'Oh, never mind the bloody car, as long as we're all right,' said Nina, and made as if to get back in. 'We'll have to turn round and go back, though – are you all right to drive, Romy?'

Though her hands were shaking, Romy said she was, but a buckled front wheel arch prevented the wheel from rotating. Nina looked up, and then down, the long, deserted road, saying it was too much to hope that someone would come by. The farmsteads were set so far away from the road that it would be as easy to walk back to the town than to one of them. Then she glimpsed something in the distance. 'Is that one of those emergency phone boxes down there?'

Whilst the other two stayed where they were, Romy went to use it.

Her trek proved a success. She came back to say there would not be a replacement car coming yet, but, given Millie's number, the nice person at the other end had promised to phone her to come and collect them. Then, for a while longer, the three stood to wait as the sun's heat increased.

Millie's arrival was not such a triumph as hoped, for her car was tiny and had only two doors.

Nina uttered a note of dismay. 'It's going be like the *Guinness Book of Records* trying to fit us all into that . . .' However, help was close behind, its little driver jabbing a walnut thumb over her shoulder at the utility vehicle that had just rattled to a halt alongside the roadkill. 'I phoned Shane when you said you'd hit a roo! He can take one of you.'

'That'll be you, Mam.' Nell felt two coaxing hands on her shoulders, pushing her towards Shane.

However, the ranger said not a word until he had bent over the corpse. 'It's a female. Somebody should've had a look in its pouch –'

'Oh, my pardons!' offered Nina. 'We were a bit preoccupied.'

Shane ignored her sarcasm. 'Yes, there's a joey in here . . .'

His audience craned around his wide back to see, making a unified, 'Ah!' as the naked pink alien was gently removed from its dead mother and cradled in outsized hands. 'There's a woolly hat in my cab, can somebody get it?'

Nearest to the vehicle, though still displeased by his tone, Nina rummaged about in the cab and finally came up with the hat. Telling her to hold it open, Shane gently poured the contents of his hands inside. Then, all of a sudden, she was left holding the baby, its pink nose jutting from the knitted folds.

'Will it be all right?' enquired Nell.

'Not sure. I know somebody who'll do a good job with it.' Shane removed the mother's corpse from the tarmac, then said, 'You need to take a bit more care along these roads. They lie in the shadows and you're on them before you notice.'

'She didn't do it on purpose!' Still cradling the joey, Nina saw her daughter's upset and was quick to defend her. 'And she wasn't driving like some of the maniacs round here – if you're interested in humans, by any chance, we're all in one piece, thanks for asking!'

The burly figure looked awkward, and asked of her, 'Are you coming with me?'

'No, you can take my mother.' Carefully holding her

woolly parcel to her breast, Nina squeezed into the little car along with Romy.

Opening the cab door and helping Nell to climb in, Shane threw their cases in the back of his utility, then went to push the wrecked vehicle onto the verge before turning his own around, and setting off with the little car behind.

'Anybody'd think we mow down animals on purpose,' muttered Nina from Millie's rear seat.

'I don't think he meant to blame you,' said Millie. 'He just sees some sick things done to animals.'

Then everyone fell silent as they headed back towards the sea.

Dropped at the holiday villa from whence they had earlier departed, Nina handed over the orphaned joey to the ranger, then turned her back as he drove away. They found the owner of the villa about to strip their beds, and spared her the trouble, asking could they move back in. Being low season, they were invited to stay as long as they liked, though Nina said it would only be a few days whilst they organised a replacement car. She was to wince at the cost of the latter, even having taken out extra insurance for such an eventuality.

'Every cloud has a silver lining,' said Romy. 'Now I can get a few more photos.'

'We came to Australia so's your Nana can look for her son,' rebuked Nina. 'Not going to find him stuck here, are we?'

But Nell waved this aside. 'I don't think another few days will make a difference.'

And they were such lovely days, strolling on the beach in the morning, perhaps sitting for a few hours under a large parasol, with intermittent dips to cool off, then just relaxing indoors after lunch, to read the stack of novels that holidaymakers had left behind.

Forty-eight hours after their accident, it was all but

forgotten as they wandered along the sands towards the headland about three or four miles away, occasionally pausing to watch vast battalions of sapphire-blue soldier crabs sweep across the wet sand, or bobbing into the sea to cool off – until they saw the ranger's vehicle heading towards them from the other direction. Nina very quickly wrapped a brightly coloured sarong around her bikini-clad figure, though Romy seemed unconcerned at being seen half-naked, Nell's busty outline already clad in a gauzy dress. Upon recognising the three, Shane made a detour across the beach, his engine ticking over as he called through the open window of his cab, 'How's the car going?'

'Same as you, a bloody nuisance,' muttered Nina, which was masked by her mother's cheery reply:

'Oh, they've fixed us up with another – how's the little joey?'

'He's doing okay! That mate o' mine has a pretty good success rate with them.'

Seeing Shane was in no hurry to drive off, one thick bronzed arm leaning out of his cab, Nell came right up to stand beside his utility truck, a smiling Romy doing likewise, whilst Nina hung back, forced to wait for them or be dubbed impolite. A usual it was Nell who upheld the conversation, though Romy inserted one or two questions about the kangaroo's habits, which Shane seemed glad to answer – then Nell suddenly stopped to point along the beach, 'Oh look! There's one . . .'

Shane turned his head, Nina too. A large kangaroo had come bounding out of the bush towards the sea, stopping abruptly at the curl of the tide to scrape one of its ears along the sand. Hovering uncertainly for a moment or two, it launched itself into the water and began to swim, at one point disappearing beneath the surface, the watchers able to see his dark form kicking out neath a turquoise wave. Nell held her breath. Then his nose broke the surface again, and on he battled against the force. Occasionally he would disappear, then come up to shake his head and twitch his ears, finally to disappear into the blue beyond.

Shane was happy to discuss the animal's behaviour, and turned off his engine for a while. 'They often go for a swim – get these mites that drive them mad, and try to wash them off.'

Nell and Romy were similarly pleased to be enlightened, exchanging looks of fascination.

'It's not always mites,' added Shane, looking not just at them but at Nina as he spoke, as if to include her in the conversation. 'They just like to go for a plunge for the fun of it. Go island-hopping too. Known them swim miles.'

'I never knew kangaroos could even swim!' Nell laughed at Romy.

'Yeah, they're strong swimmers.' Shane then proceeded to deliver more on the marsupial world.

Whilst Nell and Romy seemed rapt, Nina gave hint of her boredom by moving on, picking up shells here and there and examining them.

'Watch out, that's not a cone shell,' Shane called after her. 'They're deadly.'

'Yes, I have read the guidebooks,' came a haughty retort that was issued without a glance in his direction.

'Well, better let you folks get going.' All of a sudden Shane started his engine, and, with a cursory wave, drove away.

'Wasn't that fascinating?' said Nell to her companions.

Romy agreed. 'Looks like he's forgiven me for making an orphan of that baby the other day.'

'He's very wrapped up in his kanga-bloody-roos.' Still draped in her sarong, Nina bent to pick up another shell.

'Well, he obviously likes animals – and knows an awful lot about them.'

'Yes, and wasn't he keen to bore us all to death with his knowledge?'

'Don't be mean, he's a really nice bloke,' said her mother, Romy echoing this.

'– blaming my daughter for the animal's fault.'

'He seemed very keen on you,' teased Nell.

Romy laughed at her mother's protestation. 'Yes, I noticed that too, Nana!'

Then both began to rib Nina unmercifully about the ranger's crush on her.

With a mischievous look in her eye, Nell burst into song with her hands clutched to her heart, trilling, 'Hold my hand, I'm a *ranger* in paradise . . !'

Romy swiftly cottoned on to the idea, pretending to waltz. '*Rangers* in the night, exchanging glances . . .'

This setting the ball rolling back and forth, Nell and her laughing granddaughter adapted the words to every love song they could think of.

'You pair of daft buggers, leave off,' chastised Nina with a toss of her blonde hair. She had laughed along with them for a while, but now it grew tedious. 'This sun must have got to your brains – come on, let's be heading back, I can feel my face burning.'

And of course this drew more mockery. 'The blushing bride,' teased Romy.

'Stop being silly now.' Her grandmother adopted the air of level-headed dowager, pretending to agree with Nina's request for good behaviour, before saying. 'Lead the way, *Kimo Sabi*,' and bursting out laughing. Though a little comedic impact was lost, in having to explain to Romy that these were the words used by Tonto, the Lone Ranger's sidekick. It was not, however, to prevent more of the same all the way back to their accommodation.

'You're right,' announced Nina to her mother on their final day, as they sat in the turquoise shallows cooling off. 'About the lack of stimulation here. I'm bored to tears.'

Nell laughingly agreed. 'Yes, Shangri-La's all right in small doses.'

'I suppose it would be different if you lived here,' mused

Nina. 'You know, go out to work in town, then come home to this. That would be lovely. But to be here day after day, each one identical, the same temperature . . .' As her voice trailed away she peered up the beach to try to catch sight of her daughter, who had taken to walking to the promontory every day. 'That looks like Romy on her way back.'

Nell craned her head around the figure beside her, waved, then lay in the shallows, enjoying the feel of the water lapping over her plump thighs. They were still lazing there on the long, deserted shore, no other human in view, save for Romy coming ever nearer, when Nell felt eyes on her, and, with a little difficulty, rolled over onto her stomach.

Instantly alert, she gave an excited murmur of delight. 'Oh, look, Neen!'

Her daughter rolled over too, both of them mesmerised by the narrow-gutted dingo, who raised his muzzle and sniffed the air, then stood looking back at them with eyes that were amber and bold. In no hurry, he stared a while longer, before melting back into the bush.

'I saw him earlier!' panted Romy, as she finally splashed into the water to join them, the three talking excitedly. 'It would be on the day before we're leaving. All week I've lugged my camera around with me, and the only day I don't, I've seen all sorts! There were dolphins surfing down near the point. I might come down later and sit around for a while, see if he comes back.'

But once she had eaten lunch, having done five or six miles in the torrid heat that morning, Romy declared herself too knackered to go out again, and spent the rest of the day by the pool. In the evening, with packing to be done, she did not manage to get out again with her camera – as usual going along to the phone booth where yet another ten dollars' worth of card was eaten up on sweet nothings to Patrick – though she swore to try for a shot of the dingo the next morning.

That night, something disturbed Nell's sleep. Pricking

her ears to the horrible, bloodcurdling howl on the darkness, which caused her hair to bristle and her heart to palpate, all of a sudden she became truly aware of how isolated was her little bed, twixt the sea and the thousands of acres of wilderness, and with only a fly-wire screen to deter whatever might be out there . . .

Then the moment was over, the sound gone, and she was lulled back to sleep by the whispering waves.

'I don't think it matters what time we set off,' she said, following breakfast. 'So long as we're packed up and ready to go, we can spend a little while on the beach. I shall miss that.'

Once the car had been loaded and the bill settled, they drove all the way to the far end of the esplanade, where the road terminated in dense National Park land. Eager to find something to photograph, Romy trotted to the beach ahead of them, leaving Nina to lever Nana out of her seat, and to lock up.

Some minutes later, arm in arm, the elderly mother and daughter took the green corridor to the beach. There was an ever-present fragrance within this dappled shade, of sun-warmed eucalyptus leaves crushed underfoot, and the pungent scent of its blossom. Treading carefully to avoid stumbling over roots, Nell paused to watch some colourful finches that were darting through the swaying fronds of the sheoaks.

'Your father would love it here.'

Then she inclined her head and listened, with a look of slight alarm. 'Is that a baby crying?'

Nina stopped to listen and frowned. 'Sounds like it, but in a weird sort of way – as if it's distressed.' With the mournful laments continuing to haunt the air, she and Nell began to stoop and peer within the bushes, but could see no baby.

Nell's concern grew. The infant bleats stirred awful

memories, reminding her why she had come here. Taunting her. She and her daughter moved on, still looking for the source. Then, as she and Nina emerged from the tunnel onto the sunlit beach, they saw movement, and what appeared to be black rags flapping amongst the branches of the casuarinas.

'Oh, black cockatoos!' Nina broke into a smile of relief, Nell too, as, still arm in arm, they attempted to get a closer look at the birds – which they could see now were feasting on the woody nut-like fruit of the trees. But before they took three steps, the cockatoos lifted into the air en masse, exposing brilliant red beneath their tails, some a pale yellow, and all emitting that mournful wail that Nell had thought was a baby, flying only fifty yards or so along the beach before coming to rest again.

Faces wreathed in delight, the mother and daughter tracked their flight path, not meaning to spook them, but doing so anyway, for each time they got anywhere close, the birds would rise again squawking.

'It's nothing like a baby's cry when you know what it really is,' laughed Nell to Nina.

Agreeing, the latter wondered aloud if Romy had managed to photograph the birds – for she was quite a way ahead, standing on tiptoe, then bending right over in her efforts to spy something of interest in the dense bush to the rear of the beach.

With the gap between them widening, the elder women decided to paddle at the water's edge. 'I don't want to get too sweaty with five hours' driving ahead of us,' said Nell.

They splashed for a while, then returned to the dunes, where they sat under the shade of a casuarina, occasionally snatching a look up the beach to see if the distant figure that was Romy had acquired her coveted photos and might soon return. A vehicle was approaching from the point, though it was a mere dot at the moment, being miles away.

'Ah, she's coming back,' Nell observed quite soon afterwards, then laughed as she continued to peer through her sunglasses. 'She looks as if she's dancing!'

'About bloody time.' Smiling, Nina turned to look – then immediately stiffened, for she had seen that Romy was not dancing, but running. Running for her life towards the sea, with a dingo at her heels.

Nina screamed, startling both her mother and the cockatoos, which rose with an almighty squawk into the air. Nell cried out too, as her middle-aged daughter went racing forth, hampered by the dry sand, stumbling and tripping until she reached the damper, firmer stretch, then racing for all she was worth toward her own daughter, who was now using her camera to beat off her attacker, swinging it from its strap, back and forth between herself and the dingo. The driver of a vehicle that had been heading towards them from the other direction was now close enough to assist, and began papping its horn furiously, as it careered toward Romy, who had entered the waves in search of escape. With the ranger's vehicle bearing down on it from one angle, and screaming women from another, the dingo turned tail and, with tongue lolling and eyes bright, in arrogant fashion loped back into the National Park.

Nell felt as if she were having a heart attack. By the time she hobbled up, the ranger's four-wheel drive had ploughed to a halt, and Shane was helping Nina to assist Romy out of the sea.

'I'm all right!' Though shocked and bleeding from her calf, Romy reassured first her mother, then Nell, who arrived looking ready to collapse. 'I'm all right, Nana!'

Nina, too, whizzed round to say, 'Oh, Mam, I'm sorry for leaving you!' But she was soon back to tending Romy, at the same time berating Shane. 'The blasted thing, it should be shot! Look at the state of my daughter's leg! It's almost ripped her calf off!'

'Neen, don't exaggerate,' puffed Nell. 'You're frightening

the poor lass to death.' She drew on her nursing skills, and portrayed the calm manner that was required here – though inside her heart was pumping. 'Let me have a look at it.' Whilst Romy was supported by Shane's thick arms, Nell bent to examine the leg and offer reassurance to the victim, who seemed not half as shaken as her mother, and more bothered about her camera.

'I hope it still works – at least I got a shot of the dingo.'

Nina began to yell at the ranger again. 'Why aren't you in there shooting the blasted thing?' She speared a finger in the direction of the bush. 'It could have torn a child to pieces!'

'Calm down, Neen, it's not too serious – but its teeth have made a little puncture, so she should have a tetanus jab at least.'

'I can't understand it,' murmured Shane. 'There's been one or two instances of attacks on Fraser Island, but that's because the tourists feed them. It's never happened here.'

'Well it has now!' Nina raged at him.

The ranger was still meditative as he watched Nell tend Romy's wound with the first-aid kit he had brought from the car, and hardly seemed to hear Nina yelling at him, until she raised her voice another decibel.

'Are you bloody deaf, or as thick as the rest of them in this godforsaken place? I said go after it, before it kills someone!'

He looked at her then, his face still creased in bafflement. 'Time of the month, is it?'

'I *beg* your pardon?'

Nell thought her daughter was about to grab him by the throat, and quickly intervened her plump body between them. 'We should get her to a hospital, Neen.'

'Fat chance in this wilderness!'

Shane's attitude changed to one of mild indignation. 'I was only –'

'We'll have to get her to the car!' Nina cut him off, and

hauled her daughter none too gently to her feet. 'Though God knows how she'll manage to drive it.'

Despite provocation, Shane remained polite and took charge. 'I'll take you – where's it parked?'

'At the end of the esplanade by the toilets – we were on our way back to Brisbane.'

An expression crossed his face, unassociated with the situation here – a look of disappointment, thought Nell. But she was too concerned to bother about his attraction for Nina today. 'Best if we all go to Millie's,' she said. 'She might be good enough to drive Romy into town – I hope she's in. Can you get these girls into your cab, Shane?'

Having helped the wounded Romy into the passenger seat of his cab, Shane thought it politic to let Nina climb in by herself. Then he looked at the older woman, his posture relaying that no way would she fit in too. At that juncture he was spared from having to insult her, as he spotted another four-wheel-drive vehicle approaching from the point, and flagged it down, asking the driver if he would give this lady a lift and follow him.

Issuing breathless thanks to the strangers, Nell sought to cram her wide beam into the back seat, then remarked on how much room there was, before relating the incident to her Samaritan as they followed the ranger's tyre tracks along the beach.

Once at Millie's, after quick negotiations, Romy and Nina were transferred to her car, just as Nell was being dropped off. She gave thanks for the ride, then went to join the group in the palm bedecked driveway.

Nina was still yelling at Shane. 'Can you move that bloody thing out of the way so we can get out!'

'You'll have to forgive my daughter.' Nell gave a rushed apology as he moved to do her bidding. 'She's just worried – and thank you very much for this – what a good job you were there to scare the dingo away.'

'No worries. I reckon she got hold of the wrong end of

the stick, though. What I meant was – pardon me for asking, love,' he made a quick aside to Romy, 'but sometimes on the rare occasion a grown woman's been attacked, it's usually turned out she's been having her period. Dingoes must be attracted by it, or that's the theory. I didn't mean any offence.'

'Ah!' Both Nell and her granddaughter gave a sound of acknowledgement, Nell thinking how much things had changed when a man felt able to voice this unmentionable subject, Romy freely confessing that yes, it was that particular time of the month for her.

'Better let you get to hospital then,' said the ranger, and he drove away.

Anxious for her granddaughter to receive treatment as swiftly as possible, Nell waved them off and said she would wait there.

'Help yourself to tea,' called the spry Millie, as she sped away.

It was a very long three hours before Nell was to see her family again. She smiled her relief as Romy was helped from the car by her mother, her calf heavily bandaged. 'Did you need stitches? No, I thought not. It'll soon heal. I bet it hurts, though . . .'

Romy agreed, then was helped, limping, into Millie's bungalow. 'We were going to go straight back to the holiday house, but Millie said we could have lunch here.'

'I don't know what we'd have done without you, Millie.' Nell showed deep gratitude.

The little walnut face laughed this off, then turned as a utility truck pulled up outside.

Nina groaned.

'Look, don't be rude,' Nell cautioned. 'He was the one who saved her.'

'He didn't shoot the blasted thing, though, did he?' Nina was still grimacing when Shane twanged the fly-wire screen.

'How's the patient?'

'Better, thanks.' Romy showed him her bandaged calf.

'Did you get it?' asked Nina.

'What?' asked Shane.

She shook her head with a sound of disgust.

Nell jumped in to keep the peace. 'Did they say if it would be safe to fly home?'

'When d'you fly?' Shane asked.

'Next weekend.'

His face relaxed a little. 'So you've another week here.'

'Not here, no,' said Nina. 'In fact, we would have been in Brisbane three days ago if that kangaroo hadn't wrecked the car.' She ignored him then, to answer Nell's query. 'Yes, she's safe to fly, Mam. So we can go back to Brisbane when you want.'

The ranger looked regretful. 'Sorry your stay wasn't more enjoyable.'

'On the contrary,' said Nell. 'Apart from the bite and the crash it's been absolutely glorious, hasn't it, Nina?'

There was no way Nina could disagree with that. 'I can see why people like living here, though I don't know if I'd feel safe so far from civilisation.'

Shane questioned her idea of civilisation.

'Horses for courses,' smiled Nina, not half so antagonistic as earlier, having got over the miscommunication. 'Anyway, hadn't one of us better go round to the villa and ask if we can stay an extra night – *again*. You won't feel like driving down to Brisbane now.'

'We can stay a few extra days,' said Nell. 'After all, there's no rush.'

'But we came here to look –'

'Yes, I know.' Nell cut her granddaughter off before she could publicise the secret. 'But let's concentrate on getting you healed.' Looking at those two dear faces then, dearer to her than any others in the world, Nell asked herself how she could have subjected them to this futile and dangerous trek, to look for a son that might hate her – wishing for the moon, when she had been so blessed with Nina and Romy. 'You're what's important to me now,' she said firmly.

She saw that Shane was confused, and flashed him a smile, which he returned. He was a lovely looking chap when he relaxed that frown. 'We were just going to look up our family tree in the State Archives,' she explained with a white lie. 'One of my ancestors emigrated, but he's not important at the moment, this one is.' She indicated Romy. 'I don't know! This is the second time we've tried to set off . . .'

'Somebody doesn't want you to leave,' opined Shane, glancing at Nina as he said it. Then he had a thought. 'Is your car still parked at the other end of the esplanade?'

Both Nina and her mother looked at Romy, who was obviously unfit to get it.

'I'll give one of you a lift to collect it.'

'Neither of us drive,' admitted Nell.

He seemed taken aback.

'It's not a crime,' said Nina.

'No, no.' He scratched his jaw. 'You'll be a bit stuck for a while, though.'

'I'll be all right in a day or two,' insisted Romy.

'Yes, but all our clothes are in it,' said Nell. 'Millie, would you mind going with Shane and driving it back for us?'

'Nan, that's cheeky,' tittered Romy.

'If you don't ask you don't get,' said Nell, looking sweetly at Shane.

'I'll have to remember that one,' said the ranger, as if filing it away for the future. 'I've got something to do now, but I'll come back later for you, Millie.'

'Will you have a bite with us first, Shane?'

'No I'd better get moving.' He slapped his bare knees, and said to the group, 'Hope to run into you again later.' Then he put on his hat, touched its brim to the women, and left.

A sudden chill came over Nina. 'I left my cardigan in your car, Millie – is it open?'

'Yes, love, help yourself.' Millie set to exploring the fridge for the ingredients of lunch.

Nell said, 'I'll give you a hand, Millie.' But her attention was on Nina, who hurried through the lush garden after the ranger.

Not until they were back in their holiday villa did Nell casually mention to her daughter, 'I saw you having a few words with Shane . . .'

Nina looked blank, then appeared to recall the situation. 'Oh, yes, I was just thanking him for his assistance. I forgot earlier in all the kerfuffle. Do you want some supper? I'll just take milady something in, then I'll see to you.'

Romy was already in bed, ordered there by Nell to rest her leg. Whilst the young woman's mother went to attend her, Nell, who had been thoughtful all afternoon, turned and wandered outside.

People went to bed early here. With all the lights off it was pitch black. Nell allowed herself to be clothed in darkness, just standing there, alone, letting it seep into her. Well, you got your comeuppance, she told herself. Your granddaughter could have been killed this afternoon if there'd been no one around to help her, and all because you brought her here on your fool's errand. What kind of a woman are you, to waste all these years fantasising over a will o' the wisp? Neglecting your husband, letting Nina spend all that money on searching for her rival. Is he really more important than the one who isn't flesh, but calls you Mother just the same? How it must hurt to know that a person your mother had never met was more valued than the one who had spent all her pocket money on Christmas, Mother's Day and birthday gifts, every year of her childhood, saving all her pennies, taking such trouble to get just the right one. Especially after that business of Joe wanting a boy, and all the hurt that had gone with it. But no, you push it all aside in your selfish quest. What kind of a mother are you?

Then, her eyes attuned to the darkness by now, out of the inky blackness came a twinkle, and another, and another – and Nell remembered, that only in the blackout of that terrible war had they been able to appreciate the full beauty of the galaxy. Yes, William was out there somewhere – but she resolved there and then that she must stop this obsession before it was too late.

A cheery voice called, 'Cup of tea here for you, Mam!'

Nell turned and went in then, saying immediately, 'I'm so sorry, Neen, you must think I'm a selfish pig, putting him before you . . .'

Nina looked surprised, then started to say, with that bluff yet affectionate manner so much like her father's, 'You silly bug—'

'No, listen.' Nell's tone held determination, though her face had adopted a look of despair. 'I know you'd never complain, you're a kind, caring lass, but I'm too old to go traipsing any further. So, I've decided, I'm going to give up looking for William – don't bother to argue! This afternoon has taught me to be content with the wonderful family I've got. We're going home.'

26

Having made her momentous decision to give up her search for William, in the knowledge that she should treasure those she had, all the same Nell felt flat on landing in grey old England. Especially coming home to an empty house. Well, not empty for long. She had barely stuck her key in the door when the click of Mary's stiletto heels alerted her to the one dashing round to hear news of her sister.

'Mary, I've just this second got home!' The taxi containing Nina and Romy had not even turned the corner 'Would you mind letting me unpack these cases, or at least let me go to the lavatory.'

The beautifully applied mask collapsed in disappointment. 'Sorry, it's just been so lonely here without you,' Mary explained as she turned to go.

And then, of course, Nell felt awful. 'Oh, make yourself useful and stick the kettle on then! I'll be down in a minute or two.'

And for the next couple of hours she was forced to relay everything that Millie had said, Mary especially wanting to know if her sister had appreciated the gifts, and if anything had been sent in return, which it had.

'I knew she'd send me rubbish,' declared Mary, examining the item on top, a tea towel with an Aboriginal design. 'When I sent her all that good British stuff.'

'That's from me, actually,' said Nell through pursed lips. 'You can give it back if it's not to your liking.'

'Oh no, it's very good of you, I was just surprised it's made in China.' Mary showed her the label.

'Yes, well, I think you'll find that a lot of Marks and Spencer's stuff is manufactured by foreigners now.'

I wish to God you'd go home, thought a weary Nell, so I can ring Killie and catch up with family news.

Then as if her prayer had been answered, the phone rang. Nell pounced on it. 'Oh, hello! It's one of Joe's nieces,' she gave whispered hint to Mary.

The latter showed reluctance to go. 'I suppose I'd better make myself scarce then . . . See you tomorrow morning as usual?'

With a nod, Nell made herself comfortable to chat. But within a few seconds of Mary's departure, her smile was to vanish.

'I'm sorry, Aunty,' Nell heard the voice at the other end say. 'Bad news, I'm afraid . . . Aunty Beat's died.'

After a little weep for the loss of her dear old friend, Nell blew her nose, then rang her daughter to pass on the sombre news. 'She died the day after we flew to Oz. They thought it best not to wait for us to come back.'

At the other end there came a sniff. 'I'll come round,' said Nina. And she hung up.

Three-quarters of an hour later, she entered her mother's living room, where they both cried again.

Emerging from a red-eyed hug, Nina wiped her eyes with one hand, then held up a bottle of wine. 'I've brought this.'

'You know me too well.' Nell got out two glasses, which her daughter filled with red wine. Then she took a large glug, before enlarging upon Beata's demise. 'They had her cremated, but they haven't scattered her ashes yet.'

Nina's eyes brimmed again, and she turned away with a sigh. 'I'm not looking forward to that.'

Then they sat and talked of old times with Beata, the many kindnesses she had performed, the way she had sacrificed her own youth to look after one family member after another, the funny things she had said and done over many years. The box of photographs was brought out, that which always came out at such sad occasions, and they sifted through the old black-and-white prints, picking out ones that were especially nice, like that of Beata in her brand-new nurse's uniform, an unflattering dress maybe, but the goodness and compassion shone out of that noble, beloved face.

More wine was drunk. Then Nell said, 'I'll tell you now, I don't want to be cremated.'

'Oh, don't, Mam . . .' Nina began to put the photographs away.

'No, I'm not dwelling on it, I just want you to know. Your dad always said it was nice and clean, but it's not for me. I want to go in the good earth – don't spend heaps on a box, it's a waste of money. Cardboard will do – or wicker. Chicken in a basket.' She gave a frail smile at her joke. 'I just don't want to end up being blown away on the wind. I know it sounds silly, but I want there to be something left of me, in a particular spot, a grave and a headstone to mark where my bones lie.'

'Right, can you shut up now or you'll end up with a premature burial.'

And Nell did shut up then. But only for as long as it took for a trip to the lavatory. She brought with her another box when she returned – a hat box – though did not open it for a while, just sat with it on her lap as she stared unseeingly at the bird-of-paradise wallpaper, and commented in a flat voice, 'It's hard to grasp, life going on when you've gone . . .'

'Oh don't start again, Mam,' begged Nina, who was beginning to fear for her mother's sanity.

'No, don't be sad, I've had a good life – a useful life,

I think. And I just want to make sure you know I'm serious about there being a grave, and a headstone for William –'

'Yes, I get the picture. I'm sorry we couldn't find him for you.'

'It's not you who should be saying sorry.' Nell might well be prey to disappointment and anticlimax after the fruitless trip, but she pretended to Nina that it was only what she expected. 'I've got a wonderful daughter and granddaughter, why did I bother wasting my life chasing rainbows? I might not have found him, but I know he'll turn up one day, even if it's after I've gone. I thought about writing a letter for you to give to him – should he be interested enough to come looking, that is.'

'Course he will.' Nina looked upset at having only platitude to offer.

Nell shook her head. 'I don't think I could bring myself to write it.'

Because to do so would be to accept that they would never meet, and also that she was going to die, and Nell did not want to die. Not for many years. She had her health, and her family, and perhaps great-grandchildren to look forward to. William would know she had loved him, one way or another.

'Just give him this,' she eventually said to Nina, and, taking the lid off the hat box, she displayed the gold chain containing Bill's wedding ring and the scrap of frayed ribbon, and also showed her the watch. 'That belonged to his father. The ribbon was from one of the bootees meant for him . . .' Her eyes were slowly filling with tears, but she fought them to add, 'His father's letters to me, and mine to him, are in here too. I won't give you them yet, but that's where they'll be . . .'

'Right – now can we please talk about something else?' begged her daughter, pouring another hasty glass of wine.

* * *

There was a long period of mourning over their dear sister-in-law and aunt, and added to it was a lot of unrest over Romy and her married man – at least married in name, for he was now living apart from his wife, having immediately moved in with Nell's granddaughter, with the divorce pending. It was all very unpleasant, and Nell suspected she had not been told the half of it – but at least, having met Patrick, she could see he was not undergoing this lightly, and was a totally different kettle of fish to the roguish Hayden, and equally committed to Romy, for he had already bought her a wedding ring. Some might call it sordid. Nell did not like it either, but she could see they were madly in love, and hoped that everyone's pain would quickly be salved – especially that of the little boy. It was impossible not to equate him with William, to imagine his confusion and bewilderment at being abandoned. Nell worried about him a lot . . .

But, in the middle of all this upheaval, came something completely unexpected and pleasant.

Gathering the mail from her doormat one morning, Nell sucked in her breath as she saw that one of the letters bore an Australian stamp – had Millie found something out about William? Still in the hall, she shoved the others under her arm and tore this one open quickly.

But she was immediately disappointed. '*Dear Nina . . .*'

Concerned to have opened her daughter's private mail, she looked again at the addressee, then immediately rang Nina.

'I'm sorry, Neen, I wouldn't have opened it, but it was addressed to Mrs N Kilmaster, not Miss.'

The voice at the other end did not sound bothered. 'Never mind, see who it's from.'

'I couldn't read somebody else's mail! But it might be about William, so can you come?'

'What are you like! Can you just hold on to your excitement for an hour and I'll come round – oh, hang on! Make that ten minutes, Romy's just walked in, she can drive me.'

Nell was delighted to see her granddaughter looking so radiantly happy, the Australian letter coming secondary to their greeting. Following a round of questions and answers, she reached for the envelope. 'Look, it was addressed to me . . .'

Nina immediately turned it over, and frowned over the sender's name on the torn flap. 'S. Schneider – who the hell is that?'

Nell caught Romy's smirk. But the latter refused to voice her hunch, and just grinned as her mother began to unfold the three-page missive.

Turning at once to the back page, Nina said, 'Oh . . .'

'Who's it from?' Nell begged to be told.

Her daughter ignored her to read a few lines.

But then Nell saw her mouth fall open, and her own curiosity barked to be fed. 'What is it? *Tell* me!'

'It's nothing to do with William . . .' A punch-drunk Nina read on – then she seemed to come to her senses, and to realise how disappointing this must be for her mother. 'Sorry Mam,' she said quickly.

An inquisitive Nell continued to probe. 'But who is it bloody-well from?'

'I bet it's Shane!' Romy clapped her hands, wearing a look of triumph.

Her grandmother turned with a sound of disbelief. 'The ranger?'

'Well, he's the only person we know in Australia whose name begins with S,' said Romy.

'What the hell's he writing to me for?' Nina looked and sounded amazed.

But the others thought they knew, and immediately began to rib her in a similar vein as before: 'Hold my hand, I'm a *ranger* in paradise!'

'*Rangers* in the night, exchanging glances . . .'

'Behave, you daft buggers!' Nina reprimanded the teasers.

'No, we're not, he really must fancy you, Mam!' Romy and her grandmother were grinning from ear to ear.

'How the hell do you make that out? We only met a couple of times and on each of them had a raving argument.'

'A small misunderstanding,' corrected Romy, who was thoroughly enjoying this, along with her grandmother. 'And he did save my life.'

'No he didn't! Your nana chased that dingo away with her handbag! I hardly remember the bloke.' Nevertheless, she was smiling, and had a look in her eye that Nell had never seen before in relation to a man, as she tucked the letter away in her pocket.

But the others hadn't finished with this, Nell checking on his surname. 'What a coincidence! You naming Romy after that actress of the same name, and now you might be Mrs Shane Schneider – my, that's a bit of a mouthful, isn't it?' And, adopting a nasal speech impediment, she underwent all manner of pronunciations, having the others in stitches. 'Snane Sneider – Mrs Shnane Schneider – how will she bear it, Romy!'

'When you've quite finished, the pair of you!' scolded a laughing Nina.

Apologising, though still highly intrigued by this development, Romy gave a knowing smile. 'So, are you going to write back to him, Mum?'

'Keep your neb out – and you!' Nina warned both of them, to a final burst of laughter before the matter was put away.

Being the secretive person she was, Nina was not to volunteer any information whatsoever about Shane, though Romy and Nell shared the belief that she had set up a correspondence with him. Neither of them were to interrogate, though, and with no mention of him again, the ranger jibes were quickly to fade.

Besides, other things were to happen before summer was out.

'I'm going to be a grandma!' It was Nina who exploded into Nell's sitting room, full of beans.

Nell clutched her breast, and beheld her pregnant granddaughter who had come along too. 'Oh, how marvellous – already?'

'Yes, I told you it was Hayden to blame for firing blanks!' Nina was not one for diplomacy. 'And you'll be a great-nana!'

Exclaiming in wonder, Nell launched herself at Romy's joyful face, to give it a kiss and its owner a hug. 'Congratulations, love – you've made my day! I knew you'd finally get what you wanted . . .'

How bizarre, thought Nell, to be celebrating over an unmarried mother, but how marvellous nevertheless that this truly marked an end to such stigma as she and Nina had suffered, and that this baby would have two parents who loved it, even if they would not be married in time for its birth.

'Something else nice,' grinned an elated Romy. 'We're allowed to have Patrick's son with us for the weekend – we'll bring him to meet you, if you like?'

'I would like, very much!' Nell could have burst with happiness.

Exhilarated though their visit left her, Nell tried to subdue herself when telling Mary about her great-grandchild, for her neighbour had only ever seen her grandson in a photo – even though she might brag about him being at Harvard, or whatever the blasted place was called.

And how did Mary repay this? 'Oh, but it's a shame that it won't be your real great-grandchild,' she stated. 'You not having any real children of your own.'

Nell was so angry she did not know how to contain

herself. Knowing well enough what she had done, Mary turned up a few hours later with a box of chocolates, though she received short shrift from Nell.

Which made her feel guilty when Mary suffered a mild stroke on her way out. Then Nell was back to her old self, reassuring the poor soul and making her comfortable, phoning an ambulance and going with her to hospital.

When she got home, she telephoned the daughter in America too, receiving the answer that Rosemary couldn't come over right now . . . she had responsibilities, you see.

'And haven't you a responsibility to your mother?' demanded a furious Nell, before slamming down the phone.

That apparently did the trick, because some days later Rosemary was to appear at Mary's hospital bedside, at the same time that Nell was visiting. She was quite cool, shocking Nell with her callous indifference in stating that the house would be sold, and Mary would be moved to a nursing home. Nell pointed out that it had only been a mild stroke, and that if Rosemary didn't want to be bothered, then she herself was quite willing to care for her neighbour when Mary was sent home. But Rosemary declined.

'She only came over to put the blasted house up for sale!' Nell fumed to her own more faithful daughter. 'Didn't even ask if I'd like a memento. Just said if I saw anybody creeping around it'd only be the house-clearance people. Then she buggered off back to America.'

And still Mary raved on to her sole visitor, Nell, about how wonderful Rosemary was to put her in this lovely home, and Nell had to sit and listen, week after week.

'And I don't suppose you get any thanks for it,' said Nina.

'Never mind, I'll get my reward in heaven,' replied her mother.

Meanwhile, she was to shower her goodness on the new neighbours who had taken over Mary's house, inviting the parents and two little blond sons in for tea and homemade cakes. Though relations were to be less favourable when the boys began throwing mud at her door, just for the devilment of seeing her upset.

'It's like the blasted Village of the Damned,' she complained to Nina then. 'You tell them off, and they just stare at you with these piercing blue eyes . . . I said, "I'll tell your father!" Well, much good that did. A few days later, there they are doing it again! That Ryan's the worst – evil, he is, absolutely evil. I told him, if you do this again I'll fetch a policeman – and do you know what he said? You can't touch me, I'm only seven. My God, they all know their rights, don't they . . .'

Nina was angry. 'Move in with me,' she urged her mother, 'and leave the buggers to it. The garden's far too big for you now anyway.' Even though it was mainly shrubs, and Joe's vegetable patch had been grassed over, it was a full-time job.

But, 'No, it keeps me fit,' said Nell, though she unconsciously rubbed her arthritic shoulder. 'And they're only kids, I suppose. They'll get tired of baiting me eventually.'

Yet this was just one of many things that had begun to grind Nell's optimism. Having taken Beata's place as the last in the slot, she had no friends her own age any more. Of course, there were plenty of others with whom to chat, but it wasn't the same as having someone who could empathise. Just going into town, for instance, had become an ordeal rather than a pleasure. It was all very well if one were a little old man – shop girls loved helping little old men – oh, isn't he cute, she had heard them say, while she herself might have been invisible to the assistants whose conversation she interrupted, none of them seeing the irony in them grumbling about customers being rude, whilst one of them held out her palm for Nell's cash without any acknowledgement of her whatsoever.

York itself was no joy to visit these days. What with

most of the industry gone and tourism taking precedence, it had become like an outdoor museum in Nell's opinion. Anything that was seen to deface the ancient city had been removed – which was somewhat crass, for the Minster, which could be viewed from all points of the city in Nell's youth, was now obscured by concrete monstrosities. The Cattle Market that had been such a source of joy to little Nina had been flattened thirty years ago, its replacement built on the outer ring road – the latter being another sign of progress.

Admittedly, it prevented the old Bank Holiday snarl-ups, though Nell could not see that it had lessened the amount of delivery trucks that endangered her life as she tried to negotiate the narrow so-called pedestrian streets. Along with the market, the iron cattle pens had been removed from around the medieval walls, and replaced with grass, as had many, many more of her old haunts, all vanished under a tide of improvement.

Yes, the citizens did benefit in having all those old slummy backstreets tarted up, and the magnificent old buildings returned to former glory, but the strife involved in making one's way through the crowds, the queues that snaked all around Coppergate Square outside the Viking Centre that had replaced Joe's old place of work . . . it made Nell really cross and sad. Feeling downtrodden after another such experience, she abandoned her shopping trip and went to catch her bus home.

Alighting a stop earlier, she visited the post office, then walked the rest of the way, over the railway bridge to the estate. It was damp and dreary, the wind carrying the distinctive odour from the sugar-beet factory that smelled like a sickly blend of roast beef and sugar. Nell's stout figure puffed its way over the bridge and down again, finally to turn the corner. There were few people about, apart from a man coming towards her: an ageing teddy-boy with half-mast jeans, a greasy elephant's trunk hairdo, and a general down-at-heel appearance. What if her son was someone like this? She hoped not. She wanted better for William. Much better. But then she saw the teddy-boy suddenly turn to greet a boy who came running up to him – meeting him with such parental warmth and affection that it reversed Nell's opinion – if he *were* her son, she really wouldn't mind.

And oh dear, there it all was again: the heartache, the memories. Memories like bramble briars: you could cut them right back to earth, but a moment's complacency, the merest drop of rain, and there they were again, re-emerging into a tangle to snag at one's heart, to rip it open and leaving it bleeding.

She put on a brave smile for the man and his son as they passed, then went on her way. Alone on the street again, head down, she almost collided with a youth who appeared from a snicket. She was offering an apology into the pimpled, agitated face when he snatched at her handbag. Startled, Nell held on to it, and a tug of war ensued. She felt an almighty wrenching pain in her shoulder – then fell to the ground as her attacker ran off, taking her bag with him.

She had no idea who phoned the ambulance – did not even realise that her leg had been fractured until some very nice men came and, with some difficulty, it must be admitted, scooped her up and took her to hospital.

'Thank God it wasn't my hip,' she joked to Nina from her bed on the ward, upon hearing the fracture might take up to two months to heal. 'I suppose it's lucky I'm so fat.'

'Aye, well, you still won't be able to manage at home for a while when you come out,' said her concerned daughter, for in addition to the plaster on her leg, Nell's wrenched shoulder was supported by a sling. 'You'll have to move in with me.'

'You can't even look after yourself!' mocked Nell, which

was a rather ungrateful thing to have said, so she added quickly, 'No, I wouldn't dream of being a nuisance to you, Neen – I'll have a few weeks in a nursing home till I'm on my feet, I've got the money.'

Nina looked relieved. 'I'll pay for it then,' she said, and promptly went about finding a suitable home – preferably not the same one as Mary was in, begged her mother.

Long before leaving hospital, though, Nell was taken by surprise and humbled to find out how popular she was, attracting a stream of cards and flowers, and visitors too. Amongst them was a good-looking policeman, who arrived at the same time as Nina was visiting and took a statement. He explained that her assailant had probably been a drug addict. Her bag had been recovered, though there was no money in it of course. Nell had had the presence of mind to carry her keys in her pocket, so at least she would not be going home to a ransacked house.

'I suppose a lot of crime's committed by people on drugs,' she hazarded a guess to the constable, who looked far too young for one so cynical.

'Yes, it could so easily be solved, love,' he replied succinctly. 'If only they'd let us shoot them.'

Nina liked him. But, as every other man before him, she let him go.

It didn't take long for Nell to discover she didn't actually like being in the nursing home. As a matter of fact, she had disliked being in hospital too, and had been shocked at the way the nurses stood around gossiping. In the old days they would have been given an ear-bashing had Sister caught them – but the modern Sister was to be seen gossiping with them. It made Nell mad to think of the exhaustive work she herself had done, all that scouring of bedpans – which were disposable today, that was if anyone cared to come and dispose of them. Still, they had all been lovely to her, as were the staff here in the nursing home, all except the night attendant.

Bluto, Nell called her in private. She wasn't just rough, she was neglectful too, not caring that some of the older residents were slow eaters, hurrying them along in quite a brusque fashion, and making no effort to help them with their breakfasts. The more senile ones were given mush, which was placed so far out of reach that it was never touched. Thinking at first that this was an oversight, Nell had called out to Bluto, but had received only a telling look. Then, of course, she knew it was sheer laziness, and that made her angry. She vowed that, once able to walk, she would help the poor old souls herself.

And this is what she was finally to do. It was as she was limping round the beds by aid of a crutch, putting the bowls of breakfast within reach of those who could eat by themselves, and helping to feed those who could not, that she came across someone she knew. There was a complete lack of recognition on Sister Pike's face, and it was only after being in her company for days that Nell actually recognised her. To say she was a shadow of her former self was to overstate the matter: she was too senile even to focus. How could this fragment of humanity be the one who had instilled terror into her nurses? How far the mighty had fallen. Any residue of hatred evaporated there and then. Nell picked up the bowl and spoon-fed her, neither expecting, nor receiving, thanks.

Later, when the bowls were snatched up by the neglectful Bluto, Nell considered telling her off. Deciding it would be useless, instead she took her complaint to those in authority. It did not go down well with Bluto, though Nell was glad to see it had made her more attentive to her charges. Now that her plaster had been removed, she herself was looking forward to having a soak, and was that evening helped down to the bathroom by a friendly young nursing attendant. There were no locks on the door, but at her age Nell didn't care if anyone walked in. It wasn't a very luxurious bath, but she was enjoying it anyway, when the door opened a crack, then a hand darted in and turned the light off. Plunged into darkness, Nell thought perhaps they had assumed the bathroom to be empty, and she called out, 'Hello! Can you turn the light on please?'

She thought she heard sniggering outside. Why, someone had done it on purpose to frighten her! Then, in the next instant, she heard the rustle of clothing as that someone moved quickly through the dark and threw a pail of cold water over her, causing her to scream in shock and outrage – then they slammed the door and left her alone in the dark.

Heart thumping, Nell sat there for a moment, drenched and shivering. Then, with great difficulty, she managed to grope her way from the bath and turn on the light.

There was not much she could do but dry herself, put on her dressing gown, and retire to her bed. But she didn't sleep at all, fearing what else might be done to her.

She didn't tell Nina. She knew that she ought to, if only for the sake of the others. It was just that she felt she might cry if she said anything about it to anyone. That a nurse could be so deliberately malevolent . . .

Nina could tell, of course, that something was wrong. But, accepting the explanation that her mother was just a bit nervous of living alone since the attack, without further ado she insisted that Nell move into the annex when she came home.

'If you go back there, I'll never rest for worrying about you.' Which were exactly the right words to persuade her mother into leaving the house in which she had lived for forty years.

What might have been a difficult transition was greatly eased by the birth of a great-grandchild, Romy delivering the baby boy who was to restore Nell's sense of purpose and her zest for life. And now that she had finally let go of her obsession of finding William, she realised perhaps the true meaning behind that sign she had been given all those decades ago, when Bill's watch had miraculously started to tick again in answer to her desperate plea: not that she would hold their own son, but that she would have another little boy to replace the one she had lost, to refill her empty arms. Joe would have been so proud that they had given the baby his name – and pleased to see how happy and contented was his wife, at being so close at hand to their daughter.

Nell had a great deal for which to be thankful. But, aware that Nina's pleasure might not be as great as her own, she was very sensitive to the author's need for peace and quiet, and tried to minimise the amount of times she interrupted her. There were days, though, when it was just too tantalising to stand on ceremony; when, feeling lonely, in the middle of an afternoon, Nell would wander into Nina's kitchen in the hope of her dear daughter's company. Sometimes she would be lucky, others not. Today, her only greeting was to be the tapping of keys from the room designated a study.

She moved around for a while, hoping that Nina would hear her and break off to chat for half an hour. But when this failed, 'I won't interrupt you!' she called, hoping her daughter would take the hint and break off. 'I've just come for my bills. Are these mine on the kitchen table?' A pile of statements lay there.

Obviously having one of her out-of-body experiences, Nina made a vague reply. There was a pause, then the one in the study was to hear: 'My God! How can it be three hundred pounds? I never ring anyone!'

Nell was still fulminating over the bill when an annoyed face appeared from the study. 'That's mine, you soft bugger!' Nina's pique was due to both the interruption and the unearthing of her secret. 'Yours are those unopened ones.'

'Thank goodness!' Nell heaved in relief, but was soon exclaiming again over her daughter's extravagance. 'But how do you manage to run up such a massive amount What's this, Austral—?'

'Stop nebbing!' A frustrated Nina came to snatch the bill from her mother's hand and shoved it out of sight. 'Just worry about your own!'

'Sorry . . .' Realising she had disturbed the author's thought process, Nell took the bundle that was thrust at her. 'Shall I go away?'

Her daughter gave a sigh. 'No, you might as well stay and have a cup of coffee now.'

'I'll make it!' said Nell. 'Earn my keep.'

But when they sat down at the table to drink the coffee, she could no longer withhold her curiosity. 'Can I ask a cheeky question?'

'Will it make a difference if I say no?' Nina regarded her obliquely, then gave a half-amused snort. 'You want to know who I've been phoning in Oz – I'm sorry, it's nothing to do with William.'

'Oh, I didn't imagine it would be!' There was an entirely different reason for Nell's keenness to know. 'Is it Shane?'

As Nina caved in with a nod, her mother thumped the table in pleasure. 'I knew it!' Oh what joy to hear of Shane's persistence, of his insight in recognising the warm and sensitive person beneath that layer of shagreen.

Nell's victim looked self-conscious. 'Anyone would think I'm a teenager instead of pushing fifty!'

'Well, you'll always be a little girl to your mother – ooh, come on, tell me all about him!'

And Nina was happy to do just that. She talked and talked for the rest of the afternoon. They had been writing to each other since that first exploratory move of Shane's. The one in which he had risked being exposed to ridicule by confessing to have inexplicably fallen in love with a woman he barely knew, who had treated him quite rudely on the few occasions they had met and shown no inclination that the attraction was mutual, but he could not help his feelings nevertheless. Embarrassed, flattered, cautious, touched, Nina had then reached the mammoth decision to reply, and from then, with the subsequent opening of Shane's heart and hers, a deep affection had grown. It wasn't a huge kind of passion – Nina had only experienced that once in her life, for Romy – but she had grown to love him all the same. Like I did your father, thought Nell, but continued to listen in rapt silence, for rarely had her daughter voiced such emotional candour.

Then the letters had not been enough, continued Nina, taking anything up to ten days to arrive, and recently they had taken to communicating by phone. But apparently that was still insufficient, so, 'I've said I'll go out there and see him.'

Nell almost swooned with joy. 'My, you've really fallen for him, haven't you?'

Nina gave an embarrassed chuckle, and though she did not reply, her eyes betrayed her inner feelings. And then Nell's joy began to crumple around the edges, for all of a sudden she faced the awful possibility of losing another child to Australia. 'You're not . . . going for good, are you?'

'As if I'd leave you, and Romy and Joe! You're always jumping the flaming gun,' Nina laughed, and poured herself more coffee. 'I couldn't even if I wanted to, you have to apply for a permanent residency visa first.'

But this told Nell that she had investigated the possibility of emigrating. It was difficult to say – an utter sacrifice – but nevertheless, she must: 'Neen, you don't have to worry about upsetting me, if you want to go and live there – I know what you told me, but your eyes say different.' She wore a brave smile, but inside she was pleading, *Please don't leave me, Neen! I'll wither and die without you.* But her mouth said, 'Don't leave it too late, grab it while you can.'

'You're determined to get rid of me, aren't you?' came the flippant laugh.

'I certainly am not! I'm just so glad you've found somebody. I'd prefer it if Shane were to come and live here, but –'

'Whoa! Don't marry me off yet, I'm only going to spend some time with him, see if we get on any better than before.'

'You know well enough already how you get on!' Nell reached across the table to give her a sly prod. Despite the cost to herself, it was what she had always wanted, that Nina would find a man who loved and desired her. 'And, what's more, your daughter likes him too.'

'Oh, and she's such a good judge of character – not.' But Nina's acerbic remark soon gave way to a revealing laugh. 'All right, he's bloody lovely when you get to know him.' Her mother had never seen her so radiant. 'But I meant it about not staying over there.' She gave the old hand a reassuring squeeze. 'Honestly, don't lose any sleep, Mam – if you don't believe me, you can come along if you like, have another bash at finding William.'

'Whilst you're doing your courting – I think not!' Then Nell chuckled quietly and said, 'No, even if your offer's genuine I really couldn't face it again, Neen. It's a nightmare trip, and, as I've said, I've done with all that. I'm content with the family I have. You go and have a lovely time. I'm thrilled to bits for you, I truly am.' And again she denied the depth of her loss by quipping, 'There'll be plenty for me to do here.'

'I'm not sure I like the sound of that!' retorted Nina. 'Don't attempt any decorating or move the furniture round. I'll get Romy to call you every day to check you're up and about.'

'I don't need babying! Once a week will be ample – it'll be great if she and Patrick bring Joe to see me whilst you're away, though.'

* * *

Romy was to do better than this. Following her mother's departure for a six-week stint in Queensland, she, Patrick and baby Joe were to move into the vacated house. Patrick could easily commute, she told her grandmother, and it was a holiday for them, being a much nicer place than their own.

'I feel as if I've won the lottery,' Nell declared. 'A whole six weeks of this little chap – oh, won't your granny be jealous!' She kissed and cuddled the happy blue-eyed baby on her lap.

Romy said, 'Well, I've promised to give her regular updates by email.'

'Oh don't flummox me with all your technology stuff,' pleaded her grandmother, making the young couple laugh. 'I can't even set the video, Patrick!' She liked to include him in her conversation, not because Romy loved him, but because he was so kind and considerate to her personally, and amusing too. 'It doesn't seem five minutes ago that we thought a washing machine was something out of Dan Dare – and now they've developed a system that lets you send a letter in seconds to anywhere in the world! Honestly, if your grandad were to come back now he'd think he'd woken up in a science-fiction film. It's all wasted on me. I agree it's marvellous, though, for the young ones.'

Romy laughed. 'Wait till you hear this, Nana. While I was on the Internet I found all these Australian immigration records –'

'Oh don't, you make me feel dizzy,' began Nell. Then, when it was explained to her fully, she was to laugh at the irony of it. 'Do you mean to say, they're those same records that your poor mother spent thousands of pounds taking us to have a look at?'

'Yes – if she'd waited a few years we could have accessed them from our armchairs!'

'Ah, but then she'd never have met Shane,' said Nell,

and they discussed again how pleased they all were at the serendipitous affair.

'God certainly does move in mysterious ways.' The grandmother's smile turned a little sad. 'I don't know why He wouldn't let me find William – anyway, let's not get maudlin! We've got this little chap to cherish. Oh, he's loved!' And she planted a series of hearty kisses on the baby.

Permitted to have such access to him for the entire six weeks, Nell was on cloud nine again, and it was additionally refreshing to have young company in Romy and Patrick, her granddaughter far more generous with her time than Nina. And in donating it she happened to mention that she had recently come across an organisation set up to reunite those mothers who had had their babies or children taken away.

'They won't tell you anything,' explained Romy, 'but you can put your name down and say you're willing to be contacted.'

Willing? thought Nell. It's my heart's desire. But she said chirpily, 'Why not? It can't harm. How do I do it? It's not that blinking Internet, is it?'

Romy laughed. 'You'd have so much fun if you learned how to work a computer! The obscure subjects I've found – oh, don't get your knickers in a twist, Nan, I'll do it for you. Shall I put my mobile-phone number down as the one to contact?'

'Yes, if you like,' Nell was saying, when at that same time Patrick came home and she made herself scarce, so as to give the young parents some privacy. 'Speaking of which, your mother promised to ring me tonight, so I shall have to love you and leave you!' And off she went next door to her own little flat.

It was to be only a couple of weeks later, whilst Nina was still in Australia, that Romy brought the subject up again, but Nell had forgotten and looked baffled at the mention of the internet site.

'You know, Nan, the one I mentioned.' Romy had come in with Patrick, who held the baby and seemed in no hurry to give him up, so Nell must suffice with her granddaughter for now. 'You said you wanted your name to go down on that list of people wanting to be reunited with their babies.'

'Oh yes, I remember now,' said Nell with keenness.

'Yes, well, whilst I was at it I found another site relating to adoption, an unofficial one set up by people looking for family members, and I didn't see the harm in posting a few details on there too. Nan, I don't want to get you too excited, but I've had a telephone call.'

Her grandmother looked shocked, confused, but interested at the same time. 'So quickly . . .' After decades of futile search, Nell could not allow herself to believe the push of a few buttons had brought any result.

'Yes, well, that's the Internet for you. Anyway, I was contacted by email at first, then I received a follow-up phone call.' Romy saw that her grandmother had turned pale, and came to put an arm round her. 'Are you all right – can I get you a glass of water?'

'No, no . . . I'm fine.' She wasn't, her heart rate had taken a sudden blip. 'So who was it from? Did they have news of him?'

Romy employed a gentle tone, trying not to dramatise this, but obviously having to rein in her excitement. 'It *was* William. At least, the man who called thinks he's the one you're looking for. As I said, he first contacted me by email, and then I got him to phone me. He answered all my questions correctly – I believe it's him. His name's William Morgan.'

Nell felt as if her heart had come right up into her throat and lodged there, fluttering like a trapped bird. She could not speak, and so, holding her hand, occasionally stroking it, Romy continued.

'He asked all about you, and I told him how lovely you are, and that you hadn't wanted to give him up.' She saw tears in her grandmother's eyes and immediately they sprang to her own too; but she managed to go on, 'that you'd been forced to do it, and that you'd kept a ribbon from the little clothes you knitted him tied to his father's wedding ring – I told him that too, about him being killed before he could marry you, I hope you don't mind?' At the stunned shake of head from her grandmother, she paused to blow her nose, then gave a wet laugh. 'That's exactly what I heard him do down the phone.'

Nell uttered a laughing sob, nipped her nose with the hankie, and dashed away the brine that threatened to spill. 'So he doesn't hate me?'

'No! How could anyone hate you? Even if he hated the idea of being given up at birth – which he doesn't, he told me – he was sad, of course, and he'd always wondered why, but he said, "tell her I hold no grudge, or anything like that". I scribbled it all down, as much as I could, so I could tell you everything – well maybe not every word, but so's you'd get the message.'

Only now did Nell see that her granddaughter had been referring to a notepad, and asked eagerly, 'Did he tell you much about himself?'

'Yes, heaps!' Romy frowned over the spidery scrawls on her pad. 'Hang on. I've just put key words to jog my memory, because I couldn't write fast enough, and I wanted to be able to tell you . . . He's been happily married for twenty-five years, with three daughters, and one grandson. His wife is called Jean – she was the one who spotted my message on the Internet, apparently she's been attempting to reunite you for years – and his daughters are Angela, Mandy and Sarah. His grandson is Ryan.' She looked up into her grandmother's face and laughed. 'I'll bet you never dreamed you'd have a flesh and blood grandson!'

Nell's eyes were shining again, but with happiness now.

She reached out to Romy, to let her know she was regarded as flesh and blood too. 'He'll be your cousin.'

Then, with heart aflutter, she was pressing for more about her son. 'What else – did you ask him to write to me?'

'I did, yes, though he says he's no good at letter-writing, and he'd prefer to tell you in person.'

Nell grew more excited. 'He's going to phone?'

'No, I mean in person,' said Romy.

Her grandmother moaned. 'I can't wait that long! It could be weeks before he's able to organise a flight – oh, your mum's still over there! I could get her to call on him, take some photos!'

Wasn't life amazing – just when Australia looked set to claim another of her children, it was about to give the original one back! Yet perhaps that had all been part of God's great plan, that she must sacrifice one treasure to receive another. 'Oh, but however will I wait, Rome?' She clamped both hands to her cheeks in frustration. 'Haven't you got anything else to keep me going? Does he have an Australian accent?'

'Not really . . .' Romy had donned an odd expression. 'He just seemed keen to let you know he's had a very happy life in general, and he isn't angry and doesn't have any feelings of resentment, or any of the things you were afraid of. I made a great point of telling him how much you wanted to keep him, and that you'd been hoping to see him again all your life.' She glanced at Patrick, who remained with their baby in the background, but Nell was too euphoric to notice.

'Did you tell him about going all the way to Australia to search for him?'

'I did. He was mortified to hear we'd been to all that expense and money, especially when we were looking in the wrong place.'

'Wrong state – I knew it!' Nell smacked her knee in frustration.

'No, wrong country.' Romy stroked the papery skin of her grandmother's hand with a thumb as she deliberated. 'He loved Australia, he said, but he only stayed out there for five years. There was always something pulling him back to where he was born . . . and he couldn't understand it when he'd had so much tragedy in his early life.'

A look of devastation took over Nell's face. She stared at Romy and gasped. 'Are you telling me . . . he's been in England all the time?'

A nod. 'Not just England – in York. He said he couldn't settle anywhere else.'

Nell gave a little whimper. She could have passed him by in the street any day – he might have been any one of those males she had scrutinised and dismissed because she thought he was in Australia. Oh what absolute fluke! 'But how come he didn't see the advert we put in the press?'

'Yes, I asked him about that,' said Romy, with an ironic twitch to her smile. 'He said he can only think it appeared during one of the times he was away on holiday. Normally he'd read it cover to cover . . .'

Nell was still shaking her head at this kink of fate. Then she sucked in her breath again, as the thought impacted. 'You said he wanted to see me in person . . . ?'

Another nod, a rapid one this time, and loaded with victory as Romy saw the realisation hit home. 'I can't wait to meet him either – I'm almost as excited as you, Nana!'

Nell's eyes shone with tears of elation. 'I don't think you could ever be that, love,' she opined quietly. 'Good grief. I don't think I've had such an earth-shattering day since your mother announced she was expecting you!'

Romy turned to share an affectionate laugh with the father of her child, Patrick kissing the baby, before she turned back and said, warmly triumphant, 'You've found him at last, Nana.'

'Well!' Her grandmother heaved an exclamation, as if

unable to take this all in. But soon she was leaning forward again. 'Tell me more – what does he do for a living?'

'I don't think he told me that – anyway, he'll be able to tell you all that himself, Nan, and I'm sure you won't want an audience, so –'

'What? He's coming now?' Nell was thrown into disarray. 'But I'm not ready!'

'Sorry, I thought, well, he said he didn't want to delay the meeting after all these years . . .'

'In case I snuff it,' guessed Nell – which she felt on the brink of doing. 'Well, I can't see him right this minute!'

Romy was quick to take away that look of panic, wrapping her arms about Nell, who seemed to have shrunk all of a sudden. 'If you want us to stay here then we will. I told William I'd come and pave the way, then give him a ring.'

His name had been spoken countless times throughout their search, but to hear it uttered now from her granddaughter's lips made it more real, more immediate.

Romy looked wrong-footed. 'He's eager, so I thought you would be too . . .'

'I am!' Nell straightened her clothes, as if telling herself, *Pull yourself together, woman, isn't this what you've craved since the moment you lost him?* 'It's just been a shock,' she stammered to Romy. 'I think I might collapse with happiness at seeing him.' With every limb feeling like jelly, she didn't even know if she'd be able to stand.

Again, her granddaughter gave her an impulsive hug. 'Do I ring him then, or what?'

Nell took a deep breath, the fluttering bird in her throat making her unable to reply for a second. Then she nodded bravely, and watched her granddaughter go to the phone, somehow managing to ask, 'Where does he live?'

'Er, Holgate Road, I think he said, so it'll only take ten or fifteen minutes in the car – I'm sure he'll be as excited as you and want to come right away. Do you want to get changed or anything?' She hesitated over pressing the buttons.

'No, just tell him to come,' instructed Nell. 'He can see me as I am. I'll go to the loo, though – if I'm not being too indelicate, Patrick, my bowels have turned to water, as they say in the novels.'

A down-to-earth kind of man, Patrick laughed and helped her to rise, before sitting down to wait with Joe on his knee, whilst Romy telephoned William, and an unsteady Nell groped her way to the bathroom.

It had just been an excuse to get away from them – though it had not been a lie, her innards were bubbling with the shock and emotion of it all, every organ working overtime, and her legs so wobbly she did not know how they managed to carry her as far as the lavatory. Lowering herself onto the seat, she flopped sideways to gain the support of a cool wall as she tried to regulate her breathing. Her heart was still going bang, bang, bang against her sternum, causing a terrible dread – what if she were to collapse and die before he got here? With nausea added to the panic, she began to take deep, steady breaths, pretending she was back on the hospital wards and using her expertise to calm some frightened old biddy . . . except today that frightened old biddy was herself.

She became angry then, and asked what on earth she was so terrified of – was this not her dearest wish come true? The dream she had nurtured for a lifetime? But it did not help, for suddenly that lifetime began to reel backwards. From the tick of Billy's watch as it had sprung to life in her fist, Nell's frantic senses were dragged back screaming and protesting, sucked into a dark whirlpool to that ghastly night when their baby had been torn from her arms. The pain of it was so vivid that unconsciously she was to wrap her arms around her own ageing body and grip it for all she was worth, as if to stop them taking him – how could they, how could anyone with an ounce of humanity commit such brutality as to abduct a newborn baby from its mother?

Such fury threatened to engulf her totally . . . until, become suddenly aware of a more physical pain, Nell loosed the fraught grip on herself, relaxed a little, and began to knead the arthritic joints of her shoulders. Stop, just stop this! She rebuked herself for wasting precious time, for torturing herself in looking backwards, when in a few moments all that suffering would be put to rest.

Alert that she may have been sitting there too long, she pulled herself to order, took another deep breath, washed her hands and then her face. Studying the pale, shocked reflection, she tried to rub some colour into her cheeks, wondering what William would think of his mother. His mother. Her son. Even now, she could not quite believe he was about to walk through her door. Year after year, she had imagined this taking place, though without knowing the venue. Now she could picture an actual door as he came through it, and an actual room in which mother and son would come together, over and over again in her mind. In a moment everything would be real. After more than half a century, she would once again hold her son in her arms.

But what if it wasn't really William? How would she know? After all, with no idea that he'd been living in York all these years they might have passed each other by every day without a glimmer of recognition. She had imagined him as a cross between Billy and herself, a tall man with lovely black curly hair – but the truth hit her then that she did not *really* know. What if it was some cruel confidence trick?

And then Joe's voice entered her head, saying in that droll, affectionate way of his, 'You silly old bugger – what *possible* reason would *anyone* have to make this up? What gain would there be? Your son, who you've been dreaming about for years, is going to arrive any second, and you're up here doing your pisspotical what-ifs!'

And so, with a nervous laugh and a brace of her senses, Nell finally returned to the small gathering downstairs.

Ten minutes later, still finding it hard to concentrate, unable to sit still and twitching nervously by the window, she was to see a vehicle enter the cul-de-sac. 'I wonder if this is him . . . yes, I think it's pulling up.' Her heart had begun to thud again, and her fingers clung on to the windowsill, though she tried to sound as calm and matter-of-fact as possible. 'What kind of car is that?' she turned to enquire of Patrick, sounding completely irrational to her own ears and probably theirs – what sort of an idiot asked about a car when one's long-lost son might be in it. Yet she wanted to know everything.

Wearing an indulgent smile, Patrick came to lay his hand on her shoulder and looked out. 'An Audi, I think . . .'

'Is that a good make?' She was also keen to learn if he had done well.

'Yes, Nan.' The joint reply was warm, and with a note of total understanding.

Then they saw a man get out and straighten his tie – he had put on a suit for the occasion, saw Nell, still uncertain that it really was William – for at first sight he looked nothing like she had imagined. Then he came towards the wrought-iron gates, tugging nervously at his cuffs as he entered the drive.

Guessing how the man must feel, Patrick withdrew diplomatically from the window, and went to wait on the sidelines with Romy and their baby, leaving Nell standing there alone, her eyes on the approaching figure.

No, he wasn't at all the way Nell had pictured him. He was as bald as a coot, and looked like Magwitch from that black-and-white film of *Great Expectations*, a big, gruff, rather threatening type of man, the sort who could take care of himself in a fight . . .

But then he saw her silhouette, and instinctively put up his arm to wave and to issue a broad smile – and in that moment she saw her darling Billy.

Waving back, she turned to await his entry. Her expression was bright as her granddaughter finally showed him through to the sitting room.

'Hello, come in,' Nell said, as if it was the man come to read the gas meter – when inside her heart sang with a greater happiness than she could ever imagined possible, and tears of utter joy burnt her eyes.

Then he came to her, treading carefully over her new rug so that his big feet did not soil it, and at last they stood before each other. There were a million, a trillion things to be said between mother and son. But for now, she just held him.

Secrets of Our Hearts

Sheelagh Kelly

Niall may be poor but he is a good man. He does his best for his wife and their five children, in difficult circumstances in their small, cramped house in the back streets of York. But this loving home is torn apart when his wife dies in a tragic accident and Niall finds himself alone with only his mother-in-law and sisters-in-law for company. His five children run him ragged and, seeking solace, he finds refuge at the Angel pub.

Here he catches sight of Boudicea, the Angel's beautiful and bubbly barmaid. With his wife only gone a few months, he must suppress his feelings of passion, yet he finds he's unable to tear himself away from her warm charm and alluring looks.

But Niall's mother-in-law, the aptly named Mrs Beasty, is determined to do all she can to keep Niall from finding happiness again. And when she discovers that Boudicea's past is far from perfect, she conspires to bring about her downfall . . .

ISBN 978 0 00 721157 9